COLLISION

STEPHENLLEWELYN.COM

Published by Fossil Rock Publishing 2024

ISBNs:
Hardcover 978-1-915676-02-3
Paperback 978-1-915676-00-9
eBook 978-1-915676-01-6

For Sally, thank you for your unwavering commitment, support and for everything you do.

The author also wishes to acknowledge:
Mum, Dad and Bill. Thanks to Sally-Marie and Fossil Rock and Melanie at The Chapter House for all the reads, re-reads, marketing, publishing, IT help and on, and on, and on...

To my long-suffering friends, thank you for a lifetime of memories and for offering encouragement for my mad ideas. I dedicate this book to the ones we lost so young. Now, at the end of this series, I also feel the need to offer genuine thanks to Daniel, for introducing me to my first dinosaur at the age of seven. There is an old saying, *'Give me the boy of seven, and I'll show you the man'*, and but for Daniel's influence on that day, long ago, I may never have written these books. I'm so glad we managed to reconnect after almost forty years! For that reason, *Styracosaurus albertensis* will always be my favourite dinosaur.

Special thanks to the experts who took time out of their frantic schedules to answer my emails about our favourite subject, including Cassius Morrison (thanks for the African sauropod); sci-fi legends Stephen Baxter and Simon Guerrier, and TV naturalist Nigel Marven from *Walking With Dinosaurs*, for reading and offering endorsements, not to mention their kind words of support; and, of course, sci-fi and comedy icon, *Red Dwarf*'s Chris Barrie, for his wonderful performance of the audiobooks.

...And lastly, and most importantly, my sincere thanks to everyone who reads this book and enjoyed its predecessors. Thank you.

There is a military aspect to these stories, and so I offer my undying gratitude and respect for all those who have risked or given their lives to defend us in a dangerous world and continue to do so today.
Per ardua ad astra

Preface

"Collisions are the driving force of galactic evolution."
Brian Cox

Dear friends,

Here we are at the final chapter, COLLISION, Heidi's story, and what a ride it's been. Though I wrote the New World heptalogy to entertain – to provide an escape vector for the mind, if you will, in a world gone bonkers – I hope the series has provoked a few thoughts along the way. To all who've followed me on this journey, I hope I haven't driven *you* bonkers. You've certainly made it all worthwhile. Thank you.

Over the last few years, some of you have been kind enough to ask if Tim Norris' story parallels my own. Largely, no. All the excitements I've enjoyed and endured over the years have been of a rather different sort. However, in one respect we *are* alike. Tim is easily distracted and fascinated by almost everything, and as likely to sit staring at the ice in his glass – completely rapt, while it cracks, marvelling at how the patterns will never repeat throughout the entire life cycle of our universe – as he is to ponder the 1.65 trillion days of Earth's history; but then, as we're practically at the beginning of the universe, in the Stelliferous Era (the era of starlight), we still have it all to play for, right? I suppose it's also a fair cop that I, too, would welcome a trip back to the Cretaceous Period for a nose around. Would I stay there, given the chance? If I could live on *Factory Pod 4* or the *New World,* almost certainly, but then the grass is always greener, isn't it? I quite like the sound of the late Neolithic, too. Perhaps it's fanciful, but Skara Brae might be nice, and restful. Oh, and I nearly forgot, Tim Norris' introduction to dinosaurs as a child (revealed in this story) is a page from my own life – or should I say, a short, yet, as it turned out, extremely important paragraph.

All I can say for sure is that, when I remember back-breaking work on freezing cold, rainy building sites, or in filthy, flooded basements, I feel lucky and full of gratitude towards the people who helped me along the way to get to a place where I can now do the work I love – more than anyone, that includes all of you reading this book. I offer these stories, and hopefully many more, in thanks to you all, and so, here's to the future, our history, prehistory and time travel… bring it on!

At the beginning of this preface, I mentioned 'The End' *da-da-da-da*… Beethoven's Fifth notwithstanding, bringing anything to a conclusion is often bittersweet, if not downright painful – especially when it's something you've poured heart and soul into over several years. I always try to remember that no story truly ends. How can it, while our universe and time still exist? The best we can do is draw a line under things every now and then for neatness, which is why I chose the ending I did from several considered. There are no spoilers here, but this book does answer an open-ended question alluded to several times throughout the series – why did Heidi suddenly stop trying to destroy the *New World* during those early days?

All will be revealed in COLLISION, book 7.

However, don't plan your new bookshelves just yet… I'm not done!

Most readers I've spoken with stated that they wanted an ending, but also wanted to hear more from the *New World*'s characters. That's actually more helpful than it sounds, for within the New World universe, many stories run alongside the main narrative and rather than disrupt the flow, I often put them aside to be more fully explored between the covers of later books. I always intended to plug a few untold stories in after the series concluded, so it's a great comfort that some of my readers around the world were thinking along the same lines and approve. Thank you for the feedback. I'll do my best to oblige with a respectful expansion of the universe. Being candid, the last thing I ever wanted was to damage the legacy by dragging the saga on for the sake of it – especially when I have other projects waiting in the wings – so my upcoming NEW WORLD SLICES will flesh out some of those details by 'slicing' into the series at various points along the way, while remaining faithful to the integrity of the story arc. There are several tales I would still like to tell you, including what came before, what happened next, and what happened during the times we were all looking the other way. You may even find a few hints of stories to come among the pages of COLLISION. I hope you'll forgive an author for leaving a few loose threads to pick at later with his new series!

> *"This is not the end. It is not even the beginning of the end.*
> *But it is perhaps the end of the beginning."*
> Winston Churchill, 1942

Yep, I've a lot of work to do, in my own rather more modest way – thanks Winny. NEW WORLD SLICES will include the aforementioned REBIRTH and NEWFOUNDLAND.

Other associated adventures featuring the *New World*'s crew may be found within my NEW WORLD EXTRA series of short stories, available at stephenllewelyn.com. For all the hardcore book purists out there, like myself, I'm hoping these shorts will appear in a printed anthology in due course. I'm planning a new one called DRAGON, so watch this space. In the meantime, please download free eBook copies of ENGEL, MAPUSAURUS, GHOST and DRUMMOND with my compliments and thanks.

Please also catch up with me on my other projects, too, including the Medieval Northumbria series beginning with *The Apothecaries*. Now, I must confess that the only dinosaur in that one is the author, sorry, but there are a few chickens – specifically the Red Baron. Actually, now I consider it, birds are often termed non-avian dinosaurs, so the question is: can non-avian birds *also* be described as non-avian dinosaurs? Non-non-avian dinosaurs? Double negative? There you go, they must simply be dinosaurs, so yes, there are dinosaurs in that one, too (hope that stands up in court!).

Rest assured, I doubt I'll be able to leave the *New World* alone for long. After all, the crew have become like family – and like most families, some of them, you wish they weren't!

So, without further ado, I hope you enjoy COLLISION | Book 7 of the New World series. Thank you so very much for reading and for sticking with me to the end.

Stephen Llewelyn.

Prologue

The old man lit a few scraps of paper under the kindling. A flame soon leapt to life and began crackling happily in the hearth. His guests would arrive shortly. He had been so looking forward to seeing them.

Barely had the sigh of contentment left his lips, when he heard a bark from the kitchen, followed immediately by the sounds of breaking crockery and annoyance from his wife.

A border collie bolted into the parlour to hide behind his legs, ears flattened in undeniable shame.

The old man tousled them, chuckling as he took his seat next to the fire. "Rather you than me, my lad." Life was good, but it had not always been so. Taking the book from his side table, he removed the bookmark. "Ah, yes. That's where I was. I'd better read ahead. I'm hopeless at filling in the details from memory these days."

A log slipped from the fire, making the already nervous four-legged friend leap into his lap. "Get off, boy!" the old man laughed. "Oh, you've made me lose my place now. We were just getting to the exciting bit, too – I think. Now, where was I… ah, yes, that was it."

A knock at the door caused the cowardly hound to explode into heroic action and go tearing down the hallway at full volume.

The old man smiled, replacing the bookmark. "So much for reading ahead. Oh, well. Looks like I'll just have to wing it. It's how we did things in the old days." He chuckled again at the memory. "The very old days."

Chapter 1 | At One Time...

"Equipped with his five senses, man explores the universe around him and calls the adventure science..."
Edwin Hubble

The satellite was small, no more than a metre across. It looked like an elongated metal box – a container, for such it was. The thruster assembly, attached to what might arbitrarily be called its rear, was tiny yet powerful. Powerful enough to propel the unit around an innocent world at extraordinary speeds. The next three planetary rotations would see the satellite complete seventy-five orbits, each with incremental adjustments for latitude and longitude, to wrap Cretaceous Earth in a virtual mesh; its mission, to launch four smaller devices per orbit.

With another primed for release, a sudden burst of hydrogen left a vapour trail, dispersing almost immediately in the frigidity of space. Fuel depleted, the tiny object blasted directly for the surface of the familiar blue-green sphere far below, but whereas the satellite's mission was structured and finite, the three hundred smaller devices it was disgorging had no such mandate. Indeed, they were tasked with what might be described as an 'anti-mission' – chaos. They would simply be, and that would be enough, in just three days…

Dr Reid came round blearily. His head ached, throbbing with every beat of his heart. Disoriented, he looked about him, waiting for memory to flood his conscious mind with a sitrep. When it came, he groaned. "Oh, no."

Heidi Schultz sat in the pilot's seat of their small vessel with her arms crossed, glaring at him. "So, One, you would betray me, too." Her words had the flat tonality of statement.

"Heidi, what have you done?"

"What have *we* done, *Herr Doktor. You* built the satellite launch system we just fired into orbit."

"Has it released the—"

"Not all of them. Not yet." She cut him off. "I believe you indicated seventy-two hours for full deployment?"

He nodded, immediately regretting it. Holding his head, he asked, "Why did you knock me out?"

"You refused to launch."

He turned, painfully. "What can we possibly gain from this?"

She leaned towards him, her expression intense, savage. "*Everything.* Ah, there goes another device, and another. The satellite must be over land. Soon, all of time will be ours to access at will."

"Ours?"

"That will depend on whether you ever disobey me again."

Reid stewed, still holding his head. *Less than seventy-two hours. What can I do in that time to stop this? Perhaps the message I sent just before...* He looked around, as if remembering something. "Were we not meant to collect Benedictus Jansen before leaving?"

A strange light came to Heidi's eyes. Fleeting, it got no further than the eyes, but was something he had not witnessed before. What was it? Grief? Regret? Surely not.

"Ben will not be joining us. He made his decision. The wrong one."

"You left him to be incinerated in the nuclear explosion." Reid did not bother to frame his statement as a question, either.

Heidi looked out of the forward viewport. "Not all can be saved."

Not any, with you around, he thought, privately. *At one time, I believed our mission was to save a few – just a useful few. Believed we were the guardians of our species' future in a world ending, but now...*

Her expression hardened once more, misunderstanding his scrutiny. "The facts are all that matter. He will not bother us again."

⚬

"She shot me." Jansen spoke thickly; he had never felt so weary.

"Hey, take it easy, son." Dr Dave Flannigan was on hand to raise his pillow slightly, so that the injured man could see those around him, faces he recognised, waiting for him to awaken. His bleary mind also noted armed guards at the door to his not-so-private room.

"Thought we'd lost you, Ben," Devon stated with a half-grin. "Would have, too, if not for the quick thinking of Master Sergeant Apep Badawi, here." He leaned on the Egyptian's shoulder in a friendly manner, taking the weight off his twisted knee. "He put you on ice 'til the cavalry arrived. 'Cause o' you, I'm still waiting to see the doc myself."

"Huh?"

Flannigan smiled. "OK, guys, let's not crowd him. His heart will need time to adjust to, and accept, the new valves. If the Schultzes' med team on the ground hadn't moved so quickly to get you on life support, young fella, we'd be having this conversation via a medium – we have one, you know."

"Medium valves?" Jansen mumbled in his semi-confused state.

Flannigan chuckled. "Close enough. Don't worry, son. I only gave you *two* new ones."

"Two new valves?"

"Yeah, don't sweat it. They're fifty percent off after the first, so I can pass on the discount to my customers. I'll get my assistant to tender the bill."

"Doctor, really!" Matron Runde scolded.

Aito Nassaki began to laugh, but Flannigan was on a roll. "You're gonna need that sense o' humour, kid. Now Jansen's awake, your brother's waiting to see you in his office. Said something about following in your father's footsteps from now on, or following in Corporal Thomas' footsteps – down to the cells."

Aito stopped laughing.

⌂

"Have you seen Geoff Lloyd?" asked Mother Sarah Fellows, almost a hundred million years later in the February of AD1559.

Dr Satnam Patel turned away from the rows of seated individuals in *Factory Pod 4*'s school room and greeted her with a friendly good morning.

She smiled ruefully. "Sorry. Good morning. Excuse me for interrupting your class. I didn't realise. And Lloyd?"

"I have not seen him in two days," Patel admitted. "Though I gather he is going by 'John' now, which is a little unsettling. Just when I was beginning to trust him, too. Well, I *say* trust…"

She leaned in close, conspiratorially. "Yeah, I hear ya. He's afraid Queen Bess will find out who he is. She has an iron will, that one, and a temper to match."

"She will need that strength."

"True. The poor girl has difficult years ahead – I just hope they don't become *more* difficult, thanks to us. As for Lloyd, I understand Captain Baines' description of him left an indelible impression on the young queen. A low profile is probably wise. Still, he did save us from disaster when our crew escaped through the wormhole, so I'm inclined to cut him a little slack. It was pretty bleak for a while there, being left behind and out in the storm between three converging armies."

"Indeed, it was. Though I wonder what he is up to now. I am very deeply concerned about our continued interference with the timeline and with these people, Sarah."

She took his hand, comforting. "I agree. We must be careful. There's nothing in any way cuddly about these guys. But then, we're not going to change the world in one generation. I just hope we can set the ball in motion for a better future, that's all."

Patel sighed. "That… is a *lot* of hope, Sarah."

She glanced around Patel's class. Turning back to him, she winked. "I call it faith, Satnam. And yet, in *our* history, Elizabeth Tudor was a great monarch, but great people can also be capable of great evil. If we give her too much power, too quickly… I mean, she was hardly whiter than white, 'virgin queen' or not." She held out her hands, palms up. "I guess some decisions don't have *any* good options to choose from, but, as James Douglas once said, we walk from where we stand. The rest is in God's hands. OK, that last bit was me." She smiled, turning back to the people seated patiently behind desks. "How are they comin' along?"

Patel's lip twitched slightly. Perhaps it was a smile, or anxiety – Sarah could not tell. "Why don't you take a seat?" he invited. "Then, you can tell *me*."

He returned to the front of the class. "Forgive the delay, gentlemen. Queen Elizabeth has asked us to begin sharing our knowledge in stages to selected people within her government, as you are all aware. We will follow this with more ambitious programmes of dissemination among your younger generations and across Europe, out to the wider world. Under the Queen's strict guidance, of course," he added, to balance such wild talk about sharing. "Now, many of you have asked how we, that is, the people of the USS *New World,* came to be here – how we travelled through time, in fact. This will require a complicated explanation, but I will do my best to clarify.

"We travelled here through a wormhole in space–time. I will get to wormholes in a minute, but to help you understand the background, I will begin with singularities. Singularities, that is, black holes, emit radiation. We originally thought that singularities were totally destructive, allowing nothing to escape. Though practically of infinite density, and with enough gravity to crush even time itself, we now know that is not strictly true… or I should say, is not the whole truth."

Mother Sarah shifted uneasily in her seat. Despite being born in the latter half of the 21st century, she was already glazing over, but decided not to intervene just yet. Instead, she crossed her legs and sat back, trying to focus as Patel continued.

"*Something* does escape a singularity. From the great mind of Stephen Hawking came a theory to explain this, because, you see, when half-spent, the information sent out from a singularity as radiation, in universal ones and zeros, becomes 'one place' in space–time *with* that singularity. And by calculating the half-life of the singularity, it is possible to travel along its myriad points of egress by following that radiation in all directions. From this, it is therefore possible to extrapolate a chosen pathway, making that pathway plottable – and not merely plottable, but followable and navigable, by selecting only that information we require from the radiation.

"Once your two points are established and the half-life calculated, you can travel through the wormhole thus created. That, gentlemen, is how we travelled through time to the Cretaceous Period and more latterly to the year 1558 – last year, in fact. Do we have any questions?"

Sarah cleared her throat. Standing, she took Patel to one side. "Far be it from me to interfere, Satnam, but shouldn't you begin with something a little simpler? Perhaps explain our being here in broader strokes, hmm?"

Patel blinked. "That *was* in the broad strokes. I have not yet begun the mathematical proof."

She snorted gently. "Broad for you, maybe. Think broader. Trust me. You're giving a lecture to Tudor noblemen. Intelligent human beings, I don't doubt – and I'm sure they'll all be educated in basic numeracy – but I think we should start with something simpler, perhaps long multiplication working up to a little trigonometry by next year? Even Sir Isaac Newton won't be born for pushing another century, so go easy on 'em, huh?"

He put his back to the class and leaned in close. "Actually, I think the first thing we should teach them is a little personal hygiene. We have the extractors at maximum, and yet…"

Sarah let go a bark of laughter, covering her mouth with her hand immediately. The men behind them were growing impatient.

"What's the mo'r talking about?" muttered the once and again Secretary of State, William Cecil.

"I know not," replied Sir Nicholas Throckmorton. "Forsooth, this foreign fellow doth brandish words like a peacock flourishing its tail." He pointed to Sarah. "Beseeming, they have meaning to the hen, but are as troublous mist to the sons of Adam. An interpreter, perchance?"

"Aye," Cecil agreed, "and what's all this speak of worms? For what use have they, but to englut on England's enemies?"

Sir Nicholas chuckled. "Amen."

With more speech centres in the brain than men, women have the uncanny ability to follow several conversations at once. Sarah frowned. "Did Nick just call me a chicken? Huh! And why are there no ladies in your class, Satnam?" she added, accusingly.

"Because it is 1559," he spoke straight-faced, "and I was 'reliably informed' that the female brain is too small and too liable to overheat, often leading to fits of hysteria."

She scowled at him. "And yet they all quake in the shadow of a young slip of a girl… I see. Very well, Teacher. That's something *else* they don't know that you can put them straight on." She prodded him in the chest. "Why don't you begin by finding out what they *do* know, and work from there? Calculating the half-life of a singularity, indeed! I'm going to look for Lloyd. Have a nice day."

Patel smirked as his friend turned on her heel and left the class. His smile faded as the universe outside flipped to the inverse within his mind, firing a synapse that ignited the spark of imagination. "Sarah!" he yelled, following her excitedly out into the corridor. "I've got it!"

She stood back. "Did you get it from one of them?"

"What? No, you misunderstand me. I may have a way home for us!"

A few miles north, Allison Cocksedge was bullying Aila into packing her travel bags for her. Aila was a young Scottish girl who came 'free' with the bastle house she and Erika Schmidt stole from the girl's father. Her letter to Phillip II of Spain remained unsent. Rather than rely on one of the young men she – or more accurately, the stunningly attractive Schmidt – had hoodwinked into helping them, she had decided to take it in person to the new queen's court in London.

Turning to Schmidt, she tucked the missive safely into her jacket. "I will place this directly into the hand of the Spanish ambassador's first secretary, Erika. The current ambassador is a chap called Gómez Suárez de Figueroa y Córdoba, Count of Feria – fancy handles these oafs give themselves. I can only imagine what Gómez will be like. This whole world feels like the Addams Family to me."

Schmidt paused her own packing. "Why not give the letter to the ambassador himself, rather than his secretary?"

"I'm a politician of some experience, remember? I wouldn't trust any of the senior ministers I knew not to lose it! Besides, he will be replaced in the spring by that very same secretary. No, Álvaro de la Quadra is the man we need on side."

Schmidt nodded. "I understand. However, I am still unsure about making such a long journey through hostile territory in winter. They have nothing here that we would call a road. Delicately, Allison, you are neither fit, nor young."

Cocksedge bridled. "That's you being delicate?"

"What I am saying is, the weather alone could be deadly, particularly at night. And that is not even figuring for the other dangers of the road in these times. I understand from the girl that the reivers in these parts still take slaves."

"All the more reason to travel south. Look, I know there are risks," Cocksedge cajoled, "but think of the rewards. Besides, in this weather, the roads will be much emptier than if we waited for spring."

"Perhaps. But anyone we *do* come across will likely be the more desperate for it."

"Well... well, then, we shall just have to use these poor conditions to hide, until we choose to reveal ourselves. We must get creative, Erika."

"Make our own luck?"

"Precisely. Also, we don't want to run across any of those paragons of idiocy that Douglas left behind. This building might be proof against those unwashed mountain goats we've been trading with, but if the *New Worlder*s catch up with us, they could turn this place to rubble. *Especially* without Douglas to stop them. Remember, we're only here because Geoff Lloyd blew up our ship – he has history. No. There's much less chance of them LARPing as commandos in this weather. We should go while the going is good." She placed a familiar arm around Heinrich Schultz's personal assistant. "Come *on*, Erika. Destiny awaits. Who's to say that our letter isn't what gets Álvaro de la Quadra his promotion, eh? Douglas' clowns seem to have gotten their feet well under the table with that young girl the English have perched upon their throne, like a gilded egg. *We* have the chance to change history here."

Schmidt remained unconvinced. "And what happens if we fail to strike a deal with this Álvaro fellow?"

"My dear Erika, there's always a way to corrupt people. If not the Spanish, then we'll simply try our hand with someone like Thomas Howard, the young Duke of Norfolk. According to the histories I've been reading, he was quite negotiable, when it came to the loyalty due his queen. He ends up making a move on Mary Queen of Scots. Allegiances are so fluid here. I think we'll fit right in."

Schmidt said nothing. She had a way of doing so at volume.

"I see you still have doubts," Cocksedge continued. "Fair enough. Imagine this instead…" She waved her free hand before them, as though their names were appearing in lights. "Empress Cocksedge— No. Allison the *Great,* with *General* Erika Schmidt at her side – the most beautiful martial leader in history. How does that sound?"

Schmidt removed Cocksedge's arm. "Wordy," she stated, simply. "I advise you not to underestimate these people, Allison. They have cunning and some are surprisingly intelligent."

"Pah! They still think the printing press is news – no pun intended."

"I warn you, Allison. Do not conflate your knowledge of technology with knowledge. The people outside these walls know more about living in these times than we could ever learn from surviving scraps, captured within historical texts."

Cocksedge frowned. "I'm not exactly an idiot, you know. I do have *some* knowledge."

Schmidt raised an exquisite eyebrow. "Failed politicians do not go to the back benches here, Allison – they go to the block!"

The older woman swallowed her indignity, painting on the politician's smile once more. "Naturally, any earlier failures are to be regretted. And I agree entirely with your previous point, which is why I feel we should mingle. How else are we *meant* to learn how one should live in these times, hmm?"

Schmidt sighed. "Very well, but we had better move quickly. February is almost over. Once Elizabeth is crowned, all debate about the English Crown will be settled and any intriguing on our part will become even more dangerous."

"Yes, that would make things more difficult," Cocksedge agreed, weakly. From what she had read in the historic record, while still Douglas' prisoner, she understood that Elizabeth I's coronation was already a fait accompli, having taken place six weeks earlier in January, at Westminster Abbey. She decided not to burden her companion with that fact. Her own time in Westminster had taught her that, firstly, lies of omission were the easiest to deny, and secondly, lies to a friend or ally were the most likely to be believed.

She returned to packing and bullying Aila, while humming tunelessly. It would soon be time to once more dust off her 'spokesperson of the people' and 'kisser of babies' persona.

The shade of Sir William de Soulis watched the three women closely. Robin Rotmütze, or Redcap, as he enjoyed being called, had abandoned him again.

He felt no benefit from the large fire in the hearth, only the coldness of death. A non-feeling. Yet, conversely, he was drawn to powerful emotion in others the way a plant is drawn to sunlight – an attraction beyond his control. There was power locked within the thick stone walls of the Johnstone bastle.

The young girl possessed an innocence that was of little use to him, other than as a plaything. The beautiful blonde's aura was like surgical steel, but it was the older woman who interested him most. Her greed was fully the equal of his own – when he had been alive. Having nothing better to do, he decided to tag along.

There are crocodiles, and there are crocodiles. An unknowable plethora of pseudosuchian species have risen and fallen over the last quarter of a billion years. When the pregnant female Spinosaurus aegyptiacus was introduced to Patagonia by the New World's crew, she found herself near a river. As with the river she terrorised in Cretaceous North Africa, she immediately found that South

American rivers were also the domains of spinosaurs, and of course, crocodiles.

After the all-you-can-eat buffet of the 22nd century River Nile, snacking on hippos, large fish and the comparatively minuscule Nile crocodiles, this was a distinct backward step for her. Worse yet, she was alone. Similar species do not necessarily identify as friendlies. Indeed, friendliness was hardly a given, even within her *own* species. They would tolerate one another while there was enough to eat and when it was necessary to mate – but that about covered it. Young might be kept around until they became an encumbrance or a threat.

She was used to a world without comfort or security, and focused on her immediate need: to drink and feed. Only then would she concentrate on her next landgrab. Marking territory was all, for many apex theropods. Occasional allies never fooled, nor were they fooled *by,* anyone. The climate was humid, water plentiful, so she drew a few hesitant lines on the map in urine, to see what would happen.

Irritator challengeri were common around the *New World* camp but vastly inferior in size and power to Spinosaurus aegyptiacus. Her 'demarcation' would certainly give *them* pause. Then there were the crocodiles. Fortunately, she was all too familiar with those. Oldest of enemies, some were the greatest danger her kind could face – notwithstanding one of their own – others were prey. The question was, would she be lucky?

Her first night in Patagonia passed uneventfully, just inside the treeline near the river's edge. At least, it passed uneventfully for Spinosaurus. For the myriad creatures in her vicinity, she represented sudden demographic shock.

By morning, the respectful space around the newcomer was palpable. It seemed the whole neighbourhood was treading nervously.

The giant slipped languidly into the river for her favoured early morning bathe before the heat of the day. Just a few hundred metres downstream, a disturbance caught her attention. Visibility was poor through the murky waters bisecting the forest, but pressure sensitive receptors, connected via foramina to the nasal cavity, allowed her to detect the pressure waves caused by movement, even from some considerable distance.

She swam towards what was obviously a confrontation – a perfect scenario for the predator hunting with stealth, for it distracted both parties. If you happened to be the size of an adult Spinosaurus, that usually translated into one or the other becoming a tasty meal. Despite the saying that in war, there are no winners, onlookers often tended to do well, whether from the sidelines or during the aftermath.

Mostly below the waterline, she expelled a lungful of air from nostrils set high on her forehead. Replenishing her supply, she blinked water from large, eagle-sharp eyes before continuing her submariner reconnaissance.

Just ahead, a young Irritator challengeri was fighting with a large fish. A smaller cousin of Spinosaurus aegyptiacus, the youngster was clearly punching well above his weight to land such a leviathan. The fish had no weapons to speak of – its modus operandi was to crush small, hard-shelled creatures with a battery of denticals[1] – but its size alone was danger enough. Irritators were well adapted to their semiaquatic lifestyle, but a hard enough clout under water could easily drown the unwary, nonetheless. He had an excellent purchase, but neither the strength nor the weight to press his advantage. The whitewater turmoil took place too close to the bank to benefit the fish and too far into the flow to help the young buck.

It proved the Goldilocks zone for Spinosaurus.

She swam into the slow-moving shallows near the bank, planting her feet firmly in the muck of the bed to stand from the water like the very child of Oceanus – the Kraken.

The squabblers simultaneously panicked when she erupted from

---

1. A dentical – in this sense – is a small tooth-like, or bristle-like, structure. This method of feeding on prey with shells or exoskeletons is called durophagy.

a stinking wave of brown river water, massive head dropping like a deadweight to snap for them.

In a desperate attempt to save himself, Irritator unlocked his jaws so that he might stumble back towards the bank, his petulant roar that of terror and indignation – though mostly of terror.

The fish was less fortunate. Spinosaurus' enormous head and neck, developed over millennia to strike forward and downwards with speed and accuracy, caught the creature in a lightning strike. When her head bobbed back up above the surface, she held within the jagged vice of her jaws an old Mawsonia gigas. The five-metre-long giant of the river was cast up onto the bank like a herring thrown from the beak of a gull to slide through the ferns on its belly. That was fortunate, for Mawsonia gigas had six fins: two on top, one on each side, and a vast fin completing the tail, with a smaller one underneath. Having suffered little more than superficial bite wounds and minor blunt force trauma – it's hard to wind a fish, after all – it immediately began to wriggle; a muscular, instinctive manoeuvre to point itself back towards the river.

Spinosaurus took a step towards the shore, further backing off the suddenly diminutive Irritator, who retreated several steps into the forest running along the bank. Unseeing, he tripped over the struggling Mawsonia. Irritator challengeri was named after the fictional Professor Challenger from Conan Doyle's *Lost World,* but he may as well have been named for Chaplin that day, for he fell with a crash, looking a right Charlie[2]. It was anything but amusing for him. Struggling back to his feet, the powerful fish wriggled and slithered, almost snakelike, under him, collecting his feet once

---

2. In British slang, 'looking a right Charlie' means to look a fool. It is believed the derivation is rooted in cockney rhyming slang, possibly referring to the famous jockey Charlie Smirke, meaning berk – though why such a successful sportsman should be regarded so is unclear. The other prospect is one Charlie Hunt, rhyming with… something else. History does not record who Charlie Hunt was, though it seems he was unpopular, his nickname more frowned upon in polite society than Voldemort.

more along the way. With another crash, Irritator went down for a second time.

Blessed with no sense of humour at all, Spinosaurus aegyptiacus saw only weakness and attacked. Launching out of the shallows, her monstrous jaws snapped and barely missed the smaller dinosaur as he fell for a third time. Desperate now, he struggled merely to extricate himself from his erstwhile prey. Giant animals tend towards economy with their movements – a basic energy-saving strategy for creatures weighing many tons. Spinosaurus immediately knew she had missed the youngster and so followed the attack through to the ground, taking a large bite from the back of the fish instead.

Still in the game, this only encouraged Mawsonia on to further exertion until it felt water around its head. Its pectoral fins bit relentlessly into muck until they found free water, and with one last muscular spasm, it gained buoyancy and darted for the depths, disappearing almost without a ripple on the river's surface, despite its size.

Irritatingly for Irritator, he was suddenly the giant hunter's primary focus. Animals know a last chance when they see one, and when the final desperation is upon them, they rarely cringe, they fight – or on this occasion, flee.

He crashed through the forest, running for his life. Spinosaurus threw the pathetically inadequate bite of fish to the back of her throat and swallowed. Having not eaten since her capture, the morsel barely touched the sides. Roaring frustration, she came out of the water like Polaris, smashing into the vegetation after her much smaller quarry, but here, Irritator finally had the advantage. He slipped adeptly between the trees in a way his pursuer could not. He also knew the territory and set course for a nearby clearing. Once out in the open, Spinosaurus would have the room she needed to manoeuvre, but only if she could catch him. Wending through the foliage at speed, shattering anything in their path, the giants caused a ruckus among locals who failed to appreciate the new road where their home used to be. The treeline appeared with startling speed and Irritator at once found himself out in bright sunshine.

Several tree-dwelling dinosaurs squawked in fury as their branch snapped and fell. Already behind him, Irritator did not even notice as he sharply changed direction, swiping them with his tail to send them, and their abode, flying in all directions – metaphorically. An unflighted, arboreal species, the small family group of branch-to-branch gliders soon came down to earth in a bundle. Gravity is kinder to small creatures and they immediately leapt back to their feet, incandescent with rage, when darkness fell over them. Three of their number vanished down Spinosaurus' gullet before they even knew they were in danger, as she destroyed what remained of their tree. They provided little food value for such a beast; they were mere snacks of opportunity. The survivors caught on quickly and with an explosion of screeching and feathers, vanished into the undergrowth.

Spinosaurus ignored them, turning to follow her primary quarry, but after taking a few heavy steps, she slowed to a halt, panting hard. Lighter and faster, Irritator was well ahead now. There was no possibility of closing the gap between them, so she carefully sidestepped, taking advantage of the semi-cover the treeline provided. Lying down on her belly, she rested her chin on a soft bed of ferns and waited.

Whereas her nearest living relatives, the South American Oxalaias – also now geographically nearest, thanks to the interference of man – were coloured with reds and flame-oranges, the skin that stretched over Spinosaurus' massive sail had a greyish-green base that merged well with the murky rivers of home. Overlaid with wicked red, yellow, orange and purple stripes that mimicked a rainbow of flashing sunlight through water, she was equally aided by shafts of shifting sunlight that cut through the gently swaying canopy above. Despite her vast size, Spinosaurus blended, tiger-like, against the forest gloom, Nature's 'dazzle camouflage[3]' breaking up her lines expertly so that she became all but invisible – one with her background. The creatures of forest and clearing would soon forget the recent fracas and she would remain perfectly still, until someone came along who was not paying attention.

Dogs live in the moment. It's a useful skill from which we might all benefit at times. Human beings have a tendency to look forward, or back. Both can be distracting, sometimes even dangerous. Dr Natalie Pearson was looking forward. She had a job to do, the very next day as it happened, and was completely focused on things usually taken for granted – angles and light. Her task was outside the usual remit for a zoologist, but she was thrilled to take on the challenge, nonetheless.

Patagonia was a dangerous place, particularly in the spring of 99,198,016BC. She should have known that, more than anyone. At least, more than anyone barring Professor Tim Norris. He was the reason she was out there at all, scanning for locations, and would have reminded her, had he been there. Fortunately, someone else was there. Someone who always lived in the moment. Someone who always had his wits about him – especially where Natalie was concerned… fortunately.

Reiver went bananas, his bark erupting so instantaneously as to lack a beginning. Anyone familiar with dogs' ability to transition, instantly, from hearth loafer to ballistic missile – anyone like Natalie, for example – should have taken it in her stride. However, as always, she teetered on the edge of a coronary, while casting

---

3. Dazzle camouflage used curved, diagonal and parallel lines to break up the outlines of ships, most successfully in the First World War – when hunters relied heavily on their own eyes to find prey, although the technique remained effective against German U-boats well into the Second World War. Tiger stripes use natural daylight through the jungle canopy to similar effect. Indeed, to potentially devastating effect, even when their prey is looking, let alone when they are not…

around desperately, trying to perceive the end of the world that must surely be upon them. On this occasion, Reiver was absolutely on the money, and Natalie knew she was in trouble when his no-minute warning was almost immediately sublimated by a tremendous *roar*[4].

Had her wildlife camera not been on a strap about her neck, she would surely have dropped it, to smash on the timber retainers fronting the battered embankment that in turn supported the enclosure's D-shaped palisade.

The fact that she missed the incoming threat was indeed testament to that human proclivity to look forward and back, while forgetting to look around. After leaving Reiver sniffing about inside the enclosure, diligently answering a few urgent wee-mails, she had walked outside the gates alone. Unwise. Of the eight-metre-tall pair, a single gate still hung open after the release of their captive Spinosaurus aegyptiacus the day before. Caught climbing a pyramid in 22nd century Egypt, so far into the future, yet just a few days ago, the dinosaur had eventually been released into their old and trusted enclosure upon their return, only to find the gates closed.

Once again, humans imagining a future where the dinosaur ran free obfuscated the moment – the moment in which the gates were actually barred, making that impossible. Bluey, the Australian construction worker, had taken an armoured digger out to rectify the situation, but that was yesterday.

Today, he was back. She could hear Bluey's excavator working

---

4. This sudden and explosive behaviour is well known to dog owners, particularly during those restful, dozy hours, when all seems at peace. Even the tiniest lapdog retains the instinct to guard, passed down untold millennia from man's *first* friend. When exceptional hearing notes the falling of a leaf onto a driveway, it is always incumbent upon them – as long as *they're* not dozing – to pass on what they have learned to the management. The management rarely acts upon this intelligence, usually hounding the wolf who cried wolf instead (though sensible two-legs get up and twitch the curtains, to check whether there *is* a wolf, first).

to clear a full year's fern growth from inside the compound.

Living in the moment, Reiver realised the digger driver was not the only one to return today. The border collie made a straight-line, flat-out course for the Spinosaurus that had somehow sneaked up, completely escaping his mistress' notice.

To her credit, Natalie immediately stopped searching for the interesting backgrounds that would give Tim and Clarrie's wedding photos a wow factor, only to fall once more into the human trap of considering the future. It took almost no time at all, there being very little future left to consider, but humans also crave to leave something behind to survive them into that future. So she carried on snapping away for posterity – just in case. With no understanding of irony, nor the plurality of language, Spinosaurus opened her jaws to do some snapping of her own.

The numbness of impending doom began to clear from Natalie's mind, just as Reiver ran up the raked timbers and leapt at the dinosaur's face. Yes, it was time to scream now.

She wailed in terror as her beloved David sank his teeth into Goliath's face and hung on.

Momentarily confused by the alien sound, and by the bantam attack to her face – members of the spinosauridae were more accustomed to others running away, rather than going *for* them – the dinosaur fumbled the attack, staggering on the uneven side of the ditch that stretched around the enclosure. The soft soil, marginally compacted by heavy machines a year earlier, slipped, and so did she.

Reiver, in tune with the moment, let go and rolled down the bank into the ditch, immediately springing back to his feet.

Gravity was less kind to the fifteen-ton behemoth, and Spinosaurus roared in pain and fury as she fell sideways into the dry moat. The treacherous, shifting loam of the bank nevertheless prevented serious injury, providing instead a softish landing. Fortunately, she slid rather than rolled, otherwise the long spines that ran down her back, each fused to a vertebra, may have been broken, effectively breaking her actual spine. Quickly getting up off her side, she snapped at the space Reiver had occupied a second earlier.

Once again, with his claw on the pulse of the situation, Reiver was already deploying his four-by-paw to scramble back up the embankment to get the hell out of there.

Looking to the future, one where she no longer owned a dog, the human was rather slower on the uptake and continued to scream, right up until the Spinosaurus – now standing at the bottom of the ditch – turned to eyeball her.

Natalie closed her mouth and gulped. Should she run? Should she stand still? No. That was a stupid idea. Through her shock, she noticed the dinosaur's face was bleeding from where Reiver had taken a piece of the Cretaceous as a souvenir. In her last moments, she could not help but wonder at the little dog's courage – some might say stupidity. She decided on audacious loyalty, but then there was wisdom – dogs tended to have less facility in that regard.

As she was thinking it, she saw Reiver clear the top of the embankment and begin a second run. She knew the monstrous killer would be ready this time. "REIVER, NOOOO!"

Spinosaurus growled and drooled, almost lazily opening her jaws once more, ready to catch. The pieces were all exactly where she wanted them on the board. The little knight got lucky the first time, catching her out with the unpredictable manner of his move – the second time, he would be the first course.

A handful of dust in her eye, thrown by the *second* course, made her blink.

In that moment, Natalie grabbed for Reiver's collar, snatching him from the air.

The dinosaur shook her massive head, eyes streaming and suddenly furious. She *roared* again. Reiver barked. The second gate crashed.

Bluey's camouflaged digger shoved it aside, horn blasting. Natalie could hear shouting from the parapet above her, followed by weapons fire. "NOOO!" she bellowed again. "Don't hurt her!"

The voice that hollered back was so powerful, it could only be

The Sarge, John Jackson, her husband. His actual words escaped her, but whatever they were, they probably fell well short of her naturalist preferences, or any polite sensibilities.

Bluey raised the front actor on his machine and shoved the dinosaur back. She was just at the extent of his reach, so effectiveness was limited, but it gave Natalie the opportunity to finally live in the moment and duck underneath to run away, dragging her loyal protector snapping and snarling behind her.

The Sarge ran from the parapet, down the rear of their defences, to meet her at the gate and she leapt into his arms. "I'd b-better get b-back into the hang of this," she stuttered, shamefaced, as he pulled her back behind the gates. "At one time, I…"

He glared at her. "At one time? What's that even mean, any more? Forward, backward – it's *all* one time!"

"That's actually quite prophetic." She smiled, trying to calm her breathing *and* her husband.

The Sarge waited, rifle aimed at the open gates, while he waited for Bluey to pull them closed. With a boom they met, and the Australian once again used the front actor and bucket of his machine, this time to slide the drawbars back into place.

Natalie watched them glide through their rough hoops. When she turned back to her husband, she found him gone. It was a beautiful morning, yet The Sarge managed to storm away under a private cloud. "Oh, boy, I'm going to be in trouble for this."

Reiver gave a non-committal *woof* and ran after her husband.

"Boys sticking together, eh? Yep. That's me, Billy No-Mates."

A roar from the other side of the gates reminded her she was not the only one.

"Geoff! There you are. I've been looking for you all morning."

Lloyd jumped, in spite of himself. Tudor England was making him edgy, but then, so had 22nd century England, Cretaceous England, Patagonia and the moon. Mars, he merely disliked. He let his breath out with a *whish.*

"Caught you at a bad time?"

"No, no," he lied, obviously. "Why did you want me?"

"I hate to say it, but I'm chasin' your report."

"Oh, that." He visibly slumped.

"Somethin' wrong?" Sarah pushed. "I only ask because we agreed – all of us – that after every interaction with the 'old people' we would make sure there was a record of any discussion, or changes enacted or suggested."

"Yes, yes, I know. I was there," he snapped with more typical asperity.

"So?"

"So what?"

"So, where is it, naturally?"

"Oh, I've been putting it off," he admitted, appearing fearful beneath the habitual carapace of irritability he had long ago perfected.

Sarah softened. "What's wrong, Geoff? Somethin's been eatin' at you for weeks. Tell me…"

Lloyd rubbed his eyes, tiredly. "Not here… Oh, come on."

They made for Lloyd's quarters. "Help yourself to a drink. I always feel the need to wash after I've been around that lot." He vanished into his en suite.

"I assume you mean the locals. Rather harsh, wouldn't you say?" Sarah smiled exasperatedly. "Some things don't change."

"What's that?" came a muffled response through the door.

Sarah could hear running water, so she shook her head and made them both a coffee at Lloyd's small kitchenette.

When he returned, she suspected he was wearing fresh clothes. It was difficult to tell, as he always wore identical fatigues.

After effectively rescuing everyone, in the resulting chaos following the wormhole disaster that stranded them in Tudor England, Major White had offered Lloyd his lieutenant's insignia back. He had taken the two single bars, one for each shoulder, but refused to wear them. That had surprised everyone, though Mother

Sarah believed it to be just a small part of his self-imposed penance. Lloyd certainly had much to atone for, but he was a complicated man, capable of the most intolerable behaviour, and yet, just when you thought you had his measure, he would throw himself into the meat grinder to save the lives of others.

He sat, taking the coffee from her hand without a thank you.

"I'm listening," Sarah prompted, with a secret smile.

He took a draught of his drink, pulled a face, stood, walked to his kitchenette, and threw it down the sink.

Sarah bowed her head, shaking it ruefully.

Lloyd returned a moment later with another coffee.

"Did I pick the wrong brand?" she asked wryly.

"No. It was just disgusting," he replied matter-of-factly.

Sarah snorted. "Tell me what's wrong, Geoff."

He took a moment, nursing his mug while centring himself. "This is all getting too much, Sarah."

She frowned. "Which particular bit?"

"I expected to be left behind. Alone. I was braced for it, if not fully prepared."

"You'd rather we'd gone through the wormhole with the others?"

"No. Well, yes. I mean… as far as your well-being is concerned, I do."

Sarah's frown deepened in thought. "I… think I know what you mean. Thank you. What's your point?"

"It's just that I had a notion of being the last man – a sentinel, if you like – for the *New World*. Sarah, I planned to destroy her, and me with her."

Sarah replaced her mug on the coffee table. "I see," she hedged, carefully. "Do you still feel that way?"

"No. Yes… Oh, I don't know! Not any more. I just feel like all eyes are on me now – you, *our* lot, *their* lot. As for this crazy idea you and the others cooked up to deliberately change the future… it's just all too much. And I know Patel feels the same." He wagged an admonishing finger across the table. "He's properly worried about what we're doing here. I suppose what I'm saying is, if you *had* all gone through with Douglas and the others, I wouldn't be here now, and neither would all this dangerous technology – or temptation might be a better word for it. And I can't help wondering whether that might not have been the best outcome."

"Geoff," she began softly, then suddenly firing up, "that's all so much hogwash! For all we know, your part in this might be vital. If nothing else, you're an engineer. Heck, you may even be the guy who saves the world! Just think how much we have to offer these folks and these times. Think of the pain, disease, war and destruction we might avert."

"Yes, but that might just be the thing that *erases* the future *we* know."

"It was dying. We were *all* dying!"

"No longer cleaving to the belief that God has a plan, then?" he shot back, snidely.

"Oh, I believe. Make no mistake about that. We're here! That must be God's plan, or we wouldn't be. Perhaps he put us in this position to save it all – had you thought o' that?"

"That's a stupidly circular argument, Sarah."

The priest took a breath, internalising patience. "Actually, I'm deadly serious. When we began talking this scenario through, I'm sure God spoke to me."

Geoff's lip twisted, but before he could open his mouth for comment, Sarah cut him off. "Don't say it. Whatever it is, just don't. We have a real chance here. A chance to save everyone, not to mention the environment six hundred years from now. It *feels* right. We *must* take this opportunity and run with it – for the sake of everyone and everything the future holds."

"Oh, spare me the 'green agenda'," he chided, crossing his arms.

"This isn't the green agenda!" she snapped back. "I'm not saying we should set unrealistic goals and plough anyone who disagrees with them into the ground before they can even adapt!"

"Ah, a Republican, eh?" he taunted.

"That has nothin' to do with it! I'm talkin' about doin' things *right* this time – cuttin' straight through the hard lessons to the good times, before the world becomes so populated that every mistake we make is magnified exponentially. Think on that, Geoff. A chance to get it right!"

Lloyd fell silent. A silence that stretched uncomfortably.

Sarah's eyes narrowed. "But there's somethin' more, isn't there?"

He took another sip of his drink. "I hate this coffee."

"Don't deflect. What is it?"

"Bess wants me to go with her, to Whitehall, in London."

Sarah's eyebrows shot up. "Whoa. That's huge."

"I know, and I'm fairly bricking it, I can tell you. I'm still afraid she might find out who I really am – courtesy of the great Captain Baines. Stupid, sanctimonious bloody cow! These people are not big on forgiveness, Sarah. I doubt the Londoners of this time have much sympathy with grockles, either. Anything could happen to me!"

"Grockles?"

"Tourists. I mean, can you imagine?"

"Well, surely you could fit in, couldn't you? I mean, how hard could it be? I only understand half of what you say, as it is."

"That's because you're American. My West Country accent won't fit in half as well as you might think in Tudor London. I mean, it's the syntax. No fake BBC yokel-speak will wash with these lot." He gestured expansively to the world at large.

Sarah stared. "You've lost me again."

"Never mind. It'll be my neck, is all – if they think I'm foreign." He loosened his collar, nervously. "And then there's the… the *clothes.*"

Sarah snorted.

"Thank *you!*"

She tried to disguise her mirth. "Sorry, Geoff. It's just the thought of you in tights." She cracked, throwing her head back to laugh raucously.

"You won't be laughing if I balls this up! Let's face it, my record's not great when it comes to manipulating timelines."

She sobered. "No. Of course. I'm sorry. So, will you go?"

"She's Elizabeth the First, Queen of England. Do you really think I have a choice?"

"You know, that would have sounded real strange to me at one time."

Chapter 2 | Front Page

When the situation called for it, The Sarge had the loudest voice Natalie had ever heard – ideal in an army sergeant. Yet, he was a nuanced man. When truly angry, he emanated a silence powerful enough to gag those around without so much as a gesture. After taking her in his arms immediately, following the incident, almost crushing her in his relief, he had not uttered a word since. In fairness, she already knew how big a mistake she had made. She admired the fact that he knew that, too, and knew that *she* knew it, and so saw no point in reiterating it – but also saw no point in absolving her, either.

She was in the doghouse, pure and simple. Natalie believed this particularly unfair while Reiver enjoyed an admittedly deserved seat at the high table. He was currently devouring a steak – cooked to medium rare perfection and offered to the hero of the day by her husband's own hand – but it was lonely in the kennel.

"OK, I'm sorry."

The males in her life spared her the merest glance, before returning to their boys' night in. They had chips, too. She blew out her cheeks and drummed her fingers. Reiver had certainly been there for her when it mattered, but in peacetime, it seemed the giver of steaks was king. "I'm going to pop out."

The Sarge picked up his comm from the dinner table, scrolling through the house controls. Natalie heard a *click* as the door to their quarters locked.

She snorted gently. The Sarge would never dream of restraining her in any way; this was simply his way of saying 'don't go' without letting her off the hook. "Alright, I give up, you guys." She got up to stand behind her husband's seat, wrapping her arms around his shoulders. "I'm really, *really* sorry that I put the wind up you." She slipped into the seat right next to him at the table. "What? Apology basket still only half-full?"

The Sarge swallowed a chip. "No. It's still half-empty," he acknowledged, grumpily.

"He speaks!"

Woof!

"I know *you* speak."

Grrrrr!

Natalie blew out her cheeks again. "Tough crowd."

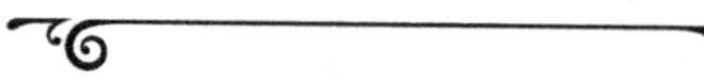

The following morning, sunrise set the eastern skies ablaze as another beautiful day bloomed over Cretaceous Patagonia. By what would be considered lunchtime – in times where there *was* a lunchtime – bright sunshine streamed through the large windows in the observation lounge, set immediately above the *New World*'s main hangar airlock. The lounge boasted views west, over plains, river, forest and the distant Petes Mountains[1] , that took the breath away – a distinct possibility when living alongside such deadly beauty.

Hank Burnstein Snr stood. "Ladies and gentlemen, guests and friends, this is a new experience for me, in two ways. Firstly, I only have *one* daughter," he smiled at Clarrie, eyes twinkling, "and secondly, because whenever I got to my feet in front of you guys in the past, it was usually to shout someone down. This time, I'm bigging someone up! My beautiful daughter, the pride of my life, Clarrie."

A cheer rose to fill the open space.

"She had a challenging childhood." He paused as laughter erupted around him. Burnstein laughed, too, for he knew they were all laughing with him, rather than at him. "And yet, she weathered it all magnificently."

Chelsea Burnstein did not laugh, but smiled up at her husband, holding back tears of pride. Her whole family had come so far to reach this moment, and all it took was the loss of almost everything they ever had.

He reached out for her hand. "I'd like to say she grew up well with our help, but the truth is, she did damned well in spite of it!"

More cheers.

Burnstein waited for the noise to abate. "As you all know, my son – that is, *our* son – Hank Jr, was sadly left behind in Tudor England. I found that hard to live with, for the longest time, but as we now know that he, and our friends with him, pretty much saved the world for us, that pain is tempered with pride. On this, the happiest of occasions, I wanna raise a separate toast to all our lost friends and loved ones."

---

1. 'Pre-Andes' is the term often given to mountains that existed before the current Andes Range that stabilised around 6,000,000BC, after a period of sudden uplift raised them as much as 3.5 kilometres in places. Tim Norris named the mid-Cretaceous range the 'Petes' (*pee-teez*), after a biblical Googling – Peter being the older brother of Andrew.

Everyone stood.

"Ladies and gentlemen, lost friends and loved ones."

The guests repeated, formally, and Burnstein waved them back down into their seats.

"Thank you." He took a moment to steady his emotions. "Forgive me, I'm not the guy I used to be." He chuckled, and it helped. "It's often said by fathers everywhere – every when, I should probably say – that I haven't lost a daughter but gained a son. Well, I must be the luckiest guy alive, because I now have two sons, and they're both heroes!"

"*Hear, hear!*" the guests agreed.

Patricia Norris dabbed her eyes, taking Tim's hand to give it a squeeze, and for once, he did not pull away in embarrassment.

"Ladies and gentlemen, I ask you once more to charge your glasses as I give you my beautiful daughter, Clarrie, and her husband, Tim. God bless them both with a wonderful life together – *whenever* that might be!"

The guests laughed good-naturedly as they stood once more to toast.

"Thank you, friends. I'll hand you over to the groom."

Tim got hesitantly to his feet. He grinned. "Thanks, Dad. I don't have a speech as such, just a few thank yous, really, but I would just like to say that this is new for me, too. Firstly, I've never been a groom before! And secondly, whenever I've had to stand up and speak, it's always been about dinosaurs!"

Laughter.

"Now, as much as I'm tempted to go on about this or that, or describe the animals on the plain out there, just to stave off the inevitability of my best man's speech a little longer…"

More laughter.

"I'd really just like to thank you all, sincerely, for everything you've done. You see, this isn't just a wedding – this is a celebration of our survival, against incredible odds, and it belongs to all of us. We have crews here from the old *New World,* and… *other* ships."

Laughter again.

"I hope I won't cause any offence by not naming *them*." Tim laughed, too. "But one thing I will never forget, or shy from saying, is that we're all *New Worlder*s now. So, I give you the *New World*."

"The *New World*," the guests repeated and cheered.

"I owe you all so much, my mum and dad especially. Thanks, Mum. I know Dad is with us."

That did it. Patricia's tears came with the memory of her long-lost husband, Edward Norris, though she smiled proudly, holding her son's hand tightly, as though it were a lifeline.

"My thank you list would take us into tomorrow, but I feel that I *must* say a huge thank you to Captain James Douglas, a man who never gave up on me, even in my darkest days. Thank you, Captain." Tim raised his glass and Douglas stood to give him a proud salute.

"I also would like to thank Captain Jill Baines-Douglas. Firstly, if I didn't, it might prove problematic for Captain Douglas' own marriage…"

More laughter.

Tim joined in with the merriment for a moment. "But seriously, I've no doubt most of us wouldn't be here now, *including* Captain Douglas – as I'm sure he would agree – were it not for Captain Baines' crazy courage and commitment to keeping us safe. Thank you, Captains Douglas and Baines, for everything."

The guests raised glasses to both captains.

"Well, that's it from me. I suppose I can't put this off any longer. Ladies and gentlemen, friends, I give you my best man, and my best friend – which illustrates just how rough a road it's been – Woodsey!"

Raucous cheers.

Woodsey stood, shoving back his chair noisily. Tapping a champagne glass with a fork, he began, "Alright everyone, it's the moment you've all been waiting for – to hear the best man, live and uncensored!

"Perhaps it's just me, but earlier, when Captain Douglas said, 'we are gathered here today', it made me wonder… could we, if we really enjoyed ourselves, go back and live it up all over again in one endless party? But then, if we've already done that, and have travelled through this day before, would we even know? But then, is that really a surprise? I mean, have you guys seen the size of the groundhogs they have here?"

Two hours earlier…

Clarrie wore a summer dress of white silk, veil streaming behind to accentuate her tanned skin so that Tim's peripheral reality was a mere white haze. For him, in that moment, there was nothing and no one else, and nothing else mattered. The angelic effect was both distracting and liberating, because though he stumbled nervously over his vows, he did not care.

Having resigned themselves to yet another delay in their wedding plans, the extreme danger of the last week threw into sharp relief the importance of seizing the day. After all, for the time traveller, fixing a date comes with baggage. Ultimately, there is only now.

Fortunately, Mrs Chelsea Burnstein was, is, and will be – depending on which period she was living through – a woman who planned, plans and will plan for the future… whenever that might be. When ordered to pack only that which they needed for their hazardous journey back to the Cretaceous, she decided that what she really needed was to see her daughter married properly, and so she surreptitiously smuggled a few 'extras' aboard, just in case. A foresight that now served her well, 99.2 million years earlier. Booking the venue had proven a nightmare unique in the annals of human history, but she was determined to make sure that, whatever their situation, her daughter and husband-to-be would be well turned out for the occasion.

Until that morning, Tim was completely unaware that the suits for which he, Woodsey and Hank Burnstein Snr were measured – several geological periods into the future – had been purchased and stored by a proud, determined mother, in cahoots with her equally committed opposite number, Dr Patricia Norris, Tim's mum. Chelsea's torture of separation from her biological son, Henry, left behind, weirdly in the far-flung future of AD1558, was ever with her as it was with her husband. Given the chance to gain a second son, she pulled out all the stops; neither pushing nor pestering, she simply remained prepared. She was, after all, the beating heart of her family – a proud and time-honoured tradition passed from mother to daughter since long before there was ever a need to write such things down.

Tim, like sons and sons-to-be everywhere, was largely unaware of all Mum's work in the background, to make sure his day continued along its rails. Clarrie, like daughters and daughters-to-be everywhere, felt Mum's involvement only too keenly, and railed against it.

Fortunately, none of that detracted from the moment for Clarrie, either. "I do." She spoke quietly, just for her husband-to-be. With more gusto, she reiterated for the whole group. "And just to make sure there are no legal issues associated with time travel – I did, I do and I will, too!"

The combined crews of the USS *New World,* and various enemy vessels that now made up the crew and passengers of the UNS *New World,* whooped with delight.

Douglas smiled down at the couple and then over their heads to the gathering before him. Eventually, he raised a hand for quiet, but certainly not for solemnity. "And so, it is my privilege and distinct honour, as captain of the UNS *New World,* to declare you husband and wife. Tim, you may kiss your bride."

A roar of approval from the two-hundred-strong assembly filled the man-made amphitheatre and was soon joined by myriad hoots and calls from the wider congregation outside their timber walls, yet still within the wondrous church of creation. Reiver barked for the sheer joy of being alive with friends and loved ones, completely forgetting about the annoying white rosette he had spent the last half an hour trying to remove from his collar. It matched the material of Clarrie's dress precisely – another point for Mum. Although, having studied the bizarre behaviour of the two-legs,

Reiver felt himself fortunate indeed to wear a beautiful black and white coat that always served, no matter the occasion. He followed excitedly, as Clarrie led Tim away, lost in a dream.

Atop the parapet walk along the timber palisade, constructed a year earlier by their people, Tim caught his breath. Looking down at his new wife, he saw the sense of shared déjà vu in her eyes.

"How...?" he managed, eventually.

Clarrie regained her senses first. "Mum probably invited *them,* too!"

Tim threw his head back and laughed, for engaging in brutal deforestation of their clearing's boundaries were several sauropod dinosaurs. Argentinosaurus huinculensis were old friends to the *New World*'s crew, but on this occasion, they were not alone. Living in harmonious destruction with their larger distant relatives was a herd of Agustinia ligabuei, an animal that carried strong emotional importance for Clarrie and Tim. After all, an Agustinia had interrupted their first kiss, by calling over the palisade at that very spot – ten years ago, for them.

Tim looked out eagerly, wondering if one of the giants might indeed be the very animal.

Clarrie read his thoughts. "You could always rustle the wrapper of a power bar to see if one of them comes over," she quipped.

The Spinosaurus they recently released back into the wild made herself scarce when herbivores, some of them eight times her mass, took over the clearing. No lone wolf would take those odds.

Clarrie stared only at her husband, waiting patiently for the 'dinosaur kid' to realise what he was missing. When he did, she kissed him.

Reiver sat patiently, looking up at them and wagging his tail.

Unaware of anyone or anything around them, Tim and Clarrie embraced on the timber walkway that looked out over a primeval world of spectacular colour and beauty, of forests, plains and high falls, while whole families of vast sauropod dinosaurs tramped the middle ground, trumpeting a fanfare to life. It was a snapshot in time.

Fortunately, despite the best efforts of Spinosaurus aegyptiacus, their photographer was still alive to catch that moment of magic, with its background that would have professional togs crying into their wedding breakfasts, if it ever hit the covers of any bridal magazines… and if their happy couples thought to feed them.

Tim surfaced with a dazed expression comical and endearing to both Clarrie and Natalie – the latter having no scruple about capturing his dumb look, reportage style, for posterity – when his eyes sharpened, his arm shooting out to point.

"Look! What the…?"

The women stared out over the palisade, searching for whatever had startled him. Then they saw it. Among the Argentinosaurus and Agustinia, there was an interloper. She – for she was categorically a 'she' – was not stalking them, but merely coexisting peacefully, living under their protection. A beautiful tan-coloured Bos taurus taurus.

"It's… it's… it's a cow!" Tim finally managed to get his mouth in gear with his thoughts.

"A Jersey cow!" Natalie cried, her knowledge of taxonomy for once outstripping Tim's own.

Tim turned, seriously. "We have to save her!"

Natalie nodded, already planning a rescue. The local flora would be lousy for a cow's digestion. "It's nothing short of a miracle she's alive," she vocalised.

"Bad diet?" Tim asked, perceptively.

"Bad diet?" Clarrie exploded. "There's a cow out there! A cow! In the Cretaceous! And you guys are wondering what she's been eating? How the hell did she get here?"

Baines appeared, as if from the air, personal comm in hand, snapping away to record the moment – infuriating the designated photographer. "Schultz," she said eventually, in awed disbelief.

"Of course!" Tim clicked his fingers as realisation struck. "I'd totally forgotten."

"What?" asked Natalie and Clarrie together.

Baines explained. "Heinrich Schultz brought cows and chickens aboard the… what was that monstrosity called?"

"The *Eisernes Kreuz*," Tim supplied, tonelessly. "Rose and I were aboard when it was destroyed. I don't know how, but at least one of the animals must have escaped when we did."

"Jerseys would make an ideal choice," Natalie explained, giving a bizarrely sensible commentary to events. "They're among the smaller breeds – a likely consideration aboard ship – but also, their milk is gorgeous and perfect for dairy produce. They tend towards curiosity, and sometimes stubbornness, but they're quite friendly. I'm sure we could bring her in safely."

"I can't believe she survived here," Tim muttered in wonderment. "It's been, what, eight months in this timeline?" Thoughts of his escape from the burning wreck of the *Eisernes Kreuz* and subsequent thoughts of Rose and Henry hurt, even on such a day, yet a smile spread slowly across his face as he watched the little cow making the best of her new home. "You clever girl."

Within minutes, a transport left the gates of their compound, moving slowly towards the Jersey and her enormous guardians. Despite their wedding attire, Tim and Clarrie insisted on joining the recovery team.

"What shall we call her?" Clarrie asked, excitedly.

"Sunday dinner," The Sarge replied, earning a slap from his wife and a scowl from Tim's.

"Belle," Tim supplied, earnestly.

"I like that," Natalie replied, still glowering at her husband. "What made you think of it?"

Tim smiled – Woodsey would have said pathetically – at his new wife. "We never got the church wedding your mum wanted, but at least we got a wedding Belle."

"Oh, Tim." Clarrie melted into his arms.

Fortunately, Woodsey had stayed within the enclosure, watching from the parapet, otherwise he might have vomited all down the front of an extremely expensive suit.

Belle proved less enthusiastic about her rescue than the

would-be dairy farmers might have hoped. She bucked when they approached and moved away. The quicker the humans moved to intercept, the quicker she loped further afield.

"She's painfully thin," Natalie fretted. "Come back, Belle. Come on, sweetie."

"Come back, you stupid cow!"

Another slap for The Sarge.

"We're never going to catch her," he stated, rubbing his arm with annoyance.

A cartoon version of their shenanigans would have seen a lightbulb pop into existence above Natalie's head. She turned back to the enclosure. Up on the parapet, she could clearly make out Woodsey, cutting a dashing figure in his best man's rig. As she expected, just to the side of him, at belly height, was an equally dashing black and white face she adored. She cupped her hands and bellowed, "Reiver!"

Dropping back to all-fours, the head vanished. Despite Woodsey's clumsy attempt to stop him, Reiver ran flat out down the earthen ramp at the rear of the palisade. Making for the open gates, and weaving between the armed guards like bollards on an agility course, he flashed out to reach his mistress, arriving at her side in seconds.

Natalie knelt to fuss his ears. "Good boy." She stood. "Away, boy. Away to me." The collie shot off in an anticlockwise arc around the animal that was clearly trying to escape, outpacing the cow easily. Natalie had taken Reiver as a two-year-old when his first master, a shepherd in her native Ireland, had sadly passed away. He always accompanied her on all her zoological trips, occasionally making himself useful to bring or drive animals out of danger. Although not fully trained, everything he learned as a pup and a youngster was retained and he was on form today.

"Take time," she called, slowing his attack. Once he was behind her, Belle became increasingly skittish. "Stand. Stand!"

Reiver stopped, but remained up on his paws, panting tonguely. Natalie motioned for the humans in their party to slowly encircle

Belle, but Belle had other ideas and bolted right.

"Come-bye," Natalie ordered and Reiver obeyed instantly, this time circling clockwise around the errant cow, bringing her to a halt, while vast mouths stripped the tree tops fifteen metres overhead, occasionally stopping to watch curiously.

"Take time," Natalie slowed him. "There!" Reiver stopped flanking and ran straight at the cow, driving her towards the ship. "Quick, corral her!"

No one reacted.

"Well, move then! Don't just stand there!"

"I thought you were talking to the dog!" The Sarge complained, but moved with everyone else to funnel Belle into the open hatch and aboard their transport, while Reiver drove her straight down the line and in.

"*Yes!*" the small group whooped.

ROAR!

The answering reply came from the river as their unfriendly neighbourhood spinosaur stood up out of the water. Sensing the sudden influx of easy prey, she climbed onto the bank and loped into a run towards them.

The humans needed no further encouragement and ran for their armoured transport, quickly turning it around to head for home.

The enormous sauropods were less willing to share their clearing with this latest newcomer, and bass bellows shook the ground as the larger females among the herd stamped and pawed at the ferns, cracking their whip-like tails. The largest male of the group watched disinterestedly, while continuing his lunch. He was far too massive to be concerned by such a thing, or *anything*. Besides, there was no need for him to weigh in; Spinosaurus was a wily hunter and positively tiny compared with the much huger Argentinosaurus. She slunk back to the river. It was a beautiful day, after all; perhaps a spot of fishing would be safer.

Now…
"Now, I have to say, I had my doubts whether this day would ever

come." Woodsey swayed slightly, expounding loudly enough to be heard by the whole gathering. "The number of appointments he missed, while the women in his life tried to arrange the most important *day* in his life… Ha! Marry him? I thought Clarrie might *murder* him!"

General merriment carried through the guests while Tim smiled, shaking his head.

"Of course, Tim would never have missed those appointments on purpose, he's far too noble for that – *hic!* – oops. Sorry. Bit of the old hiccups. Better have another drink – hang on. Right, where was I? Oh, yeah – nobility. No, Tim would never have missed those appointments on purpose. It was usually because something had driven the engagement from his mind. Almost always life and death situations, I might add, like one of his students having placed a ceratosaur metatarsal in the drawer with the megalosauroid fragments. Or his post-doc assistant," Woodsey took a theatrical bow, "causing totally accidental damage to a university vending machine, and then promising to sort it out, but forgetting about it. By the way, talk of police involvement within the department was overplayed, on that occasion." He grinned at the blushing groom. "And you were worried I might embarrass you."

Woodsey paused to take another gulp of champagne while the laughter subsided. He retained just enough sobriety to suppress a drunken belch, thumping a closed fist to his chest. "Fizzy, this stuff, ain't it? What I'm trying to say is, there may, on occasion, have been mitigating circumstances when Clarrie was left waiting for a Tim that never came. Luckily, much needed help arrived when the poor girl, having stood patiently by, for years, waiting for him to notice all that was right under his nose, decided enough was enough. Tim needed rescuing, but she knew he would only be satisfied if everything was done properly and to the letter – though he often forgets that *when* you do things to the letter, 'do' is the important bit." He chuckled, taking another drink. "But those of us who love him understand the geological nature of Tim's decision-making processes, so Clarrie took the initiative. And so, on the 29th of

February, 2120 – having waited years for him to wake up – she took advantage of the leap year tradition and proposed. Thankfully, the bumbling professor *finally* realised what he had right in front of him, and the rest *was* history – now prehistory, as it turns out!"

Woodsey raised his glass to the whole gathering before taking another draught. "Well, that was pretty much the end of my speech, but Tim, being Tim, opened a whole new avenue for me this morning. I mean, getting married in the Cretaceous was pretty wild, so what did he get the new missus for a wedding present? You may well ask. Was it a pretty dress? A trip to a tropical paradise? OK, he may have accidentally snagged that one."

Further merriment from the guests.

"But no. Miraculously, and sticking with frontier tradition, Tim somehow managed to get his wife a *cow* for her wedding present!"

A roar of laughter.

"OK. So, I think I've embarrassed the skinny Pom for long enough."

"Hear, hear," Tim spoke up, also slurring ever so slightly.

"Although, there was that time… No, I'd better not," Woodsey concluded, hanging on to his chair to stop himself from swaying. A grin curved his lips up at the ends, resembling a rum sot in a hammock. He replaced his glass on the table before his tongue was forced to show a leg. Clumsily topping it up, he held it aloft once more. "So! It is without further ado – *hic* – that I ask you to raise your glasses and join me in a toast to the happy couple. Ladies and gentlemen, I give you the most sanctimonious boss in *any* epoch – my best mate, Tim, and his Sheila, Clarrie Norris. Here's to a…" he started laughing, "a very, very, *very* long and happy life together – Tim and Clarrie!"

The wedding party and entire *New World* crew stood and responded, "*Tim and Clarrie!*"

"Because," Woodsey continued into the hubbub, checking his notes blearily, "when we get home, you'll then have to join me in wishing them a happy ninety-nine million, two hundred thousand, one hundred and thirty-eighth anniversary. Talk about a life sentence, that's gotta be a record!" Woodsey winked at Tim. "Worked that out all by m'self, mate. And so! Coupled with the happy couple, ladies and gents – and Belle the cow, of course – I raise one last toast to the future… all of it!"

Laughter, cheers and spirited cries of 'The future!' filled the observation lounge.

Thousands of miles overhead and two-thirds of the way through its mission, a satellite spat out yet another device. The tiny plume of vapour vanished instantly into the black, propelling the small piece of technology towards Earth. Following preprogrammed coordinates, it headed straight for a target destination just west of the wedding celebrations below, to the crash site of a battleship named the *Last Word*.

Chapter 3 | Sail Away

"I assume, as we weren't invited to the wedding, that we're prisoners?" asked Devon, seriously.

Douglas considered. "Let's say, ye're our guests, but there *will* be restrictions."

"Such as?"

"Such as, ye'll be under close surveillance at all times and will only be allowed to gather in small numbers until we get home. As for retaining your weapons… Ah think ye can guess the answer to that one."

"So, like a 'gentlemen's prison', then?"

"If that's how you want to sell it to yer people, fine, but dinnae expect me to trust you blindly after everything your group has caused."

"And exactly what have we caused, Captain?"

Anger flashed in Douglas' eyes. "Speak to ma crew, they'll tell ye about everything they've been through because of you people. Ask them about those we've lost!"

"Captain Meritus was allowed to join you. He, too, worked for the Schultzes. Have you forgotten that?"

"No. Ah haven't, believe it or not! However, he took a huge risk in coming over to our side – they all did. We were ridiculously outgunned at that time. *You* seem to have turned when ye had nae choice. That said, why don't ye tell me what the difference is?"

"That's unfair, Captain. Some of us have been working for many months – since before you left the Cretaceous, in fact – to break the Schultzes' stranglehold, and prevent them from disrupting the future."

"Ah believe ye, and ye'll be fully debriefed in due course, with full opportunity to tell us your side, make no mistake. But not all your people were against the Schultzes. So once again, Lieutenant, tell me, how should Ah know who to trust and who to lock up? Ah think we're showing an extraordinary level of goodwill as it is. You disagree?" The last was a challenge.

Devon smiled slowly. "That's a trap, Captain. If I argue the point, then what? You'll more easily justify banging us up and keeping us locked down?"

"Ah dinnae have tae justify ma actions, laddie. Yer people worked for terrorists and murderers. The fact that you're here at all, and werenae abandoned to that nuclear disaster is testament enough to *our* good faith."

Devon bowed his head. "We're not your enemy, Captain. When you hear our story—"

"Aye," Douglas cut him off. "Ah'm reserving judgement until then. Ye've ma word on that. And when we get home, assuming we do get home, after all the damage your people have wrought on the timeline, your part in what has happened, and any role you may have played in your alleged resistance, will be taken into account."

"We'll be judged fairly?"

"Believe it! We're no' the Schultzes. If ye've done yer best in a hard situation, it will be noted. If ye've aided and abetted a group trying to rub out our entire race and all our history, ye'll wish ye'd never been born. But all of that is a conversation for a future date. Now, Ah'm more concerned about others of your number who may be keeping their heads down, hoping tae avoid us."

"Captain?"

Douglas snorted derisively. "Very slick. Dinnae play games, Devon. Yer loyalty, if that's what it is, does ye credit, but we know all about the base in Britain – or what *will* be Britain, one day. We hacked yer wee satellite net the first day we arrived, so let's no' dance around the floor again."

Devon leaned forward in his seat. Elbows on knees, he rubbed his face tiredly.

"Come on, laddie," Douglas prompted, with a little more kindness. "Ye must know, we cannae leave anyone behind. The timeline's in enough trouble as it is."

"I don't suppose there's any point in telling you that base was abandoned?" Devon tried, without much hope.

"None." Douglas' response was firm, but not harsh. "Next, ye'll be expecting me to believe that the USS *Newfoundland* – a completely ruined ship, already hollowed out for spare parts by our people – somehow fixed and then autopiloted herself to Britain and then North Africa?"

"Is that so impossible?"

"Am Ah to believe it moved for the climate? And the *Newfoundland* also built that... that, what should Ah call it, wormhole catcher, as well, did it?"

Devon smiled. "That's what we called it, too."

"Aye. A very clever piece of improvisation. Ah'll even give ye 'may have saved the planet', but dinnae play me for a fool, Lieutenant. We continue to monitor the satellite feeds. Unless we're somehow tapped into a rerun, there seems to be a number of people who're carrying out what Ah can only describe as farming."

Douglas leaned forward, too, fixing Devon with an ice-blue

stare.

Devon sighed, puffing out his cheeks. "OK. Plan B. You have us, but can I possibly talk you into just leaving them alone? That's all they want, you know."

Douglas leaned back, crossing his legs comfortably. "Ah'm no' unsympathetic. It's a beautiful, clean world we have here, but it's no' our world. We have nae rights to it."

"But, Captain—"

"Hear me out," Douglas forestalled him. "Ye havenae seen the 2122 we just left behind. It was the world we *should* have created – no' perfect, nothing ever is, but it was *close,* Devon. Ah'd go as far as Heaven *adjacent.* A mostly fair world, mostly at peace. We lived it for ten years."

Devon frowned, interest piqued. "How did they achieve that?"

"In all kinds of ways. For a start, their technological advancement stayed ahead of population expansion, so they were always in front of the curve when it came to managing energy and environment, crop yields and pollution, that sort of thing. That's no' surprising, if the people we left behind in the 16th century gave our ancestors access to advanced knowledge and more efficient solutions to their problems. One stark difference we noted immediately was the lack of social media, so no aggressive censorship, proscription, nor social engineering either."

Devon considered. "And the population?"

"Shared out among several worlds. Out of everything, the thing most noticeable was that folks from the alternate timeline – in the main, at least – *liked* one another. Honestly, it's a future worth saving, laddie. If Ah leave people behind in the here and now, it could change everything. D'ye no' understand? We rolled the dice – were *forced* to roll the dice, by Schultz's actions – and by God, somehow, we won! Ah willnae throw all that away. We cannae bring back the world in which you and Ah grew, but Ah'll fight to ma last breath tae protect the people we just left behind. Humanity was close to fulfilling its potential, our population spread out amongst the stars. Infinite room for people to achieve their goals and dreams. We're talking Star Trek, here!"

Devon was impressed. "That's incredible. I didn't realise. We had a prisoner from that world. Badawi. He escaped to steal the tank that destroyed the *Heydrich,* but I never interrogated him and knew little of his background, until the end. Doubtless Heidi kept all the good news to herself, so that more people didn't start to question just what the hell the Schultzes were playing at!" Anger flushed Devon's face. "They hoodwinked us, Captain, but for many of us, it didn't stick." After a calming breath, he continued, "But we were talking about the people at Crater Lake. Don't they equally have the right to live how, where and when they choose?"

Douglas smiled sadly. "Ah wish it was so easy, son. Really, Ah do."

Devon sat back, crossing his arms. "So you're going to decide their fate and drag them out of their home, so *you* can live in Star Trek world? And your approach differs from Schultz's how, Captain?"

"That's harsh, Devon. And Ah dinnae think ye really believe it, but either way, it doesnae matter. In a way ye've answered yer own argument."

"I have?"

"Aye. How many people are there at Crater Lake?"

Devon shrugged. "I'm not exactly sure. Forty, maybe?"

"Forty," Douglas repeated thoughtfully. "And the fate of those few tens, if they're to be uprooted, is to be set against the lives and well-being of the billions in that future we've already seen – in which we *lived* for ten years, in fact – not to mention the billions who came before them."

"I fail to see how I've answered my own question, Captain."

"OK, Ah'll tell ye. Star Trek world, ye called it? We both called it. A perceptive choice of words, Lieutenant. Makes me recall that beautiful phrase by Gene Roddenberry. 'Logic clearly dictates that the needs of the many outweigh the needs of the few.'"

"Or the one," Devon completed the well-known quote. "I've seen that movie. Although another phrase from literature springs to my mind, Captain. '*Plus ça change, plus c'est la même chose.*'"

Douglas smiled ruefully. "Touché. Do Ah take it ye disagree?"

"In principle, no. But I'm concerned that sentiment might be used – or abused – to sanitise the removal of anyone inconvenient, where the numbers dictate. Living in the age of the 'managerium' also has its dangers for anyone who doesn't want to be deleted from someone else's spreadsheet."

Douglas sighed. "Ah'm a military man, from a military family – dyed in the wool. But during ma time as Training Director at UNASA, Ah learned first-hand that which Ah'd hitherto only suspected: politics is imperfect, even when well-intended – often, *especially* when well-intended. We frequently have no choice but to rely on the character of those implementing policy. Bad results happen, but you're right in that bad actors can make them a given. Ah accept that, but also believe that if you *genuinely* approach problems through the prism of helping as many people as ye possibly can, it usually leads you to at least make the hard calls in good faith. Aye, it's broad, it's flawed, but it's the best we have."

"I can respect that point, Captain. History may even prove you right, but I've learned a lot from working under the Schultzes, too, and it's a lot more difficult when you're living it, believe me. And for the people of Crater Lake about to be snatched from the home they've built, difficult hardly cuts it.

"I'm a weapons specialist. You might argue that's the most prejudicial job anyone can have. I never wanted to be a leader, but…"

"What is it, Lieutenant?"

"I kept the existence of their base from you, so they could retain control over their own destiny. I feel like I've failed them."

Douglas nodded. He understood. "Ye didnae give up their secret, laddie. It wasnae a secret! Still, Ah want you with me, when Ah meet them. That'll give you a chance to help them, 'cause Ah'd prefer a reasoned argument – to convince them to join us, freely. We'll see…"

It was a rare day, when the tall windows streamed sunlight across low tables and chairs grouped like little islands across the high-ceilinged classroom. Teacher's voice was a distant drone, largely indistinct from the general hubbub as she busied herself with another group. Tim approached a red-headed boy. Standing in the pool of light from a window, completely engrossed with what he held in his hands, he did not notice Tim, but placed the object on the windowsill to view it from several angles.

Ever curious, Tim edged closer to look over the boy's shoulder – no, not 'the boy', his name was Daniel. "What's that?" he asked, intrigued.

Daniel turned in surprise, not realising he had an audience. He stepped back slightly, allowing Tim to admire the model he had brought to class that day. Tim thought it was the best toy he had ever seen. "It's a monster!" his seven-year-old's voice squeaked in awe.

"No," Daniel corrected, abruptly, as only a little boy can when he *knows* he knows something. "It's a *dinosaur!*"

Tim looked blank. "What's that?"

Daniel explained. "They weren't *monsters,* they were animals."

"You mean they're real?"

"*Were* real. They lived millions of years ago."

Tim looked more closely, studying the green plastic rhinoesque figure on its base, standing next to an equally plastic and equally fake green palm tree. A massive horn sprouted from the tip of its nose, and it stood stockily on four stout legs, but there the similarities with a rhinoceros ended. It had many more horns around the top of its head, like a jagged frill, and a long, meaty tail. Although the shape of the snout was broadly rhino-like, it culminated in a hard, parrot-like beak.

Tim was transfixed. Not looking up from the model, he asked, "How big were they?"

"This one wasn't that big," Daniel explained mischievously, "but it would have filled most of this classroom."

"Whoa… And there were other ones? Even *bigger* ones?" Tim was incredulous, and although he did not yet know it, hooked for life.

Daniel nodded, smiling proudly down at his model. "It lived about seventy-five *million* years ago."

Tim's eyes widened further. "What's he called?"

"The name's on the base," Daniel pointed out.

Tim leaned closer. "Sty-rase—"

"Sty-rack."

Tim tried again. "Sty-rack-oh-say… sow?" He looked to his friend for help.

Daniel laughed. Little boys also love to know things others might *not* know. "Sty-rack-oh-sor-us. Styracosaurus!"

"Styracosaurus…" Tim repeated, his child's mind drinking in the knowledge and memorising it easily. "Can I have him?"

"No."

"Go on."

"No."

"OK." Tim leaned in again to pick up the model, viewing it all the way around before replacing it. The windowsill was at chin height, which suddenly struck him as unusual. The chairs and tables behind them appeared normal size – at least to him.

Teacher called for everyone's attention. She was freakishly tall – why had he never noticed that before? In fact, why did the room in general seem so big, its ceiling so far away? He turned back to the model dinosaur, choosing to ignore Teacher's requests until he had no choice. It was far more interesting than doing counting and stuff.

Styracosaurus' head moved to stare balefully up and then down at the little boy. Immediately, it was huge, and Tim was standing right in its way. The size of an African elephant, the creature was terrifying. Lethal horns as tall as he was, with a savage beak powerful enough to easily snap a small tree trunk, it took a step towards him. He felt the footfall through the ground and cried out as that beak opened to gobble him up, only to close his mouth disgustedly when the stinking wet tongue slapped across his face.

"No. *No.*" Tim tried to break away, but it was impossible, like falling into a warm vat of urine-flavoured bubble gum. "Stop! Leave me alone!" His voice was smothered, the tongue asphyxiating him. No matter how he tried, he could not make himself heard, when the bubble gum bubble *popped* and eyes, already wide, somehow opened again – had it been a dream? More importantly, was it *still* a dream?

"No! God, *stop!*"

Arms pinned by his duvet, he had no defence against the onslaught that followed him into the waking world. Desperately freeing an arm, he pushed back. The scaly face and hard-horned parrot beak of Styracosaurus transformed into a black and white, furry face he knew all too well. "Reiver! Oh, yack! Stop it, boy. *Please.*"

His pleading fell on deaf ears. There was no escape – no sympathy, either. Laughter filled the room. "Good morning. I thought you were gonna sleep the day away," the tone turned disapproving, "after all that booze you and Woodsey put away last night!"

Tim wiped his face, his look of disgust morphing into a fragile smile as his blurry mind recognised Clarrie – no, not merely 'Clarrie', but his new *wife.*

She leaned in to kiss him but recoiled, laughing again. "Why don't you go wash your face, before we get any further?"

Reiver *woofed* indignantly. Had he not just spent ages trying to achieve that very goal?

Tim wiped his face and sniffed his hand, laughing ruefully. He sat up and groaned. "Oh, my head. Woodsey, if you survived last night, I'm going to kill you." He applied pressure to his temples, speaking from between his hands. "Why is our guest here?"

"Natalie dropped Reiver round earlier. She's off doin' somethin' or other. I agreed to mind him, last night."

"Last night?"

She laughed again. "Don't worry. I'll let you know all the stuff you did wrong, later. Captain Baines would like a word about breakages, by the way."

"Breakages?"

"Mmm, yeah, it gets worse, too. You lifted her dress."

"*No?*"

"Yes. Apparently, the sequins were stitched into a pattern resembling the foramina within a Spinosaurus skull you once excavated."

"Oh, *nooo,*" Tim groaned, head in his hands.

Clarrie chuckled, mercilessly. "I'm not sure if she was more offended by what you did, or by your dispassionate appraisal. I promised I'd send you round to apologise as soon as you could stand."

"Actually, it was a Baryonyx skull," he muttered between his fingers.

"Seriously? That's the hill you're choosing to die on this morning?"

"Erm… S-sorry?"

She giggled. "Better. Maybe now it's time for you to do somethin' right – that is, after you've cleaned yourself up, of course."

She rose from the side of the bed to lead Reiver into their suite's lounge area. "Come on, boy. You can wait in here for a while." She turned to her new husband and winked. "After all, this ain't a peep show."

<hr>

Britain, AD1559

"Do you think we have the power resources to pull this off, Satnam?" asked Major Ford White, concerned.

"I believe so," the astrophysicist explained. "Bear in mind, last time, we needed to keep a wormhole open for three whole minutes."

"Three *whole* ones?"

"Yes," answered Patel, missing the sarcasm. "While making sure it retained its integrity for that period. The reason the wormhole shut down last time, before we were all through, was not because we had used up all our power."

Ford shuffled in his seat, leaning forward with interest. "I thought that was exactly why it shut down."

"No. We simply dropped below the line for being able to keep the wormhole open *safely*. When we designed it, we thought it would be best not to kill our people as they stepped through."

"I can see why that made the specification list," added Mother Sarah, drily.

"So what's your answer… *this time?*" Geoff Lloyd asked in a bored voice.

White turned to him. "Why do I get the feeling you're not really down with the programme here, Geoff?"

"John."

"What?"

"The name's John, remember? Please try not to forget it when in company. It's only my life on the line."

"Don't start with me, Lloyd!"

"Gentlemen, gentlemen, please." Sarah smoothed ruffled feathers. "Can we just hear what Satnam has to say?"

"Of course. Sorry, Doc. Please continue," White apologised.

They all turned to Lloyd, who leaned back in his seat huffily. "I didn't start it."

Sarah tried not to roll her eyes. She smiled, sweetly. "Satnam, please. Continue."

"Although it's almost dead at the moment, we have plenty of replenishment fuel for the *New World*'s core. Sealing off the cave before we evacuated back to *Factory Pod 4* should have protected our equipment from the elements and any unwanted guests. Even if it was handled in the roughest way possible…" He skewered Lloyd with a glare.

"You ungrateful… I came back for you – in the middle of an

invasion by several armed and highly agitated forces at once, I might add!"

"I'm sure you acted quite courageously, parking your locked and heavily armoured transport, while we climbed up that treacherous mudslide in little more than our shirtsleeves, amid a rain of arrows!"

"Crossbow bolts," Lloyd corrected pedantically, ignoring his barb. "But you're right. I did all that and still found time to block the entrance to the *New World*. Anything could have happened!"

"You fired a pair of fifty-calibre machine guns into an unstable situation right on top of a vast nuclear reactor," Patel clarified, pointedly.

Lloyd had no compunction about rolling his eyes. "Details."

"OK," White interjected. "So how do we use what we have, to travel forward in time?"

"Firstly," Patel explained, "we will need to go outside and check our wormhole drive has not been damaged. Unfortunately, when Geoff—"

"John!"

Patel sighed. "When *one* of our number collapsed the tunnel to the *New World*'s core, this did nothing to protect the plant and equipment further down the hill. Obviously, with bands of brigands running amok in these hills, we had no choice but to beat a hasty retreat."

"With *my* help," Lloyd asserted. "No need to thank me."

White ignored him and whistled softly. "You wanna go out there? We don't have many security personnel, Satnam. Besides, that kit has been out for a full winter. It gets pretty harsh up here, and that assumes none of those 'brigands', as you called them, decided to take out their frustrations on our gear, after they failed to get to us."

"The Queen still has a large force camped outside. Why don't we ask her commander for a security detail?" Patel suggested.

White sighed heavily. "Alright. Assuming we can reconnoitre safely, and we find that our equipment is still functional, or at least salvageable, well… then what?"

"We will have to repair and refuel the core, repair the power conduits linked to the wormhole drive and possibly the WHD itself. It will not be a quick fix. Especially with the limited team now at our disposal. It is fortunate we still have Jim Miller with us – that is, fortunate for us, not for him – but I believe, all things being equal, that we could send a person through."

Concern played across Sarah's face. She replaced her teacup on the table. "Erm… just one?"

"I'm not going," Lloyd stated. "And that's flat."

"Why, thank you, *Geoff*," White responded with a hard, humourless smile. "Finally, somethin' we can both agree on!"

❦

Close to the same spot, almost a hundred million years earlier, Dr Harry Bismarck was engaged in worries of his own. "Can we trust them?"

Commander Ally Coleman shrugged. "What choice do we have?"

"We have two orbital attack craft. The new one *mostly* works."

Coleman snorted. "Gnats to a falcon. I *could* send them up – if I wanted to get everyone killed."

"You think they won't kill us anyway?"

"Calm down, Harry. Lieutenant Devon said Douglas wants to talk. That's all."

"Oh, yes. Talk. That's alright, then. Did you happen to notice Devon's arm up his back when he spoke?"

She turned away from the viewport to stare at him. "No."

"So it couldn't have happened, then, could it?" Bismarck snapped, tetchily.

Coleman smirked. "You're starting to sound like our dear friend Dr Alba. Where is Brian, by the way?"

"Checking we have everything fully charged, in case we have to run for it."

Coleman laughed. "Run where? Surely he knows that's a hopeless plan – he *is* the most intelligent person among us."

Bismarck smiled for the first time. "So he tells us."

"At length." Coleman took his hands in her own. "Look, Harry, there's nothing we can do but wait."

He looked out of the viewport. "Looks like the wait's over. Better order our people back inside before the noise and downwash kill anyone."

The UNS *New World* flew low over the jagged peaks that ringed Crater Lake Base. Douglas had allowed Devon to call ahead, hoping to prevent any overreaction from base personnel. It also gave them some time to clear an area large enough for the leviathan to land nearby.

All creatures, great and small, scattered from the colossal shadow overhead, and its seismic rocket noise. One such creature was well known to Coleman's group. It was well known to her personally, too. It had very nearly succeeded in killing her. The constant ache in her ribs still marked the occasion.

Sigilmassasaurus brevicollis ran for the safety of the water. Crater Lake sat in the bowl of an extinct volcano. The river that wended its way south, through the only pass leading out, had been turned into a raging whitewater monster by torrential spring rains. *Sigilmassasaurus* would not usually have entered the river at that point, not at that time of year, but sheer panic, created by the arrival of the *New World,* scattered all caution to the wind.

It was a wild ride, filled with the sort of excitement animals normally have the sense to avoid. The dinosaur was an exceptionally powerful swimmer, born to a semi-aquatic lifestyle. Nevertheless, the power of water can be terrible, even to such a beast. Submerged, she fought to remain upright in the water, giant sail on her back working like an inverted keel, while her vastly muscular tail acted as rudder, keeping her true. Her direction was predetermined by the flow, all control limited to which way she preferred to face and which way up she wanted to be when she arrived. The sail helped; it was a strength, but also one of her greatest weaknesses. She knew that, should any of the elongated spines that gave her sail its shape be broken, it could severely damage her vertebrae, effectively breaking her back.

Many times, she was bashed into rocks and cried out, the bubbles created by her roars inconsequential amid the maelstrom. Had she any way of marking time, it would have seemed interminable. Yet even in times of disaster, opportunities sometimes arise. A large fish, also caught up in the wild current, flashed silver in front of her. She snapped instinctively, fear and anger adding force to her attack. The fish died instantly, but Sigilmassasaurus held on to the corpse. Instinct drove her to navigate for deeper, safer water. It also guided her to retain her catch. She would require rest, possibly even healing, after this adventure. A free and easy meal would be of great value once the ride was over.

She was, of course, absolutely right; animals often are, when it comes to their own well-being. However, on this occasion, she would need that meal more than she could ever have realised.

They met on the beach between the *Newfoundland*'s rescue pod and the gargantuan *New World*, impossibly huge on the ground. After checking the satellite net in orbit for a gap in the weather, both sides had agreed to wait out the driving rainstorm before venturing outside.

"I take it this is a courtesy conversation, Captain?" Coleman led.

Douglas took her measure. "You flew the *Newfoundland* to Egypt to remove the wormhole into space?"

"I did. With a small team." She glanced at Devon, surmising that Douglas had brought him in case he proved useful. After their shared involvement in the anti-Schultz resistance, she was disappointed that he had given them up.

"No." Douglas read her thoughts. "Lieutenant Devon didnae give ye away. We hacked yer own satellite net a long time ago. We saw everything it saw. The lieutenant here tried to cover for ye." With a raised eyebrow, he added, "Told me a porky pie, in fact."

Coleman had no idea what that meant, but nodded, processing the rest of the information. "And I assume you intend to uproot us, Captain? From our home? From the crops we've cultivated?"

"Careful, Commander. If ye play it any harder, ye'll break yer wee violin. Ah seem to recall that *we* initially planted those crops, ye just looked after the place after trying to blow us out of the sky."

She smiled, but then sobered. "We don't want to leave, Captain."

Douglas nodded slowly. "Ah know, lassie. And Ah also know that *you* know that Ah cannae let ye stay."

Coleman sighed heavily. "We can't fight you, nor do we wish to try. There's been too much of that already. So, I ask you… reconsider. Please."

Douglas' comm beeped in his pocket. "Excuse me." He turned away, stepping back within the ranks of the *New World* delegation. "Reading you five by five, Jill. Go ahead."

"James, something's going on here. Two things, actually. Both concerning. First, Hiro has found a rogue program in our operating system. It wasn't there before. He thinks that when Weber took control of our systems and forced us to land on the moon, there must have been a second worm that we didn't find. Hiro believes it's been unpacking over the last few days."

"What's its purpose?"

"We don't yet know. Like I said, concerning."

Douglas kicked at the sand angrily. "OK. So what's the other problem?"

"I don't know if this one's even worse, James. We're sensing the opening of a wormhole, just two klicks south of our position."

"What? How?"

"We're gonna have to get back to you on that. I suggest you ask our new friends if they know anything about it. In the meantime, be careful, honey. Something's goin' down, I can feel it. Baines out."

Douglas swore under his breath.

"Trouble, sir?"

Douglas span round to find The Sarge, magically at his elbow. "Ah don't know, Sarge, but if Ah had tae guess…"

"They're all open." Reid could hardly believe the readings he was getting. Despite the horror of what he and his team had created, he could not deny the sense of pride and achievement he also felt. "All three hundred, ma'am."

Heidi returned to the cockpit from the rear of their ship to look over his shoulder. A smile turned her lips up at the ends. "Excellent, Dr Reid."

He fidgeted uncomfortably.

"Whatever is the matter, man? Do I make you nervous?"

"Only when you're this close, ma'am."

Heidi giggled girlishly. "Well, you had better get over it. This is a small ship."

"I'd noticed, ma'am."

"Now for the next part of my plans."

"You have… erm, plans, ma'am?"

"Of course, you silly man." She giggled again, clearly in a good mood. It was terrifying. "I always have a plan – you should know that by now."

"I just thought…"

Her eyebrow rose, daring him to continue. "Well?"

"I just thought that… you know… that you wanted to… erm…"

"Spit it out, Reid!"

"To… er… destroy everything. You know, bring the final chaos because we… erm…"

"We what?" Her tone turned icy.

He swallowed. "Lost?"

"*Herr Doktor,* we have not lost. We are barely getting started."

"Once we've *encouraged* this lot aboard the *New World,* are we heading back to South America to exhume the bodies of Captain Meritus' people, sir?"

"We are, Sarge," Douglas replied. "Sadly, they're not going anywhere, so we'd better deal with the more pressing business heading our way first." He quickly reiterated Baines' dual warnings of crises.

"Never rains, sir."

The first drops hit the ground hard enough to make loud *splats* in the already saturated sand, then it began. Total deluge.

Douglas turned miserably to The Sarge. There was nothing to be said.

"Commander," Douglas hollered over the sudden storm. "Ah'd like you to come back with us. Ah guarantee your safety."

"Yeah? Throw in a towel and you got a deal."

"Reid, Douglas' people obviously have control of our satellites. You proved that, before we lost our factories at the wormhole head, when you discovered that carrier signal being bounced from our network up to their ship around the moon. Because of that intelligence, I have not used the system thus far, to avoid detection, but the time has come to be bold."

Reid swallowed hard. "Really? Again?"

"Indeed. I need to know where Douglas' ship is, currently."

"You're right, they'll almost certainly detect us, ma'am."

"I know. Hence the word *bold.* I intend to try out your new navigation system. You say we can use the wormholes to travel through time and space?"

"As long as we have accurate coordinates for our destination, yes, ma'am."

"Excellent. How were the time periods chosen?"

"At random, ma'am. As per your instructions. You asked me to cast the net wide, to allow maximum potential for gathering resources and for escaping unwanted attention. That's what I've done. We have a small number of fixed points, each forming an anchor for a spaghetti of interlinked wormholes – a manifold, if you will. Each manifold intersects with its fellows, so that we could, in theory, go almost anywhere."

"Excellent, excellent. It seems we cannot fail, Dr Reid. We have but one primary concern."

Reid raised an eyebrow, clearly thinking, *just the one?*

Heidi continued, "Douglas' new ship and support craft hugely outgun and outclass our technology, thanks to their sojourn into the alternative 2122, so this will likely be a rough ride. We dare not fly around the planet to our destination – they will launch an attack squadron and cut us off. Therefore, we must pick our route via the new network of wormholes we have created. Call up a three-dimensional map of the wormhole manifold. Good. We shall enter here and exit… here. Got that?"

"Understood. Accessing the net for the coordinates of Douglas' ship. Downloading…"

"You've found a what?" Coleman looked genuinely astonished and turned to Bismarck, always at her side.

"A wormhole," Baines elucidated. She spoke tightly, from across the table in Douglas' briefing room, clearly trying to force a calm into her voice she did not feel. "Care to explain?"

Bismarck shrugged. "We have no way of creating anything like that, Captain."

Baines' eyes bored into his.

"Seriously, Captain," Coleman chipped in, her inner soldier taking the towel and folding it neatly on the table before her, as if for inspection. "Even if we had that kind of technology, why would we use it? Firstly, we want to stay exactly where we are, and secondly, we want you to go away – no offence."

"None taken," Baines replied frostily.

"Something like this," Coleman continued, "would be certain to catch your interest. Am I wrong? So, it's the very opposite of our best interests."

Baines looked to Douglas.

He shrugged. "It's a fair point. We're hardly going to let this go, are we? And we certainly can't leave without finding out what's going on. Who knows what effect this is having on the planet – or the future."

"How long has the wormhole been there?" asked Bismarck, obvious concern playing on his face.

"Just minutes," Baines replied, studying his reaction.

"*Minutes?* And it's *still* open?" He turned to Coleman in fear. "Ally, this is bad. We've only ever seen a sustained wormhole once before, and that was the one we just closed down, because it was eating the world!"

"Actually, that's not quite true," Baines corrected him. "We created one ourselves, in order to leave Tudor England. We sustained it for three minutes."

Bismarck's jaw dropped open. "Tudor... *What?* Look, never mind. If these things are popping up all on their own now, and with no obvious power source, we are in *big* trouble, people!"

"OK." Douglas rose from the table. "Ah'll lead a scouting expedition to check it out. We'll send a probe through. Jill, make the arrangements. Commander Coleman, you and Dr Bismarck should come with us. Your local knowledge may come in handy. It's no' an order, ye'll understand, but your willingness to help would go a long way towards winning ma trust and sympathy."

Coleman smiled lopsidedly. "After a loaded invitation like that, how could we possibly refuse?"

<hr>

The river turned, only gently, but enough for the current to shove Sigilmassasaurus towards the bank. Seizing the opportunity, she added her own strength to the equation and lurched out of the whitewater maelstrom.

Head and shoulders free, she panted, with the dead fish still in her mouth, and began clawing at the soil with her forelimbs. Her back legs kicked, her powerful tail muscles contracted and pushed. Gradually, she swam and scrambled from the rapids onto the land, where the rain whipped and the wind tore at her – catching the sail on her back. Legs shaking from exertion and shock, she staggered sideways and promptly vanished…

The orbital troop carrier launched from the *New World*'s hangar, clearing the snaggletoothed ridge surrounding the Triassic caldera that was Crater Lake in seconds. The wormhole lit up on their instruments like a Belisha beacon. Corporal Thomas brought them in slowly, pointing out the anomaly to Douglas.

"Got it," the captain noted from the co-pilot's seat. "We cannae land right beside it. Look, see that small hillock, the one sticking up out of the jungle canopy, Corporal? Put us down there."

The wormhole – at least, the shadow that existed in three-dimensional space – was located immediately beside the river that drained Crater Lake. Though their devices showed it clearly on the eastern bank, it was difficult to discern with the naked eye, showing itself as no more than the merest distortion in light – a *wrongness* within the observer's field of vision.

Thomas set them down carefully, in the high winds, approximately a hundred metres from target. They would have to chop their way through the jungle to reach it.

"Full kit, everyone," Douglas called through to the passenger compartment. "Just in case we run into trouble trying to get back to the ship. Ye'll understand, Commander Coleman, Dr Bismarck, that ye'll no' be given any kind of weapon."

"I don't care," Bismarck replied with a mixture of tetchiness and fear.

Coleman merely shrugged.

Douglas nodded to the pilot. "Wait for us here, Corp."

"Yes, sir."

"Do we have Douglas' ship?"

"Ma'am," Reid acknowledged, searching through several menus to call the information she requested. "Oh."

Heidi looked across to his console. "What is it?"

"It's just that your entrance point seems to be almost exactly where the USS – I'm sorry, the UNS *New World* has landed. It's within a couple of klicks according to the IFF, ma'am. UNS? Wonder what that stands for? Never mind. I'll find us another vector."

"*Nein.* Follow my flight plan. Immediately. Do it!"

He obeyed and their ship dropped from orbit, diving to Earth.

"I expected this, Reid. Douglas will want to scoop up any of our people left behind. The closer *they* are to where we are heading, the better. After we accessed the net, they will be tracking us now, so we must strike quickly. Anywhere else on the planet below, they would launch fast ships to catch us. They will not expect this. We must dive faster, to catch them on the ground before they launch a fighter screen. Hand over control to me."

"Ma'am." Reid turned to her as she took the pilot's seat. "You can't mean… We're not going down there to poke the bear?"

"What an interesting metaphor. I suggest you fasten your crash webbing, *Herr Doktor,* in case they awake from hibernation with a sore head! We are going in."

Singh sent a message through the ship's tannoy to the captain's briefing room. "Sorry to interrupt your meeting, Captain, but we're in trouble. The *New World* is going through an engine startup sequence, all on her own!"

Baines jumped to her feet, spilling her coffee. "How?"

"Hiro doesn't know yet. But that's not all," Singh continued. "We have incoming!"

"Who?" asked Baines.

"I can only give you the where and the when, Captain. Right here, right now! Thirty seconds out."

The *New World* lurched as massive thrusters fired, raising her from the ground.

"Sandy, what the hell is going on? Get back control of this ship!" She ran from the briefing room onto the bridge. Outside, the ground was going away rapidly, when a sudden *boom* shook the whole ship.

"What the hell was that?" she demanded.

"Something hit us – a missile! Oh, crap…" Singh turned to face her. "Captain, we have no control. I don't know where she's going, and I can't stop her."

Baines slammed her fist down on the nearest console. "Heidi," she spat. "I'd lay odds."

Heidi saw the *New World* lift and turn due south as they shot past on a similar heading. The missile she launched on her run caught the behemoth on the starboard flank. The fireball was immense, though her instruments showed only superficial damage.

With no time to worry about that, Heidi poured on the power and shot over the rocky ridge, heading for the first of their artificial wormholes. There was no way the *New World* could catch her, nor launch any kind of pursuit in time to make any difference. She felt a thrill of exhilaration. Everything was going just as she had hoped.

⁓๑⁓

"Send the probe, Sergeant," Douglas ordered.

They stood on a narrow strip of riverbank, facing south, barely safe from the raging torrent on their right that threatened to break its banks any moment. Sergeant Prentice placed the drone on the ground at his feet. The wormhole swam before them, like a distortion at the edge of vision, almost impossible to see – a corner of the eye phenomenon disallowing close scrutiny.

Prentice took the remote control from his backpack, activating it. The drone also activated. Buzzing to life, it shot forward through the anomaly to boldly go… splitting dimensions and infinitives as it went.

Douglas, Sergeant Major Jennifer O'Brien and Sergeant Dewi Jones huddled around a small screen on the device Prentice held in his hands.

"Will we retain control of her via the wormhole, Adam?" asked Douglas.

"We're about to find out, sir. If not, the drone will activate its onboard artificial intelligence and continue to broadcast. This is all," he searched for the words, "*next frontier* stuff, Captain."

"No' final frontier, then?"

"Hopefully not, Captain. I'd like to get it back," Prentice replied earnestly, going full Yorkshire[1] . "Honestly, sir, we just don't know— Oh, wow!"

"Is that—"

Prentice cut Douglas off, in his enthusiasm. "Grass!"

They all shared a single grin of wonder. Veteran time travellers they may have been, but now they were actually looking *through* time, to an age far into the future, where grass was commonplace.

Continuing with the no-nonsense approach of a Yorkshireman, Prentice broke into their reverie. "Too light. We'll have to wait to get a fix on t'constellations, though it does look like dusk's on t'way. Hopefully, Lieutenant-Commander Singh will be able to work out *when* we're looking at, sir, after we're able to transmit footage back to t'*New World*."

Coleman and Bismarck craned to see over their shoulders. It

---

1. Yorkshiremen have a certain reputation for *frugality*. This is, of course, wise, but we British do enjoy our regional banter.

was a moment of wonder, of magic. Unfortunately, it was *but* a moment.

The strafing hit before they even heard the shots, or the swell of powerful rocket engines closing on their position. Large calibre bullets tore up the ground right behind them and out into the violent waters.

There was absolutely nowhere to run, and no way to survive the next attack that must surely come. The trees would provide little or no protection from such powerful weaponry, while the river offered only variation to the theme. For the merest instant, Douglas and Prentice locked terrified gazes. Each arriving at the same conclusion, they bellowed simultaneously, "JUMP!"

Chapter 4 | Rust

Six bodies in military fatigues appeared as if from the air to roll down the grassy hillside. The slope steepened into a shallow ravine, but their tumble ended at a craggy outcrop, near the mouth of the wormhole that spat them out. Untangling himself from the others, Douglas scrambled to his feet. "Take cover," he cried. Matching action to words, he half-ran, half-stumbled the last few metres to hurl himself behind a jagged rock.

His team dove after him, with no time to get their bearings before the wormhole birthed something much larger – a wicked-looking, sleek, black fighting machine. It shot through, soaring skywards.

"Get down!" Douglas hissed, checking everyone was out of sight, though he knew the pilot must have seen them plunge through before following them. *No prizes for guessing who's flying that ship!*

he thought, angrily. It was a bitter pill to swallow, especially while his people were so completely at the pilot's mercy, but who else *could* it be? "Damn her! What's she up tae!"

Coleman scrambled to his side. "You think it's Heidi?"

"Oh, aye! This whole situation has her fingerprints all o'er it!"

"What's that?" Coleman asked quietly, hesitantly reaching out to point back up the hill, and then up again. Something unnatural was happening high in the sky.

"We're in trouble, boy," was Jones' take on the situation. Barely had the words left his lips when the unthinkable happened.

"Do we hunt them down, ma'am?" Reid enquired.

"They are an irrelevance," Heidi stated uninterestedly, already focused on the next issue. "Unless they come directly under our guns, save your ammunition. We must now manipulate the wormhole to take us to our final destination. Here are the…" Her words hung in the air as both she and Reid stared out of their front viewport in shocked disbelief.

"Oh, my God…" Douglas murmured.

A hole in the sky hatched another intruder into what barely passed for their reality these days – whenever those were – this one, a giant. Lovecraftian and godlike, she hovered, dominating the heavens to throw deep shadows across the hillside. The UNS *New World* had arrived.

"What the hell is going on, Sandy?" Baines spoke softly now, a tremor of fear in her voice.

"We seem to have opened a wormhole and jumped, Captain."

"Jumped? To another time, another place? Give me something!"

Singh blew out a deep breath, shaking his head. "I don't even have the 'where' this time. I'm completely lost."

A comm call made them both jump.

"Bridge," Baines answered.

"Captain. This is Hiro. What's happening?"

Baines shook her head, astounded. "I wish I knew."

"Th-that's your ship, Captain," Coleman stuttered.

Douglas' mouth was open, but speech eluded him.

The gap in their conversation was suddenly filled by another voice, cutting through their shock to fill up the corners – just in case they had any room left in their lives for fear. Even above the rocket noise, they heard it.

Coleman swallowed, slowly turning. "Oh, no."

Bismarck joined them. He recognised it, too. "I know that sound," he called above the apocalyptic roar overhead.

Coleman shook Douglas to his senses. "We have to go!"

"Wha...?"

She turned his head slowly. Refocusing, he saw movement in the distance, though less far into the distance than he would have liked. "Oh, crap!"

Sigilmassasaurus brevicollis roared again. Even apex predators knew fear, and after the last few minutes of her life it was hardly surprising that she, too, was in a state of terror. Unfortunately, her coping mechanism was to spread it around.

Desperately, Douglas weighed his options. Hide in plain view, when several tons of muscle with a front end made of teeth bore down on his position, or show himself to Heidi? It was no choice, but fortunately, he never had to make it.

"Quickly! We cannot stay here! Feed these coordinates into wormhole navigation. Do it, before they fire on us!" Heidi screamed.

With fumbling fingers, Reid complied as quickly as he could.

The wormhole shimmered, ripples crossing the event horizon from the outer edge inwards to a central vanishing point. For the observer, it was like watching the rings on a pond after a pebble splash, but in reverse.

"N-now. It's done! Go, go, go!" he called back, frantically.

Their little ship banked sharply on a return vector for the

wormhole. Meanwhile, higher in the sky, the *New World* also turned, the giant ship's movement strangely following Heidi's attack craft like she had it on a string. She tracked it on her instrument panel, but with no time left to ponder the enemy's behaviour, she focused all her attention on threading the eye of the needle. If the *New World* launched missiles, Heidi's small vessel would be obliterated, and they would fly through the wormhole in a million charred pieces. Indeed, she could only assume their reluctance to fire on her, thus far, was because they had a team on the ground. If she was right, then her own reticence to fire on the people below had proved prescient, but it was a mystery for later. Whatever her captain's reasons, the *New World* did *not* fire, allowing Heidi to navigate into the wormhole, albeit at breakneck speed. Reid's cry of fear choked off, instantly, as they shot through the nothingness outside four-dimensional space–time.

As Heidi's ship vanished, Douglas immediately ordered his people to hide on the opposite side of the rocks sheltering them.

He pulled a small electronic telescope from his jacket pocket, the better to see what the dinosaur was up to. Dusk would be upon them soon, but he could make out the animal clearly enough as she tore at something on the ground, pinned under a massive, taloned foot. Ripping gory chunks of meat, bone and innards from the corpse, she threw them to the back of her throat in a bird–like manner, never chewing, merely swallowing – a muscular action, often with jaws wide. He had seen footage of chicks in a nest eating that way and imagined a nest full of Sigilmassasaurus. He shuddered. The animal had no table manners at all, but the disposal of her dinner was certainly efficient. Zoom and digital enhancement helped him clear up the image enough to see a long, silver, tubular something… "Is that a fish?"

O'Brien moved close. "What's it doing?" she asked, urgently.

"Eating," Douglas replied dumbly. "Oh, no."

"Captain?"

"It's eating a fish, but no kind of fish Ah've ever seen." He handed her the scope. "Ah dinnae think we're back in Kansas, Dorothy."

O'Brien accepted it, adjusting for her own sight. "That's probably good for us."

"Aye. At least it's eaten."

She shrugged. "That too, I guess."

Douglas frowned. "What else?"

O'Brien returned his telescope with a wry grin. "If you'd called me Toto, we'd *really* have had a problem."

Douglas snorted, but their gallows humour was short-lived when the *New World* manoeuvred above them to face back the way she had arrived. Douglas pulled out his comm. "Douglas to *New World. New World,* come in."

"*James?*" Baines sounded frantic. "*What are you doing here? We left you at Crater Lake.*"

"We had tae jump for it. Ah thought *ye'd* followed *us.* Did ye no'?"

"*James, we have no control of the ship. None! Some kind of worm has unpacked within our operating system, just like the one Weber unleashed on us, around the moon. We seem to be tracking—*"

"Jill!" Douglas was on his feet, screaming at the heavens, "*Jill!*" but the heavens were empty, the *New World,* vanished.

"Captain, get down!" O'Brien grabbed him roughly, dragging him back behind their cover.

"Ah'm sorry," he muttered, stunned. The sudden silence was all encompassing.

"Captain?" Prentice hissed, crawling towards him, whispering now the ships were gone.

"Adam. What is it?"

"Did you notice how our ship moved, sir?"

Douglas shook his head blearily, trying to clear his thoughts. "No, laddie. Ah was focused on that monster down the valley."

"Sigilmassasaurus brevicollis," Bismarck supplied tonelessly.

Douglas whished anxiously. "Thanks, but Ah think we already met once before… briefly… the first time we evacuated Crater Lake. Just one of the many occasions Ah felt sure Heidi was done for." He cursed under his breath.

"Aye, I know the feeling," Prentice continued. "Anyroad, I was watching t'*New World,* and she matched vectors with the Schultz vessel exactly – as if she was *slaved* to Heidi's ship, sir."

"Not a term you throw around lightly when dealing with the Schultzes."

"No, sir."

"So you think Heidi may have taken control of ma ship *remotely?*" Baffled, Prentice shook his head helplessly.

The ship's departure had prevented anyone but Douglas from hearing Baines' communication, so he quickly disseminated what he knew. "Ideas, people?"

"Look at this, isn'it." Jones gestured up the opposite slope of the ravine they were in.

They all turned, Douglas using his telescope again. "OK. That's better news. Here." He passed the scope once more to O'Brien.

She scanned the opposing bank. "Goats! But that must mean…"

"That we're within a few *million* years of civilisation," Bismarck rained on their parade.

"Look." Prentice pointed down the valley. "The dinosaur's got wind of 'em."

"He's not the only one," Jones replied nasally, holding his nose. "They're not subtle, boy."

"It's following them," Prentice continued. "Hope they're fast."

"Better lamb chops than long pig, Sergeant," Douglas stated, darkly.

"Aye, sir." Prentice turned onto his back, leaning against the sloping rock face that was their shelter. "We should check on the wormhole, Captain. It's still there."

"Perhaps we could make it back to Crater Lake?" suggested Coleman.

Douglas nodded. "OK, Adam. Go alone. You'll attract less attention. Be careful, laddie, and stay low."

Prentice set off, crawling across several metres of grassy hillside. When they gambolled through from Crater Lake, they had been fortunate. Bordering the short grass that softened their landing lay a scree of sharp quartz and granite to one side, with ankle-breaking heather to the other.

He moved easily through the goat-nipped middle way, reaching the wormhole, so far, without incident. To the naked eye, it was a perfect circle, roughly seven metres in diameter. Easily big enough for Heidi's small craft, but an order of magnitude too small for the *New World*. He could only surmise that whatever took over their ship had indeed linked the two craft in some way, feeding space–time coordinates from one to the other.

If Heidi has somehow taken control of… Prentice could not bring himself to finish the thought. It was too awful.

As the daylight faded, it became increasingly difficult to pick the wormhole out from its surroundings – an incredibly dangerous new feature to the landscape. He shivered at the thought, and was considering what might happen to anyone, human or otherwise, who just happened by in the darkness, when something else snagged his attention – something at the foot of the wormhole mouth, something seemingly, impossibly, *within* the event horizon. A device of some kind. It shimmered. He could barely make it out, the technology so far over his head that all he could think to do was reach out for it.

It was not there.

He crawled around the back of the anomaly. It had no thickness at all, hanging in mid-air, in all its two-dimensional weirdness. Once around the other side, he looked again. The device was still there, as before, only perceivable at the periphery of vision. He reached out for a second time. Pointless. He may as well have tried reaching into a mirror. There was a slight tingle, like a tightening of his skin, but nothing more. Frustrated by failure, he scrambled back to make his report.

After listening carefully, Douglas asked, "Where's the drone?"

"Don't know, sir." Prentice admitted. "When we jumped through, I hit the park command. Didn't want it giving away our position, sir. It's taken itself off somewhere."

"Can you recall it?"

"Yes, sir. Recommend we wait until that dinosaur is well away first, though, sir."

"Agreed. Once we're alone again and clear, we'll send it high, to look around and then through the wormhole, before we step back through. Ah'd rather not assume Crater Lake's still on the other side. Somehow, Ah cannae see Heidi just going for a wee peek before shooting straight back again."

Prentice nodded. "'Appen so, sir. There's something else, an' all." He gestured back to the wormhole. "Did you see that ripple effect cross the event horizon before they went back through? Something changed. For all we know, it could lead anywhere now."

The little ship shot out into bright sunshine, very obviously a world away from where they were but a moment before.

"That's the… the *Last Word?*" Reid's confusion was clear in his voice. "I thought I recognised the coordinates, but I wasn't sure. Why return here?"

"Because there is something aboard that ship that I need." Heidi explained. "A diary."

"A *diary?*"

"Of sorts. We'll set down here." She landed quickly, undid the clasp on her flight harness and stepped into the rear compartment to arm and equip herself for a climb. "You remain with the ship."

"Yes, *ma'am,*" Reid replied, sardonically. He was yet to recover from the idea that Heidi had kept a diary. Somehow, he doubted it contained angst about acne or boys.

A smile quirked her lips. "Not really the sporting type, are you?"

"No, I am *not,* ma'am."

Heidi opened the side hatch. "I won't be—"

"Wait!" he interrupted. "There's another— Oh, my God!"

"What?"

"The *New World!* She's here!"

High above, Baines was at a real low. "Do we know where we are *now?*"

Singh stuttered and tripped over his words. Eventually, he managed, "The *Last Word!*"

Various sensors and cameras clearly showed Heidi's ship far below them. "What the hell is she playing at? No, scratch that." Baines changed her mind as the light of murder entered her eyes. "Can we launch missiles?"

Singh turned, sadly shaking his head. "We still have no control, Captain."

Baines hailed engineering. "Hiro, I still have no control over my ship! What do you propose to do about it?"

"Take off!" Heidi ordered. "Come back for me when I call."

"I… *What?* Fly away? What if they start shooting at me?" Reid shot back, the edge of hysteria in his voice.

Heidi's smile spread to a grin. "What if they fire while you're *not* flying away? Go!"

Without further ado, she leapt from the ship and ran to the edge of the escarpment. She heard Reid take off behind but could spare none of her attention for that. Below, down the steep-sided embankment, lay what was once the most powerful ship in the Schultz Dawn Fleet – the *Last Word.* Captain Baines' attack left her a broken husk, but hidden somewhere within her darkened corridors, there remained a piece of information that might prove far more powerful than a mere battleship. It might just be the missing piece that would allow Heidi total freedom from the society she despised. Even out here, a hundred million years before the dawn of man, it was a fuel economy. *Time to change that,* she thought as she stepped over the edge to slide down the loose surface.

Nature was already reclaiming the area. Green shoots were everywhere, all across the steep embankment. Within a couple of years, the ship would be practically indistinguishable from the hillside where she lay.

The noise of the ships above was growing painful. Leaning against the hull of the dead ship, she produced earplugs from a vest pocket and inserted them. That was the first time she looked up. What she saw puzzled her.

She expected to see Reid running for the hills, hoping to lose his tail among the smaller, tighter valleys. Instead, he flew to and fro across the wider basin where the *Last Word* lay. For a spacecraft, the few miles were a mere hop and took no time at all. Harder to understand was why the *New World,* in a clumsy, elephantine way, seemed to follow, while appearing to have no weapons trained. She deployed no fighter screen, either. It was odd. More than that, it was an unknown. Heidi hated those, but had no time to ponder the situation now. She had a job to do. Finding a suitable crack in the hull, she vanished inside.

<hr>

"It's knackered!" Prentice spat. "Must have gotten caught in the downwash from the ships, Captain. Sent it off."

When the drone failed to answer their call, they began a search pattern of the local area. The device was quickly found, but, as Prentice so succinctly described, several of its multiple rotors were damaged, perhaps from the colossal downwash itself, perhaps from when it hit the ground.

Douglas leaned over his shoulder to take a look. "Can it be fixed, Adam?"

"Not sure, sir. Probably, but not here. We'll need parts. I can give it a try, sir."

"OK. Well, for now, what about the camera? Did that survive?"

Prentice considered. "*Maybe.* I'll check, sir." After a few moments' tinkering, the onboard cameras and sensors came back to life.

"Good job, laddie." Douglas turned to the rest of the group. "Right, listen up. We have the drone's eyes and ears, *but,* if we pop it through the wormhole, we'll have no way of retrieving it, bar stepping through ourselves. Of course, that willnae be a problem if the wormhole leads back to Crater Lake. However, if it leads somewhere else, then we'll have a decision to make. So, before we take our single shot, Ah want to find out more about where we are right now. God alone knows what's going on here, so the more we can find out, the better. We still need to record the constellations for Sandy to examine, anyway, and it'll be a wee while before full dark, so we've time to kill. That said, and before we lose the light completely, we'll climb to the top of this hill we're on and take a look around.

"Adam, stash the drone under the heather there 'til we get back. Any questions? No? Good. Let's move out."

A thought struck, and Heidi was tempted to contact Reid, ordering him to attack. If the *New World* was indeed a sitting duck – or at least, in some way incapacitated – they might have a golden opportunity. The idea was seductive, but then maybe an attack would be shortsighted, especially when she considered the pilot. Reid was a man fashioned by nature to run away, rather than to fight. He might lose her ship through incompetence or cowardice, but there was more to it than that. The *New World* was behaving strangely, and this fed a suspicion growing in her mind. She sighed, once more pushing the idea aside. Her environment was extremely dangerous and warranted her full attention.

Climbing through the split in the *Last Word*'s hull required dexterity *and* concentration. The honeycomb construction provided great strength and many voids through which engineers could run their myriad conduits. Unfortunately, it also provided many treacherous voids to fall into – and then there were the jagged edges. Eventually, she struggled through to the interior, suffering no more than a torn sleeve.

A *bump* sounded from within the ship. Not a heavy sound – more like something, or someone, alighting onto a hollow surface. The scratches and rustles that followed from deep inside the darkened heart of the dead vessel would have sent a shiver down the spine of even the hardiest soul, but not Heidi Schultz. No one would ever accuse her of being faint-hearted, but more to the point, she still wore the earplugs.

The light was falling fast as they reached the summit. Douglas took out his telescope, scanning the horizon in a full 360-degree sweep. Whether they were technically at the summit was open to debate, as the mountaintop was given over to relatively flat moorland for some miles in every direction.

He looked again, taking it all in more slowly this time. Facing just a little east of due north, he froze.

"What is it, Captain?" O'Brien queried.

"Not sure." He zoomed the device to maximum, holding it two-handed to limit shake. "The light's not quite good enough to see, but dead ahead of me, there," he raised his arm to point, "it looks like there may be a settlement of some kind. Here, Jen, take a look. Your eyes are younger than mine." Again, he handed her the scope, this time with a heavy sigh. "That was such an old man thing to say."

She grinned, closing one eye to squint into the lens. Handing it back, she was forced to admit, "I can't say for sure, either. Tried night-vision, too, but we're sort of in the twilight 'in-between'." Turning to the group at large, she asked, "Any of you guys have any theories about where we are?"

"Looks like Yorkshire, before everything was built over," Prentice suggested, just as Jones said it looked like Wales.

Douglas smiled. "Ah was just thinking it looked like Scotland, in the Borders."

Prentice looked at him, strangely. "You don't think...?"

"That this place looks like the Cheviots?" Douglas completed the question for him.

"Could we be back at the *New World?*" Jones asked excitedly.

"That is, the *old* world, *New World?*"

Douglas scratched the new stubble on his chin. "Ah don't know. Might just be wishful thinking. Let's face it, this type of grassy upland covered most of northern Europe, that wasnae forested, for untold millennia. We could be anywhere."

"Or any when," O'Brien added, darkly.

"I might be able to narrow that down." Prentice bent to pick something up. "Look at this. Metal, sir." He handed a small block to Douglas, who tossed it a few times in his hand.

"Aye, it's heavy. Badly corroded, too." He rubbed it between finger and thumb, sniffing the residue. "Scratch that, badly *rusted.* It's iron. Question is, who fashioned it? It doesnae look natural."

"And who dropped it, and more to the point, why?" Prentice added. "It might have little or no value to us, but for earlier cultures…"

"What are you saying?" asked Douglas.

"We've picked up no kind of radio or digital traffic, Captain. I'm simply saying that making this much iron would have been a lot of work for someone from a primitive society. They wouldn't have discarded it lightly. They may have dropped it accidentally, but if they didn't, that might suggest that, wherever we are, there are dangers in this land."

O'Brien took out her own comm to search for any signals or broadcasts. "You're right. Doesn't seem like these guys, whoever they are, have discovered radio waves yet. Assuming that *is* a settlement over there, and not just a bunch o' rocks, and if what you have in your hand there represents the limit of the tech in these parts, I don't think we're gonna be finding a hotel tonight, Captain."

"Well, it's no surprise," Bismarck allowed. "The technological age covers an almost immeasurably tiny slice of the world's history."

"Can we try and stay a little glass-half-full, guys?" Coleman interrupted. "And what do you mean the old-world-new-world?"

Douglas briefly explained their short stay in AD1558.

Coleman whistled. "So, it really was you guys who changed the future. 1943 Germany was certainly a surprise for the Schultzes. Not that it stopped them from taking what they had and breaking it anyway. Guess you can't keep a good nut-job dictator down, huh?"

"You could argue that, by taking us back through time in the first instance, they gave us an opportunity to save the human race that we wouldn't otherwise have had," Bismarck postulated.

Douglas glowered at him. "Ye may as well thank the snake that bites the lion that's about to bite yer head off!" He rubbed tiredness from his eyes as the recent adrenalin broke down in his system. "Look, this is getting us nowhere. We'll head back to the wormhole, before we lose the light altogether. Dinnae want any twisted ankles adding to our woes. We should be able to grab some footage of the stars easily in a wee while. It's looking like a clear night."

"Sounds cold," Bismarck noted.

"At least it's not raining," O'Brien chipped in. "The way it was going back at Crater Lake, I only hope we get back before your guys get washed out!"

Douglas merely nodded, accepting Bismarck's assessment. "We should send the probe through this evening. See where we stand, eh?"

Behind a number of boulders deposited by an ice age, a watcher hid, waiting for them to leave. Understandably cautious, the scout evaluated the situation – the age-old conundrum when facing creatures unknown: Assess? Ambush? Retreat? Stealth was the thread that bound all three, and it had been working pretty well, thus far. After all, there was no need for haste. This was their territory, so they followed.

"It's been hours!" Dr Brian Alba stated, slamming his fist down on the table in frustration. The continued absence of both

Commander Coleman and their glorious and masterful civilian leader – as he referred to Bismarck – was making the inhabitants of Crater Lake anxious.

It was worthy of note that they no longer considered themselves *crew.* Perhaps the loss of the USS *Newfoundland* had dealt the final blow in that regard, though Alba still hoped they might find a way to fix the old ship in orbit and retrieve her, but all that was for the future. For the moment, they had other problems.

"Well?" Alba continued. "Do we go looking for them, or stay here and do nothing?" As a marine and irrigation engineer, he was recently tasked with the laying of a pipeline out into the lake. Hardly an unqualified success – grave markers in their fields bore silent witness to that – yet their efforts *had* prevented a water shortage from killing last season's crops.

This season had so far handed them the reverse problem. Without significant and immediate attention given to drainage, their crops might be destroyed, washed away by the monsoonal weather. The idea of taking time out to go looking for people stupid enough to get themselves lost annoyed Alba.

One of his engineers raised a hand. "If we do go looking for them, perhaps we could wait until the rain stops?"

Alba hung his head. "Give me strength. I never thought I'd miss Bismarck. Sergeant!" He skewered the NCO Coleman most trusted with a glare. "What do you say?"

"I can have a team geared up and ready to go in ten minutes, sir. If Lieutenant McBride agrees."

"Finally!" Alba slapped the table again. "Someone's awake!"

"But that's not what the commander told us to do," the sergeant continued. "She said we should not come after her or Dr Bismarck, and should look to ourselves, if anything went wrong on the enemy ship. Well, I would guess – as the ship lifted without warning just after Coleman's party left, and rushed off in pursuit of Schultz – that something *has* gone wrong, wouldn't you, Doctor?"

Alba calmed. "She said that?"

The sergeant nodded. "I'm not saying we should do nothing. I'm just saying that we have limited resources. So, if the *New World* people are in trouble, despite their frankly vast resources…"

"What are you saying?" pushed Alba. "By the way, what's your name again?"

"Zimmermann, sir. Sergeant Helmut Zimmermann."

"Alright, I don't need your whole family tree, damnit! What's your point, Zimmermann?"

The sergeant eyed Alba wryly, but without rancour. "Simply this, *sir*." His inflection made others seated around the table smirk. "If we're going to make a plan, it had better be a good one."

Baines paced her bridge like a caged bear. "Extreme times call for extreme measures."

"Captain?" asked Singh, distractedly, though he was getting nowhere with the controls.

Baines opened a channel. "Sergeant Jackson?"

"*Ma'am,*" came the immediate response.

"Put together a security detail and bring Richard Weber to the bridge. On the double, Sarge."

"*On our way, Captain – out.*"

Baines forced herself to sit. "Are we still tracking Schultz, Sandy?"

"Yes and no, Captain. We're tracking her ship. However, just as we arrived, she ran out of it, towards the wreck of the *Last Word.*"

"Still no weapons?" she asked, frustratedly.

He turned in his seat, shaking his head. "What could she be up to?"

"I hate to think. Maybe Weber will give us some answers."

"Might need some persuading, Captain."

Baines glowered. "We can hope." She opened a second channel to Chief Nassaki.

"*Engineering.*"

"Hiro, I need something from you. I need you to scribble a note for me, too."

Due to the orientation of the ship, Heidi walked across the wall of a large room. The fuselage of the vessel had settled facing mostly down the slope leading into the ravine. Hitting the bottom broke her back, making it possible for Heidi to gain entrance – and for Douglas to escape, she remembered furiously – but at least she was in.

The *Last Word.* Her grandfather's masterpiece, now no more than a rusting ruin, hollowed out by her enemies. Down in the core of the ship, the only illumination came from the flashlight fixed to her assault rifle and the head torch she wore.

A chittering echoed around the walls, rebounding off every hard surface. It would have been next to impossible to guess its source or location, even if she had heard it. Running the torchlight over and around her environment cast fast-moving shadows everywhere. She stopped walking to steady the beam and checked again. Nothing.

Something touched her face. She recoiled instinctively, shining the light up above her head. Cracks in the superstructure allowed dripping water to fall into the room. She assumed they ran all the way to the upper hull. Though, as the weather was fine outside, she reasoned it to be a long-term issue. Stepping blindly into a fetid pool in the darkness would not enhance her day, so she made a note that somewhere above, there would probably be a room holding an unknown volume of water.

She tasted it, as it ran down her face and over her lips. Rust. *Could be worse. Better keep moving.* A crash from behind made her spin, torchlight flashing wildly. *Did I cause that?* She could see no movement. Her heart hammered. Were she more spiritual in temperament, she might have considered how many people recently lost their lives inside the vessel, and how angry they might be – quite possibly at her. However, Heidi dismissed all such thoughts as nonsense. As far as she was concerned, the dead were merely threats ticked off her to-do list.

She was about to move on when another crash, much louder this time, stalled her. She span round again, peering ahead. Despite herself, these crashes in the darkness were raising the hairs on the back of her neck. She moved forward cautiously, towards the latest.

A protracted *hiss* susurrated past her, flowing around corners as it rebounded from surface to surface. Again, earplugs deprived her of the sensitivity to hear it. Then there was another sound, just loud enough for her to react. She stopped in her tracks. It was hard to make out. Could it have been a voice? *Impossible,* she thought, bolstering her confidence with logic. *If Douglas' people had managed to land, I would have heard well in advance of any incursion into this ship.*

Heidi despised cowardice, but she was only human. The claustrophobic darkness, coupled with strange bumps and bangs, was beginning to gnaw, even at her resolve. *Let us get this over with.* She started forward again with purpose, heading for the crew quarters. Despite her loathing for the man, she was grateful to Meritus for the diligent way in which he had cleared the corpses from the ship. She had trip hazards enough to deal with.

The central corridor was a problem. She shone her torch upwards and up again, near fifty metres. Though not actually vertical, it was much too steep to climb unaided – a high-traffic area deliberately designed with smooth floors and walls, free of any protrusions or safety risks to menace the crew.

She sighed. Leaning her rifle against a wall with its light shining upwards, she pulled a rope from over one shoulder and unpacked climbing anchors and carabiner clips from her vest pockets. She had come prepared for this. The anchors were military spec and came with small blast caps that allowed them to fire into a rock face – or a mild-steel floor. Like an expansion bolt, they used a central pin, widened at the end, to spread a pre-split outer sleeve. When *in situ,* the more pulling force a user applied, the more secure the fixing became.

Heidi reached as high as she could to tap an anchor against the almost vertical corridor floor. The bang was deafening within the metallic confines of the ship. The plugs she still wore protected her hearing, muffling both the bang and the rebounding echoes. They also subdued the other sounds that woke up around the ship, sounds of agitation and skittering.

Unaware, Heidi assembled her equipment, stepping into a climbing girdle and knotting the rope securely through its loops. Taking a second anchor, she blasted it into the metal surface at hip height and stepped onto it, pulling herself up by the one above her head. Securing the rope, and using carabiners, she worked her way upwards, securing small but immensely strong titanium anchor points every couple of metres.

By the time she reached the room she wanted, she was feeling the strain. The constant loud bangs in a confined space, along with the exertion of climbing, had given her a thumping headache. Silently, she cursed herself for not bringing a drinking flask. Never mind, it would only have added weight. Besides, she was close to her goal now, and certainly had no intention of hanging around, literally or metaphorically.

Every cop show there ever was has used the phrase 'the room was turned over', but in this case it was the literal truth. Hanging from the door frame, lowering herself down onto what was once a wall, she walked across the sloping surface with care, holding on to anything that remained secure. With the rifle strapped across her back, she relied on the head torch to see. This task required a different kind of rifling, that of going through her own spartan belongings. Heidi felt little or no emotional attachment to objects, and precious little to people, but even to her, it felt uncomfortable. Almost like she was going through her things after she had died. When she boarded the wreck more than seven months ago, to send the signal that summoned her grandfather from the future, it never occurred to her that she might need this data pad and its contents. After all, despite the *New World* having dragged them over the edge, there were three other warships on the way to assist them. A sudden fury burned through her – so much waste. *Never mind.*

They will pay. They will all pay. One last mission, one last acquisition, and I will be unstoppable. Who knows, perhaps overhead I have even been handed a serendipitous superweapon?

Baines pushed Weber down into a seat on the bridge and leaned forward on its arms, menacing. "What have you done, Richard?"

Weber drew away from her, as much as he was able, but said nothing.

"We know you created the worm that shut down our operating system, almost crashing us into the moon. We got rid of it, so what have you done now?"

"If you have rid your systems of my work, then I fail to see how I might help you?"

Baines smiled. "I thought you'd say that. You know, when I took this post – that is, on the old *New World* – I never thought I would end up interrogating people, but it's surprising what you pick up along the way. Now, I'm asking nicely, Richard, tell me what you've done."

"Or?"

She stepped back, thoughtfully. "You've met my chief engineer, I believe? Hiro Nassaki? Yes, I thought you'd remember him. He's a great guy, always fixing and building things – always tinkering – he loves it. Some years ago, he built something that, I gotta admit, took me by surprise. I have it here." She produced a small taser from her pocket. "He put this together, on his own dime," she explained matter-of-factly, "so that he could use it to find out what had happened to his brother, Aito. I *know* you know him. The information was hidden from us, you see, locked away inside the head of another old friend of yours, Bevel Lemelisk, remember him?"

Weber's face twisted into a sneer. "I heard he escaped."

"Oh, no. We let him go. With Del Bond – you *must* remember how that went down for your side. Of course, that was after he recovered."

"Recovered?"

"From this." She waved the taser under his nose. "That Hiro, he's such a character. You know he offered to draw me a graph to scientifically explain how this thing delivers the pain. It was all well over *my* head, but luckily, all you need to know in order to use it, is which buttons to press. Am I pressing any of your buttons yet, Richard?"

Weber swallowed. "I will never betray my cause."

"*Your* cause?" She laughed. "The Schultz cause never made provision for you, young man. And you're still a young man, Richard. It doesn't have to end this way."

"Are you threatening to kill me, Captain?"

She smiled again. "Not yet. Not while we have other fun choices."

"Oh, come on!" Prentice snapped crossly, kicking the heather. "It's gone, Captain. Some animal, or summat, must have come along and taken it."

"Or someone," Douglas added, quietly.

Prentice stopped ranting to look at his captain quizzically. After a moment, he realised that Douglas was looking not at him, but over his shoulder. He turned slowly. "Oh, well. That explains that, then."

There were ten of them. In the failing light of dusk, it was difficult to make out fine detail, but their garments were of a coarse cloth, possibly wool, dyed a dark colour. Difficult to be certain, Douglas suspected it might be blue. He felt a creeping horror across his shoulders and neck, making every hair and nerve stand up on end. If he was right, and their clothes *were* blue, that might imply they were dyed with woad. That was suggestive. Add the rawhide shoes they wore, of soft, untanned leather, and a picture began to emerge – their iron-headed spears made it almost conclusive.

Added to the spear, one of the men also wore a short sword at his belt and carried an oval shield fashioned from timber, faced with a skin of hammered bronze. Clearly a high-status item, the shield displayed a supporting rib running top to bottom, bisecting a roundel at its centre, with two smaller, decorative roundels at each end. A beautiful piece of workmanship, it obviously marked him as an elite and it was he who stepped forward.

Though not tall, the word 'brute' tripped uncharitably across Douglas' mind before he could stop it. The man spoke. It was a completely unintelligible string of guttural aggression and phlegm, though for all Douglas knew, he may have been commenting on the fair weather they were having.

"Their poetry must really be something," O'Brien quipped.

Jones' jaw dropped. "Did he just accuse us of bringing the dragon?"

They all turned to him in astonishment. "You understood that?" Douglas demanded, urgently.

Jones shrugged, not quite sure *what* he had heard. "I think I caught *ti* and *draig.* I… I don't know, sir."

"*Dragon?*" O'Brien asked in disbelief.

Douglas waved her down. "Hang on. Jones, could they be speaking a form of ancient Welsh?"

Again, Jones shrugged. "Not like any Welsh I ever heard, isn'it. Still…"

"But isn't Welsh from a Brittonic root?" Douglas tried again. "If these men are Celts, might you be able to communicate with them… just a wee bit?" The desperate hope in his voice sounded pathetic, even to his own ears.

The spearmen looked from one to another, surreptitiously moving to surround the newcomers.

"This doesn't feel good," O'Brien noted, taking her rifle from around her shoulders, readying to fire.

"If it is Welsh, like, or Brittonic, or whatever," Jones continued, "then *draig* might also mean warrior. I mean, we *are* soldiers, right?"

"Aye," Prentice joined the discussion, "but I wonder if they know that."

"Oh, man," Coleman groaned. "They won't recognise our weapons, will they?"

"They will in a minute," O'Brien retorted, moving to a fighting stance. "These stone-age guys probably won't tolerate *any* strong-looking strangers on their turf, Captain."

"Ah think we're in the Iron Age, but Ah take your point. Easy, everyone," Douglas calmed them. "Stand easy – but stay ready. Now, Commander Coleman, what was your point about our weapons?"

"Just that, maybe, they really were talking about a dragon."

Douglas looked round sharply. "Oh, crap!"

Chapter 5 | Here be Dragons

Dr Alba's comm binged. Interrupted from his work, he glared at it, answering crossly. "What is it?"

The call was from Lieutenant McBride. *"Doctor, we have incoming. It's the dropship that Commander Coleman was riding."*

The group around the meeting table visibly relaxed. "That's good news, Lieutenant," Alba answered for them. "Send them a landing vector. Alba ou—"

"Wait, Doctor! There's a problem."

The dropship was painted in greens and khaki camouflage markings, with the UNASA logo on its sides. Rain bounced off it hard enough to blur its edges as the craft landed alongside Crater Lake in mid-Cretaceous Britain.

"Perhaps I'll give it a minute," Corporal Thomas announced.

No one aboard the *Newfoundland*'s rescue pod blamed him, but eager to interrogate the pilot, McBride sent their personnel carrier to pick him up. The all-electric four-wheeler, stolen by Heidi from Captain Baines, just prior to her one-legged race with a hunting Tyrannotitan in Patagonia, was almost as well-travelled as the man it rescued from the weather. Thomas leapt aboard gratefully, yet the second or two between vehicles was still like walking through a waterfall.

The truck slipped and skipped, wide tyres designed for fine Martian sands working like paddles to dig through the mud and deliver Thomas into the pod's hangar. Rainwater sluiced from its sides as it left a trail of mucky 'elevens' across the deck plates.

Thomas jumped out of the passenger door. "Thanks for sending a lift, Lieutenant. Permission to come aboard, sir."

McBride returned Thomas' salute stiffly. Though he was in camp Coleman, and no Schultz fanatic, working with enemy combatants was still new to him and chafed. "You're not a flight officer?"

Thomas relaxed with a smile. "I left the military ten years ago. Believe it or not, I spent most of the last decade working public transport – airbuses, mostly. When Captain Douglas recalled us all, to stop Heidi from destroying the future, it was a small matter to transfer my skills."

"I wish you had not returned," McBride stated tersely.

Thomas scratched his ear. "As I understand it, if we hadn't, that wormhole your ex-bosses opened would have consumed the entire planet."

"We closed that wormhole! Through our own ingenuity and courage!"

"True. But had our people not caused a massive distraction, yours would have been a courageous suicide when those tanks turned and blew you out of the sky – not to mention the fact that we hauled most of your side out of there, immediately before the place was turned to ash."

"I—"

"*Lieutenant.*" Thomas waved the younger man down before he could bluster further. "Can't we just agree that we all had our parts to play, and we need each other now?"

McBride bit his lip, swallowing his resentment. "Very well, Corporal. You had better come with me and tell us what happened out there."

Thomas' face clouded, and when he spoke, worry brought his native Birmingham accent even further to the fore. "I'll tell ya worra can, but it ay much."

⸺ ◎ ⸺

Patagonia

The battery was dead. No surprise after several months. Unable to transfer the information, Heidi tucked the precious data pad into her combat vest before making her way back to the door. She jumped, lithely, to hang from the frame. Using her legs to scramble up the wall, she pulled herself up to stand in the threshold over a deep drop. Her earlier climb up the near-vertical central passage had revealed an open door into a large room, not far below where she now stood. Although mostly in shadow, a crack on its far side showed daylight. She had noted the split, higher up on the hull, on her way down from the escarpment above. Inaccessible from the ground, it might yet provide a reasonably safe exit point, if she lowered herself to full stretch before dropping. She wondered if Douglas made his escape that very same way, all those months ago.

Knowing the geography from the outside and comparing it with the inside, she now felt confident enough to try. It would greatly shorten her dangerous climb back down in the dark. Carrying her pack up the rope with her might have made the climb torturous, but it had proved the right decision.

Reattaching clasps on the rope to the loops of her climbing girdle, she began her descent. Five metres and two doors down the steeply sloping corridor, she easily spotted the crack of daylight and, feeding herself some slack, swung until her feet landed on the hatchway that led through. Standing on the side of the aperture – what, for a traditional doorway, would have been the jamb – she tied off the rope and moved to lower herself into the room. With everything oriented through roughly sixty-five degrees, her floor was once again a wall, a wall that was at least three metres down. She considered a moment. Once down, she would be committed, for better or worse. Rethinking her strategy, she reconnected the rope to her girdle before sliding down the room's actual floor to stand on the wall below.

Untying the rope, she let it hang into the room, just in case she was unable to escape the way she hoped. The rocket noise of the *New World* filled the wide valley outside. It was naturally louder by the split in the ship's hull, and through her ear protection sounded like the constant mewing of a snared beast. Yet, on the cusp of hearing, she sensed something else, too…

The room was littered with furniture, storage cabinets and all manner of supplies Meritus had not deemed necessary for their survival in a prehistoric world. In the poor light, it presented a minor gauntlet to cross. Almost everything she climbed over shifted under her.

That noise again… What was it?

With a huff of annoyance, she reached to remove one of her earplugs. The rocket noise magnified instantly. Balancing on a cabinet with her trigger hand away from her weapon, the timing of their attack could not have been more perfect. Heidi screamed.

High above, Reid was in a state of abject terror. He knew that any second the *New World*'s weaponry would vaporise him – he simply knew it. It made no sense. His craft should have easily outmanoeuvred the *New World,* but he just could not shake them. Even when he flew low into a dangerously tight canyon, the vast ship simply hung in the air above, waiting him out.

Despite his fear of tempting fate, the words burst out of him anyway, "Why aren't you firing on me?"

Several hundred metres above Reid, Captain Baines followed a similar line of enquiry. "I'm losing patience, Weber. *You* are putting all my people in danger. Do *not* think that I won't hurt you! *What the hell have you done to my ship?*"

No response.

She raised the taser. "Last chance. I'm not fooling around here…"

Weber kicked down, activating the communications device in the heel of his shoe. "I only have seven letters for you, Baines. Three of them are 'F', can you fill in the remaining four?" He grinned triumphantly.

With regret, she fired. Two wires shot across the space between them, but not before a signal shot from his concealed micro device to the Schultz orbital attack craft below them.

Reid's console lit up with a message. He activated it and all hell broke loose across his instrument panel.

The benefits of increasingly ubiquitous computer interfaces show themselves by the ease with which even marginally complementary systems can interact, and with ever more complexity and effectiveness. Earlier systems were messy – a tumbled Tower of Babel, eventually flattened and repurposed by digital convenience to make things much easier for everyone… including any bad guys wishing to learn the lingo. Reid's years of working for the Schultzes had left him so captured that he rarely even recognised the bad guys any more. What he did recognise was a virtual simulacrum of the *New World*'s bridge and was not about to question his good fortune. He could see it all, almost every major system on the heavily armed ship above him. It was neither within his power nor remit to scrutinise the how, let alone the why. All that mattered was the when, which was now, and could not have been more timely. Still shaking with anxiety, his grimace, almost rictus with terror, gradually turned to wonder. He might just make it through this.

She missed the creature's approach, darkness, ambient noise from outside and earplugs stripping her to the three remaining senses, of which scent was blunted by the residual burnt-metal smell lingering after the ship's death in fire; taste was consumed by the blood in her mouth, leaving only touch – now working overtime to make sure she felt every single claw that tore through her fatigues to gouge her side.

Heidi screamed again. Balling a fist around her earplug, she brought it down to hammer the animal that clung to her side, before it could scramble up to tear out her jugular. Buitreraptor fell away, among the detritus littering the room. Heidi slipped too, falling onto her back as the vicious little dinosaur rolled immediately to its feet and leapt for her again.

The rattle of her assault rifle was suddenly painful within the enclosed metal box where they fought, but nowhere near as painful as the gashes down her side.

The predator's death offered little comfort when its companions weighed into the fray. Heidi knew they were pack animals. Severely disadvantaged by human senses, she was also injured and without backup. Having narrowly avoided the jaws of death many times, they had never felt closer than at that moment. She fired indiscriminately, into the near darkness. Agonised screams filled the room as her spray of bullets sporadically found their marks, though some of the screams were her own. Her sense of touch outdid itself as another set of excellent teeth pierced her flesh, jaws clamping tightly around her right calf like a pint-sized iron maiden. She fired again, into the dark, offering up a prayer of the godless that she would miss her foot.

Several percussive thuds and one abbreviated squawk suggested a lucky hit. Less fortunate was the *click* that terminated her rapid-fire frenzy. The clip was empty. Would the remaining creatures in the darkness realise, or had she done enough?

Heidi hated to bluff; she believed in overwhelming, crushing force, with no room for ambiguity. Should she risk changing the clip? She would appear vulnerable. Adjusting for the intellect of her enemy, she opted to threaten – like she had them right where she wanted them. All those thoughts flashed through her mind in the moment it took to get to her feet. Burning agony shot up her leg as she waved the empty weapon, bellowing the menace of a wounded tigress.

Far above Heidi's existential crisis, the wide basin teemed with life. Vertebrates, invertebrates, plants, fungi and bacteria all existing as they always had, in a balanced, harmonious, symbiotic state of total war. Even when all seemed calm in macro, there was always the microscopic battlefield raging just beneath. Planet Earth, and the universe itself, had no concept of peace, but occasionally there was distraction.

The vast, roaring juggernaut, hanging in the sky like an inverted volcano, caused everything that *could* move to do so. The howling, growling and chittering of a million calls, everything louder than everything else, would have been extremely concerning, were it not for the all-pervasive rocket noise, drowning all.

There was terror. There was agony. There was death. There was always death.

The abused, when fearful, kick downwards – sometimes losing their footing and going down themselves. Visible from above, for any blessed with the gift of flight, there was movement through the forest. The canopy obscured the cause, but the effects were clear, like a school of fish, just below the surface of murky waters.

The flow through the swaying canopy was towards the escarpment plateau, irrelevant to those hanging in the air above, but to anyone caught on the ground…

Heidi had bitten her tongue in the first attack. By screaming at the remaining Buitreraptors, she also spat blood all over them. Though little more than a fine mist – virtually undetectable to dull, human senses – it was a mistake. Re-energised by the scent of gore, they tensed to spring at her, when a roar from outside the ship got their attention.

The *New World* must have retreated along the valley, because the constant growl of massive rocket motors attenuated enough for this latest calamity to cut through. While Heidi assumed Reid was leading their enemies away, there was clearly something else going on outside and its fortuitous timing made both surviving Buitreraptors leap for the split in the ship's hull. They vanished.

She had no idea how they found their way into this room in the first place. She doubted even they could have jumped up as easily as they jumped down. Despite the tools and equipment she carried, her own ascent to this level had been a muscular venture, but then, the whole ship took its strength from lightweight, honeycomb design. Broken as the *Last Word* was, there could be dozens of entrances and exits to any number of rat-runs through her structure. It was reason enough to get out of there. However, the burning questions for Heidi were, firstly, *could* she get out of there, weakened as she was by injury; secondly, what manner of creature had frightened away her attackers; and thirdly, could she get past it to reach her ship?

She took a deep breath. Answers were the future. As a veteran time traveller, Heidi knew she could only rely on the now, for then would be too late. She made the most of it, moving as quickly as possible, as carefully as necessary, towards the gash in the *Last Word*'s outer hull. It cost her, every limb stiffening from exertion and injury. She was also going into shock. By force of will, she pushed past the fog in her mind to reach daylight and assess the damage to her side. Her flak jacket had borne the brunt of the attack. There was some blood, and she was sore, but the injuries did not feel serious. Of greater concern was the bite to her lower leg. If she was immobile… She left that thought hanging, instead, taking a knife to the leg of her combat trousers. Cutting it off at the knee, she flung the scrap of cloth back into the room behind, not wanting the scent of blood to bring whatever was outside right to her.

Her calf was covered with blood from multiple puncture wounds. Taking an antiseptic wipe from a pocket, she tore open the packet, gritting her teeth against the pain as she cleaned the wounds. Tears streaming down her face, she opened her eyes and released the breath she had been holding. Shrugging out of her backpack, she delved inside for a bandage. Within moments, she had her leg bound and tied off expertly.

Within Heidi's vicinity, it tended to be others who bled. Nevertheless, she had undertaken many missions for her grandfather, long before she boarded the *New World,* and was not completely unacquainted with injury.

Fixing herself up hurt, but she knew a slide down the ship's outer hull would be worse. Gritting her teeth, she lowered herself out of the crack to full stretch, taking two more deep breaths to steel herself before letting go. The slope, three metres below her feet, sent her into a natural roll. Loose soil reduced the shock from her fall, though enough remained to make her yelp, the cry irresistible, despite the danger of her circumstances. Fortunately, whatever was making all the noise up on the plateau above showed no sign of calming down, and covered for her.

She removed the remaining earplug to hear clearly. If she had to guess, she would say that whatever it was had brought its family, too.

She breathed a heavy sigh. *Time to face the next challenge.*

The climb back up the escarpment was torture. Slipping and sliding on the uncompacted loam was frustrating and tiring. Worse, it felt like a cheese grater against her injured leg. Eventually, she hunkered down just below the top.

The roar of the *New World* was some way off, maybe a few miles, but the constant rumble rebounding off hillsides and down the valleys surrounding the plateau made it hard to be sure. Of greater moment were the plateau's latest visitors. There was something unsettlingly familiar about them.

Ducking and flattening herself against the slope, she sighed again. The plateau was the only place for miles where Reid could set down. Assuming he had found a way to stay hidden from the *New World,* he would now have to land in the lion's den.

She snorted. *If only!* Her leg throbbed. It felt weak. The idea of a long hike to avoid the immediate danger was unappealing.

At least the monsters before her had not yet noticed her presence. They appeared to be involved in some sort of domestic strife, perhaps born out of fear from above. Some of their spats were vicious. Heidi could only hope they would move along once they sorted themselves out, but it would have to be soon. She could not wait there forever.

She popped her head above the crest of the steep slope to steal another quick glance. At that moment, her comm crackled to life, at volume, making her jump. *"I've got some great news, ma'am!"* She grabbed it, silencing it immediately. Whatever Reid had to tell, it was not great news for her. Suddenly a mouse in a nest of eagles, Heidi wilted under the combined glares of a full pride of Mapusaurus roseae.

"Ouch! Aaarrgh!"

Baines slouched casually, one hand on her hip. "I haven't fired the charge yet, Richard. That was just the two little pins."

"They really hurt!"

Baines shook her head with disgust. "Imagine what this will feel like, then. Oops – no need." She raised the taser theatrically, preparing to incapacitate him.

"WAIT!"

She paused, taser held high in readiness. "Well? What have you done to my ship?"

"There's nothing you can do!" he blurted.

"I disagree." She raised the taser again.

"No! I mean, it's too late."

"Richard, if you don't spill, I swear I'm gonna zap you just for the hell of it."

"I wrote a program that got past your security. It allowed another program to unpack and eventually shut down your operating system."

"We already know that. You nearly crashed us into the moon! Hiro was able to clean it from our systems. Tell me something I don't know. *Now.*"

"He only found the bits he was supposed to."

Baines hesitated. "OK. You have an audience."

"I knew Nassaki would reinstate a backup. It's a new ship – he would have little or nothing to lose, right?"

Baines' eyes narrowed. "Go on."

"I wrote the worm to copy itself into a completely compartmentalised environment, so that it could reinfect any reboots you tried." He grinned again. "That was the clever bit, but here's the *really* clever bit. I only took your systems down last time as a blind. Granted, I knew you were in trouble and thought it might take you down, but my plans were not contingent upon that."

Muscles bunched in Baines' jaw. "Go on," she repeated, stiffly.

Still grinning his magician's reveal, he continued, "The second time my program was activated, it was to go into full stealth mode. Don't feel guilty about not noticing it, Captain. The software I have written is, if I say so myself, quite brilliant. You see, one of the reasons the people in the alternative 22nd century were further along than us, was because they had less crime and corruption to deal with. Ironically, that made their more advanced tech easier to infiltrate and affect. My program simply lay dormant within your systems until triggered. Then it moved into phase two."

"Phase two?" Singh prompted, with concern.

"Indeed, Commander."

"And what *was* this trigger?" Singh pressed.

"When your sensors detected Schultz technology, obviously."

"Obviously," Baines stated sardonically. "So do we surmise correctly that you have somehow slaved the *New World* to that orbital attack craft down there in the valley?"

"Oh, it's better than that, Captain. Your computers have just sent the final signal to them. Think of it like cloning tech. What happens next is up to the pilot of that ship, now."

She leaned forward again. "What do you mean?"

Weber's lip curled nastily. "Simply that, whatever the people down there have planned, this ship will not merely follow, it will now obey, too. Ours is to watch and learn. Every day's a school day."

Baines scratched her cheek in thought. "It is, isn't it? You know, Hiro explained to me how this device works. This unique taser delivers its shock at a very specific frequency that affects the… hang on, I had him write it down so that I didn't miss anything – I can tell you're a man who loves detail…" She unfolded a small piece of paper from her pocket. "Ah, yes, here we are. The shock affects the primary and secondary somatosensory cortices, anterior cingulate cortex, prefrontal cortex, insular cortex, amygdala, thalamus, cerebellum, and the peri… er… periaqueductal grey areas of the brain – I think I got that right. However, its real genius is that it singles out those areas but attacks them simultaneously. In case you were wondering, those are the structures within the brain most associated with the perception of pain. The highly synchronised—"

Fear crossed Weber's face. He cut her off. "What possible use would that be as an interrogation tool? It will completely incapacitate, maybe even kill me!"

"Yeah, it's pretty efficient."

Perspiration appeared at his brow. "*Do* you wish to kill me?"

Baines raised a wry eyebrow at that. "How I feel right now, Richard? It's complicated. Perhaps we're all learning what we're capable of today, wouldn't you say? And while we're back in school, memorise this – a long, long time ago, corporal punishment was used to control naughty boys like you. You've heard of experimental archaeology? Think of this as an experimental history lesson." She raised the taser once more.

"No! Please. Don't."

"Then *tell* me how to get control of my ship back!"

"By taking control of the control ship."

Baines stepped back slightly. "And how are we meant to do that? We can't even land this boat, let alone fire our weapons."

"Captain," Singh called out. "We're moving again. The Schultz ship has left us behind." He called up a display. "We seem to be flying some kind of holding pattern."

They both turned to glare at their prisoner.

Weber raised his cuffed hands sheepishly. "Er… don't shoot? Please?"

～⑥

Lucky to escape the raptors, Heidi believed her goose well and truly cooked this time. The gaggle facing her numbered fourteen, and ranged in size from disconcertingly large up to terrifyingly massive, and they attacked like piranhas – as one.

She slumped, turning onto her back on the steep slope, holding the rifle to her breast until the last moment. She would be lucky to take even one of them down, but that would not stop her from trying. Braced, waiting for the end and expecting to die alone, the dual explosions from the plateau above and behind took her by surprise.

She was not alone. The detonations did nothing to improve the mapusaurs' day, either.

Both missiles struck with a speed that left their rocket noise hanging in the air. Immediately on their heels, Reid arrived before the booms' final report even died away.

The dinosaurs forgot all about Heidi and ran north. She climbed over the edge to limp onto the plateau, just in time to see them disappear, tails swishing and flicking angrily.

"Oh…" Seemingly anticlimactic, her subdued comment was actually an admission. When journeying there, Heidi knew that opening pathways through time and space might affect the planet's magnetic field and would certainly interfere with the natural order of things. The team on the ground, that she followed on their first jump to the Iron Age, proved that. She had *not* expected to be followed in turn by the *New World* – though their failure to attack her ship proved beyond doubt that there was something strange about their pursuit. Even if Douglas was given to mercy, Baines would surely have blown her back to stardust. However, the full potential scale of their interference with Earth and the natural order became clear, as the last tail vanished through the wormhole.

Whoever we left back there is about to have a worse day than I have had. I wonder if the New World *will leave us to save them.* She smiled, slyly. *I suspect they will spend several days going through dinosaur dung looking for dog tags.*

"Everyone, calm down!" Douglas shouted. "O'Brien, no shooting!" The situation got away from him so quickly that he had no time to react, but as always when things were in motion, he was at least able to see the trajectory. The spearmen and their leader were posturing, brandishing their weapons, openly hostile now, but their aggression was not directed towards Douglas, nor any of his people.

"*Dreigiau!*" their leader screamed.

Douglas turned to Jones, also shouting now, amid the fracas exploding all around them. "Dragon again?"

Jones was shaking his head and it occurred to Douglas, in that white hot second of action, that he had never in all their adventures seen any sign of fear in the giant Welshman. He saw it now.

"Not *draig* – *dreigiau*. Dragons! There's bloody loads of them, isn'it!"

Monstrous roars from right behind Douglas forced him to miss that subtle distinction. "Everyone, behind those rocks!" he cried, running for his life without even bothering to look round. His team followed immediately, soon crouching on the outcrop's opposite side where they hid from the Sigilmassasaurus earlier.

Their more recent prehistoric friends bellowed in fear and rage, waving their spears. It was a bantam defiance, and Douglas could certainly understand their terror, yet he marvelled at their courage, too. It was only a pity that it would get them killed. Used to hunting comparatively large game, like wild cattle and even bears, the men were no strangers to danger, but these were like no game they had ever faced before. Neither game nor bears, they were apex killers, Mapusaurus roseae – the Earth lizard – and even worse, Douglas felt sure he recognised them, too.

All those years ago, from his perspective, he had stepped outside the *New World* with The Sarge and a few others, only to come face to face with a hunting pack – *this* hunting pack. The largest, and certainly the alpha, leered over his diminutive prey and *roared*. Douglas would never forget that furnace stare. It was the very same animal. He was sure of it. Perhaps with a few extra scars, but if anything, the creature was even larger. *Do these damned things ever stop growing?* he wondered, his wits utterly scattered.

Jones tugged Douglas' sleeve, breaking into his moment of terror. The Welshman held a couple of grenades in his large hand. Slowly regaining his senses, Douglas nodded affirmative.

The dinosaurs were also in shock. A moment ago, they were hunting in a hot Cretaceous jungle on the other side of the world; suddenly in the cooler hills of the north, they were confused and afraid, despite their size. Faced with a new and aggressive prey, they hesitated, uncertain. If Douglas was correct, and these were indeed the animals he met when he first stepped outside the USS *New World,* then this pack had confronted humankind before. However, this new quarry, when viewed through the prism of a hunter's senses, would seem quite different from Douglas' people. Despite being approximately the same shape, their diet and lack of modern hygiene products would surely give them a radically different scent.

Regardless, Douglas knew the mapusaurs' hesitation would not last long. Any fear or disorientation they felt would only make them even more dangerous, as they took that fear and disorientation out on whoever was closest.

Jones looked over the jagged top of their hiding place and picked his mark, aiming for one of the dinosaurs furthest from the suddenly tiny figures waving spears. He pulled the pins and threw both grenades together, with all his prodigious strength.

It was almost dark, adding to the terror of the altercation, yet even as Jones released, Douglas could see the distraction would come too late for one of the men out there. He closed his eyes as a vast head dipped, bird-like, to snatch the luckless victim from the ground. The massive jaws closed with a crunch, cutting off the man's scream immediately as the dinosaur threw back its head and swallowed. At the same instant, a metre-wide, three-clawed foot kicked out to stamp another man to the ground. The head of the second animal dropped to tear the man's head and shoulders clean from the rest of his torso.

The man with the sword bellowed at the top of his lungs. Douglas could recognise an order to retreat in any language, but the men did not run. Instead, they grouped with spears raised and backed off as one. It was brave, but about as useful as the hedgehog's defence from the badger.

Fortunately, Jones' grenades landed more or less on target, but the animal he was aiming for moved. Instead of landing behind the creature to frighten as intended, they actually came down right on its head and exploded.

The double bang sent the pack running down into the ravine below. The detonation of two grenades would have virtually disintegrated a man. At least that would have been quick. Jones winced, actually glad that the flash temporarily affected his vision.

The giant took the damage and staggered. It was incredible that any creature could sustain such an horrific injury and live. It mewed unnaturally, unable to see or understand. Left alone by its pack, it was harrowing for everyone. Douglas could not stand it. "For God's sake, Jonesy, put that poor creature out of its misery." A majestic creature destroyed; two men killed. He could hardly begin to imagine the damage they had unleashed on the timeline already, without factoring for a pack of colossal killers running free in an unsuspecting world. Then there was the Sigilmassasaurus that vanished into the hills earlier.

Jones pulled a hand-held rocket launcher from his pack and loaded one of Commander Gleeson's tank-buster shells. "Cover your ears!" he shouted, and then shouted it again in Welsh for good measure. He had not meant to hit any of the mapusaurs and hated to do it, but watching the creature suffer was too much. He fired.

The mountain goats of Iron Age Britain proved too fleet of foot for Sigilmassasaurus brevicollis, and they were remarkable climbers, too. After enduring a succession of shocks, she needed to keep up her energy levels. She ate the fish, caught in the Cretaceous, hours ago. Fortunately, water was plentiful. Though colder than she was used to, an abundance of mountain streams kept her hydrated.

However, blind luck decreed that the shock of relocation was not nearly as severe as it might have been. She lacked any understanding of the period in which she now found herself. Even Douglas' small team were unable to establish that with any accuracy. Yet there *were* pointers and telltale signs. Early Iron Age Britain suffered a protracted interval of unusually cold and harsh weather that pervaded across the whole North Atlantic region – a period known as the Iron Age climate pessimum[1]. Fortunately

---

1. 'Pessimum' meaning worst or lowest point. Although that period was long gone, it was as good a way as any to describe the life of anyone unlucky enough to stumble upon *Sigilmassasaurus brevicollis* while strolling through the heather.

for Sigilmassasaurus, she arrived during a summer in the warmer cycle that followed. The Christian calendar to be used the world over would not be invented for centuries, but historians and climatologists know it as the Roman Warm Period that extended roughly from 300BC to AD450.

Sigilmassasaurus headed north into mountainous territory that, superficially at least, more resembled the craggy peaks and deep lakes of her home. Significant changes in flora, and particularly the abundance of grass, mattered not a jot to the carnivore. She was a skilled fish hunter, but meat was meat, and as abundant as the new grass. She was also large – essential for retaining a stable core temperature. The ambient temperature, though cooler than her Cretaceous home, would have to drop significantly and for a protracted period to seriously affect her. Such large animals found it harder to stay cool than to generate heat. The hills she headed into, while not yet Scottish by name, were relatively warm and inviting; warmer than they would be in some later centuries, possibly due to the obliquity of the Earth's axial tilt, and the variable orbital path around the sun that so affected the planet's ever-changing climate. Essentially, she would adapt, she would survive; she would lay the eggs she carried, and they would thrive.

The day's trials were already fading from memory when she came across something she recognised. She sniffed. Fire – the forever enemy – but there was also something else. Her massive stomach growled. Whatever the little creatures ahead were up to, it smelt delicious. She drooled disgustingly onto the heather.

Maybe she would stay a while before moving on? She marked the area liberally with urine – making the most of the seemingly endless supply of water in the area. The scent would drive hunting wolves crazy, at first, but they would soon learn that there was nothing they could do about it, and it would be suicidal to try.

She raised up on hind legs to her full and considerable height for a better view. The smell of cooking meat now had her full attention.

A distant roar made her turn. Sniffing the southerly wind, she snarled, spraying more urine. This was hers now. All of it. No interloper was going to take it from her, but then the roar came again, this time joined by several others.

Animal thoughts are difficult to comprehend from a human perspective. The closest verbal description would be to say that Sigilmassasaurus brevicollis *reassessed*. Whatever was coming sounded at least her size and even dinosaurs could count up to 'many'.

With regret, she continued north, and just a little west. This elicited all manner of screams, shouts and calls from the little creatures within their circle of ditches and stones. She cared not.

One of the younger men knelt by the severed torso. He cried soulfully. Douglas watched in dismay. It was so easy to think of our ancestors as mere unthinking, unfeeling savages – to believe their lives, often so short and so brutal, somehow mattered less than our own. From his experiences in the 16th century, Douglas already knew that was not so. Clearly, it was not the case here, either. Jones was still attempting to communicate with their leader in some kind of pidgin Welsh, while two other spearmen rallied around their friend to offer comfort in his hour of need. It was all so familiar.

"You OK, Captain?"

He turned to see O'Brien studying him with concern. Taking a deep breath, he let it out slowly. "Everywhere we go…" His words, though mumbled and enigmatic, were understood perfectly.

Her smile in response was tinged with sadness. "We're the guys tryin' to fix all this, remember?"

"Aye." He shook his head gloomily. "Though Ah sometimes wonder if we're up to it – even fit for it. When we came upon these men, we viewed them as dangerous animals – little more than that – and yet they understand loss just as we do, they care as we do, they suffer as we do."

"True. And watching their courageous stand from behind our rock was kinda embarrassing." She smiled again, this time with chagrin. "History records all the big events, and the terrible ones, but unless you actually get to meet these guys, to live with them, it's hard to appreciate how similar we are, in many ways. We have differences, too, of course, and they seem to steal all our focus. So we just demonise them and the things they did, and the decisions they made, like we're somehow better, more enlightened." She snorted bitterly. "It was the people of *our* time that caused this, this… whatever this mess is. Nothing these guys do is gonna end the world." She placed a comforting hand on his arm. "But don't beat yourself up, Captain. After all, they *were* pretty aggressive when we arrived back here. And it seems they stole some of our equipment, too. If those dinosaurs hadn't shown up…"

"There are evil men and there are evil days," Douglas replied stoically, "and they don't necessarily coincide. Ah can only wonder how we'd fare in their shoes. *We* may remember times like these as dark, or unenlightened, but Ah refuse tae declare war on the dead for the hard decisions they were forced tae make and the way they had tae live. Look at these men. They're just doing the best they can with what they know. Many lesser leaders since, men and women who *should* have known better, have made things far worse by shying away from the tough calls. For all these fellas knew, we might well have come here to rape, pillage and murder."

"Whoa there, big fella."

Douglas smiled, gently. "What Ah'm trying to say is, weakness can be an evil too, and we're no' going tae gi' in tae it. We *must* fix this. We have tae." As always, when upset or agitated, his accent thickened.

"Perhaps that's why we're here, Captain? Assuming that *was* Heidi Schultz in that ship, she'd have had no way of knowing that we'd go gambolling through the wormhole she created – even though she was firing on us. It was a pretty desperate move on our part."

He nodded. "Aye, mitigated slightly by the fact that it was our *only* move. And now we owe it tae these people tae sort out the mess we've brought down on them, because if we don't…"

"There may never *be* an 'our people'," O'Brien completed for him. "Two have already lost their lives, after all. What might that mean for the future?"

"That's a whole new can of worms," he concurred. "If they were going tae have bairns, we'd better hope they've already done so, or some of our number could even disappear from time – we just don't know. Then that leaves the other elephant in the room – that the actions of people from our time may have just created orphans. Damn it all!" He kicked at the heather. "And damn the Schultzes."

"Amen to that," agreed O'Brien.

Douglas took another breath and straightened. "Come on, lassie. Dwelling on this is no' going tae help. Any action is preferable. Let's see how Jonesy's getting on."

"He's probably trying to buy a sheep for his dinner," O'Brien quipped.

Douglas waved a hand over towards the Mapusaurus corpse. "Ah dinnae think these folks'll be going short o' meat for a while. At least there's that."

"Yeah. Must be, like, a million chicken sandwiches on that thing. Plenty of leather, too. Not to mention some pretty spectacular ivory. Talk about your full set of steak knives! When the *New World* comes back, perhaps we'll be able to lift it for them – help them move it, maybes?"

Douglas stopped, turning to her, slowly. "We dinnae know what caused our ship to jump here. If Prentice was right, and she was slaved to Schultz's craft…"

Concern crossed O'Brien's face. "You think we might be stuck here?"

"Whether we are or no' is nae longer down tae us." He spoke calmly enough, but the emotion was clear in his voice. "Jill willnae stop trying tae find us, ye can believe in that. Though Ah think we'll have tae chance our arm with that wormhole soon – if we can find that drone. Hopefully, Jonesy will have answers in that regard. Ah want tae see where it leads – and that means rounding up that dinosaur pack and sending them back through. Then, we'll consider *our* next move.”

O'Brien nodded, but remained silent.

“Ye OK, lassie?”

“Yes, sir. I was just thinking about the animal that came through with us – that sigil-wossname-opotamus.”

He smiled wryly. “Aye, some of the names Tim has given us are almost as frightening as the beasties themselves[2]. Ye're thinking that creature was from Cretaceous Britain and these latest critters are from Patagonia?”

“Yes, sir. If that wormhole goes more than one place, that could be a big problem.”

Douglas puffed out his cheeks. “Aye. That occurred to me as well. So let's just take one problem at a time, Sergeant Major. One foot in front of the other, eh?”

“You're injured!”

“I see nothing escapes you, *Herr Doktor*. Help me aboard.”

“You've lost your trouser leg!”

Heidi rolled her eyes as Reid helped her up into the ship and then on to the cockpit, all the while babbling about his big news. Heidi received the revelation thoughtfully, falling stiffly into the pilot's seat with her leg outstretched.

“It is fortunate that these things do not require pedals to drive,” she noted drily. “I have new coordinates for you. Your news about the *New World* could not be timelier. Full control, you say? And who do we have to thank for this development?”

“Ah,” Reid explained drolly, “there's no subterfuge there. He

---

2. Technically, Hippopotomonstrosesquippedaliophobia, but Douglas was afraid to try it. Sergeant Dewi Jones might have made a stab, having grown up in Gwynedd, North Wales, and not so very far away from the village of Llanfairpwllgwyngyllgogerychwyrndrobwllllantysiliogogogoch – but that would have been showing off.

made it quite clear who we should credit for this – pinning his name to the top of the accompanying communiqué and crowbarring it in wherever possible. And in the third person, too. I can see why he made the grade to join one of your grandfather's schools." He muttered the last.

"What was that?"

"Er… He was obviously no fool, ma'am. Weber, Lieutenant Richard Weber."

Heidi wore a rare look of astonishment. "Really? Interesting. I assumed he was lost along the way. *Mein Großvater* said his popularity among Douglas' people was not all it might have been, after his failed attempt to break them both out of prison. Indeed, *mein Großvater* said he was an imbecile. Wrong again, *Opa.*"

"He may not have been much of a strategist, but he's certainly no imbecile," Reid concurred. "At least, not in a strictly intellectual sense. This is an outstanding piece of programming. Especially when you consider that ship's military prowess. It must be cutting edge and would almost certainly have been constructed under the highest levels of security. Then there's the fact that he dovetailed it to work seamlessly with our less advanced tech."

"That would seem almost impossible," Heidi agreed. "Or, at least, it would in a normal military environment."

"Ma'am?"

"Looking at the way they run their so-called society," she elucidated, "they probably gave one of their most dangerous enemies a job on the project, out of some ludicrous sense of egalitarianism. Especially if he told them he was sorry! I was unaware that Weber possessed such high-level technical skills?"

"He didn't. You're right. They must have trained him."

Heidi snorted, his words taking her by surprise. "You are probably correct." She winced, and then smiled, her beauty marred only slightly by the stab of pain from her leg. "Are you beginning to see why they will never stop us?"

Reid nodded. He saw it, and it terrified him. *They* terrified him – both sides, but especially the Schultzes. The only way he could continue was by selling it to himself that he was better off inside the tent peeing out, than outside peeing in, though it still gnawed at him.

"What is it?" Heidi demanded.

"Nothing, ma'am. You have coordinates?" he deflected.

"I do, but first we must program the *New World* to follow us, but not directly."

Reid's brows knitted in confusion.

"Their vast ship has a wormhole drive," Heidi explained. "Our small craft does not. We must use the manifold system we have seeded around the world. I intend to take us through one of our 'fixed point' wormholes, adjusting for my own timeline there – I do not wish to meet myself, nor come face to face once more with an angry spinosaur. With those modifications made, I intend to cross the world in that timeline. The *New World* must hold position here, while we make that journey. We must make the calculations accurately, *Herr Doktor*. Timing will be everything."

Reid absorbed her words, trying to see where her plan might be leading them. "You're thinking that, if the *New World* followed us directly, it would attract so much attention that we might never reach our destination?"

"Correct. Someone in that timeline may even find a way to deprive us of that asset, and I intend to use this unlooked-for gift, Reid. And use it well."

He sent her a questioning look.

"I thought we would need stealth and…" Heidi soured, "a little luck." She smiled again, wolfishly this time. "However, that flying arsenal above our heads provides us with *other* options."

"I've got an idea!" Prentice declared.

"Well, dinnae keep it tae yersel', laddie." Douglas was upset and worried, making him curt.

"The Schultz ship came here, to Iron Age Britain, as far as we can tell. We've no idea why, but that doesn't matter right now. What does matter was that t'*New World* was somehow forced to follow. Schultz barely stayed here for the time it took to turn around before entering the wormhole again. I thought they, whoever they are – probably Heidi – were running from Captain Baines, but the arrival of those beasts changes things."

"Go on, Adam," Douglas encouraged.

"What if Schultz has control of not just *this* wormhole, but has created some kind of technology that can manipulate worm*holes,* plural. A ship that size fits easily through these portals, almost as if by design. The *New World* would have been destroyed if she'd followed, but the *New World* can create wormholes for herself. If someone *has* slaved her to that little ship, they could be leading her by the nose."

"That tracks," Douglas allowed, "but how does it help us?"

"I'm not sure it does, *but* if Schultz changed the destination of the wormhole over there," Prentice pointed vaguely behind him, "then the chances are, it now goes to the home of these latest beasts. Pretty sure that's Patagonia, sir. We all recognised them – those of us from the *New World,* at least. I doubt very much that we would find Crater Lake if we stepped through it now. So I'm just wondering, if the *New World* did follow Schultz's little ship, could she still be there?"

"More to the point, can we join her?" Douglas completed, enthusiastically.

"Exactly, Captain. Although, I was going to suggest we try this first." He pulled his comm from a vest pocket, wobbling it side to side for emphasis. "The signal *might* carry through the wormhole and back to us."

"Brilliant! Make the call, Sergeant. Let's give it a whirl."

Prentice configured his comm for analogue radio waves, to give his message the best chance of being received.

"*Sergeant Prentice! Thank God!*" The response was almost immediate and from Lieutenant-Commander Singh.

"Good to hear your voice, Commander," Prentice replied

heartily. "I have Captain Douglas for you." He handed over the comm.

"Sandy! We're pretty relieved you're there, Ah can tell ye! Can ye confirm where exactly there *is*, and your status?"

Singh explained their predicament and loss of control, briefly noting Weber's involvement.

"Oh, my God." Douglas hung his head. "When Dave Flannigan was bellyaching about leaving him behind, Ah should have listened."

"*Sir?*"

"Nothing. Sandy, Ah want to come through to join you, but we've a situation here Ah cannae walk away from." He explained in turn about the missing Sigilmassasaurus and the now-distant pack of rampaging mapusaurs.

Singh listened patiently. "*I would have advised against you stepping through anyway, Captain. It's probably safer where you are. You may have a group of large theropods on the prowl, but we have zillions of them this side! Worse yet, we've no way of picking you up. We can't even launch any of our support vessels. We're completely at their mercy!*" The disgust in his voice was clear, despite the crackling of their cross-dimensional signal. "*We* have *sighted Heidi. Worryingly, she had some business aboard the ruin of the* Last Word, *sir.*"

"It gets worse. Any idea what she was up to?"

"*Negative, sir. On a slightly lighter note, I can tell you she was injured…*"

"Really?" Douglas brightened.

"*But, as far as we can tell, not seriously.*"

Douglas swore.

"*Captain, the Schultz vessel is making a run for the wormhole.*"

"She's coming back here?"

"*After what I've seen today, sir, I've no idea. She seems to have an almost supernatural ability to control them these days. Just in case we lose contact, remind Prentice that the dr—*"

"Sandy? Commander Singh? *Sandy!*"

Douglas looked to Prentice, who was shaking his head.

"They're gone." Douglas spoke dumbly.

"Or perhaps they're still in Cretaceous Patagonia, but that wormhole has been redirected elsewhere, sir."

They both turned irresistibly towards it.

"So where does it go now? That's the question," Douglas pondered aloud.

"It may still go to the *Last Word* crash site, sir. Even if we're correct and Schultz *has* altered it to go to another point, we've always assumed wormhole travel is two-way, but now…"

"What are ye saying, Sergeant?"

Prentice puffed out his cheeks. "I don't know, sir. The whole playing field has changed."

Douglas was forced to agree. "Not for the first time in the last ten years am Ah missing the sage advice of Satnam Patel. OK. Park that for a minute. What do ye think Sandy was trying to tell us when he said 'remind Prentice about the…' then what sounded like *gr* or *dr… br,* maybe?"

Prentice was silent a while, thinking hard. "Dr, dr, dr…" He snapped his fingers. "Could he have meant *drone*, sir?"

Douglas shrugged. "Possibly, but what about it?"

Prentice thought some more. "They have tracking devices, so we can find them. You know, if they go down…" His words lacked certainty.

Douglas understood, pointing out, "But the Argentinosaurus in the room, here, is that they cannae send a signal that can be picked up from anywhere in time and space."

"Ha! That's it, Captain. It doesn't need to. We're assuming – and let's face it, it's all we have to go on – that the *New World* is slaved to that orbital attack craft, yes?"

"Aye. And?"

"Well, it seems Heidi needs the wormholes to travel. If you recall, I saw a device, somehow *within* t'wormhole, that I assume was responsible for generating the portal – though where it gets it power, God alone knows. Didn't those lunatics tap into t'power of the Earth's core, t'last time they nearly destroyed t'planet? Anyway, it seems that this wormhole is now a permanent fixture, so if there *are* others…"

"They might go anywhere or any when." Douglas took a shuddering breath, the full horror hitting him like a train. "There might be hundreds."

"Aye, sir, but in t'good news column, there's a chance that, if that wormhole up on t'hill here tracks her ship, then the *New World* might be able to send a signal via that wormhole, from wherever they happen to be when they catch up."

Douglas looked sceptical. "That suggests this wormhole, here, is doing a lot of heavy lifting. Surely that would only work if she departed directly *from* this wormhole? And what if the *New World* doesnae follow her? Ah'm really no' sure about that."

A slow smile crept up Prentice's face. "Fair enough. Let's try something more substantive, sir. The *New World* might have a record of our location that our enemy doesn't – as she's clearly generating her own jumps. Captain Baines *will* eventually regain control of her – I don't think either of us doubt that." His smile turned to a grin. "Now, you know Commander Singh far better than I do, Captain. You tell me, is it likely he's recording every minute detail about the jumps they're being forced to make?"

Douglas' lips twitched into a smile of his own.

Weber cringed in his seat under The Sarge's baleful gaze.

Still standing taser in hand over him, Baines demanded, "Where's she gone, Sandy? Can you track her?"

Singh shook his head with annoyance. "Our hands are completely tied, Captain. All I can do is record – so if you ever want to look back, I've got you covered!"

"OK," she replied calmly. "What *can* we do?"

Singh unlocked his seat to spin it around. He glared vengefully at Weber. "I'm for giving *him* the shock of his bloody life, ma'am!"

"They were on a hunting trip," Jones explained. "They sleep rough in the heather during the summer months, when they're out in the field. Apparently, they kill other tribes' cattle to preserve their own for a rainy day – a bit like having your cow and eating it, sir, isn'it. Of course, sometimes they just steal them." He grinned. "Says his name is Catgualatr, sir. I think that's like the old Welsh for Cadwaladr."

"Catgualatr *yr uchel!*" the short, barrel-chested man insisted.

Jones covered his smile with a hand as he towered over his ancient forebear.

"What is it, Dewi?" asked Douglas. "What did he say?"

"He said, that's 'Cadwaladr the Tall', sir."

Douglas looked down at the man in astonishment. "The tall?"

"It might also mean 'high', sir."

"That's no' really any better, is it?"

Annoyance flashed in the Briton's eyes. He may have been short by modern standards, but the man was not stupid. Language barrier notwithstanding, he clearly read their thoughts and stood straighter – though it made little difference.

Indignation came off him in waves and so, not wishing to lose control of the situation, Douglas suggested, "Would it be better if we... er... sat?"

"Doesn't look like the sitting around type, Captain. He probably thinks he's a king, but you can try it."

Douglas sat slowly on some open grass between patches of heather, gesturing for the Briton to do likewise. "A king? Ye think so? Have ye asked him?"

Jones tried to lower his stature, respectfully – an equally vain effort. Deciding that his strange stoop was not working, he sat, too. Eventually, after checking his men had his back, the chieftain did likewise. "*Dach chi'n frenin?*" Jones queried.

The Briton sat straight-backed, his chest swelling with pride.

"*Dwi yn.*"

"Ah take it that was a 'yes'?"

"Yes, sir. Catgualatr Brenhin. King Cadwaladr."

"Right. OK." Douglas pondered, collecting his thoughts. "So, how many subjects does he have? We should probably know how much of a threat they might pose – but don't be obvious."

"No, sir, I'll do my best, like, but…"

"What?"

"Just wondering how high he can count, isn'it."

"He's no' a simpleton, Jonesy. The man'll know how many spears he commands, Ah'll wager that."

Jones nodded and did his best.

"Jones?"

The Welshman scratched his stubble in the torchlight. "Not really sure I understand fully, Captain."

"Ye're doing yer best, laddie. Ye're doing grand, and it's all we've got, so go ahead. What do you think he said?"

"There's an old word, or unit of measurement, really – *cantref*. It means a hundred villages or settlements – although *tre* technically means town, so… well, anyway—"

"Like the 'hundreds' in the old English shires. Aye, Ah ken. Excellent, Dewi. Go on."

"Yes, sir, but I think we're here before land was portioned like that. Thomas Beckett, our old historian, would probably know better, but I *think* what he said sounded like *cant o dai* – a hundred houses. So I'm guessing a town – or what they would call a town? He's probably more a local chief than an actual king, but that hasn't stopped him from thinking big, sir." He grinned again. "Even at one and a half metres."

Douglas smirked and then coughed, throwing Jones a disapproving look. "Hearts and minds, Sergeant. Did ye glean anything else from what he said?"

Jones turned back to the small band's small chief and spoke again.

Douglas listened carefully. It was almost entirely incomprehensible to him, sharing none of the Latin or

Franco-Germanic roots of the English he was familiar with, but one word did snag his attention. "Did he say Yeavering?"

Both Jones and Cadwaladr looked at him with interest.

"Does that mean anything to you, sir?" asked Jones.

Douglas smiled ruefully. "Aye, it rings a bell."

Jones frowned, confused.

"Sorry. Ah've just realised where we are. Yeavering Bell is a prominent hill just north of Great Cheviot – where we left ma last ship, nearly two thousand years from now, as it happens," he added wryly.

"So that was a joke, sir?" Jones asked, deadpan.

Douglas shrugged. "Ah said Ah was sorry. In our time, ye could see the ruins of a great hill fort on the top. Maybe this guy's the head honcho. Can ye ask him how far away his settlement lies?"

Jones snorted. "Do you remember the trouble we had with the Tudor people and their 'miles', sir?" he noted, breaking out the inverted comma bunnies for a run. "These boys are way more primitive even than that."

"A little respect, Jonesy. This guy might be yer great-great-grandaddy. It's worth a try."

Jonesy dutifully obeyed.

"I think he said half a day's march, sir. I'm guessing ten k, maybe a bit more, isn'it? They travel light, after all."

A roar erupted from higher up the valley. Cadwaladr jumped instantly to his feet, drawing his sword.

"Aye," Douglas concurred, getting up stiffly. "Ah'm a wee bit concerned maself, laddie."

An hour passed and Douglas turned to look down the hill at Jones, still persevering in his attempts to commune with the locals. "Ah left him to it," he admitted to Prentice as he joined him on the rocky outcrop. "There wasnae anything Ah could bring tae the conversation. The language has been through countless variations over millennia, but he's doing his best tae learn the lingo. At least Jonesy's been able to give us a head start. Thank God he was with us."

"Aye, it does seem like someone's looking out for us sometimes, don't you think, Captain?"

"Are you a believer, Adam?"

Prentice shrugged. "I'm willing to accept there's more we don't understand than we even dreamt of before all this, sir. Yet, after my recent experiences, I've also realised that faith can be undermined. That said, I've made the decision to live in a world where God *does* exist. If I follow that moral framework, then, whatever the truth is, I've got my bases covered."

Douglas nodded thoughtfully. Eventually, he said, "So you either live the best, most decent life you can and that's all there is to it, or you live the best life you can *and* get your reward. Ah like that. A plan with no drawbacks." He smiled. "And while we're on the subject of things we dinnae understand, Ah wonder if Jonesy has found the ancient Brittonic for 'Aerial Analytic Sensor Drone'?"

Prentice laughed.

Douglas smiled. "More tae the point, if they dae have the AASD, will they freely hand it back tae us?"

"Suppose that depends on whether they can be *aasd,* sir."

They looked at one another a moment, and both snorted. Sometimes, gallows humour can save a man, even when it seems nothing else can.

Chapter 6 | Woman Steals Spaceship
From 'The Man'

The terrain outside Heidi's orbital attack craft instantly passed from mountainous jungle to dark forest, with the smashing of tree trunks heralding their arrival. Fortunately, the collision occurred at low speed.

Outside, the darkness was almost impenetrable under the canopy. "Is this it?" Heidi asked sharply.

"Not sure. I think so." Reid turned to her. "Not what you expected?"

She unclasped her flight harness. "I *expected* a desert."

Reid checked his instruments. "Pretty sure it's not that."

"Yes, I noticed the trees almost immediately when we crashed into them! Clearly, our new technology comes with surprises."

"Tetchy. Might I remind you the whole system was launched untested? There are bound to be kinks."

She threw him a glare and he looked away.

"Come. Let us see where we are." She jumped out of her pilot's seat and was immediately reminded of her injured leg. Hissing, she limped with purpose into the rear compartment to quickly and immodestly change into a new pair of combat trousers. Relacing her boots, she opened the side hatch and removed two powerful torches from their clips on the inner bulkhead, handing one to Reid. She gave her own a squeeze to switch it on and stepped outside into a frigid woodland.

Changing the focal point of the lens for a wide beam, Heidi cast about, taking in their new environment. Her breath coiled in the air like smoke. Snow fluttered down where it found a space between the boughs – obviously deepest winter. The forest around them looked old, too. Several varieties of deciduous trees were in evidence, typically types found in northern Europe. *A natural forest,* Heidi mused. *This is no timber farm. Suggestive, but not evidential.* She sighed. "Come, Reid. It looks like we must explore, if we are to find out where and when we are, or alternatively, if we are to find out what you have done wrong."

"*Me…?*" Reid mouthed. He swallowed, daring a look out between the gnarly, twisted shapes, swaying gently in the gloom. Instantly, he judged their location: terrifying. "Erm… looks lovely. After you, ma'am. While we're at it, perhaps we should split up, too? We can cover more ground that way."

"No need for sarcasm, Reid."

"I disagree."

Heidi sighed, but she was still learning to listen to others' opinions, before crushing them utterly… it was a journey. "Very well, we need to get our bearings. What would you suggest we do?"

"Something cowardly and without overthinking things. Definitely without overthinking things!"

Heidi shook her head disgustedly. "It is only darkness, Reid. In the daylight, the same view would not trouble you. You might even find it appealing."

"In the day I'd *have* a view. It's what might be in the dark that worries me."

"You can see me, can you not?"

"Of course."

"Then perhaps you should worry more about what you *can* see. Now move!"

They stumbled through the encroaching night. Where they glimpsed the sky, it was darkest blue. Within minutes, it would be completely black under their leafy roof. Eventually, Reid plucked up the courage to ask, "What exactly are we looking for, ma'am?"

"A road, a glade, a small hill – anywhere we can clear the forest to get our bearings. If there are no signs of civilisation or technology, we might at least get pictures of the night sky to cross reference with our navigational star maps. If the coordinates for our last jump were incorrect, we must plot our findings on the system. Especially if you believe we might experience further anomalies within the wormhole manifold. Hmm…"

"Ma'am?"

"No radio signals."

Reid sighed. "We're in the wrong time."

"Perhaps. I wish to know for certain. After all, it would not be the first time we found a future timeline altered." She stopped, turning back. Reid stumbled into her. "Then of course, it may actually be as simple as you botched our flightpath!"

"Me? I… I…"

"Indeed. We shall see. Come."

Less than ten metres and Heidi stopped again, shushing him as he stumbled once more.

"What is it?" Reid whispered.

"I heard voices. *Shh.*"

Listening hard, they picked out a man and woman speaking in hushed tones. They sounded nervous.

Before Reid could comment, Heidi hushed him again. "They must have heard you stumbling around like an ox in heels!" she hissed. "*Listen!*"

"Erm, is this forest perhaps… *haunted?*" asked the male. He sounded young.

"Don't be such a big girl's chemise. I brought you here to look after *me*."

Heidi rolled her eyes in solidarity.

"I am. I mean, I will," the male retorted, if a little unconvincingly.

"So why am *I* holding *you* protectively?" the girl bit back.

"You go left," Heidi whispered. "I'll go right. We'll come at them from both sides. Don't do *anything* without my order. Clear? Good. Go."

As they spread out, it became more difficult to make out the whispered conversation of their quarry over their own movements. Heidi stepped on a twig, cursing herself. Almost immediately, Reid made a similar blunder, out in the darkness. The couple they tracked were definitely aware of their presence now. The man mumbled something incoherent.

"What are you doing?" asked the girl.

"Praying," the man replied.

"With your eyes shut? It's hard enough to see in here as it is."

"I don't want to see!"

Heart of a lion, clearly, thought Heidi. *This will be easier than I had hoped.* Circling left and just behind the couple, Heidi switched on her torch, flooding them in a cone of unnaturally brilliant light.

The man whimpered, calling out the girl's name in fear. "Matty?"

Recognising the pair were no threat, Heidi called out, "Reid? You can move in now."

"Yes, ma'am," he answered from the blackness to their right. The couple jumped, holding on to each other.

Pathetic! Heidi thought as she peered into the murk. "Reid, where *are* you?"

"Over here, ma'am." He activated his flashlight to show his location.

Heidi was close enough now to see that the couple were indeed youngsters, probably no more than twenty years old. The man had a dishevelled look. The girl was pretty, in a simple, natural kind of way. Their style of clothing added to Heidi's misgivings, as she stepped out from the shadows and around them, to block their path.

Both jumped again, clutching each other even tighter in fear, when the young man's whole demeanour suddenly changed. He loosened his grip on the girl. Heidi wondered what had come over him.

"Are y-you an angel?" he asked.

Heidi shook her head, not in answer so much as disgust. *Lamentable.*

There was something strange about his mode of speech, too. *Ohhh,* she groaned inwardly, as the final penny dropped with a pitiful *clink* into her empty piggy bank of patience. *I hope this is not what I think it is.* She flashed the torch in the young man's eyes, pulling her sidearm. "Answer my questions or I will certainly introduce you to the angel of death."

Terrified, neither spoke.

Unsure whether they understood, Heidi spoke plainly. "What year is this?"

Again, they stared, dumbly.

"The date?" she demanded angrily, raising her gun to threaten.

The man studied it curiously, trying to look down the barrel. Innocently, he enquired, "Is that a hammer for pressing dimples into plate?"

Heidi let out an exasperated sigh. "Clearly, a demonstration will be necessary."

"Ma'am, perhaps we shouldn't—" Having taken up a position behind the couple, Reid dropped suddenly to the floor as a deafening *bang* rang through the forest. Getting back up slowly, he spoke in anger. "Heidi! Others may have heard that!"

The young man belatedly covered his ears. "Ouch."

"The year?" Heidi demanded, peremptorily.

He obviously had no idea what the gun was, but was not a

complete fool. Reid's reaction proved how dangerous the device in Heidi's hands might be. Clearly terrified, it was the girl who spoke next. "Why, 'tis the year of our Lord 1399, my lady."

Heidi's eyes narrowed, not at Matty, but at Reid. "Imbecile! What good is this? These people still think the Earth is flat!" She holstered her weapon and grabbed the young man by the neck of his rough garments. "You have not seen us, yes?"

He stared, baffled.

Heidi sighed again, speaking slowly as if he were simple. "Do not tell anyone you have seen us. Do you understand?"

He nodded quickly, too afraid to speak.

"Reid," Heidi snapped, "we must get back to the ship."

"Ahem." The young man found his voice. "Excuse me, my lady, but the sea is that way." He pointed east. "If you're looking for a way back to your ship, I mean."

Heidi rolled her eyes and stalked out into the night, torchlight flashing wildly as she negotiated the rough going with her injured leg. Reid followed, stumbled and fell. "Fool!" she spat. "I should *leave* you in Chaucer world, for this incompetence! Now hurry – and find me another wormhole."

Soon after, a terrible rumble shook the ground as flames, impossibly bright, lifted high into the night sky, vanishing almost instantly with a sonic boom that rolled and rebounded across the darkened medieval landscape. The young couple were left in total darkness and silence.

"Harry, was that an omen? A portent of doom?" Fear shook Matty's voice.

"I don't know, but can we go home now? I think I've had a wee."

The *New World* rose out of the wide valley, leaving the escarpment and the wreckage of the *Last Word* far behind. "Are we snagged again?" Baines asked both Singh and Weber.

Weber shrugged. "The control is out of my hands now, Captain."

Singh checked his instruments before turning to face her. "Looks like we're heading for space, Captain. Orbit, maybe?"

Astonished, Baines handed the taser handset to her security. "Keep him in line, Sarge." Approaching Singh's station, she peered over his shoulder at the display. "This is new."

Singh stroked his chin thoughtfully. "I don't understand. Why aren't we opening a wormhole to follow? We haven't regained control, so what's she up to?" He nodded over his shoulder towards Weber. "Do you think he really does know?"

Baines shook her head. "I think he's right. The control's in Heidi's hands now. God help us."

"I'd like to put us on full alert, though there's practically nothing we can do, Captain."

"True. Still, it's not a bad shout, Sandy. Order the crew to battle stations. Should our circumstances change, I want everyone ready to take maximum advantage of any opportunities that may arise, and at a second's notice. Can we scan the wormhole she entered – find out where it leads?"

He shook his head, frustrated. "Passive scanners only. Sorry, Captain. I can tell you that we recorded minor fluctuations in the quantum foam that provides the wormhole with its structure. But as that foam is part of a sub-atomic structure of matter and antimatter particles that exists throughout the known universe, each constantly being created and destroyed, and a billion trillion times smaller than the nucleus of an atom, all I can say with certainty is—"

"Something's changed?" Baines predicted, drily.

"Pretty much."

She sighed, angrily. Turning back to Sergeant Jackson, she pointed at Weber. "Get this creep off my bridge, Sarge."

"Can you at least get these probes out of me?" Weber cried.

"If you make a fuss, they might fall out all on their own when you hit the deck," The Sarge explained. "So walk carefully, sunshine. Move!"

"I'm your prisoner. I have rights!"

"Funny how everyone breaking the law remembers that, and seeks its protection when they're caught, ain't it? Don't worry, me old fruit, we've got you your very own suite – *and* it's got a bar."

"It's got *bars!*"

The Sarge shrugged. "You'll have quite the weekend then, you lucky little Herbert. Now shift it!"

Back aboard their ship, Heidi continued to berate Reid.

Not daring to gainsay her completely unfair assertions, he argued instead, "Something obviously went wrong on the last jump. I believe our safest course may be to retrace our steps and try again with new coordinates. I might be able to use your personal wormhole generator to open a way back, as it's one of our fixed points. Might be preferable to crashing through the forest again."

Heidi nodded affirmation, and within minutes, their ship vanished to reappear once more at the *Last Word* escarpment in Cretaceous Patagonia. The *New World* no longer growled above, clearing the sky for the return of the local pterosaurs and birds to whom it belonged. "At least our backup seems to be following my instructions," Heidi allowed, moodily, as she turned them slowly about. "Are they in orbit yet?"

Reid checked their instruments. "Yes, ma'am. That was a good call, by the way." He doubted favour could *be* curried with Heidi, but he tried anyway, just in case their next jump turned into a complete masala, too. "At least when they jump in space, they stand less chance of causing any of the complications we've witnessed when ships jump near the surface of the Earth."

"I am glad you approve," she replied frostily. "As a matter of fact, I have been thinking about that. I believe we should take space out of the equation."

"Ma'am?"

"We should use another of our fixed points to take us *when* we want to go, if not exactly where." She sent him the coordinates from her console. "Prepare our route."

"You wish to travel across the world?"

She stopped typing. "You have a better way?"

"Not necessarily better, but certainly quicker. If we continue retracing our steps, we could shave thousands of kilometres off the trip."

She considered. "Very well. That would be quicker, naturally. Why would it not also be better?"

He shrugged. "Call me old-fashioned, but I consider travelling in the real world safer than jumping through space–time distortions."

Heidi agreed. Yet, despite their time machine giving them all the time in the world, their fuel was still finite. "Plot our backward course through the wormholes." She hesitated a moment, as uncomfortable with praise as she was with favour. "You are correct. The island chain of Cretaceous Britain is much closer to North Africa than Patagonia – even in the Cretaceous. Good idea, Reid."

Hiding his surprise, he merely nodded and got to work. Just a few minutes' number-crunching and they would be ready.

Presently, Reid signalled for Heidi to proceed, and their ship slipped slowly through the event horizon to vanish once more.

Douglas stood on the highest rock in the outcrop, gazing upwards. The waxing gibbous moon was only two-thirds lit, but visibility was surprisingly good across the upland moors, thanks to the clear, starlit skies of a place that would one day be known as Northumberland. It was beautiful. Yet, he could not enjoy the experience. His team was hopelessly lost somewhere in time. Now, before they could even think about finding their way back, they must return the dinosaurs to theirs.

He had taken first watch for himself and turned to gaze down upon their little camp at the foot of the rocks. The Iron Age men slept apart from his group, keeping a watch of their own. That seemed only sensible; obviously, they would not trust Douglas' people. More interestingly, they lit no fires. That gave Douglas pause. So far, these men had shown themselves to be cautious, at least, if not actually reasonable. He could not help wondering what the neighbouring tribes must be like, if giving away their position was a greater danger than discouraging nocturnal hunters. Especially after the day they had all had – the day when dragons became real. For all he knew, the myth may even have originated right there and then[1] . Regardless, he could certainly sense the natural order of things unravelling – with Heidi's reckless interference at the bottom of it all. How many other breaches in the continuum had she thrust upon an unsuspecting world?

He took a deep breath of wonderfully fresh air. He could almost feel it cleansing every cell in his body as he tried to hang on to the moment, but within seconds, darker thoughts returned.

Just before turning in for a few hours' sleep, Jones had imparted what Cadwaladr told him about the wolves. They were always a threat, especially when his people hunted their neighbours' territory and camped without a fire. Yet this evening, not a single howl nor growl had been heard by anyone.

Almost certainly, the pack of Mapusaurus represented a serious problem – both to them and to the local ecosystem.

---

1. He was unaware that the earliest known and recorded dragon myth came from Mesopotamia, circa 2100BC, almost two millennia earlier. The dragon is believed to have been first adopted by the Welsh kings of Aberffraw in the early fifth century. It became a symbol of their power after the Roman withdrawal from Britain. By the seventh century, it became known as the Red Dragon of *Cadwaladr,* king of Gwynedd. Coincidence? Was Douglas on to something with his musings? Or was it simply that royal dynasties around the world have very little imagination when naming their offspring? In Europe, we would eventually resort to assigning numbers to differentiate them. Perhaps one day, when the numbers are high enough, they will be given barcodes – or even Quick Regnum codes.

Thank God we seem to be in Britain well after the Storegga Slide tsunami[2] , so at least the beggars cannae migrate, he thought. His father had always been interested in geology. He remembered many trips around his native Scotland and its borders to go rock collecting as a boy. He closed his eyes, sadness threatening to overwhelm him. *So much is lost… and so many.*

Unfortunately, the bad news kept coming, for there was also the possibility of getting mixed up with inter-tribal squabbles between the peoples of this time. That was perhaps even more concerning, as every involvement risked the integrity of their timeline still further. *Everyone must have seen the* New World, *and heard her, for miles around,* he reflected. *Maybe they're all hunkering down behind their walls, in fear for their lives. Ah cannae blame them for that, but they'll get curious sooner or later.* He smiled, fleetingly. *It's in our nature. Trouble is, if they come and we have tae defend ourselves… a small, local effect like that in the here and now might bring down the future we're trying to protect like a house o' cards.*

A distant roar pierced the night; clearly the cry of a massive animal, a primal sound that had no place there. Douglas exhaled anxiously. From his vantage point, he kept an eye not only on the locals, but also the wormhole. The last thing he needed was further incursion, but what could he do to stop it? Animals were also curious. It was practically a given that other creatures would cross over.

Another roar echoed through the valleys, disturbing the Britons' rest as much as that of his own people. Douglas noted that, despite their distrust, they stayed close. Clearly, Jones' prowess with hand

---

2. Great Britain has been constantly moving north for half a billion years. However, throughout more recent prehistory, the island was a peninsula jutting out from continental Europe. Around 6200BC, a submarine landslide off the coast of Norway created a vast tidal wave. The catastrophe known as the Storegga Slide tsunami flooded the connecting lowlands known as Doggerland, creating the North Sea and the English Channel, separating Britain forever – 'forever' meaning until the next grand shakeup, though no one should be advised to sell their boats just yet.

grenades had impressed on them that there was safety in more than numbers alone.

Obliquely, the close proximity of the dinosaurs also provided a terrifying comfort of sorts, for though every bone in his body told him to stay as far away from them as possible, the closer they remained to the wormhole, the better his chances of sending them back. Unfortunately, it was but a small leap to also imagine the sharpening of swords and spears within the local hilltop strongholds. If he did not act quickly, lives would be lost.

"What a mess," he muttered, tiredly, but stayed on his feet, lest weariness overwhelm him entirely. After all, bringing himself up on court martial charges for dereliction of duty simply would not do. Where would he find a court? He snorted, gently. All such concerns seemed so petty in the visceral world outside the human bubble of manufactured stress. At least it was quiet here. A man could hear his own thoughts and give them structure.

He enjoyed a whole three seconds of that contentment before the stillness was shattered again, this latest roar so loud, so close and so sudden that his weariness evaporated. Spiked with adrenaline, Douglas drew his weapon, while the soporific majesty of clear, starlit skies erupted with scorching fire as the wormhole birthed another monster.

"Sensors are picking up life signs, ma'am."

Heidi dismissed the news. "That is of no consequence."

"They're human, ma'am," Reid stressed.

"Anyone we know?" Machine-gun fire pinged off the hull. "I guess that answers that."

"You do have a way with people, ma'am," Reid offered with a grin. "Should we engage?"

"They nibble like gnats. Ignore them and feed our next coordinates into the nav-computer."

The Iron Age hunting party were living through interesting times, of late. Earlier, dragons had appeared, eliciting a spear-brandishing frenzy. Now, the chariot of the gods hovered overhead and they dropped to their knees in the heather, following Cadwaladr's lead, apotheosising.

The ancestors lacked understanding enough to separate the cracks and rattles of Douglas' assault rifle from the overall chaos of light and noise, whereas the descendants jumped up from their sleeping rolls like they were on fire.

By the time they joined their captain, Heidi's ship had vanished once more, back through the wormhole, leaving absolute silence in its wake. The darkness returned more slowly as embers in the grass submitted gradually, one spark at a time, to the breeze. Douglas blinked, his night vision temporarily blown.

The ancient people remained kneeling and struck up a chant.

"Shut the hell up!" O'Brien bellowed. Though they did not understand the words, her tone was surprisingly effective. She spoke into the new calm. "You hear that?"

"Water?" Douglas suggested, sceptically.

"Look out!" O'Brien called, pointing her rifle's flashlight at the wormhole. *Through* the wormhole appeared not merely water, but white water. Almost immediately losing most of its kinetic energy, it spread wide to form a disconcerting mini tsunami that streamed relentlessly down the hillside.

"Get our gear!" Douglas hollered.

As one, they half-scrambled, half-jumped down the crag to save their belongings. Jones and Prentice arrived first and desperately began throwing everyone's possessions up to them while they were still climbing down.

The Britons also scrambled onto the rocks to escape the sudden flood.

"What the hell's occurrin', like?" shouted Jones, outraged, his voice high, sounding almost comical in the circumstances.

"Maybe the wormhole leads back to Crater Lake," suggested Prentice. "Perhaps Heidi's retracing her steps?"

"Ah dinnae remember being followed here by the Euphrates!" Douglas called back, rattled.

"Sergeant Prentice might be right, Captain," offered Bismarck. "The river was uncomfortably close to overtopping the bank where the wormhole was called into being."

"And that rain was showing no sign of letting up, boy. It might have burst its banks any second," Jones added, jumping onto a rock, out of the flow that crashed around their island at knee height. "Oh, that's just champion!"

"Did ye get everything, Dewi?" Douglas called down.

"No. I dropped my power bar, sir."

"I thought you were asleep?" O'Brien queried.

He rounded on her. "So I get the munchies, isn'it!"

"Alright, calm down, everyone." Douglas considered. He turned back to the wormhole, shining a torch at the steady stream of river water running down the hill. "At least we don't seem to be getting the entire river through. Still, who knows how many alien creatures and plants have slipped through into this time with the water."

"Let's just hope they're small," O'Brien remarked, thoughtfully.

"Even genetic material could…" Douglas tailed off. "Oh, no. Did we lose the drone?"

Prentice sagged. "We let them keep it for a while, to show good faith, Captain, remember? When they jumped up on t'rocks to save themselves, they didn't bring…" He tailed off with an angry sigh.

Douglas seethed. "So, we've no way of knowing if that leads back?"

"It hardly matters, Captain," Coleman stated, flatly. "There's no way we'd be able to push against that current, anyway. Even if we got through, we'd wash straight back – and I, for one, am miserable enough, without being soaked to the skin."

"Dr Alba, a ship has appeared on our sensors," Lieutenant McBride reported. "We should get our birds in the air, including Corporal Thomas' troop carrier, if he's willing. We noted its armaments—"

"Yes, yes," Alba agreed. No one moved. "Well, scramble, then –

or whatever it is you people do!"

There were no fighter jocks among the Crater Lake community, so Thomas and two of their best transport pilots ran for the three craft at their disposal.

The rescue pod's main hangar doors opened slowly, as did the outer hatch. His ship already outside, Thomas was in the air first, tearing towards the wormhole where he set Douglas' group down earlier in the day. The river was higher than before, the constant deluge breaking its banks. Visibility was appalling through the torrential rain, but his instruments told him the wormhole was taking storm water from the raging river. "Oh, my life," he muttered, full of concern. "I hope the captain's well out of that."

His heads-up display tagged the enemy ship as the one that shot the place up earlier, forcing Douglas' desperate escape through the wormhole. He lined them up and fired a missile.

The ground erupted right beneath Heidi's craft. "Bit more than a gnat?" Reid cried out in alarm.

Cool as always, Heidi answered with an economical, "Do you have the coordinates ready?"

"Yes, ma'am."

"And the time of our arrival? It is critical. You have checked it?"

"Yes, ma'am."

Thomas circled for another run on the enemy ship which, for some reason, was making no attempt to defend itself and merely hovered before the wormhole. He knew he would never get a better chance to inflict some serious damage when two similar ships flew across his targeting box, peppering the enemy ship with a withering fire that largely tore into the fierce whitewater maelstrom behind and beneath their objective, barely inflicting a scratch.

"Get out the way!" Thomas bellowed across the airwaves. "I 'ad 'em in me sights!" Forced from his attack run, he circled again, when a thought struck him. If that ship had just returned, then maybe Douglas was just the other side of the anomaly? It had not worked last time, but he nevertheless sent a radio signal, directed at the wormhole. "Captain Douglas, do you read?"

Almost a hundred million years later, Douglas' comm crackled. He fumbled for it in the dark. "Thomas? Is that you?"

"*Yes, sir. I see the river flooding through the wormhole. Are you all safe?*"

"A loaded term, Corporal, but we're OK at the moment. What's happening your end?"

"*The enemy ship is lining up to go through the wormhole again. I'm about to engage and then I'll come through and get you. I've done the sums. She should fit, sir – just about. Engaging the enemy now, Captain.*"

Douglas' comm fell silent. Not merely the silence of no one speaking, but the total silence of no signal. "Thomas? Corporal?"

"Sir, look!" O'Brien pointed her flashlight at the wormhole. Almost imperceptible ripples worked their way across the event horizon, from the outside into the centre, just as Prentice had witnessed them previously. The raging water abruptly stopped – a weird spectacle to behold, behaving like a long string of spaghetti, suddenly bitten off. For a split second, a low wall of water butted against the wormhole and then crashed to earth with a splash before running harmlessly away down the hill.

"Thomas?" Douglas cried, anxiously. He turned to his people. "Theories? Anybody?"

Bismack put a hand up, as though in class. "All I can suggest is that Heidi reconfigured the wormhole to go elsewhere."

"So that torrent is now flowing into someone else's back yard," Douglas agreed, catching on. "And our rescue just went up the spout!"

AD2122, El-Shaikh Ebada, Egypt

A box canyon, set within a craggy, desert landscape; there was no warning, no hint to presage the aggressive irrigation to follow. Heidi's ship slipped through the portal, just above the water. Incoming fire struck almost immediately, the heavy rounds bouncing and pinging off their hull like biblical rain.

"What the hell!" Reid screamed, hanging on to the arm of his seat as the ship shook around them. "It's those damned gnats again!"

"Return fire!" Heidi retorted, without missing a beat. "Do it!"

Hands shaking, Reid primed the little ship's automated targeting system. "Parameters?"

"Anything that's firing on us, *Dummkopf!*"

The river flooded through the wormhole, spreading to fill the wide space available to it. Four main battle tanks, moving into an arc formation around the wormhole, were caught in the flow. Low bow waves broke around them as they opened up with heavy machine guns, while heavier weapons were brought to bear on the slow-moving target. Behind the armour nestled a whole host of support vehicles and a veritable village of field tents. Cries of alarm filled the canyon as the flood waters, though only a few inches deep, turned over tables and swept away equipment.

The Schultzes had no compunction about integrating artificial intelligence into their targeting systems. Heidi's ship returned fire almost immediately, painting and selecting victims with terrifying speed and accuracy.

Superheated explosive gases ballooned against the tanks' heavy plate, sending shrapnel flying in all directions, yet did little to prevent their turrets from turning ever closer towards a firing resolution.

"Get us out of here!" Reid screamed again.

"I am trying. They hit us before we had even fully materialised."

"Those helicopter gunships are prepping to take off, look!"

"*Shoot* them, then!"

Reid complied, sending two missiles into the chopper with rotors already spinning. Less heavily armoured than the tanks, its cabin vaporised, while angular momentum carried sheared rotors with deadly effect into the tents.

"Good shot!" Heidi acknowledged enthusiastically. Pulling back on the stick, she lifted the nose of their craft and engaged its main engines. Blasting skywards, they left fire, water and earth in their wake as they leapt for the air.

Two further gunships took off vertically from the valley floor below. They had no hope of catching their quarry, but they did not need to.

"Missiles incoming!" Reid cried out, frantically.

"Countermeasures, idiot!"

"Already engaged," he spat back. "They won't be enou—"

Bang!

***

Crater Lake, Cretaceous Britain

"*We should fire after her!*" one of the pilots suggested.

"Belay that!" Thomas ordered with more authority than he truly held. "We don't know what or who is on the other side. That witch might have reintegrated in a school playground, for all we know. Hold your fire. *Please.*"

"*Corporal Thomas is right,*" Lieutenant McBride joined the conversation from the rescue pod. "*If the enemy has left theatre, return to base.*"

"*But sir,*" the pilot tried again, "*we'll be letting her get away.*"

"*Far away, I hope,*" McBride admonished, flatly. "*Let's count our blessings. Return to base. That's an order.*"

***

Heidi's control console turned almost entirely red. "Damage report!"

Slack-jawed, Reid stared in horror.

"What is it? Speak up, man!"

"Er… damage report is offline, ma'am."

"*What?*"

"They must have taken out the sensors that tell us when things aren't working."

"So do we have any *actual* damage?"

"I don't know, ma'am. I believe it was a glancing blow." He lowered his voice. "Wish I could say the same about my underwear."

"What was that?"

"Nothing, ma'am."

"I no longer have full power, Reid! Without it, we cannot make orbit. What the hell is going on?"

"If the sensor that tells you something is wrong stops working, it prevents other systems from working, too – you know, to safeguard them, in case…" His voice wavered under her glare.

"So rather than protect its crew, you programmed my principal war machine to protect *itself* by going into *limp home mode!*" she scathed, completely incredulous.

His hands shot up. "I can fix it! I was concerned about the potential lack of spare parts in the field. Don't shoot me!"

"Wise. Were we in a *picnic* field, you imbecile! You seriously built a fighter craft that cannot fight if the sensor designed to check for battle damage is damaged? Override that nanny state rubbish, this instant! Those gunboats are closing and will soon be within firing range again."

Reid leapt from his seat and began removing hatch covers behind the cockpit.

Heidi seethed as she stared at her instruments, watching the enemy gain on them. "Hurry!"

"I am, I am. Just looking for my thousand-volt snips…"

"You will receive a shock you will never forget in just under ten seconds' time – when they hit us again!"

Several days earlier, in 22nd century Egypt, Master Sergeant Apep Badawi was abducted by Heidi and forced through a wormhole to North Africa in the Cretaceous Period. His comm was later found in black box mode, half-buried in the sand and still recording, by a fellow police officer. Although details were sketchy, the device tipped off local authorities to a possible military incursion from an unknown aggressor.

The chopper pilots, stationed at the mouth of the wormhole near El-Shaikh Ebada, had endured days of boredom and jobsworth maintenance, but that was all in the wind now. With a chopper destroyed and its crew killed, they were out for blood, pushing their craft to the limits. A steady tailwind helped them, and they gained quickly on the stricken ship – so quickly, in fact, that one pilot chanced a ranging shot.

It exploded close enough to Heidi's stern for them to feel the buffeting. "*Reid?*" she cried.

"Almost there," he called back, panicked.

On a closed channel, the lead helicopter pilot signalled her commander, who followed just off to port, below and behind. "I have a resolution, sir," she stated in Arabic.

"Don't wait for me to catch up. Fire when ready."

"Yes, sir."

A missile dropped from beneath each of the gunboat's stunted wings. The rocket motors fired, immediately leaving the chopper behind.

"*Incoming!*" Heidi screamed, the timbre of genuine fear in her voice now.

A *zap,* a *crack* and an "Ow!" came from behind her. "Go now – *hit it!*" Reid shouted, sucking his burnt fingers.

The red lights relinquished their stranglehold on her console immediately, as full power returned. Heidi pulled back on the joystick to climb steeply.

The missiles shot beneath them.

"Whoa. That was close," Reid noted, rejoining Heidi in the cockpit.

"They have not missed us yet. They are turning and triangulating our course."

"Heat-seeking, or AI-guided missiles, probably. That's what we'd use," Reid postulated.

"Regardless, we have lost too much ground. Unless we escape atmosphere, they will catch us."

"Not this ship, sister." Reid grinned.

She glared at him.

"Sorry. It's a line from… never mind. Look, I made a special addition to this ship for you. It's experimental but… yep. Engaged. Right. Keep a tight grip on the stick."

"What are you *dooooooiiiiing?*"

The ship shot almost vertically for space, pressing them so hard into their seats that Reid blacked out.

He came around a few minutes later. "Where are we?" he asked, blearily.

"Orbit," Heidi replied, tightly. She was still furious.

"Oh, good." He straightened up in his seat. "ETA?"

"Twelve minutes."

"Oh. Not so good."

"Indeed."

Reid had set a countdown before leaving the Cretaceous. It currently read nine minutes, thirty-three seconds. The *New World* would arrive before them. "We must have lost a couple of minutes in the firefight."

"So it seems. Before we go into the next firefight," she asked pointedly, "can you guarantee that we will have no further problems with damage control? I only mention it because war zones do not typically come with a hard shoulder, or breakdown lane."

"Well, we'll have limited diagnostics, because of the…" He withered under her blowtorch glare. "All disabled now, ma'am. Yes. I, er… see the b-boost function I installed got us out of trouble, though," he added, groping for a way out of his personal crucible.

Heidi turned full square towards him. "And when was it your intention to inform me of that? Any other upgrades I should know about? Or must we be seconds from death before you share? The G-forces from that stunt almost knocked me unconscious, too. What a fine mess that would have made."

Reid shifted in his seat uncomfortably. "The moment never came up, ma'am. The boost function was intended only for the direst of emergencies where we would have nothing to lose. It saved us, and your physical strength was enough. So, in the minutes we have remaining, perhaps you would be kind enough to tell me what we're doing here? From the satellites I can see on our sensors, this seems an advanced society, but not *our* society."

"Correct. But there are similarities. I am here for a device that is, and was always, outside *our* timeline."

"Outside?" he asked, nervously.

"In a way. Our biggest problem going forward will be refuelling our vessel, yes?"

"Ma'am," he replied, noncommittally.

"Below us is a device. According to the details I studied some years ago, it focuses three amplifiers to negate gravity, utilising vacuum-space to—"

"Are you serious?"

She looked at him. "Have you ever known me not to be?"

"You're talking about Area 51?"

"I am. That device could completely negate our need for fossil fuels."

"It was a hoax! One that didn't even work, because hardly anyone took it seriously!"

"Indeed, it was not. *Mein Großvater* had a scientist in his pay who actually worked on the propulsion system."

"Alien devices!" Reid spat, dismissively. "Seriously, Dr Schultz, this is too far."

"I hope for your sake you are wrong, Dr Reid, because after I have stolen it, you will install it to drive this craft."

"What? How…? Where?"

"Do not worry yourself with the details, yet. I have planned for everything. The e-diary I retrieved from the *Last Word* also contains the device's precise location. Appended are all the research notes from the scientists involved. I never considered them important when we were originally forced to leave the ship, given our situation at the time. Even until recently, we had all the power and resources we could desire from our link with 1940s *Deutschland.* However, the treachery among our people forced me to devise a plan B. Did you not wonder why I requested extra load space built into the design of this ship?"

"I thought it would house supplies, for long-term, deep-cover missions…" He tailed off. He *had* thought it odd at the time, that Heidi ordered the ship stocked without taking advantage of all that extra capacity. Returning to the now, he huffed, incredulous, when a thought struck him. "Just one minute. What do you mean 'precise location'? This is an altered timeline."

Heidi shrugged. His point was not without merit. "True, but as I said, this technology is from a source outside that altered timeline. We have no reason to suppose the captured devices will have been treated any differently."

"I can think of a few!"

"Very well. It is my *hope* that the device will not have been treated any differently. It does make sense."

To you, maybe. Reid kept that thought to himself, instead moving on to the other elephant in the room. "OK. Let's say all this wasn't just a massive hoax dreamt up by the Pentagon, and that it wasn't just a story released to calm the militant camps threatening world peace in the 21st century – by *bringing humanity together,*" he scoffed, "while creating an environment of fear that drove the masses into the 'protective' arms of the global elite, who conveniently promised that, so long as everyone stayed in their little boxes and did as they were told, they would all be kept safe—"

"Why, *Herr Doktor,* I had no idea you were such a radical."

Reid chewed indignantly over her insult before continuing, "I *read,* Dr Schultz. The *only* conspiracy is that there are no conspiracies! You've lived in the shadows all your life – you know this. And let's not forget how many of mankind's greatest achievements *began* as stupid ideas that no one credited, until someone did them – take time travel, for instance! Anyway, that's all beside the point. All this came out a century ago, for us, at least. OK, so I get why Heinrich Schultz would have interests in such organisations, and profit by them, but surely—"

"None of that matters in the here and now, Reid."

"*OK,*" he replied, patiently. "Even accepting that you're right, and there was no hoax, nor conspiracy theory, nor whatever, and it was all for real, here's something that *does* matter in the here and now – Area 51 is still likely to be one of the most secure facilities on the planet!"

"You are forgetting one very important aspect, *Herr Doktor.*"

Reid crossed his arms belligerently. "Am I?"

She smiled coldly. "Indeed. An argument you yourself made, in fact. Area 51 was one of the most secure facilities in *our* world. This 2122 is not part of the timeline we knew. I questioned that policeman – the one I captured from 22nd century Egypt – thoroughly."

"Badawi?"

"The same. Since Douglas' meddling in the 16th century, much has changed. Surely there can be no doubt about that, having seen 1943 Munich for ourselves? These people are much more trusting and, consequently, will present a much softer target. If nothing else, we shall prove one thing, Reid."

"And what might that be?" he asked, cautiously.

"If the antigravity drive is there, and in a form that is still beyond the indigenous people's technological understanding to reproduce, that will be your proof."

"Proof of what?"

She giggled her strange, tinkling little laugh. "Why, proof that the hoax was, in fact, true, of course. Proof of extraterrestrial interference. Honestly, Reid, after everything you have seen, I expected more open-mindedness."

He stared in disbelief at the brass neck of such a comment from a Schultz. "One *small* point, ma'am."

"Yes?"

"Yes. If this technology exists, and is beyond the people below us – who are more advanced than we are – then how the hell am I meant to adapt it to this ship?"

She smiled again. "Reid, you will do yourself an injury with all your worrying. We must secure the technology first. Besides, you will not need to understand how it works, only how to *make* it work – and if my plan succeeds, you will not be alone in the endeavour, either. I know just where we can find some top minds to help with our groundbreaking research."

Reid placed his head in his hands. "We're going to die."

Soaked, miserable and terrified, the Iron Age hunting party had had enough.

"Cadwaladr is taking his men home, Captain," Jones announced. "Think they've given up on sleep, isn'it."

Despite his bone-weariness, Douglas could see their point.

"He's asked if we want to go with them, sir."

"He has?" Douglas considered. Leaving the wormhole behind would make it more difficult for any rescue to find them, but then, that assumed there would *be* a rescue. On the other hand, a concern had been growing in his mind for a while. He knew, from his own meagre grasp on the history of his home region, that the hills around them were also home to others – others who may not be as friendly as Cadwaladr's people. He almost certainly had Sergeant Dewi Jones to thank for the relative ease with which they had made their acquaintance, but the people of other forts might consider themselves entirely separate tribes – might even be at war with Cadwaladr, or at least, on a perpetual skirmish and raid footing.

Douglas rubbed his temples to relieve a mild headache. The Britons would certainly have enemies, so it made sense that they would have an agenda, too. Regardless of the century of his birth, Cadwaladr seemed intelligent. He might not possess the superior understanding of the time-travelling interlopers, but lacked none of the basic conniving inherent to the human psyche. Douglas' people carried some impressive toys, after all – toys Cadwaladr would not want to find in the hands of his enemies. It was reason enough for Douglas not to trust him. They might be walking into a trap, should Cadwaladr have designs on their weapons himself. He had a duty to protect not only his own team but the indigenous people, too. He was wracked with doubt. If they upset the timeline…

"Sir?" Jones interrupted his thoughts.

Douglas nodded. It was a risk, but their options were limited and all equally unpalatable. Putting a stout wall between themselves and the mapusaurs was also front and centre in his mind. "We'd better take what hospitality we can find, until we can figure out the rules of the game. Thank him and tell him we accept."

Jones relayed the message. "*Rydym yn derbyn, diolch yn fawr iawn.*"

Cadwaladr squinted in the moonlight. Still struggling with Jones' modern Welsh, he seemed to get the gist and ordered his men to retrieve the partial cadaver of their fallen man, before moving out. Swallowed whole, the other man who fell to the Mapusaurus pack left no remains to collect.

The hike was exhausting. Sixty years old, Douglas felt every one of them after the day he had endured, and without rest to replenish him. The oldest of their group, he fell to the rear of their party with Dr Harry Bismarck. Bismarck, although not yet forty, was happier in the classroom or workshop rather than in the field.

"Ah'm sorry for how this has turned out, Dr Bismarck. Looks like my guarantee on yer safety wasnae worth very much."

Bismarck replied haltingly, short of breath as he fought to keep up with the brutal pace set by the local hunters and military types in front of them. "I suspect, Captain, that if we tried, we could spend all night leapfrogging back over one another, to previous events, to apportion blame for all this. I prefer to look forward. That's all any of us at Crater Lake want."

"Was that rebuke or acceptance, Doctor?"

"Please, call me Harry. Not a rebuke, Captain. Just an explanation – one I hope you'll consider before reaching your final decision."

"You're assuming we're no' stuck here, then?"

Bismarck smiled, the pale moonlight casting shadows across his features. "After everything we've seen, who knows what might be just around the next corner?"

Douglas returned his smile, deciding to like this man, while struggling to understand how he ever became embroiled with the Schultzes. They, like the Iron Age people, were clearly of more than one tribe.

Saving their breath, they travelled the next couple of miles in silence. At first, they had used flashlights to pick their way through the ankle-breaking carpet of heather and rabbit holes, but their guides had taken fright at their control over incoherent light. Whereas the moderners' first impulse was always to shine a light into darkness, the ancients adapted to it. Their natural night vision was excellent, both broader and further reaching than the range and scope of a torch beam when out on the moors. Douglas' people found it easier to trust them. Indeed, all Cadwaladr's people seemed to possess superior senses – probably because their lives so often depended on them.

Cadwaladr dropped unexpectedly to one knee, raising his spear horizontally overhead. His men followed him down to crouch expectantly. Douglas' people, slower to realise and react, eventually did the same. Jones' enquiry was summarily hushed as the king of Yeavering scanned the moonlit landscape ahead.

Keeping low, Douglas moved along the file to where Jones knelt. Jones placed a finger on his lips, nodding to where Cadwaladr stared, completely focused, sniffing the air. There was no breeze to speak of. No rustle in the heather. All was silence. Then they heard it. A snort and low grumbling. Straining their ears, they tuned in to the night. The sounds overlapped, suggesting more than one source.

Cadwaladr's head snapped right, immediately zoning in on the sound.

Prentice had heard similar sounds in the night on previous occasions. *Oh, why do I always get the weird ones?* he thought, also not for the first time. He bent close to Douglas and whispered in his ear. "They're asleep, sir."

Douglas turned to him. The moon provided just enough light to read expressions, close to. "Who's asleep?" he mouthed, almost silently.

Prentice shook his head. "Not who. What."

"*What?*"

The Yorkshireman stared north-east, across the tenebrous, undulating landscape. "Something big, sir." His voice was so low, Douglas hardly caught it, yet Cadwaladr turned furiously, waving them down. Two and a half millennia of linguistic fluidity separated the group, but it turned out that the gesture for 'shut the hell up' was the same any time, anywhere.

When Cadwaladr made a second gesture, his spear describing a circle in the air above his head, Douglas guessed that he was ordering them to go around. The Briton's free hand made a gentle, downward wave, almost certainly adding a 'quietly' on to the end of the unspoken command. Douglas nodded understanding and they set off on a north-westerly heading, keeping low.

The locals moved swiftly but absolutely silently through their homeland, completely at one with their surroundings. Douglas' people followed as best they could, with variable success, until Bismarck went down. Anglo-Saxon should not have been heard in those parts for at least another six centuries. However, it arrived early, when Bismarck let fly a string of startlingly coarse invective. The only noun to make it out, unmolested by the sweary adjectives, was 'ankle'.

Douglas winced. It was not merely that a sprained ankle might seriously compromise them at that moment; it was also a matter of the volume.

Cadwaladr was waving his hands about madly for Bismarck to shut up, but the man was in a private world of pain, refusing to listen until one of the hunters grabbed him from behind, gagging him with a rough hand.

Everyone remained low and motionless, listening for a change in the texture of the night. East of them, they heard another snort followed by several thuds and a whine, culminating in a *clop*. Douglas and Prentice eyed one another with concern. It sounded for all the world like a dog waking up, shaking, yawning and snapping its jaws shut, but on an altogether greater scale.

"Oh, crap!" Douglas hissed. "Jonesy, how far are we from their fort?"

Jones queried Cadwaladr, who lay flattened to the heather. He bit out a curt response. Jones crawled back to where Douglas was also lying on his belly. "Not sure, boy. They seem to have more words for valley than the Welsh! I think he said it's the next hill over, isn'it."

Douglas pulled out his telescope. Setting it to night-vision mode, he could see across the valley, north of them, to the rounded top of the next hill. "Yeavering Bell," he muttered. "Oh, wow."

Rather than the time-eroded lumps of ancient earthworks and tumbled, robbed out stones, there were robust walls. It was difficult to be sure over the mile or so distance, especially in the dark, but they appeared two, maybe even three metres tall – an enclosure perhaps three hundred metres across. He activated the device's electronic distance measurement and geometrical suite to fix the lowest and highest points on the walls. It was a fascinating resolution to a question posed by generations of archaeologists. However, Douglas' reasons for seeking answers were more prosaic: if they ran to the fort, would the fort keep whatever slumbered in the nearby hollow out, or would their group simply be leading whatever slumbered in the nearby hollow into a larder?

Numbers scrolled up and down at the sides of his vision, adjusting with his every slight movement. Distance to the top of the wall from their location was 16,784.00023 metres, to the bottom of the wall 16,784.00001 metres. The inverse cosine gave an angle of 0.009277 degrees. The sine of that angle, multiplied by the distance to the top of the wall gave him a height of 2.7175 metres. He whistled softly.

"What's wrong, Captain?" Jones asked, urgently.

"Ah dinnae think we should go back tae the fort," he whispered, anxiously.

Cadwaladr watched them closely, trying to work out what they were doing and saying.

"Why not?" asked Jones.

"Because their walls may no' be high enough."

"You think we should lead them away, sir?"

Douglas nodded seriously. "Or at least some of us."

"Split up, like?" Jones clarified, clearly with misgiving.

"Ah cannae see any other way of getting Bismarck out of here."

A roar came from the near distance, due east of their position.

"They're waking up, Jonesy. Better explain it all tae wee man – and quick. See if he'll take Bismarck with him."

"Yes, sir."

Douglas crawled over to Coleman. "Commander, we're going tae lead those beasties away. Jones is asking Cadwaladr tae take Bismarck with his people. Hopefully, he'll be safe there. Ah want you with him."

"You think it's a good idea to separate, Captain?"

He raised an eyebrow. "Ah'll no' go that far. Here." He took his sidearm from its holster, handing it to her. "Stow this away. Just in case."

"Yes, sir. Thank you. Good luck."

He grinned, encouragingly. "What could possibly go wrong?"

AD2122, high orbit, 38,000 kilometres above the Earth
UNS *New World* appeared in space. Almost a tenth of the way to the moon, she was well clear of most artificial satellites, and yet, even from three diameters away, the Earth hung vast in the heavens.

Deep within the giant ship's heart, the prisoners had no such frame of reference, their galaxy shrunken to three-metre-square cells with bars on three sides and solid walls to their rear.

"It's Lieutenant Nassaki, isn't it?"

"Actually, that's Captain." Elbow on the table before him, Aito's voice was slightly muffled as he supported his chin with a hand. "Heidi promoted me after the *Eisernes Kreuz* debacle. Richard, isn't it? Lieutenant Weber?"

Weber nodded affirmative. "I thought that ship was lost?"

Aito got up from the small table in his cell to sit on the side of his bunk instead. "It was. Hence the debacle, but I prevented Captain Emelia Franke from finishing the job."

"Congratulations, Captain."

Aito grunted, miserably.

"So why are you in here?" Weber asked, gesturing around his own cell, adjoining Aito's.

Hands now dangling between his knees, Aito looked up. Wearily, he straightened. "Have you met my brother?"

"Oh."

"Yes. He's just like our father. Thinks locking me up for a bit to contemplate my *many* sins will somehow make me toe the line. Once, our sister Himari stole Father's favourite saké. She blamed it on Hiro. The idiot didn't even complain, but when I told Father who had really stolen it, he talked Father into grounding me, too, for being a snitch!"

"And your sister, Himari?"

"Free as a bird!"

Weber snorted, despite his situation. "So what will you do when they let you out?"

"Other than strangle my brother? Not sure. I'm concerned about the effects this mission will have on the world below us – whether successful or not. Humans are bad news. We're just so darned interfering!"

Weber's interest was piqued. "You wish to stop them?"

Aito sighed, considering. "I did. It's why I joined the Schultz movement. Even falsified my own death, so I could just...

disappear.”

“Your intention was to stop the Schultz Dawn Fleet, too?” Weber stiffened slightly, suddenly distrustful of his fellow lag.

Aito frowned. “What’s that to you? None of it matters now, anyway.”

“I disagree.”

“You have a plan?”

Weber smiled. “I always have a plan. I was well trained.”

Aito leaned forward, rousing. “What can you do from in here?”

“Haven’t they told you? This ship is now under the full control of whoever piloted that Schultz orbital attack craft – I assume Heidi.”

“*What?*” Aito stared, eyes wide. “What’s she planning to do?”

“I don’t know.” He smiled again. “But I intend to enjoy the ride.”

Aito lapsed into thought. His latest reunion with Hiro had gone about as well as all the others. Memories of his original purpose to prevent the human race from *ever* becoming dominant resurfaced. He had grown up in the cradle of capitalism and rebelled, turning to extreme Marxism for answers. Eventually, he realised he had no stomach for either. The Schultz programme offered a third choice – a decisive choice. Meeting up again with his long-lost brother – a hundred million years lost – had tempered him, but now…

Bitterness stirred within him.

The ship shook.

Weber sprung up from the edge of his bed. “Did something just hit us?”

“Felt like heavy buffeting to me,” Aito replied, trying to rationalise and calm his nerves after Weber’s revelation. “Maybe re-entry? Perhaps whatever it is Heidi’s planning is about to happen to us?”

“Can we open a channel to Canaveral?” asked Baines, anxiously.

Singh shook his head sadly. “We don’t even have comms any more, Captain. So far, we still have life support, but I’m worried we might lose control of that, too."

"Any idea where we are?"

Singh huffed, undoing his harness to rise. He waved a hand over his instruments. "All this is dead. May as well go and look out of a window!"

Baines' eyebrow rose in mutual irritation. "I may as well join you."

They looked out of one of the viewports.

"North America," Singh stated, tonelessly.

"Didn't I see that movie?"

"That's *every* movie, Captain."

She sighed. "True."

"I think we're coming in over Nevada."

They looked at each other. "What the hell is she up to?" asked Baines.

"I... I think we should strap ourselves back in, Captain."

"Do we have internal comms?"

"Er... maybe. They worked last time."

"Better try to warn everyone, Sandy. This might get rough."

The UNS *New World* re-entered the Earth's atmosphere and descended with little fuss to come in low over the desert. The air displaced in front of her created low pressure behind, sucking the russet and yellow sands hundreds of metres into the air, to fall in billowing vortices that could be seen from miles away.

"I've got a bad feeling about this," Singh wailed, plaintively. "They're hailing us, Captain."

"Can we respond?"

"No, Captain. Must be one of Heidi's sick little jokes."

Baines puffed out her cheeks, exasperated. "Well, what are they saying?"

"What are our intentions, ma'am?"

"Hell, if I know!"

"Oh, no."

"What is it, Sandy? *Sandy?*" she repeated, urgently.

"Our weapons are coming online."

The first animal stood like an avenging leviathan – an effect only slightly marred by its stopping to yawn, hugely.

"Time to go!" urged Douglas. "Jones, Prentice, O'Brien, on me." They ran due west.

Taking Coleman and Bismarck with them, Cadwaladr's men ran broadly north, after a slight detour around the no longer sleeping giants.

The Mapusaurus sentinel sniffed the air, powerful eyesight tracking the little creatures predictably running before it. He could have awakened the others to go hunting, but that would mean relinquishing this important spot. To a human observer, the slight dip the dinosaurs held would have looked like almost anywhere else in the vast moorlands, but to the mapusaur pack, it was the area marked by Sigilmassasaurus. She was long gone, headed north, but they intended to test that. No, this was no time for chasing; this was time for consolidating. The young male watched with interest as the strange two-legged things ran off in different directions. They reeked of fear. Some of them reeked of other things, too. Sickly, cloying aromas; still, it all went down the same way in the end. He yawned and lay back down.

One of his sisters stirred. Stretching languidly, she stood to take her turn in an unspoken changing of the guard. She sniffed the night air. So many new scents to experience as she turned in a full circle, checking their surroundings for threats.

Douglas slowed, looking back over his shoulder. "They're no' interested in us." He could hardly believe it. Was this a little good fortune, at last? He could just about make out Cadwaladr's party heading over the brow of the hill, about to descend into the valley.

The female Mapusaurus saw them, too, and *roared!*

"Oh, for crying out loud!" Douglas spat, angrily, his good fortune lasting no more than a second. "We'd better make some noise."

"Are you kidding? You'll get us killed!" O'Brien scathed.

"Are you kidding, you'll get us killed, *Captain*," Douglas retorted. "If we dinnae distract them, those people have had it."

"But we've no place to hide, *Captain!*"

"Oh, crap!" Douglas pointed east. "They're chasing Coleman."

"What should we do, sir?" asked Prentice.

"Run after them!" Douglas led the way. He was exhausted. They all were. The only ones fresh and rested were the rapacious theropods – rabbit holes and heather hardly seemed to impede them, either.

"We'll have to shoot them!" Jones called after him. "We'll never catch them up, boy!"

Douglas knew he spoke the truth, but every instinct told him he needed to get the remaining animals back to their time intact. They had messed things up enough already. "Alright. Fire over their heads."

They did as ordered, but if anything, their shots only encouraged the dinosaurs to continue along the vector they had already chosen, away from the noisesome bangs.

"What's the range on that small rocket launcher?" he asked Jones.

"It'll do, sir."

"A warning shot, then, in front of them before they head down into the valley."

Jones checked the ground ahead through infrared scopes. Making sure their colleagues and new allies were clear, he fired and the explosion lit the night for brief seconds, throwing the terrible Mapusaurus pack into silhouette. The rocket worked as expected, diverting them. Like a flock of geese, they darted north-eastwards as one.

A horrible thought struck Douglas. *Anyone seeing that will be convinced they breathe fire now, as well. Damn!* He waved overarm for the others to follow and set off again. The dinosaurs vanished out of sight down the slope. There was no edge as such; the hill merely rolled downwards. As they arrived at the point where the mapusaurs disappeared, the valley opened before them in the silver moonlight. It was beautiful, though of more immediate concern to Douglas was that it was empty.

They pulled up, panting hard.

Douglas took a deep breath and blew it out. "OK. No' as bad as Ah expected, but where is everybody? And where the hell did the dinosaurs go?"

"We could track them?" suggested Prentice.

"You any good at that?" asked O'Brien.

"They leave three-toed footprints a metre across," he explained, sardonically. "The biggest thing we've seen up here, so far, is a goat. Pretty sure they'll stand out, Jen."

She rolled her eyes. "I was talking about tracking the *people.*"

Prentice bent over with hands on his knees, taking deep breaths. Straightening, he shrugged. "We might pick up boot prints if we use our torches."

Douglas' comm crackled. He jumped and swore.

"Captain, this is Coleman. Do you read?"

He grinned ruefully. "Aye, we read. Glad to hear ye're still in one piece. Where are ye? Surely ye havenae made it to the fort already?"

"No, Captain. Cadwaladr's men have a small hide dug into the hillside. They threw us inside and pulled a trellis over the entrance, covered in turf and heather. Saved us, Captain. Are the dinosaurs gone?"

"Aye, but we dinnae know where. Ah suggest we get out of here before they come back. Jonesy's rocket spooked them, but Ah cannae say how long it'll last. They woke up in a hell of a mood! Where are ye?"

They saw torchlight a hundred metres down the slope and to their left. In their haste and in the darkness, they had overshot. They made for it and got there as Cadwaladr's men were replacing their trellising. Douglas gave a short bow of respect to the Britons' chief. "Thank ye."

"*Diolch,* sir," Jones reinforced.

"What?"

"Means thank you, sir."

"Right. What he said."

The stocky little man was unfamiliar with the words, but understood well enough. He nodded and turned, calling his men after him. They made a last push, across the shallow valley and up the opposite slope to the gates of Yeavering Bell Fort.

Heidi watched the *New World* approach their target as though she were on the bridge herself, instruments accurately mimicking the *New World*'s to place the giant ship's full power at her disposal. The missiles she launched struck precisely where she intended. Though still a few minutes out, her plan was otherwise proceeding better than she could have hoped.

The voice sounded frantic, even over the comm. When the *New World* launched rockets, the line died, as fuel and accelerant were turned into light and noise.

"Oh, my God," Baines muttered, as her stomach fell away.

"One of the hangars has been torn wide open, Captain," Singh reported.

"Casualties?"

"Unknown. It's like our controls have been routed to a virtual bridge somewhere else – everything's on, but nothing's responding."

The *New World* came in, to hover over the base.

Baines moved to stand behind her pilot. "Still no control?" she asked.

"No, Captain. But we have incoming. Three fighter craft. They must have been stationed nearby and scrambled as we approached. They're hailing us."

"Comms?"

He sighed. "That's still negative, Captain. It's hard to imagine how we could look any more guilty."

"I know. We're a sitting duck, too."

He turned to her. "I just don't understand the point to all this. I mean, where *is* Heidi? It's just so…" He tailed off, completely frustrated, when a second hail snagged his attention. "They're warning us to clear the area and set down. What should we do, Captain?"

"Hope they don't shoot."

"Wait. What's that?" Singh pointed to an object on their limited, passive scanners. "It's coming in hot. On a collision course."

"IFF?"

"No, but maybe I can… no, I can't even get a visual. Perhaps it's Heidi?"

"Looks like we're going to find out what this party's all about, after all."

"Maybe not. Our weapons are arming again, but we can't defend ourselves. No, wait! Oh, no."

"What is it now?"

"Targeting resolutions acquired for the three fighters incoming." He turned to her. "Careful what you wish for."

"Damn it!" she shouted, suddenly furious. "There must be some way we can warn them!"

"They must've detected it, Captain. All three are taking evasive action. Unfortunately, that's all the good news."

Heidi's ship tore past them in a swell of rocket noise.

"That answers that! Definitely Heidi," Baines spat.

The *New World* launched a full spread attack on the incoming aeroplanes, who broke formation and returned fire.

"Oh, this is *so* not good," Singh whimpered. "Brace for impact!"

Missiles bloomed against their starboard flank in half a dozen places, shaking the entire vessel.

"Good. The *New World* performed within acceptable parameters," Heidi noted with satisfaction. "I'm taking us inside that hangar."

"They're taking heavy fire, ma'am."

"Of course they are. Meanwhile, we are free to act. A real stroke of luck. I expected this to be difficult, but then, who needs stealth when you have a battleship?"

Reid stared at her in disbelief, but her concentration was fully given over to precision flying as they penetrated the tear in the side of the building. Ahead was a pair of extremely heavy-looking steel doors, easily twelve metres tall.

Machine-gun fire rattled off their outer hull for the second time in the last few minutes. For the moment, it was only small arms fire, but that would soon change as the base fully woke to the threat.

"Quickly, Reid. We don't have much time."

"What do you want me to do?"

She glared at him like he was an idiot. "Surely even you can hit a barn door. Fire!"

It took four attempts to break through. Heidi moved the ship into the next chamber, ignoring the rings and pings off their hull. She turned slowly in place, situating them for a quick evac as she lowered their hydraulic landing struts. The ship kissed the concrete lightly; a perfect landing, despite the chaos all around. Heidi could see men approaching quickly, firing as they ran. Her eyes narrowed.

Heavy, gatling-style, multi-barrelled machine guns appeared from behind protective armoured panels in the nose of her ship. She fired. The soldiers dove for their lives behind any cover they could find. Any caught in the open were shredded into bloody mist.

Reid covered his eyes.

"Get a grip!" Heidi admonished, sharply. "We have work to do. The machinery we are after was kept in a unit over there, in our time." She pointed across the hangar to a substantial-looking storage container. "That one. The working parts were removed from the alien ship last century."

"We don't know that—"

"And we won't, if you don't get going!"

He gulped. "Me?"

"I have an injured leg. I will slow you down. Besides, someone has to stay and continue persuading our new friends out there to leave us alone. You do not seem to have the stomach for it. Now, go! Wrap the heavy straps around the unit and attach them to the hitch underneath the ship. I will hold here and prevent anyone from stopping you."

Explosions boomed from the sky battle raging above as Reid stepped out on shaking legs. He half-tripped, half-ran to the container, dragging high-tensile-strength, lightweight webbing behind him.

Closing the distance, he was already fumbling to unwind the straps as he ran around the container, throwing himself against the side wall, panting hard. Eyes shut, he took a last deep breath before feeding the straps through hoops along the sides of the robust container, hitching them together to a single, self-locking steel ring. Connection complete, he attached the final, heavier strap, that would be used to tow their cargo.

Not so long ago, they had used a similar arrangement to tow a large boulder, so that Heidi could launch it into a comet, deflecting it to collide with the moon. Such memories he had. "Father was right. I should have followed him into accountancy. Spreadsheets might lie, they might steal, but no one ever actually died of boredom!" A high-speed round rebounded from their ship to *ping* off the container, right by his ear. "Come on, Reid, focus, or this'll be your final depreciation!"

After one last check, he ran back to their ship, carrying one end of the tow strap with him. He closed the distance at a sprint, terrified as bullets zinged off the concrete and steel surfaces all around him. Further explosions came from outside the building – not that he needed any encouragement to hurry. He quickly slipped the loop of the strap into a self-locking hook on the winch that hung beneath their ship. Giving his final connection a tug, he hid behind one of the stout hydraulic struts that supported their tough little craft. He closed his eyes again, breathing heavily, while steeling himself to break cover and leap back inside.

Sounds of combat grew even louder. From the ground-shaking

rumble, he guessed the *New World* was right above them, too. If it fell out of the sky…

A thrill of terror made him shake uncontrollably. They had but moments to save themselves, he knew it in his bones, but terror froze him, and now he could hear heavy vehicles approaching, too. Reid could only hope the defending security force's innate protectiveness of the hangar's contents would prevent them from launching an all-out strike. Collecting himself, he briefly ducked around the strut, immediately jumping back as a hail of bullets strafed the concrete right next to where he crouched.

Heidi's return fire backed the defenders off again.

Whimpering unashamedly, he forced himself, with every ounce of resolve left to him, to step out once more. Small arms fire continued to *zing* off the side of their ship, but each time Heidi returned fire, it became more sporadic as the defenders hunkered down behind their cover. Another loud *ping* rang off the hull right by his head, sending him diving back under her belly. "Heidi!" he screamed. It was all too much. Though not really sure what he wanted her to do, he was nevertheless desperate for her to do it. Whether she heard him through the open side hatch, he could not say, but she launched a missile at a stack of containers, behind which sheltered the last man to fire. The whole stack, racking and all, went up. Whatever was inside the crates was clearly combustible, because the whole hangar lit up in white-hot fire and shrapnel. The screams were terrible as Reid hid beneath the ship, curled up in a ball. Had the hangar not been constructed in segments, he would surely have been incinerated, too. Even through the aperture they blasted on their way in, the heat was intense.

"Reid! Are you still there?"

Heidi's shrill call brought him out of his shock to react, if not actually to answer. He stumbled back to his feet and jumped back in through the side hatch, closing it behind him.

"We're g-g-good to g-go! *Go!*" he called through from the rear compartment.

"Excellent." Heidi spoke quietly to herself. Smiling, she opened up again with deadly swathes of machine-gun fire, keeping any survivors or reinforcements suppressed behind their cover as the flames died away. "Reid, how robust is the container we have in tow?"

He struggled to answer, shock and exertion taking his breath away. He swallowed. "V-very. As you'd… as you'd expect. Why? W-w-what… did you have in mind?"

Two armoured cars moved in to block their way out. Punishing fifty-calibre rounds joined the assault on their ship.

"More to the point, what do *they* have in mind?" he added.

"They probably hope to hold us in place until heavier weaponry arrives. I am afraid I cannot allow that." Again, Heidi switched to missiles and fired. They crossed the distance almost instantaneously, once more filling the hangar with fire and screams. The Schultz ship edged forward, shoving the burning steel hulks out of the way.

High above, Singh cried, "We can't take much more of this!"

The Sarge joined them immediately after the shooting started and now sat at communications, hoping the Schultzes' stranglehold over their controls might loosen. Captain Meritus waited patiently in a fighter within the *New World*'s main hangar, ready to launch his squadron the moment they could open the hatch. They were all living in hope, so far, denied.

"Captain." The Sarge drew the bridge crew's attention. "We have a message. It's from… it's from Captain Arnold Bessel, ma'am!"

Baines sagged. "Oh, man… really? Think, everyone. There must be a way we can get through to him!"

"I may have something." The Sarge spoke thoughtfully. "I've been running through our security systems."

Baines turned hopefully. "And?"

"We *can* open a couple of the pedestrian airlock hatches. With the ship fully under their control and airborne, that's hardly of much use, however…"

"You have an idea?" she prompted again.

"We could send someone out with a parachute, Captain."

"At this height?"

He shrugged. "Higher than most BASE jumps. If we pre-release the chute and—"

"They've stopped firing at us, Captain," Singh interrupted.

"Thank God for small mercies," Baines muttered to herself. "Do we know why?"

Singh checked his instruments. "Because we have stopped firing on them, I'm guessing. The Schultz craft is leaving the compound and seems to have a large container attached via cables." He turned to them, baffled. "What the hell is she playing at?"

"I don't know, but we may jump again, any minute. Sarge is right. We should parachute someone down there."

"They'll be captured, Captain," Singh stated, doubtfully.

"Or shot," The Sarge added, gruffly.

"It's our only chance to explain our situation, guys – not to mention our actions here. Fortunately, I know just the man to send – courage of a lion!"

⌖

"You want me to what?" Master Sergeant Apep Badawi cried in dismay.

"Return to your own time – right here and now – and to explain our current predicament," Baines explained as patiently as she could with the clock ticking against them. "Captain Bessel is one of the best, but we can't get a message to him. He knows James Douglas would never behave this way – it's probably why they've stopped firing on us. He will know something's wrong—"

"*You think?* Let us rewind a moment, to the *manner* of my return to my own time."

"Sorry, Apep. Will you do it?"

Head in his hands, he whimpered softly. "Well, of *course* I'll do it," he replied in muffled tones. "As to whether your message gets through… that I cannot promise!"

She smiled warmly. "Good man. Thank you and Godspeed. I

hope we can meet again after all this and—"

He nodded, taking a deep breath for courage. "*And… the drinks will be on *you*!*"

Baines clasped his arm. "Bet on it."

The Schultz orbital attack craft came about. Singh followed her as best he could with passive scanning instruments. "What the hell is she up to now? Oh, you have *got* to be joking!"

He opened an internal comm channel. "Captain, you won't believe what Heidi is doing. She—"

In the middle of his explanation, the *New World* opened a wormhole and jumped, trailing fire and smoke from several missile strikes.

A thousand klicks out, en route from Canaveral, Captain Arnold Bessel watched several camera feeds out of Area 51 from the passenger compartment of a UNASA executive jet. He was under no illusions. Having failed to communicate with the *New World,* it was obvious that something was seriously wrong.

His mind raced. Douglas behaving this way was unthinkable. He would never believe it. So what *had* happened? Had his friend lost his ship to the enemy they returned to the Cretaceous to defeat? When the *New World* jumped, he cursed. Whatever had happened, it was over. The smaller vessel, that penetrated their facility, was also gone. Aside from the damage left in their wake, the only proof they had ever been there was a solitary figure, drifting to earth under a parachute of the larger type normally used by pilots.

Bessel sat back, shaking his head with disbelief, wondering who it might be and what they could possibly say to explain all this. "Oh, this had better be good." He knew that two and a half thousand miles away, the president was being given 'the news' and fancied he could feel the heat of the man's fury all the way from the Oval Office.

⸙

Badawi hit the desert sand with a crunch. Hit hard, rolling as best he could, in line with the full twenty seconds' instruction imparted by The Sarge just moments ago, on the art of parachuting.

He was an extremely unhappy man at that point, but he was alive, largely uninjured, and closer to home than he had any right to hope, after surviving a week spanning a hundred million years and several geological periods.

A motorcade of military vehicles drew up in haste, fanning out, tyres biting into the sand as they skidded to a halt. They immediately disgorged troops. Shouted orders filled Badawi's world as a shock team surrounded him in seconds, assault rifles aimed, very pointedly, at every part of his anatomy. He had survived the falling, even the landing. Would he survive the questioning?

As first impressions went, it was not one he had hoped for. Hands rising gingerly, he addressed the newcomers. "I… I can explain." As he uttered the words, the chute wafted down to cover his face, entangling him in its cords. A breeze caught it, dragging him. He gagged, staggered and fell over again. "I'm OK," he assured them, muffled by the canvas.

The soldiers relaxed slightly, but made no move to help. Clearly, this incompetent terrorist was not all *they* had hoped for, either.

Chapter 7 | Magnet, Making Molehills
Out of Mountains

The *New World* arrived back in the real world, or at least, the nearest approximation space–time offered.

"Sandy?" Baines demanded. "Where are we… this time?"

He threw his hands up, miserably. "Somewhere dark?"

"Give me strength! Can we get a read on the constellations?"

Singh turned to his instruments. "I'm taking an image from the passive sensors still answering my commands." He picked up a tablet. "I'll run comparisons on this, until we get the ship's computer back under our control. In the meantime, there's something you should know, Captain. We have a hitchhiker."

Heidi powered down her negative attitude thrusters. Normally for making corrections in vacuum, she used them to increase the ship's mass within Earth's gravity, effectively 'sticking' them to the upper surface of the *New World*'s starboard wing. Of the three hundred artificial anomalies created by Reid's devices, none were geographically close enough to provide them with an escape vector – especially when hampered by their unruly cargo, tethered by straps and cables. Successfully transitioned through the wormhole created by the larger ship, she separated from their beast of burden and shot away at high velocity.

"Schultz has detached herself from the ship, Captain, and... she's gone."

"OK," Baines replied, slowly. "Do we know where?"

"No."

"So what's next? Do we have a new course?"

"Not so far."

"So... what? This is goodbye?"

"I just don't know, Captain. All I *can* tell you is that we took a lot of damage during that firefight. Rather than hit the ship's more populated zones, they seem to have focused on disabling our main engines."

A chill passed through Baines. "Bessel," she murmured.

Singh stared quizzically.

Baines defocused for a moment, considering, before returning eye contact. "Captain Arnold Bessel, that is, *our* Arnold Bessel, from the timeline we were born into. Remember what Hetfield told us? How Bessel disabled the *Newfoundland*, so she could land safely on thrusters but would be incapable of reaching orbit again? He did that via internal sabotage, stranding his small crew in the Cretaceous for forty years to save *us* from Schultz's goons. I'd bet the orders to disable our main engines came from him. He's still Arnold Bessel, after all. I got to know him well over the last ten years. James said he was the same man – a fixed point, was how he described him." She whistled softly. "Talk about 'the more things change'. The last thing he would want to do is take this ship down, killing everyone aboard. He did what he could."

"Well, he did enough."

"What do you mean?"

"I mean we're in trouble, Captain. We may not be *able* to follow Heidi on her next jolly through time, wherever that might be."

His tablet binged – operation complete. He powered up the screen.

Baines approached his station. "Let's hear it."

Singh swore.

⁓◌————————

The spearmen called down from their stone rampart. Lit by torchlight flickering from sconces above the gates, they stared out hard, into the darkness. A brief greeting from Cadwaladr sent one of them down a ladder behind the wall, calling to others, presumably to let them in. Hidden guards swung open the gates of Yeavering Fort for their king. At least, that was their intention. Like any fort the world over, in any time, the gates opened inwards – a defence strategy that allowed them to be barred and braced in times of strife.

In theory.

In reality, they could only be opened fully when cleared of obstruction. After transporting a large cask of mead to the night watchmen, the stubborn, belligerent pony, harnessed to the meathier's small delivery cart, refused to budge. Cadwaladr was already in a foul mood. He had lost two men, failed to steal any cattle from their neighbours and spent many hours as a plaything of gods and monsters.

He squeezed through the semi-open gates, roaring his indignation, which, to Douglas at least, sounded like his normal speech but at a higher volume.

Jones was laughing.

"What?" Douglas asked, confounded.

The giant Welshman shook his head in merriment. "I caught some of that, sir. Probably best it doesn't really translate, isn'it." He strode up to the entrance, swung his rifle over a shoulder, placed both plate-sized hands on one of the gates and pushed.

The gate creaked open noisily, driving the obstruction forward. The pony snorted and complained equally noisily, as she was shoved forward up the earthen ramp by her own cart.

Cadwaladr watched in slack-jawed amazement as Jones swept into their settlement like the march of progress, shoving aside the good, the bad, and the troubling. Douglas followed in his wake without so much as a raised eyebrow – after all, he had watched Jones play rugby.

The people within the village gathered in a curious arc around the gates. After strange and terrible portents in the sky, and monsters abroad, no one was sleeping that night.

Terrible, heartbreaking cries split the night air as wives and mothers were presented with news and what little remained of the Mapusaurus victims.

Douglas bowed his head, closing his eyes tight against the sound, but a roar in the distance made him spin round to stare out into the darkness as the heavy wooden gates closed.

The women were guided away by caring hands. None of the men followed. Related to the victims or not, they remained near the main gate – near their king.

Douglas could not quite believe where he was or what was happening. It was impossible to know the exact date, but he suspected they might be staying with some of the ancestors of the very people he met when the first *New World* crashed, roughly ten kilometres south and perhaps two millennia ahead of where and when he stood. He wondered about all that might be going on, out in the world. Could Hannibal be crossing the Pyrenees with his fabled elephants at that very moment? Despite the horror, it was intoxicating, too.

As that thought surfaced, a horn of strong mead was pressed into his hand, solidifying irony's contribution to the fate of mankind.

Douglas failed to recognise it, naturally increasing its power.

It sloshed down his combat vest. He held it away from himself to prevent further spillage. "Thank ye." He spoke awkwardly, though it occurred to him that receiving a social beverage from the king's own hand must represent a considerable honour. He forced himself to smile warmly and gave a slight bow in return.

Cadwaladr seemed content with that and turned to address his people. Douglas tried the mead tentatively. He need not have worried. Sweetened with honey, it tasted not only good, but wholesome. He drank again, feeling vigour return to his weary muscles. As a 22nd century man, he knew the evils of sugars and carbohydrates, but to anyone standing by grit and determination alone, it was just the fuel injection he needed. Combined with the alcoholic relaxant, he began to feel human again.

Looking around his people, he watched the honey hit revive them, too. Jones was already on his second. "Perhaps we should keep our wits about us," he warned, sensibly, while taking another long pull on his mead in what, for him, was fast becoming the irony[1] age.

He stepped closer to Jones. "Steady on, laddie. Tell me, what's our new friend saying?"

"From what I can gather – and it's like, one word in three – he's telling them how he faced a monstrous pack of terrible dragons and sent them away."

"Did we help out, at all?"

Irony often flew under Jones' radar, too. "I think he's coming to our role, sir."

"Peripheral, was it?"

Jones listened.

Douglas heard his own name mentioned, or at least, a fair approximation of it. He brightened. "Ah got a mention."

Jones sniggered. "Yes, sir."

---

1. Sorry.

Douglas glowered. "Out with it!"

Jones fought to control his mirth. "He said that, while *he,* their king, courageously faced the dragons with the men of their town at his back, you stayed in the rear, using your – I'm going with 'fire stick', to make loud noises that eventually helped drive the monsters away. I think that was the gist, Captain."

"Happy to have been of service," Douglas conceded, sourly.

A male scream, followed immediately by a loud *boom* from the gates, turned all heads. A bridge across the opening created a four-metre-high portal and fighting platform. It creaked ominously. One of the guards had fallen from the top to lie winded and groaning on the earthen ramp below – all sounds that were entirely lost beneath the *roar* of Mapusaurus roseae. The giant buck stood tall, to leer over the timber structure. Poor light limited vision, but the sounds of imminent failure from the timbers were impossible to miss.

The Earth Lizard[2] blinked in the light of many fires. He sniffed, unsettled by the smoke, despite his awesome power and size.

The people of the settlement exploded into movement, but though panicked and crying out fearfully, there was nevertheless an order to the ensuing chaos. Every baby or small child was grabbed by a mother and snatched out of harm's way, while every man and boy grabbed a weapon or farming implement that could be used as such, ready to do what they must, no matter the consequences.

Douglas looked around in alarm. He had brought this desperate situation down on these brave, simple, yet noble people. He had to prevent further disaster, hopefully without destroying animals that were as much a victim of their situation as the rest of them.

The rough overhead platform cracked and partially fell. Jones dashed in, bodily removing the injured man from where he lay, a split second before a ton of timber crashed onto the ramp.

Coleman grabbed Douglas and span him round. The exact same

---

2. Literal meaning of 'Mapusaurus'.

idea struck them at the exact same moment and they both shrieked, "FIRE!"

Douglas found Jones in the mêlée. "Dewi! Fire! We need fire! Tell them!"

The Welshman caught on immediately. Despite his size, he had an unusually high voice for a man, and it cut across the fracas easily. "*Tân!* Cadwaladr! *Dod â thân!*"

Wild-eyed, the Briton was unsure what Jones was trying to impart. So, as the gates creaked, the heavy bar across them cracking, the Welshman darted forward again. This time, he picked up one of the fallen torches from the shattered fighting platform and waved it furiously, right under the creature's nose.

It bellowed ferociously, but backed away[3].

Cadwaladr also caught on immediately and leapt into action, shouting orders left and right.

The spearmen and older boys gathered in a crescent around the tortured gates. Women brought large earthenware pots, while younger children distributed bundles of torches to the men, who lit them from braziers. Used to relying on one another absolutely for their very survival, they worked as one. Despite the terror at their gates, the women emptied their pots, soaking the smashed remains of their fighting platform with linseed oil, a prehistoric accelerant more generally used for cooking[4].

The sweet smell of the oil carried on the night air, and giant, demonic heads soon popped up along the wall at several points to investigate the enticing new aroma. They drooled and salivated, roaring at the conveniently corralled food hiding within. The giant buck at the gates pushed and the drawbar *cracked* loud enough to

---

3. A dragon afraid of fire – another irony that flew under the radar, which in itself was a feat, because Mapusaurus had no wings either – but then, the ancient Britons had only recently mastered iron, and still looked to the Greeks for the 'y'.

4. They also used linseed oil as a laxative – unnecessary on that night.

be heard over the commotion. The gates gave way, opening with an ease that mocked Jones' earlier efforts.

"Light the bloody fire, isn'it!"

Jones may have forgotten to translate, but it hardly mattered. A firestorm of burning torches rained down on the broken defensive structure. With a *whoomph,* an instant conflagration lit the night, its flames licking well above the height of the walls as tongues reached hungrily for the closest dinosaurs' faces.

The alpha gave an angry snarl before twisting away from the bearers of fire to lead his pack away, back down the southern slopes of Yeavering Bell.

⟡

Warning lights lit up everywhere. "We need to land, right now!" Singh barked, reaching for the controls. "Ha!"

"What?" Baines demanded, anxiously.

"We have the controls back, the computer, everything! We lost control when the *New World* sensed Schultz tech, according to Weber. Her program must have run its course. So, if she found another wormhole and left us behind, then… Never mind, I need to drive!"

Baines strapped herself back into her captain's chair. Identifying their location would have to wait.

When leaving the Cretaceous the first time, the original *New World* had ended up inside a mountain and totally ruined as a vehicle. When they left Crater Lake for the second time, earlier that day, they had done so from high altitude, reducing the risk of a recurrence. However, when they left Canaveral, the *New World* was less than two hundred metres above the desert. By a stroke of blind luck, the ground was a similar distance below them now.

Singh fired the landing thrusters and brought them down to rest gently onto another desert. Powering down, he released a heavy sigh of relief. "We're on the ground, Captain. I recommend we stand everyone down from red alert. We need to take stock before taking any further action."

Baines agreed. She made the announcement, enlisting everyone to help. Everyone but their latest arrivals – Lieutenant Devon's people. They were still locked in their quarters and Baines dared not trust them, so precarious was the *New World*'s situation. She summoned her senior personnel to the bridge.

"OK, Sandy, where are we?"

"Shall I start with the good news?"

"Why not?"

"I don't think we've moved. Though we are on both a different latitude and longitude."

"How's that work? It's been a hell of a day, Sandy. Break it down for me."

He rubbed his eyes, tiredly. "I know. I'll start again. We're in Pangaea."

Baines swore.

The officer strode into the interview room with two armed guards at his back. Already seated was a tired-looking, dust-covered man of Arabic descent. "Has the prisoner been fed yet?" he asked the guard already stationed inside the door.

"No, sir."

He looked back to Badawi. "Any special dietary requirements?"

After the stress of the last several hours, Badawi's stomach growled. He smiled weakly. "I'm quite partial to food, sir."

Bessel's lips turned up at the edges. He nodded to the guard. "Better get somebody to fix us some sandwiches or somethin', OK? Oh, and somethin' to drink."

The man saluted and turned to leave.

"And bring two plates," Bessel called after him.

"Yes, sir."

"And two glasses!"

"Yes, sir."

He returned his attention to the prisoner, taking the seat opposite. Placing some files on the table between them, he proceeded to ignore him, while pointedly checking his notes. "When dealing with James Douglas' associates," Bessel spoke without raising his eyes from the papers, "it makes a nice change to have documents from *this* reality. That may *sound* strange, but trust me, it's not any more. So, Master Sergeant Apep Badawi, I believe you told these gentlemen you could explain?"

"Yes, sir."

"Good. I'm Captain Arnold Bessel. You may not have heard of me, so I'll just explain that Captain James Douglas is one of the best friends I've ever had." He glanced up from his notes. "*So...* your story had better be worthy of a Booker Prize, son."

Badawi explained everything he knew, beginning with the brutal killing of a young palaeontology student in Egypt, by a time-travelling Spinosaurus that itself ended up slumped across the Red Pyramid. Soon after that incident, Heidi Schultz had captured him by the first wormhole, discovered near El-Shaikh Ebada, imprisoning him within an enemy warship, somehow parked in Cretaceous North Africa. Eventually, he got to his daring escape with *another* Heidi Schultz – that one from 1940s Germany – in a stolen tank, and their eventual rescue by Captain Baines and the crew of the *New World.*

Bessel's ears pricked up at the mention of his friends. His eyes bored into Badawi's as he listened intently.

As a policeman, Badawi was no stranger to prisoner interviews, though being on the other end of one was unpleasant. He tried to lighten the mood by describing Tim and Clarrie Norris' wedding, but Bessel's stare did not waver. The man barely blinked. So Badawi explained Douglas' expedition to round up the last of the Schultz company in prehistoric Britain, up to the point where another wormhole had opened nearby. Some of his story was hearsay, but he did his best to tell how Douglas' small reconnaissance party had been driven through the wormhole under fire. That was when Richard Weber activated the program that took control of the *New*

World's computers for a second time.

Bessel cursed, rubbing a hand down his face in distress. "Looks like James was right all along."

"Sir?"

"He said we should hold Weber within a high security facility – that he was indoctrinated, a zealot to the Schultz cause. Unfixable."

Badawi leaned forward on the table. "You mean, you *believe* me?"

Bessel ignored the question. "James was furious when Weber was transferred to an open prison and put through university."

Badawi sat back, deflated. There was a hint of laughter in his voice, but certainly no amusement. "You put him through *university?* Might I ask what he studied?"

Bessel placed his elbow on the table, miserably, supporting his brow with a hand. "A gamut of micro-electronics, software engineering and artificial intelligence studies. That type of thing."

"That type of thing?" Badawi repeated in dead tones, closing his eyes. "I assume he passed?"

"And then some. James argued that he was – they *all* were – not from this world, and some of the values from their timeline were…"

"Different?"

"Close enough. Damn it! They should have left Weber behind, but James insisted they all had to go. Just in case some unforeseen situation required their presence to fix the timeline. It was a crazy episode, the way they all appeared out of nowhere on that hill in Britain. I guess we just decided that Douglas was the closest thing we had to an expert and let him lead. Looks like we were both wrong. Weber should have stayed here, and he should have stayed in a dark hole! Sorry, Badawi. Please continue."

"There's not much more to tell, Captain. After several jumps through time and space, seemingly under the Schultz vessel's control, we ended up here. I can assure you that no one aboard the *New World* instigated that attack against your people. They were powerless – not even able to send a radio signal."

Bessel scratched his cheek while he thought. "No. I didn't think that any of the people I knew could be behind that. Others might take more convincing, however.”

“Captain, I’m a policeman. You’ve seen my record.”

“It’s exemplary. What’s your point.”

“I *swear* to you, Douglas’ people had no part in the actions that led to the damage and loss of life within this facility. What did Schultz take, by the way?”

Bessel blew out his cheeks, just as the refreshments arrived. “I think we’ll need a little fortification before we get into that story.”

“It’s going to take us at least three days just to patch up the hull, Captain, without the systems damage and replacements we need to carry out,” Hiro stated, mournfully.

“We can’t just sit here for three days, Hiro. Must do better.”

“Why can’t we?” asked Meritus, reasonably.

Baines stared at him. “We’re sort of on the clock here. Who knows what Heidi’s up to, or how much danger James and our people are in.”

“No. Captain Meritus is right, Captain,” Hiro explained. “If Heidi *is* travelling through time, then we can follow her to wherever she’s gone and arrive just after she did – or before – relativity has nothing to do with it. Same goes for wherever or whenever Captain Douglas is. But, of course, that all assumes we can *find* Heidi. At the moment, I can’t think of a way to do so. We don’t even know where she went geographically in *this* time, let alone where she went after that – assuming she *has* left this time. Though, I doubt she would want to hang around here.”

“It might be quite nice out,” Singh replied, half-heartedly.

“I wouldn’t bet on it, Commander Singh.” Tim spoke for the first time. “According to your own work fixing the constellations, and allowing for stellar drift, we’re right at the end of the Permian – more specifically, the Changhsingian Age of the Lopingian Epoch of the Permian Period.”

Singh sighed. “Well, that’s elucidating.”

Tim brightened. "Is it?"

"No."

"Perhaps," Baines stepped in, diplomatically, "Tim might tell us what's so bad about this period?"

Tim glanced at her. "You mean, like, if we're stuck here?"

She nodded.

"Well, temperatures outside are hotter than we could survive, for anything other than the shortest time. At least, that will be the case within the interior of the continent. And there is a *lot* of inland, I can tell you. Assuming that, when we left Area 51 and Nevada, we moved through time only, and not space. Pangaea won't fully form until later in the Triassic to come, but it already makes up most of the world's land mass. We might fare slightly better near the coast, *perhaps,* but that could be a long way from here. So, I suggest we get gone, and quickly."

"OK," Baines acceded. "We need to work quickly, so—"

"Oh, I'm not finished," Tim continued, every inch the professor, these days. "If we *are* staying, anyone working outside will need to keep their wits about them. There are some particularly nasty predators in this era – sabre-toothed gorgonopsians, therocephalians, and so on."

"Gorgo-*what?*"

"Think sabre-toothed tiger, but larger," Tim explained. "On the upside, you most certainly won't feel tempted to stroke their fur. Firstly, they might not have any, we're not sure, and secondly, they'll be some of the most vicious-looking brutes imaginable – and *we've* all lived through a small part of the Cretaceous! Trust me, you won't need me around to tell you they're not friendly."

"OK. That's useful knowledge." Baines tried again. "So, if we *do* need to step outside—"

"Sorry, I'm still not finished, Captain," Tim pressed on relentlessly. "We seem to have landed right at the very end of the Permian Period, too."

Everyone around the table waited for more.

"You know, the end of the *Permian?*" Tim repeated for

clarification.

"I think you'll need to explain, darling," Patricia Norris prompted her son.

"Two hundred and fifty-two million years before our time, in the 22nd century, at the end of the Permian Period, was the greatest mass extinction the world has ever seen. Approximately ninety-five percent of everything died. And when I say *everything,* I mean plants, animals, sea life – even life at the microbial level. Life almost ended on this planet. It was one of the most volcanic periods in the Earth's history, centred around what we would call Siberia. Please note, Siberia is a lot closer to Nevada in this time than many of us might realise. We could find ourselves close enough to the epicentre to have ringside seats. Volcanic eruptions, vast beyond anything we can imagine, will send ash and a cocktail of gases into the atmosphere over thousands of years." He counted on his fingers. "Sulphur dioxide, chlorine, fluorine and carbon dioxide, to name but a few. The acid rain to follow will kill most of the plants. Of course, when the monsoon finally comes, the dead vegetation will be swept away, but without the root structures to bind it, the soil will eventually get washed away, too, over the years, leaving bare rock. The baking heat will leave almost nowhere for life to recover. Reduced oxygen levels will stress any survivors still further. All the dead plants and animals, billions upon billions of tons of organic carbon will eventually be washed into the sea, smothering the seabed and poisoning the oceans themselves. As it rots, it will consume oxygen and give off hydrogen sulphide, poisoning any reefs that are left. Elevated toxic gases in the air will penetrate the surface of the ocean, killing all the plankton and everything that feeds on that, so—"

"I think we kind of get the picture," Baines interrupted. They were depressed enough.

"But, Captain, I haven't got to the biggest danger yet. Hydrated gases, once locked up at high pressure in polar ice, will be released in vast methane bubbles. As the years go by, some recovery will take place – sometimes over periods of two or three thousand years at a time – but volcanism will return again and again. The greenhouse gases created will drive a cycle that will keep spiking the temperature. Unfortunately, those spikes will, in turn, keep melting glaciers – at least periodically – releasing ever more hydrated gases to take temperatures even higher. Locked in this loop, the environment will suffocate this world, killing almost every living thing – a process that will take millions of years to fully recover, with most species not making it past this point in time."

The room fell silent.

"Are you saying," Baines asked, quietly, "that we've come full circle? That this will be very like the world we were born into, thanks to man-made pollution?"

"Not at all, Captain," Tim explained sincerely. "I hate to burst humanity's bubble, but the effects we wrought upon *our* world are laughable compared with what's about to happen here." He leaned forward, meeting her eye with an intensity that hammered his words home. "We really need to get out of here. If this ship is capable of flying and creating a wormhole, we should go, and worry about repairs at the next stop."

Silence again.

"Assuming you are correct," Hiro interjected, "and I don't doubt that you are – when is all this meant to start, exactly?"

"Could be a hundred thousand years," Tim suggested.

Everyone relaxed.

"Or it may have begun this morning. The good news is, it will probably take over a hundred thousand years for almost everything to die."

"So we can afford a day or two, then?" Singh suggested, drily.

"Not necessarily. This is a cycle due to begin," Tim checked his wristwatch theatrically, "ooh, roughly now. OK, now*ish*. We have no *idea* how far we're pushing our luck at this moment. Ringside seats, remember?"

Baines stood. "OK, Hiro. Create a schedule. Put everyone to work. If we have to effect repairs outside the ship, we're going to need protective equipment and security details on rotation. Sarge,

Tobias, I'd like you to take care of that."

The Sarge and Meritus nodded acknowledgement.

"Well, let's get to it, people. Before the world ends!"

⌒⊙───────────

The earth shook beneath Reid's feet. "Whoa! That was a big one."

Heidi scanned the horizon north. "I suspect the epicentre is some considerable distance from here. Lucky for us." She turned to him, smiling cruelly. "Not so lucky for our friends."

Reid failed to see the funny side. "We should get our work done as quickly as possible. I've a bad feeling about all this."

"We are well south of the event."

"I'm not so sure. Please, let's hurry."

"Very well," Heidi agreed. "We do, indeed, have much to do. I will use our cutting equipment to remove the container's locks. You set up the hoist. As it turns out, this antigravity equipment is surprisingly heavy. Swinging below us on straps, it felt like piloting a safe."

She broke out a small oxyacetylene tank with a cutting torch and got to work. Reid vanished back inside, assembling as many of their hoist components as he could within the relative safety of their heavily armoured ship.

Heidi wiped her brow. The heat was unbearable, and she perspired freely. In the dull realm of human senses, fresh trousers were enough to hide any outward sign of her injured leg.

South of Heidi, a decidedly non-human hunter stopped in his tracks to sniff.

The disruption in the north had already forced most creatures in the region south, away from an approaching cataclysm. Consequently, there were very few large animals still in the area. Those that were, were starving and afraid. Prevailing winds driven by the events in the north carried the scent of fire and destruction, but also something else. Inostrancevia latifrons was the largest gorgonopsian to live in Laurasia – the northern half of the

188

supercontinent of Pangaea. It roamed the vast lands that would one day become North America, all the way across to European Russia, west of the Ural Mountains.

Typically, Inostrancevia benefitted from a hunter's superior olfactory sense. To him, Heidi's bandaged wound, mixed with female mammalian sweat, flashed like a beacon, advertising a free meal. He turned, sniffing the air again. There had been so much noise of late, but all was still, now, except for the breeze. He sniffed a third time, getting his bearings and zeroing in on the specific scent that invited him to retrace his steps north.

Animals have no concept of 'a mile', only understanding how much effort is required to return to a place they have smelt before. The three-and-a-half-metre sabre-toothed giant growled softly, his stomach grumbling in counterpoint over the universal rhythm of hunger. Nature's mathematics, the type understood instinctively without need of expression *or* expressions, was built in to all her creatures, and for Inostrancevia, the numbers tallied.

Decision easily made, the monstrous quadruped leapt into action, quickly gathering speed to lope economically across the desert sands. The scent grew stronger with every step, as did his desire to feed.

With no one watching her back, Heidi had no warning at all.

252 million years later…
Dawn came early. It was high summer and the cockerels within Yeavering Bell Fort were in good voice. Douglas groaned, taking a moment to remember where he was. As memories flooded back, he groaned again. Once the previous evening's turmoil had calmed, Cadwaladr's people showed his group extraordinary generosity, considering their limited resources. Their king ordered a roundhouse given over entirely to them for the duration of their stay as honoured guests.

As well as the cockerels, there was also the coughing. It sounded like a child. Douglas winced – a child not long for this world, if he was any judge.

He stepped through the doorway, set into the low walls, facing east. A small porch raised the level of the door head so that a man could walk though without crouching – a local man. Douglas was no giant compared with the likes of Sergeant Dewi Jones, but he was a solid six-footer, which was enough to put him head and shoulders above the tribesmen. The Welshman was already up and about. Contentedly ingratiating himself with the locals, he was currently helping them remove the debris from the previous night's fire in the gateway, so that the structures could be rebuilt. He was easy to spot – like Gulliver on holiday.

Douglas snorted at the thought. Then the terrible wracking cough came again. He approached the sound and called into one of the neighbouring roundhouses. "Hello?"

A woman appeared at the door, almost instantly. Fearfully, she held a young child perched on her hip. The little boy could have been no more than four years old. He coughed again, a lung-shredding bark.

"Ah may be able to help ye." Douglas spoke softly, so as not to intimidate.

The woman barely came up to his chest and was clearly afraid, while trying not to show it. Douglas opened a Velcro pocket. The ripping sound made her squeak in alarm, and she jumped back. Grabbing a wooden ladle, she held it in front of her like a weapon.

Douglas smiled disarmingly and held up a hand to calm her. "Sorry if Ah frightened ye, lassie," he apologised, kindly.

She answered. Though Douglas had absolutely no idea what she was saying, he gradually realised that it hardly mattered, as she was not speaking to him. He turned to see a short man standing a metre behind him, his spear held at a relaxed angle, but in a tight grip, nevertheless.

Douglas recognised him as one of Cadwaladr's hunting party and pointed to the child, who was coughing exhaustedly again. He took a sachet of high dose, broad spectrum antibiotic powder from his pocket. He mimed 'by mouth'.

Obviously suspicious of this stranger visiting his wife, the man had already witnessed several instances of Douglas' group's 'high magic', and the light of understanding came to his eye. He gestured, inviting Douglas in.

The roundhouse was dark and smoky, smelling faintly of earth and damp. *Ah can see why the bairn's coughing his wee lungs up,* he thought, sadly.

A large clay pot sat on the central hearth. He could see it contained water. Moving slowly towards it, making no sudden gestures that might alarm, he took the pot and made to place it over the fire. The father shook his head, no.

Douglas sighed. *This will be harder than Ah thought. Ah'd better get Jones.*

The man spoke briefly to his wife, who took a pair of iron tongs and removed a couple of egg-shaped pebbles from within the fire. Douglas watched, mystified, as she dropped them into the water with a *plop, plop.*

Instantly, the water began to bubble and in no time at all was boiling merrily. Douglas smiled and nodded, making a mental note to stop underestimating his ancestors. Less sophisticated certainly did not mean stupid. The hot stones boiled the water quicker than a kettle.

He took a smaller pot, looking to the woman for permission. She merely looked to her husband. *Dolt!* he thought. *When in Rome, Douglas, ye damned fool.* He looked to the man, instead, who nodded consent.

Douglas dipped the small bowl in the water, careful not to scald himself. He tore open the packet, causing the mother to take a sharp breath. Waving a hand gently to calm her again, he poured the sachet's contents into the bowl, stirring it with the foil wrapper. He had no idea about the quality of their water here, so he erred on the side of caution by boiling it first. However, he now had to explain that it must be allowed to cool before imbibing. Would that be obvious? Probably, but he would rather not take a chance, either with the child's well-being or with their burgeoning relationship.

He held the bowl well in front of him and pretended to blow on it, keeping it away from his mouth as much as possible. The child was already desperately ill, who knew what alien germs his people might have brought with them from the future – or the past. Better to let the mother do it.

She put the child down and took the bowl, blowing as instructed. As the steam reduced, she risked sniffing it. Her nose wrinkled and she spoke to her husband. Douglas could smell nothing, but what more could be expected of a 22nd century man?

He gestured for her to give him back the bowl. She did so. He took a sip, proving the drink was wholesome. Making sure he turned the bowl from where he drank, he knelt to where the child sat, coughing once more. Moving into a cross-legged sitting position, he smiled at the little boy opposite. "This will make ye better, wee laddie."

The child looked to his mother, terrified, refusing to let the bowl anywhere near him.

Douglas sighed. *What's that old saying about animals and children? Here Ah am, in the Iron Age with a child who doesnae understand a word Ah say, hiding from eight-ton carnivorous dinosaurs! There has tae be an easier way tae make a living, Douglas.*

Mum came to the rescue, perhaps unsurprisingly. She walked to a rough wooden cabinet with boxes and shelves. Taking down a small pot, deliberately stored well out of the child's reach, she returned to take the small bowl from Douglas' hands. He caught a whiff of something sweet. Some kind of conserve?

He sniffed again and smiled, making appetising noises. "Blackberry and blueberry jam."

She had no idea what he was saying but smiled in return, adding the confection to the water, stirring it with a rough wooden spoon.

Douglas nodded, respectfully. "Just what the doctor ordered, lassie. Well done."

She took the bowl back and offered it to the child. This time the liquid vanished, the added vitamin C doing no harm at all.

Douglas chuckled, as did the parents. The father offered his hand. Douglas stood to take it, but the tribesman grabbed higher up on his forearm. Douglas returned the grip, with a small, respectful bow. He had been found in the man's house with his wife, after all.

He took out his comm, causing the tribesman to step back, nervously. Douglas made another placating gesture. "Jonesy. Ah need ye."

"*Yes, sir. Where are you?*"

The family balked, the man raising his spear threateningly. "The roundhouse next to the one where we slept." Douglas turned to the couple, speaking softly. "It's alright." He held out his comm to show the father, when a thought struck him.

He flicked it to camera and took a quick snapshot of the family together. Turning the comm to face them, he moved closer, cautiously. Man and wife leaned in, all curiosity, and then exclaimed loudly.

Douglas jerked back, in spite of himself, momentarily imagining that vicious-looking spear providing him with one more hole than he was comfortable with, when they both turned to him, beaming.

The man gestured for Douglas to pass the comm to him. He did so. The father knelt to his son and showed him their family portrait. The child gurgled happily, completely enchanted.

At that moment Jones arrived. "Sir?"

"Morning, Dewi. Thanks for coming on the run. Ah've given the wee lad some antibiotics for a serious chest infection. Ah need to explain to them that he'll need the same again tomorrow and possibly the next day. Ah dinnae feel comfortable leaving the medicine with them, just in case they misunderstand."

"Is that all, sir?" Jones asked wryly. "Your faith in my translation skills might be over-optimistic, isn'it."

Douglas snorted, gently. "Do yer best, laddie." He leaned in close to the little boy, offering his hand. The boy clasped his index finger in a tiny fist and Douglas shook it. "Ye'll start to feel better in a wee while, son. Ah'm James." He placed his other hand on his own chest. "James."

"Jemz, Jemz."

"Just James."

"Jemz, Jemz."

"*No, just*—"

"Sir?" Jones was smirking.

Douglas looked up at him. "Aye, ye're probably right." He turned back to the boy. "Jemz, Jemz, it is then."

He stood slowly, smiling at the Welshman, keeping his tone light. "A word of that to anyone, Sergeant, and it'll be *Private* Jones."

Jones' face, not naturally given to smiling, contorted painfully as he tried not to laugh.

Battles between heavily armed warships, unarmed combat, mortal combat with dinosaurs, time travel, crashes and bombs, Heidi had seen it all – survived it all. The sixth sense is a very real phenomenon, particularly heightened within experienced warriors. Like a change in the wind, Heidi sensed something was wrong. She moved the cutting torch away from the lock and turned slowly, raising her blackout visor with her free hand.

"Why, you cunning—"

Whether her words were respectful, as one proficient killer to another, or a barb would never be recorded. The predator had successfully sneaked to within four metres of his intended prey – very nearly to within his own body length. Ready to pounce, his jaws parted hugely, hippopotamus-like, to almost a metre high. The six-inch canines dripped disgusting saliva, promising imminent death.

Heidi tensed, also ready to act or react, but the speed of Inostrancevia's attack took her completely by surprise. The giant gorgonopsian was on her instantly, clearing the distance between them in a single leap. She dove right, twisting in the air to bring the oxyacetylene torch to her left side. She caught the quadruped across his shoulder, making him bellow in rage and pain. He landed awkwardly, shaking like a dog and taking a moment before turning to face her again.

Heidi rolled to her feet at full reach of the pipes that connected her impromptu weapon to its canister of fuel. She calculated the distance to her ship. If she dropped the torch to make a dash for it, the creature would certainly run her down. No, she would stand her ground. Taking a wide stance, she was ready to dive out of the way again. Perhaps she could outwit the animal and fall back to her ship incrementally? He was hurt, but there was no blood. By its very nature, her attack had cauterised the deep wound. She waited, dialling up the gas on her torch, increasing the length of its white-hot flame. Inostrancevia circled left, cautious now.

"Reid!"

Reid was tapping a cotter pin into position with a small hammer and looked up irritably, not sure if he had heard anything.

"REID!"

"What?" he called, as an afterthought adding, "Ma'am?"

"Some assistance here!"

He poked his head from the side hatch of their ship, crossly. "What is i— Aaargh!"

Inostrancevia's head snapped immediately to face the new opponent.

"I need a distraction," Heidi called. "Get out and make some noise."

"You… *what?* You have *got* to be kidding!"

"*Reid!*"

Before her compatriot could do anything, the gorgonopsian took advantage of Heidi's distraction, using it against her. Again, he cleared the distance between them in the blink of an eye, this time taking her hard in the stomach with his nose, flicking her high into the air. At barely a sixth of her attacker's mass, all Heidi could do was land with as much grace as possible. The torch was snatched from her hand as she flew.

Reid wailed in terror, but Inostrancevia paid him no heed. He had his prey now. This time he came at her slowly. Once again, using the mathematics of nature, he calculated her strength and speed, taking her measure, knowing she could not match his own. Just one well-aimed snap or claw would seal her fate. He stepped on the oxyacetylene torch, accidentally reigniting it. Although he suffered no injury, it spooked him, and he took out his fear of the unknown on the nearest thing he could bite. The pipe hissed as his powerful jaws and savage teeth snapped closed around it.

Heidi staggered to her feet after landing hard. Her blond plait had come undone. She brushed hair from her eyes, breathing heavily. Stunned by the fall, she nevertheless reached instinctually for her faithful nine-millimetre sidearm. Groggily, she remembered replacing its holster with a tool belt. Never mind; most tools can be weapons in the right hands, and she certainly had those. She drew a posidrive screwdriver and waited.

Reid was also coming to his senses. After rummaging around the back of their ship, he leaned back out of the hatch. "Heidi! Catch!"

Still unsteady, she turned, but not quickly enough. The gun cracked her on the side of the head, knocking her to the ground once more. She rolled down into a small depression, momentarily out of sight.

Reid swore profanely, profusely and profoundly – it saved Heidi the time.

She was furious. Luckily, the pistol was at the end of its trajectory, and caught her only a glancing blow, to land just a couple of metres behind her. Rising on all fours, where she had fallen, she dove to retrieve it, screaming back at him, "Could you not have simply shot the creature? *Dolt!*"

Inostrancevia tossed Heidi's cutting rig up in the air, roaring ferociously and catching the twenty-five-kilogram gas bottle in his jaws, trying to crush it in dumb fury. The canister was far too strong to give, even to his prodigious bite force, and realising the futility of his efforts, he turned a baleful eye back towards the food that had caused him so much pain and trouble. Drool splashed onto the sand. When Heidi's head popped back up above the shallow depression, the scent of blood was almost too much.

She stared right back at her ancient ancestor, for the gorgonopsians were among several species distantly related to later mammals. "Two birds, one stone," she announced.

Reid was gripped by terror. "What? What are you talking about?" he called from the ship.

Indeed, the gorgonopsians were mammal-like in many ways, though Inostrancevia truly bore the mask of a gorgon, as he poured all the pain and rage from his wound into destroying the container.

Heidi knew she had mere seconds before the creature gave up and took his fury out on her. She fired from where she lay on the ground. The shot caught the hapless predator in the shoulder wound she inflicted earlier, driving him back towards the shipping container she had been working on when he came upon their camp.

She stood and fired again. Inostrancevia roared in agony, the gas canister slipping around in his jaws to show Heidi the nozzle. She fired a third time.

The gas bottle exploded with enough force to lift her bodily from the ground and blast her another five metres back into the depression. The ancient creature's head vapourised, along with much of his torso. By design, the explosion also blew the hinges from one of the shipping container's doors.

Once the dust settled, Reid dared to look back outside. "Whoa! Didn't I see that stunt in a movie once?"

Heidi got back to her feet, massaging her ringing ears. Brushing dust from her fatigues, she climbed out of the hollow and blew a stray lock out of her eyes to glare at Reid. "Like I said – two birds, one stone!"

"I thought it was a shark?"

***

AD1559, Great Cheviot, Northumberland
"The idea of going home has an almost magnetic draw," Jim Miller admitted, as he scrambled down the hillside. "However, after the

impact we've made on this time, I have some scruple about just leaving them to it now."

"You think our impact has been positive?" asked Satnam Patel, sliding next to him.

Miller caught the physicist by the arm to prevent him from going down.

"Thank you, Jim."

"You're welcome. In answer to your question – I don't know, and I doubt *we* will ever know. If we leave, the chances are our civilisation will collapse in the way we've already seen."

"And if we stay?"

"If we stay, we'll not see the results of our work, anyway. The benefits will be for others to enjoy, but will be of no less value for that – assuming there are any benefits at all."

"Hmm," Patel considered, "and there lies the problem for me. Whether our contribution here proves beneficial is a *large* assumption."

Miller shrugged. "It's possible we might make things worse. But we may have already done that. Let's face it, we've crashed into this time in so many ways. I'm erring towards making the best fist of it we can. Ultimately, our own actions are the only thing we control. We can second guess ourselves 'til the cows come home and achieve *exactly* nothing. We categorically know the future is bleak if we don't act, so ultimately, what have we to lose?"

"Some of the time allotted to our race," Patel answered, darkly, unwilling to be swayed.

Miller turned to face him. "We might shorten our time a little, yes, but we also have the chance to win thousands of years, maybe much more. Come on, Satnam. Let's first see if this machinery is even salvageable. The future will just have to get along without us for an hour or two." He smiled.

The wormhole drive was exactly where they had left it, still bolted to its concrete slab partway down the slope. Major Ford White and Geoff Lloyd descended the hillside just behind them, escorted by two armed guards from the remnant *New World* staff and sixteen of Sir Nicholas Throckmorton's soldiers under a Captain Fear-God Barebone – a man, perhaps unsurprisingly, with no sense of humour at all.

Lloyd puffed out his cheeks with disgust. "It's totalled. I expected nothing less."

"What a surprise," White jibed.

Lloyd turned on him. "Of course, you're right, Ford. What was I thinking? I'll just harness it to a brace of unicorns, and we'll have it out of here in no time. I'm sure it'll be magically fixed by the time we have it back indoors!"

"Gentlemen, let us focus. We may yet be able to salvage our equipment," Patel countered, reasonably.

Miller caught Patel's eye, communicating silent misgiving without publicly pouring cold water on his colleague's show of optimism.

Patel shrugged. "We can try."

Miller moved in closely to inspect the device, standing on the reinforced concrete slab laid by Bluey and his team during that fateful storm, just a few months earlier. The slab certainly seemed to have fared better than the machine. There was clear damage from hacking, as though from an axe; someone had even fired upon it. He found lead shot both embedded in the machine itself and lying around on the slab – as evidenced by the discs, flattened upon impact. Some were less damaged and easily identifiable as balls fired from the wheel lock pistols the locals favoured, the weapons known colloquially as daggs.

The drive housing seemed to have borne the worst of the violence, protecting most of the equipment beneath. That was good news, but Miller still cursed silently, wishing they had been more thorough with their protective plating.

"There's nothing we could have done differently," Lloyd broke into his thoughts, perceptively. "This was meant to be a one trip enterprise, remember? The less that remained for…" he eyed Fear-God Barebone suspiciously, "for *this lot* to find, the better. I decided to stay behind and had just plucked up the courage to destroy the *New World,* when *you lot* started popping up over the brow of the hill and back onto the road, looking like mud-men." He snorted, ruefully.

Miller frowned. "If you'd destroyed our ship, where would you have lived? Can't see you going native, Geoff."

Lloyd stared balefully back at him.

"Oh…" Miller uttered softly, understanding Lloyd's intention. "Well, for what it's worth, I'm glad you didn't do that. Maybe that single decision will be written down somewhere, one day, as the turning point that saved civilisation." He smiled, disarmingly.

"Or the moment when history died," Lloyd replied, moodily.

Miller chuckled. "Don't worry. If that's the case, no one'll be around to remember it was your fault. Right, to the job in hand. We'll need some tools to unbolt the drive from the slab. Then we'll need the shuttle out here, to lift and take it back to the plateau. If we're going to try Satnam's plan, I want it in our manufacturing bay."

"It's all the devil's work," Barebone told his men, loudly enough for the *New Worlder*s to hear.

Lloyd rolled his eyes. "God help us. Stupid, primitive ba—"

"Geoff," Miller cut him off, sharply. "We're trying to help these people, remember?"

"The name's John! And will you keep it down?" Lloyd's annoyance slowly morphed into a malevolent smile. "Let's get on with it, then. I'm keen to bring the shuttle over. That'll *certainly* put the fear of God into our friend over there."

252 million years earlier…

"Any signs of the wildlife?" Baines' voice was loud and clear through the comm built into Hiro's helmet. The last time he had tied himself to the outer hull of the *New World* was just after the explosion that killed Mario Baccini and began their crazy journey through the history of Planet Earth. This time, he was not alone, but

with Mario's twin brother, Georgio. The circumstances were quite different; he was in no danger of floating off into outer space, after all, and this was not even the same ship, yet it felt eerily familiar. He sighed. Perhaps it was just the sense of impending doom that struck a chord with him.

Sensing Hiro's reticence, Georgio replied for him. "Very little, Captain. A couple of small lizards. It's-a pretty lifeless out here."

"It's extremely hot," Hiro spoke at last. "My suit says 51.4 degrees Celsius, ambient temperature. And there's another problem, Captain. The atmosphere has less oxygen than our traditional arc welding equipment needs to create the highest temperatures required for strong connections. Efficiency is way down, and our high-energy, electron-beam welding machines are better suited to vacuum environments, so we're split between the beams, Captain."

"Was that a joke, Hiro?"

"I don't know, Captain. Was it funny?"

"Not really."

"No, then."

Baines laughed. *"Can you help your equipment along with oxygen from your environment suits?"*

"Not without wrecking our suits, Captain," Georgio chipped in, "or risking immolation inside them."

"That's also a 'no', then."

Georgio shook his head sadly, within his helmet. "Pretty much, Captain. We didn't expect the oxygen levels to be so poor. We must be closer to Tim's extinction level event than we thought."

"This is no good." Hiro gave up. "I thought arc welding would be suitable enough. It's the quickest-easiest for a really strong fixing, but it looks like we'll have to go with TIG. It will be harder work, hanging on to the side of the ship like this."

"TIG?"

"Yes, Captain. Tungsten inert gas welding. The electric arc provides heat between a non-consumable electrode and the steel to be welded. The molten pool created to form the fixing is shielded by gas, deliberately excluding the surrounding atmosphere from the weld area. We're coming back in."

"*Thanks, Hiro. I'll try to remember all that,*" Baines replied, without a hint of sarcasm.

"You're welcome, Captain," Hiro replied, without a hint of awareness. "Georgio, bring the machine."

Georgio was nonplussed. "Of course. No problem! Are you sure you can manage that pencil-sized welding rod all on your own?" Shaking his head again, he pulled on the winch ropes and swung the welder away from the hull, so that it would rise unobstructed. Hiro hauled himself up on a similar system and waited by the open hatch for their equipment to come within his reach. "This is hot work, you know!" Georgio added, pointedly.

"Yes," Hiro agreed. "I've just dialled up the environmental controls within my suit. Much better. You should try that."

"Why didn't I think of that? I'll just-a use my third hand!"

While Hiro swung their equipment inside, the ground shook violently. Fortunately, the tremor sent him, and their gear, flying backwards into the airlock. After absent-mindedly disconnecting his suit from the winch, he might have been thrown to his death. He cursed his own inattention and unforgivable failure to follow safety procedure as the ground shook again, so fiercely that the whole ship lurched.

This time, it did pitch him out of the hatch. Hiro screamed in terror as he faced the ground a hundred metres below, headfirst.

Georgio reacted immediately, securing the grip on his ropes with his left hand while reaching for Hiro with his right. He caught his falling friend on the way down, in the crook of his elbow. Hiro hung, winded, draped over his friend's arm like a pair of saddlebags. "Whoa!" Georgio cried, gritting his teeth with effort. "You really put-a the weight on, during your soft life in 2122!" Pulling Hiro in to himself, he allowed the chief to connect to his line.

"You're fat-shaming me? Here? Now? I tell you, I'm exactly the same weight I was ten years ago!"

"No, you're not. You're fat, and I agree, it's a shame."

"I'm your superior officer," Hiro retorted.

"You're superior in weight, too."

"*What the hell is going on out there?*" Baines demanded.

"I think the ship might be falling into a hole in the ground, Captain," Georgio supplied. "But I'm-a sure it has nothing to do with Hiro's BMI."

"I am *not* fat!"

High-pressure volcanic geysers split the earth around them, ending their squabble immediately.

"Captain, we need to get out of here, *now!*" Hiro screamed.

Bubbling lava spat from jagged rends in the desert floor.

Georgio joined his superior officer in screaming. "Captain, if we don't-a lift off right now, we're all dead!"

Another rumble and a deafening blast caused the ship to lurch again, this time righting herself as her landing thrusters broke gravity's embrace to raise the *New World* from the tortured earth.

Hanging from a shared rope outside the *New World*'s hull, the engineers would have preferred a far greater rate of climb. "Get us out of here, Sandy!" Hiro bellowed.

Another geyser erupted a kilometre off their portside, with a tremendous *clap* of cracking rock, followed by an explosion that completely drowned the men's terrified screams.

The Japanese archipelago has always been notoriously volcanic, but this was like nothing Hiro had ever seen back home. Technically, they were in a place that one day would be southern North America, another place with a violent volcanic history. "To shoot that high, that must be a very, very deep eruption." As the ship rose, he made his observation quietly now, numbed by shock and awe. "Look at that. And when I say deep, I mean possibly even as far down as the transition zone between the upper and lower mantle – four or five hundred miles." Inspiration struck. "Sandy, scan the properties of that magma!"

"*What? Now? Get us out of here, he says. Scan the magma. Anything else I can get for you? How about a sandwich?*"

"Sandy, just fly the ship!" Georgio shouted, desperately. "Hiro! Help me pull us in! We don't have-a the time for sightseeing, or geology, or philosophising!"

Something had gone wrong with the winch. They could see it smoking above, struggling to lift the two men. "It must be the heat," Georgio noted, anxiously. "Even your increased weight should be well within payload specifications."

Hiro helped, oblivious to the barb, because, as his biceps burned, his engineer's mind was already working on the next problem. They had to close Heidi's wormhole network – Earth's future and the stability of space–time itself depended on it.

Swinging Tarzan-like from the *New World*'s side as Singh turned them about, Hiro cried, "Captain! I've got an idea!"

<hr>

Iron Age Britain

The Cheviot hills were wonderfully peaceful. It was a place made for thinking. Douglas' thoughts drifted back to his time spent – ten years ago, for him – in these very hills and to the people he left behind. There had been nothing he could do to prevent it, but the pain never went away. With everything they had experienced recently, thoughts of those lost in the 16th century filled his mind more than ever. They were so close now, separated by time alone, but what could any mortal do about that? It was inconceivable that he and five others could have gotten themselves stranded, once again, in this exact place, albeit two millennia earlier than Patel, Miller and the others – but then, since setting off from Canaveral on an ill-fated journey to Mars a decade ago, inconceivable was less safe than it used to be.

If Baines and the *New World* managed to find and come back for them, Douglas would have the power to travel forward to Tudor England and bring his people home – but at what cost? He knew that was the one thing he must not do, and it ate at him. Whatever Lloyd, Miller, White, Patel, Mother Sarah and the rest did in the year of our Lord 1558 and counting, it was responsible for the new, better future he had seen. If he prevented them from doing it, he would doom that future, possibly even the entire human race. It was the hardest choice of his life – so cruel, yet so necessary. "If only Ah could leave them a message," he whispered to himself, but saying what? 'No, you cannae come home. Still, good job, chaps. Carry on!'

No, perhaps it was for the best, but as always when a decision is made, the doubt demon immediately jumps up and down on the thinker's left shoulder. What if they give up, thinking there is no hope? Or decide to back down on their plans to encourage future events? He knew Patel was dead against interference, and he would certainly be a strong voice among those who remained.

A message? he considered again. *Just to let them know some of what's happened and to reinforce their will to proceed. Ah could skirt the issue of coming back for them, just out of kindness. The last thing they'll need to feel is abandonment.* Pain struck at his heart. *God help me, but Ah want tae go back for them… and yet, we may end up stranded here ourselves, so it willnae matter.*

He stood atop the stone walls that ran 1200 metres, tracing a rough parallelogram around the crown of Yeavering Bell. Three metres high in parts, they were possibly even greater in depth. He marvelled at the determination and sheer industry of the ancients. Their equipment barely passed for tools by modern standards, and yet they had managed to quarry thousands of tons of the local andesite, igneous rock.

Douglas scuffed his boot on the hard, grey, volcanic stone. Memories surfaced. This time of his father. They had not only visited the Saxon abbey at Abb's Head, built from and onto the Coldingham rock strata; his father had once brought him here, too. He took a deep, shuddering breath. So much was lost. So many connections. The very andesite itself was named after the Andes Mountains. He had stood in Patagonia, in the Cretaceous, on the very ground where those mountains would eventually rise ninety million years later – perhaps as much as nine million years before *when* he found himself now – though in his personal timeline, he had stood there just yesterday morning. He whistled softly; it was mind-boggling.

Equally mind-boggling was the amount of labour that must have gone into building the structure beneath his feet. Antler picks and wooden shovels – that was all they had. If they were lucky, some of those shovels might have been tipped with iron. Incredible. Some things, while perhaps not forever, were certainly close, and that gave him an idea.

"Is the witch doctor in?"

Distracted, Douglas turned to find Dr Harry Bismarck just behind and to his left. He smiled. "Ah wondered how long that would take."

Bismarck returned his smile. "Sergeant Jones is very keen for you to know that it wasn't his doing. He's surprisingly good at carpentry, by the way."

"Really?"

"Yes. Give him an iron hand-axe and watch him go. Look, he took a minute away from helping with the gate repairs to make this crutch for me."

"How's the ankle?"

"Hurts like hell. How are you?"

Douglas snorted, turning back to the view. "Dewi's one of the best. Ah'm certainly glad he's here."

"Yes. Might have been tricky, otherwise."

Douglas frowned. "But why are *you* here, Doctor?"

Bismarck looked surprised. "Has the terror of the last couple of days driven the memory from your mind, Captain?" he replied jovially.

"No. Ah mean with Schultz. Ah cannae see ye as a Nazi."

"That's because I'm not one. I despised the Schultzes, and all they stood for."

"But then how…?"

"Because I couldn't take any more. The world grew more dystopian every day. My options were to suffer, or do something about it – choices as simple as they were limited. I could either join Heinrich Schultz's deranged plan to begin again, or…"

Douglas looked sharply at him. "Or?"

Bismarck smiled again, this time without humour. "Or find a tall building and long drop. I chose the former. I remember the very day that pushed me over the *metaphorical* edge like it was yesterday, though it was three years ago for me, personally."

"What happened?" Douglas asked, gently.

"The windows to my apartment were controlled by the building's climate computer – and networked to the local authority's servers, naturally. Whenever there was a possibility of heat loss, they locked down."

"No override?"

"Yes, we had overrides. Whenever you wanted to open a window, you were forced to enter a reason why. I'm sure you're familiar with similar systems, Captain. Fire, noxious air, escape, other. Those were the choices. If you typed 'other', and then opened your window, and if they disagreed with your stated reason, the authorities would deactivate your apartment's heating for twenty-four hours for wasting energy – with longer penalties for repeat offences.

"Schultz's offer came in the week before. I didn't like the sound of it, but decided to keep the message anyway – I don't know why. Then, on that day, I spilt some concentrated cleaning fluid all over my clothes from a faulty, barely fit-for-purpose, recyclable container. The chemical smell was burning my lungs, so I opened the window – *tried* to open the window. The building's computer scanned my apartment's environment and found that the parts per million were within acceptable parameters, and so…"

"Denied?" Douglas guessed.

"Indeed. That was the moment I realised the hell we were living had deprived us of all autonomy or self-determinacy – our freedoms and choices, gone. But it got worse."

"How?"

"As you might expect, I wanted to wash that muck off me and my clothes. Imagine how it felt to be told by my washing machine that I had almost used my water allotment for the day. With less than half a litre left, it could not comply with my *request* to wash my clothes. Told off by a household appliance! That was a pretty low moment. My washing machine was my master! Then, and I will never forget this, the dead machine voice of my *shower* said, '*Dr Bismarck, you cannot shower for another nine hours, forty minutes. Your remaining allowance should be consumed as drinking water. Your drinking water intake is below optimal today. You must remain hydrated to remain a functional unit of society.*' A functional *unit* of society! What the hell is that?

"I opened my tablet and accepted Schultz's offer immediately. The offer was via one of his legitimate subsidiaries, naturally. Many of us have similar stories, Captain. We didn't even know what we were getting involved with, but once we were in, there was no getting out. Besides, it hardly seemed to matter."

Douglas was appalled. "Ye cannae mean that?"

Bismarck sighed heavily. "Captain, you seem a good man, but you're a high-ranking military officer. For most of us… well, let's just say that when life under the heel of a criminal maniac is less totalitarian than the rules of your own society, or government, you welcome the enema!

"Having not travelled for years, I had saved enough transport tokens to get to South America, so I packed and left. Within days, I was eating real food for the first time in my life, instead of the processed filth forced on us by our masters. I was inside the most insidious criminal gang on Earth and therefore, bizarrely, safe. Safer than I'd *ever* been in the city where I grew up. Aside from weekly trips to my office and workshop, dodging every kind of violent beggar and criminal, I never went out. I was already dead, Captain – just going through the motions of existence. As I never married, and neither of my parents had qualified for the few places set aside for later life care, I was completely alone with nothing and no one to lose."

Douglas considered. He knew many of his own people joined the military for the food rations, which were far better than the fare 'enjoyed' by the average citizen, since corporations had taken over many of the duties traditionally assigned to government. Most decisions were taken on *behalf* of democracy by bodies outside electoral responsibility or accountability. Those multinationals believed, quite literally, in hostile takeovers and in guarding their interests. Some corporations had stronger forces than many nations. He had heard that said many times and knew it to be true. It made him more determined than ever to save the altered, positive future his people in Tudor England had somehow created, and he himself had stumbled into.

Letting the thought go, he took a deep breath of exquisitely clean air and tried lightening the mood. "Ah sort of got the impression that you and Commander Coleman…"

Bismarck's smile returned. A genuine smile. He, too, sniffed the air, so fresh, it was sweet. In through the nose, he breathed deeply, his chest expanding to hold for a moment before breathing out through his mouth. "Let's just say that's a work in progress, but I have hopes. So, you see, if I'm stuck here, Captain, I'm totally fine with that. These people probably only have a couple of hundred words in their whole language – how hard can it be?" He smiled again. "I took a course in Greek once – I'm afraid of nothing! I might even be useful to them. I'm a fair engineer, you know."

"Aye, that's what Ah'm afraid of."

"Further interference?"

Douglas nodded. "Even saving that child's life from a dreadful chest infection was interference."

"How could you not have acted?"

"Exactly my point. That's all it takes to change the future. We find ourselves in a situation where a simple act of kindness might be all it takes to sow disaster. That child will grow to a man now, hopefully – may even have children of his own. All of whom might have been deselected were it not for my interference. Will they make the world a better or worse place, Ah wonder? And if not them, then what about their progeny a hundred generations down the line?" He blew out his cheeks. "We don't belong here, Doctor."

"Harry."

Douglas nodded. "Sorry. You did say. And please, call me James. But you understand why we should fear any intervention here?"

A distant roar echoed around the hills and through the valleys – a primeval, bestial sound from an alien world.

Bismarck adjusted the crutch under his arm, hopping backwards slightly. "I feel bound to say, *my* fears are more contemporary, James."

Cracks appeared all around, zigzagging across the desert for miles in every direction. Hiro and Georgio hauled themselves back inside the airlock. Tying on to secure anchoring points just inside the hatch, they immediately began packing down their winch system to bring it inboard after them. Focusing on their equipment provided a useful distraction from the premium-budget disaster movie unfolding outside.

Georgio shoved some of their welding gear further into the hatch and returned for more when he committed the cardinal sin of looking down. He fumbled, hands shaking.

"Don't look at it!" Hiro shouted, still using the comm system built into his helmet. Struggling with a fixing, he unthinkingly removed his gloves, throwing them behind him, into the airlock. Comparable to a hot bath, the sudden heat on his skin was shocking and it took him a moment to adapt.

"Hiro?" Georgio called, wild-eyed.

Forcing himself back to the moment, Hiro took advantage of the deftness gained from bare hands. "I'm OK," he said, returning to work. Some of the connectors and fixings were hot to the point of endurance. He made to blow on his fingers, instantly realising how stupid that must have looked through his visor. He waved his hands around instead, before reaching a second time for the last connection. He recoiled, crying out. In the intervening seconds, it had grown even hotter.

"I've got it," Georgio assured him. Protective gloves made

him clumsy, but he offset losses in tactile dexterity through the application of strength, pulling the connections apart with a confidence that would have cost Hiro his fingerprints.

The *New World* continued to rise. At a thousand metres, they were still within reach of the flying magma that shot from ultra-high-pressure geysers. The flat desert below them extended for several miles, bookended by mountain ranges to the north and south. Singh turned the ship around to point east, leaving Hiro and Georgio looking north from their portside hatch, when several flat-topped mountains exploded. Dormant no longer, they spewed forth all the ingredients that would one day give the region its next facelift – a spectacle not lost on the engineers. Both knew, at a subconscious level, at least, that they were at the end of an epoch and that the Triassic was coming to a desert near them, yet their conscious minds lagged behind. Shock held them. Most who see such things are moments from death. Even those endowed with flight require oxygen to make use of their gift. They were witnessing the worst climatic disaster of the Phanerozoic Eon of complex life. It would make the extinction of the non-avian dinosaurs at the end of the Cretaceous look like a middling affair. Their only hopes for escape lay with the cleverness of man, and his rocket engines, powered by so-called fossil fuels that may not even have formed yet.

"This would be a really good time to seal the hatch!" Singh's scathing comment in their ears woke them to their danger. There was no popcorn with this show, and Georgio reached out a shaking hand to follow the order. The outer set of heavy doors slammed shut from above and below, immediately followed by the inner set, which closed from the left and the right, with a finality that would have left earthbound health and safety officers in apoplexy[5]. The tip of Hiro's welding torch was crushed as the inner doors met.

---

5. Spaceship design stands firmly in the one-for-all camp, because when the atmosphere is blasting out through the door, an all-for-one approach becomes simply M.A.D.

Georgio turned to his friend. "Erm…"

Hiro was removing his helmet and environment suit. "What?"

"Nothing. Perhaps we should just leave everything for now, and get down to engineering."

"Agreed. Maybe you could ask Sam Burton to get some of his people to fetch all this later. I suspect we're going to be busy." Free of his helmet, he pulled his personal comm from a pocket. "Bridge?"

"*Go ahead, Hiro,*" Baines answered.

"Captain, we really mustn't push the engines hard. I was only able to get a cursory look outside. Are Sam Burton's teams back aboard?"

"*Yes. You were the last. The damage reports are still coming in… It's not good reading.*"

"All the more reason for Sandy to take it easy with those engines, Captain."

"*You're absolutely right, Hiro,*" Singh's voice burst into the channel. "*I'll take it nice and steady while the world detonates around us!*"

"Push them too hard and we won't get to where we're going," Hiro retorted.

"*And where exactly is that? Anyone?*"

On her bridge, Baines was thinking hard. It had all happened so fast. Desperately worried about her husband and friends, lost who knew where, she was now faced with an existential crisis. They would be exceedingly lucky to escape, with the *New World* limping so badly. "How far must we travel to find safe haven from this?"

"I hear Mars is nice this time of year!" There was the edge of hysteria to Singh's voice.

"Going to Mars has never really worked out for us, has it?" Baines replied, forcing herself to regain a measure of composure. They all needed to calm down if they were going to get through this and it was their captain's job to lead. "Can we create a wormhole?"

"*If we're lucky, we might survive* one *jump,*" Hiro explained. "*So we'd better get it right and make it count. We might be stuck there for weeks before we can fly again.*"

Singh turned to Baines. "Alright, assuming we've got one jump in us before it all goes to hell. I need to know where, I need to know when, and I need to know now!"

Her eyes bored into his. "Sandy, find my husband."

"You mean retrace our steps?"

She nodded. "If that's what it takes."

Singh ran his fingers through his hair, desperately. "I don't think we'll survive that many jumps, Captain. If it goes wrong while we're outside normal space–time, that might be the last anyone ever hears of us."

"*There may be a way,*" Georgio chipped in, thoughtfully.

"Make it fast!" Singh bit out. "I'm not sure how much more of this flying casually through the end of the world we can survive!"

"*According to the information Tim gave us earlier, Gondwana does exist in this time. Therefore, Patagonia should be easy enough to find in the southern hemisphere.*"

"You want to fly south? Halfway around the *world?*" Singh could hardly believe what he was hearing.

"*Stop being so three-dimensional!*" Georgio snapped back. "*Think, Commander. We're dealing within a framework of hundreds of millions of years, here. On the maps Tim showed us, South America is close. We're just above the equator, in what will be North America – way too close to Siberia, it seems – and South America is just below the equator. I think-a we can make it.*"

"How will that help us?" Baines prompted.

"*Georgio might be onto something, Captain,*" Hiro rejoined the conversation. "*We can make one wormhole jump, before we really will be pushing our luck. If you want to plot a direct course to Captain Douglas, then our best way is to follow a wormhole that already exists. We have no idea how many of these permanent wormholes Heidi has created. The only two we are sure of are located in Britain and Patagonia. I really wouldn't recommend any attempt to cross the ocean – even if we can work out where Britain is in this time. Besides, as Georgio correctly says, South America is virtually on the doorstep in the here and now. A thousand miles, maybe, as the pterodactyl flies. I think we can make it –*"

if we're gentle *with her.*"

"You're referring to the artificial wormhole Heidi opened near the *Last Word*," Baines stated, catching on. "But we can't travel through those permanent wormholes. Our physical dimensions preclude us from—"

"*No, Captain. The* New World *can't travel through. Not the same thing.*"

Baines was sceptical. "You're suggesting we leave the ship and take our chances? Thus, stranding ourselves wherever we end up?"

"*Again, no. We have no idea how far this devastation has travelled through the early Pangaean continent. For all we know, we may have arrived during a lull in the middle of an ongoing event. It's possible we won't survive outside long enough to escape. No, I'm suggesting we send a probe, Captain. If it works out, we may be able to extrapolate a direct course back to… to… er… wherever Captain Douglas actually was… I mean, is… that is, will be… I think.*"

"We get it, Hiro." Baines opened a ship-wide channel. "All crew and passengers, secure yourselves in any way you can, immediately. We're expecting a bumpy ride. There will be no further warnings. Secure yourselves *now!* Message ends." She looked to her pilot. "What do you think, Sandy? Could that wormhole still connect to when and where we left James?"

Buffeting rocked the ship. Singh swore. "I'm still climbing and something *hit* us! I think we'd better pick a direction and fast, Captain. This is going to be really close. Shall I set course…" he checked his instruments, "south-south-west?"

"Do it."

Douglas finished speaking into his comm. He had recorded as much as he remembered – as much as he dared – for posterity. He could only hope and pray that someone got to hear it – better yet, the ones he *hoped* would hear it, got to hear it. He removed the small data clip and wrapped it in the foil that, until recently, had contained the antibiotic powder administered to the sick child with the chest infection. The small boy was doing well, and Douglas marvelled at the little machine-manufactured packaging. Such a small, inconsequential thing to his eyes, yet in his hands, it literally held life or death for these people.

He shook his head. *Mankind has come so far. It cannae be for nothing. Not now.* He folded the foil securely around the clip to keep out air and moisture. "Maybe ye can perform one further miracle," he muttered to the small sachet.

There was very little timber on the local hilltops. Most of the trees had been stripped away with much of the deep soil by extreme and protracted bad weather in the late Bronze Age. Further deforestation was carried out by man to create pastureland and terraces for crops. Consequently, by the late Iron Age, all firewood and organic building material was culled and carried up from the valleys below. Douglas strolled over to a stack of logs, harvested recently by their appearance. Fortunately, pine was common in Britain and Northern Europe from about 8,000BC onwards – long before Douglas found himself this time – a softwood that, while less robust or long-lasting, was in some ways easier to work than the local hardwoods. It was certainly easier to cut, if less controllable to carve. Taking a knife from his belt, he scraped and gouged through the outer and into the inner bark, near the base of the trunk, assuming the best source of resin would have been near the tap root, prior to felling. He sniffed and inhaled deeply the fresh and distinctive scent of pine.

Filling a second foil sachet with resin, he placed the one containing his data clip inside it, using the resin to seal the opening. He squeezed and wrapped them together tightly. Those were the materials at his disposal, and he hoped they would be enough. Now it was all about finding a permanent vessel and the right place to leave it.

Douglas was no historian, nor an archaeologist, but growing up in Hawick, in the Scottish Borders gave him an edge. He did know a little *local* history, and no matter how far he travelled, no matter when he found himself, his destiny seemed irrevocably tied to this place.

He wracked his brain, when a slow smile spread across his lips. He made his way back up onto the fort's walls, where he had spoken with Bismarck earlier that morning. Raising his hand to shield his eyes from the noonday sun, he gazed south-west.

<hr>

Ten miles south, a metallic cylinder appeared in mid-air. A shaggy, Mephisthophelean head rose from the grass, curiously, though it continued to chew its mouthful of cud. Dull eyes studied the cylinder, while being studied in turn. Within a millisecond, the goat was categorised and slotted into a space–time framework within the known universe, as was the grass on which it chewed. The probe analysed every aspect of its surroundings.

The goat lost interest and lowered its head to nip another mouthful from the hillside. It would check again in a while, to see if the new arrival became interesting, if it remembered to do so.

The next metallic cylinder to appear was rather more difficult to ignore. Its shadow fell across the whole mountain, arrival heralded by the loudest roar the goat had ever heard. Whatever passed for rational thought in the mind of a goat, this one was beyond it. It bolted in terror, merely selecting a course that led away.

The hornèd observer was not the only one in trouble. High above, Baines cried out over the klaxons and alarms that wailed across her bridge. "Did we make it?"

"I'll let you know if we survive the crash!" Singh bit out, anxiously.

"Oh, man – not again," Baines groaned. "James is gonna kill me."

"He might not get the chance, Captain, if I can't keep her in the air. The magma that struck must have burned into our hull – or entered one of the new holes those fighter jocks ripped us. Something that worked a few minutes ago, doesn't now. Atmospheric controls are all over the place."

Baines gripped the arms of her captain's seat, letting him concentrate.

"I'm correcting… coming about…" Singh continued his running commentary. "Oh, crap!"

"What is it?"

"I'm *over*correcting! We're going down!"

Douglas realised that his personal horror was not so personal. Most of the settlement's inhabitants were suddenly ranged along the fort's walls, gawking at the leviathan in the sky ten miles south. Doubtless, the Iron Age folk thought it was the end of their ancient world. Douglas was terrified it might be the end of his *New World*. Initial shock forced him to look inwards, his higher brain functions, and reason, focused on loss and never considering the potential environmental disaster that half a kilometre of nuclear-powered spaceship might wreak in the pre-industrialised landscape.

"No' *again*," he moaned, attracting nervous glances from his audience. Two millennia from now, the USS *New World* would appear *within* Great Cheviot, upping its height to mountain status. As the UNS *New World* fell towards that very same hill, Douglas was trapped in a dual nightmare, for he could neither turn away, nor bear to watch.

A colossal boom shook the earth. Many spectators fell from the wall in the ground quake. Fortunately, the inner edge of the wall was little more than a metre above the earthen bank ramped against it. The unlucky few near the outer edge fell three metres. Of those, some were less fortunate still, as they fell into a ditch filled with nettles.

Douglas barely noticed their cursing – he was too busy cursing himself. While the *New World* had not exactly crashed, it had certainly landed with enormous prejudice, this time scalping the top *from* Great Cheviot. What the *New World* giveth, it now taketh away – though not necessarily in that order.

It was all Douglas could do to picketh himself up. Barely avoiding a fall, he stood once more atop the wall, watching with horror as soil and debris flew high into the air all around his ship, easily visible at the distance. Furiously, he roared, "That mountain is a bloody magnet!"

Chapter 8 | 1588

Approximately 1800 years later, in AD1559, and inside Great Cheviot Mountain, Jim Miller was struggling to believe what he was hearing. "So, if we can jury-rig this thing to work again, you want to open a wormhole *inside* the ship, this time?"

Patel held up his hands. "I'm simply postulating that if we could open a small, man-sized wormhole within our walls, we would control our environment and reduce risks of interference – both from the local people, and *to* the local people, should we—"

"Mess it up?" Major White interrupted.

"I'm just putting forward an idea," Patel assured them. "Alfred North Whitehead, the English metaphysician, said that the purpose of thinking is to let the ideas die, instead of us dying."

Miller pulled a face. "Well, in my humble opinion, we should let that one die, then! Besides, I preferred his earlier work as a mathematician. Worrying about whether the world is matter or a sequence of processes won't exactly help us if, as the major so eloquently puts it, we mess it up."

White, too, stared at Patel in frank disbelief. "Are you serious, Satnam? I thought there was a very good reason we opened the wormhole outside last time. And that was when this equipment was good. It's had all hell beaten out of it since then!"

"That was one of the reasons," Patel acknowledged. "The other was simply a matter of altitude. If you remember, Lieutenant Singh's camera probe appeared in mid-air from our current location, so we set up further down the hill to be on the safe side."

"So what's changed?"

"We now *know* there is a ten-metre drop on the other side, Major, and can therefore prepare for it."

"What are you suggesting, a jetpack?"

Patel and Miller looked at one another, a slow grin spreading from one face to the other. They would never have dreamt of saying 'out of the mouths of babes' when referring to the major, but it was clearly what they were thinking.

"That would allow whoever goes through to get the lay of the land for miles around." Miller vocalised his thoughts as he warmed to the idea.

White was now astonished by Miller, too. "Are you kidding? Have you two been at Maxwell's single malt already this morning?"

"We cannot simply do nothing, Major," Patel explained, patiently. "We have been working on the drive for almost a month now. There is only so much you can do before you must test your work. And I, for one, am still unsure about our continued presence in this time. I can hardly claim that my education programme is proving an unqualified success, either."

White chuckled, wryly. "Yes, Mother Sarah mentioned your classes."

"Oh?"

"Only to say that your initial syllabus needs work."

"Oh."

"I'll need a few days to build a jetpack," Miller cut in, not really listening to them as his thoughts forged ahead. "We have everything we need, but—"

"I was joking!" White exploded. "And if you succeed in this crazy scheme, who are you suggesting we send into the future, huh? If I understand correctly, won't this be a very short window lasting no more than a handful of seconds?"

"I'll go," Patel stated, immediately.

"Look, wait a minute," White insisted. "There are only a handful of us left. More than ever, each life is precious, but even accepting that, surely, we should send someone further down the food chain. I mean, I know it's a zillion-to-one shot," he added, sarcastically, "but what if we should totally screw this up? We're going to need you here, Satnam."

"You would send one of your men instead, Major? I could not allow it. If we do 'screw this up', as you say, then I could not have that on my conscience."

"Actually, I wasn't going to order *anyone* through to the future. I was putting myself forward."

"Laudable, Ford, but there really is a high factor of danger this time. As Jim says, this time, our equipment is jury-rigged[1]."

White subsided into thought. Eventually, he said, "I'm really not sure about this, Satnam. It's been growing on my mind that maybe our friends…" He tailed off.

"You think they might all be dead," Patel finished the thought;

---

1. Not to be confused with jerry-rig or jerry-built. To *jury-rig* is to make something as best you can with what you have; to jerry-rig is to make something badly – possibly a reference to the walls of Jericho, which famously fell after Joshua's followers blew their trumpets at them (a slightly earlier, roughly contemporaneous – if narratively useful – earthquake may have had something to do with the collapse). The mud brick construction on top of stone footings was not well made. For modern equivalence, the people inside the walls probably wondered why they bothered paying their taxes.

it was not a question.

White looked to Miller, who was busying himself at a workbench. He took Patel aside. "Jim's wife went through with the others, comfortably in the middle of the herd. He stayed until the end to make sure they got through, so I don't want to throw around doubts like that. The guy's lost enough."

Patel glanced at Miller. "His daughter had the courage to stay here with her father. Call me heartless, but I don't think he lost anything of any great value."

"I agree, but I wouldn't wanna tell him that. The thing is, Satnam, if they did get through, back to our own timeline, why didn't they come back for us?"

"You have a theory?"

"I have three," White confessed. "One, they didn't make it. Two, they made it into a future world that was changed in some way, and had no way of coming back for us. Or three…" He hesitated. "They left us back here for a reason."

Patel mulled his words over. "Your logic is hard to argue against, Ford. All I can ask in return is this – should we not find out for sure?"

"And if it turns out to be a one-way trip? What will we have learned then? We'll have lost the finest mind among us for nothing."

"Are you saying you would prevent me from going?"

White lapsed into thought again. "No. What I'm saying is, this affects all of us – hell, it might affect the entire future of our race. I think we should put it to the vote. At the very least, we should hear everyone's thoughts before we do anything perilous. You can make your arguments to the group."

Silent a moment, Patel eventually conceded. "Yes. That is both democratic and fair. I agree."

252 million years earlier, Gondwana
"The wormhole has gone," Reid reported solemnly.

"Impossible!"

He turned to his mistress. "Impossible? What does that even mean any more? It's gone. I don't know what else to tell you. Despite existing outside space–time, the device that opened the wormhole... *Whoa.*"

"What?"

"Obviously, the colossal volcanic activity in this region might be masking our readings. Either that, or... our device has somehow been swallowed. This was no ordinary magma chamber, after all – it seems to have vents stretching across twenty percent of the world's landmass. Ha! Of course..."

Heidi glared at him. "Again, what?"

"The wormhole popped us out of the manifold at the Permian–Triassic boundary."

"Explain."

"I thought Tim Norris' notes might have helped you there?"

She shook her head. "There was a vast amount of information. I read only that which pertained to the middle Cretaceous."

"Fair enough," he allowed. "I know very little about this time, either, but from geology classes taken in my youth, I believe this to be the greatest period of volcanism recorded in the fossil record over the last half-billion years. Perhaps it's no surprise that it was also the greatest mass extinction. We need to get out of here."

"That much is true. How do you suggest we do that?"

"The closest wormhole that I can detect is the one we opened in Patagonia, ma'am."

"That will be in the same location in this time?"

"The *wormhole* is in the same location, it's the *location* that's someplace else, due to a hundred and fifty million years of tectonic movement and continental drift. But we can track it."

"Better look to it, Reid. Even at this altitude we are no longer safe. We pushed our luck putting down yesterday."

On that, at least, we agree, Reid thought, darkly, bending to his task.

⌒⊙‿‿‿‿‿‿‿‿‿‿

White's face was filled with concern. "Are you sure about this, Satnam?"

Patel smiled. "I am. We managed three minutes last time. I will give myself just sixty seconds to take a look around, at height, while sending out an open broadcast on every frequency our equipment can produce. If I find nothing and no one, I shall return."

"Are you sure about the date?" Ford pressed.

"AD2114. Yes. One year after our companions stepped through into the 22nd century – I hope. There is no point arriving right on their heels. Firstly, if…" He leaned in closer. "If they met with some sort of misadventure, I would merely be adding to the casualty list. Secondly, one year should have given them chance to find their feet and hopefully gather the help they would need to come back for those of us left behind."

White blew out his cheeks. "That's a whole heap of suppositions, my friend."

Patel took him in a solemn forearm clasp. "Science and achievement have always required leaps of imagination, Ford."

"And leaps of faith," Sarah added, joining them. She embraced Patel. "Take care, Satnam. God be with you."

He smiled again. "I am sure He will." He turned to his small group of time-travelling companions. "I'll see you in about sixty seconds, or six hundred years, my dear friends." He nodded to Miller.

A wormhole opened in the heart of *Factory Pod 4,* at the centre of the main hangar.

"Yes! It worked," Miller exclaimed, punching the air. "You're clear to go, Satnam. Good luck."

Patel nodded farewell, fired up his jetpack and vanished.

The rocket motor's roar drowned Miller's warning. "*Wait!*"

White and Sarah ran over to him. "What's happened?"

"I… I don't know. Something…"

"Jim!" they cried together.

"The wormhole. Something strange happened just after it opened. It took me a second or two to notice. Oh, I just don't know!"

"Did he get there?" White pressed.

"He got *somewhere*. I'm sorry, that's all I can tell you."

⁂

"It's still there. Thank God!" Reid exclaimed, enthusiastically. "Setting up our run… what's this?"

Heidi looked over at his instruments. "Ionisation in the atmosphere?"

"Yes, and it's localised above the wormhole. I would have chalked it up as an artifact of the vast disturbance north, except that this is *very* localised. Ma'am, I think a wormhole has already been opened here. A large one."

"You think the *New World* arrived here before us? I thought they sustained heavy damage in the firefight in Area 51?"

"They did. After we travelled through from Nevada, I didn't think they'd have another jump in them. Not without repairs – and good luck with that, the way that whole place lit up when the eruptions began. We were fortunate to be well south of them."

"Could they have passed us unseen, or unheard?"

"We weren't scanning for them, ma'am. Perhaps they flew by while we spent the last day moving that heavy equipment aboard our ship – and fighting for our lives, of course. Still, I'm surprised. After all, we came here thinking they'd be trapped, so far back, and in such a harsh environment that…"

"That we would not be troubled by them again," Heidi completed.

He shrugged. "Shall we proceed? The epicentre of all that volcanism is far to the north at the moment, but its effects will soon be felt the world over."

"Very well. I wish to head back to Crater Lake. Make the adjustments and feed the coordinates to the wormhole."

"Yes, ma'am."

Their ship vanished.

<hr>

"Not again!" Dr Brian Alba complained, noisily.

"What's happened now?" asked Corporal Thomas.

"Another ship has come through the wormhole," McBride reported.

Thomas walked over to see the instruments for himself. "Is it Heidi, Lieutenant?"

"Looks like. I'm going to need you to launch again, Corporal."

"On my way, sir." Thomas left the control centre at a trot, muttering, "Up and down, up and down. Honestly, I feel like I'm flying a yoyo!"

Instantly leaving the Permian–Triassic boundary, Heidi's orbital attack craft appeared once more in the torrential rain of mid-Cretaceous Britain. It climbed rapidly over the jagged cliffs of the Crater Lake caldera to fly over the small base, tearing out across the lake before any ships were scrambled to answer the threat she posed.

"Is there a second part to your plan, ma'am?"

"Of course."

"Of course," he muttered, deadpan.

They came in low, just above the windswept water. Spray flew high into the air in their wake.

"We're slowing, ma'am," Reid stated the obvious. "I only mention it because…"

"Yes?"

"We're very low, ma'am, and there are some extremely large and dangerous predators in these waters. Also, the base commander will certainly launch their ships to intercept us again."

"Why, Reid, you are becoming quite nervous."

"My nerves were all burned out months ago, ma'am. This is just learned behaviour from sharing your adventures."

She grinned. "Believe me, travelling at speed would be unwise where we are going."

"And where is that, exactly?"

"Off grid. Douglas' people – or Baines' people, depending on who's left alive – may yet work out a way of mapping our wormhole manifold. They survived the Permian extinction, it seems. Who knows what they might try next. I have learned from bitter experience never to underestimate their tenacity. So, I am taking you to a place I am convinced they will not follow, and would have no reason to suspect. Soon enough, they will have no way of knowing *where* we are, so you can work in peace on our little gravity drive project."

"How can I possibly convert that technology to work with this ship? We have nothing more than basic tools aboard."

"Again, you are worrying, Reid. I promised you help and help you shall receive, when we arrive at our destination. The people there may need a little coercion, perhaps, but we know how to accomplish that, do we not? I want you to set the self-destruct on this ship and link it to my comm." She winked.

Reid could hardly believe it; she actually winked at him. He had no answer, so he just gripped the arms of his seat and hung on.

"Do it now, and do not worry," she continued. "I have been there before, very recently. My mission failed, as it happens." She spoke lightly, matter-of-fact.

Reid closed his eyes.

"Our sojourn to the 22nd century proved that," Heidi continued. "And it is fortunate that I did fail. Otherwise, we would have lost this option. Now, obey my order and prepare the self-destruct. Give me fifteen minutes on the clock. That should be long enough to get the locals to see things our way."

"The locals?"

"Hurry! I do not wish to be shot down. As you noted, a swim for the shore would be most inadvisable."

AD1588, year of the Spanish Armada –
inside Great Cheviot Mountain

Despite his eighty-three years, Geoff Lloyd had lost none of his finesse at the stick. He brought the Schultz orbital attack craft down inside *Factory Pod 4*'s main hangar, to land gently, just inside the huge steel doors.

He, Major Ford White, Henry Burnstein Jr and Rose Burnstein-Miller disembarked, congratulating one another on a job well done. Less than an hour previously, Heidi Schultz had popped up out of nowhere, right in the middle of their ship, only to promptly vanish again – who knew how – leaving them with a turkey-mayo sandwich and a tactical nuclear warhead to disarm.

Henry and Lloyd quickly demolished the sandwich but just as quickly gave up on disarming the bomb, calculating the chances were high that any tampering would only set it off right in their faces. Rose's plan to fly it out over the North Atlantic and dump it at sea had been bold. Unknown to them, their actions had not gone so well for the Spanish galley *San Juan de Sicilia*. Ill-fated in both timelines, she circumnavigated Britain after the failure of the Spanish Armada, never to return home.

Closing the heavy vehicular hatch behind them, Lloyd and his companions turned their thoughts to hot showers and hot meals – possibly even hot toddies – when their peace was shattered again.

In the centre of the main hangar, Satnam Patel appeared from a shimmer in the air, attached to a jetpack. He crashed into the lorry Heidi's ship had so recently pushed out of the way.

"What the hell!" White shouted, running to help. "That's Satnam!" He could not believe it. "But we lost you thirty years ago!"

Patel tried to pick himself up, but his pack prevented him. "Ouch! Ford? Is that you? Oh, no. I failed." It was then that he noticed his friend's face. "My God, Ford. What has happened to you? You look thirty years older! What year is this?"

White was speechless. He bent to help his long-lost friend back to his feet, when the prow of a ship appeared. Though moving at no more than a walking pace, it shoved them aside with an inexorability no man could resist.

The vessel stopped when it hit the lorry, its side hatch opening to reveal Heidi – *again.*

Lloyd swore loudly. "What the f—"

"For the second time, Geoffrey, what *are* you doing in those tights?" Heidi greeted, smugly, gesturing to the ship Lloyd had just landed. "Ah, I see you saved my other ship." She then slapped the hull of the vessel in which she arrived. "Snap. How did you dispose of the warhead I left you? Never mind, you can tell me later. We are, *ahem,* on the clock." She smiled. It was terrifying.

Lloyd swore again. "Later? What do you mean, *later?*"

She ignored his question. "And is that Dr Satnam Patel, India's foremost astrophysicist, I see, under that *remarkable* backpack? What *are* you doing? No. No. That, too, can wait." She lowered herself down to the hangar deck, still favouring her injured leg, and clapped her hands, foppishly. She turned to Reid, still lingering in the open hatch. "What an unexpected bonus. *Now* do you believe in our destiny, *Herr Doktor?*"

The remaining crew of the USS *New World,* left behind in Tudor England, gathered in the main hangar. Heidi recognised them all. Though thirty years older, they appeared fit enough. The benefits of a simple, non-processed diet and fresh air, she assumed. Major White had taken some convincing before he agreed to line his people up for her address, but the powerful self-destruct mechanism aboard her ship had convinced him.

Heidi walked along their ragged line, like an inspecting officer – an officer unimpressed by their ragged line. She curled her lip. "I see your people still lack discipline, Major. Small wonder we beat you at every turn."

"Didn't we beat *you* at every turn?" White responded, wryly.

"Despite all your military hardware and malice. And you lied when you were here earlier. At least, you partially lied. You told us the Allies never got it together. The fact that you're here at all suggests either that they did – or that they never needed to. Perhaps there was no World War Two, maybe no world wars at all, huh? Perhaps our instruction of Queen Elizabeth and other leaders of this time has taken your dark future away, replacing it with a more hopeful one?"

Heidi's eyes were like ice, though her smug smile remained. "Some recollections may vary."

"That's funny," White noted, his expression suggesting it was anything but. "Nice quote, but wrong Elizabeth. Why don't you cut to it, Heidi? What do you want?"

"Why, do you have to be somewhere, Major? We, quite literally, have all the time in the world." Again, smug Nazi arrogance.

White's expression hardened. "You have the time it takes me to work out how to disarm the self-destruct on your ship. Then you will face a decidedly Tudor-style justice system – and it will be swift!"

"Temper, temper, Major. I can assure you, I will not be hung, drawn and quartered today[2] ."

"Actually, no you won't. Since being here, we've learned that the practice of drawing a prisoner to the gallows, hanging them until near-death, emasculating them and burning their entrails," White's typically lopsided grin returned as he rubbed it in, "before

---

2. An invention of Edward I of England; the unfortunates were 'drawn', or dragged, by horses to the place of their execution and literally 'hung' by the neck until nearly dead, before the rest of their awful sentence was carried out – not to be confused with 'hang', where death was *caused* by hanging. Death finally came as the still-living body was 'quartered' as an expressive warning to any like-minded potential offenders. The first recorded victim of the 'hung, drawn and quartered' method of execution was Dafydd ap Gruffydd, younger brother of Llewelyn ap Gruffydd, Prince of Wales – whom he betrayed time and again throughout his life, and was constantly forgiven. In the October of AD1283, Edward I proved *less* forgiving.

quartering their body and sending the parts all around the country to hang above town gates as a warning, though quaint, was reserved for men only." He laughed lightly. "Believe it or not, for the sake of decency! No. You are most certainly a woman, Heidi, and a beautiful one. Think of the spectacle when they burn you at the stake – and a more fitting end for you, I cannot imagine. *I'll* certainly be asking the queen to reserve me a ringside seat. I'll bring a fork and marshmallows!"

"Enough!" she ordered, dangerously. "I see Jim Miller is still alive, too. Good. All your remaining science and engineering crew are hereby conscripted to work under Dr Reid, here, to build a project for *me.*"

Uproar and outrage ensued.

"Must I remind you all that you stand before a ship primed to explode," she checked her private comm, "in a little under three minutes? Now, what is your answer?"

White looked around the faces of his people before replying. "That would depend on exactly *what* you wish us to do," he answered, cagily. "Some things are worth dying for, in any time."

"Two minutes," was Heidi's response.

White tried a different approach. "Let me elucidate. Having witnessed some of your earlier *work*," he poured a disgust into that single word that represented the views of all but Heidi herself; even Reid was in agreement, "we might weigh our approaching demise as a worthwhile price to pay, just to stop you. So I ask again, what the hell do you want?"

She told them.

Patel let go an unintentional bark of laughter. "You are not serious."

Heidi glared at him. "In the times where our paths have crossed, Doctor, have you ever known me to be anything else?"

"You want us to retrofit your ship," Patel paused to take in his companions, showing his clear disdain for the notion, "with alleged *alien* technology?"

"Mock all you wish, Doctor. You have just over a minute to

enjoy it."

Jim Miller instinctively stepped in front of his daughter, like that would somehow protect her from what was about to happen. "Perhaps we should consider Heidi's request in more detail, people. Of course," he turned to Heidi herself, "We'll need rather longer than a minute to do so."

"I need a 'yes' from you, Dr Miller. Or you, your daughter and this entire vessel will become the epicentre of an ecological disaster unique in the annals of history. One syllable and thirty seconds to give it. Good odds, no?"

"Always so fair," Lloyd sniped, waspishly.

"Twenty-seven seconds."

White stepped forward. "Alright, we agree to look at your plans, damnit!"

"Detonation paused at T minus, let me see, *eighteen* seconds," Heidi confirmed. "I do hope you are sincere, Major, or I promise you, eighteen seconds of regret *will* feel like a lifetime."

AD1588, historical context

On February 8th of the previous year, 1587, Mary Queen of Scots was beheaded on the orders of Elizabeth I. Mary's death proved a catalyst for the famous Spanish Armada of 1588, while the Pope's excommunication of Elizabeth signified to the princes of Europe that England was also an enemy of Catholicism and thus fair game. The execution of Mary, a Catholic monarch, was all the justification Philip II of Spain needed for his final failed attempt to invade England – though his Armada was initially delayed by Francis Drake's expedition to destroy Spanish supplies at Cadiz, known as the 'Singeing of the King of Spain's Beard'. The Spanish Armada of 150 ships was itself defeated in the main by Drake's fireships, their engagements culminating with the brutal Battle of Gravelines on August 8th, AD1588. Elizabeth survived three attempts on her life and her throne, in favour of Mary Queen of Scots. The final 'Babington Plot' of 1586 showed evidence of Mary's own hand in the scheme to usurp Elizabeth, as stated in coded letters uncovered by Francis Walsingham.

The arrival of castaways from the 22nd century changed some events, but not all. With deadly threats mounting at home and abroad, she felt the loss of her friend, Nicholas Throckmorton, keenly, after his passing in 1571 following long service in England and Scotland. With the Spanish threat seemingly behind her, she made her way swiftly north, to protect not only her greatest asset, but as she saw it, the future of mankind: the USS *New World.*

❦

"Oh, my God," Lloyd groaned. "How am I going to deal with this? The whole world was a powder keg last year, after the Queen executed Mary of Scots. She didn't want to, you know."

"I understand, Geoff," Mother Sarah spoke kindly. "But what does that have to do with our current difficulties?"

He showed her the letter in his hand.

She squinted. "The scratchy writing these guys use doesn't work for me. Could you?"

He took it back. "Would it have killed you to familiarise yourself with their primitive cursive?"

"That has nothing to do with it! The corrective eye surgery I had was over forty years ago. I'm no spring chicken, you know."

"Indeed, you're considerably older than I am. Makes a nice change. Your God has a sense of humour after all, it seems. And will you please call me John?"

"The letter?" Sarah asked, patiently, tapping it with a finger.

He huffed. "Elizabeth writes that she will be here tomorrow. And if her entourage has almost caught up with her fast messenger, she'll be in a right mood, I can tell you. So the last thing I need right now is for her to hear you calling me Geoff or Lloyd, OK?"

"OK, Geoff. I'm sorry."

"John! Are you trying to get me executed? Elizabeth bears a grudge like no one I've ever met – saving that crazy German woman who's forcing our people to build a hybrid alien spaceship!"

Sarah was thoughtful. "Perhaps Bess could help us? With *her*, I mean."

"With Heidi?" He considered. "No. Good Queen Bess has enough problems at the moment. She's coming here both for her own safety and to protect her investment – which has been considerable, by the way. How do you think she's going to react when she finds out the *New World* might detonate at any minute, taking the ancient kingdom of Northumbria with it?"

"The bomb on Heidi's ship is that powerful?"

"Probably not, but it will be when the dual reactors on the *New World* and *Factory Pod 4* go up. Not to mention that we're now working for one of the people Elizabeth specifically joined our cause to prevent from coming to power in the future. I think she might take umbrage with that, don't you?"

Sarah frowned. "OK, so that's not a good look for us. What do you suggest we do? Jim, Satnam and that loathsome Reid guy," she raised her eyes to Heaven, "forgive me, Lord – barely started with Heidi's crazy scheme a week ago. I'm guessing it's gonna take longer."

"Of course it's going to take longer! Damn, damn, *damn!*" Lloyd swore. "What the hell am I going to do? Liz'll go barmy!"

"You could try telling her the truth, Geo—John." She caught herself just in time, remembering his request.

Having worked with Elizabeth for nearly thirty years, he looked at Mother Sarah as though she were mad. "Arguably the main thing I've learned at the Tudor Court, Sarah, is that you never tell anybody the truth. Don't tell them anything, in fact, unless it gives you a clear advantage, or you simply have no choice. 'Heads will roll' is not a metaphor here, remember? Or has your memory faded with your eyesight?"

"There's no need to be like that."

"I disagree!" Lloyd was half out of his wits.

"Calm yourself, Geoff—"

"*John!*"

"Sorry, sorry. But since James and the others left, you've spent years at the Royal Court. You've dealt with Elizabeth on numerous occasions, regarding all sorts of crises. They've always blown over. You've never let it get to you like this."

"Those problems were barely a ripple – a slight freshening in a mouse's teacup. *This* is a crisis! Heidi is here, with a fully armed nuke! And, if Elizabeth ever got wind of *my* part in all this, how I blew up the wormhole drive on the *New World,* leading to all this interference…" He tailed off, running fingers through his scant remaining hair in agitation. "I caused this whole situation, Sarah, all of it! But Elizabeth is yet to find that out. I've lived for decades with the fear that some idiot might let something slip, but now Heidi's here, she'll tell Bess just for fun, should they ever meet. The Queen has trusted me to advise her on all manner of things over the years. She refers to me – affectionately, for her – as 'my astrological advisor'. She'll see Heidi's presence here, and our helping her, as a betrayal and me as a traitor."

"Calm yourself, Geoff."

"John!"

"Oh, sorry, but I'm too old to start renaming things."

"I've been going by John for thirty years, Sarah. Thirty years! And what do you mean renaming *things?*"

"Details," Sarah admonished, crossly. "Time goes by so fast these days."

"Was that a joke?"

"What I'm saying, *John,* is that there's always the third choice."

Lloyd subsided slightly. "Explain."

"You don't want to tell her the truth because you see no advantage in it and you don't want to tell her the truth unless you really have no choice, so…"

"So…?" he prompted.

"We lie," she replied simply.

Lloyd blinked. "You're a weird priest."

"Who are you, fellow?" Elizabeth demanded imperiously.

"Captain Billy Maxwell, Yer Majesty," Billy replied coolly, whilst not offering overt offence.

"Maxwell? Any relative of that rogue David Maxwell?"

"Aye, yer Majesty. *Lord* Maxwell's ma uncle."

Elizabeth soured. "Still not dead, then? We art surprised the worms hath not madeth better use of that gent afore this date."

Billy smiled wryly. "Nay, Yer Majesty. Ma uncle enjoys rude health. Should Ah pass on yer regards when Ah see him?"

Her lip curled into the ghost of a smile. "You may. And remind him, he still owes Sir Nicholas' heirs a fine stallion for the one he did steal thirty years hence!"

A wide grin split Billy's face. "Ah wish Yer Majesty luck in that endeavour, but Ah'll tell him. Ah've this tae show ye." He held aloft one of the communication devices used by the *New World*'s crew.

The Queen leaned forward slightly, taking it from one of her servants, who appeared as if by magic to take it from the Scotsman. She held it before her, like it might turn into a biting ferret.

Lloyd's voice crackled to life. "*Your Majesty?*"

"Ye hold doon tha' wee button on the side there," Billy supplied helpfully.

"I know what to do!" Elizabeth snapped. Still holding it at arm's length, she depressed the button on the side. "John? Is that you?"

"*Yes, Your Majesty.*"

"Ope' these doors, this instant! We are bitter cold, wet, filled with pangs of hunger and crave time alone in one of your warm rain engines."

"*Warm rai— oh, a shower, of course, Your Majesty.*"

"Well? We appearest yet outside thine doors, sir!"

"*Yes, Your Majesty. About that. We have a problem, you see?*"

"I do not, and our patience hath limits. Pray, explain, this instant."

Inside *Factory Pod 4*'s hangar, Lloyd massaged his temples; he had never known a woman with more limited patience, and when the lie came, it sounded weak, even to his own ears. "The doors aren't working, Your Majesty, because of... technical... erm... things." He winced. "But we can pipe some relaxing music outside, while you wait. How would that be?"

"She's been outside a whole day, Jim. A whole day!" Lloyd exploded. "Do you know how bad that's going to be for me?"

"I know the Queen can be fiery," Miller placated, reasonably, "but you'll just have to turn the other cheek."

"That's easy for you to say! Over the last thirty years I've turned the other bloody cheek so bloody often I've barely anything left to bloody sit on!"

"Calm yourself. We can't work any faster, Geoff—"

"John!"

"We can't work any faster, *John.* You know what we're up against here. This technology is like staring into the sun – we just don't know what we're doing! You're an engineer, Geo— John, I mean, John! You know what Heidi's asking us to do is impossible."

Lloyd turned away angrily. "I don't remember her *asking,* but I know what she *needs,* the little..." He turned back. "Jim, I can't keep Bess outside much longer. I don't think she believes me. She thinks we're up to something."

"We *are* up to something."

"Don't I know it! And worse..."

"There's worse?" Miller demanded, nervously.

Lloyd nodded slowly. "She's getting so angry out there, that she no longer wants to listen to the Sex Pistols."

Miller whistled. "They're her favourite, aren't they?"

"Thanks to young Mr Woodsey, yes," Lloyd replied. "If *God Save the Queen* won't soothe her, nothing will."

Miller smirked. "Does she still believe 'she ain't no human being' is a statement of deification?"

"Probably. All I know for sure is, sod England, I wish *I* was dreaming! I need a better excuse, and I need one now, or we're going to have our very own Anarchy in the UK right outside our doors!"

"Maybe you should get Heidi to explain it to her."

"That was a joke, was it? Only I couldn't tell because your delivery was so slick," Lloyd spat, bitterly. "Besides, if anything happens to our dear *Führerin,* that ship goes boom – taking northern England and half of Scotland with it, remember?"

"Do you know, I'd clean forgotten – thanks for the reminder! Maybe you should explain *that* to Elizabeth, then?"

"No," Lloyd responded quietly. "At least, not yet. She won't understand. Not really. To them, gunpowder is still news – even after thirty years of everything we've been trying to teach them. We knew this would be a long-term project. I mean… the scale of this is just so…" He tailed off, taking a different tack. "It's not like we can call Heidi's bluff, either. She wouldn't be here if she had any other choice, so she *will* blow us all to hell rather than let us beat her."

"You think things are going badly for the Schultzes, in the future, or the past, then?"

Lloyd shrugged. "Who even knows any more? Regardless, I think the possibility is our only silver lining, but it doesn't help us here. Very much the reverse, in fact. Have you had *any* breakthroughs with her ship?"

"Some. Working with the engineers' notes she brought with her, taken from people who'd studied it for years, we've managed to activate the antigravity drive and even worked out some of its basic functions. Still, that's a long way from understanding how it works, let alone retrofitting it to jive with human technology."

"Jive?"

Miller shrugged. "That was how Major White described it."

Lloyd slumped. "Human technology," he repeated, dully.

"I know," Miller acknowledged. "Hard to wrap your head around, isn't it? Even after everything *we've* been through."

"Dad?"

Miller turned as his daughter approached. "Hello, darling. What is it?"

Rose had grown into a beautiful woman. Now in her mid-forties, she looked fifteen years younger and glowed with health. Only the frown of concern gave away her maturity. She held out a comm to Lloyd. "Glad you're together. This is for you, Geoff."

Miller coughed, hiding a smirk. "John," he whispered.

"Oh, yes. I keep forgetting. Anyway, we have another visitor outside our doors. He has something for us, and it sounds important."

"Who?" asked Lloyd, suspiciously.

"Lord Maxwell."

Lloyd sagged even further. "Him and her? Together? Oh, who'd be me?"

Miller threw him a quizzical look. "Oh, come on, stop blubbing, Lloyd. What do you mean, him and her together? What's wrong with them? They've both always seemed rather nice to me."

"David Maxwell and Elizabeth Tudor? Nice to *you*, maybe. To the rest of humanity, they're just two over-mighty nobles, both capable of starting a fight in an empty room and they loathe each other. How much food do we have?"

"Food?" Miller was taken off-guard. "I'm not sure. Quite a bit. Why?"

"I'm wondering if we could just lock ourselves in and wait for them all to go away, or die of old age, or something! They're knocking on, you know."

"Ha! So are we!" Miller reminded him. "No. We don't have years of food. You're going to have to grasp the nettle, Geoff."

Lloyd gave him a long-suffering look.

"John," Miller corrected. "Better find out what he's brought us. Especially if, as Rose says, it's important."

Lloyd took the comm. "Hello," he said, wearily.

"*Who is this?*" demanded an imperious voice with a strong Scottish accent.

"This is John."

"*Who? Speak up, damn ye!*"

Lloyd rolled his eyes. "Doesn't improve with age, does he? Deaf as Drake's gunner! Better cover your ears. I'll need to shout." He toggled the talk button for analogue communication. "It's *John*. Go ahead, Lord Maxwell." With the expression of a man about to search a cesspit for lost jewellery, he added, "It's good to hear from you again."

Rose smirked at the obvious lie.

"*Open this damned door, rot ye! Ah've an important delivery and it's addressed to ye.*"

"To me?"

"*Aye. Ye in especial. Now, open up.*"

"We can't open the doors right now. We're working on the problem so that the Queen can enter, too."

"*Aye, Ah spoke to the lassie. She's no' happy with* ye, *Ah can tell ye that! What's that ungodly din?*"

"The Sex Pistols," Lloyd informed him, distractedly.

"*What's that?*"

Lloyd looked to Miller. "Jim, can you switch off the music. It's making things worse. Probably scaring the horses, too."

"Sorry, Geoff. I thought I had."

"It's John, *bloody* John! Stop calling me Geoff!"

"*Aye, Ah kenned it tha first time!*" Maxwell retorted. "*Ah didnae call ye Geoff. Are ye dense, man? Who in Hades is Geoff?*"

Lloyd winced. "No," he mouthed, silently.

Rose snorted. "Oh, you silly thing. You've really gone and done it now."

Miller took the comm from Lloyd. "Lord Maxwell, this is Jim Miller. Apologies for the delay," he explained smoothly. "We're close to having the problem fixed and will have the doors open again within the hour. Miller out." He gave it back to Rose. "Better continue monitoring that, darling. Just in case. Well, *John*, I've bought you an hour. What do you suggest we do with it?"

"*Nein!*" Heidi's response was unequivocal, requiring little understanding of the German language to perceive.

"Be reasonable, you stupid girl!" Lloyd raged.

Heidi merely raised an eyebrow. "Reasonable? *That* sounds like me!"

He pointed at the vast steel doors blocking the hatch to the outside world. "You have a very close and personal relationship with arrogance, so you'll get this. If we keep messing them about out there, they're likely to bring up cannon and start attacking the airlock! Now, try using your imagination to see what happens next!"

"It would take them weeks to break through those doors with 16th century cannon, Lloyd. And you know it."

"Yes, but it will take weeks – at least – to do what you're asking of us. If it can be done at all – which I doubt!"

"Better work quickly, then."

"And what about if they merely damage the doors, so they won't open again?"

"As you have already observed, Geoffrey, I have my own 'front door'. I do not need the main hangar airlock to leave here."

"We do!"

She smiled coldly, leaning forward slightly. "Yes, but I do not care about that – or you."

With a gargantuan effort, Lloyd reined in his anger. "Look, Heidi, all we're asking is that you stay in the manufacturing bay, with your ship, and that you keep yourself scarce. I can soon fob them off and we can continue as planned."

She gave him a sideways look, calculating. "Any tricks, and up she goes."

"We *know.*"

"And with her, all of you, your precious queen and the future you are trying to build."

Lloyd gave her a sideways glance. *Surely she has no intention of letting us continue with our plans to change the future. What does she know?*

"Your mouth is open, Geoffrey. Are you trying to catch flies?"

He closed it. "So, we can rely on you to stay out of the way?"

"I just said so. Do not make me repeat myself. You forget, I have seen the future you are attempting to create. It fails. So, by all means, continue. Now, better open those doors, Geoffrey. I will be with my ship." She drew her comm from a pocket. "With my finger on the big red button of doom, remember?"

Lloyd nodded stiffly.

Rose raised her hand. "I have a question."

"What?" asked Lloyd, grumpily.

"How come *she* gets to call you Geoff?"

Jim Miller opened the main hatch to the *New World*'s hangar. He made a show of opening and closing the heavy steel doors a couple of times, causing them to judder, so that it looked like there were indeed problems with the mechanism – subterfuge enough to placate the Elizabethans. He left them open just enough to allow horses and riders to pass, two by two.

Elizabeth entered first with a small entourage, leaving her main forces camped outside. Maxwell followed in a similar fashion, though one of his men also drove a small cart through the semi-open doors, after them.

Elizabeth was helped from the saddle by one of her aides. At fifty-five, she was still a striking woman, though grey now flecked her long, fiery red hair. The *New World*'s crew had been careful to conceal much of her personal life story from her, offering only guidance – which she usually acted upon. She was unaware that smallpox, developed at the age of twenty-nine, forced her to use copious amounts of white lead to cover the scars on her face, which in turn led to hair loss – a side effect of residual lead poisoning. The arrival of the *New World* meant she would never need her famous white make-up and collection of eighty-eight wigs to disguise disfiguration and premature aging. When she fell ill, Private Tomás Suárez, an American army medic stranded with Lloyd and the others, simply travelled to Hampton Court by air at night, in the October of 1562, to treat her condition with powerful, 22nd century antiviral drugs. Lloyd's intercession at the Tudor Court kept her healthy beyond her years, though her commitment to remaining unmarried never wavered.

She had a naturally ruddy complexion, and never more so than when she was angry, which was most of the time. Lloyd ducked and bobbed obsequiously. It did not come naturally to him, but he had realised, years earlier, that it was necessary for a quiet life – or at least, a quieter one. Indeed, she was one of the worst-tempered women he had ever met.

"Stop dithering, man! 'Tis *We* who hath been left outside for a night and a day with the horses!"

He knew for a fact that the suffering of huddled masses outside in the cold would not have registered with her, and so fought the urge to roll his eyes at the use of the royal 'We'. "Your hot rain engine awaits, Majesty," he placated simply, and watched her follow Rose – whom he knew Elizabeth liked – towards the exit leading into the Pod's residential area. As they passed close by a bin, its lid popped open automatically, causing the Queen of England to jump with a squeak of surprise. "We hadst forgotten about those magical midden barrels. We liketh them not!"

Rose picked up a small piece of packaging from the deck and dropped it in. The hatch closed immediately and, sensing the increased weight, the bin automatically opened at the base to empty into *Factory Pod 4*'s garbage disposal and recycling system. Bess glowered at the machine as though it were a demonic invention.

Lloyd sighed heavily and turned away. *On with the next…* "Lord Maxwell, what a pleasant surprise."

Maxwell grunted. "Ye've been toadying at that slip of a lassie's skirts tae long." He stooped low from his mount. "*Geoff*."

Lloyd stiffened.

"Oh, aye. Ah know who ye arrrre." He rolled his 'r's majestically, in that marvellous fashion of the educated Scots. "And whit ye did, laddie." Maxwell winked. "All in the past, eh? Dinnae worry. Ah forgive ye. After all, if it wasnae for ye, Douglas would ne'er have crashed here." He patted his generous belly. "It's been a beneficent relationship, Ah swear." Flashing a grin, he eased himself out of the saddle, while an attendant stood ready to support him if necessary. Maxwell was technically Lloyd's contemporary – in that he was also in his eighties – although Lloyd would not be born for another six centuries. Theirs was a ripe old age by 16th century standards.

"And you've told no one my real name?" Lloyd asked, quietly.

"It's known tae a few." He slapped Lloyd on the shoulder – his rheumatic one – making him wince. "Dinnae worry, laddie. We'll keep it our wee secret, eh? And o' course, ye'll keep reminding the young queen[3] how important ma friendship is tae her and tae England – ye ken?"

Unfortunately, Lloyd did ken; he kenned all too well. "What do you have for us, David?" he deflected.

Maxwell darkened. "After tha De Soulis incident, thirty years ago, Ah decided it was safer tae make ma new chapel within tha walls o' Hermitage Castle, rather than doon tha valley. Between reivers and armies a-marchin' aboot, it seemed canny."

Lloyd nodded. Personally, he would not have bothered with a chapel at all, but he understood the sentiment well enough. After all, 16th century magnates had a duty to keep their religious credentials well polished. Their lives often depended on them.

"Well," Maxwell continued, "Ah decided tae clear tha remains o' th'auld chapel and turn tha land o'er tae crops. After tha priests said their mummery, tae desanctify tha land, we got tae work."

"And?" asked Lloyd, interest piqued.

Maxwell winked again. "We found something." He beckoned Lloyd over to the small cart his contingent brought with them. "Ye'll have been here lang enough tae have heard tha tale o' tha Cout o' Kielder?"

"Would it surprise you to learn that I haven't?" Lloyd replied, deadpan.

---

3. At Maxwell's age, everyone seemed young.

Maxwell laughed. "Now, that's tha man Ah remember!" He slapped Lloyd's aching shoulder again.

He rotated his arm, painfully. "So, what's a cout?"

"The Cout o' Kielder was a local chief – a Tynedale baron, in tha time o' Sir William de Soulis' forebear, who also bore tha same accursed name!" He spat on the hangar floor to dispel the curse.

Lloyd stepped back slightly, causing another bark of laughter from Maxwell.

"Ah cannae say Ah really believed he ever lived. Ye ken how tha peasants hae their wild tales! But while clearing tha land we found this…"

Lloyd leaned over the side of the cart to look in. On the load bed was something resembling a shroud, wrapped around a roughly man-sized shape.

Maxwell gestured for one of his men to unwind the cloth that protected their cargo. Lloyd stared wide-eyed. "What the f—"

"Found it in the ground, aye," Maxwell continued over his outburst. "Tha story has it that tha Cout o' Kielder was a giant, see? Aye, Ah know what ye're thinking, when are these types no' giants, eh? Anyways, he was caught on tha lands o' tha first Sir William de Soulis with a small band o' his friends. De Soulis offered him traditional border hospitality—"

"Killed him, did he?" Lloyd interjected, sourly.

"No… Well, aye, but no' at first."

"Naturally. That would have been rude."

Maxwell clapped him on the shoulder again. "Now ye're gettin' it. Tha cout, and his companions, worked oot that De Soulis planned on a-murderin' tham all—"

"Really? Lucky guess, was it?"

Lloyd's sarcasm was wasted on Maxwell. "Aye, maybes. Anyways, they ran, and De Soulis sent men a-chasin' after them. They caught them up near tha chapel that yer Commander Gleeson blew up, thirty years since."

"Oh, *him*," Lloyd mumbled, bitterly.

"Aye, as fine a man as ye'll meet," Maxwell reminisced,

obliviously.

Lloyd rolled his eyes.

"Tha Cout o' Kielder was driven intae tha river at Hermitage, at a place the peasants call Drowning Pool. De Soulis' men couldnae take tha giant doon, so they pushed him intae deep watter and held him doon wi' lang spears 'til he drowned."

"Do all your local stories have such happy endings?"

"Aye, as ye'll see. There's a low mound just outside tha ruined chapel's enclosure. Tha locals call it 'Tha Cout o' Kielder's Grave'. They say it's a burial mound and that tha giant rests there tae this day. Ah thought it was all rubbish, ye'll ken, but when we levelled the area for growing, including tha mound beside Hermitage Watter[4], we found what ye see here. As ye can imagine, Ah thought tha legend must have been true, but then Ah saw the carvings and…"

Maxwell tailed off, at a loss for words to describe his find, for within the cart was an enormous thigh bone. Lloyd immediately knew it was no remnant from a giant chieftain – the idea was ludicrous. Unfortunately, the truth was no better.

Almost two millennia earlier…

"Jonesy!" Douglas bellowed. "Calm these people down. Tell them we'll take care of it. Prentice! O'Brien! Get everyone together, full kit. We're going back for ma ship!"

"What about Dr Bismarck, Captain?" asked O'Brien.

---

4. 'Hermitage Water' is the river that flows beside Sir William de Soulis' ancient haunt, Hermitage Castle and its ruined chapel, to this day. In Northumberland and the Borders, water is often referred to as 'watter' or 'witter', depending on local tradition and dialect, and is quite close to the West Midlands' 'wairter', that may even hark back to the dialect used by Shakespeare himself. Visitors to Britain may be forgiven for wondering water we all talking about.

"He'll have tae limp. Let's move it, people!"

It was slow going. Though Bismarck did his best, he required help. It was Douglas' turn.

"It seems conclusive that we're in the Iron Age, Captain, but did you know the Proto-Indo-European root word for 'iron' means blood? Possibly because of how iron looks in its molten state, or maybe it's because of the taste of iron in our blood. Who can be sure?"

Douglas was in the mood to brood. "Ah just hope it's no' because of what we've unleashed upon this simpler time."

Bismarck stumbled slightly. He winced but came back with a smile. "I wouldn't worry too much about that, James. These people seem old hands at killing one another already."

"Aye," Douglas accepted gloomily, "but it's a matter of scale."

"And talking of scale," Bismarck changed the subject, "that is a very impressive ship you have. It looks like a vast, matt black Thunderbird II."

Douglas soured further. "Ah wish people would stop saying that."

Bismarck laughed, lightly.

Another hour's march and the shadow of UNS *New World* loomed over them. Douglas breathed a huge sigh of relief when he saw many people moving around on the ground, doubtless checking the ship over. More concerning were the obvious signs of battle scarring that clearly predated their rough landing.

"This oughta be a fun debrief," O'Brien drawled.

"Aye. Ah cannae wait."

His mood brightened immediately, as he spotted someone running towards them.

Baines leapt into his arms, bowling him over. They rolled in the heather like a couple of laughing teenagers. Commander Coleman and Dr Bismarck shared a secretive smile and turned away, back to the *New World.*

Douglas got to his feet, pulling his wife up after him. She held on like a limpet. "If you try to leave the ship again," she said breathlessly into his ear, "I'll shoot you in the leg!"

He smiled. A genuine smile, full of relief and passion in equal parts. "Better aim low, lassie."

She giggled before turning serious. "For a moment there, I thought…"

He held her close once more. "Thanks for coming back for us." He looked up at his crashed ship. "Although Ah wish ye'd learn to park."

She slapped his shoulder, joyful tears brimming. "I love you, honey."

"Ah love you, too."

"Yeah…? How much?" she teased.

"More than yesterday. Nowhere near as much as tomorrow." Baines melted.

"But that doesnae mean Ah forgive you for bending ma ship out of shape – nice try, Captain!"

She grinned, wiping her eyes. "Come on, we have the debrief from hell ahead of us."

"Aye, we'd just said as much."

She stroked his cheek, affectionately. "Welcome home, James."

He snorted. "There's no place like it. Ah take it ye just stopped off to make a few repairs?"

Baines pulled a face. "It wasn't my fault."

He laughed again. "It never is. Look, before we get into that, Ah've an idea that might at least bring a little comfort to those we left behind."

Her brows knitted. "Go on."

"Ah need an armoured transport, saws, knives and any instruments of butchery we have."

Baines was taken aback. "Planning a lads' weekend?"

He chuckled. "Ah have a message, and Ah intend tae send it."

She was horrified. "James, what are you saying?"

He laughed. "Not that sort of message. Trust me."

She looked at him askance, wondering if she had left him in the Iron Age too long. "Right… no problem."

"This is the place," Gleeson called from the cockpit of one of the *New World*'s dropships. "Although, it looks a little strange without the buildings."

"There willnae be anything built here for fifteen hundred years," Douglas replied from their rear compartment.

Gleeson set them down. "Those folks you made friends with, back at Bellowing Yell, seemed happy with all that dinosaur meat we delivered."

"Yeavering Bell," Douglas corrected. "Aye, once they got over the 'chariot of the gods' landing on their village green."

Gleeson laughed. "No worries. I missed the duckpond, didn't I?"

Douglas smiled. Gleeson had made first contact with the Elizabethan people, not too far from where they found themselves now, even opening the first dialogue with the then-Princess Elizabeth herself. Douglas read the written account that followed, of course, but imagined the event itself was rather more nuanced than Gleeson's report suggested. However, that was all in the future. There would not even be a Kingdom of Northumbria for another eight and a half centuries, and no England for three hundred years more. The Elizabethans would not arrive until six centuries after that. Small potatoes when compared with deep time, yet Douglas still shook his head at the marvels he had seen – had been *fortunate* enough to have seen. Though the Australian was as brave a man as he could hope to meet, Douglas doubted Cadwaladr would have responded so warmly to a simple 'G'day', no matter how sincerely intended – nor how slowly repeated. He thanked his lucky stars that Jones had been with him on their most recent first contact.

Still lost in his musing, he undid his crash webbing, got to his feet and took a breath before ordering their next task. "OK, everyone out. And dinnae forget tae bring tha shovels!"

They stepped outside. The early evening sun was dipping behind the mountains in the west, bathing the lush, green valley in ultraviolet velvet. The river that rushed by, just ten metres south of where they landed, was noisy and bloated from recent rains in the hills, yet the scene was movingly peaceful. As a local man – one day – Douglas felt a *twang* on his heartstrings. "Ah love this place," he murmured.

"Maybe we should stay."

He turned to find Baines at his side. "Dinnae tempt me."

She looped her arm through his and breathed deeply of the mountain air. "I can think of worse places. The end of the Permian Period, for one." She shuddered.

He held her close and spoke emotionally. "We cannae stay. For everyone's sake. Everyone who's here and everyone who will be. We've been given an incredible gift tae see all that we've seen, but it's no' ours tae keep."

She smiled with pride, but also with a tinge of sadness. "We'd better get digging then. Don't want any industrious doggies to find our prize, do we?"

After an hour's spirited digging, they lowered the vast femur from the dead dinosaur, along with its treasure, hidden within. "Wait." Douglas jumped down into the hole. "Ah nearly forgot. That would have ruined everything."

"James, what on the moon are you doing[5]?" asked Baines.

He flashed her a grin, took out his knife and began to carve.

Almost two millennia later…
Lloyd blinked, hardly believing his eyes. "That… that's a dinosaur

---

5. Baines was the first human soul born on the moon and spent most of her early life there. So often, sayings learned as a child are baked in. Douglas' behind sticking out of a hole in the ground had nothing at all to do with her turn of phrase.

bone."

"A whit noo?"

Lloyd gave a resigned sigh; this would be an interesting explanation. "Millions of years ago, there were giant creatures… everywhere… reptiles."

"Dragons?"

Lloyd shrugged. "Close enough. I think I know what this femur – that is, this *thigh bone* – belonged to, as well. Mapusaurus roseae."

Maxwell was awestruck, despite himself. "How dae ye ken such things?"

"Oh, I was killed by one once. At least, that's what they all believed, anyway – when they abandoned me to my fate!" Lloyd puffed out his cheeks, remembering. "It wasn't so far from the truth, I can tell you. Also, the name is written on it. See? If this message was for *me* to find, then it's either a joke in poor taste, or one of the world's great ironies."

Maxwell was baffled.

As his men turned the femur over with great effort, Lloyd tried to explain – to throw the Scotsman a bone, so to speak. He pointed to its underside. "Someone carved it laterally along the shaft, just under where it says, 'Whoever shall find this bone must take it to Geoff Lloyd of the USS *New World*'. You surely read *that* bit."

"Aye, Ah recognised *New World*." He patted Lloyd's rheumatic shoulder again, making him wince. "Good job Ah knew who ye are, eh? The rest looked perilously close tae Latin. Ah dinnae bother masel' wi' it. That's what priests are f'r. If Ah didnae get 'em t' read tae me, and keep ma accounts, tha lazy cloister loafers would dae nothin' at all."

They continued turning the bone, to flop it over against the upright side of their cart, fully revealing a second line, stating, 'This Mapusaurus roseae bone is a <u>not</u> the leg of a giant'.

Lloyd rolled his eyes again. *Bloody Douglas,* he thought. Had to be. He could see further writing carved deep into the bone, too, still in shadow underneath. "Look, there's another line. It's well preserved. You two, turn it again!"

The men struggling with the bone gave him a withering glance but did their best.

"It says there's something hidden inside. I'll need to get it under a scanner. There's one over here in the medical ward we built years ago, just across the hangar. Well, come on!" Lloyd snapped his fingers. "It's on wheels, isn't it?"

Maxwell smiled wryly and nodded for his men to follow Lloyd's instructions.

Within an hour, the time capsule was found and cut from the bone. "My God, it's a data clip wrapped in foil and resin." Lloyd was flabbergasted. "How the hell? I've dated this bone to no more than two thousand years old. But that animal lived half a world away, a hundred *million* years ago."

"Dae ye want tae keep it?" asked Maxwell, slyly.

"Of course. I need to see what's on it."

"Ah meant tha bone."

"Oh, no. I don't need that. Why? Do you want it?"

"Aye. Ah'll hang it on tha wall in ma great hall at Hermitage."

Lloyd viewed the bone with distaste. "Help yourself."

He plugged the data clip into his comm and within moments, they heard a voice lost to them for thirty years – and who knew how many epochs.

'*Major White, Mother Sarah, Dr Patel, Dr Miller and everyone of the USS* New World, *this is Captain James Douglas.*'

"Notice he didn't mention me on this bit!" Lloyd chuntered bitterly.

'*Ma dear friends, things have no' gone quite as we expected, but Ah can tell ye this, what ye're doing in Tudor England matters – is vital to the future of humanity. Ah cannae overstate the importance of yer efforts, or how proud Ah am of each and every one of ye – that even goes for you, Geoff, if ye're listening…*'

Lloyd stiffened, pausing the playback; it was like being teased by a ghost. He glanced around surreptitiously to make sure none of Elizabeth's people overheard the name 'Geoff'.

Coast clear, he breathed a sigh of relief and continued with Douglas' monologue.

Chapter 9 | Über Alles

Kill one man, and you are a murderer.
Kill millions of men, and you are a conqueror.
Kill them all, and you are a god.
Jean Rostand 1939

"…And though it's been over a decade for us, ne'er a day goes by that we dinnae think about ye all – and Ah really do speak for every one of us in that regard. Ah cannae make ye any promises. Ah don't know if we can ever meet again, without destroying the future ye created for all humanity, but Ah can promise ye that we'll no' give up trying to find a way. Godspeed, ma friends. This is Captain James Douglas, signing off."

The schoolroom aboard *Factory Pod 4* fell absolutely still. Aside from the mandatory guard left to monitor Heidi, her ship and their other guests overnight, the entire remaining *New World* crew were present.

"Well, that was a load," Lloyd complained. "How that man does like the sound of his own voice."

Rose glared at him, wiping a tear from her cheek. Deciding to ignore his comment, she spoke quietly, reverentially, into the silence that followed. "At least we know Heidi was lying about the future."

"I never doubted it," Lloyd responded from the front of the class. He turned to Patel, specifically. "It seems we *did* make the right decision, to interfere."

Patel blew out a long sigh. "Yes. It seems I was wrong. It also means any attempt to get ourselves home now would be folly."

"We lost you, thirty years ago," White added, also speaking to Patel. "It's a miracle that we got you back." With his customary lopsided smile, he added, "And looking so young. We should be content with that. And that brings me to my next point…"

Everyone turned to White. Realising he had their full attention, he stepped to the front of the classroom to join Lloyd. "Knowing that we somehow manage to pull the biggest rabbit from the hat of all time, and fix the future, I'm more convinced than ever that Heidi must be dealt with here and now. She must not be allowed to continue to… to… well, who the hell knows what she's up to."

Lloyd nodded agreement. "Ford is right. The fact that she might even be *willing* to simply leave, once her ship has been upgraded, scares me. It means she no longer cares whether we improve the future, erasing many evils from the timeline, or not – many of those evils that are, in fact, *our* history. That suggests one of two things to me."

Mother Sarah frowned. "Go on, Geoff."

Lloyd sighed. "*Please* call me John. Elizabeth is just a few corridors away and her people are all over the place. Her spymaster, Walsingham, has ears *everywhere.* Thank God we haven't advanced them to the point of building electronic bugs yet."

"About Heidi, John?" White urged.

Lloyd nodded. "Thank you, Ford. My point is simple. Heidi either has no intention of leaving us alive in this century – though, I haven't figured out how she plans to kill us yet – or, and this might be even worse, she doesn't care what our intentions are because she already has a plan to corrupt our efforts. It's the only answer."

"Or she wants to destroy humanity altogether," Patel added, darkly. "I would not put that beyond the realms of her insanity, either."

"OK," Lloyd acceded. "That's the third possibility."

"There might be a fourth," Rose suggested.

All eyes turned to her, so she stood from her seat to speak. "According to Captain Douglas, she's already been forward through time and seen the changes we make. He said that a Ben *Jansen,* was that his name?"

Lloyd nodded affirmative.

She continued, "Ben Jansen told the captain that Heinrich Schultz was loose in the 1940s. Perhaps a different 1940s from the time we were taught about, but does that really matter?"

"What do you mean, honey?" asked Henry, still seated at her side.

"I mean that I wouldn't trust that scumbag, Schultz, in *any* time."

"That makes sense." Henry rose to stand next to his wife. "We may have created an altered timeline, but you can bet most of the main players are still there. What if they have the same, shall we say, character flaws, the second time around? What if Heidi is quite happy to let our new future unfold, so she can jump off in the 1940s and destroy the future Captain Douglas spoke of, to replace it with…"

"Something far worse." Patel picked up the baton. "I believe Mark Twain put it best when he said, 'History never repeats itself, but it does often rhyme'. The impression Douglas gives us, based on the intel he himself had been given, was of a more *innocent* 1940s society – I believe that was the word he used. Prime material for Heinrich Schultz's manipulation. Especially when he has superior military and interstellar hardware to offer them."

Major White whistled softly. "That's a dark road, but ultimately, we can only guess what Heidi's true intentions might be. She's just so unknowable."

"And unflushable!" Lloyd added, waspishly.

White snorted. "Yeah, I'll give you that one, Geoff."

"John," Lloyd grumbled, rolling his eyes. "Look, she's bloody mad, is all, and you can't reason or anticipate a mad dog. Even if you love it, you have to put it down. As, on this occasion, we most assuredly *don't* love it, the decision should be an easy one. We certainly can't let the mad dog off the leash."

White agreed. "No. We can't let her leave here. So, unless anyone has anything else to add, I say we draw a line under that point and call it agreed." No one spoke up, so he asked, "OK, so *how* do we stop her?"

"Do you mean stop her from leaving, or breathing?" Lloyd qualified.

"That's a can of worms," Jim Miller spoke up for the first time. "If we kill her, the nuclear device aboard that ship goes up and so do we. On the other hand, if we manage to separate her from the self-destruct device, will we be able to disarm it permanently ourselves? Added to that, if she's to remain here among us, can we make *her* safe? Bearing in mind that we may hold the entire fate of humanity in our hands, I suggest we do not even *try* to detain her."

Rose looked at him sharply. "Dad? What do you mean?"

"Something I never thought I'd say," Miller confessed, sadly. "I think we might have to dispose of her."

Lloyd nodded approval. "I agree."

"We can't go around killing people." Mother Sarah was on her feet, at last. "We're not executioners!"

"Oh, spare me!" Lloyd admonished. "After the things I've witnessed at Elizabeth's court this last thirty years, and purely for personal gain or grievance. We're talking about the entire future of not only the human race, but all the creatures and environments we share. Surely you remember the dead world we left behind in *our* 2112. If, by our bumbling efforts, we somehow manage to create a better world, then we cannot allow Heidi to mess it all up. She must die!"

"Strong words from one of her ex-associates," White noted, drily.

"You really want to bring that up now?" Lloyd exploded. "I've been through this many times, but for the *last* time, I did what I did for the money... the *money!* Money I never received, by the way. There was no ideology for me. I had no idea what I was getting into—"

"Getting us *all* into," White interjected.

"Fine! Getting us *all* into. It was wrong, but I can't take it back. I've spent the last three decades of my life trying to educate and coerce a whole generation of violent thugs into a more, shall we say, progressive way of thinking – at great personal risk, I might add. So I'm saying – no, I'm *telling* you – this is no time for wet liberalism at the expense of everyone and everything! We extend the same rights to our enemies that we do to our friends – or ourselves – and we die. It's that simple."

Heidi's heart had missed a beat when she learned Jansen was still alive. How did she feel about that? Had they potentially been granted a second chance at some sort of future together, or had she simply been granted a second chance to kill him? With Lloyd's chilling summation, she removed the earpiece and clipped it back into her comm. "Well, it seems that is about it for me. Fortunate, that I bugged Miller's jacket."

"Ma'am?" asked Reid. They had retired for the night, and he was already wrapped up in one of the three bunks in their small craft's rear compartment.

"They plan to kill me. A bold strategy, for them. They are learning."

Silence from Reid's bunk.

"Did you not hear me?" she demanded.

"Erm... Did they mention me... at all?"

Might she have just made a mistake? Miller thought. A spike of adrenaline shot through his system. Heidi was the most dangerous individual he had ever met. If *he* made a mistake, it would probably cost him his life, but her comm was right there in front of him, lying forgotten on his workbench.

His mind screamed at him that it was too easy, that Heidi would never be so careless. He took a deep breath. *Come on, Jim. Empires can be won or lost on single acts of courage.* The phrase triggered a memory of a conversation held with Thomas Beckett, the *New World*'s historian, long ago. Beckett explained how Pompey the Great's final, and arguably worst, defeat at the Battle of Pharsalus was in no small part due to a lack of confidence imbued by an *overconfidence* in the omnipotence of his enemy, Gaius Julius Caesar. The memory spurred him on. *Funny, the things you pick up along the way.*

He looked around nervously, one last time, and seized the comm. The device's memory was encrypted. Of course. However… his heart leapt… the device *itself* was not. He could simply copy everything, all of it, including the encryption and work on breaking it later in his own time. *Fortune favours the bold!*

He drew a fresh data clip from his desk and synced it to her comm. The data transference took mere seconds, but it felt like he was losing years off his life. Any second now, she would realise her mistake and return for it.

The data clip beeped to signify that the transference was complete. He quickly removed any evidence that the comm had been synced and returned it to his workbench, heart hammering in his chest so hard that the blood boomed in his ears.

Within moments of Miller returning to his task, Heidi returned from her ship. She picked up the comm, appearing cross with herself as she looked around to see if her slip had been noticed. Miller watched her, slyly, in the reflection granted by a darkened screen. She seemed content, if annoyed, and returned to her ship.

Miller sat down, his legs feeling like they might collapse. He was not cut out to be a spy. His actions gave him a new appreciation for just how much courage Geoff Lloyd had shown in recent years, surrounded night and day as he was by potential deadly enemies at Elizabeth's court.

"Did it work?" asked Reid as Heidi entered their ship.

"It did. Eventually. I thought he might have a crisis of confidence, but he got over it. He will no doubt tell the others and they will spend tonight trying to hack my information to learn my plans."

"You've made it easy for them?"

"No need. It will be more convincing if they break into it themselves. You forget, some of these people are geniuses, after all."

Reid looked surprised. "High praise."

"No. Just a fact. Despite their obvious weaknesses, they have proved extraordinarily difficult to kill."

He nodded thoughtfully. "Assuming they do crack your security, do you think they'll take the bait?"

"Initially."

"And after that?"

"That will not matter as we will not be here."

Reid shifted uncomfortably.

"What is it?" she asked.

"It unnerves me that they guessed where we're heading and, in a way, what we intend – that is, what *you* intend."

"Yes. Douglas' message from the Iron Age was unexpected. An extraordinary display of prescience from yet another man who simply refuses to die!" Belying the savagery of her words, her wry smile was very nearly one of admiration. "*Mein Großvater* was wrong to underestimate Douglas and his gaggle of righteous fools."

"Perhaps not fools?"

Heidi shrugged. "We shall see. Either way, I intend for us to be on our way by tomorrow."

"What about the stolen technology?"

She shrugged again. "You assure me there is no way to implement it in the time we have."

"So we just *dump* it?" He sounded pained.

"It is just so much extra weight, and our fuel resources are finite, even after refuelling from *Factory Pod 4* stocks."

"But all that effort, the *lives…?*"

"Regrettable, but not insurmountable. Besides, we know the alien devices will be recovered in 1947. So, we can be well placed to get there first, should it amuse us to try again, no? We also have our fixed points to guide us. And of course, we still have our ace in the hole."

Reid looked uncomfortable again. "We haven't tested that theory."

She clapped her hands, giving one of her tinkling, girlish laughs. "It is just so delicious that you and I, and more importantly *Mein Großvater,* share the same blood group. If he had ever found out where his transfusion came from, after his brush with the dinosaurs in Cretaceous Egypt, he would have probably ordered your removal."

"Don't I know it." He shuddered.

She laughed again. "*Mein Großvater* always did love the phrase 'blood will out'. He has certainly let enough of it out in his time. Of course, there may come a future time when I must prove his theories of genetic predisposition, and let *all* his blood out. Either way, we cannot stay here. They might just find a way of depriving me of this ship. As my only defence against them will bring about my own destruction along with theirs, I think it is time for a new strategy."

AD1944, The Berghof, Obersalzberg, Bavaria

Above all, Heinrich Schultz breathed deeply of the wonderfully fresh mountain air. His glass charged with another fine, crisp white, he gazed out across the Bavarian Alps. *The way things are proceeding, I shall soon be the richest man in the world.* He resisted the 'again' adverb of frequency. In his previous life, he had accrued so much wealth that it was hard to know its exact value. Every trillionaire in the 22nd century probably felt the same way, as they eyed one another, waiting for their opposition to blink... and fall.

A short walk down the hill was Mengele's laboratory. His granddaughter's extraordinarily daring exploits had secured four eggs from the Cretaceous, large eggs, and as a similarly rich oligarch, Reinhard Heydrich had bought them all – two to hatch, and one for his mad geneticist to experiment with. The fourth had been broken during Heidi's desperate escape but still provided an excellent yield in genetic information. Heinrich had been present when the two creatures chosen for birth broke through their shells, opening their cold reptilian eyes on a world they simply assumed was theirs to own. Heinrich respected that – even when he had to destroy those who believed it. His granddaughter was also such a creature; equally beautiful, equally deadly. Regardless of all his training and the elitist, weaponising education his granddaughter received as a child, he still marvelled at her courage and audacity. *I'm lucky to be alive.*

Heinrich sipped the last of the excellent vintage. His host was most indulgent. Of course, that would change once Reinhard Heydrich wrung him dry of information and technology, but by then the old man would have his own plans in place. For the first time in his life, those plans leaned towards defence rather than conquest. For the first time in his life, Heinrich Schultz considered retirement.

The world in which he grew was a frightful place. A damaged world, teeming with damaged people; some revelling in it, others so repressed that they did not even consider it. This world was wholly different. In this world, mankind lived harmoniously with his surroundings; everything was plentiful. No one had yet poisoned the well. Indeed, he did not mind admitting, albeit to himself, that he marvelled at the achievements of Douglas' rabble. Such changes they had wrought through time. Naturally, it would not do. The world would not be perfect until he sat on top of it. He smiled at that thought as he looked down from his elevated position. No, it would only be perfect when he sat *über alles.* There *were* men and women like him in this world, of course. His host was one of them, but not Mengele; Heydrich's pet geneticist wore a different kind of insanity. Yet, looking around at the beautiful world they had created, he sensed that the Heydrichs of this time lacked the joined-up vision of *his* ambitions. They were empire builders, certainly, but he was the man to yoke those empires together and rein them in, under his sole, godlike command. *Let all men share, steal and barter their meagre possessions, up and down their pre-agreed societal structures, for I would own the men themselves. Yes, the ultimate penthouse suite encompasses all the world but should berth only one. Hmm,* he pondered, *perhaps retirement is overrated. Perhaps I should…*

"*Herr* Schultz."

Heinrich turned away from the view and his machinations to find his host approaching with a glass in one hand and a bottle in the other.

"Top up?" Heydrich offered. The bottle dripped condensation from the ice bucket onto the flagstones as he poured first Schultz, then himself another glass.

"You have a beautiful world, here, Reinhard," Schultz began, obliquely.

Heydrich glanced out briefly, across the mountainous Alpine vista. "Yes, it is."

"How much of it do you control?"

The younger man turned, eyeing Schultz appraisingly. "Much."

"But not enough?"

"Nothing is *ever* enough, Heinrich. You know that."

"Indeed, I do. During my brief stay here, I have been studying the politics of your world, to gain an understanding of this timeline."

Heydrich's interest was piqued. "And what observations have you drawn?"

The old man shrugged, neutrally. "Largely, you have what I would consider egalitarian states, with little to distinguish one political movement from another."

"Interesting. And what do you infer from this?"

"That they're ripe for indoctrination and subjugation, naturally."

Heydrich had seen the information and propaganda the Schultzes brought with them, had seen many evils his world rejected centuries ago – and others it was yet to consider. He was a moth to the flame. Forcing himself to be cautious, he argued, "Our people have built their very identity on freedom. Our country—"

"Of course they have," Schultz interrupted, knowingly. "You must break them of that, stealthily, without letting them realise you're doing it. I'm paraphrasing, of course, but remember this – all the world's a spreadsheet, and we are merely numbers. Well, I say we…"

Heydrich smiled. It went without saying that such a philosophy did not apply to them.

"As for your country," Schultz continued, "is that truly the limit of your vision?" He placed a hand on the younger man's shoulder, a rare, almost human gesture. "Think bigger. Control their money, control their energy, control their movement, control their food, control them."

Heydrich's eyes narrowed. "You have some experience?"

The old man returned his smile, indulgently, though his stare remained hard as granite. "On that, you must trust me, my young friend."

Heydrich never trusted anyone, but he would certainly listen.

"You already possess the technology to do this. You are simply not using it to effect," Schultz continued. "First, you begin with subtle attacks on what your people believe. Or, I should say, you set up those attacks – never engage directly. This is relatively simple. You merely allow a larger platform for the voices of grievance – they will be there, trust me, and easy to cultivate. Then you stand back until a groundswell begins to stifle the old orthodoxy. Once this gathers momentum, you will find it relatively simple to undermine what people 'know' – and you'll do it in the name of those freedoms they hold dear."

Heydrich frowned. "How do you replace what people know?"

"You begin by allowing them to replace the truth with *their* truth.

Many regimes have tried to replace what people know with what the regime *wishes* them to know. This is a fragile construct, for your people will constantly compare what they see and hear with what you're telling them. Within those systems you'll rarely garner more than a handful of true believers. Most will remain unconvinced, and they'll hate every minute of it. Doubly dangerous."

Heydrich nodded, thoughtfully. "Yes, I can understand how such a regime would have a limited life cycle."

"Ultimately ending in revolution," Schultz explained further. "Such a strategy will eventually drive them together, against you, when you need to drive them apart, and *to* you. No. You allow them the freedom to replace what is accepted by the majority, with a chaotic 'anything goes' philosophy. In short, you offer them *total* freedom. From there, society will break, and quickly, looking to the state for salvation – and then, you will have them."

"Enough rope to hang themselves?"

Schultz nodded. "Indeed. No one on the ground will believe that their very reality is being reconstructed by cabal." He inclined his head slightly. "Or by one guiding hand."

"This can be done?"

"Certainly. A well-placed favour or party donation here, an incriminating photograph there. I'm sure you already have many politicians and other useful authoritative figures under your control. Once you have them hooked, you reel them in over their heads and *squeeze* those resources of their usefulness. There are many issues and pressure points – though, I prefer to term them control mechanisms – that you might create for them to promote, for others to follow. Your world hasn't fully explored this yet, not to the scale I'm describing, but if you build the maze and give them a few road signs, the mice will soon push the truth outside the accepted window of belief, along with the cheese! And they'll do so willingly – aggressively, even."

"Leaving themselves poorer and trapped."

"With you, richer and in command."

"A totalitarian state."

The old man smiled again. "Exactly. I knew you'd see it. Subjugation, as stated. And the more freedoms you take away in order to restore their safe little world to what it was, the more power they'll grant you in return to go still further."

"That is quite bizarre. Such action could never take the world back to what it was. Surely, many will see what is upon them?"

"They will, and that's where *indoctrination* comes in. I am old – I have observed the cycle. You see, freedom is not the natural order of things. People think it is, but it isn't. It must be fought for, every few decades. It is quite remarkable how much can be forgotten within a generation – and innate intelligence provides surprisingly little protection against indoctrination. The whole system will very quickly become self-policing, too, requiring no more than the occasional nudge to stay on course. Dissenting voices will be swept aside and ridiculed – perhaps even destroyed."

"So, total freedom becomes its very antithesis – in a very real sense, slavery."

"Yes. Everything is but a point on the great wheel, my friend. Delicious, isn't it?"

Heydrich pondered a moment. Realisation dawned that his successes, though impressive, were really just a nibbling at the edges. The monster within him came fully awake to the possibility of a larger bite, and yet… "It sounds too good to be true, Heinrich."

"And yet I've seen it, though it began a little before I was born – next century for you. It gained extraordinary power over a relatively short space of time, too. Once this whirlwind of confusion and fear becomes manifest, you'll find ever more opportunities to build wealth and power, far exceeding anything you might have found among a cohesive society. Their wealth must become your wealth, their freedoms must become *your* freedoms. But here is the real icing on the cake – anyone standing against the current thing will be taken down by radicalised people who used to be their own. Leaving you clean-handed and ready to… *help.*"

"I must think on this, Heinrich." Heydrich was no stranger to politics, but always his lobbying had been towards some strategic end – a new hyper factory, some mass-housing development – never had he sought political power in and of itself. Never had he sought to control at *scale*. Like a junkie who had tried it all, suddenly, he was being offered something new and simply had to have it. He eyed the old man guardedly – his sick messiah – while schemes swirled and collided within his mind. No longer content with everything he ever needed, Heydrich realised he might be able to get the rest, too – simply everything – and if he had to share, it would only be for a little while. The old man could not live forever, just long enough. He smiled and raised his glass once more.

Schultz lifted his own to *clink*. "Of course, you must think it over, my young friend," he replied, smoothly. As with a good wine, he knew when to let an idea breathe, allowing it to grow within the minds of those he wished to coerce, and so changed the subject. "Now, I assume, as you're here, that you've some news for me."

Heydrich hid his surprise. *I must be careful, even with my thoughts, around this man.* "I do. Interesting news, in fact. Would a trip to Munich amuse you?"

"That would depend upon your news."

Heydrich's blue-grey eyes twinkled with intrigue, hard and bright as chromium steel. "It seems your wormhole in the Old Academy vanished in an explosion earlier today, destroying the whole building. At least, we assume the wormhole has gone. Until the rubble is removed, we will not know for sure. However, perhaps of more interest to you will be the names of those who came through."

Schultz's eyebrow rose slightly, but otherwise, he remained impassive.

"One of your forebears, Dr Heidi Schultz, was among them. My sources are as yet unsure whether it really is her, or your granddaughter masquerading as her. Her companion was a Corporal Heinz Engel."

There was the merest tightening around the eyes as Schultz processed the name. *One of the traitors under Meritus, who betrayed me. Yes, I remember him. A promising NCO... once.* "Indeed, you do interest me, Reinhard. When do we leave?"

Heydrich smiled again. "Within the hour. My helicopter is en route. Until it arrives... well, there is no sense in wasting such a particularly excellent vintage, is there?" He raised his glass once more, in salute, and Schultz returned the gesture before drinking to the future.

***

AD1588 – Tuesday 22nd November, 0700 hours

"I want to finish my work."

Heidi stared.

Reid adjusted the collar of his geography-teacher white shirt with brown checks, uncomfortably. "I mean, I would *like* to..." He tailed off.

"To what end?"

"It's the ultimate puzzle – at least, it is for a man like me. Technology from another civilisation, so far ahead of our own – from another galaxy, perhaps. Don't *you* want to see it work?"

"And what if the technology of which you are so in awe turns out to be man-made?"

He shook his head. "No way. We have nothing even *approaching* that level."

Heidi raised an eyebrow. "Yet."

His jaw dropped. "You think it might have been left by... by time travellers from our future?"

"There seems to be a lot of it about," she answered, dismissively.

"But the bodies – they were so alien."

"I thought you didn't believe the so-called hoax?"

He smiled ruefully. "You've forced me to reconsider."

"Surely you do not believe we will exist in this form forever. You are a scientist, after all. Do you not accept the – albeit incomplete – theory of evolution? If you do, then you must accept that these bodies are transitory."

He admired her perfect form for a mere second before turning away. "I suppose we'd better enjoy them while we have them, then."

She glared at him. "Don't get any ideas, Reid. Burke and Hare would not want yours!"

Despite his fear, he laughed at that, which actually elicited a grudging smile from Heidi in return. "I am afraid, *Herr Doktor,* that I cannot leave you behind, even to achieve such a noble goal, because, you see, were I to do so, then you might change the soft-headed future these circus fools are about to create."

"I thought you wanted that?"

"Limited vision, Reid. Better to stick to the path we know. The altered future is full of opportunities for someone with my knowledge and," she smiled again, "skills."

Reid shivered in spite of himself. He nodded acquiescence, deciding it was better to speak of it no more. Changing the subject, he asked, "Exactly when do you intend to leave?"

***

AD1588 – Tuesday 22nd November, 0730 hours
In the pre-industrial age, people's routines tended to be based around daylight hours. Natural early risers, Elizabeth R and Lord David Maxwell sat in the small lounge originally created as a waiting room outside the infirmary, to one side of *Factory Pod 4*'s main hangar. The seats were a little worn these days, though still more ergonomically comfortable than anything they had in their castles and palaces. They discussed the politics of the region and the recent failure of the Spanish Armada. They discussed, they schemed, they plotted, they promised, they lied. They *were* allies, after all. Major White and Mother Sarah did not join in the conversation so much as they kept score.

Jim Miller, Satnam Patel and their small engineering staff greeted them with a wave and a 'good morning' from across the hangar as they entered the manufacturing bay through a pedestrian door.

Before they had even entered the workspace, they were bickering about the project – each instinctively sure that his or her theories were the correct ones. Consequently, it took a full thirty seconds before any of them noticed the security guards bound and gagged in the corner.

"Look!" Miller shouted, cutting through their argument. "What the…"

As he spoke, Heidi's ship fired up lifting thrusters and rose from the deck, turning to face them menacingly. A loudspeaker boomed across the bay. "*Dr Miller. Open the vehicular doors through to the main hangar. Open them now, or I will destroy this place. If you recall, you have eighteen seconds to comply.*"

"What are you doing?"

"*Seventeen, sixteen, fifteen…*"

"OK, OK. I'm doing it."

He ran to the massive, seven-metre-tall doors and hit the open stud. As hugely powerful hydraulics drove the enormous steel slabs apart, Rose and Henry appeared at the pedestrian hatch. "Dad?" Rose called. "What's going on?"

"Get back! Get clear!" he screamed at the top of his lungs.

Henry reacted immediately, pulling his wife back through to the main hangar and closing the door behind them. He held her close as they sheltered behind the eight-wheeled lorry, still parked where Heidi's ship had collided with it.

Heidi edged her attack ship forward, passing easily through the colossal doors with room to spare. Using her wrist device, she activated another wormhole at the exact spatial coordinates as the one that carried them there.

However, just as she prepared to jump, she noticed the small gathering across the hangar, as they leapt up from their seats in alarm. She had no idea who Maxwell was, but she recognised the older versions of Mother Sarah and Major Ford White. Moreover, she noticed a red-haired woman, in her middle years, standing with them. Queen Elizabeth I appeared quite different from any historical preconceptions Heidi might have had. She wore no white-lead make-up, nor did she require a wig. Had Heidi not spent the last twenty-four hours eavesdropping on Jim Miller, she would never have known who she was, or indeed, that she was there. In that instant, she gazed in awe at the extraordinarily influential woman and monarch before her. She gazed, and she fired.

"Heidi, no! What are you doing?"

Before Reid's outburst was even complete, the people and the infirmary behind them evaporated in a fireball of white heat.

Reid unclipped his safety harness, jumped out of his co-pilot's seat and ran for the little ship's side hatch.

"Reid!" Heidi screeched, furiously, but it was too late; he was away.

Landing heavily on the steel hangar floor, Reid staggered as a gunshot ricocheted from the hatch closing behind him. However, his troubles were far from over. Heidi fired her ship's weapons again and again, incinerating many of the vehicles in the hangar. Fire, smoke and noise filled *Factory Pod 4.* Open hatches closed automatically, but not all of them in time. Flames shot down corridors, igniting anything they touched.

Jim Miller watched in horror as the vast steel doors closed with all the slowness of nightmare, to protect the manufacturing bay – a horror that was barely getting started. He saw Henry and Rose run for the hatch that led back to the Pod's habitation zone, but fire suppression systems sealed the door ahead of them, barring their escape.

Rose turned to see Miller standing in the closing doorway. He leapt into action, to get to her, when two events happened simultaneously. First and worst, the truck behind which his daughter and her husband hid exploded. The last thing he saw was Henry enfolding Rose in his arms to protect her as flames engulfed them both.

Miller screamed, when the second event overtook him. Reid, running flat out to escape the inferno, dove through the narrow gap left between the massive closing doors, collecting Miller on his way through.

The doors *boomed* with a finality that echoed Miller's world coming to an end. The deck beneath him shook as secondary explosions ran through the Pod, severely damaging their home and refuge, though Miller hardly noticed.

Reid tried to help him up, but Rose's father merely turned and retched so hard that he was soon fighting for breath and eventually blacked out.

For any observers in Cretaceous Britain, Heidi's fortnight in AD1588 never happened. Her ship simply vanished to almost immediately reappear facing in the opposite direction.

On the shores of Crater Lake, alarms continued across the *Newfoundland*'s rescue pod and control centre, without missing a beat. "She's back again," cried Lieutenant McBride.

Halfway across the lake in his dropship, Corporal Thomas observed Heidi's craft vanish from his instruments. Barely had he come about when she reappeared from nothingness, into the driving monsoonal rain.

"What the…" He opened a comm channel. "I have her this time, Lieutenant. Should I engage?"

"Yes, Corporal. All ships – engage immediately!"

Thomas lined up his sights and fired.

Heidi's instruments screamed for her to jink to port, which she did, leaving Thomas to strafe nothing more than the open waters below.

She, too, opened a channel. "Nice shot, if your intention was to catch fish!" She fired a missile from an aft launcher.

Thomas expected immediate retaliation. No one got a second

chance with Heidi Schultz – most never got a first. So, even before it was clear his shots had missed, he made sure he was already somewhere else. One of Crater Lake's other pilots was less experienced and less fortunate. The heat seeker sensed their ship, just behind Thomas, and locked on to them instead.

"*Evade! Evade!*" McBride screamed across the airwaves.

The pilot was quick, and the missile scored only a glancing blow as it exploded. The tough little ship's armour took the brunt of the damage, but as the vessel had recently been rushed into service to escape Heidi's nuclear strike in Cretaceous Egypt, many of the drive systems were yet to be installed. Among the missing systems were some of the self-repair mechanisms. The ship bellyflopped onto the lake, creating a splash that rose tens of metres into the air.

Heidi's attack ship was already going for altitude, climbing steeply to leave them behind.

"Lieutenant," Thomas called. "Do I give chase or help your pilot? It looks like his ship is taking water."

"*I can continue pursuit, sir,*" the second of McBride's cargo pilots confirmed.

In the control centre aboard the *Newfoundland*'s rescue pod, McBride looked up to Dr Brian Alba, standing behind his console.

Alba shook his head with misgiving. "These guys aren't fighter pilots. She'll eat them for breakfast. We can't afford to lose anyone else, or any more ships."

McBride nodded. "That's a negative. Return to base. Corporal Thomas, does your ship have the capability to lift our damaged craft out of there?"

"*No, sir,*" Thomas replied, thoughtfully. "*However…*"

"What do you have in mind, Corporal?"

"*Order your pilot* not *to climb out, sir.*"

McBride struggled to hide his disbelief. "I thought you said he was sinking?"

"*Yes, sir, but there are some ginormous crocodile things already circling him,*" Thomas answered, urgently, his Brummie accent coming to the fore. "*I wouldn't get out if I was him!*"

"So what do you suggest?"

"I've got a plan, sir. Erm… erm… gimme a minute."

⌇

Heidi dropped sharply down the opposite side of the craggy mountains that encircled Crater Lake, back towards the artificial wormhole created for her personal use. In this timeline, the wormhole had been open mere hours, the white waters of the river still flowing through it.

Using her instruments, she checked the last location it linked with. The *Last Word,* as she had left it. She programmed new co-ordinates, another place recently visited, albeit briefly. From there, it would be a simple matter to travel north, to the area where her fixed-point wormhole had once existed.

Slowing, she came in to hover, just above the raging torrent. The last time she had travelled through this wormhole, she had been attacked brutally by the military force waiting on the other side. The sudden influx of river water would give her away, so she prepared to move swiftly once through. Cautiously, she entered the portal.

⌇

Thomas hovered just above the downed ship as it listed to port, taking on water. Several grinning *crocodilianesque* maws surfaced, opened and snapped closed again in anticipation, forming a circle around the slowly sinking vessel. The creatures were anything between four and eight metres in length, more than large enough to trouble the pilot.

This is bad, thought Thomas. *If that bloke gets out, he's dead. And as the Schultz vessels don't have a top hatch, he'd sink the ship an' all.* He opened a channel to the man below. "Do those ships have any lifting points?"

The answer was immediate. Although Thomas did not know the man, he could hear the nervousness in his voice. "*The original attack ships had crane loops so they could be moved around in the hold of our capital vessels. What are you thinking? Surely you don't have the power to lift me out of here?*"

"No, but you're floating – mostly. I could drag you to the shore and possibly some way up the beach before you lost all buoyancy. I can't see any loops or hooks. Where am I looking?"

"*They're hidden for aerodynamic purposes. Hang on…*" Three small compartments revealed themselves, all in a line along the top of the fuselage. Two more appeared, immediately after, one on each wing.

"I can see a few small hatches. Where are the lifting loops?" asked Thomas.

"*Internal. Our cranes were designed to connect with them.*"

"Aye yi yi." Thomas sighed with frustration. "I'll lower the winch to see if I can hook one. Cross your fingers!"

As a child, Thomas once visited a 'Museum of Primitive Entertainment' with his mother. There he played a claw crane grabbing machine, filled with impossible to obtain items he never wanted but had to have. Naturally, the coin slot had long been replaced by a more sophisticated, digitally index-linked form of pickpocketry, but otherwise the game remained the same. As the hook, hanging from steel cables beneath his ship, slipped and slid over the target, never making meaningful contact, he was irresistibly reminded of those wasted minutes, so long ago. He was also painfully aware that, rather than digital fiat currency flowing out, water was flowing in.

"*How's it going?*" the stranded pilot asked, nervously.

You don't want to know, me old mate, Thomas internalised. "Nearly there," he lied.

Natalie Pearson once hypothesised that the freshwater mosasaurs common in Crater Lake might be ancestors of Pannoniasaurus inexpectatus – named by palaeontologists because all mosasaurs found prior to that discovery were marine reptiles and so the unearthing of a freshwater mosasaur was unexpected. Conversely, there was plenty of expectation to go around that day, as the creatures surrounding the stricken ship waited to see what might fall out of it. The way things were going, Thomas also expected nothing less.

No pressure! he complained within the privacy of his own head.

He zoomed his ship's belly camera in on the connection point nearest the bow of the vessel, reasoning that it would be best to drag the ship forward, rather than spinning it, potentially forcing it to take on even more water. If he could lift the nose, so much the better. There was no sound – the storm was far too violent – but he fancied he almost heard it *clunk* into place, as the hook caught.

"Yes!"

"You have it?"

A sudden, powerful gust tore at the dropship, forcing it back a few metres. The hook slipped free. Thomas swore.

"You don't have it."

"I'm working on it."

"Thanks. It's just that my feet are getting wet."

"That much is coming in?"

"'Fraid so."

Thomas swore again. "Well, at least we know it's possible now, right?" he offered, encouragingly, while redoubling his efforts. He took the ship lower. Pointing downwards, rocket engines beat the lake's windswept surface to a mist, eventually scaring away the wildlife. A dozen variously massive heads vanished beneath the waves. Accepting the temporary no-score-draw, Thomas concentrated on the chromium steel hook as it flapped about in the wind, sliding across the hull's sleek surface. Every time it caught, it slipped free. Again, he could not help but remember a claw closing around a fluffy bear within a glass cabinet, only for it to slip back among the pile of plastic rubbish and outrageously past its 'sell-by' chocolate. His own anxiety grew by the second, but he resisted the urge to slam his fist down on the controls. An unfortunate surge of testosterone would be unlikely to help his companion. He knew he was on the clock, because when the ship flooded to the point where it began to lose buoyancy, its greater mass would prevent him from towing her to shore.

The autopilot fought the wind, while he focused all his concentration for one last attempt. It was a balancing act, because if the hook connected, he would quickly have to disengage the autopilot and take the ship forward to keep tension on the cables. The flight computer reacted quicker than any human being, but had no setting for 'take up the slack while being buffeted by the completely unpredictable eddies and vortices slamming us from every direction'. The people who built it had long ago decided that artificial intelligence in a war machine was far too dangerous and should largely be kept on a leash, correlating data. Thomas understood their concerns, but that hardly helped him now.

"This water's really cold."

"I'm almost there, mate." Thomas saw the hook slide into the slot atop the ship and catch. Restraining his whoop of delight, he carefully took back his control of the ship and edged her forward. The sudden resistance on the cable elicited an almost tactile relief, like he was pulling the load himself. Everything lined up, he gradually altered the angle of his rocket motors and increased the power.

Both ships moved forwards steadily. Crater Lake Base was a tropical paradise, but on that day the storm-ravaged shore looked like holiday-hurricane hell. Nonetheless, it was Shangri-La for Thomas and the stranded pilot. If only they could reach it.

Thomas could feel the drag of his cargo increasing as they went. "How's it going down there?"

"C-c-cold."

"We're almost 'ome, lad."

They were still half a kilometre from safety, but this was no time for honesty. The bow wave they cut through the choppy waters was obviously increasing the rate at which the ship was sinking.

"I hope the ship's OK."

Thomas smiled. Pilots were the same everywhere. He knew Dr Alba was a marine engineer but had to wonder whether repairing a flooded spaceship was mixing apples and oranges. His belly cameras showed the ship lying ever lower in the water, but so far, the incredible cacophony of wind and rocket noise was at least keeping the predators away.

Inside the sinking craft, the pilot was now sitting in water. He unclipped his flight harness and stood, hanging on to his seat, as water sloshed around with every jerk of the cable connecting him to his unlikely sky-tug. He opened a compartment, taking out a helmet and flight suit – there had been no time to change when they scrambled. Normally, pilots of spaceships would dress appropriately, should disaster strike, but trying to don a spacesuit – even a lightweight pilot's suit – would be quite a feat, waist deep in water.

As they neared the shore, the choppy waters turned into two-metre rollers creating a swell within the ship that shoved him from one end of the rear compartment to the other. Trying to hang on, he fought his legs into the suit, along with the lake water – there would be no comfort, but fully kitted out, at least he would not drown.

The attack craft lurched. It had struck bottom. The pilot fell into the rising water within the cabin, but despite his cold, wet misery, he also felt elation – it could only mean that they were close to the beach. Fighting the wave sloshing fore and aft, he got back to his feet to look out through the forward viewscreen. Though the white crests rolling away obscured his field of vision, every now and then a trough allowed him to see the shore. He was buoyed by the sight, but the same could not be said for his inundated vessel. Thomas' dropship was clearly struggling now, too, the operation suddenly more akin to dredging than towing. As the pilot wondered how close to the shore they might make it, his ship juddered to a halt with depressing finality – about fifty metres, it seemed. He fastened up the top half of his suit, donned the helmet and fished out an air tank from a storage compartment. He was safe for now.

Thomas realised he was going nowhere at the exact instant the alarms sprang to life in his cockpit, warning him that he was about to destroy the ship's winch. Rated at just five metric tons, all he could do was let out slack and continue cautiously for the shore, keeping the cables under tension so that he did not lose his purchase on the flooded craft. He landed high up the beach, not far from the rescue pod at the heart of Crater Lake Base.

***

AD2122, Egypt

"I do not know. I do not understand it," Master Sergeant Apep Badawi confessed.

Captain Arnold Bessel could see that his passenger was as baffled as he was. After the UNS *New World*'s attack on Area 51, he had obtained clearances from his superiors and a flight plan, agreed with local forces in Cairo. He and Badawi flew a UNASA-registered private shuttle from Nevada straight to El-Shaikh Ebada.

Below them was a military field base in some considerable disarray. Despite its location deep within the desert, at the heart of a box canyon, it looked for all the world like much of their equipment had been washed away by a flood. It was completely inexplicable, as far as Bessel was concerned. "This is just getting weirder and weirder."

It got worse. A wave appeared mid-air to crash over the sands, washing away the tidy-up crew's efforts. Suddenly there was a river running through the middle of the camp.

"What the hell!" Bessel was about to find a place to land, when a ship appeared, seemingly riding the magical wave that appeared from who knew where. With varying levels of success, much of the hardware on the ground – including four main battle tanks – were again moving away from the wormhole before they bogged down.

Heidi scanned the scene quickly before plotting her course north. She was heading for the location of a base she had incinerated with two tactical nuclear warheads almost a hundred million years earlier, in Cretaceous North Africa. That was her fixed point and the place that would lead her where she wished to go next.

She shot skyward, straight past a small, hovering shuttle, while its pilot dithered about whether he should land.

Bessel felt the wash from Heidi's much more powerful engines buffet his shuttle and fought with the controls to compensate. "Would you care to tell me just what the hell is going on? What was that?"

"Heidi," Badawi seethed. "I would recognise those deadly black ships anywhere. I cannot tell you what she is up to, Captain, but a month's salary says we will not like it! We should follow."

"Are you kidding? We've no weapons on this boat!"

Badawi turned to him and spoke seriously. "The last time we lost track of her, that is, Captain Baines lost track of her, Area 51 happened – and those were a most uncomfortable few minutes for me, I can tell you. Now, would you rather find out what she is up to now, or wait to see it on the six o'clock news? Oh, and by the way, if we do follow her, does this shuttle have parachutes?"

Bessel swore and set off in pursuit of Heidi's ship.

The rain poured, obscuring Thomas' view. He was unsure what to do next. Between him and the stranded pilot, wind-driven breakers as tall as a man crashed high on the shore, and beyond those lay choppy waters filled with a whole gamut of freshwater predators. He informed control of their situation, but what could they do? Bringing heavier winch equipment from the pod was all well and good, but connecting stronger cables to the semi-submerged ship would be incredibly perilous. The pilot's message, explaining that he now wore an environment suit with an eight-hour ceiling on breathing, relieved some of the pressure, but the storm alone might continue past that deadline. Worse yet, he knew for a fact that the predators had tens of millions of years to wait them out. He sighed. It was probably time for something heroic.

Floods often strand animals and people alike. The way into Crater Lake was difficult for non-aquatic creatures, but not impossible. During drought periods, the river draining through the only valley to lead out from the extinct Triassic caldera was shallow enough to walk. Occasional swims across pools left behind by the flow were not merely easy, but often desirable during the baking summer months. That, along with the scent of the lake itself, regularly encouraged those that the inhabitants of Crater Lake Base considered undesirables. Of course, when the monsoon returned, many such visitors found themselves trapped and hungry, within a large game vacuum. Under the surface, the lake was naturally plentiful, but was unquestionably the domain of the mosasaurs. Only the matriarch Sigilmassasaurus dared fish there with impunity, but now she, too, was gone.

The jungle that wrapped the inner walls of the extinct volcano teemed with life. Most of it relatively small. Most, but not all. This particular Robinson Crusoe had stayed alive over the last several weeks by foraging the shores for dead fish, missed by the mosasaurs in the water or by the giant pterosaurs that ruled the local skies. It had not been enough, and the carcharodontosaurid was extremely hungry and stressed, his blood sugar low, his system flooded with cortisol and adrenaline. He was *hangry*. Just one more in a long list of undesirable traits beach walkers hoped to avoid in an eight-metre-long, one-ton killing machine.

Thomas was oblivious as he stepped from the rear hatch of his ship. The weather was so appalling, he could barely squint at what was right in front of him as he walked towards the crashing breakers. Intellectually, the finite nature of a lake took away the threat from the raging waters, though it still felt counterintuitive to stand before them – almost like tempting Neptune.

Thomas shook his head. If the stranded pilot ran out of air, he would fly out there, lower a line and hope for the best, but it would be extremely dangerous for the man caught in the water. He snorted. *Where isn't it dangerous in this place?* That thought jogged a memory and he looked around warily. When the *New World*'s crew originally colonised Crater Lake, their have-a-go farmers often narrowly avoided sticky ends at the teeth of crafty mosasaurs. Though not directly related, they bore all the cunning of crocodiles with the size and ferocity to match. Almost immediately, Thomas realised his puny human senses had let him down, as a huge maw opened to reveal upwards of thirty crooked teeth. Perhaps even more terrifyingly, a second set of pterygoid teeth lay at the rear of the palate to conveyor prey down the gullet.

As wrapped up in his thoughts as he was in his jacket, Thomas screamed – as manfully as possible. The only thing going for him was that the mosasaur was not one of the largest denizens of the deep, but it was big enough. He fell on his backside, desperately scrambling away in reverse, as the creature tensed to launch for him. Mosasaurs were not at home on the land, but their flippers were more than up to the task of carrying their weight and propelling them across the sand and gravel of the lakeshore.

Thomas had less than a second to live. Just time enough for one last nightmare.

A vast head ducked down, straight over him, to snatch the mosasaur off the beach.

The winded soldier lay on his back, looking up in disbelief as his would-be killer was lifted bodily into the air and thrown further up the beach by a dinosaur he had never seen before. The rain hit so hard it stung. His eyes streamed, but from what he could make out, the newcomer was not dissimilar to the giant predators of Patagonia. He was no expert, but his saviour looked like one of the monstrous carcharodontosauridae that seemed to hold the whole world in their claws during this time, though he could not name the species.

He opened his mouth to cry out. Fortunately, the winding he

suffered when he fell took away his breath, saving him from doing anything so stupid.

The giant turned to follow his prey up the beach. Covering the ground in an instant, he pinned the mosasaur to the sand with one massively taloned foot, while his head dipped to tear the throat out of the smaller creature. The combat was one-sided and over quickly. The larger mosasaurs certainly would not have been on his menu; the dinosaur had picked his mark well.

In shock and awe, Thomas watched dumbly as the predator tore chunks off what he assumed was now a corpse. Fortunately, his hindbrain woke up before he did, and propelled him, staggering, back to the safety of his ship. He closed the hatch behind him and slumped down the wall to sit on the deck, panting hard. "I–I'd forgotten what this place was like. I think I'm ready to go 'ome now."

AD1944, Munich, Germany

The helicopter set down at the centre of a wide street. The rotors slowed, allowing Martin Ludwig Bormann, head of the iNazi Party Chancellery, to approach safely and greet its passengers.

Reinhard Heydrich stepped out first, shaking the politician's hand. Heinrich Schultz followed, though he was far more interested in the ruins of the Old Academy. His last visit had seen the building in all its 16th century glory – once he had left the stockroom in which their wormhole appeared the previous year, in November 1943.

Brushing Bormann's pleasantries aside, he asked, "What caused this?"

Bormann gestured for the two men to follow him towards a group of large vehicles, and what appeared to be a field headquarters and crisis centre. "We can talk in here."

They stepped up into an articulated trailer. "This is one of our observation pods. Our field command centre is parked next to us."

The inside of the trailer looked more like the plush boardroom of a multinational than a container on the back of a truck. Most of the walls were actually one-way structural glass, completely opaque from outside. Heinrich stepped onto a thick-pile carpet and allowed himself to be ushered towards the luxurious sofas at the far end. A smartly dressed butler offered them drinks before retiring into a small galley behind a bar.

"Very nice," Heinrich noted drily. "Are we going glamping?"

Bormann's smile was smug. "We cannot always bring the field to the office. In those circumstances, I prefer to take a little of the office out into the field." It began to rain heavily outside, reinforcing the advantages of such privilege.

The soporific drumming on the roof and windows drew Heinrich back to the palatial quarters among his beloved *Eisernes Kreuz*. He was forced to agree.

"Now, to why you are here," Bormann stated, down to business. "As far as we can tell, the wormhole your people created from Cretaceous Egypt has gone, *Herr* Schultz."

Schultz tensed, imperceptibly to his colleagues. *So, my way back is closed forever. Never mind. This time and these people amuse me. I'm sure I shall find something with which to busy myself.* Outside the privacy of his thoughts, he asked, "Do we know *how* it was closed?"

"Theories vary. There was certainly a powerful explosion – as you will have seen. Our engineers believe that to be the cause, *but* our instruments are picking up strange readings from the locus of the wormhole – or perhaps what used to be the locus—"

"Strange?" Heinrich interrupted.

"Ionising radiation and a strong residual magnetic field," Bormann elucidated. "I do not pretend to understand wormhole physics, but our experts believe that a strong magnetic field was either directed at, or used to cocoon, the wormhole before it closed. However, neither the explosion nor that residual magnetism seems to explain why the wormhole closed. Ultimately, we may never find out what happened from the evidence remaining in the rubble."

Schultz leaned forward, interestedly. "You have witnesses," he stated.

Bormann nodded. "Or rather, we *had* witnesses. They have disappeared, too. My men are combing the city for them now. They will not get away."

"Who?" Heinrich demanded, forcefully.

"A young lieutenant named Gunther Sonne – a nobody, as far as we can tell. He's unlikely to be involved with this – a low priority. Party Engineer Fritz Todt—"

"No bodies have been found among the wreckage?" Heinrich interrupted again.

"*Nein, Herr* Schultz."

The old man sat back in his seat, stroking his chin thoughtfully. He knew from his own timeline that Todt had become distant from the *Wehrmacht's* commanders, taking a particular dislike to *Reichsmarschall* Hermann Göring. In the end, the pressure he applied on Hitler to end the war with the Soviet Union was followed by his death in a suspicious plane crash. The man was an agitator – not to be trusted, as far as Schultz was concerned. *Blood will out,* he internalised one of his favourite mantras. "Continue."

Despite Schultz's curtness, Bormann smiled amiably, though he raised a wry eyebrow towards Heydrich, who shook his head almost imperceptibly.

"The other missing persons become each more interesting than the last. Herbert Frahm—"

"The political agitator!" Heydrich snapped. "That vermin has set himself against just about every project I ever put a hand to."

"Yes," Bormann agreed, coolly. "Though he goes by the handle of Willy Brandt now, I understand. A nom de plume. However, the next names on the list may be of especial interest to you, *Herr* Schultz. Corporal Heinz Engel, Colonel Hans Schultz and last, but by no means least, Dr Heidi Schultz."

Heinrich sat forward again, abruptly. "Which one?"

Bormann held out his hands, palms up. "As yet, I cannot say."

Heinrich stood and paced, his mind working frantically. If this

Heidi Schultz was his ancestor – a mere weak celebrity – it hardly mattered whether she was found or not. If, on the other hand, it turned out that the missing person was his granddaughter, then it was imperative that they find her – he would hate for Heidi to find *him*. She had become more volatile than he ever could have envisaged when he created her. Always his creature in all things, she had, since the Tim Norris incident, become dangerously independent and quite extraordinarily vindictive – even for a Schultz. The fear he felt was tinged with pride for the perfect monster he had bred.

He turned sharply to Bormann. "Somewhere within that rubble lie the remains of the Spinosaurus aegyptiacus dinosaur that my ingenious granddaughter tracked through time to bring us here. All traces of it must be recovered and stored in a very, *very* strong and secure cell."

Bormann glanced out of the window. "Surely there will be nothing left of it. Hundred-million-year-old fossils? They will be dust."

"No!" Heinrich bore down on him. "Any remains of that animal might be enough for my granddaughter to get a lock on these space–time coordinates." He straightened to look out of the window, over the sea of rubble. "*Never* underestimate that girl, Bormann. It may just be the last thing you ever do. Find your runaways, and until you know which Heidi Schultz you have, exercise the utmost caution." He turned to Heydrich, still seated across the lounge. "Reinhard, I assume a man in your position has the very best security."

Heydrich shrugged. "Of course."

"Quadruple it!"

⁓❦

AD2122, Egypt
"Where are your forces?" Bessel harangued Badawi, angrily. "We need birds in the air to stop her!"

"Our forces are limited, Captain," Badawi argued, equally animated. "There has been no war in this part of the world for two hundred years!"

Bessel seethed, completely exasperated with the limitations of their vessel. "We'll never catch her in this bucket – and frankly, God help us if we do!"

"We just need to keep her in our sights."

"What sights? We don't have any guns!"

"You understand my meaning, Captain. My superiors have requested help from our neighbours. Fighter craft are on their way."

Bessel blew out his cheeks. "That's generous, but it'll take them some time to get here. We don't even know where she's going."

"I think I do."

Again, Bessel turned to him. "Well, don't keep it to yourself."

Badawi sighed. "When Heidi captured me, she took me through the wormhole at El-Shaikh Ebada and then flew north."

"How far north?"

Badawi shrugged. "Maybe four hundred klicks?"

"About the same distance your neighbours' pilots will be travelling. This could get interesting."

They flew over the Red Pyramid, Heidi approximately a kilometre ahead of them. "We're gaining," Bessel observed. "She's slowing down."

Badawi leaned forward excitedly. "Excellent. We may catch her yet."

Bessel raised an eyebrow. "Got her right where ya want her, do ya?"

Badawi's arm shot out. "Look!" Ahead, Heidi's craft was not merely slowing, it was pulling several gs of deceleration. "Better hit the brakes, Captain!"

As Bessel slowed them, using the shuttle's air brakes to assist in deceleration, a pair of fighter jets streaked across their path, barely a hundred metres overhead. "Whoa! Keep your distance, boys. This ain't no air show!"

The jets circled to come about while Heidi's attack ship was already just metres above the ground.

"The pilots are asking how they can assist, Captain," Badawi translated.

"Tell them not to let that little black ship escape under any circumstances. Use any force necessary. The UN has granted us full autonomy on this matter."

Badawi relayed the message as Bessel lost altitude, better to see what Heidi was about. Bizarrely, she appeared to have stopped, hovering barely two metres above the desert sand.

Bessel whistled. "Ballsy little minx, isn't she?"

Badawi swallowed. "You have no idea. The pilots are ordering her to land." He winced.

"What is it?" asked Bessel. "Why are you cringing?"

"Nothing. I am not sure she will understand the message. After all these years, you would have expected someone to be able to create a better translator. *I'll* open a channel…"

"She's not landing, though, is she?"

Badawi paused, hand outstretched. "No."

"What *is* she doing?"

"I believe she is opening a wormhole, Captain."

"Tell those guys to fire. Fire at will!"

The rockets hit the ground, throwing sand hundreds of metres into the air, but Heidi was no longer there.

Bessel and Badawi looked at each other. Bessel powered forward and their tiny shuttle vanished, leaving only the ghost of a bellowed expletive hanging in the air.

Circa 99.2 million years earlier, Egypt

The land was scorched for many, many steps in all directions, for as far as Ouranosaurus nigeriensis could see. She was a herd animal, yet the recent enormous explosion had scattered her brethren to the four corners of their lands, leaving her alone but for one other creature.

Her giant companion had also been left alone, separated from her kind. While Ouranosaurus was an ancestor of the hugely successful duck-billed dinosaurs, her new friend was simply huge. Rebbachisaurus garasbae was a barrel-bodied, long-necked, long-tailed sauropod of the diplodocid family. At twenty metres long, and more than twenty tons in weight, she was little more than an adolescent and not yet fully grown. Ouranosaurus was notable for the spiny sail running along her back. Lacking the sail of stretched skin, Rebbachisaurus also had unusually tall dorsal vertebrae that appeared as pronounced ridges along her high back, differentiating her from most other sauropods.

Walking in the shadow of such a creature, Ouranosaurus found security of sorts, if not actual safety. Necessary, in such a harsh environment – made exponentially worse by the recent detonations of two tactical nuclear warheads in the vicinity. Most creatures had since avoided the area entirely, so unnatural was the place after the Schultz-German incursion into the prehistoric world. Yet even shocking change lives only so long in the memories of animals, and a few opportunists from outside the blast zone were already beginning to trickle back, seeking the bounty that always follows mass death. The threat of scavengers and hungry predators forced the females together in common cause, naturally falling into step as they sought out surviving plant life for food within a broader search to find their herds.

A small flock of Afromimus tenerensis ran across their path. Ostrich-like, they cut in front of the giant and her relatively diminutive three-ton sidekick at an alarming clip. Although the runners offered little or no threat to the mismatched pair, their instincts screamed that if one group of animals was fleeing the area, then perhaps they should, too.

Unsettled, both females snorted and pawed at the ground in their nervousness, though neither could pinpoint the cause. Ouranosaurus, much closer to the ground than her giant counterpart, scratched at sand that was melted and strange, in places reflecting the sun, like water. She sniffed, thirsty. The sea breeze, coming from the north, brought the smell of lush vegetation in the middle distance and with it a sense of relief. She would be fine. After many, many more steps, all would be well. She would doubtless find more of her kind there, too, if the eating was good. Her agitation began to subside.

Sensing the change in her companion, Rebbachisaurus also calmed, the smell of lush food ahead driving out her own recent anxieties.

However, the freshening from the north completely masked another scent sneaking up on them from the south. Despite his vast size, some fifteen metres in length, the wily old Carcharodontosaurus saharicus had not reached such impressive proportions without knowing how to fool the herd-dwellers.

He was close now, almost within striking distance, when Ouranosaurus turned, suddenly, a primeval sense of foreboding shocking her into action. By far the easiest quarry of the pair, she would have been done for, her life ending there and then, were it not for the large, black, flying boulder that forced itself between them.

Both animals balked in terror as the monstrosity appeared out of nowhere, seeming to float as it scorched the air. Yet unaware, her head high above and forward of the altercation, the giant sauropod plodded on for several steps before she, too, dully realised they were in trouble – at which point, she began to bray and honk and stamp in fear.

Heidi's ship almost fell foul of that stamping, and she was forced to take immediate evasive action, wending her way between the legs of the massive creature, scraping her hull between the vitrified sand and the sauropod's underbelly. Rebbachisaurus bellowed at the indignity of being lifted and moved aside, like an indolent hound from the hearth.

Heidi glided away gently, slowly slipping from the crush zone, her technological magic mocking the gravity every other creature had to live by.

Ouranosaurus bolted north, as fast as she could, in a flat panic. She would have been far safer to remain with her walking companion. Rebbachisaurus could have broken the predator's back with one well-placed crack of her massive tail, but in a time before logic, there was only fear.

Carcharodontosaurus bellowed his own fury, retreating warily as he swished his own tail in a show of aggression – he knew only too well the risks of attacking such a massively powerful prey alone – when another flying boulder appeared from the air to confuse the situation further. This one, white. He roared again, backing away.

Completely inaudible through their bulkhead and over the rocket noise, the men inside the white ship roared, too – in absolute terror.

Gripping the arms of his seat, Badawi eventually regained some control of language. "Oh, this was a bad idea!" he cried.

"You said we shouldn't let her go!" Bessel retorted.

"I was hoping those pilots would shoot her down!"

Bessel turned the shuttle to get a view of their surroundings. "I think that fate might yet be ours when she turns arou— WHAT THE HELL IS THAT?" The shuttle bucked as his hand slipped from the controls in terror.

"It's a-a-a a dinosaur!" Badawi cried the obvious, heart in his mouth. "What? You thought I was making it all up?"

In a panic, Bessel reacquired the stick and controls as he yawed their tiny craft to the right, narrowly slipping beneath a vast, whip-like tail – clearly aimed for them – while fighting to prevent their shuttle from ploughing into the sand. Off to their left they could see the skeletal remains of a large ship, all that was left of the *Heydrich* after the nuclear explosions. Not far in front of the capital ship lay Heinrich Schultz's escape pod, almost intact. "Wow!" Badawi exclaimed. "They really built those things."

"Never mind that! What do we do?"

"Get out of the way!" Badawi screamed.

A second wormhole opened almost as the old one closed and Heidi brought her ship in to hover next to them. She winked and waved to the terrified men in their defenceless shuttle.

"Oh, my God," Bessel muttered.

"What?"

"She's hot, like seriously *hot!*"

Badawi glared at him, incredulous. "Please focus, Captain Kirk! Watch out for the dinosaur!"

"Which one?"

"I would start by avoiding the one with all the teeth!"

Heidi programmed her next jump, this time using the anchor points already existing within the time frame she required – her fixed point, the fossilised Spinosaurus aegyptiacus, whose remains were so recently spread around among the ruins of the Old Academy, Munich, 1944. Despite the destruction of the spinosaur's fossilised remains, the uranium 235 isotopes were still very much present and traceable.

The massive wormhole the *Heydrich* generated had stayed open for many months, weakening the fabric of space–time itself at this location. When she opened her new wormhole over the same coordinates, the portal generated was larger and more defined than any her wrist device alone could have produced.

Carcharodontosaurus eyed one vessel, then the another. The rocket noise was terrifying and hurt his ears, but as they effectively bracketed him in, he was unsure which way to run, or which he should attack. His fear grew, and so did his anger.

"No, no, no!" shouted Bessel. "Not us, not us! Look at that one. Look at the pretty girl!"

"He's not a puppy!"

"This is all new to me, OK? Give me a break!"

Heidi moved towards the wormhole, shoving the dinosaur aside for a second time before she vanished once more. The Carcharodontosaurus patriarch, seeing his way clear at last, ran for it.

"No, no, *noooo* – you stoopid animal!" Bessel raved. "Not that wa— Oh, my God…"

The men looked at each other in stunned silence.

"He went through." Badawi spoke in hushed tones, once more stating the obvious.

"I got that, Master Sergeant! What do *we* do now, is the question?"

"I suggest that wherever she is going will be better than here. Believe me, I have seen this neighbourhood – you do *not* want to live here!"

"But… but… we don't know where that leads."

"It leads to Heidi. Go! Quickly, before it closes or goes somewhere else. She seems to have these things interconnecting all through space and time. We could end up on Mars!"

"Now, wouldn't that be novel if it worked out, just once!"

"Go!"

"I'm going. I'm going!"

***

AD1944, Munich, Germany

Bormann pulled his overcoat tight about him, while his aide covered him with a large umbrella. "As you can see, *Herr* Schultz, very little remains. I cannot imagine how any possible use could be made of—"

"Your lack of imagination is of little interest to me, *Herr* Bormann. I want that rubble gone through immediately. Tell your engineers to search for evidence of uranium 235 – there may even be traces of strontium 90."

"Uranium!" Bormann was horrified.

Heinrich eyed him sternly. "You would do well to carry out my instructions, *Herr* Borma—"

Heinrich's warning was interrupted by a loud crash from the wreckage and ruins a few dozen metres away, at the heart of the devastation. Three things happened in rapid succession that caught everyone's attention.

Heidi's orbital attack craft rose from beneath the rubble of one of Munich's hitherto most prominent buildings like the fabled phoenix. Stone, timber and glass cascaded down the sides of her ship, as plumes of dust billowed out from the debris.

Her heavily armoured ship cleared a route for others to follow. The first was an enormous carnivorous dinosaur. Anyone not already screaming for their lives joined in quickly, as the creature stepped from the remains, also roaring in terror for his own life – a distinction entirely lost on those running away.

By comparison, the third arrival, Bessel's shuttle, had all the impact of a taxi pulling up for a fare.

Bormann could not see. His aide had dropped the umbrella on his head when he ran away. Brushing it aside, his anger immediately turned to self-pity. "I will be fired for this."

"You'll be killed, you fool. Run!" Heinrich, as good as his word, was already away.

Reinhard Heydrich was halfway to his helicopter when he realised that he still needed the old man. He swore, looking around for inspiration. The chopper pilot was already powering up, rotors gaining speed with every second. He could see the terror in the man's face.

Heidi scanned the area. Spotting her grandfather, she zoomed in on her heads-up display to be sure. It seemed likely the chopper was his getaway vehicle. "I do not think so, *Großvater.*" A single rocket turned the civilian helicopter into superheated gas and shrapnel.

Heydrich dove for the paviours.

Heidi recognised him, too, both from her time in this Germany and her extensive teachings of the Third Reich's lead players and their exploits. She brought her ship in low and opened the side hatch. "*Herr* Heydrich, get in," she called through the ship's public address system, "if you wish to live."

Heydrich weighed his options immediately, and dove for the opening to roll inside.

Further back, Heinrich Schultz stumbled. His heart was weak.

He should have taken the surgery months ago, but did not wish to sully himself with implants not constructed from his own DNA. He almost fell, staggering back to his feet.

Carcharodontosaurus saharicus *roared.* Now on a firm footing, his claws tore up the small paviours as he ran at Heidi's ship – the reason for all his pain.

Heidi watched the monstrous predator approach quickly, easily gaining on the old man, who clutched at his chest while he ran. There was no way he would reach them before the dinosaur did and Heidi needed her vessel intact. She closed the hatch and powered up the thrusters. *"Auf Wiedersehen, Opa."*

Chapter 10 | Time and Again

Cheviot Mountain, Iron Age – 3rd century BC
The Sarge delivered Aito into Hiro's office and backed away to stand by the door, arms crossed disapprovingly.

Hiro continued to stare at his screen, ignoring both men.

"I'll have a seat, shall I?" Aito pointedly scraped a chair across the hard floor and sat.

Hiro continued to ignore him. "I'll be fine, Sarge. Thank you."

The Sarge nodded and left the room.

"Well?" Aito pressed. "Did you bring me here just to ignore me?"

Silence.

"I see," Aito continued. "And I thought, after all the recent damage, you might want my help fixing the ship, but maybe we first need to work on fixing our relationship, hmm?"

Hiro closed his screen and eyed his brother with sadness. "I…"

Aito waited… and waited. Exasperated, he snapped, "Hiro! I can talk to myself in my cell!"

Hiro nodded, mostly to himself. "I've been busy, and not just with the ship. I've been talking with your former colleagues among the enemy personnel. I suppose they're no longer enemies, but… well, never mind. I've been piecing together your actions over the last few years. Perhaps you could fill in a few gaps?"

Aito grunted. Hiro's was clearly one of those questions that was nothing of the sort. "Good. So you know how I worked with Devon and Jansen, and others, to bring down the Schultzes."

"Hardly a resounding success on that point, was it?" Hiro scrutinised his brother. "I want you to answer me honestly on three points. Firstly, why on earth did you run away to join such a regime in the first place, letting us believe you were dead? You broke Father's heart!"

"I had reasons… at the time, and Sargo Lemelisk gave me an opportunity to make a difference—"

"Make a difference!" Hiro was suddenly on his feet, shouting. "Schultz tried to erase everyone who ever lived!"

"Sometimes saving the world comes with hard choices," Aito replied, calmly. "And costs."

"Hard choices?" Hiro leaned forward onto his desk, lowering his voice menacingly. "What kind of a choice is the total destruction of human history and the removal of all our people from the timeline?"

"The only choice, if the world is to be saved."

"Oh." Hiro breathed the word, bitterly, slowly sitting back down. "Saving the world, were you? May I ask, for whom?"

Aito did not answer. Instead, he changed the subject. "And your second question?"

The muscles in Hiro's jaw bunched. "If you think I'm finished with the first, then think again. But as you're a glutton for punishment, answer me this – did you murder Sergeant Denholm Haig on the moon?"

Aito's eyes widened with shock. "Who told you about those allegations?"

"Allegations?" Hiro glared at him. "For your information, all your ex-buddies have been only too willing to help with our enquiries, now they're facing life in prison."

It was Aito's turn to jump out of his chair. "Many of those people worked to bring the Schultz paradigm to an end – risked their lives! You can't blame everyone, just because their overlords were monsters! Some were gangsters, sure, a good many, but others were victims, trapped within a regime that demanded their expertise and knowledge – forced labour on the Old Man's pet science projects. It's an old story, that comes round again every now and then. You can't just…"

Hiro sat back, a half-smile tugging at his lips. "So… there *is* still a little decency left within that shell of my brother – my father's son."

Aito swallowed, unable to continue.

"Sit, brother, and tell me the truth – did you murder that man?"

Aito sat. "He was a bad man, Hiro."

Hiro leaned forward quickly, banging his fists down on the desk. "Did you kill him?"

Aito closed his eyes, bowed his head and nodded slowly. "I sabotaged his space suit, so that the air tank blew, while he was working out on the surface of the moon. I had to, brother."

"Had to?"

Aito nodded again. "Remember the private conversation we had, just before I left the old *New World* to rejoin Heidi, as part of the deal Captain Douglas struck to get Tim Norris back?"

Hiro sat back again. "Go on."

"Apparently, it wasn't so private. Haig overheard us. Somehow, Heinrich Schultz found out that it was Haig who gave Del Bond the materials he needed to turn a simple pen into a gun, in exchange for some voyeuristic pictures of the young girl he had with him. When the Old Man questioned Haig, he gave me up, trying to save himself. He would have said anything. All pointless, of course. When a Schultz marks you for death, there's no appeal process. Heidi was summoned to the Old Man's cell – despite him being her prisoner at the time. They're a great family! She was ordered to *deal* with Haig. However, to avoid an even greater stink among a crew already grumbling about mutiny, she decided that it would be *amusing* to let me tackle the problem to save myself. She promised me that she would speak with her grandfather on my behalf and persuade him that Haig was merely lying to save himself. The way she saw it, that might even be true. Naturally, *I* knew that no flimsy promise from Heidi would save me, because they could never be sure of me, whether they believed Haig or not. I was a loose end, and the Schultzes abhor those.

"It was only a matter of time before Devon was on my trail. Heidi knew he would do it, too. Knew he would seek justice for Haig, a simple soldier – at least, according to his *official* record – who was murdered in a cowardly manner. What she didn't account for, was that Devon's sense of justice, and his search for truth, might outweigh his thirst for revenge. An easy mistake for a Schultz to make, I know. They weigh everyone against their own standards. It's a blind spot and by far their greatest weakness, in my opinion.

"Despite cracking my deception, Devon shielded me. I don't know exactly what he told her, but I'm guessing he gave the impression that his investigation had gone nowhere. Again, not all of Schultz's people are bad, brother."

"I know. We've lived with Captain Meritus' crew for years." Hiro considered, absorbing the answers his brother provided. "So, you set out on a one-man crusade to save the world by erasing all its people, and committed murder to save yourself…"

"You make it sound so shabby." Aito tried a youthful smile.

Hiro glowered, unimpressed. "Your actions disgust me. And they would have disgusted Father. I'm ashamed of you. If you hadn't managed to redeem yourself with a few selfless acts of courage along the way, I would be campaigning for you to be thrown, top down, into a room without a door! But at least, I hope, you've answered me honestly now. Have you?"

Tears welled in Aito's eyes, but he nodded solemnly.

Hiro held his gaze a moment before continuing. "Regarding the conversation we held, all those *eons* ago, the one Haig overheard, the one that got him killed, I still await your answer."

"That was your third question?" Aito asked quietly, knowingly.

"Indeed. You already know the question. Now… how do you answer?"

Aito looked away. "I don't know, brother."

"I see. In that case, you leave me no choice. I cannot leave you free to act. Not if at any moment you might turn on the people I care about, Aito." Hiro's voice cracked with emotion. "Why must you be like this?"

"Because I've seen the world of men."

"Is the natural world, away from men, any different, or better?"

"It's more honest. You may not have asked your third question outright, but I want to explain my reasons, nonetheless."

Hiro sighed deeply, wiping his own eyes. "Fine. Let's debate your secret cause. Again."

Aito leaned forward on Hiro's desk, urgently. "As I told you, I joined Schultz's mission because I saw a way to return the world to herself, without the blight of humanity. He was glad to have me – Old Man Schultz, I mean – possibly because of some sad delusion about resurrecting the Axis Powers alliance of old, but mostly because our father was such a powerful industrialist. I believe he kept me around in case he ever needed to play a trump card that would either bring our father down, or deliver him neatly into Schultz's pocket."

"And you went along with it? Knowing that!" Hiro scathed.

"It never happened in the end, did it?"

"Oh, that's alright then!"

"Look, aren't you beginning to see why I believed it was necessary for us to go? And the only way to be sure was for everyone to go!"

Hiro was beseeching. "You can't still feel that way?"

Aito slumped back in his chair. "Not the way I once did. I was young and idealistic. I have seen such evils, brother, but also some of mankind's greatest traits, too. I feel like I've lived many lives—"

"Join the club."

"Exactly, and now… now I'm just confused."

Hiro reached across the desk for his brother's hand. "Come back to us, Aito. *Please.* Come back to *me.*"

❧

AD1588 – Cheviot Mountain, Tuesday 22nd November, 0735 hours

Jim Miller lay curled up in a ball on the steel deck of his manufacturing bay, calling his daughter's name. His order had sent Rose and her husband, Henry, out of the bay, when Heidi's ship lifted off. By trying to protect them, he had got them killed in the most horrific manner. With all his heart, he wished for nothing more than to join them.

Satnam Patel reached down to pull his friend into an embrace. There was not a single thing he could say, so he simply held him.

"Dr Patel."

He turned to see Dr Reid standing awkwardly to one side. Patel looked away, bending his head down to lay his cheek on the top of Miller's head, eyes closed.

Reid walked around to his back. "Dr Patel, I really must speak with you. It's about Heidi's wormhole manifold."

"It can wait," Patel replied, curtly. "If you had not just saved my friend, I would have ordered you shot!"

"I understand, but no, it can't wait. You see, I *built* it."

Patel stiffened. Anger surged white hot through his veins. Gently lowering his friend back to the deck, he began to rise and did the least Satnam Patel thing he had ever done in his life. Fury drove his arm back as he turned. Closing his fist, and with all his weight behind it, he delivered Reid an uppercut to the jaw.

The lab coat formerly known as 'One' flew across the chamber like a broken swan, skidding to a stop three metres away, unconscious.

Patel screamed in agonised rage. Rose, Henry, Mother Sarah, Major Ford White, even old Lord Maxwell gone – and were that not enough, Heidi had murdered Elizabeth R, too, their one great hope for the salvation of man's future. He howled, tears streaming down his face. He was so angry, he no longer knew what to do with himself, marshalling all his control just to stay his hand from killing the unconscious man. Reid's machinery threatened the end of everything; a mechanism that negated the natural laws of the universe to distort fate itself. Falling to his knees, he sobbed, soulfully, no longer wanting to live in such a friendless world.

Reid stirred groggily.

Patel glowered through his tears, though he suddenly had neither the strength nor the will to get back to his feet and attack him again. He closed his eyes and wept.

"Dr Patel?"

Patel's eyes snapped open, bloodshot.

Reid stepped back sharply, holding his hands up to defend himself. "I… I guess I deserved that. Please, let me speak. I can help you – all of you."

"You have done *enough!*"

"You don't understand. I can make it right."

Patel jumped to his feet, suddenly furious again. "Make it right? You have given the tools to destroy the natural order of time itself to a mass murderer – can you make *that* right? She has butchered some of the finest people I have ever known – can you make *that* right? Why, you…" He grabbed Reid by his lab coat and drew his fist back once more, his knuckles already bleeding.

"No. Wait! Yes, I can make it right. Some of it, maybe *all* of it. Hear me!"

Patel waited, fist shaking with the power of his wrath. Through clenched teeth, he forced the words that would bounce along with Reid for some time. "Speak. Quickly."

AD1944, Germany

"You destroyed my helicopter!" Reinhard Heydrich spat,

venomously.

"Get another one," Heidi retorted, from the attack craft's cockpit. She pulled back on the stick, sending Heydrich barrelling into a wall.

"You also killed my pilot!" he shouted angrily, from the rear compartment.

"Get another one," she repeated, coolly.

He shrugged, acceding to the logic of her point. As the ship began to level off, he risked heading fore, dropping into the co-pilot's seat. "Dr Schultz, I presume?"

She glared at him. "That was not funny centuries ago."

"Centuries?"

Heidi rolled her eyes. "Perhaps not for you. Never mind. Someone down there will wake up sooner or later, and alert your air force. Where should we go to talk?"

"I have a small mountain retreat, off the beaten track. Set your course south-east-by-east."

When Heidi set off two simultaneous nuclear explosions in Cretaceous Egypt, Carcharodontosaurus had been more terrified than ever before in his life – despite that life being one of extreme and unending violence. His current situation would have ranked second, had he the ability to count. He *roared* defiance at the world – a world he no longer understood. Someone would simply have to pay. All that mattered was the need to sink his teeth into something, to take out all his rage upon it, then all would be well, balance restored.

One rapacious predator to another, Heinrich Schultz read that very need in the creature's eyes as he, pointlessly, raised his arms to cover his head.

That end never came.

Suddenly realising he was not, in fact, dead, his other senses worked overtime to report the news. Firstly, the roaring grew louder. Much louder. Then there was a deep, percussive thud.

Bessel's shuttle hovered just three metres above the ground. From the co-pilot's seat, Badawi cried, "No! Don't save *him!*"

"Why the hell not?"

The Egyptian bellowed the first Americanisms he could muster. "Because he's the… the… the bad guy – the *son-of-a-bitch!*"

"What?"

"Never mind. Take us up before that thing turns back on *us*. This shuttle has no armour and I've seen what these creatures can do, especially when frightened!"

Lying prone on the paved road below them, the old man risked opening his eyes. Lowering his arms, he immediately raised them again as he dove away from the downwash, narrowly avoiding incineration from Bessel's rocket thrusters.

The small, white shuttle that followed his granddaughter's ship through the wormhole had miraculously interceded on his behalf, shoving the dinosaur away. Heinrich could barely believe his luck. Against all hope, *his* end of the seesaw of life was rising again. On the downside – literally, and in so many ways for the person on the other end – someone had to pay to restore universal balance. Martin Bormann screamed and ran.

Deprived of his bite therapy, the theropod turned on this new chew toy and lunged. Bormann screamed again as he was lifted from the ground. Carcharodontosaurus saharicus bit down – *hard.*

Remarkably, from Schultz's fascinated perspective, the man continued to scream, despite the crunching of bones and cartilage. The dinosaur threw back his two-metre-long head, completely engulfing the iNazi Party Chancellery's Head, who vanished from sight, a screaming, bloody mess, cast into darkness to burn in acid.

"No need for decades of conspiracy theories this time, old chap," Heinrich noted thoughtfully. "There will be no doubt whatsoever about what happened to *this* Martin Bormann. Perhaps less dignified than a glass capsule of cyanide, but *so* theatrical. Well played."

Vehicle sirens filled the city centre as armed men surrounded the petrified animal[1] , firing into the air to corral him and trap him. One of the vehicles that drew up with a screech of tyres was from the City of Munich Animal Control Unit. Were they ever in for a surprise.

Perhaps unsurprisingly, Carcharodontosaurus was having none of it, and ran east along *Neuhauser Straße*.

Captain Arnold Bessel brought his ship down to rest upon the paved roadway, also facing east. He watched the dinosaur make its way through the city's main pedestrianised zone, taking giant steps, his tail rigid behind him to retain perfect balance. Nosy bystanders suddenly woke to their danger. Show over, they ran screaming, desperately forcing their way into shops.

Bessel shook his head as animal control dashed for their vehicle to pursue. "How many times are they going to remake *that* movie?" He leaned forward to glance left and right.

"What are you looking for?"

"Japanese tourists."

"What? Look, never mind. Maybe we should help?" Badawi suggested. "Air support?"

"Right, and get shot down as enemy combatants? You saw what Heidi did to that chopper. No. I think we'll leave this one to the locals. God knows we're going to have enough explaining to do as it is."

"Seems that is all I ever do, these days," Badawi agreed, moodily.

---

1. The word 'petrified' on this occasion is a mere narrative device. By the most unlikely of flukes, this particular *Carcharodontosaurus saharicus* was not, in fact, turned to stone over millions of years, but merely scared and confused. His fossilised remains would never now appear in the same collection as Ernst Stromer's other discoveries, including the recently destroyed *Spinosaurus aegyptiacus* that shared the same recurring fate as the Old Academy in Munich.

AD1588 – Cheviot Mountain, Tuesday 22nd November, 0740 hours

Reid pulled a device from his pocket. "This," he spoke loudly over the sounds of distant secondary explosions, tearing through the ship, "is how Heidi is travelling through time without the huge power plant required to open a wormhole in the usual way."

Patel lowered his fist. "That is not possible. You would need to…" He tailed off.

Reid nodded. "You understand?"

Patel let him go. "You tapped into the power of the Earth's *core?*" Incredulity and fear pervaded his words in equal measure.

"Yes. That's why she can only open pathways through the manifold in the immediate vicinity of Earth. However…"

"What?" Patel prompted, his anxiety notching up to eleven.

"Just an idea, really, but if she knew of a wormhole elsewhere – a guaranteed link, so to speak – it might be possible to connect with it, using the power of our planet to travel to *another* planet, or anywhere, potentially. Not sure how she'd get back, but…"

"Sterling work, Dr Reid, and like I said, you have given this godlike power to an insane terrorist!" Patel shouted in his face. "What is your encore? Use the power of Earth's mantle to blow up enemies on other continents? Imbecile!"

"Can I go back?"

They both looked around to see Jim Miller picking himself up from the floor. He looked like hell. "Can I go back, Dr Reid?"

"Yes, Dr Miller. That is my whole point. I made two of these wrist devices. Heidi has the other. She doesn't know about this one. I doubt she would have allowed me to keep it. It's very similar to the devices we launched from orbit, but with one essential difference."

"Explain," Patel demanded, tautly.

"Those devices, all three hundred of them, can no longer be accessed in our three-dimensional space."

Patel shook his head in disgust. "How could someone so obviously brilliant behave *so* foolishly? Where do these three hundred wormholes lead?"

"Everywhere. That is, all over the world. We had little time in the end, what with the attack on our base by the *New World*'s support ships. I was ordered to simply scatter them all over the Earth, each anchored to a different time chosen at random. Although they can be redirected to join with other times and places, each individual device is fixed in space."

Patel hung his head. "You have triggered a collision in space–time that will destroy causality. I have said it before, I will say it again – *imbecile!* I am sure you come from a long line of Nazi lunatics, Doctor, well, guess what? You have surpassed them all. Congratulations!"

"Actually, my father was an accountant."

"Really? Pity you did not follow in his footsteps!" Patel snapped, still furious. "You might have tallied up the mess you were about to make and advised your client to buy a timeshare instead!"

"Actually, those aren't good investments – not long term."

"Why, you…" Patel blustered, raising his fist again.

Miller placed a gentle hand on his friend's chest to forestall him. "Satnam, wait. Dr Reid, tell me honestly, can I use your wrist device to save my daughter?"

Reid nodded. "I'll show you how."

Almost two thousand years earlier, practically on the very same spot, Baines studied Hiro carefully. She was worried about her chief engineer. "But can we trust him? I'm sorry, Hiro, I know he's your brother, but his history's chequered to say the least, and we have troubles enough right now."

"I understand, Captain. I would have him working only with me, and make no mistake, if he steps out of line, I *will* stop him."

She sighed frustratedly. "You really think he's sincere with this, his nth reversal? Because I can't deny the idea of having another Nassaki around engineering at this time is attractive, but by the same token…"

"He's my brother, Captain. I have no choice but to believe him – at least, I must give him a chance to prove himself."

Baines considered. "Have you spoken to James about this?"

Hiro nodded. "As overall mission controller, I went to him first, Captain. No offence."

"None taken. What did he say?"

"He sighed deeply, like you just did, and said, 'Ye'd better take it up with ma wife'."

Baines soured. "*Did* he? Marvellous. OK, Hiro. I don't trust your brother, but I'm willing to trust you. If he screws up, the costs might be unthinkable, so you're gonna have to be all over him like cheap aftershave – are we clear?"

"Yes, Captain."

"Don't jump into this, Hiro. Are you *sure?*"

"I will watch him like a razor, you have my word."

"I think you mean 'like a hawk', but never mind. I got it. I want you to liaise with The Sarge on this, too. I want more than one pair of eyes on him, at all times. Understand?"

Hiro nodded. "*Hai.*"

"But that raises another problem, doesn't it? While you're watching every step he makes, you won't be fully on the case, will you? And we need you, Hiro. God knows what Heidi's up to, or when. I need this ship ready for anything, systems completely clean of Weber's hacking."

"Yes, Captain. I have spoken to Weber on that point."

Her eyebrows shot up in surprise. "You have?"

"Yes. The Iron Age people outside have some interesting ways in which they honour their dead, Captain. Captain Douglas recently attended one such funeral for two men who were killed by the Mapusaurus pack that travelled through the wormhole. They bury them in disused grain pits, apparently, but only for a while, and then they retrieve some of the bones to keep, or for use in family or tribal rituals—"

"Hiro," she interrupted, "is this going anywhere?"

"Yes, Captain. I'm sure I had a point… er… ah yes, here it is. The local people were deeply affected by the loss of their tribesmen, especially to what they believe was an evil god, or something. They understand that Captain Douglas and his team were as much the victim of their situation as they were themselves – they're surprisingly *un*primitive in their sense of empathy, actually, I—"

"*Hiro…*"

"Yes, Captain. What I mean is, Jones explained it to them – in basic terms, naturally, their language is—"

"Hiro!"

"Yes, yes. He explained that there are a group of evil people from the future who have brought this down on them – on all of us, in fact. I wonder what they would do if they caught anyone responsible for killing their kin and releasing these 'dragons' into their lands?"

"I don't follow?"

"Weber did, when I explained that I would hand him over to them, unless *he* explained his coding to me. It is quite brilliant, by the way, that coding. I don't think I would have cracked it on my own, even with the next two and a half millennia to play with."

Baines blinked. It was not the first time he had shocked her this way. There was an underground stream of malice running through the veins of that bumbling teddy bear of a man they all knew and loved. Bizarrely, and perhaps fortunately, she was almost certain that he was completely unaware of it himself. "You told him he would be given over to the savages?"

"They're categorically *not* savages, Captain. I just neglected to tell *him* that. However, I doubt they're particularly enlightened when it comes to crime and punishment. Your husband seems to really admire them."

"*He* would. They're practically family."

"And worthy of respect, Captain."

"Of course, and quite rightly so. Did that *really* work, though? On Weber, I mean?"

"His help has allowed me to hack further into the problems than I ever could alone. Yes, I would say he's helping. Our main problem is that the software he created is more or less self-aware, and constantly working to hide and defend itself – practically reinventing itself to avoid detection within our systems. Without his help, I wouldn't even know what to look for."

"What did you actually say to him?"

Hiro blinked. "Captain?"

"Come on, Hiro. He's a Schultz zealot – a nut job. How did you convince him? That knowledge might prove useful, going forward."

"I told him the area outside was being terrorised by a ravaging pack of Mapusaurus and that there was even an escaped spinosaur, of some sort or other, out there too. So, if we handed him over for punishment, without speaking a word of the local language, and he used his superior intellect to escape the old people, he would be eaten in very short order. Of course, if he didn't escape them…"

"Go on."

"I told him they hang criminals from their gates to die of exposure, unless they're preyed upon by the wildlife or pecked by the crows first. Thanks to his masters, the crows in these parts are rather bigger than they used to be. He got the hint."

"But he flat refused to crack, no matter how *I* threatened him."

"Captain, Captain," Hiro explained, gently. "What would you – or any of us – have really done to him? Us, with our 22nd century moralising and softness." He pointed north, gesturing through the bulkhead of their ship. "Those people have much simpler ideas about the treatment of enemies and those who hate them. Their ancestors walked here, before there even was an English Channel. They've thrived for ten millennia. For some reason, in just two centuries, we brought our world to the brink of destruction. Perhaps we should show them more respect, because whatever they did, it worked."

Baines sat back, taking her chief engineer's full measure – a man, after all, separated by a paper-thin slice of time from the noble samurai. She nodded to herself. "OK, you've sold me. *But* keep a tight rein on him *and* that brother of yours."

"Thank you. I'll have him fetched from his cell and put to work. Oh, by the way, I think I may have solved the problem with Heidi's multiple wormholes, too. Good day, Captain."

"*What?* Hiro! Come back!"

***

AD1588 – Cheviot Mountain, Tuesday 22nd November, 0750 hours

Overworked fire suppression systems battled frantically to bring the flames under control. More than thirty years old, the USS *New World*'s remaining crew were too few in number to fully maintain such a vast network of technologies. A breach of the power core would be an ecological disaster for the region, even if an explosion was avoided. Of course, if they survived that, they would then have to explain to the English how, after pogoing from one ruler and religion to another over the last half-century, they would now have to start all over again with a new monarch.

Tuning out the booms and portents of doom, not to mention the warnings and klaxons screaming in his ears, Jim Miller strapped on the wrist device.

"Are you sure you fully grasp the controls, Dr Miller?" Reid checked, anxiously.

Miller nodded, but Patel was less sure. "Jim, maybe it would be better if I went? You have been through the worst imaginable shock..."

"No, Satnam. Thank you, but no. I must do this. I caused..." He choked.

Patel grabbed him roughly by the arms. "You caused nothing! This was the fault of Heidi Schultz, and no one else. If you insist on doing this, you must focus on the job in hand, Jim – not a misplaced sense of guilt. Are we agreed? Deep breaths, my friend."

Miller complied, taking large gulps of air and releasing them slowly. "Thank you. I'm OK, Satnam. I can do— *will* do this. It's not just Rose and Henry. We lost many of our oldest friends today, and without this ship…"

Patel nodded. "Quite so. Good luck, Jim. God go with you."

Miller took another breath. "Good luck to us all. OK, Dr Reid, I'm ready, and Dr Reid…"

"Yes, Dr Miller?"

"Thank you. I'm not sure exactly what part you played in all this, I'm sure Heidi gave you little choice, but nevertheless, you didn't have to stay with us – or save my life when the hangar exploded, for that matter…" He tailed off again, his voice breaking.

"Focus, Jim," Patel assured him. "If this works, you'll be able to make sure none of it ever happened."

Tears streamed down Miller's face, leaving white lines in the soot from the explosion that almost incinerated him. He nodded, the sorrow in his eyes replaced at once with a look of determination.

Reid stood off to the side. "Thank you, Dr Miller, for your understanding," he stated quietly, just loud enough to be heard over the noise all around. "I wish you success."

<hr>

AD1588 – Cheviot Mountain,
Tuesday 22nd November, 0600 (two hours earlier…)

Heidi listened carefully, her eyes narrowing.

"What is it?" asked Reid.

"The listening device I placed within Miller's jacket is no longer working."

"Are you still planning on leaving this morning?" he asked, tentatively.

"Yes. However, I would have preferred to do so knowing where my enemies were and what they were up to. This complicates matters."

"We could postpone…?"

"*Nein.* They are up to something. Better we leave before they have chance to stop us."

"They wouldn't dare, surely? Not while you hold that detonator in your pocket."

"Perhaps they will call our bluff?"

He looked at her askance.

"You disagree?"

"Only in so much as I would say they know better than to underestimate you, ma'am."

"Very diplomatic, *Herr Doktor.* You are, of course, correct. And yet… something feels wrong about this."

Dr Jim Miller woke with a start. Anyone waking abruptly might wonder where they are, especially if they are frequent travellers, but confusion and concern usually melt quickly away to be replaced by normality as memory returns. Perhaps unsurprisingly, time travellers have similar experiences, but with the added complexity of wondering *when* they are, too – a disorientation often making the drive to work feel like 4-D chess.

For reasons he could not fathom, Miller had awoken curled up on the deck of *Factory Pod 4*'s main hangar, still in his pyjamas, with no idea how he had arrived there. "What the…?" It was all he could manage, while he waited for his language skills to boot up. He got stiffly to his feet. Everything around him was scorched and several vehicles were on fire. Smoke made him cough.

Standing to either side of him were Satnam Patel and Dr Reid. They looked almost as surprised as he did, before they and everything around him began to fade.

Miller stood in the bedroom of his quarters, hands on knees, panting. Bundling his sleeping self into the wormhole he had just travelled through from the future had winded him. Now in his seventies, he was getting old; added to the shock of seeing his daughter and son-in-law incinerated, he felt fit to collapse. Unfortunately, he still had much to accomplish and very little time.

Straightening, he stood before the mirrored doors of his

wardrobe. He was black with soot, his clothes dishevelled and filthy, but Reid's device had worked.

He remembered waking in the bed behind him a little over an hour earlier. Twisting to look back at the bed from which he had just turfed out his sleeping younger self, the room suddenly shifted alarmingly around him. He leaned against the bedstead to stop himself from falling. He closed his eyes, taking deep breaths. Memories of the last hour flashed behind his lids. He could not live through that nightmare a second time. Swaying drunkenly, he bolted for the door as quickly as he could.

Rose Burnstein-Miller woke to loud banging on the hatch to the quarters she shared with her husband.

"Henry? *Henry!*"

"Wha'?" he groaned, irritably.

"Can't you hear that?"

"Wha'?"

"The *door*, Henry."

He pulled the duvet up over his head and turned over. "Yeah, sure. I'll fix it, baby, I promise."

She slapped him on the rump. "Henry!"

He sat bolt upright. "Where's the fire?"

The banging intensified.

"Who've you invited round this time?" Henry asked groggily, mussing his hair and yawning.

"*Me?* I haven't…" She pulled the duvet up to her chin. "Never mind. Go and see who it is."

"Gee, thanks."

A pillow flew across the room, connecting with his head, while he fumbled with his dressing gown. The banging on the hatch grew ever more urgent – there was shouting now, too.

"Alright, I'm comin' already!" Henry dragged his feet across the lounge carpet to answer it. "Give me a break," he groaned.

He opened the door and was surprised to see his father-in-law, smoke-blackened and highly agitated.

"Henry!" Miller burst into the room, grabbing him, virtually lifting the tall, squarely built American off his feet. "Oh, son. Thank God you're safe, my boy."

Henry was at sea. "Wassup, Dad?"

By that time, Rose had made herself respectable and joined them in the lounge.

"Rose!" Miller streaked across the room to snatch her up in his arms, spinning her around. "Oh, my little girl!" he repeated over and over, tears smearing the mess across his face still further.

"Dad! What *have* you been doing? What have you been *drinking?* Put me down this instant – you're filthy!"

Miller was laughing and crying now.

"I think Dad's havin' a breakdown, honey," Henry pointed out, gently.

"Nonsense. I'm sure there's a perfectly rational explanation for his behaviour, even if it involves Lord Maxwell's whisky, isn't there, Daddy?"

"I've come from the past!"

"OK, perhaps not. Come on, let's sit you down – *wait!*" She ran to a cupboard and fetched a towel. Once it was laid across the sofa, she allowed him near the furniture. "Right, *now* you can sit. What's this all about?"

AD1588 – Cheviot Mountain,
Tuesday 22nd November, 0615 hours

Major Ford White sat on the opposite couch in Rose and Henry's quarters, listening attentively to Dr Jim Miller's description of the worst couple of hours of his life. From the state he was in, he did not doubt the veracity of the man's tale. "Let me just get this straight, Jim. Are you suggesting that we simply do nothing and allow Heidi to leave?"

Miller anxiously ran his fingers through filthy, soot-blackened hair. "I don't know. I suppose I am, yes."

White lapsed into thought for a moment. "Look, I can understand you've been through hell. I can't imagine how that must have felt, but surely, the very fact that you're here now must mean we can avoid all that this time round. For one, Sarah and I won't meet with Maxwell and Queen Bess in the main hangar. That'll tick *that* box, by removing Heidi's target of opportunity—"

"But that's exactly my point, Ford," Miller interrupted. "If there's no reason for her to shoot up the hangar, maybe she won't. Maybe she'll just… go!"

"*Maybe?* This is Heidi we're talking about. Who knows what the hell she'll do. I don't like it. Sarah, Satnam, what do you think?"

Mother Sarah and Dr Patel looked at each other before either spoke. Patel gestured for Sarah to go first.

"Horrifying as Jim's story is, I still think we should prevent her from leaving. Thanks be to God, we seem to have been given a chance to fix the terrible events Jim witnessed. If we let Heidi go, we may be squandering that chance."

"But, Sarah—"

"Jim, please," she cut through Miller's interruption. "Rose and Henry are safe now. They should stay here – I think we can all agree on that."

"And I suppose if we do get it wrong, we could always go again," White pointed out. "I mean, now you have Reid's wrist device…" He tailed off under Patel's glare.

"We are discussing the timeline, Ford, not Saturday morning reruns over cornflakes! A little respect?"

Miller averted his eyes, lost in a private hell. "I saw you, Ford, and Sarah. I saw you both…" He looked to his daughter, drinking in her image, so full of life. "I can't go through that again. I just can't."

Mother Sarah cleared her throat and spoke into the awkward silence. "Yes, well, we'll just have to avoid that, too. As Ford says, we'll keep everyone out of the hangar. Thanks to you, we know that in a little over an hour, Heidi will attempt to leave. That gives us a window of opportunity. Now, how do we use it?"

Patel nodded agreement. "Sarah is correct. We *must* stop her."

"But why?" Miller tried again. "Wouldn't we simply be better off shut of her?"

The astrophysicist reached out to place a friendly hand on Miller's shoulder. "Jim, I think the appalling experience you have suffered might be clouding your judgement. It's completely understandable, but you – *we* – are neglecting to ask the main question here."

White leaned forward with interest. "Which is?"

"Simply this. If Heidi is willing to leave behind that extraordinary *alleged* alien technology – especially after what she must have gone through to get it – then she must have something even bigger planned."

"Bigger?" asked Miller.

"Worse," Patel elucidated. "She came here for two reasons, the way I see it. Firstly, she genuinely thought her pet scientist, Reid – with our help – would be able to make her ship into a hybrid and get it working. We now know that, if even possible, the project will take time. Far longer than she will have hoped or planned to stay here, I suggest, which fails on two fronts, potentially. It gives us plenty of time and opportunity to come up with a way of stopping her for one. For another, she lacks the patience to see it through, especially as it looks likely to fail anyway. The second reason she came here – again, in my opinion – was because she needed time off grid, to collect herself and regroup. I noted she was limping when she first arrived – clearly, she suffered an injury somewhere along the way. My guess would be that Captain Douglas et al have the Nazis cornered – or on the run, scattered. Despite his message from the Iron Age stating that he was stranded, he remained hopeful of rescue, and vouched that Captain Baines was still out there, somewhere, some when, giving them hell from the bridge of an immensely powerful warship. I could be wrong, of course, but I believe these hypotheses fit what we know."

"Alright." White spoke forcefully. "So how do we stop her *and* avoid the disaster Jim witnessed?"

"We play the ace up our sleeve," Henry Burnstein Jr stated,

quietly. "The one we never knew we had."

Rose smiled at her husband. Over the last thirty years together, they had become one, able to finish each other's thoughts, and this occasion was no exception. "Of course. Who better to prevent Heidi from leaving than the one person she trusts?"

***

AD1588 – Cheviot Mountain, Tuesday 22nd November, 0645 hours

The message appeared on Reid's private comm silently. He frowned. Sitting on the lavatory within the tiny hygiene room aboard Heidi's modified orbital attack craft, he wondered how the *New World*'s crew had gained access. Perhaps when Miller had downloaded the bogus information from Heidi's own comm? It did not matter. What did matter was the content of the message. Fear and adrenaline spiked within his system. His mind raced in time with his pulse. How did they even *suspect* he had thoughts of betraying Heidi?

Talk about timing. It was fortunate that he was already on the toilet.

The tone of their message was strange, too. Beyond assumptive, it was like his betrayal had already happened. He shivered. Something was off here – very off, and yet… there *had* been a plan growing in his mind. The reason he kept putting off its execution was because it would be suicide, but maybe that was no longer the case? *Three hours should do it. That way, wherever she goes in the timeline, she will have moved on from her point of access and the wormhole, almost certainly… at least, I hope so. It's a gamble. But then, why not? I'll never have a better chance.*

When Heidi knocked him out and launched the probe that spat forth hundreds of wormhole generators from orbit, he had known from the moment he regained consciousness that he must do what he could to stop her. Unfortunately, he was a natural coward. He was not alone. So are many, possibly most, until they reach that moment in life where they are forced to meet themselves. Some shy away, some push forward, some die – all are changed. *His* moment was upon him. He felt it. More than any creature alive right here and now, or there and then, he held the future of causality in his hands. Only he could stop Heidi Schultz. At least, that was his intention and hope; more importantly, it was what he *believed.* He was shaking. *Can I do this? I must do this.*

He typed a timed message on his spare comm – the one he would leave behind. The message would be sent in three hours' time. It included a short execute program – he smiled at the irony of that – one that would unpack automatically, the moment she opened the message.

AD1588 – Cheviot Mountain, Tuesday 22nd November, 0715 hours

"I'm leaving now," Heidi stated with finality. "I thought to destroy them for plotting against me, but never mind. Perhaps another time. We should leave before they spring their trap. We must protect this ship."

"I want to finish my work."

Heidi stared.

Reid adjusted the collar of his geography-teacher white shirt with brown checks, uncomfortably. "I mean, I would *like* to…" He tailed off; something felt incredibly familiar about this conversation. "You're thinking, 'to what end,' aren't you?"

Heidi stared at him. "How did you know I was about to ask that?"

"Erm… lucky guess?" His sense of déjà vu was crushing. It felt like he was reading their conversation from a script. "It's the ultimate puzzle – at least, it is for a man like me. Technology from another civilisation, so far ahead of our own – from another galaxy, perhaps. Don't *you* want to see it work?" He paused. "You know, there *is* something awfully familiar about all this, ma'am. Have we had this conversation before?"

Heidi looked momentarily unsettled. Even to her, it felt like they had become living echoes. "*Nein,*" she lied in all honesty. "We're leaving. Right now."

"Wait!" Reid studied his instruments, frowning with concern. "We have a problem."

"Explain. Quickly."

He blinked. Another massive déjà vu shock, but something was different this time. The words 'explain, quickly' seemed to retrieve a memory engram he had never made, and there was something else, too. He had it. Wrong voice, wrong face. Someone else had said that, only, he knew they had not. *What on earth is going on?* he wondered fearfully.

"Reid!" Heidi barked, bringing him back to the now – as far as he could tell.

"Sorry, ma'am. In the main hangar next door, I'm picking up a massive magnetic field."

"*What?* How?"

"I don't know, but their original mission was to colonise Mars. Perhaps they took magnetic field generators to help them predict space weather events, such as geomagnetic storms or solar flares. They would have used them to mitigate the effects on NASA technology and infrastructure. More importantly for us, such a machine will make any wormhole we open – *if* it allows us to open one at all – incredibly unstable. We're going nowhere," he stated with finality.

"How could they possibly have known we planned to leave this morning?"

"Don't look at me," Reid snapped defensively. "You only just told me!"

"True. Suggestions?"

"I have *one…*" he ventured, hopefully.

"Go on."

"They must have set up their magnetic field generator in the main hangar—"

"Obviously! What is your point?"

He sighed. *I won't miss this.* That thought stunned him. *Am I really planning on leaving her? More to the point, can I pull off such a thing before she shoots me?*

"Reid!" she snapped again, with growing impatience.

"There are no life signs in the main hangar. I could just step outside our ship, walk in there and switch it off."

She blinked. "Well? You had better do it, then!"

He opened the hatch and stepped out into the Pod's manufacturing bay. There was no one around yet. However, work was scheduled to begin at 0730 hours, so people would be drifting in at any moment. He strode quickly to the main vehicular hatch. The heavy steel doors parted with a slowness that reflected their mass, opening in readiness for his mistress' escape. He stepped through.

Sure enough, a large machine, perhaps two metres cubed, sat in the centre of the hangar. It hummed.

Reid made his way towards it. *Something's wrong here.* What little remained of his hair was standing proud of his scalp. It might have been an effect of the magnetic field being generated, though he suspected it was just plain old terror. He tried to focus, but found it hard to imagine Miller or Patel just dropping a single machine in their way and leaving it. It was too obvious. He looked around. *There must be other generators,* he thought. *This one must be sacrificial – they know she'll blow it to pieces.*

He dropped low, to look under the large lorries parked at the edge of the hangar. *Ha! Thought so. They've hidden other, smaller generators around the perimeter. I wonder…*

Reid stepped up to the centre generator. If he left it alone, Heidi *would* blow it to pieces. Dangerous bait, because who knew how much else she would destroy, simply because she could? If he switched it off, the other generators would prevent her from leaving, but then, what would she do if cornered? He shuddered, and then shuddered to think. Whatever it was, he doubted it would end well for anyone – especially him, if he was standing exposed in the middle of it all. He sighed. He was trying to second guess the workings of an insane mind. It could not be done. Normal probabilities did not apply with Heidi. No, it would be best to let her *think* she had gotten away. If she was in enough of a hurry, she might just *leave.* Of course, she would expect him to go with her…

He studied the machine's control panel when an idea struck. He read 'polarity'. *Hmm… that ought to do it.*

A few seconds tinkering with the controls and he ran back to signal for Heidi to lift off and move into the main hangar. He had already stowed his second comm in the shuttle, hidden among a few personal effects. He was ready.

Heidi lifted off and approached him. As she entered the main hangar, she activated her wrist device to open a portal in front of their ship.

Reid smiled to himself. Reversing the polarity of the largest machine negated the effects of the smaller ones – it had worked. He took a deep, steadying breath. Now for phase two.

The wormhole opened. Heidi called through the open hatch, "Get in!"

He stepped up to the hatch and called inside. "Do not fire on the generator. They have many. I programmed that one to counter the others. If you destroy it, you will be trapped here."

She turned in the pilot's seat. "Noted. What do you mean, *I* will be trapped here? Surely you mean *we, Herr Doktor?*"

Reid swallowed. "I'm staying. To finish the work. I'm sorry."

"Traitor!" she snarled, drawing her last faithful friend, her nine-millimetre pistol.

Reid leapt away from the hatch as sirens and klaxons sounded all over the Pod's hangar. Probably due to Reid's interference with the machinery, he noted peripherally.

Heidi screamed in fury and fired once, twice.

Reid cried out in agony.

Heidi was torn between making sure of him and making her escape. She chose the latter and closed the hatch. Her ship vanished.

Suddenly a hive of activity, the hangar was filled with running people as hatches opened in the walls along both sides. White, Patel,

Miller and Mother Sarah ran to Reid's side as he lay on the deck, rocking gently and clutching his arm. He let out a gasp as blood welled between his fingers.

White pulled out his comm. "Private Tomás Suárez to the main hangar on the double – and bring your med kit."

Receiving an affirmative, he knelt at Reid's side. "So… you actually came through for us, but you were meant to deactivate her ship. Instead, you seem to have deactivated our trap. Explain. Quickly."

Reid gritted his teeth. Those same wretched words again. "I did better than that, Major, I assure you." He noted Miller's blackened and dishevelled state. "What happened to you?"

"I was nearly blown up the first time she tried to leave."

"The *first* time?"

"Never mind. How are you?"

"I've been shot!"

"She missed you, last time."

"*Really?*" Reid spat, angrily. "Well, that just goes to show what you get for helping people then, doesn't it!"

Two millennia earlier…

"For the record, Commander," Baines spoke over an open comm, "I think this is the craziest idea we've *ever* had – and I include that time we tried to round up a Spinosaurus while it climbed the Red Pyramid in the Giza Desert."

She heard Gleeson's laughter through her headset. "*It's just a little déjà vu, Captain. You'll get over it. It's a great idea – a plan already tried and tested!*"

Strapped into the backseat of one of four small reconnaissance helicopters, Baines shook her head and looked to her fellow passenger, Tim Norris. "You look concerned, Tim."

"Of course I am," he retorted. "*I'm* still sane."

In Giza, they had flown a new breed of fully electric choppers.

However, after considering the drawbacks of flying the Cretaceous skies – and the very real possibility that crews might, on occasion, have to fly for their lives – the UNASA, NW2 mission project designers expressed natural concerns about range and recharge times. They therefore dabbled on the energy futures market and opted for fossil fuel equivalents.

The noisy, fumy jet-fuel engines would provide the pilots a secondary advantage in the coming engagement – that of terrorising the creatures below them. At least, that was what Commander Gleeson, their current mission planner, hoped. Baines equated it to the spider argument – the one where 'who was more afraid of whom' was open to debate. Indeed, she believed human imagination probably gave advantage to the spider.

She knew the argument was academic, of course. They were not hunting spiders. They were hunting a pack of Mapusaurus roseae, still thirteen-strong, so the 'who was more afraid' argument was already decided – although with Commander Gleeson, one never knew for sure.

She sighed. "OK, listen up, everyone. We need to split up. I'm assigning numbers and directions. My chopper will take call sign one, and head north. Commander, as this was your idea, and just in case the whole mission turns into a complete number two, you have that privilege – also in keeping with the metaphor, you can head south!"

Gleeson laughed again. "*Bon voyage, Captain. I'll call if I spot them.*"

"Take care, Commander. We haven't even paid for these things yet! Captain Meritus, you take three and head east.

"*Leutnant* Hartmann, thank you for offering your services as a superior pilot. I want you to take chopper four, west. Are we all clear?"

"*Yes, Captain.*"

"Good luck."

The helicopters shot off to the four points of the compass and began prearranged search patterns. The challenging terrain within the Cheviot Hills made it difficult for the grounded *New World*'s sensors to build a complete picture without satellites. Even so, Baines doubted it would take long to find their quarry. They would almost certainly stand out in the landscape.

"This is really silly," Tim broke into her thoughts.

"You don't think it'll work?"

"I'm sure we'll find them," he answered, cautiously. "Just follow the death. I just can't help remembering that the only psychological response our helicopters elicited from the Spinosaurus we hunted – the *single* Spinosaurus, I might add – was annoyance, as it went for us. There are *thirteen* mapusaurs, by Captain Douglas' count. I'm just not sure what we're hoping for here."

"Gleeson's idea comes from his experiences working the vast cattle and sheep farms in the Australian Outback. They use choppers to drive the cows—"

"*Cows,* exactly!" Tim snapped, anxiously. "These animals are more likely to see us as sport than a threat."

Baines expelled a deep breath. She suspected Tim might be right, but it was the best shot they had. Short of killing these creatures, pushed out of their natural time through no fault of their own, it was the *only* shot they had. "Here we go again…"

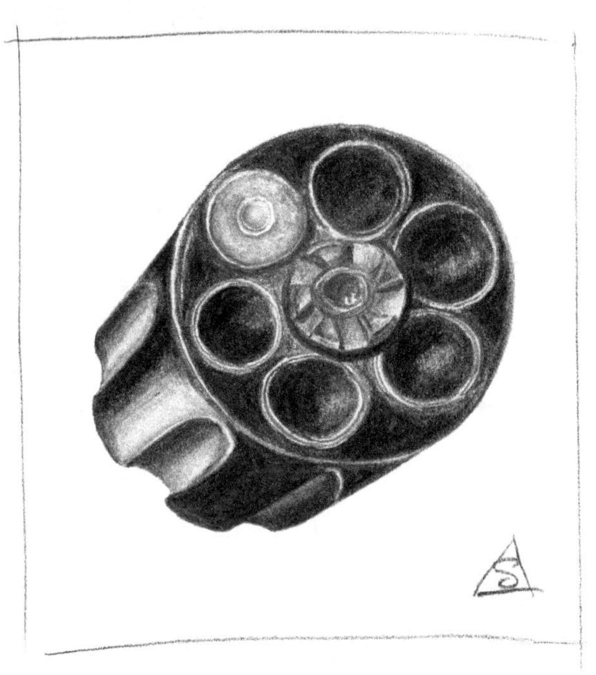

Chapter 11 | The Quality of Mercy

Munich, Germany, AD1944

Heinrich Schultz possessed eight decades of memories on Planet Earth. Some of them were out of sequence as far as the rest of humanity was concerned, yet all flashed before his eyes now.

Martin Bormann, head of the iNazi Party Chancellery, had died an impressive death, though with little dignity. When Bessel's shuttle arrived in the middle of things, shoving the Carcharodontosaurus away, Schultz dared to believe that he was saved, but it was not to be. The old man felt that now, as he walked east along *Neuhauser Straße* in the wake of the dinosaur, his heart hammering irregularly. The latest had been one shock too many. He stumbled, caught himself, and carried on, walking past the rubble of ruined buildings with all the stateliness and grandeur his failing body would allow. Heinrich Schultz was a moving island of calm amid the running and shouting all around him. Some acted with purpose, while for others, their only purpose was to get from there.

The dinosaur darted left, two side streets down the road. A piercing scream marked its passage as it moved out of sight.

Heinrich slowed. His heart slowed, the edges of his vision blackening. *So,* he thought, *it's time…*

Dragging his feet now, no one around him seemed to notice. *They never notice what's right in front of them.* He smiled painfully. *That's what made it all possible.* Time slowed, too. At least, it seemed to for him. In the real world, outside his head, things moved apace. *Or perhaps inside my head* is *the real world, and all else is a dream.*

His mind was wandering, he knew it, no longer able to perceive time. Moments strolled by, or perhaps longer, when he heard a colossal *roar.*

Standing at the junction of the *first* left turn off *Neuhauser Straße,* he stepped cautiously to face the sound. The side street was signed *Ettstraße.* Chunks of perception were going missing; he tried but could not hold on to them. After running around the block, the dinosaur now approached him from several hundred metres away, then several dozen, then several. Heinrich blinked and, suddenly, he was looking up into a giant face that stared right back down at him. Blood and gore dripped from steak-knife teeth. The old man had always prided himself on the naked power of his stare and its ability to terrorise. He smiled. "It seems there really *is* always someone better. Hello, old chap. We've travelled a long way from home, you and I. Shall we finish our journey together?"

Carcharodontosaurus saharicus bowed his head to sniff the strange creature before him. He was not used to prey stopping to chat. He smelt no fear on the man. It was interesting, but then animals are often curious. Yet when the chips are down, they always do what they must. This morsel may have intrigued the giant, but it was also an easy meal in a terrifying new world.

Heinrich Schultz's mind sharpened for one last hurrah. All senses heightened, he stared, iron grey eyes boring into the soul of the beast – a soul who knew only violence. For the predator, mercy meant only death. It was him, or his prey; the best he could do was make it quick. The old man understood. "You know," he drawled, "there was a time where, at the snap of my fingers, you and half your continent would have been vaporised. But all times end. So let's end it. You are a truly magnificent creature – I shall feel no shame." He straightened, reaching into his jacket to remove a small hold-out pistol from the inside pocket. Opening his arms wide, he dropped it. He was struggling to speak. "I will not scream. *I*… will allow *you* to live, will *help* you to live, to continue our great work. So, come, my friend. I am ready."

The old man's heart stopped, though his consciousness dallied just long enough for his powerful mind to exert its last control over a body shutting down. Standing by the indomitable force of his will alone, his body never fell to the ground, but was caught in one final embrace as Carcharodontosaurus saharicus bit down. Heinrich Schultz smiled at the exquisite pain, smiled into the darkness. He could not and did not scream. His body no longer responded, the pain evaporating, yet his mind held one last thought. *Until the next time…*

The dinosaur threw back his head to swallow his food whole and immediately looked around for more. By obeying his coding, and the coding of all life, even of the universe itself, he fulfilled a dying old man's last request, and continued the business of killing.

Chapter 12 | Bake Off at the Berghof

Munich, Germany, AD1944

Captain Arnold Bessel and Master Sergeant Apep Badawi stepped out of their shuttle into a mob. A frenzy of journalists and television cameras pushed in on them from all directions. However, even these strangers from another time were not the big story. *He* lay unconscious in the middle of Munich's first and largest pedestrian zone – a fifteen-metre-long, seven-ton predator from mid-Cretaceous Africa.

Several police vehicles surrounded the sleeping giant. Animal control units in Germany were understandably ill-equipped to take on and capture such a beast. Consequently, the dinosaur resembled the world's largest porcupine, so many tranquiliser darts had it taken to bring him down.

A massive tongue lolled from the side of his mouth, still covered in blood and worse.

Bessel bobbed and moved to get a clear view through the crowd around him, hoping to avoid looking even more dumbstruck than the dinosaur to the millions of people doubtless watching him on TV, all around the world. He turned to Badawi. "This is going to be an interesting political situation for someone. You know, when I woke up this morning, I never imagined… You know what, never mind."

Badawi nodded sagely. "Welcome to my world."

Across the city, in a private apartment registered under an assumed name, Dr Heidi Schultz screamed. She was *not* the granddaughter of an old man half the world had just watched disappear down a dinosaur's gullet. She was, in fact, his great-great-grandaunt, who was known fashionably as H and held a PhD in sociology. "Apep!" She jumped to her feet.

Her brother, Colonel Hans Schultz, pulled a face. "Whatever is the matter with you? What is a *pep*? One of your subversive charities?"

"Not what, you fool!" she rounded, spitefully. "Who! Apep is a man. He's the man who saved me from my great-great-grandnephew and his insane granddaughter, my fourth-great-grandniece – the other Heidi."

"I know who they are," the colonel replied, irritably.

Fritz Todt scowled. "How do you keep up with your family tree?"

Colonel Schultz rubbed his face, tiredly. "It is not as easy as it used to be."

"Would anyone care to tell me what is going on?" asked Herbert Frahm, known professionally as Willy Brandt.

"No!" they shouted together.

Lieutenant Gunther Sonne was young, and after surviving the total destruction of the Old Academy earlier that day, somehow looked even younger. He was completely at sea.

Corporal Heinz Engel took the young man and Frahm to one side. "I'll try to explain – that is, I'll tell you the bits I know. I'm not sure anyone knows the full story."

While Engel brought them up to speed, the Schultzes and Todt bickered around the television about what they should do. After imparting what he knew, Engel returned to others. "We should pick them up before they disappear into a military enclosure somewhere. Hopefully, without getting ourselves captured and sent there with them… Not the reunion we're after."

"Why should we interfere?" asked Todt.

Engel shrugged. He looked more presentable after taking advantage of H's shower and picking from the wardrobe of male clothing he thought it best not to ask about. "Out of all of you, I'm the only one who does not belong in this time – or indeed this timeline. Maybe I'm just lonely."

"What timeline are they from?" asked Colonel Schultz.

"This one," H supplied. "At least, Apep is. I don't know the other man. Master Sergeant Apep Badawi was captured by my fourth-great-grandniece – whom I shall call 'Evil Heidi' – and taken back to the Cretaceous. He is *from* early 22nd century Egypt."

Frahm blew out his cheeks. "I should never have agreed to meet with you, Todt. I want to go home now."

The colonel rounded on him. "You don't have a home – not any more! None of us do. If you have any funds hidden away from my inheritance that you stole, dear sister, I suggest you secure them now. We are on the run from the moment we leave this building – and we had better not dally here too long, either. No matter how clandestine your purchase of this place may have been, there will be a money trail somewhere. And if the authorities find us, they will put us somewhere safe for a very, very long time, as Corporal Engel suggests. After all, no matter how sound our reasons, we are still the people who destroyed the Old Academy. As soon as the dust settles, we are going to have some very uncomfortable conversations, if they catch us. We can prove our innocence, of course, but it seems that our proof is in the Cretaceous a hundred million years ago and on another continent. Our lawyers will have to be *exceptionally* diligent to dig up the evidence and witnesses we need!" He turned to the corporal. "You are right, Engel. We should pick these men up as quickly as possible, which means acting while the area around the explosion is still in chaos. As for that ship that blasted out of there…"

"*Heidi,*" Engel spat.

"Yes?"

Engel waved H down. "Not you, the other Heidi – *Evil* Heidi. That's her ship. It must be, and if she's free and clear in this time, let me tell you, we're in trouble. Who was the man she picked up before she left?"

Colonel Schultz's face curdled with disgust. "Reinhard Heydrich."

Engel's jaw dropped. "Oh, my God. Reinhard Tristan Eugen Heydrich? The Reich Security Chief?"

"So I have been led to understand. He is more industrialist than politician here. However, regardless of his alternate life, we must take *these* men now. Somehow, we few will have to work outside the system to prevent whatever our government and my descendants are up to – you all agree?"

"Why outside?" asked Frahm.

"Because the Schultzes have already sown their corruption through our government, offering them all kinds of dangerous advancements. We have no idea who to trust."

"But we just saw the old man die," Frahm argued.

"Did we?" Engel replied earnestly. "I don't even trust my own eyes where that man is concerned. Even if he *is* gone, we still have Heidi to reckon with, and from my experience, she's the more dangerous of the pair."

Frahm took a seat, his brows knitted with concern. "Truly?"

Engel nodded. "The Old Man is, or was, cold and unemotional – a textbook psychopath and political irredentist. Because of that, we could usually rely on him serving his own interests, with a certain structure to his approach. In short, he had a cause. I was trained to think just like him, but it didn't take. Heidi behaves like an *angry* psychopath – which perhaps is an oxymoron, meaning she's something else. I'm no analyst, so I can only describe her as someone trained *into* psychopathic tendencies, but who's prone to spats of hyper-emotionality. Though she seems to care nothing for others, it would be a mistake to assume she cares about nothing. I've seen her go from cold calculation to explosive fury in a heartbeat. We should have no preconceptions where Heidi's concerned. She's dangerously insane and a case study in unpredictability, if nothing else."

Colonel Schultz stood. "That's useful intelligence, Corporal. It is vital we understand as much as possible about how our enemy thinks and behaves. It seems we are in this together, people – like it or not – and must no longer trust *anyone* outside this room."

Only the young lieutenant answered. "I understand, sir."

The colonel's expression softened. "I am sorry you were dragged into this, Gunther, but if you return, I fear they will only place you under arrest and whisk you off somewhere extremely secure – quite possibly for the rest of your life."

"He might give us up, too," Todt spoke harshly.

Lieutenant Sonne jumped to his feet. "Never, sir!"

Todt waved him back down. "Alright, alright, Sonne. I did not mean deliberately. No offence was intended. However, the risk remains."

"He's right, Gunther," the colonel agreed, in gentler tones. "Our people are not savages, but if any of us are caught, interrogation will be intense and designed to trip us up."

"I'm with you, sir."

"Good man. Right, this is what we are going to do."

"Hold on a moment," Todt interrupted. "Who put you in charge? I brought you into this, remember?"

"Indeed, you did. Forgive me, for not having found the time to thank you," Schultz replied, coldly. "Nevertheless, I am the senior officer here."

Todt shook his head. "I am not military. Not any more, and

neither is Frahm – nor your sister, for that matter. I am a Party member and an engineer, used to overseeing huge contracts. Frahm pretends to be a journalist—"

"How dare you!"

"And your sister is a… whatever she is."

"I am a world-renowned celebrity!"

Todt scowled distastefully. "Never mind."

"I am in charge here," Colonel Schultz restated, "both because of my prowess as a senior campaigner – skills we will need to survive this crisis – and because it is my money that will finance this expedition, wherever it takes us."

"I think you mean *my* money, brother," H corrected him. "Father left it to *me, remember?*"

"Doubtless that is, of course, what I meant," he replied blandly, with the barest veneer of sincerity. "Right, as I was saying, this is what we will do."

❧

Heidi flew through the breathtakingly beautiful Bavarian Alps to land at Heydrich's private helipad, next to what used to be the *Hotel zum Türken,* until he made it his base for secret genetic experimentation. The hotel was a mere hundred metres from his luxury retreat, known as The Berghof.

"You have deprived me of the greatest military assets of our time," Heydrich rumbled menacingly, once they were on the ground.

Heidi powered down the ship before answering. "What did *mein Großvater* promise you?"

"The full specifications of wormhole capable warships."

She smiled coolly, unplugging a one zettabyte hard drive and slipping it into her pocket. Capable of storing a trillion gigabytes of information, it held all Schultz technologies developed in her original timeline, and also included those of Dr Reid's team in the Cretaceous. "He would have betrayed you, you know."

"And you will not?"

She locked eyes with Heydrich. His piercing glare almost rivalled her grandfather's, when he was alive. *When he was alive…* That thought struck hard. She was, as yet, unsure what it meant to her, or might mean to her, in due course. She focused her attention on the job in hand. "That depends on how sensible we are all willing to be. In my timeline, you had a reputation for being the hardest man in the Reich, so maybe it is you who is not to be trusted. The man with the iron heart, Hitler called you."

"Did he?" Heydrich moved closer, appraising her in a way that would have made a normal woman uneasy. "Perhaps you could apply enough heat to melt it?" His words were soft, though his eyes remained hard as Saxon steel.

Her comm beeped, breaking the moment before she was forced to break his nose. She looked up angrily. "What is this?"

He looked surprised. "What is what?"

"*Mein Großvater* was injured in the Cretaceous. He required a blood transfusion. I controlled the situation, securing a donation from one of my scientists. We gave *mein Großvater* his life back, but with a little extra on top – something he was unaware of."

"You intrigue me."

"Give the wrong answers to my questions and your fascination will pass swiftly, *mein Herr*. On that, you *can* trust me."

He blinked. *What a woman this is!* "Interesting, though you have, as yet, neglected to ask me anything."

She nodded, accepting the fact. "I saw to it that *mein Großvater* was injected with nanites that would not only track his movements, but also…" She caught herself. Perhaps it would be best to keep the full potential of her grandfather's blood to herself, at least, until it suited her to divulge further.

Heydrich eyed her curiously, obviously noting her caution, though he did not press the point.

She continued, "Know this. As long as we shared the same time, or I had an open wormhole to when and wherever he might be, I could track him anywhere in the world. He was, in fact, mine, whenever I wanted him."

Heydrich felt a stirring. The Old Man had grandsired a truly exquisite creature. He was both entranced and terrified. "Continue, *Fräulein*."

She glared at him. Unlike the frigid cold of the Old Man, the violence in her eyes almost seared him. "You may call me *Doktor Schultz*."

He bowed, smiling slightly. "My apologies, *Doktor*. Please…" He gestured for her to continue.

"No, *Herr* Heydrich. *You* explain."

"I am afraid I still have no idea what you expect from me?"

"No? My comm has detected *mein Großvater* in that building over there. I suggest you consider *very* carefully, before attempting to lie to me. Now, explain."

Heydrich was confused. Although he made no attempt to hide that confusion, he also knew she would not take it at face value. "I do not understand," he admitted at last. "We both saw the Old Man die."

"*Nien.* We both saw *mein Großvater about* to die. You do not know him."

"But even if he miraculously survived, there is simply no way he could have reached here before us."

Heidi's eyes narrowed. His confusion seemed genuine – for what that was worth. "You have a hangar here?" she asked, changing the subject.

"Of course."

"This ship must be hidden. Others may come looking for us."

He nodded. "Of course. But before we do anything further, I notice that information drive you carry – do you have access to the specifications of the hardware *dein Großvater* promised me?"

She raised an eyebrow. "Promised you?"

His expression darkened.

Heidi sensed another fork in the road as she assessed the man before her. Eventually, she said, "I do."

He smiled again. "Then, please, would you care to follow me

inside? I will have your ship moved into safe, secure storage. It has been a most trying day for us all. Perhaps we should freshen up and replenish ourselves before talking further."

Heydrich led the way into the *Hotel zum Türken* and down into the concrete corridors beneath.

"This is your bunker?" asked Heidi.

"Merely insurance," he replied over his shoulder. "I do have some particularly ill-tempered competitors – you know how business can be. Considering the nature of our exit a little while ago, I suggest we take no chances."

"Indeed."

"This facility will stand proof against an explosion equivalent to fifty thousand tons of TNT—"

Heidi's comm beeped again, making her stop dead in her tracks.

"What is it?" Heydrich asked, cautiously.

"Fifty thousand tons of TNT? You are sure?"

"Yes. Why?"

"Seal the hatches, *now!*"

"What?"

"DO IT!"

Heydrich reached out to a large red button on the wall in the corridor where they stood. "Now, would you care to explain why I have just sealed myself within my own facility, young lady?" he demanded crossly.

The message Heidi had just received was from Reid. It simply read, "Goodbye." Attached was a self-expanding file that reactivated a program already running on her comm. The self-destruct restarted at fifteen seconds.

She opened her mouth to explain but changed her mind. What would be the use? He would find out soon enough... in nine seconds' time, to be precise. Instead, she simply murmured, "Cover your ears."

Thrown into absolute blackness, both Heidi and Heydrich hit a floor that felt alive as an indescribable *boom* violently shook the ground beneath and everything around them.

The stretched SUV limousine parked in the basement garage of H's apartment was perfect for the colonel's purposes. As one might expect for celebrity transport, the rear windows were all blacked out.

"Perhaps I should drive," Engel suggested, "as no one knows me here."

"A good idea in principle. However, should we be stopped…" Colonel Hans Schultz considered. "Explaining your lack of identification, or even a driving licence might be problematic."

"I do have one, but…"

"Exactly. It is from the 22nd century and a timeline that may not even exist any more. Our *Bundespolizei* are often accused of having little enough imagination as it is. No point in taxing them. No. Lieutenant Sonne will drive. He is the least conspicuous of us and has all the right permits. No one will be looking for him yet, other than as a potential casualty of the disaster we inflicted upon Munich."

"Actually, it was your great-great-grandkids who caused this, brother," H pointed out.

"You deny that it was you who carried the bomb back from the Cretaceous – the one we used to destroy the Old Academy, sister?"

"I am just saying *we* were all forced into this. I was trying to be kind."

He glared at her. "Of course you were. While insinuating that my descendants' dabbling with time travel and their involvement with organised crime a hundred years after my death is somehow *my* fault."

"I am not blaming you *directly* for bad parenting, Hans."

"I am yet to become a father!"

"Siblings, siblings," Todt intervened. "We must go! Lieutenant, please drive. The rest of you, in the back. Quickly. Come on, Hans, we must leave." He ushered the prickly colonel towards the vehicle.

They pulled out onto the main road and headed for the broken remains of the Old Academy. It was not far, and the roads were still relatively quiet after the emergency services' efforts to clear them earlier that day. Munich was a city in shock.

"Pull up here, Gunther," Hans ordered.

"Yes, sir. Shall I go in alone, sir?"

"I think you had better. Will you recognise them?"

"I saw them on TV earlier. I believe so, sir." The young officer flashed a smile. "Besides, they will be the men surrounded by cameras, sir."

"Fair point," Hans agreed. "Tell them—"

"Tell them H sent you," H interrupted. "Say that to Apep. He's the Egyptian, not the American."

Sonne looked to the colonel for confirmation.

He shrugged. "As likely to work as anything," he acceded. "Be quick, Gunther. Good luck."

"Yes, sir."

❧

Heidi opened her eyes and wondered if she had. Eventually, emergency lighting flickered to life. Despite all she had seen and endured, never was she more surprised to be alive.

Heydrich coughed and turned over slowly, groaning. "What happened?"

"You chose your builders wisely," Heidi noted wryly, also coughing. "That explosion carried the force of a tactical nuclear warhead."

"You fly around with nuclear ordnance?" Heydrich asked, astonished. "Is that usual?"

"It seems *I* have made some ill-tempered enemies, too." She was seething. "Reid…" In the privacy of her thoughts, she wondered, *How could that little worm of a man have gained the upper hand over me so completely, and without my even suspecting it? It seems so incredible that he even possessed the courage.*

Naturally, if she caught up with him, he would regret ever being born. Nevertheless, this latest *incident* did spark a kernel of admiration for her lab coat, formerly known as One.

"How long before we can go out?" Heydrich interrupted her reverie.

"Not long. The radiation should be minimal. Do you have air quality sensors to sample the outside environment?"

"No. Why would we?"

"You built a nuclear bomb-proof shelter – is it not obvious?"

"Our people do not use nuclear ordnance. We developed the technology for power generation. Some scientists have theorised about *other* uses, of course, but they were always deemed far too dangerous. In fact, they framed the idea as M.A.D. – that is, mutually—"

"Assured destruction," Heidi completed for him. "Yes, we had the same acronym."

"And you built them anyway?" Heydrich was at once appalled and intrigued by the thinking of these newcomers who offered him the world. "But what if everyone…" He tailed off.

Heidi merely raised an eyebrow. "We're not going to give them to anyone else, are we? It is fortunate that I brought the specifications for the Dawn Fleet with me."

"Dawn Fleet?"

"All in good time, *Herr* Heydrich. Perhaps we should take a look outside—"

They were interrupted by further coughing from down the corridor. A dark-haired man rounded the corner. Silhouetted by emergency lighting, he staggered slightly, leaning against a wall to recover his balance. Seeing Heidi and Heydrich, he stopped. "Reinhard? What the hell just happened?"

"Ah, Josef. I am pleased you still live. I would have hated to explain all this to Irene."

Heidi snapped round. "Irene and *Josef*?"

"Indeed," Heydrich drawled. "Dr Heidi Schultz, may I introduce you to my lead geneticist, Dr Josef Rudolf Mengele."

Heidi did not show surprise often – it was all in the training – but that day was an exception. "The Angel of Death," she breathed, reverentially.

Mengele was left standing with his hand outstretched, blinking with surprise. "My pleasure, I am sure," he answered tersely, winding his arm back in. "Seriously, Reinhard, what just happened?"

Heidi answered for him. "A nuclear explosion, Dr Mengele." She gave a shallow nod of respect. After several shocks in succession, her mind was beginning to catch up. "Did you meet with *mein Großvater?*"

Mengele blinked again. "I did. A charming man."

"Are you sure it was him you met? Never mind. Did he happen to leave you anything?"

Mengele looked shifty. "Such as?"

Heidi's blue eyes bored like starlight into his black holes. There was nothing to read there, yet she knew he was hiding something – sensed it – and guessed what it was he was hiding, too. She made a mental note to fully explore this genetic playground Heydrich had fashioned for himself and his pet monster, under the mountain. "We should see what, if anything, is left outside, *Herr* Heydrich, and I suggest using your contacts to throw a total security blanket over this whole area. The last thing we need is the media, or government busybodies, poking around to see what caused the disaster."

"We have satellites, you know," Heydrich responded, irritably. "Just how do you suggest I prevent *them* from seeing the crater where my beautiful mountain retreat used to be?"

"I suggest you get creative. Tell them you are remodelling for a pool. Just get it done, Heydrich. Or did I place my trust in the wrong man?"

He held up his hands, placating. "I will see it done."

"That is better. Come. Let us evaluate what is left. And rather than complaining about your pretty house, perhaps you should view this as the first example of the power I can bring to bear.

Power I might be persuaded to share with you, if you cooperate." She walked back through the warren of subterranean concrete tunnels towards the entrance where they came in.

Heydrich and Mengele eyed each other in frank disbelief. Mengele puffed out his cheeks. Both extraordinarily dangerous men, they were used to dealing with others of their kind, yet even for them, the 'other world' Schultzes were next level. Equally unsettling was the fact that Heidi and her grandfather seemed to know so much about *them* – or at least, what they were and might yet become. They followed.

According to Heidi's comm, they had been unconscious for nearly an hour. "Do you at least have cameras to *see* outside?" she asked Heydrich, witheringly, as they stood before the heavy steel door to the bunker.

"Of course. Though whether they are still operational after—" She glared at him.

He held up his hands again. "Yes, yes, I will look." Everything was on emergency power, but he was able to activate a security panel on the wall, toggling through several cameras until he found one that still worked. The equipment was obviously damaged, but they could see that the dust had mostly cleared. The extreme high-pressure zone created by the explosion itself left a low-pressure vacuum in its wake, sucking immediate and violent winds in from every direction. The maelstrom was fed by a sudden extreme drop in temperature following the flashpoint. Indeed, a storm still raged outside, with heavy rains complementing the lingering gales.

Heidi gave a satisfied nod. "Good. The rains will dampen the dust cloud and further lower any residual radiation. On our approach, my instruments detected a high-pressure front, moving up from the south. It will soon calm things."

She was right. The rain subsided almost immediately, though strong winds still gusted sporadically. They stepped outside. Heidi was impressed. The motors that opened the enormously strong steel door still worked perfectly. Looking around, she was irresistibly reminded of her walk across the surface of the moon, almost a hundred million years earlier. That had ended in a colossal bang, too. The crater – formerly the helipad – was easily two hundred metres across, though it was irregular, both in shape and depth. The topsoil had vanished, in all directions from the look of the place, coating everything remaining in a heavy dust which the rain now turned to mud. The ragged bedrock exposed was blasted razor-sharp and treacherous.

Heydrich brought up the rear, speaking animatedly into his comm, while Mengele looked around, black, fathomless eyes crinkling at the edges as he smiled at the devastation before them.

Even Heidi could sense the man's inner madness.

"I was very fond of that house," Heydrich spoke sourly, joining them.

Mengele laughed. "There is still one retaining wall standing, Reinhard. Perhaps you could rebuild." He walked off, cackling to himself.

Heydrich's eyes narrowed. He was not laughing. "You have caused me a lot of trouble, young lady."

Heidi's lip curled. "Trust me. I am worth it."

Heydrich glared, all pretence of sophistication and charisma dropped. "If I did not believe so, you would already be dead, my dear."

Heidi pulled her faithful nine-millimetre and held it to his head. "Likewise." She pulled the trigger.

Heydrich jerked with shock, though the pistol merely clicked – empty.

She let the clip fall and replaced it with a full one. "*Never* threaten me again, Heydrich. It would be such a shame if you did not live to see my new world order." She turned her back on him, contemptuously.

His steel-eyed stare bored into her back, but there was nothing he could do. He did not dare assault her, hand-to-hand. Her grandfather had taken great pride in describing her impressive skillset only too well. Indeed, Heydrich was fairly certain that, along with that pride, the Old Man held a deep fear of her, too. Yet that was not the only reason he stayed his hand. He craved the knowledge held on the drive in her pocket, and would need her to access it. Added to that, all his local security personnel and most of his staff and sycophants were dead, killed by the weapon of mass destruction she had brought down upon them. No. He could, and would, wait.

<hr>

Ruins of the Old Academy, Munich, AD1944

Bessel was at sea, the shock of his predicament falling on him all at once as the adrenalin broke down in his system. His legs felt close to collapse. There was no fight or flight this time, and as for *which* time… His career had taken him all over the world, even to other worlds. Being a foreigner in strange lands was nothing new to him, but being a stranger in foreign times would take some getting used to. In a way, time was becoming like currency, interchangeable – and like currency, he would need more of it, if he was to adapt and survive. He wondered if he would get it. "Er… do you know where we are, or when exactly, Master Sergeant?"

"I believe we are in 1944. I suspect this is Munich." A shadow of regret stole across Badawi's open features.

"What's wrong? That is, what specifically? And how can you be so precise?"

"Nothing is wrong, Captain. Just a memory. I once knew a girl from here. More precisely, captured from here by the Schultzes. That is how I know."

A small detachment of armed soldiers split from the force brought in to secure the area. They immediately pushed back the press, holding them at bay to form a circle around Bessel and Badawi.

"Oh, good. We're saved," Bessel noted sourly.

The soldiers ordered the two men from the future to simply stay where they were until someone came to take custody of them.

Bessel did not like the sound of that, but there was nothing he could do about it. When pressed, none of the men seemed to know precisely *when* someone might take custody of them, either. The fiasco around them was distracting everyone. "We might be standing here a while," he continued, and was surprised when an army lieutenant pushed through the ring of security, almost immediately. The young man acknowledged the salute of the sergeant in charge before stepping forward to salute Bessel.

"Captain Bessel, Master Sergeant Apep Badawi, I am Lieutenant Gunther Sonne. Please follow me, gentlemen."

Bessel and Badawi exchanged looks of astonishment.

"How do you know my name?" asked Badawi. Unlike Bessel, he was out of uniform and wore neither name badge nor insignia.

Sonne's smile was enigmatic. "My superior wishes to speak with you. Please…" He gestured.

Bessel was instantly suspicious. "Hey now, wait a minute, Lieutenant. Where are you takin' us?"

Sonne ignored him, instead leaning close to Badawi. "H sends her greetings. You must come *now,* or you will be detained."

Badawi nodded understanding. "Captain Bessel, we should follow this man without delay."

Exasperated, Bessel let out a long sigh. "Fine! Lead on."

They stepped through the ring of guards. To show correct form, Sonne ordered two of the men to escort them through the crowds. Once away from the blast zone and the rubble, Sonne turned to the soldiers. "Thank you, gentlemen. I will take them from here." He took his sidearm from its holster, giving Badawi a secret wink. "You will come with me."

Seeing the lieutenant had things in hand, and was obviously engaged in something well above their paygrade, the privates left.

"I apologise for the strongarm tactics, gentlemen," Sonne explained. "We must keep up appearances. Please head for the black stretched SUV on the corner."

One of the rear doors opened as they approached. Another German officer stepped out to greet them – a colonel. "In here, gentlemen, please."

He bundled them into the back of the vehicle, while the lieutenant jumped into the driver's seat and drove them out of the city without delay.

<hr>

Heidi sat on a rock, considering her next move, while Heydrich's people drove or flew in to take control of the situation. Looking around the destruction, she sipped from a can of beer taken from the bunker that saved her life. As she flicked its ring pull into the crater where her ship had been, with a *ping*, she was irresistibly reminded of the time she sat with a similar beverage, looking down over the wreckage of the *Last Word*. An artefact just like it had been discovered a little over a decade ago – in her personal timeline – during the summer of AD2102, down in Patagonia. Preserved in tree resin turned to amber, it had taken the long way around, through millions of years, and she often wondered as to its provenance. Could *she* have started it all? Could the man-made, yet somehow one-hundred-million-year-old relic that began the race for time travel have been hers?

In a way she could not entirely explain, it felt like coming full circle. Much of her childhood had been spent in Germany, in the late 21st century and, although this was not home, it was close. In so many ways, it was better. The Germany she remembered was a broken place of extreme poverty, where burnt-out wrecks and murderous gangs reflected the city state. In her pocket, she held a wealth of technology from that broken world. Technology that would make her the richest woman alive in this one. Unfortunately for mankind, Heidi cared nothing for money. She had other priorities. Obviously, Douglas' people, left behind in the 16th century, had changed the world enormously, despite her two failed interventions. There was no point in trying to reverse their achievements; she saw that now. She must continue her journey from here. Heydrich would pay anything for the knowledge she possessed, while trying to take it from her. Doubtless he already nurtured plans to dispose of her. Her grandfather held huge respect for the Reinhard Heydrich of their timeline. It meant nothing to Heidi that he was reviled as a monster by most of the world. They would come to think of her in the same way soon enough – she would see to it – for such was the rebarbative nature of absolute power. No. That did not concern her at all. The question was, could *this* Heydrich become the man they had learned about?

"Dr Schultz?"

She turned. Heydrich was behind her, his approach silent – she would have to watch out for that. "*Herr* Heydrich?"

"We must leave here. I have another facility in a converted salt mine, two kilometres west. Dr Mengele's research and equipment is being packed to follow, including the infant dinosaurs I bought, to prop up your efforts in the Cretaceous."

Heidi raised an eyebrow. "You bought them all?"

He smiled icily. "Two have been allowed to live. You will be pleased to learn that they survived your… *event.*"

"An expensive token to prove your wealth, *mein Herr.*"

"Not exactly. More an investment. I have plans. Come… please."

Apep Badawi grinned like a fool. He was quite unashamed about it, too. He never thought he would see H again. He held her hand as they spoke quietly in the rear of the limousine.

"Colonel?" Bessel conversed with H's brother.

Hans Schultz, bemused by his sister's behaviour, returned his attention to their guest. "Captain?"

"Where are you taking us?"

"My family has a lodge in the Chiemgau Alps. My father bought it many years ago. No one knows we have it, and no one there knows who we are. It is as safe as we can hope for, for now – though I doubt we shall be able to remain *there* long, either. The man the other Heidi…" he rolled his eyes, "*Evil* Heidi, abducted, was Reinhard Heydrich."

Bessel did not react. In his altered timeline, Heydrich's memory survived as barely a footnote into the 22nd century; just a wealthy, little remembered industrialist.

Hans studied Bessel with interest. "You have not heard of him? Apparently, he was the Reich Security Chief in the alternative timeline. Though, as far as I am aware, he has held no such post here. Corporal Engel will doubtless explain later. For now, all you need to know is he is a business mogul – one of the richest men in the world. He is also a total sh—"

"Schultz and Heydrich together…" Engel shook his head in horror, speaking his thoughts aloud. "Sorry to interrupt, sir, but for context, they named one of their ships after him. The Schultzes, I mean. Heinrich Schultz made us study all the 'great Nazi leaders', as he called them. Heydrich was one of the evilest men from our history, sir."

The colonel's interest was piqued. "Hmm, seems to do well for himself in any timeline. Like I said, he is a total sh—"

"Surely," Bessel interjected, "whatever he may have been in the original timeline, Douglas' people changed all that, when they stranded themselves in the 16th century? This man couldn't possibly…" He tailed off. "Oh, my God. If Heidi Schultz – the other one – has him, then…" He shook his head, deep lines of concern furrowing his brow. "Look, James Douglas told me she was the most dangerous individual he'd ever met. If this Heydrich is a man with such potential and with such a predilection for evil—"

"We must stop them," Engel completed. "Whatever it takes. Or your future, Captain Bessel, may be destroyed forever. For all we know, Heidi may have set things in motion that have changed things already."

Bessel placed his head in his hands. "I think I'd like to go home now."

"But what would you find, I wonder…?" Colonel Schultz tailed off and then exclaimed, "What in the *world?*"

"What is it, sir?" asked Engel.

"I have been downloading everything I can before taking my

comm offline. They will surely remove my access soon and begin tracking it. Gentlemen, it seems there has been a development – an explosion, in fact. Of quite biblical proportions, if these reports are to be believed."

Bessel leaned forward. "Where?"

"At the luxury retreat of the business mogul, Reinhard Tristan Eugen Heydrich."

Bessel blinked. "He's dead?"

"Unclear. It seems there is a complete security blackout over the whole area. That must have come from on high. Indeed, if I cannot access the data – right from the top."

Engel sat back, deep in thought.

"What is it, Corporal?" Schultz asked.

"I'm just wondering if she's dead, sir – the other Heidi, I mean. Maybe it's over."

"We can't assume that," Bessel asserted. "If those two get their act together…"

"Quite," Schultz agreed. "From what I have learned, my fourth-great-grandniece is nothing if not resourceful. As for Heydrich, he is a complete sh—"

Beep. The electronic interruption was followed by Lieutenant Sonne speaking over the intercom from the driver's cab. "Lady and gentlemen, we have left the city limits and should arrive at our destination in two hours."

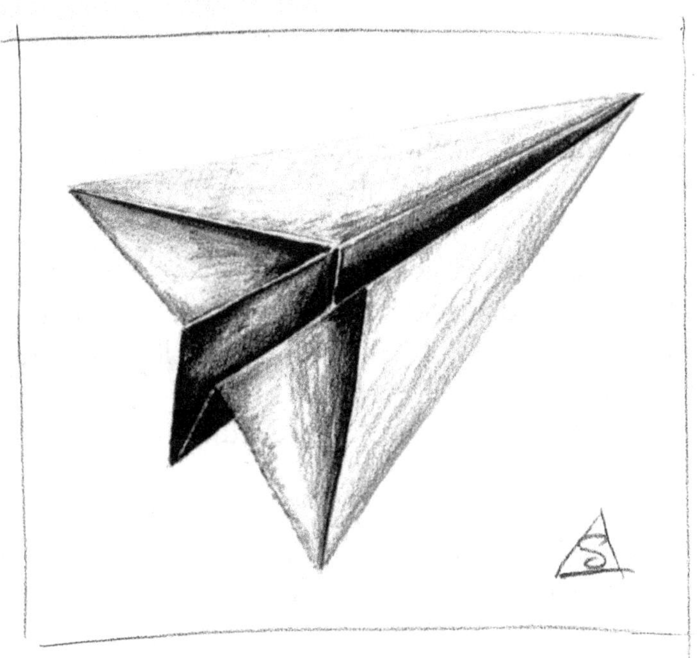

Chapter 13 | Blue Sky Trying

Blessed are the Peacemakers (Matthew 5:9)

Iron Age Britain, Great Cheviot

Sergeant Adam Prentice stared down at the remote controller in his hands. Douglas looked over his shoulder to watch the probe's video feed on its small screen. Both were awestruck by the miracle of technology that delivered images through time and space via the wormhole, all the way from Patagonia, almost a hundred million years into the past.

On the other side, the probe hovered over the plateau above the wrecked *Last Word.* Douglas blew out his cheeks; despite his wonder, the memories he had of the place were far from pleasant.

Prentice glanced at him. "It's good news, Captain. We can send them back."

"Aye," Douglas admitted. "Ah have to admit to misgivings about our plan B. Sedating that many giant predators, and keeping them under, would have caused us no end of problems."

Prentice agreed. "And even if it had worked… well, then what? I understand the need to take them off the board, for t'safety of t'local people and ecosystem, but we all know how that would have gone down in the end."

"Aye. Ah hope this allows us to save them – vicious brutes that they are! Something doesnae look right, though. Look over there, towards the edge. Can ye zoom in? The whole place looks like a flood's been through there."

"Aye, it does at that," Prentice agreed, adjusting the camera for a closer look. "Oh."

"What?"

Prentice flew the probe out to where the land dropped away sharply, down to the ruined battleship. The edge had been completely washed away.

"Where's the bank?" Douglas asked, puzzled.

"Mostly at the bottom, piled up over the enemy ship, sir. When the *Last Word* went over, she will have loosened all the soil, making it ripe for a sudden flash flood to wash it away, but more importantly, Captain, where're all the bodies?"

Douglas blinked. It took a moment for realisation to dawn. "Captain Meritus' dead were buried there, weren't they?"

Prentice sighed, sadly. "Aye, Captain, they were. If they've all washed down the bank, many will've been exposed…" He left the sentence hanging, the awful ramifications running through his mind.

"Poor souls," Douglas muttered. "If we dinnae get back there ourselves, and soon, their remains will be—"

"Eaten, sir. Yes. Almost certainly. Although it was a decade ago for us, in t'Cretaceous, only nine months have gone by at this point. Scavengers will certainly find them interesting."

Mixed emotions washed over Douglas. Those were the bodies of enemy combatants, hard to reconcile with Meritus and his people, valued friends, and comrades of many years. He rubbed a hand down his face to relieve the tension. "Must have been a fair storm since we were last there."

"Perhaps, perhaps not, sir. I have a theory. Remember when the river came through to us here, into the Iron Age, from Crater Lake – the flood waters?"

"Do Ah ever. We were nearly lost with all hands."

"Aye, sir. Just think, what if it washed through there instead?"

"But the wormhole was connected here. That's how Jill managed to find her way back to us, remember? She sent the probe, just before she crashed ma ship again."

"Yes, sir, but she said Heidi was loose in that time, an' all. What if she took the same route out and went to Crater Lake? Hang on. I'll get the probe to sample the soil. We can run a correlation with readings we took from the water when *we* lived at Crater Lake."

It took a few minutes, but sure enough, the technology joined the dots and proved a ninety-nine percent match with the bacteria present in Crater Lake, half a world away from the probe's location on the *Last Word*'s plateau.

"It's close, sir. Unnaturally close – excepting a few contaminants. I'd say close enough."

Douglas scratched his head. "But if Heidi sent the wormhole back to Crater Lake, and presumably travelled through it to that destination herself, then how come our probe went back to the *Last Word* plateau?"

"I can only guess, there, sir."

"Go on, Adam."

"All I can surmise is that she then used the wormhole at Crater Lake to go somewhere else. Thus severing the connection to the *Last Word*."

"Right." Douglas was catching on. "So you think that when a connection is severed, the wormhole jumps back to its previous connection."

"It's just a idea, sir, but then, where else would it go – assuming the connections aren't just made at random?"

"Well, that's a big assumption. Nevertheless, it's a good working hypothesis, Adam. And let's face it, we've nothing better to go on. Quicker we get those animals back home, the better. Then we'll have to see if we can retrieve the bodies of Meritus' fallen. Ah think Captain Meritus will be pretty put out, having his dead disturbed like this. Ah would be."

"Aye, but on the flip side, we should take the positive, sir. At least we *can* send these animals home – as long as nobody messes with the connection."

Douglas turned a full circle, scanning the horizon. "Better hope they find them soon, then, and get them back here *tout de suite.* Bring the probe home, Sergeant. We've done all we can for now."

Thomas Beckett took a deep breath of fresh mountain air. He could see Douglas and Prentice intently discussing something in the near distance. *What now?* he thought. *Can't we enjoy a minute's peace?*

"Beautiful, isn't it?"

He spun to find Natalie Pearson admiring the view alongside him – and alongside her sat Reiver.

"It is, indeed, my dear. Hello, boy." He tousled the collie's ears. "I could grow some wonderful tomatoes here."

She smiled. "Still missing that wheelbarrow of yours, left at Crater Lake all those years ago? You probably abandoned it not far from here, you know."

"I'm not sure I'd go as far as 'abandoned'. I don't seem to remember having a choice, but no, I don't miss it. I have another one now."

She laughed. "Have you met any of the locals yet? Captain Douglas seems to hold them in high regard."

"Not yet, but I'd like to. I have spoken to our giant Welsh colleague, however. He's been telling me all about them. I must say I'm fascinated. As a historian, I've seen more of our planet's history than I've any right to, I don't doubt, but to actually meet people from our past. It's all so…" He ran out of words.

"I know. The Elizabethans were weird enough."

"My dear girl," he rounded on her, irritably, "we've been greatly honoured."

She laughed again, lightly, completely unoffended by his schoolmasterly tone. "Well, you knock yourself out, Thomas, but they give me the creeps. It's unnatural."

"But as a scientist, surely you appreciate what an incredible opportunity we've been handed? We alone have the chance to learn, not from scratching in the dirt, or sifting through tangled messages and cryptic clues in dusty old libraries, but from our ancestors themselves?" He was clearly in awe.

"Hmm. Maybe." She was distracted, watching Douglas and Prentice piloting the probe back to the ship.

"*Maybe?*" Beckett was outraged.

"Boys and their toys." She grinned. "Got to admit, flying one of those things looks fun. What? Oh, the locals, right. Well, they look sort of *savage* to me. If it's all the same to you, I think I'll keep my distance. I'm better with animals, anyhow."

"Ah, child, it's not for us to place our standards, indeed, our very thinking, over theirs and try to match them up. That's a palimpsest that will never correlate on any schematic, believe you me. But, just occasionally, we *can* match the odd line here and there, and *from* there, we begin to understand the journey we all travel through time. Superimposing our values onto our forebears is to create a collision, a blurring of the lines, obliterating their mistakes so that we can make them all over again, like helpless children, endlessly stumbling through year zero."

"That's pretty deep, Thomas. I thought you were going to run out of breath there," Natalie replied, wryly. "And here I was, thinking it was a lovely evening to walk the dog. It just goes to show… still, I don't know. I'm really not convinced. Did you know these guys keep bits of their dead family members in their *homes?*"

Beckett chuckled. "And where do *we* keep the trinkets and keepsakes of ours? Natalie, we may see little of ourselves in these folk, but we forget, these early societies are the *original* thinkers, the people who found ways *to* think and understand the world. What we consider to be our standards and morals are nothing more than a process. We would do well to at least try to understand our ancestors, the better to understand ourselves. Our ideas will be equally backward and ludicrous to our descendants, you can be assured of that."

"I suppose…" She stared off into the west, shielding her eyes from the low sun. "I think we should go back inside the ship."

"What do your young eyes see?"

"I'm thirty-six, you know."

The old historian grinned broadly. "You're starting *that* early."

She frowned and then laughed again, as the penny dropped. "Come on, Thomas. I think they've found the mapusaurs. I hope they can get them home safely, without hurting them."

"Or them hurting others," Beckett added, darkly.

"Let's hope so. Reiver! Heel, boy. We'd better get inside quickly – they're coming on the run."

⎯⎯⎯⎯ ❧ ⎯⎯⎯⎯

AD1588, Great Cheviot

Dr Reid sat up in a hospital bed within the Pod infirmary, nursing a bandaged arm. Private Tomás Suárez, the *New World*'s last field medic, had expertly removed Heidi's bullet and now berated Reid for constantly fiddling with the dressing.

"It itches!" Reid complained.

"Alright, enough!" Major White commanded. He held Reid's wrist device, turning it over in his hands. "We're going to need to know more about this thing, Dr Reid."

"You plan to use it again, Ford?" asked Jim Miller, doubtfully. "I'm not sure we should."

White mulled the situation over for a moment. "Maybe. We saved your daughter and son-in-law, thank God – me and Sarah, too, apparently – but that got me thinkin', what else could we do with this thing?"

"*That* is the kind of thinking that got us all into this mess!" Satnam Patel retorted sharply.

Geoff Lloyd rounded on White. "Patel's right. I didn't spend thirty years learning my lesson just so you could forget, young man!"

White guffawed. "I'm past *sixty!*"

"I know. Don't rub it in, boy!"

White held up his free hand. "Look, just hear me out, OK? I'm not saying we go wandering through time like Doctor-Who-screwed-*this*-up. I was thinking more along the lines of controlled contact with the rest of our people in the future."

"What, like shore leave?" asked Mother Sarah.

"Not exactly – though that's an interesting idea, too. Visiting loved ones and friends might be good for morale. Even if we decided it was imperative for the protection of the future that we stayed here, they could potentially come to see us, once we'd set things up. But no, that's a separate issue. I was thinking more about sharing intel."

"Wait right there, Ford," Patel interjected again, cutting to the heart of the matter. "What do you mean by 'controlled'? No contact is the *only* control we should rely upon."

White answered obliquely. "Perhaps, but before deciding anything, we need to know more about how this thing works. Dr Reid, Jim used this to go back a couple of hours to save his daughter. Presumably, that was because we had a set of coordinates to follow, yeah?"

Reid nodded. "Correct, Major. The device cannot take you just anywhere. To use it, you will need either an anchor or another extant wormhole for the device to detect."

"An anchor?" asked Miller.

"Yes, Dr Miller. We developed markers, built into explosive caps that could be blasted into a rock face, so that we could retrace our steps through time. Heidi used them a few times. Some are still in place. The device can sense them through the manifold, once a wormhole has been created."

"Manifold?" Patel looked horrified. "These pathways are permanently open?"

Reid nodded sheepishly.

Patel was aghast. "I should have punched you harder!" He held up bandaged knuckles. "I still have another fist!"

Mother Sarah snorted, immediately feeling guilty for seeing the funny side of two lab coats squaring up to each other. She wrapped both hands around her friend's raised fist. "Dear Satnam, we must work together now."

Patel exhaled loudly. "Forgive me, Sarah, all of you. It has been quite a year. For barely a year has passed for me, since I was last in my university in India. Since then, I have lived across entire epochs, running from dinosaurs and lunatics with every kind of weapon from nuclear powered warships to muskets, and all my dearest friends are suddenly thirty years older than when I met them. Added to that, apparently everyone in the future is relying on us to save the world! It has all been rather trying, I am afraid."

"Well, when you put it like that…" White drawled, wearing his usual half-smile.

"I never did see Mars," Patel grumbled on.

"I've been there, several times," Lloyd pointed out. "It's rubbish."

"I'm not even sure how I came to be here," Patel murmured, not registering his comment. "I opened a wormhole that was meant to take me forward almost six centuries."

"I think I might be able to help you there," Reid answered, tentatively.

Patel refocused on him. "You know what happened?"

Reid shifted uncomfortably, fidgeting with his arm dressing again. "Perhaps. I think you may have opened a wormhole at the exact same spatial coordinates Heidi chose to bring our ship through. Perhaps it was wild coincidence, or maybe Heidi's earlier wormhole created a weakness in space–time at that point – I don't know, it's a matter for further discussion – but, somehow, we hooked you. Travelling through a fifth dimension, our ship would have been the largest mass available. This is just a theory, you understand, but I think it may have simply attracted you, a smaller mass flying through the same dimension."

"A smaller mass," Sarah interrupted, wryly. "I guess it pays to work out, huh?"

Patel smiled, weakly. "I need to consider it. Though at the moment, I confess, I have no better hypothesis."

White waved them down. "Back up a minute." He turned to Reid, holding out the wrist device. "So you're saying this thing can sense other wormholes, huh?"

"Yes, Major. But there is also a third way the device can be used to travel through time and space…"

"Go on, Doctor," White encouraged, gently.

"You probably won't like it."

"It's OK, Dr Reid," White assured him. "We need to hear it anyway."

"Only if Dr Patel promises not to hit me again!" He gingerly stroked a growing bruise on his jaw.

Everyone turned to Patel. "Oh, fine!" he hissed, scathingly.

White smiled again. "Please, go ahead."

Reid swallowed nervously. "There are also the fixed points."

Miller shifted uncomfortably. "Fixed points?"

Reid nodded slowly. "I know of at least four. It's possible more have been created, but that's conjecture."

"Very well, tell us about the four you *are* sure of," Patel demanded.

"The first was what we called the master wormhole, the one we created in Cretaceous North Africa – Egypt, if you prefer. That was the strongest. It was an aberration. Frankly, it was a mistake. The Old Man, that is, Heinrich Schultz, forced us to open it, totally disregarding our warnings. It is my belief that we created another weakness in space–time at that point – a much more serious one that may never heal. The second lies at the opposite end of that anomaly. In the physical world, it's located in Munich, Germany. Since Commander Coleman's people – rather brilliantly, I might add – managed to close the master wormhole back in the

Cretaceous, thus saving the world, I no longer fully understand its relationship with the one in Munich." He shrugged, helplessly. "It should never have been. The wormhole, when created, cut a secant line through the Earth's mantle, you see? That's when and why it gained its superpowers."

Patel fumed, offended by the Schultz expedition's total lack of scientific probity or even basic respect for the fabric of the universe in which everyone and everything lived or existed. "And the third?" he spat between gritted teeth.

"Some miles south of the master wormhole, also in Egypt. That's where Heidi broke through to the future, to AD2122, setting in motion the events Captain Douglas described, on that memory card you discovered, within the dinosaur bone he buried in the Iron Age. I must admit to being fascinated by the fossilised Spinosaurus that vanished from the rocks on young Mr Norris' dig, and how its destiny was completely altered – notwithstanding how they caught it climbing a pyramid." He smiled. "I should turn that into a graphic novel!"

"That's *Professor* Norris," Rose corrected him, glowing with pride for her long-lost friend's achievements.

Henry smiled and squeezed her hand. "I love the idea of seeing those guys again, Major."

White nodded thoughtfully and then jerked his head up to glare at Reid. "Hang on, how the hell do you know about James' message from the past?"

"Heidi bugged Jim Miller's jacket. That's how she knew you were coming for her..." He tailed off as the temperature in the room dropped noticeably. Everyone glared at him. "I'm sorry. I thought you'd worked that bit out. I only listened to Captain Douglas' monologue, mind you – and not all of that. I must confess, I found it rather long and went to bed. I heard nothing of your conversations afterward. Heidi, on the other hand... Naturally, she... I mean... I just went to bed..." He was not winning his audience over, so he shut up.

The muscles bunched in White's jaw. "Alright, let's leave that for now, shall we? We can't change the past—"

"Yeah, right!" Henry Burnstein Jr sounded unusually like his father.

White sighed. "OK. Bad choice of words. Let's just agree that any time-related anecdotes are no longer fit for purpose and move on."

"Into the future, you mean?" Henry taunted.

White snorted, despite himself. "Enough, already. Dr Reid, you said there were at least four of these fixed points. Where and when is the final one?"

"The final one that I know of," Reid amended. "Actually, number four is technically the first. It's where Geoff Lloyd blew up the *New World*'s wormhole drive, creating the very first portal back through time."

Lloyd shrank back as all eyes turned on him.

"But that's in space," Reid continued, "most of the way to Mars, so I doubt we'll have to worry too much about that one."

They continued to glare at Lloyd.

"Do I need 'sorry' tattooed on my brow before you'll all back off?" he snapped, waspishly. "It's been thirty years!"

"For you, maybe!" Patel snapped right back.

"Satnam," Mother Sarah spoke quietly, "Geoff has worked tirelessly—"

"John!" Lloyd interjected. "It's the most common English name! Why will none of you remember?"

"I thought that was *Dave?*" Henry argued.

"Don't start with me, boy. Look, it's John, OK?"

"I'm forty-eight," Henry mumbled, grumpily.

"As I was *saying*," Sarah continued her explanation, "Geoff has worked tirelessly—"

"John! Bloody John!"

"—and at great personal risk for many years to save the future. We've all accepted that, Satnam. If he hadn't done what he did, we would never have had the chance to save humanity and the world we all share."

Patel glared balefully at Lloyd. "Why *do* you go by John, these days?"

Lloyd scowled. "Never mind, just please try to remember it."

"I am more than a little surprised you did not go with 'Jesus'."

"That's enough!" Sarah admonished, hotly. "Both of you!"

"Me?" Lloyd answered plaintively. "What have *I* done?"

"*You* started all this!" Patel shouted, angrily.

"I said, that's enough!" Sarah repeated. "Honestly, Satnam, whatever has gotten into you?"

"Yes, and he punched me!" Reid piled on.

"You deserved it!"

"In the face!"

"Stop!" White shouted.

Patel sighed, hanging his head as he banked the fires within. "I apologise for my behaviour, but I came here thinking it was my way home – to the future. Now I realise I can never go home. I must stay. We all must."

Sarah placed an arm around his shoulders. "I understand. I guess we've all had a lot more years to come to terms with it."

"We may not be completely cut off from our people," White suggested. "We have this, after all." He held the wrist device aloft again at the centre of the circle around Reid's bed. "If we're destined to change the future and bring peace to the world, can we really turn up our noses at help?"

Sarah smiled. "Ford is right. Blessed are the peacemakers, for they will be called children of God."

Lloyd rolled his eyes. "If I understood the brief correctly, we were meant to force that change, not pray for it!"

Sarah regarded him, thoughtfully. "For the peacemaker, Geoff, both are sometimes necessary."

"*John!*"

Two millennia earlier…

Hiro stole a surreptitious look at his brother, working quietly at the next workstation. He, too, was trying to broker a peace. They had quarrelled. Indeed, they had always quarrelled; that was the problem. He sighed, gently. Sometimes, it was possible to love someone while wondering why. At least their latest quarrel had been about wormhole physics, rather than one of his little brother's deranged ideologies. Things were looking up.

As he thought it, his brother did look up. "What?"

"I've been thinking about what you said."

"And?"

"I still think you're wrong."

Aito stopped scribbling notes and threw his pen down on the desk before him. "*Really?*"

"No, hear me out, brother. I think you're wrong about the *location*."

Aito sat back, relaxing slightly. "Go on."

"Georgio suggested that, if we're going to do this at all, then Patagonia might be the place to try. It's where all this began for us. And, if we *are* to do this, I'm coming round to the idea from the standpoint of stability."

"Stability or destiny?"

Hiro shrugged. "It's a large continent separated from the other large continents… for what that's worth. We're in over our heads, I don't deny it."

"Talking of Georgio, where is he?" Aito asked, looking around engineering.

"Oh, somewhere. He took himself off. Said something about not being able to think because 'we were-a doing his head in'," Hiro impersonated his friend. He smiled.

Begrudgingly, Aito smiled back. "Egypt is stronger, Hiro. We already made the connection, and the power it drew was terrifying."

Hiro agreed. "That's what I'm afraid of. Stability is what we need. I don't want to eliminate the wormholes at the cost of a global tectonic disaster. The wormhole you and Schultz's people opened in Egypt, back in the mid-Cretaceous, was so strong you couldn't control it." He leaned forward, spreading his hands on the desk. "Well, you couldn't, could you?" he added, reasonably.

Aito chewed his lip irritably. He hated it when Hiro was right, and especially when he was reasonable about it. It was just another tool in his 'older brother psychology kit'. Hiro had employed it since they were children.

He pushed his agitation aside. "So how does Patagonia help?"
"Magnetism."
"Fabulous. We can all go home."
"Aito!"
"Oh, sorry, brother. Forgive me, I thought the world was vast and the wormholes small and far apart – what was I thinking? Please do carry on. Magnets, right, I'm all ears."

Hiro half-sighed, half-growled. "In the middle of the Americas there is a little place – you may have heard of it – called Bermuda."

Aito's eyes opened wide, but he suppressed his laughter, instead placing an elbow on the desk to lean on his hand in dumb insolence.

"What?" Hiro prompted, annoyed.

"Nothing. Just waiting for what I'm sure will be one hell of an explanation. Please, continue."

Hiro soured further. "Why do you always have to make things so difficult?"

"It's a talent. Come on, just spit it out, will you?"

Hiro bunched his fists in exasperation. "Must I send you back to your cell again? Bermuda, as I was saying, before I was so rudely interrupted—"

Aito rolled his eyes.

Hiro was fit to explode. "Will you just listen and pay attention! You might just learn something."

"If I can stay awake."

Hiro's eyes narrowed. Georgio had also quarrelled constantly with his twin, Mario, but theirs was always good-natured banter. The relationship with his own brother had always been strained.

Despite his love for Aito, he often found it hard to like him. "Don't make me reach for my taser. Now, please listen. Bermuda sits on exceptionally magnetic bedrock."

Aito straightened, his curiosity rising just a notch. "Go on."

"Lava in what we call the Bermuda Triangle is enriched with extra minerals, including titanium oxide and iron oxide, which combine to make a mineral called magnetite. But, of course, you already knew that."

"Of course," Aito agreed, drily.

"At least, you would have *if* you'd studied and paid attention to the metallurgy component of your engineering education. Anyway, magnetite is the most magnetic naturally occurring mineral on Earth."

"I never would have guessed from the name."

"Aito! Bermuda rock contains eighteen to twenty percent magnetite, as opposed to the one to five percent found in most other rocks and soils elsewhere in the world. The cause was a hugely powerful volcanic event and the reason for such unusually high magnetic readings was because the lava came from deeper below the crust. *Much* deeper. Perhaps four hundred miles down. As you *may* be aware, the deeper one goes, and the closer one gets to the molten core, the more powerfully magnetic the material."

"But four hundred miles would take it below the upper mantle, surely?" Aito was interested now, despite himself.

"Exactly. Into the transition zone between the upper and lower mantle – I'm glad you paid attention to something."

Aito huffed. "OK. So, where are you going with this?"

"We know that in the year…" Hiro waved his hands about, "for want of a better term, I'll call it thirty million BC, this eruption happened, for whatever reason. Four hundred billion tons of, amongst other minerals, titanium oxide and iron oxide were blasted out and deposited in the sea. By the end, the event had covered a vast area – some 250 miles in diameter, with Bermuda at its centre – essentially remaking the whole region into a giant magnet, so powerful that it changed magnetic north by several degrees. In our time, the magnetite bed was – is, I suppose – in excess of a hundred and fifty metres thick, too."

"OK." Aito spoke slowly, digesting the information. "So, we know that the wormholes are attracted and affected directly by magnetism, but as I said, how does that help us on a global scale? The reason I suggested reopening the Egyptian wormhole was because its power was practically beyond measure. This single event would not have anything like that sort of juice, even if we went back to the time when it occurred – which would probably be unwise, based on your description."

Hiro considered a moment before answering, getting his thoughts in order. "The Bermuda Triangle in this time – the Iron Age, ironically, as we're talking about magnetism – is further south than in our own. It continues to move north, which is suggestive of a long-term instability."

"Oh, I get it, and you think making it even more unstable will… help?"

"If handled sensibly, I hope so." Hiro rarely spotted sarcasm. Even when dealing with his younger brother, his success rate was patchy. "What I'm saying is, the area is one of natural instability, but despite this, the world has functioned with relative normalcy for millions of years. Remember, we saw that massive eruption back in the Triassic—"

"Or the Permian Period," Aito chipped in, "depending on what day of the week it was."

"Right," Hiro answered hesitantly, again not quite sure whether he was being mocked. "We were on the periodic boundary, I agree. Well, my point is—"

"That region has history, as far as instability goes. OK, I'll buy that. So you're suggesting we create another wormhole, cutting a second secant line through the Earth between South and North America?"

"Maybe. Through the Bermuda Triangle region, certainly. Professor Tim Norris uploaded extensive palaeo and geological research into our computers – almost the sum of human knowledge on the subject, pre-time-travel. Thanks to Tim and his years in academia, our group now knows more than ever before about the Earth's deep past. I've been looking through some of this research and I think I've found a connection."

Aito was genuinely interested now, and nodded for his brother to continue.

"According to what I've read, and the geological maps I've seen, I believe that the place where we landed in the Triassic – and were almost destroyed – and the lesser event in thirty million BC, actually share the same location."

Aito frowned. "Same place, different time?"

"Exactly. Separated by upwards of two hundred and twenty million years, but essentially the same place."

"Wow," Aito murmured, puffing out his cheeks. "Another coincidence?"

Hiro snorted softly. "The universe seems to run on them. So much so, that I no longer believe in such things."

Aito frowned again. "Now you've lost me."

"Never mind. The essence of my plan is – or at least, my *hope* is – that the vast magnetism generated at either end, when opened within the same space, will increase the magnetic effect massively, drawing all the wormholes to one place."

"Or two places."

"Possibly."

"Through time?"

Hiro winced slightly. "I'm not sure what will happen. There's no map for this. However, we believe that all these wormholes are connected in some way we're yet to determine. It does make sense, though, if Heidi was planning on using them like some kind of inter-dimensional subway system. We're not dealing with someone rational, or sane, here."

"That's comforting. OK, let's say you're right and it works. What then?"

Hiro blew out his cheeks. "One step at a time. I'm doing my best. Unfortunately, for any of this to work, I believe our best chance would, indeed, be to go back to the point of that eruption, thirty million years ago. Once there, we could open our wormhole. I think that's the Oligocene Epoch of the Palaeogene Period."

Aito sat back, pointing accusingly. "*You* didn't know what that period was called."

Hiro shrugged. "I already told you, I spoke with Tim Norris about it."

"And what did *he* think of this plan of yours?"

"Never mind that," Hiro bit back, irritably. "*I* believe it's our best chance."

"Whoa, hang on there, brother. You're talking about interfering with an already catastrophic event and multiplying it by two. Can't we just go back a little further and blow Heidi out of the sky, before she did whatever she did?"

"We've considered that, ad nauseam."

"And?"

"If we go back before we left, we risk creating the mother of all paradoxes. At least, that's the consensus. It's something we're desperate to avoid. We could all end up going round and round forever!"

Aito raised an eyebrow.

"Tim did agree with me about that part, at least," Hiro admitted, sheepishly.

Aito huffed. "I assume he didn't think much of the rest of your plan, then?"

Hiro looked pained.

Aito pressed him relentlessly. "And such a paradox would be worse than blowing up the planet, would it?"

"*Potentially* blowing up the planet, and..." Hiro considered. "Well, honestly, I don't know. I wish Satnam Patel were here. This was always his bridge, really."

"You mean wheelhouse."

"I'm not a fisherman!"

Aito smirked. Poor old Hiro, still socially awkward after all these years. "I'm telling you, Hiro, we should consider creating our master wormhole in Egypt. It's a known quantity. A terrifying quantity, I agree, but we have experience with it. I'm sure your Dr Patel would agree."

"I doubt that," Hiro replied, witheringly.

Aito tried again. "Here's a thought. We have a time machine – couldn't we just ask him?"

"Who?"

"Patel."

"No. Captain Douglas has completely forbidden any interference with the efforts of our people in the 16th century, barring the message he sent them – which they probably won't even find."

Patel listened to Captain Douglas' message again, trying to find anything within the tale that he could navigate by. Major White's idea to open some form of dialogue with the future seemed perilous. It was damned attractive, too – a temporal honeypot that might just get them stung to death.

If Douglas was correct, then all they had to do was continue one foot in front of the other, doing whatever it was they were doing. It had already worked; the captain had seen it – lived in that world for ten years. Contacting the future might – *would* – complicate things and the ramifications if they got it wrong might be dire for the whole of humanity.

He sighed, rubbing tiredness from his eyes. Then there was the counter argument that Heidi's last visit, and Reid's defection, was all part of that perfect future they were now charged with bringing about. There was no doubt that their presence there had changed things – but changed them how? Was the future now contingent on them using what they had learned from Reid? It was a nightmare. How could any mortal truly comprehend the effects their cause might propagate, let alone grapple with them?

He took a sip of coffee. At least, he tried to. His mug was empty. He put it down, not even noticing. The wormhole manifold Reid described terrified him. He knew Douglas and the others would be working on some way to shut it all down, and that terrified him, too. Patel had nothing but the greatest respect for his former crew, but of all of them, his was, without question, the most profound understanding of astrophysics – and he was not there. Not that *he* had a plan, but he might at least offer guidance as to what they should and should not try.

He considered Reid's wrist device again. So much temptation. What should he do?

Intelligence was failing him. He sought wisdom, and thankfully, knew where to find it.

Thunder rolled across the moors, heavy, slow, less frenetic than the rumble of wild horses, yet the ground shook beneath the baker's dozen as they pounded for the *New World*. Massive creatures, out of the westering sun, ran through the Iron Age hills fleeing an aerial terror. The 22nd century jet-fuelled helicopter popped up over the brow of the hill behind them, whirling around the runners, herding them, driving them on. Leutnant Erich Alfred Hartmann had found his quarry.

Each time a lone Mapusaurus broke from the pack, the noisesome flying machine brought them back, dipping and intimidating, dancing around the stampede. With extraordinary skill, this undisputed lord of the flies carved an arc in the air behind the runners. The buzz of rotors, coupled with the scent of exhaust, infected the beasts with a dangerous fear of the unnatural.

Hartmann[1] was soon joined by two similar helicopters, approaching from north and south. They flanked the running dinosaurs while Hartmann brought up the rear, terrorising, but

---

1. The greatest fighter ace of all time, Hartmann's nickname in the *Luftwaffe* was 'Bubi', pronounced 'boobie', equating loosely with 'The Kid'.

always retreating before losing his advantage. Any contact on this chase would kill hunter and hunted alike. The *wop wop* of vicious blades grew louder as they approached on a shallow descent, each chopping through the vortex created by the last, attenuating as they slowed or pitched forward to manoeuvre out of the way. The mapusaurs leapt for the aircraft whenever they came close, often taking frustrations out on one another when their attacks failed. Huge talons gouged the earth, flinging turf and heather in their wake. Bellows of fear and rage heralded their arrival as they neared the wormhole.

Baines could see people in the distance running to find safety within the vast citadel that was the *New World.* She opened a channel to Hartmann. "Bubi, do you read?"

"*Go ahead,* Kapitänin."

"Don't know if you can see from the rear, but it looks like our people are clear. If we don't get this done soon, these guys are gonna kill one another. I can see bloody wounds on some of the smaller ones already – they're being bullied."

Gleeson buzzed a rogue Mapusaurus back into line along their southern flank. "Where's Meritus?"

"*One minute out,*" Meritus broke into the channel. "*I'll meet you at the wormhole.*"

"Good. Hold that position, Tobias," Baines ordered. "I don't want them to overshoot, or we'll have it all to do again!"

"*Roger that,*" Meritus replied.

"*Woohoo!*"

"Clear this channel, Commander!" Baines snapped, crossly.

"*Wasn't me, skip.*"

She frowned in confusion, then noted Tim was bouncing up and down in his seat beside her, calling into his helmet microphone, "*Look at them go!*"

Gleeson was laughing. "*Think you'd better calm the professor down, Captain. He'll do himself an injury.*"

Baines was shaking her head. "When this is all over, I'm gonna find myself the most boring job in existence and enjoy every moment of it!"

A mile ahead of the pack, four armoured vehicles left the *New World* from her main hangar at ground level. They drove noisily over the rough terrain, bouncing towards the wormhole, their tracks chewing up the soil and shale. Douglas was at the controls of the first. He spoke across an open channel to the other drivers. "Everyone line up on me. We're to provide a wall of steel, to stop those beasties running past the wormhole, nothing more. Leave the rest to the aerial team. Is that understood?"

Three affirmatives came back as Douglas brought his armoured carrier in, perpendicular to the wormhole. He halted just east of the anomaly, on the right-hand side as he faced it. Although the approaching Mapusaurus pack could technically enter at any angle, he knew his pilots would first drive them a little to the south before sweeping them back into line, giving his people chance to funnel them in. With a little luck, the dinosaurs would run straight through the portal without even noticing it was there.

Meritus buzzed overhead in chopper four, as the remaining ground vehicles parked nose-to-tail behind Douglas. "*Meritus to ground crew – close up those gaps, people.*"

"Aye, nudge the vehicle in front, if you have tae," Douglas added. His anxiety was growing. "If we leave so much as the crack of daylight between us, they'll try tae break through. Those animals will be terrified – let's no' make it worse. Oh, and be sure tae keep yer engines running and yer brakes on – or we'll be shoved out of position. Jill, do ye read me?"

"*Five-by-five, James.*"

"Make sure you have that northern flank covered. Ah dinnae want them splitting up at the wormhole and running back west, the way they came."

"*Understood.*"

Gleeson to the right of them, Baines to the left of them, Hartmann driving from the rear, the mapusaurs came on flat out and panicked.

Douglas could feel the ground shaking through the tracks of his vehicle. From the tiny viewport on his left, he watched the pack's approach, faster than any man could run, when Gleeson opened the right flank for them to escape. First one, then another mapusaur took advantage of the opportunity to split away. Within moments the whole group had darted right, like a migrating flock. Baines and Hartmann immediately pushed in, to drive the stampede south as planned, as they began their run on the wormhole.

Meritus drifted his chopper a hundred metres south, to help Gleeson close the door on them when the time came.

Baines and Hartmann backed off as Gleeson cut an arc through the sky to the right of the dinosaurs, gradually nudging them back to the left, edging north. The dinosaurs described a sweeping curve as Meritus blocked their way west, further encouraging their turn, corralling them. Eventually, the pack was oriented towards the wormhole and Hartmann moved in to close the box, and any retreat west.

Douglas' convoy stretched out thirty metres from the portal, funnelling the animals towards the almost invisible event horizon and, hopefully, Cretaceous Patagonia.

Baines' pilot brought their helicopter in close to the wormhole, to its left, opposing Douglas' group on the ground. Tim loosened his crash webbing to lean forward between the front seats, completely awed by the view ahead.

Mapusaurus roseae, the Earth Lizard, did not belong in Iron Age Britain. This was, of course, a human perspective. The alpha male belonged anywhere he damned well pleased. It was an understanding he had literally grown into. His pack followed his lead, more or less, and would continue to do so until the mating cycle was over, or food became scarce. From there it would be every killing machine for him or herself again, but until that day, they would follow their programming; they would follow the strongest – and none came any stronger than the alpha. He was massive, scarred and monstrous. A wondrous nightmare, yet he had no more concept of cruelty than a housefly. He was driven by an empty stomach, the need to perpetuate his kind and nothing more. He was, in fact, innocent.

Humankind can imagine so much worse; indeed, our descriptive writing relies upon it. So, whereas Tim might have interpreted the alpha as being no more evil than a glossy-haired spaniel, greeting his master at the gate, Baines viewed him as the grotesque leader of a demonic horde, bringing chaos, death and destruction. Opinions, like recollections, do indeed vary.

The dinosaurs' estimation of the technological terrors that harassed them from the air was equally low. They *roared* ferociously, deafeningly.

Tim's jaw dropped. Even within the cabin of the helicopter it was loud. It made his headset rattle. He had seen these majestic creatures many times throughout his travels. He, most blessed among palaeontologists, had seen so much, but never before had he placed himself in the path of a hunting pack of apex predatory theropod dinosaurs. Had he stood in their way on the ground, it would have been the last thing he ever did. Fortunately, his pilot kept their craft just out of reach of the jaws of death – no metaphor required.

The push and shove within the pack launched some of the creatures into Douglas' armoured barrier, nudging the twenty-five-ton machines out of line.

"Keep it together!" he bellowed across the comm.

Meritus moved in overhead, driving the creatures away from the personnel carriers, while Hartmann prevented them from straying too far from their escape vector. Baines' pilot still hovered just to the left of the wormhole, and that left the animals just one direction to run. Gleeson brought up the rear to make sure, driving them forward and through. "Yeehaaaaah!"

His yelp of elation was cut short as he followed the mapusaurs through the wormhole to pop out into the brilliant sunshine of a jungle world. He was back in the Cretaceous. "Oh, crap! I may have gotten a little carried away."

Hiro and Georgio watched the dinosaurs vanish through the wormhole in ones and twos via a monitor in engineering. Hiro heaved a sigh of relief.

"Have they done it?" asked Aito.

"It seems so." He frowned. "Although, I wasn't aware of any plan to follow them."

Aito walked around the desk to see for himself. "Who went through?"

"Commander Gleeson, I think," Georgio informed him. "Maybe he just wants to be sure they clear the area and don't come back through?"

Aito looked up in surprise. "Is he crazy?"

Georgio stroked his chin thoughtfully. "You know, I'm not actually sure."

Aito blinked. "Was there a selection process when your side put this mission together? Or did Douglas just hire using a 'you don't have to be mad to work here but it helps' philosophy?"

Hiro smiled tiredly. "I barely remember how any of this even began. I doubt *any* of us would pass a psych test now. Commander Gleeson was – *is* – an explosives expert. He probably doesn't understand fear the way you or I would."

Aito stared at his brother. "So glad you brought me over to the winning side! Look, now Georgio's here, have you given any further thought to my plan for the time and location where we should bring the wormholes together to neutralise them?"

"I've told you, thirty million BC, Patagonia."

"No, brother, that was the first plan – the unrefined and incorrect plan."

"I'm not getting into it again here, Aito. Lieutenant-Commander Singh needs us to stay sharp in case we have to help our people out there."

Aito nodded. *I see,* he thought. *Perhaps I should seek help elsewhere?*

"Where are you going?" asked Hiro.

"To powder my nose!"

Hiro watched him go, shaking his head. "Father let him spend too much time in America."

In almost the exact same spot, two millennia later, Satnam Patel waited outside Mother Sarah's quarters aboard *Factory Pod 4*. He was far underground, the Cheviot Mountain being two hundred metres taller than it had been during the Iron Age, thanks to the sudden and violent appearance of the USS *New World* and *Factory Pod 4* at its heart.

Sarah opened the hatch, greeting him with a smile. "Satnam, what can I do for ya? Won't ya come in?"

Patel allowed himself to be ushered to a sofa while Sarah placed a glass and pitcher of water on the coffee table before him. "Or would you prefer something hot?"

It occurred to Patel that he was indeed thirsty. A vague recollection surfaced of him trying to take a drink from an empty cup. "Perhaps a little tea, Sarah, thank you."

Sipping on a much-needed beverage, he placed his conundrum before her. "Well? What do you think I should do?"

"I have to say, I'm surprised, Satnam. You, of all people. I mean, ever since we got here thirty years ago, you've been telling us not to get involved, and now you want to risk everything by going forward to the future. More than that, you want to find Captain Douglas and – forgive me – very definitely interfere!"

Patel slumped. "That is the argument with which I have berated myself, ever since we took possession of Reid's wretched wrist device, and yet..."

Sarah poured him more tea from the pot. "Go on, old friend."

He leaned forward, anxiously. "To couch it in familiar terms, perhaps sticking to my guns, hoping to prove I was right would be the sin of pride, Sarah. After all, sometimes wisdom is to *change* one's mind. And this wormhole manifold certainly changes things.

At least, I feel that it does. In theory, if we keep doing what we're doing, we should create the future Captain Douglas wishes to keep intact. It must be important. So important that he was willing to sacrifice us to protect it."

"Is that what you think he did?"

"Not willingly. And might I add that I hope any one of us would have shown similar fortitude in his situation. It must have torn him and the others apart knowing they had to abandon all hope of rescuing us – especially where families have been separated. Imagine if it were the other way around and the choice had been ours?"

Sarah stared solemnly into her teacup. "Poor James."

Patel smiled wryly. "Not poor us?"

She looked up at him. "I wouldn't have wanted to make that decision – to take that responsibility. You're right. It must have been awful."

"I agree. But Reid's presence here changes things."

"Does it?" She eyed him, guardedly. "It might all be part of the plan. Reid built that monstrous tech a hundred million years ago. How can we be sure what affects what, or in which order, any more?"

"Again, I agree. At least, superficially. The problem, you see, is that that may just be a lack of imagination on our part. I feel certain that James and the others will be trying to undo the damage Heidi has unleashed upon space–time."

"Do you think they'll succeed?"

"I believe it unlikely."

"Even if you found them and joined them?"

Patel considered. "I will not stand on false modesty. I do have considerable expertise within the field of wormhole physics, though I'm not sure how I could help them solve this problem. No. My focus would be on stopping them from trying."

Sarah replaced her teacup on the table and sat back. "I see."

"So what do you think I should do? Try to help them? Try to *stop* them? Or just stay here and hope for the best?"

She considered a moment. "There's no stigma attached to failure, only the failure to act. If you feel you can do this, then you must."

"The odds of me fixing things are not good, Sarah."

"Alone, perhaps." She leaned forward again. "But what if there was a fourth option?"

Chapter 14 | Wheels Within Wheels

"Captain Nassaki. I didn't expect to see *you* again any time soon. You'd better come in. Oh, and be advised, Douglas' people will be spying on us. Please do whatever you wish, but don't say anything that might incriminate me."

"Why, Dr Hemmings, I see your reputation for generosity is well deserved. And *Aito* will do. Rank hardly matters any more. We're all prisoners."

"Really? I was led to understand that you'd been freed… by your *brother*." She spoke the word as an accusation, not even deigning to look at him.

"I thought you'd be a fan of nepotism, what with *your* family connections?"

She looked up, sharply. "What do you want?"

"Advice."

"Really? About what?"

"You may not be aware of this, but after we were taken captive by Captain Baines – just before Heidi nuked our factories in Cretaceous Egypt – our illustrious leader went on to launch a satellite into orbit."

Hemmings sat, grudgingly inviting her visitor to do likewise. "I must caution you, Aito. If Douglas' people wanted us to know this, I'm sure they would have mentioned it."

"I'm sure they would. The trouble is – largely because of my brother – I think that *they* think they've got a handle on the situation."

"And you don't?"

"Correct. I'm not here to intrigue, so much as to save them from hubris."

"How high-minded of you," she commented, drily. "And what exactly is this situation?"

Aito leaned forward. "Heidi's satellite launched multiple wormhole generators down onto the planet. Each opens a portal to a different time and place, drawing its power from the planet's core while remaining out of phase. A nice touch that makes it impossible to simply collect them all up – or even to tamper with them." He looked around her comfortable yet small quarters. "I assume they have you on an information blackout down here?"

"Let's just say, they only tell us what it's good for us to know."

"Hmm. Well, we've already encountered a few of these wormholes, though we don't know how many there are. My brother suspects they might number in the hundreds."

"And all based on the miniature generator technology Dr Reid was working on." Her reply was a statement of fact.

"You know of it?"

She nodded.

"How *much* do you know of it?"

"Only the premise behind his work. Heidi deliberately divided our efforts. She obviously feared we might work together to overthrow her, after we all took the decision to close the first wormhole and strand her in 1940s Germany with her grandfather. You may recall we entirely failed to do so. I certainly don't know enough about Reid's project to reverse the problem. I assume these devices tap into the power of the Earth's core by cutting secant lines through the mantle?"

"That's our hypothesis."

"So what do you expect from me? You already seem to know as much as I do, perhaps more."

Aito studied her. "I believe my brother might take an unstable situation and turn it into an extinction level event."

Hemmings blinked, surprised in spite of herself. "Thinks big, does he, your brother?"

"Yes. While remaining consistently small-minded. Ironic, no? So, of course, he's rejecting all contra opinions."

"You mean he's rejecting *your* opinions?"

"Perhaps. But what if I'm right? All I want to do is throw this out to the floor. Genuinely. If Hiro has it right, great, but *I* think we should bring every scientific mind we have to the table. Our past differences really won't matter if he gets this wrong."

"What if he's right?"

Aito considered. "My brother is brilliant. He certainly understands these concepts better than I do, but I know he's distracted. I think it might be because I'm here. Trouble is, if he's not right, we're dead. All of us and everything, dead. In fact, this might prove the most dangerous and disastrous event in billions of years, if it goes wrong. Certainly in our neck of the galaxy. That's a lot of faith to put in one man who's not listening to contra opinions."

She snorted. "Family. You should have seen what I had to work with."

"I did. Isn't it about time we stopped them, once and for all this time?"

She gave him a secretive look. "I thought you were all in favour of the end of the world?"

He sat back, appraising her. "What's that supposed to mean?"

"It means I've read your file – your *secret* file. So don't waste my time, young man. What do you really want?"

Aito considered. "I may have had an agenda. Once. But that most certainly did not involve the death of our planet. Everything I did, I did, not for man, but for the Earth. I'm concerned that the natural world might go up in smoke if my brother gets this wrong."

"So you think mankind can save the day in the end, do you?" She smiled, but with little humour. "Fine words from the poster boy for ecomentalism."

He returned her smile, coolly. "Actually, I was thinking, perhaps womankind might save the day? After all, you know more about the wormhole we created from Egypt to Munich than anyone, alive or dead. You oversaw its creation. And it was *your* niece who caused all this. To some extent, this is on you."

"Ha! Man creates the modern world, woman ends it. How beautifully circular. Ever heard of nuance, young man?"

The door chimed, interrupting Aito's response.

Hemmings rose. "Ah, that will be our eavesdroppers, coming to separate the inmates."

"At least they knocked."

"Yes, Douglas is very civil," she replied sourly, opening the hatch. "Sergeant Jackson, how lovely to see you again."

"Away from the door," The Sarge ordered. Pointing a stun pistol at Aito, he added, "You, with me."

"Am I in trouble with my dear brother again?"

"Oh, it's worse than that, lad. Captain Baines would like a word."

"I thought she was flying around after dinosaurs."

"My, my, how well informed we've become," The Sarge allowed, drolly, his cockney accent coming to the fore. "You're right, lad. And let me tell ya, she weren't happy when I interrupted her with this, neither. Still, don't worry yourself, she'll be back soon enough, and until then, I've got a lovely little room picked out just for you."

Aito glanced at Hemmings. "At least I won't have to unpack. My things are still there."

"Enjoy it while you can, sunbeam," The Sarge taunted. "I wouldn't be surprised if you're for the Spanish archer this time."

Aito frowned. "I'm to be shot?"

"For the 'El Bow'," The Sarge replied, witheringly. "Sorry, am I not making myself clear? Now, get a move on."

***

"Commander Gleeson?" Baines called into her headset's microphone. "Commander? Baines to Gleeson, come in – over."

"Still here, Captain. Hearing you loud and clear – over."

Baines sagged with relief. "I'm glad to hear that, but I'd like to know why you're not *here*? Over."

"Bit of a problem there, Cap. These guys have blocked the door – over."

"Eh? Over."

Wormholes link points in space–time, making journeys that would otherwise be impossible to any mortal as simple as stepping through a door to the next room. Consequently, implausibly, Gleeson found himself almost 13,000 kilometres and 99.2 million years away, even though his radio transmission travelled no more than a few hundred metres to reach Baines, thanks to the magic of wormhole technology. However, stepping through a door to the next room becomes a lot more difficult when that door is guarded.

The Mapusaurus pack milled about, checking every new scent laid down in their absence. For Gleeson, it brought to mind how a family dog checks every blade of grass in the garden after a holiday. Not that there was any grass, and there were certainly no dogs. He would have been heartened by this understandable and recognisable behaviour, would even have been happy to wait for them to get bored and wander off, but for two things. Firstly, he possessed very little understanding of how Heidi's wormhole manifold worked – his gateway home might just as easily lead somewhere else, if he left it too long – and secondly, the Mapusaurus alpha, unlike his underlings, seemed less interested in sniffing about on the plateau and all *too* interested in Gleeson. Despite living with dinosaurs for some time, the *New Worlder*s still had very little understanding of how the Earth's early masters thought and perceived the world around them. Maybe they *could* count? After all, in a very real sense, the mathematics that described everything were also used *by* everything to describe everything else; an innate calculator that guided every interaction and decision, and while Gleeson hovered, he could certainly believe the alpha Mapusaurus was the calculating type. He strutted back and forth, guarding the wormhole and flicking his tail excitedly, almost daring Gleeson to pass him, never once taking his piercing gaze from the pilot suspended, for now, just out of reach. Clearly, the fear factor his helicopter instilled was reduced significantly now the animals were back on their home turf[1] , and Gleeson was alone, outnumbered thirteen to one. He knew he was on borrowed time if he stayed where he was. After all the erratic stunt flying employed to hunt and drive the dinosaurs back through the wormhole, his fuel gauge was dipping dangerously low. Even as he considered the problem, the reserve warning flashed up on his control console.

His comm crackled. *"Commander, how are you for fuel? Over."*

"Funny you should ask that, Cap. It was on *my* mind, too. Twenty minutes, maybe a little more if I'm careful – over." He closed the channel, speaking instead to his machine, "Come on, baby, sip gently, there's a good girl."

"Do you require assistance? Over."

"Negative, Captain. The big guy, that real ugly rooter, is right this side of the portal. Anyone coming through will crash straight into him." Gleeson glared at the creature, who seemed to glare right back. It was weird, almost as though the giant male understood that he, Gleeson, was the cause of all his pain, and that the helicopter was just a thing.

---

1. As stated, there was no turf, but home ferns just hasn't the same ring to it.

"Bagger! These guys were bad enough when I thought they were just vicious monsters. The last thing I need is to be outwitted by a bladdy dinosaur!"

"*Commander?*"

"Nothing, Captain. I'm working on it. Do nothing, unless I call, OK? Over."

"*Understood – out.*"

The Australian brought the chopper forward, threateningly, dipping the rotors at the last minute and backing away.

Mapusaurus roseae swished his tail, head swaying gently from side to side as he followed Gleeson within the transparent bubble. He had no idea how lethal the rotors would be if they touched him. His eyes were on the prize. Gleeson did know. He also knew that if he made contact, his machine would be smashed to pieces, quite possibly by those very same rotors, when he dropped out of the sky.

"Not falling for that any more, eh? OK, let's try a different tack."

He backed the machine off, quickly gaining altitude. He was recording everything – all their vehicles did – so it made sense to gather intelligence while he was stranded there. Perhaps the dinosaurs would lose interest in him, and the wormhole, if he stopped behaving in ways that intrigued them? He began a slow circle of the plateau. Following the helicopter's natural inclination to drift used less fuel than hovering in place, so it was a plan with no drawbacks.

Out over the plateau's washed-out edge, he recorded the semi-buried *Last Word* with interest. If he became trapped there, the wreck might be his only refuge, might even become his home for a while, until a rescue could be mounted.

He blew out his cheeks. "Well, that's unappealing." The Mapusaurus pack's sudden re-emergence, notwithstanding his smelly, noisy chopper, had sent most of the wildlife into hiding, but Gleeson was not fooled. He knew they were still there, all manner of dangerous critters, just lying in wait for him to put down, and that led him to the next obvious question – *where* should he put down? He had ten minutes' flight time left, ten minutes to get home or, at least, to safety.

He rotated the chopper on its axis, facing east, back towards the wormhole. The alpha predator had moved a little further from the gateway, but still seemed transfixed on the flying machine and the goodies locked within. Gleeson adjusted his collar uncomfortably; he was getting better at reading the creature's mind. It was most disconcerting.

"Commander?"

Baines' sudden query made him jump, and he worked swiftly to bring his machine back under control before it piled into the bank to join the *Last Word.*

"Still here, Cap. Next time we should take the attack choppers – over."

"You insisted on superior aerobatics, Commander, remember? Just like herding cattle in the bush, you said."

"Don't remind me. Next time I recommend stealth and agility over firepower and brute force, shoot me – it'll save time!"

Baines laughed. *"Is the dinosaur still covering the mouth of the wormhole? Over."*

"Yeah. Bagger's taken root! What're you thinking? Over."

"Sergeant Prentice has a plan to get you back. He's coming through. Are you well clear of the anomaly? Over."

"Affirmative. Has he missed this month's psych evaluation? He'll be killed!"

He hovered, drifting back towards the wormhole, thinking, *Better stay high and well back. Who knows how this'll go down?* His fuel gauge sounded the decidedly ominous, Death's doorbell *bong* of doom. "Oh, great! Captain, five minutes before I'm outta juice – over."

"Don't worry, Commander. Help's on the way – over."

"Who's worrying?" Gleeson muttered to himself. "Every time I say 'over' it feels like a prediction."

The nose of an armoured personnel carrier erupted from the event horizon of the wormhole, reintegrating into a space already occupied by another. The giant Mapusaurus *roared* with indignation as he turned on the interloper.

Prentice kept the power on, shoving the animal aside in a way that would have led to catastrophe with a helicopter. Unlike the less advanced Schultz APCs, the ones the *New World* carried had a small, rotating turret, allowing the driver to fire the quad-mounted fifty-calibre machine guns in any direction, even vertically straight up. Learning from the enemy's proclivity for attacking from the air, Douglas had insisted on it. Prentice fired a volley, high, well over the animals' heads.

Gleeson's fuel gauge was now screaming at him – were it a reversing sensor, he would have long driven through the rear wall of his garage and already been on the phone to a builder. "I'm going down!" he cried to everyone and no one in particular.

The angry dinosaurs bunched together, forming a united front against the new, seemingly unassailable aggressor. They were becoming acclimatised to the strange sounds, smells and bangs, too, each having less and less effect. Slowly, they backed away, en masse, but not far. Even in the Cretaceous, even when hopeless, territory has never been yielded easily.

Heading for a clear space away from them, and Prentice, Gleeson put down. He landed hard, though the only serious damage was to his dignity.

The alpha saw that he was, at last, within reach and launched for him at a run. "Prentice…!" The rest of Gleeson's cry for help was lost between his chronic, stress-driven inability to articulate and an overdriven microphone.

Fortunately, Prentice was reading the situation and already moving on an intercept course. Once again, he biffed the alpha aside, his twenty-five-ton machine relentless and unstoppable. Spinning the right track, his machine turned left, so that its rear faced the hastily landed chopper. He unlocked and opened the tail hatch by remote, bellowing over the comm, *"Commander, leg it!"*

Gleeson did not need telling twice. Already unbuckled from his safety harness, he had not needed telling once. Torturing a metaphor, his rifle was riding shotgun, so he grabbed it from the co-pilot's seat and ran for his life towards the open carrier.

Diving through the hatch, he yelled for Prentice to close it behind him.

Complying with the order, Prentice applied the parking brake and stepped into the rear compartment to check on his colleague. "Still in one piece, Commander?"

Gleeson checked himself over. "I reckon so. I'll check the rest when I go to the dunny." He extended his hand. "Thanks, Adam."

Prentice took it, pulling Gleeson to his feet. "Gets the heart pumping, eh?"

Their transport shook. Even through the armoured hull the animals sounded angry. They, too, had had a hell of a day, after all, and were hopped up on a massive adrenaline surge.

"How close are we to the edge?" asked Gleeson, concern reigniting in his chest.

"Fairly," Prentice admitted, cautiously. "The edge is a lot closer than it used to be. All the loose soil's been washed away. I reckon by the river from Crater Lake."

Gleeson considered that. "I noticed what looked like flood damage when I hovered over the plateau."

The APC shook again. This time it felt like it moved, too.

Gleeson got back to his feet. "We're a threat on their turf. Quick, let's get out of here, before they push us over the edge, 'cause I gotta tell ya, I saw that movie, and it didn't end well for anybody!"

"Right." Prentice darted back into the cab. "What about the helicopter?"

"Did you bring any jet fuel?"

"Do you know, I totally forgot."

"Alright, alright, fair enough," Gleeson acknowledged. "We'll have to come back for it when these guys have baggered off."

The powerful diesel engine roared to life, startling the mapusaurs again. They backed away cautiously, but aggressively, as Prentice turned the APC on the spot to face back towards the wormhole. "Let's go home."

The heavy machine lumbered easily over the rough ground and

disappeared through the wormhole.

Gleeson let go a huge sigh of relief. "A hot shower and an early night for me – maybe a sherbet or two. What'll it be, Adam, a brown ale?"

Prentice grinned. "Sounds like a plan, sir— What the hell!"

They rematerialised, not on the green slopes of Great Cheviot, but in a desert canyon. Weirdly, there were signs of flooding there, too, where a military field camp appeared to have been smashed by a storm.

Four main battle tanks sat in an arc around the mouth of the wormhole, surrounded by washed up detritus. Each one turned their turrets to face the intruder.

"Back up! Back up!" Gleeson shrieked.

Prentice was already on it, throwing the machine into full reverse. The APC lurched backwards through the wormhole, returning to the Cretaceous, where thirteen mapusaurs slowly turned their heads towards the intruder.

Gleeson swore. "Back into the frying pan, Sergeant! What the hell happened?"

"Dunno, sir, but I'm not waiting here to find out!" He practically fell on the left control stick, causing the carrier to lurch hard to the right. Engaging both tracks, the heavy machine leapt forward as a terrific explosion erupted behind them.

"What the hell was that?" Gleeson bawled.

"They're firing on us!"

"Through the wormhole?" Gleeson could hardly believe it. "Do they have any idea how dangerous that might be?"

Prentice gave him a look. "Not for them! Suggest you try talking to them, sir. Like, *now–ish!*"

"*Me?*"

"It'll be an officer on the other side, sir."

"So what? You're talking to me!"

"You're special, sir. You have an open channel."

Gleeson gave a strangulated huff as he switched immediately into civil mode. "This is Commander Gleeson of the UNS *New World,* please desist – repeat – please desist in your attack. You're blowing all hell out of our forest here, fellas!"

There was no answer, but the shelling stopped.

The two men looked at each other. "Now what?" asked Prentice. Gleeson shrugged.

"At least the explosions sent the dinosaurs away."

"Small mercy, but I'll take it," Gleeson agreed. "Where the hell *was* that? North Africa? The Middle East?"

"I don't know, but it certainly wasn't the Iron Age – those tanks were seventy tons of steel!"

"No way back to our friends, then," Gleeson muttered. "This is bad, Adam. Can't see how it could be worse."

It began to rain. They looked at each other and sighed.

Also in the mid-Cretaceous, but far to the north, Corporal Thomas was a man with his own problems. After slaying the mosasaur, the dinosaur had eaten his fill and now settled down to sleep next to his kill. The deluge drummed the dropship's hull loud enough to make Thomas wince, but the animal just hunkered down, curled up and waited it out. In a way, Thomas felt sorry for him.

That emotion caught him by surprise. A few minutes earlier, he thought he was a dead man and would have done whatever he could, whatever he had to, to survive. Now, he simply saw an animal, an innocent, trying to stay alive in a brutal world with no toys or helpful gizmos to take away the pain. Many of his crewmates had spoken of similar epiphanies, but this was the first time he saw it for himself. Thomas had grown up in a world of concrete and steel, yet from the safety of his cocoon – indeed, in spite of it – he now understood a little about nature in all her cruel irony. He knew that, should he step outside, the creature would seek his death, but only as a means to survive. He felt a new respect for the predator, and the prey, but none of that helped him save his comrade from the lake. He could scare the giant away with engine noise, or blow a hole in the beach, but that might lose him his connection to the stranded ship. He knew his winch had only the most tenuous grip on the sinking craft as it was.

Fortunately, he did not have to wait long for an answer. The dropship's comm binged for his attention. It was Dr Brian Alba. Thomas rolled his eyes – that was all he needed – but Alba surprised him with a glass-half-full moment. *"We have portable air pumps aboard the Pod."*

After his shock, it took Thomas a moment to understand where Alba was going with that statement. Suddenly sceptical, he realised Alba's glass was half-full of something he would only drink in the direst of emergencies. He sighed. *Like this one.* "Right," he answered, cautiously. "And you think it'll work?"

"Of course."

"Won't the pressure give the pilot the bends?"

"No. These can pump air in, or water out. I doubt we could seal the vessel well enough to force the water out by pressure alone, anyway, so we'll pump it out instead, understand?"

"OK. How do we get the pump in?"

"Well, that's the other bad news. He's going to have to get out before we do this."

"The *other* bad news?"

"Yes. We have plenty. For one thing, we need to lower the equipment to him, and he will have to put it all together. Otherwise, we'll be putting others at bite height, too. We're hoping the rocket noise will scare away those crocodile things – or whatever they are – for long enough, while we carry this out. You'll need to keep tension on that winch of yours. Losing your grip would be bad – we saw how difficult it was for you to connect in the first place. We thought you were wasting your time, frankly, but there you go. If you lose the connection now, this storm will probably drive him off the shelf where he's stuck and sink him."

"You're welcome," Thomas replied, sarcastically. "Any good news?"

"Yes. The pump will work perfectly, even when fully submerged, in the right operational mode."

"It'll need to. We've got a large predator on the beach, an' all. Must have found his courage, as we haven't seen that big spino-wossname for a while."

"Yes. We watched your completely ridiculous walk in the rain. For someone so oblivious to his surroundings, I'm surprised you're still alive, Corporal."

Thomas exploded. "You saw all that? Saw them coming my way and said *nothing?* That crocodile thing and that, that… whatever he is?"

"You haven't checked your personal comm, have you?"

Thomas deflated slightly, drawing it from a pocket. His screen lit up with a dozen missed calls. "Ah."

"Indeed. Silent mode, perchance?"

"No. The storm was battering. I didn't hear. Look, never mind. We need to get this plan of yours moving. The pilot can't stay out there forever."

"The equipment is being loaded into our one remaining ship as we speak. You must stay put. And don't forget to man the winch! When she floats free – if she floats free, before the pilot gets eaten – she might well drift forward and loosen your connection. Got it?"

"Funnily enough, I understood the first time. Get on with it, Alba." Thomas was running out of patience with the pompous engineer.

"Just be ready to reel her in – Alba out!"

The ship left from the Pod's opposite side and circled back towards the lake. The unknown carcharodontosaurid jumped to his feet in alarm. Spinning on the spot, he searched his surroundings to identify the threat. Grabbing the corpse at his feet, he tried to carry it away, but dropped it in his panic. It was still heavy, even for the one-ton predator. Fear overriding acquisitiveness, he ran along the beach with the chunk of flesh torn from the cadaver still in his mouth before disappearing back into the jungle, throwing one last wistful glance over his shoulder at the meal he was leaving behind.

Again, Thomas felt sorry for him. Before his recent windfall, the dinosaur had clearly been starving and would be lucky to find another such meal any time soon. Nonetheless, Thomas hoped the rocket noise had the same effect on the creatures of the lake.

The ship roared overhead to hover above the stricken, half-submerged vessel below. Thomas heard Alba give a similar explanation of their plan to the pilot, who naturally balked at the idea of getting out and climbing on top of his ship. Alba gave him a speech promoting the virtues of doing or dying, eventually falling back on the tried and tired 'needs must'. Unable to stomach any more demeaning platitudes, the pilot eventually gave up and agreed.

Thomas decided that Alba was even worse at positive reinforcement than he was at diplomacy. It was impressive. Suddenly with time on his hands, he briefly wondered if Brian Alba might actually be more unpleasant even than Geoff Lloyd. Could they be long-lost kin? *What an appalling idea. Still, bringing them together would be box office on the reality TV circuit.* He shook his head at the thought. *Not much call for that in Cretaceous Britain – what a waste.*

The pilot opened the side hatch to his half-submerged ship and was immediately knocked back inside by a wave. No giant predators were necessary to make his task incredibly difficult; the fact that he had those to contend with, too, was merely a bonus. He sighed within his environment suit and reached forward, clutching for any handhold that would allow him to pull himself outside. His rescuers hung in the air above. Despite the rough weather and the choppiness of the waves, he could feel the vibration of their rocket motors through the water. It was comforting in that he suspected the local fauna would hate it. As a parallel, he knew crocodiles and alligators often shied from the sound of an outboard motor. The engines of the Schultz attack craft would be far more intrusive. Now he just had to climb. Again, easier said than done. Everything about his ship was designed to be sleek.

"Throw me a rope!" he shouted into his comm, as he bobbed

about in the swell.

The pumping equipment was already on its way down. "*Grab the pump!*" someone answered through his headset.

The ferocious winds grew in intensity, increasing the amplitude of the swell, and his ship rocked. It skipped forwards towards the shore as Thomas kept the tension on the cables.

The pilot was left bobbing about, suddenly finding himself well aft of the side hatch. Another wave caught him, crashing him against the half-submerged vessel. Had it not been for the helmet, he might have dashed his brains out against the hull. As it was, he was seeing entirely the wrong kind of stars from within his spacesuit.

"*Are you alright?*" someone called.

He turned away from the ship and saw the mosasaur. "No," he answered, bleakly.

A *boom* shook the water and the very air around him. The pilot above had fired a missile into the lake like a depth charge. A vast plume of lake water rose high into the sky before crashing down again. The pilot's glimpse of death lasted a moment only; the mosasaur's jaws opened to an impossible angle, briefly revealing two rows of teeth ready to work together like a dual conveyor belt to draw him in, crushing and destroying his flesh until he was swallowed whole. Above, the pilot's quick action not merely prevented that fate, but also created another wave that drove the stranded man back towards the open hatch in his ship.

Giving up on the idea of climbing onto his ship, he simply swam into it. Damn the machinery, he would rather risk knocking it about than go out there again.

The heavy pumping equipment clanked heavily against his hull before splashing into the lake just outside the hatch. He grabbed it one-handed and pulled, while hanging on to the hatch frame with the other. Still suspended from the ship above, the pumping machinery was almost weightless. "Feed me some slack," he cried.

Thomas opened a channel to control. Alba answered. "*What is it?*

We're a little busy, you know!"

"What's his name?" Thomas asked.

"Who?"

"The man we're trying to save."

"He's… he's, oh, someone or other. How the hell should I know?"

Thomas scowled. "You've lived with him for months!"

"I've lived with a lot of people. You'll be asking me what he looks like next!"

Thomas opened his mouth and closed it again, lost for words.

A new voice broke into the conversation. *"His name is Matteo, Matteo Kitzler."*

Thomas recognised the voice of Sergeant Helmut Zimmermann. "Thank you, Sarge. Well, he'll be tickled pink, if he gets through this one."

"Was that a joke?" demanded Alba.

"An observation. My German's not that good." Thomas opened a channel to Kitzler. "Matteo, this is Corporal Thomas. I'm feeling a lot of bucking through the line."

"The wind is getting worse," Kitzler replied, breathlessly. "The swell is getting bigger. Please keep tension on the cable, I'm about to begin pumping – if I can put all this together and find a way to rig the door so that I can keep it open a crack at the top."

He sounded understandably stressed. "Take your time, mate. We're not going anywhere."

The side hatch employed two sets of doors. The inner set closed laterally, while the outer set closed vertically, meeting in the middle. Casting about for inspiration, the pilot took a crowbar from the ship's basic tool pack and moved closer to the hatch. Head under water, he looked cautiously, right and left, holding the bar up to defend himself if necessary. The turbid waters churned the bed as the waves rolled towards the shore. He could barely see a couple of metres ahead of him, doubly disconcerting as the mosasaurs could sense his every movement through the medium of their environment. He reached out onto the lakebed and scrabbled around in the silt until he found what he wanted – a stone, about the size of his fist.

He drew back inside. Hoping his ship's electrics were well insulated, he placed the stone on the crook at the end of the bar and held it out to the point where the doors met. He activated the hatch. It slammed shut immediately, crushing the soft siltstone instantly, and jamming his bar. Kitzler swore.

Crossing his fingers, he activated the open stud. He breathed a sigh of relief when the hatch opened again, seemingly none the worse for wear.

It would take something more substantial to keep them open. He briefly considered shorting the circuit as the doors closed, to make it impossible for them to complete their action, but it occurred to him that he would probably electrocute himself while doing so.

He was just about to reopen his toolkit when Alba spoke loudly into his earpiece, making him jump. *"It just occurred to me, Martin—"*

"Matteo," Zimmermann interjected.

"Close enough. It just occurred to me that you're within a few metres of our medium density polyethylene water pipe. We never did fit the filter on the end of it. It must be nearby. Don't suppose you could…?"

"Of course! And would you like me to catch you a mackerel for dinner, while I'm out there?"

"Well, I…"

"This is Lieutenant McBride. Belay that! Just find a way to save yourself and the ship if you can, Kitzler. You're doing great."

The pilot blew out his cheeks, allowing some of his stress to escape. He checked his toolkit again. He opened a channel to everyone. "I need to close the hatch, leaving a hole for the pipe leading from the pump. Any ideas?"

"Use a Brummie screwdriver," Thomas suggested.

"Come again?"

"A hammer. Put a hammer in the way! Put your pipe through and put a hammer in the way. It'll pinch the pipe but not enough to stop such a powerful pump, surely?"

"He's right," Alba chipped in. *"Better get to it, Kettler. It'll take*

hours."

"Kitzler, sir."

"Whatever. Get on with it."

<hr>

AD1588, Great Cheviot

"You have got to be joking!" Reid snapped, nervously.

"Do I look like I am joking?" Satnam Patel retorted, sourly. "You caused this mess, Reid. I, for one, think you should be given the *opportunity* to fix it."

"I agree," White seconded. "Who knows, maybe fate has, just for once, given us the whip hand?"

"Heidi shot me!" Reid argued.

White frowned. "And you betrayed her. What's that got to do with anything?"

"I betrayed her to work on the alien device. It might be mankind's greatest endeavour."

"Fool! Arrogant fool!" Patel raged. "I will tell you what mankind's greatest endeavour will be, shall I? Saving mankind! The wheels you have set in motion could destroy this very planet. What good will knowledge be then?"

Reid opened his mouth to reject Patel's prognosis, only to close it again. He had to admit, his perfectly valid argument – that knowledge was never wasted – fell apart on that occasion, when no one was left to know it.

"Please, gentlemen," Mother Sarah calmed them. "Satnam and I have already discussed this, and we believe that… Well, why don't you explain, Satnam?"

"I've been wrestling with the idea of using Reid's wrist device to go forward in time, potentially, to find the rest of our crew. I say potentially, because we've no idea where or when they are."

"Perhaps…" Reid hesitated, not sure whether he should commit himself.

"Go on, Doctor," White encouraged.

"I was just thinking that, perhaps, my device could locate them, if they are in a time where the manifold has an open wormhole."

"I was hoping for that very thing," Patel allowed, calming slightly. "I considered finding Captain Douglas and the others to either help them disassemble Reid's manifold, or failing that, discourage them from trying, if the situation looked too perilous. The last thing we need is to damage causality further. The third option was to simply stay here and hope for the best. Sarah came up with a fourth – to take Reid with me."

Reid eyeballed her. "Thanks."

She smiled disarmingly. "Welcome."

"Just one fly in the ointment," White noted.

"Just the one?" Reid queried, sarcasm his only shield against the fear stabbing for his heart.

White ignored him. "If you leave us, Satnam, who's to say we'll pull all this off?"

"You mean changing the future, to create the world Captain Douglas spoke of?"

"Exactly. At the risk of causing embarrassment, you've a brilliant mind, possibly the most brilliant among us. You're also a generation younger than most of us, thanks to your thirty-year jump. It's not much of a stretch to see how we might need you."

"You're suggesting this might be a one-way trip?" Patel asked, hesitantly.

White shrugged.

Patel nodded, acknowledging the point. "I had intended to leave Dr Reid in my place—"

"Reid? Are you kidding?" White burst out. "Bit of a moral deficit on that transaction, don't you think?"

"Regardless, anyone who could create such monstrous technology might be of immeasurable use to our efforts, so long as *his* efforts," he glared at Reid, "are directed by *us* and not a psychopath. But then Sarah suggested that I take him with me. After all, who better to tear all this down than the man who built it?"

"I have a better idea," White countered. "Why don't you stay here, Satnam, and we send *him?*"

"Because, should he find our friends, they will be unlikely to trust Heidi's number one mad scientist and partner in crime."

"I'm not mad," Reid countered.

"We'll remember you said that for your trial," White quipped.

"*Trial?*"

"Yeah. Perhaps Satnam's right and we should send you. Hell, you could sure use a little mitigation!"

"So, it is agreed, then?" Patel looked around them all in turn, lingering on their latest recruit. "Friends… and enemies, working together to save the world. Dr Reid, have you anything to add?"

"Canned laughter?"

"Come on, guys," White interjected smoothly. "We can do this."

"Makes you proud of the human race," Sarah added, enthusiastically.

"What could possibly go wrong?" Reid added, acerbically.

"Well, when you get there, Captain Baines might just shoot you," White added, jovially.

"If there are no further questions, we should move quickly," Patel added, encouragingly.

Reid slumped in his chair. "I've nothing more to add."

99.2 million years earlier…

Just a few short metres from where Patel made his decision to save the future, cargo pilot, Matteo Kitzler, dared to look forward from a long, long way back into the past. His prospects were improving as the water level inside his ship dropped back down to around his knees. He removed his helmet to save the oxygen in his tanks, when sudden buoyancy pitched him forward into the cold water. Raising himself into a press-up position, he expelled a spout of silty lake water, cursing as soon as he had the breath. The ship jerked again, and this time there was no doubt that he was moving forwards.

Out of the front viewport, he could see the beach approaching – no more than thirty metres now. Despite the terrible weather, he was elated. Immediately, the ship grounded again, pitching him forwards once more, but he was ready for it this time and managed to keep his feet. "Corporal Thomas?"

"*Thomas here. Go ahead – over.*"

"We're on a sandbar at this point of the beach. The water's much deeper just a few metres to our right – that is, *my* right – over."

Thomas understood. "I'm prepping to take off. Stand by – over." He locked down the winch and launched carefully. Keeping the cable taut between the two vessels, he allowed the dropship to drift due west, describing a compass arc.

Gradually, Kitzler felt his ship begin to lurch right. He could hear dragging and scraping as the hull ground across silt and pebbles, the pump still working to lower the water level inside the cabin. Within moments, he was floating again. Moreover, he was moving into deeper water, and this was a good thing. The direction Thomas was towing him would allow his vessel to be pulled right up to the beach.

Cutting swiftly through the water now, the tug ship applied just enough power to keep him moving without stressing its winch and cable. Buoyant, Kitzler's ship was a fraction of its tare weight and soon mounted the beach, carving through the shale and sand. Thomas landed, still keeping the cable taut.

Sergeant Zimmermann moved a tracked personnel carrier in close as men attached Kitzler's ship to a front hitch via heavier cables. Before he knew it, he was being dragged up the beach onto dry land. He opened the hatch and watched the remaining water gush out to run down the saturated sands straight back into the lake. He switched the pump off and stepped out to a soggy but heartfelt round of applause.

AD1944, Bavarian Alps, Germany

"Plush for an abandoned salt mine," Heidi noted, wryly.

"We have standards," Heydrich replied airily, with a foppish wave of his hand around what, for all intents and purposes, looked like the underground palatial headquarters of a supervillain. "Besides, 'abandoned' is such a narrow interpretation."

Heidi looked around. "Helped the previous owners to leave, did you? All that is missing is a vast pile of gold and jewels."

Heydrich smiled. "You refer to the recent work of that *Engländer* – I forget his name – the *kinder* author, yes?"

"Tolkien," she supplied the answer.

Heydrich nodded. "Yes. As it happens, I do also have a dragon – two, in fact."

"I know. I ran through a Cretaceous jungle to secure their eggs, chased by their parents."

"So *dein Großvater* told me. Another fantastic story. You must tell me about it, and how they were, in the wild."

"Not friendly, but while we are addressing the subject of standards, our history records that you were marred by an apparently unknown, hypertensive and atherosclerotic cardiovascular disease, with significant left ventricular hypertrophy. Accepting the differences between our timelines and the advances your people have made, are you now aware of this condition?"

Heydrich was both surprised and affronted, but forced a hard smile. "Those *minor* abnormalities were all fixed when I was a child. My genetics are quite *pure,* Dr Schultz, I assure you."

Heidi nodded brusquely. Seemingly satisfied by his response, she demanded to see Dr Mengele's research.

For the second time, Heydrich was forced to swallow his surprise. "Might I ask why?"

"Of course you might."

He sighed, the muscles in his jaw bunching with annoyance. He was not used to taking orders, nor tolerating anything less than total deference and was placing himself well outside his comfort zone for this woman. *You had better come through with all that you have promised, Fräulein,* he thought bitterly. He cleared his throat. "Very well. I will call down for him to expect you. He is unpacking his new lab. Now, I must speak with my security people. After what has happened…"

"Quite. I will not detain you." Heidi made her way down to Mengele's lair.

Mengele leaned over the side of a large glass tank, dangling a rasher of bacon. The baby Carcharodontosaurus saharicus jumped for the raw meat immediately, soon to be joined by his sister, who nipped at him, knocking him out of the way to jump for the morsel herself.

Mengele giggled merrily at the chicks' antics, testing and evaluating, to see how high they could jump. The wall of the tank was 1.2 metres; the dinosaurs were already clearing a metre.

"You will need a larger tank very soon, Josef."

Mengele turned in surprise. "Dr Schultz, you sneaked up on me."

Heidi smiled frostily. "Then imagine what *they* will do, a month or two from now."

"You have seen them, in the wild?"

"Déjà vu."

"Doctor?"

"Nothing. I have had this conversation already. How do you think you came by those eggs?"

"Quite so. How big was the mother?"

"Very. I suggest you find somewhere more secure than a fish tank, and soon. Are you planning to sell them?"

"I am not party to that information," he lied.

Heidi looked down into the tank. "I can picture it now. Some obese oligarch with their spoilt offspring, hopping up and down, demanding the one with the red stripe on his head."

Mengele's eyes crinkled at the corners with amusement. "Perhaps I should let the child into the tank, to choose."

Despite herself, Heidi shuddered. "I see you have already been considering this."

He laughed. "Not at all. How may I help you, Dr Schultz?"

"You have *mein Großvater* here," she stated unequivocally.

He blinked. "I can assure you that I do not. I understand he is dead. My commiserations." He bowed slightly.

"Perhaps. But that is not what I meant. I suspect you know this, *Herr Doktor*. It would be unwise to test my patience. You have… *material* from *mein Großvater* here."

"Ah… that."

"Yes. That."

"How did you know?"

"Simple. I saw to it that the lifesaving blood transfusion he recently received contained a little extra."

He studied her. "The nanites?"

Heidi was impressed. "Very good, Josef, for 1944."

"Ah, yes. I understand *your* 1944 was rather more primitive than our society."

"Yes, and no. Less technologically advanced, certainly, but they had higher philosophies that your culture seems to entirely lack."

Mengele's smiled broadened, teasing. "Perhaps you will teach us."

"I intend to. Now, tell me, what are you planning to do with *mein Großvater's* blood?"

"He demanded I take it."

"That sounds like him. Now tell me *why*."

Mengele shrugged. "I assume he foresaw his own demise. He had a weak heart, no?"

Heidi nodded. "You examined him?"

"There was no need. You, too, are a medical doctor, I understand?"

Heidi nodded again.

"So you will know the signs – the blueness of the lips, clubbing of the fingers."

"Very well. I believe you, that he foresaw his end. Now, I ask again, why did he demand you take a sample?"

"I have a certain… *reputation*, Doctor."

Heidi snorted, gently. "You have no idea, Josef."

He stared at her intently. "Perhaps you could enlighten me about that, too, some time."

"Perhaps. Why do you have his genetic material?" She stared deep into his intense, black eyes.

He smiled back with the bright brittleness of insanity. "Why, to make him live again, of course."

***

A shimmer appeared in the air, barely three metres above the lake's surface. A probe slipped through, silently, to hover just above its choppy waters.

Brian Alba strode quickly through the *Newfoundland*'s rescue pod, answering an urgent summons to the control centre. "What is it, Lieutenant?" he demanded brusquely upon entering. "Another wretched crocodile trying to eat our rescued ship?"

McBride turned in his seat. "It's a probe, sir."

Alba stopped in his tracks. "From where?"

"Don't know yet, sir."

"From whom?"

Again, McBride merely shrugged. "We're being hailed. Should I answer?"

"Yes, yes, of course!"

The lieutenant complied. "This is Crater Lake Base. Who are we speaking with, please?"

"*Crater Lake, this is Dr Satnam Patel, of the USS* New World. *We are in need of your assistance.*"

Alba and McBride stared at each other in shock. Returning to his senses, Alba snapped his fingers to get Sergeant Helmut Zimmermann's attention. "You, Sergeant Whatsyername. Get Corporal Thomlinson up here on the double!"

"You mean Corporal Thomas, sir?"

Alba waved a hand. "Just do it, will you?" He leaned on McBride's console, signalling that he wished to speak.

McBride nodded. The channel was open.

"Dr Patel, this is Dr Brian Alba, of Crater Lake Base. How may we assist?"

Patel's voice rang clear across the control centre. *"We are transmitting from the future, far into the future, but we need to get back to you urgently. It is imperative that we locate Captain Douglas or members of his crew – the very fabric of the universe may depend upon it!"*

Alba frowned. He made a cutting gesture across his throat.

"Muted, sir," McBride confirmed.

"Bit overly dramatic, wouldn't you say, Lieutenant? Where *is* that Brummie corporal?"

"Do you mean me, Dr Alba?" Thomas jogged into control. "What's happening?"

"It appears we have a friend of yours on the line. Open the channel, Lieutenant."

"Yes, sir."

"Dr Patel, Alba again. I have with me one of your crewmen, a corporal Thomkins."

"Thomas, sir."

Alba rolled his eyes. "Will he do?"

"Corporal Thomas? Truly?"

"It's me, Doctor." Thomas' smile travelled through the transmission; he could hardly believe it. "Please go ahead."

"Corporal, it's wonderful to hear your voice." It was unusual for Patel to show high emotion; he really had not been himself since journeying forward thirty years on a jetpack. He laughed openly. *"This is remarkable. Corporal, we must catch up with James Douglas. Can you help us?"*

Thomas winced slightly, stress bringing his native accent to the fore. "I'd like nothin' better, Doctor, but I doh know where he is, or any on 'em, for that matter. He went through a wormhole that we think was opened by Heidi Schultz, and that was the last we saw of 'im. The *New World* jumped soon after. I'm 'ere on me own."

"Is the wormhole still extant? Is it still there, Corporal?"

"Ar, I think so."

McBride checked his instruments and confirmed that it was.

"*Excellent! We may have a way of tracking them, if that is the case. Corporal, I cannot help noticing that our probe is hovering above the lake. My fellow traveller and I are reticent to step through, knowing the sort of creatures that inhabit the waters in that time. We have ships, but cannot afford to lose them. I myself am not a pilot and my companion... well, that is complicated. Do you have a vessel small enough to pass through the wormhole and taxi us back through to Crater Lake?*"

Alba nodded agreement.

"I'll be with you in a few minutes, Doctor," Thomas replied. "Keep the door open!"

"*Thank you, Corporal. Oh, and by the way, enter the wormhole very, very slowly!*"

A whoop of delight rang from *Factory Pod 4*'s main hangar, a sound that had not been heard there for many a year.

Thomas was greeted like a conquering hero, tearfully by some, boisterously by others. "How the hell are ya, Thomas?" White wrapped his arms around his old comrade, slapping him on the back enthusiastically. "Man, but you look so *young!*"

Thomas was at sea. He could hardly believe where he was, or when. He had not seen any of them in over a decade, and yet, for his long-lost crewmates, it had clearly been longer.

Rose Miller hugged him tightly. "How are you? And how's Tim and Clarrie and Woodsey and... oh, everyone?"

"Tim and Clarrie were married," Thomas tried and failed to keep up with her questions.

Henry Burnstein whooped for joy. "That's great! When?"

Thomas shook his head in disbelief. "A few days ago, I think. It's all been a blur!"

"Give the corporal some air," Patel interjected. "Unfortunately, we have work to do and must leave immediately."

"Actually, I can take us back any time," Reid pointed out. Unused to being around people who shared love and comradeship, he found himself wrapped up in the moment. "An hour or two would literally make no difference, Doctor."

Patel smiled. "Very well."

"Hey, we got the Mud Hole all fixed up – mostly," Henry cried. "One for the road, Corporal?"

"Not while I'm flying through a wormhole just a few inches bigger than me ship, Henry, but I'll definitely join you! I'll give Pete Davies your regards. He'll be sorry to have missed you. He hasn't arrested you in years!"

"Hey, tell him he's welcome any time!"

The old friends jostled and bantered their way to the Mud Hole for a brief reprieve from crisis, and for old times' sake.

Unbeknownst to them all, they were followed along the corridors by a dark, watchful presence that remained cloaked and hidden, also fascinated by what was happening.

❧

"You will take a sample of my blood, also."

Mengele was taken aback. "I will?"

"Indeed. I have unfinished business."

He was curious. "Elsewhere?"

"Would be one way of putting it. Else*when* might be another."

"I see. And when do you propose to leave?"

"Soon."

"I think *Herr* Heydrich might be, er… *disappointed* to learn this."

"He will get over it. Do not worry. I will leave him a little something to make it all worth his while – and yours."

"I will need to discuss your request with him, naturally, before I—"

"Did you discuss *mein Großvater's* request with him?"

He was about to lie, but reconsidered. Heinrich Schultz was a man who, at one time, held the world in his palm, yet feared his own granddaughter – perhaps he should, too. "I see you are as perceptive as *dein Großvater*."

Heidi allowed her lip to twitch, showing good humour. "You will show me the same courtesy?"

"You are an incredible woman, Doctor. For a small flask of your blood, you have my silence."

"And you will get to work straight away?"

He considered again. "When it is safe to do so, yes. You wish me to work on both *projects* simultaneously?"

She nodded. "My blood also contains nanites. Have you been able to establish what they do?"

He shook his head. "Time has been against me."

"You and me both. My nanites do not merely make us visible to our specialist equipment, they also record our memories. Allowing for redundancy, it would take a sample of several thousand to reconstruct them completely. A five cubic centimetre sample should easily suffice. I will leave you two vials of ten, to be sure."

His eyebrows rose in surprise. "Genetic memory? *Dein Großvater* knew you had this technology?" He glanced away from her, lost in an intellectual treat. "We have theorised, but I never…"

"He oversaw its development, though as I have stated, he did not know that he carried nanites within him." She shrugged. "At least, I assumed he did not. One could never be sure with Heinrich Schultz. You see the potential of this, Josef – where it might lead?"

He was clearly awed. "Indeed, I do. Genetic memory is but a step from…" He faltered, placing his hands over his mouth. He could hardly believe what was being offered.

"Genetic control," she joined the dots for him. "Total submission of an entire population, controlled at the cellular level, yes." She had learned much on her perilous journey through time. The Schultz approach of stick first, last and always, occasionally failed – not so occasionally, as it turned out. She had seen it more than once. Whereas Douglas' preference for the carrot could, on occasion, prove the weapon of choice. She pushed down the impulse to threaten Mengele with a painful death if he failed to carry out her wishes. She needed this, and needed *him* on side. Her enemies were closing in. Between the surprising resilience they had shown and the treachery of her minions, her ability to control destiny had once again been, if not actually thwarted, then at least considerably curtailed. No. She would not threaten this man – not yet. She would *buy* him first, allowing self-interest to do the heavy lifting. "*Mein Großvater* had geneticists developing just such a project, back in the old world. Perhaps *you* are the man to complete their work? Eventually, you will be able to control whole societies with a simple injection."

"You paint an interesting picture of the future, Dr Schultz."

She smiled, charmingly. "Interesting. Some might call it dystopic. You may call me Heidi."

"Thank you, Heidi. How would we disseminate such a treatment?"

"You are a clever man, Josef. I'm sure you will come up with something."

He pondered no more than a second. "By piggybacking it onto something beneficial, perhaps?" he postulated.

"Or allegedly so." She spoke seductively, satisfied that he understood. "Our knowledge is worth more than *Deutschland's* gross domestic product. Complete this work and you will find that *mein Großvater* will be very generous. Bring him back and he will provide you with every resource you could desire."

He considered. "But not for many, many years. I can create a clone, but again, despite theorising, we are far from any viable maturation process. And then we must consider my friend and current sponsor. Heydrich already gives me every resource I desire. He will respond badly to what you ask of me, I think."

Heidi produced the zettabyte drive from her pocket. "The information on this device will advance your understanding by many decades – in all likelihood, well beyond the dreams of your own lifetime. My family will give you what you need to know, to make this work."

"And for my friend? Dear Reinhard does so hate to feel left out."

"So *loyal,*" she mocked.

"So *sensible,* Heidi. My continued existence might weigh in the balance, should I err."

"Have no fear. Reinhard Heydrich is also important to my plans. Rest assured, he will receive more than enough to justify his investment, until I return. We shall all benefit from this, Josef."

"You will give him *enough?*" he queried. "I am unsure whether my colleague upstairs understands the meaning of that word."

"I thought he was your friend?"

He smiled his insane smile again. "You tease me, *Frau Doktor.*"

"Perhaps. Now, allow me to offer you something more solid. A warning." She leaned in close because too much carrot was bad for any donkey. "I *will* return and am liable to pop up anywhere at any time. No lock nor security will keep you safe from me, so if you fail me, or try to betray me, or *mein Großvater,* Josef, you *will* die." As she spoke, she wondered if she would return. No matter, her message was understood.

The drop ship appeared above Crater Lake. Corporal Thomas signalled his approach to the control room.

Patel shook his head in wonderment. "I never thought I would see this place again."

"Snap!" Reid grumbled.

"It was ten years ago for me, since we were all of us here together, I mean," Thomas noted, "but as I recall, the weather was a lot nicer."

Torrential rain beat the surface of the lake to a mist as high winds continued to drive the two-metre swell up the beach in white-crested waves.

Patel remained silent a moment. Eventually, he admitted, "And yet, regardless of the storm, it is, in many ways, a place of peace."

"And danger," Thomas countered. "Great danger." He piloted them into the rescue pod's hangar, gently setting them down. "I think we should bring these people up to date before we take off again. Just in case, you know."

Patel agreed. So far, theirs had been a journey from the known to the known. The next leg would be less certain. They were also unaware that they carried a stowaway from the 16th century with them. Still cloaked and hidden from mortal eyes, the malignant spirit of Robin Rotmütze smiled.

It is a myth that evil breeds in the darkness. It also breeds in the light, its purposes hidden and revealed both in the abstract and the commonplace, its artillery most effective when ranged in plain sight. Evil is constant, *using* structure, never needing it. The emperor's new clothes are its camouflage, rendering it invisible to those unwilling to look. Evil sees all, measures all, though it never stares inwards. Like the classic vampire, it has no reflection. Mostly, it just goes about its business, through the motions of life like everyone and everything else, waiting for alignments, for those special days when it all makes sense.

Heidi removed her clothes and slipped into the shower cubicle. The hot water washed away a fraught several days. For the first time, her bite wounds did not sting. She checked her side and right calf. Two weeks aboard *Factory Pod 4* in 1588 had helped the healing process along. There would be no lasting scars from the raptor attack aboard the *Last Word*. Despite being surrounded by enemies, that fortnight was one of the safest times she had spent since leaving Canaveral – for her, a mere nine months ago.

She closed her eyes and sighed with pleasure as the water ran through her blond hair and soothed knotted muscles in her shoulders. Her plans for 1944 Germany were looking good so far, but they were, after all, merely backup plans. The original Schultz strategy, to colonise the Earth of 100,000BC, had been derailed by the incompetence and cowardice of Geoff Lloyd. Since then, her life had been an endless string of violent compromises – a constant journey of machination and forced reinvention. She was proud of her achievements. Her survival alone had been a battle against the odds. However, with every hand now dealt, she could see where things had gone wrong – all the potholes and pitfalls laid out in hindsight. It was time to fix them.

For months, she had blamed Tim Norris for clouding her judgement, their short time together in the Cretaceous forcing her to reconsider, perhaps even re-evaluate, the true meaning of family. His later betrayal cut deep, still. Nevertheless, an important lesson about trust and weakness had been learned that day, and nothing since had changed her mind – until she witnessed the death of her grandfather. Any distant relatives who still lived were either Douglas' captives or long lost in time. Tim's message about the importance of family replayed in her mind. Her own family were a pit of snakes; Heinrich had eradicated any who thought differently, and yet there was still a bond…

Should she go through with her final option? Reid had been quite specific about avoiding certain time frames – had even refused to assist her in visiting them. His fear of such a paradox was even greater than his fear of her. She now recognised that to have been the first turn of the worm, but now he, too, was gone. She was harnessed to no one.

Heidi was made of much sterner material than her tame lab coat. However, the fact that Reid had absolutely no idea what might happen in such a scenario gave her pause. Yes, it was a last, desperate roll of the dice, but if she won, she would win all.

It was time to decide. Continuity was everything, she could see that now, but trust was important to that continuity. If her plan failed, she would return to 1944 and personally see to the indoctrination of both her own and her grandfather's clones. Yet that was still a plan B.

No. Not enough.

She *would* go through with her primary plan, and return to where it all began, taking with her the one person in the world she could trust absolutely – her own child.

Her mind retraced every step back to the moment where she shot Ben Jansen through the heart. He could have been the one, an excellent specimen, but though he seemed to have survived, she felt it was not to be. In the end, all that truly mattered was the quality of the genetic material. Fortunately, she was in exactly the right place at exactly the right time – assuming Heydrich had spoken truthfully. Ultimately, all such decisions were a leap of faith.

She had summoned Heydrich before getting into the shower, telling him that she was willing to deal for the information her memory drive contained, but there would be a price. She would keep the original device, of course, only allowing him to copy enough to get him hooked, keeping crucial final steps back as security. There was no doubt the temptation would prove irresistible for such a man. Yes, she felt confident she had him on a string for the moment. Doubtless he already awaited her in the next room.

Heidi stepped from the shower, refreshed and ready to begin a new life. She smiled at that, while drying her hair, and the timing could not be more perfect; she could *feel* it.

Staring into the mirror, she could hardly ignore the gifts nature had bestowed. Going through the bathroom cabinet, she found and applied a little make-up. Clearly Heydrich was a man who entertained. She smiled again. The Aphrodisian reflection smiled back. She looked *incredible.* This would be easy.

Perhaps unsurprisingly, the guest suite's bathroom within Reinhard Heydrich's underground citadel was luxurious. Her bare feet sank into the thick pile of a carpet that probably cost more than the average household income.

She stepped from the bathroom into the suite's large, open plan living and sleeping area.

Heydrich was indeed waiting, pouring himself a scotch from the room's small bar, with his back to her. "I have with me several of our most advanced storage drives, so that we may copy the information you promised. They're on the side, over there. I wish to begin our exchange immediately."

"As do I," she answered, alluringly.

He turned slowly, dropping his glass. Heidi's feet were not the only things bared. Yes, all too easy.

Chapter 15 | Lost and Found

The small helicopters were out of fuel. Meritus landed first. He squinted, looking ahead. "What's happening to the wormhole?"

Sure enough, the now-familiar concentric waves flowed across the event horizon towards its centre.

"*Look sharp, everyone!*" Douglas' voice cut across the channel. "*Stay with your vehicles!*"

Before they could even move, white water appeared mid-air, to crash down the hillside. It was more ferocious than any time before, suggesting that the other end of the tunnel through time was at least half under water. A wave smashed around the three remaining armoured personnel carriers, still parked in a row near the mouth of the wormhole.

"*I don't think you should get out of your transport, James,*" Baines called, unhelpfully.

Fortunately, the raging torrent turned sharply downhill, missing their lightweight reconnaissance helicopters, or they might have been smashed to pieces in the shallow but steep-sided ravine below.

Douglas and the drivers of the remaining APCs fought against the sudden floodwaters, their tracks carving the hillside into channels as the water drove them downhill. Luckily for them, the further downhill they slipped, the less forceful the water became. Eventually, they settled for remaining stationary. Like three islands of steel, they waited, as the torrent broke around them.

"*We're no' winning this battle,*" Douglas called across an open channel.

"*Just stay there, all of you,*" Baines replied. "*We'll tow you out when the waters stop.*"

"If they stop!" Douglas retorted. "*We'll have been washed away by then!*"

All their comms binged.

Still seated with Tim, in the rear of their chopper, Baines picked up. "Corporal Thomas? Is that you?"

"*Oh, thank God. Yes, it is. Is that Captain Baines?*"

"Recognised the dulcet tones, huh? Yeah, it's Baines. What's going on, Corporal? We're being flooded out here!"

"*Sorry, ma'am. The mouth of the wormhole's in the middle of a river that's burst its banks, but we think we can solve that. We expected Captain Douglas to be there – is he? These were his last known coordinates.*"

"He's here. Most of us are. Look, it's a long story. Can you come through?"

"*We're hoping to fly our dropship through, ma'am. Are we clear your end?*"

"Yes – all clear."

The *New World* dropship appeared amid the flow, more whitewater rafting than flying. With a blast of fire and noise, Thomas went for altitude, while Reid realigned his wrist device. As previously, the water seemed to break off mid-air and smash to the ground before running away.

Tim Norris climbed out of the helicopter to join Captains Douglas, Baines and Meritus beneath its now-stationary rotors.

Corporal Thomas landed fifty metres west of them, his dropship scorching the heather beneath its side-mounted rocket motors as they twisted and locked into landing positions. Once powered down, the ship's rear hatch opened and three men stepped out.

Sharp-eyed, as always, Tim caught Douglas' elbow. With his other hand, he pointed towards the trio in astonishment. "Captain, look!"

As they drew nearer, Douglas' jaw swung open. "It cannae be?"

Always more expressive, Baines launched herself into the arms of their long-lost friend. "Satnam! Dr Satnam Patel!"

"As opposed to?" Patel answered, voice muffled in Baines' shoulder but grinning ear to ear.

Everyone spoke at once, gabbling excitedly in the pure joy of reunion.

After their initial shock and emotion, Douglas turned from Patel to shake Corporal Thomas' hand. "Ah cannae tell ye how glad Ah am to see ye, laddie."

"Likewise, sir. I thought I was going end up part of the commune for a while there."

"Aye, we'll have to deal with that soon enough, but first things first, who's this with ye?"

Thomas' expression darkened. "I'd better let Dr Patel explain, sir."

Douglas frowned slightly, calling for calm. "Satnam, who's our guest?"

"This is Dr Reid." He took a deep breath – and so did Reid. "Until recently, Dr Reid was Heidi's chief engineer – the man who built the wormhole manifold that has corrupted our continuum."

Douglas glared, but before he could act or react, Patel continued, "Wait, please. Dr Reid tried to prevent Heidi from launching those devices. Moreover, if we are to stand any chance of fixing this, we will need his help, James." Patel looked up at the behemoth behind his friends. He spoke enthusiastically – his attempt to deflect the sudden tension. "I see you have a new ship. My, what an impressive vessel. She looks—"

Douglas pinched the bridge of his nose. "Like a matt black Thunderbird II, Ah know."

Baines smirked.

Patel blinked. "I'm sorry, Captain. I'm not sure I understand the reference. No. I was going to say, she looks powerful."

Baines laughed.

"Anyhow, as I was about to explain," Patel continued, "Heidi found her way back to the *New World,* twice actually, the second time hoping to exploit our manufacturing facilities to retrofit her own ship. She held us to ransom with a nuclear device—"

"She's developed quite an affinity for those, recently," Baines interjected, sourly.

Patel frowned. "I see. Well, Dr Reid took a risk and left her. She winged him for his trouble. Fortunately, Private Tomás Suárez was on hand to dig the bullet out – a change from the musket wounds he has become more familiar with over the years. Dr Reid has already been of some service to us, after Heidi killed several of our people, including…" He tailed off, registering their reaction. "Perhaps a story for another time. Rest assured, we fully corrected a particularly nasty incident and everyone is safe and well in 1588, now."

"Fifteen-*eighty*-eight?" Baines queried. "It was 1559 when we left you, but…" she studied him closely for the first time, "but you haven't aged a day."

"No. *I* haven't. Another story for another time."

"Fine." Douglas held up his hands to stop them getting sidetracked. He glared at Reid. "So why have you brought Heidi's collaborator-in-chief to me?"

Despite attempts at mitigation, Patel's introduction had obviously gone down like a cup of cold sick with everyone, so he cut to the heart of the matter. "He understands the threat better than any of us, James. God knows, we have little enough idea about what we're dealing with. We must accept his assistance."

Douglas' face was taut with anger. "Ah think ye'd better start from the beginning. No. Wait. Before we get into that, we've a couple of men trapped in Cretaceous Patagonia – Ah can only assume it happened because you activated the wormhole from a different location, cutting off their connection."

"We're sorry, sir," Thomas apologised. "We couldn't have known…"

"No need, Corporal. It wasnae your fault, and we're glad to have ye. What Ah'm getting at is that Dr Reid was able to close the connection from Crater Lake." He eyed Reid directly. "If ye've some control over these abominations ye've unleashed, can ye no' take us to our friends?"

"Possibly," Reid allowed, cautiously. "If you have the correct space–time coordinates. Do you know which part of Patagonia and when, exactly?"

"You mean there's more than one in that area?" Douglas asked, furiously.

"Three hundred worldwide, Captain."

"Why, you…"

"James," Baines cut in, before her husband fully erupted. "We believe they're marooned near the wreckage of the *Last Word,* but as you can see from the battle damage, we're in no position to take the *New World* anywhere just yet."

They all turned to Reid.

"In that case, I believe I can take you to them. If the information you've given me is correct."

"Then get to it," Douglas ordered, gruffly.

Patel believed that Reid's desire to repair what he had set loose upon the world was genuine; nevertheless, he wore the wormhole wrist device himself – just in case Heidi's right-hand man felt tempted to take his leave of them. He held out his arm for Reid to work it.

Numbers scrolled across its tiny screen. "See here?" He spoke to Patel. "We can see the last time a wormhole was activated to those coordinates from the wormhole we have here. I will open the wormhole immediately after—"

"No," Tim interrupted.

Everyone looked at him to explain.

"They should be quite safe for a time, inside one of our APCs. If we open the wormhole where we left off, so to speak, then those mapusaurs might run straight back here again. I'd rather avoid that – especially while we're standing out here, lined up like a buffet."

"Good point, laddie." Douglas winked. He turned to Reid. "Give it an hour."

Reid nodded, returning to the device strapped to Patel's wrist. Within moments, ripples crossed the event horizon, working their way inwards to the centre once more before disappearing.

"I think that's it."

Douglas stared balefully at him. "You *think?*"

Reid shrugged. "Occasionally, they take you somewhere you don't expect. Once, Heidi and I programmed a wormhole to the Egyptian desert in 2122."

"And where did ye end up?"

"The Middle Ages. England, I think."

Douglas sighed, pinching the bridge of his nose again. "Jill, send a comm message. Let's see if anyone's listening."

She complied and almost immediately a signal came back. Her expression darkened.

"What is it?" Douglas demanded.

Baines looked sick. "We have a voice link, but my German's not great."

Douglas was taken aback. "German?"

She nodded. "I think we may have another crossed line."

They all turned to Reid again.

He backed away. "Let me work on it. Please!"

Baines pulled her husband aside. "Assuming Sergeant Prentice got to Commander Gleeson, what supplies do they have?"

"The chopper carries emergency long-life rations and basic supplies for two, the APC, for ten," he answered, immediately.

"But for how long?"

"Fourteen days."

Baines nodded. "OK, that's good. So they won't go hungry while we search for them. Two men could stretch those rations for months, if they had to. And, like Tim said, they'll be safe enough within their armoured transport."

Douglas was less sure. "Aye, but you're assuming they're no' injured. Gleeson was out of fuel – anything might have happened. Leaving it an hour was prudence for all our sakes, but *months?*"

"Then we'll just have to hope they made it and they're safe for now, at least," Baines argued. "What choice do we have? Hiro's got everybody working round the clock to fix the ship. That's all we can do." She turned back to the group. "I'm concerned about what actually happened to our connection. The wormhole jumped who knows where, which suggests to me that someone might be tinkering with the system again. Dr Reid, what do you say?"

He looked uncomfortable. "Not necessarily. There may be glitches in the device's navigational system. After you attacked our factories in Cretaceous Egypt, Captain Baines, Heidi launched the devices from orbit without a single live test."

Baines rounded on him. "You're saying it was *my* fault? Why the hell didn't you try to stop her?"

"I'm not saying that, and as Dr Patel already explained to you, I did – she knocked me out! My surprise was that I woke up at all, after defying her – but as it happened, she still needed me."

Baines' eyes narrowed.

Reid continued nervously. "She stole an alien device from Area 51 – had a crazy idea about installing an antigravity engine to our attack ship—"

Baines exploded. "So that's what it was all about! You used *our* ship to carry out a heist on one of America's most famous 'secret' military facilities!"

"But if we only understood the technology. Antigravity is…" Reid tailed off under her blowtorch glare. "I programmed her ship to explode. Do I get points for that, at least?"

Baines closed her mouth, scrutinising the lab coat. "Go on."

Reid shrugged. "She held the ship's self-destruct over the heads of your people in 1588. I programmed it to restart its countdown once she was far away. She may even be dead by now."

"Aye, and Ah'm Robert the Bruce," Douglas scoffed.

Reid leaned into Patel. "I thought you called him James?"

"Ah mean, we've thought she was dead before. The woman's a damned cockroach!"

Patel remained pensive during the confrontation.

"What is it, Satnam?" Baines asked, more calmly.

"Gravity, Jill. From what little we understand, the wormholes are affected by three things, all linked – the extreme energy generated by our planet's core, magnetism, and gravity... just a thought."

Douglas shook his head. "Ah'd like you to come up with a way to get our men back before we consider any broader issues, Satnam. Gleeson and Prentice are out there somewhere, and we can only guess at their condition. Ah'll have Hiro assign you a workspace." He pointed at Reid. "Take him with you."

He turned to leave when Baines called him back. "But, James, what about the Germans? Should we try to make contact?"

"Oh, aye, and say what? Hello from the Iron Age? No." He nodded to the wormhole. "Unless someone falls through that damned thing, we'd better leave those people alone. We've interfered enough as it is."

"James, wait. What about Bubi? Leutnant Eric Hartmann?"

Douglas stopped in his tracks, his shoulders slumping. "Crap!"

More recently known as Redcap, the dark spirit of Robin Rotmütze watched and listened with interest. His power was diminished in this time, though it was still a force. There were enough human souls living in terror for their lives, from portents, predators and their neighbours, to feed his needs. He used the intense spiritual energy of the 16th century like an engine, but it was also a drug, and like all users, he craved a bigger, better hit. Travelling through open wormholes offered all manner of potential rewards. He was glad he had hitched a ride with Thomas and planned to explore his good fortune by finding out how to use them.

***

On the 'other side'…
In 1940s Germany, Engel's arm shot out towards the television. "Wait! Lieutenant, hit the pause!"

Sonne complied.

"What is it, Corporal?" asked Colonel Schultz.

"Look there, sir. See that woman? The one in uniform. Are those the pips of a major she's wearing?"

"Yes." Schultz leaned forward. "Zoom in, Lieutenant. Oh, my God, it's her! But how?"

Engel was shaking his head. "We must stop her, sir."

"Care to share?" asked Bessel. "Hey, wait a minute. I've seen her before – back in dino world!" He stared at the woman on the screen and then turned to H. "Whoa – that's you!"

H was unimpressed by his suggestion. "A lot of people have made that mistake, Captain. I can assure you that it is not!"

He groaned. "Douglas told me about this. She was an officer aboard his ship, right – the original *New World,* in the original timeline – a doctor, yeah?"

"More than that, Captain," Colonel Schultz explained. "She is my fourth-great-granddaughter."

"Fourth? You have *four* great-granddaughters? But you don't look a day over… erm, you look great," he finished, weakly.

"No, Captain. Fourth, as in great, great, great, great. She will not be born for another century and a half."

Bessel's jaw dropped in bafflement.

"With respect," Engel interjected, "that sounds like a long story, and we don't have time for explanations, sirs. We must *do* something."

"Again, the corporal is right," agreed Hans Schultz.

"But what?" Bessel threw it out to the room.

"As long as my name is not completely sullied, yet, I might still be able to call in a few favours and organise some transport," Schultz suggested. "We must move quickly. According to these news feeds, your shuttle is still on *Neuhauser Straße,* outside the ruins of the Old Academy."

"You're suggesting we take it?"

Schultz nodded. "Clearly, *Evil Heidi…*" He glanced at the sister he loathed, checking the comparison.

H crossed her arms and glared back at him.

He tried again. "The *other* Heidi obviously survived that massive explosion and the destruction of her ship. The only reason she would have returned to Munich and the wreckage of the Old Academy is to access the wormhole site, surely?"

"That makes sense," Bessel agreed, "but this footage is probably an hour old, at least. Maybe more. She may have gone through by now."

Colonel Schultz had many friends. Within the hour, a military helicopter met him and the others at a crossroads, five miles from their hideout in the Chiemgau Alps.

Bessel, now dressed in a German captain's uniform, was ready to go.

"I'm staying," Badawi announced.

Bessel turned on his heel. "*What?*"

Badawi looked down into H's eyes and took her hand. "Did you ever consider that some things might simply be destined, Captain? The circumstances that brought H and myself together the first time were outside a lottery win – I would not even know how to describe the odds of it happening twice. Besides, something is going on here. Heidi may or may not have left, but she was up to something. Whatever it was must be stopped, or the future in which we grew may cease to be. I owe it to my friends and colleagues – everyone I ever knew – to prevent that."

"If Heidi has *anything* to do with it," Engel joined the conversation, "whatever she did will be huge, far reaching and completely despicable. I'm staying, too. I may not belong here, but neither do I really belong with Douglas' people, either. There's a war to be fought in the here and now, Captain, and my knowledge of Heidi and the original timeline might be invaluable." He extended a hand.

Bessel shook it and returned to Badawi. "Well, you're hardly my prisoner any more, Master Sergeant. I've no direct authority over either of you, so I'll just wish you luck." Such a short time they had known each other, but what a ride it had been. They embraced and Bessel repeated, "Good luck, Apep."

"Thank you, Arnold. God go with you, my friend. And thank you for believing me."

Bessel snorted softly, looking around at the world of an earlier century, long before he was born. "Your evidence was compelling!" He took in Badawi and H by his side. Like her fourth-great-grandniece, she was uncommonly beautiful. He winked. "Godspeed, young man. And goodbye, all of you." He shook hands briefly with Brandt, Todt and Sonne before embarking with the colonel, bound for Munich.

Back at her lodge in the hills, H worked frantically at a terminal. Badawi looked over her shoulder. "You're moving money around?"

"Yes." She sighed. "Thanks to my brother's progeny, it looks like my old life is over – at least for now. I knew he would ruin everything for me."

"I think you're being a little unfair, blaming him for what his descendants technically have not even done yet."

She sighed and sat back. "I know. I am just…"

He gently stroked her hair. "I understand. I am sorry all this has happened to you."

She turned a dazzling smile on him. "I met you, so it is not all bad, I think. I am happy for our reunion, Apep."

"Perhaps your reunion with your brother should also be given a little time and care," he suggested.

She sighed again. "My brother…" She straightened. "If he intends to go after Reinhard Heydrich, we will need a lot of money, a great deal of luck and a very good plan."

"I will let you work." Badawi kissed the top of her head and joined the men in the sitting room. They would indeed need a good plan, one that might prove to be their life's work. He could only hope that would be as long as it sounded, for there could be few things more dangerous for everyone than messing around with history.

⁂

Heidi mingled – just another German officer in combat fatigues. No one questioned her right to be there. She had the build of a lithe soldier and looked every inch the major she purported to be. Most of the military personnel saluted her without question. A whole army of construction workers, both military and civilian, crawled all over the wreckage that was the Old Academy. There was no obvious sign of the wormhole, but she knew it was there. At least, she knew it was *potentially* there, under the rubble.

Unsure whether it would give away any obvious signs of its presence, Heidi erred on the side of caution and reactivated it from a distance, transmitting new coordinates surreptitiously. The last thing she needed was to be drawn into the centre of everyone's attention. Now it was just a matter of waiting patiently, until the rescue teams, builders and combat engineers were elsewhere, before moving in.

As she understood it, Reid's theory suggested that their original wormhole – created to link Cretaceous Egypt with Munich – had left what he described as a permanent weakness in space–time at both locations. Although that wormhole had been closed when the *Newfoundland* dragged it into space, breaking its connection with the power of the Earth's core, Reid prophesied the effects of that weakness would become more prevalent – particularly if the problem was exacerbated by the creation of further wormholes at the same location. On the flip side, the weakness of that fixed point made it the *ideal* place to create further wormholes – especially for anyone indifferent to the risks or ramifications.

Using her own wrist device, she zeroed in on the exact spot where her ship had broken through the rubble the previous day. The passage of her ship, and then Bessel's – not to mention a fully adult Carcharodontosaurus – had left a perilous-looking overhang among the ruins.

Impatiently, she waited for the area to clear, going through the motions as she pretended to investigate the rubble for evidence or survivors. She found a shoe, sticking out from under a pile of broken masonry. More than that, she had found a body. Glancing around surreptitiously, she moved a few stones to rebury it. Avoiding scrutiny was essential. It mattered nothing to her whether the victim still lived or not.

Eventually, the search teams moved on to another section, and she moved in. Although risky, it was possible to step inside, beneath the rickety overhang that hid the wormhole. The precarious cover in no way resembled any part of the beautiful building they had destroyed, but it allowed her a few moments' privacy from the workers – and more importantly, from the cameras. Making one last check for prying eyes, she examined her wrist device. It was difficult to see it in the shadows, but the wormhole was there and, assuming everything was working properly, now led to her chosen destination.

The dangerously stacked rubble above her began to tremble. By climbing in, she must have dislodged something. Smaller pieces of masonry and building material started to fall. Quickly, she stepped through as the whole structure collapsed behind, hiding all evidence of her departure.

The sharp smell of lime plaster, cement, brick and stone dust vanished instantly. Heidi took a deep breath of air that was fresh and sweet – though her new location, chosen for its relative safety, was less comforting than it might have been.

It was dark. She had arrived at night. That was unfortunate, but many of their wormholes led to far worse places, so she accepted it stoically. When Reid detonated the nuclear device aboard her ship, he left her without transport, limiting her options. She could have asked Heydrich for a suitable combat ship, but it would have taken time to organise. Besides, a stealth approach suited her purposes on this occasion, so she had contented herself with palming several smaller gadgets from his personal collection of lethal toys instead. She knew her enemies had visited this place previously and suspected they might be there still. A firefight would ruin everything.

A cool, gentle breeze kissed her cheeks while her eyes adjusted to the darkness. The moon resembled a balled-up tissue, hanging damply from a sky heavy with cloud. It would rain soon. There were no stars and very little light, so she sensed, as much as saw, the *vastness* before her. Something huge dominated the landscape. She frowned. Whatever it was, was unnaturally black – even at night. The last time she passed through that place, there had been no cliffs nor peaks to speak of. She rummaged in her backpack and withdrew a pair of night-vision goggles. Settling them onto her face, she activated them and almost stepped back through the wormhole in surprise. The edifice blocking her view of the hilltops ahead was the UNS *New World.*

Prowling the corridors of the *New World,* Robin Rotmütze sensed Heidi's arrival immediately. She fell into his perception like an obsidian ball onto a taut blanket, hard and dark. Her presence there could only mean trouble for Douglas' *gang,* and he was only too happy to assist.

It was an old habit, for he had no flesh in the material world – let alone a face – yet he smiled as he left the ship to meet her. More than ever, he recognised Heidi as an agent of chaos, and Redcap *was* chaos. Outside, he watched her don the night-vision goggles. She could not see him, of course. Few could.

Of those few was medium Beck Mawar. Still aboard the ship, neither she nor any of her spirit sidekicks had yet discovered his presence. Redcap had spent years learning how to shield himself from sensitives, and Mawar was the most powerful he had ever met. Remaining hidden from her was a benchmark of success for him, but now he had a new project, it seemed.

He studied Heidi closely, waiting in anticipation to see what she might do next.

***

"We must be quick." Colonel Hans Schultz marched Bessel along a floodlit *Neuhauser Straße*. The daylight was failing, but the activity on site showed no signs of abating, nor even slowing.

Bessel's small shuttle was where he had left it, cordoned off like a crime scene. It gleamed white under the powerful lights. Schultz hid them behind a lorry. "It is probably best you wait here. I will reconnoitre, to see if the wormhole is still in place."

"Surely someone would have found it, if it were."

"Not necessarily. It may be buried. Also, we are the only ones who suspect it may still even *be* there. Those of us in the know hoped the explosion that destroyed the building also collapsed the portal."

"True," Bessel acknowledged. "But if it is there, and this plan doesn't work, I might end up… well, *anywhere*."

Schultz frowned with concern. "You do not have to do this, Captain. The risks are—"

Bessel raised his hand with a smile. "Please, no need to spell it out for me."

"I wish I could come with you."

"Thank you, Colonel, but it looks like you'll have your hands full here. If Heidi's even half as bad as I've heard…" He shook his head. "You guys are the only people on this planet who know that something bad might be coming down the track. If I fail and can't get back, then who'll stop it, if not you?"

Schultz nodded. They were military men. They knew the risks and accepted them. He pressed a sidearm into Bessel's hand and tucked four spare clips into his combat jacket pockets. "Do what is necessary, Captain. If the wormhole is still there, I will send a message on this device." He placed a mobile phone into Bessel's other hand. "See those men over there? The ones who guard your ship? I will tell them to expect a Captain Bessel, directly, and that you will fly the shuttle to Neubiberg Air Base. Do you have any German?"

Bessel winced. "*Ja und nein?*" he offered apologetically.

Schultz shrugged. "Hopefully, your name will be enough." He smiled. "Once you hear from me, make your move. Do not hesitate. Good luck."

Bessel tucked the pistol and the phone into his jacket. "To us all. I hope to see you soon, but if I don't… thank you."

They shook hands and parted.

<hr>

Back in the *New World*'s captain's quarters, Douglas landed on the sofa, completely exhausted.

Baines placed a hot drink before him and walked around the back to rub his neck and shoulders. He groaned pleasurably. "Been a hell of a day again," she stated, tiredly.

"Just tell me it's over," he muttered softly. "We got the dinosaurs home and Thomas, and even Satnam, back – an unbelievable stroke of luck. Ah'll take it."

She smiled. "All true, but our day's not completely over. Not yet."

She felt the tension return to his shoulders. "What now? Problems getting Leutnant Hartmann home? Did the wormhole not go his way?"

"No, it's OK. *Relax,*" she urged him, soothingly. "As a matter of fact, he asked to stay on – now we've the means to return him, without half a kilometre of spaceship suddenly appearing in the sky above one of their cities. He told me that, what with so much at stake, he'd rather see it through."

Douglas nodded approvingly. "A brave young man. He's certainly one hell of a pilot. So why's ma day no' over, then?"

"Firstly, how's Tobias? He couldn't have been happy to hear about the bodies of his fallen comrades being washed away by the flood from Crater Lake."

"Ah told Meritus they'd been washed down the bank of the escarpment to the *Last Word* below, when the wormhole diverted. Even after ten years, he still carries the guilt. He feels that he failed his crew. Ah wouldnae be able to forgive maself, either."

Baines walked back around the sofa to sit opposite her husband. She bowed her head in silence.

"It was no' your fault, either, lassie. You saved our people when you destroyed the *Last Word*. It was war."

She nodded, slowly. "What did he say?"

Douglas shrugged. "Not much, really. Ah tried to suggest that they're all resting now, together, but it was a platitude and we both knew it."

"We'll still try to recover them, though?"

"Aye. If there's any way at all. Ah gave him ma word on it. But first things first, we need to focus on the living."

"Hmm." Baines appeared nonplussed.

Douglas held her with a piercing blue stare. "Now Ah find out why ma day's no' over, right?"

"Well, while we're talking about the living, it seems Aito Nassaki has been plotting with Dr Anne Hemmings – Schultz's *other* evil scientist – telling her all about Heidi's wormholes."

"Plotting?"

"Perhaps that was too strong. Soliciting her help, at least."

"Where was Hiro while this was happening?"

"On station, in case Sandy needed him. He had no idea Aito intended to meet with Hemmings."

"Ah dinnae doubt it, but it illustrates the problem we have with regards to his relationship with his wee brother, doesn't it?"

"Hmm." Again, Baines was pensive. "I wonder."

"Wonder what?"

"Whether Aito might not actually be right about this one. At least, partially."

Douglas slumped, head in hands, sighing deeply. "Which reminds me, Ah still need to have that wee chat with Dr Hemmings ye promised when ye captured her. About how her…" He faltered. "About how her daughter, Lieutenant Elizabeth Hemmings, died."

Baines' brow furrowed. "Another casualty of the mess I caused when I sent the *Last Word* down that hill. It was a lot easier when they were just the enemy. Now I…"

He got to his feet and walked around the coffee table. Sitting next to his wife, he took her in his arms. "All of this is on the Schultzes, not you, ma love. And Tobias knows it. Ah'll make sure Hemmings understands, too. God knows what Heidi told her."

"That you killed her daughter."

He stiffened.

"Don't take it too hard, James. It was no more your fault than mine, or any of ours. We were all dragged into the schemes of Heinrich Schultz. I think she knows that, too. She's no fool. I sensed that she didn't believe Heidi. At least, she suspects there may have been nuance."

"Wise," he acknowledged, quietly. "Now, why do you think Aito might be right to involve her, behind his brother's back?"

Baines considered, ordering her thoughts, and they sat in silence for a while, just holding on to each other. When the red alert sounded across the whole ship, they both jumped out of their seats.

"For the love of… What now?" Douglas cried, opening a channel to the bridge. "Sandy?"

"*On a rest cycle, sir. It's Hiro.*"

"What's happening, Chief?"

"*A shuttle has just come through the wormhole, Captain. We're being hailed— Whoa! That, I did not expect.*"

"What is it? Never mind, Ah'm on ma way!"

Douglas and Baines left their quarters on the run.

Outside in the deepening night, Heidi was knocked to the ground. Something large, and fortunately blunt, struck her in the small of the back. She rolled to the side instinctually, coming back to a crouch, astounded by what she saw.

The small shuttlecraft that followed her to Germany from Egypt, via the Cretaceous, now extruded from the wormhole – the UNASA logo emblazoned along its side clearly marking it as from the altered future. She had flown alongside it, during those fleeting moments in Cretaceous North Africa, intending to strand its occupants in the deep past. Having glimpsed Master Sergeant Badawi and, even more incredibly, Captain Arnold Bessel, or at least *a* Captain Bessel – the one she had known captained the USS *Newfoundland* and was long dead – she could only assume it was them again.

Bessel was alone this time, but as he crept forward, he heard and felt a small bump through his starboard bow. He craned to look out.

It was entirely likely that he would have missed Heidi in the darkness, but Robin Rotmütze instantly moved to shield her from sight, nonetheless – another trick learned over the last thirty years.

Bessel saw only blackness. Though, even under the cloudy night sky, it had an unnatural quality. He activated a night-vision camera, just to be sure, but received only a screenful of white noise. He frowned, then shrugged it off. The little craft had been through a lot, after all, and who knew how wormhole travel might have affected its electronics.

The ship continued forward, but for Heidi there was no time to ponder, either. Staying low and acting immediately, she reprogrammed the wormhole for her next destination the moment Bessel's ship reintegrated fully into real space.

As soon as her wrist device signalled the portal was ready, she dove through, hoping she remained undetected.

Rotmütze felt a thrill of excitement and made to follow, only to be shoved back. He tried again, but the wormhole was completely blocked to him. Unnerved, he summoned all his power for a third attempt, but it was no good. Was he trapped there? Dread seized him, for despite the psychic force at his disposal, fear is the constant companion for those who seek to make others afraid, so he fell back on anger. Furious, he returned to the ship. Clearly wormhole travel was a more dangerous toy than he had bargained for.

Douglas and Baines arrived on the bridge in under a minute. "OK, Hiro, what's going on?" Douglas demanded breathlessly.

"You made good time, sir. We have a visitor."

On the screen was a man in military fatigues. Douglas did not recognise the uniform, but he certainly recognised the man. "Arnold!" He felt faint, weak at the knees.

Baines helped him into his captain's chair. "Arnold?" She could barely believe it, either. "How…?"

Bessel grinned broadly. "Permission to come aboard, Captain?"

<hr>

The *Last Word* plateau, mid–Cretaceous Patagonia
Heidi rolled through the wormhole alone, coming to her feet in an instant. As before, it was dark. Unlucky again, but at least this time there was a bright moon and a sky full of stars. She span round, scanning her surroundings and recognising them instantly. So far, so good, but then she spotted something that did *not* belong.

"They're obviously having trouble renewing the connection," Gleeson rationalised, downplaying his concerns.

Prentice merely nodded, happy to play along. He, too, knew they were in trouble. Until the *New World* was fixed, they were stranded, barring interventions. They had no idea that Drs Patel and Reid were working to make a connection aboard their ship in Iron Age Britain.

They were also unaware that a third person stood outside their protective steel hull, while they considered the situation.

Completely confounded, Heidi realised that Douglas' people were one step ahead of her again. Incredibly, a tracked personnel carrier sat bathed in moonlight on the *Last Word*'s plateau, and next to it was, of all things, a helicopter. The temptation to larceny was almost unbearable. She deliberated, unaware that the chopper was already out of fuel.

Ahead lay a trek through many kilometres of jungle, filled with some of the deadliest predators ever to have lived. She had made that journey before, more than once, and most unpleasant were the memories, so taking the easy option was extremely appealing to her.

Mildly exasperated, she shook her head, no. Assuming she escaped Bessel undetected, it would not pay to give herself away now. If Douglas got wind of her purposes here, it might ruin everything – and not just for her. She looked up into the celestial majesty of the starry night and sighed. If *her* stars were aligned, she might soon be carrying a child. Counterintuitively, this was no time to become risk averse. It was certainly no time to become sloppy. She wanted her second chance – a chance to put everything right – and so, she tightened the straps on her backpack, hid a small transmitter within a hollow of a nearby tree trunk, and stalked off towards the treeline.

As she passed by the wormhole, Heidi noted something, invisible by the light of day – reflections. She paused for a moment, lost in the wonder of wormholes and a natural universe that somehow tolerated them. Rather than the almost invisible, minute distortions she was used to seeing hanging in the air, the darkness at both ends of the tunnel through space–time made it possible to see moving reflections within the quantum foam that gave the wormhole its structure. Heidi was momentarily entranced. If she had to guess, she would say that Douglas' people were moving about on the other side, lighting up the whole area around their ship – probably due to the arrival of the shuttle that recently hit her from behind. Although no discernible image could be made out, lights came from several sources and appeared to swim across her field of vision. Unlike the view through a traditional tunnel, the appearance was more akin to light bouncing and rebounding off the interior surfaces of a liquid bubble. It was bewitching, and brought into sharp relief that she knew almost nothing about such miracles that, until now, at least, were becoming almost commonplace for her.

A rustle and a low growl across the plateau brought her back to her senses and her purpose there. With one final, wistful glance at the magic before her, she vanished into the jungle.

After the reunion with one of his best friends in any timeline, Douglas caught his second wind. Assigning quarters to Captain Arnold Bessel, he engaged him in a jovial catch-up before checking in on another long-lost friend, also returned to him that day.

Entering engineering, he made his way to the office Hiro had allocated to their old crewmate, Dr Satnam Patel, who, at Douglas' behest, was working late. He was about to knock when the door slid open automatically – his chief engineer programmed all doors on the engineering decks that way. It saved time, and also saved him from having to remember to be courteous. Douglas stepped into the room. "It's getting late, gentlemen. Have ye worked out what went wrong with our connection to the *Last Word* plateau?" he asked Patel and Reid.

"I can't find *anything* wrong, Captain," Reid replied. He was tired and obviously exasperated.

Patel shrugged. "I do not understand it either, James. Based on what Dr Reid has explained about the workings of the device, it should have worked. We are, of course, well aware that Captain Bessel came through from Germany, but that was many hours after we tried to contact Commander Gleeson at the *Last Word* plateau. The timing doesn't add up. Unless..."

Douglas frowned. "Unless?"

Patel stroked his chin, considering. "Unless someone else coincidentally opened the wormhole from Germany, much earlier."

"Coincidentally?" Douglas queried again, doubtfully.

Patel shrugged. "From Captain Bessel, we now know your suspicions were correct, and that Heidi still lives. He saw her near the wormhole and followed as quickly as possible on her heels, but suppose she opened the wormhole hours before finally stepping through."

"Why?"

"There you have me, James, but were I to guess, I would say she might have been biding her time to slip through unseen? I suggest the most important question is, where is she now? Bessel should have virtually run her over."

"Aye. Ah've been wondering the same thing. She's slipperier than an eel in a bathtub full of axle grease." He shook his head, trying to think, tiredness creeping up on him once more. "So you're suggesting that these wormholes can, what, give an *engaged* tone, maybe?"

Reid reflected for a moment. "You're suggesting a scenario where we're trying to pass, or send a signal, through the wormhole, while someone else is trying to come through to *us* from a third location? Hmm... That's not impossible."

"The double negative meaning it's possible," Douglas retorted.

Reid sighed. "Captain Douglas, I can understand why you have a strong dislike for me. I don't blame you, under the circumstances, but please believe me when I tell you that I was in no way ready to launch this system. I'm not even sure it's complete. As I told you already, it was certainly never tested. Used properly, the devices should create a stable manifold, allowing travel through time and space. It was not *I* who chose to launch it half-cocked and use it for evil!"

"You knew who you were working for!" Douglas countered, angrily.

Patel moved between them. "We are all tired, gentlemen. If Captain Douglas' 'engaged' theory carries water, then perhaps my idea is also correct. That said, we should simply try to reconnect with Commander Gleeson's location again in the morning."

"The hell we will," Douglas snapped. "If you think your idea might work, we'll damned well go outside now, and Dr Reid can try it. Ah've two good men in extreme danger, lost a hundred million years ago – sleep can wait!"

Good as his word, Douglas marched them out to the wormhole with a security detail. He ordered the three remaining armoured personnel carriers moved, to create a box at the mouth of the wormhole. The vehicles' spotlights floodlit the area. Armed men and women kept vigil in the spaces between the APCs as Douglas stood in the centre with the scientists.

Patel raised his arm and the wrist device for Reid to work the controls, when he stopped suddenly. "I do not understand."

"What is it?" asked Reid and Douglas together.

"According to Dr Reid's device, the wormhole is already connected to the last known location of Commander Gleeson and Sergeant Prentice, in Cretaceous Patagonia. It certainly does not lead to Germany – not in *any* time." He turned to Douglas. "Captain, I suggest you—"

"Ah'm already on it." Douglas produced his comm from a pocket and opened a channel. The technology fired an analogue signal at the wormhole. "Commander Gleeson, Sergeant Prentice, this is Captain Douglas. Gleeson and Prentice, come in – over."

"*Bladdy 'ell, you beauty! Are we glad to hear from you, mate!*"

Relief spread across Douglas' face in a weary smile. "Commander, thank God. Are ye both safe?"

"*As houses, Captain, thanks to Adam coming through to save my bacon. I'd have been stuck out here like a galah, otherwise. I managed to put down without carking my bird, but I'm out of petty, and a hundred million years from a servo. Can you render assistance? Over."*

"Servo? Petty?"

"Service station. Petrol. Fuel. Y'know? Over."

"In a manner of speaking, aye – over." Douglas nodded to Sergeant Jackson. "Ah'm reasonably certain he's asking for a fuel truck. Make it happen, Sarge."

"Yessir."

He reopened the channel. "Douglas to Gleeson. Ah'll send a convoy with fuel as soon as we can unload one from the ship. In the meantime, get yourselves back here, just in case we lose the connection again. And come through carefully, Commander, dinnae charge it – we've boxed off the wormhole – over."

"Understood, Captain. We're on our way – over and out!"

The next day dawned over a hive of activity. Work crews moved through the UNS *New World,* fixing battle damage and refitting compromised systems within the main computer, and they did so with renewed vigour. Weber's help, though grudging and limited, had provided Hiro with the head start he needed to get his bearings. The addition of Dr Patel to his team was a massive bonus. Astrophysicist and polymath, Patel was highly tech savvy. Originally hired to oversee the building and maintenance of atmosphere-altering machinery on Mars, he was as at home with a spanner as he was at the delicate controls of infrared astronomical equipment.

Patel worked with a small team of engineers from both the original *New World* and *Last Word.* He also worked under the close scrutiny of The Sarge, not because he was under any suspicion, but because he had pressed Dr Reid into service at his side. Douglas accepted the argument that Reid's help would be invaluable, but that was a long way from trusting the man.

"This ship has some impressive technology, Dr Patel," Reid noted.

Patel was forced to agree. "It has. Some of which, I confess, is beyond me – for the moment, at least."

Alongside them, Georgio Baccini worked to bring them up to speed, explaining divergences between their new technology and that aboard the original *New World*. As Hiro and Georgio were heavily involved with the new ship's development, many of the changes were handy shortcuts and improvements. Repairs would likely take some weeks, so Patel was determined to learn all he could.

"How were the others?" Georgio asked, referring to those they left behind in Tudor England.

"They seem to have adapted to their new lives well over the years. Their morale is understandably low, but that has not diverted them from their task. The real surprise – for me, at least – was Geoff Lloyd's contribution. If the alternative future you have witnessed in the 22nd century is to be, or to continue, then it will in no small part be down to him."

Georgio smiled. "I long ago forgave him for my brother's death. I know it was what Mario wanted. He also saved my life from that dinosaur, the one that almost killed him. It might have been me who went over into that ravine and the forest below." His gaze lost focus as he stared into the past. "Mario knew. He saw it all." He sighed. "Seems so long ago now."

Patel understood, though for him, it had been just a few months. "I believe we should go back."

Georgio refocused on Patel. "To where?"

"To our friends in the 16th century. I believe it would give them hope and bolster their belief in what they are doing. There is also the matter of the antigravity drive Heidi stole from Area 51."

"You think you can use it to manipulate wormholes?"

Patel was impressed. "Indeed, Georgio. At the very least, it belongs in a secure facility in the 22nd century. Our friends have made progress, but that time and place should not be exposed to such things for many centuries. On that, I have *not* changed my mind."

"I know it's been a while, but I don't remember the people of that time as *all* bad," Georgio argued.

"That is because you never met Captain Fear-God Barebone! He believed we were all devils! No. That alien technology, if such it is, has no place in our past, but it may just save our future."

⁓❦⁓

Tim and Clarrie entered UNS *New World*'s main hangar. Several hatches, of various sizes, led to smaller adjacent holds. They headed for a heavy steel hatch labelled '3B'. Unlocked, the hatch slid to the side as Tim pressed the open stud. Once inside, they faced an array of purpose-built animal enclosures. Their new ship was expressly designed to return them to the Cretaceous, so they could find and capture all remaining Schultz personnel – thus preventing any further interference with the timeline. However, experience told Douglas and his engineers that they might have to rehome other creatures, too – even house stowaways.

Mayor lived in one of the large pens. Near the outer hull of the ship, the animal bay benefitted from natural daylight via several portholes. Each was circular for strength and bathed the pens in morning sunshine. Natalie doted on the little dinosaur, exercising him daily with Reiver, though he was not allowed off the ship in case he bolted and was lost. Despite the earliness of the hour, she was there already, mucking out Belle the cow.

"Hey, Natalie," Clarrie greeted.

Natalie leaned on her muck shovel and blew a stray hair out of her face. She smiled warmly. "Hi, guys."

"How's our new recruit?" Tim asked, walking over to pat Belle gently, on the nose.

"She's very underweight, but Thomas and I have been bringing her loads of fresh grass to eat – one of the benefits when crashing in Iron Age Britain."

"Thomas Beckett?" asked Tim, sceptically.

Natalie laughed. "I know. The library loafer, helping out on the farm – who could have seen that one coming?" She winked. "I think he just wanted an excuse to use his new barrow. Look."

Behind her, leaning against the wall of one of the enclosures, there was indeed a wheelbarrow adorned with the name 'BECKETT' hand painted in block capitals along its side.

Clarrie laughed, too. "Guess he doesn't wanna lose this one, huh?"

Tim brought them back to the purpose for their visit. "Actually, Belle's the reason we're here."

"Don't worry, Tim, she's OK," Natalie assured him, brightly. "I'll make sure she's fattened up again."

"For now," Tim added, darkly. "There's talk about us going back – a long way back – to fix all this."

She frowned. "The wormholes?"

He nodded. Seeing the bond Natalie had already formed with the cow, he spoke with reticence. "So I, that is, *we* thought that, well, perhaps… I mean…"

"We think Belle might be better off here," Clarrie stated for him.

"That's what I was trying to say," Tim agreed, relieved. "They may not have any Jerseys yet, and certainly not up here, but at least she could live with other cows – or perhaps even live with the villagers Captain Douglas has befriended? They have a beautiful and entirely appropriate environment for her."

Natalie considered. "A long way back, you say?"

Tim nodded again. "Well before grass. It's nothing short of a miracle she survived for months in the Cretaceous – the diet being the least of her worries. If she hadn't tagged along with those sauropods, she'd never have made it in that time and place."

Natalie regarded Belle sadly. "I'll miss her."

"We all will." Clarrie moved in to tousle Belle's ears. "Especially after how she came into our lives, on our wedding day. We'll never forget you, girl."

"It's for the best." Tim laid a comforting hand on her arm.

"Besides, the excellent milk she'll provide, when she's breeding fit again, will be of great benefit to the tribe on Yeavering Bell. A fittingly named place to leave her, don't you think?" He smiled.

Natalie smiled back. Though there were tears in her eyes, she knew Tim was right, and that the animal's welfare must come before her own attachment.

With so much to do, it proved a long day for everyone. Nevertheless, late that afternoon, Douglas listened courteously to Patel's arguments. "And ye think paying our old shipmates a visit will help?" he asked, gently. "What if they decide they want to leave with us? We cannae allow that, Satnam. Do ye no' think we'd just be reopening a wound?"

"I have considered that carefully, Captain, but once the decision was made to effect changes in the timeline, beginning in Tudor England, it became a question of making the best job of it we could. I have no idea whether I was even intended to stay there – or in which period, 1559 or 1588. Everything has become confused. I can only suggest that, knowing what we know now, we offer any and all assistance we can from 1588 onwards. Who knows, perhaps we were meant to. It is impossible to know any more. The only thing about which I *am* sure is that our friends need us, and miss us desperately."

Douglas sighed. "Aye, and we miss them, but Ah'm still no' sure about further interference, Satnam."

"I understand, James, but all that Major White suggested was that we keep the door open – under controlled circumstances, naturally. No one else in the world, outside our group, need ever know. Now or in any other time."

Douglas blew out his cheeks. "Ah don't know. The future they created is a good one, Satnam – a great one! If we start tinkering now…"

"James, we have already tinkered – and tinkered, and tinkered!"

Patel retorted, passionately. "It is impossible to foresee where this will take us. It might alter the future, or it might confirm it. We just do not know, we really do not."

Douglas laid his hands flat on his desk, between them. "Alright, supposing you're correct and this willnae mess up the future, that leads us to the second part of your suggestion – keeping a lid on it. How do we do that?"

"I have been led to understand that you held a senior government position in the future, Captain."

"Aye, but they didnae make me emperor! Ah still have superiors tae answer tae."

"Then perhaps our future does not lie in that direction."

Douglas sat back. "Whoa now, wait a minute…"

Patel sat forward, earnestly. "James, I understand you all found your Elysium there, in the future, but perhaps we do not belong there – none of us. It is not *our* future, after all."

Douglas leaned his elbows on the desk, hands cradling his head wearily as he exhaled deeply. "Ah thought we'd found a home. A better one than we left behind. That was the whole reason for us leaving Canaveral in the first place. To build a better future. Ah cannae deprive our people of their dreams, Satnam. They've already lost so much – all of them."

"You did so for the people left in 1558, James."

Douglas looked up sharply, wounded by his words.

Patel held up his hands, placatingly. "That was not a rebuke, Captain, but a compliment. Upon realising the importance of our changes, made in the past, you did what had to be done. I only hope I would have shown such fortitude, to do as you did. I understand that your own family no longer exist in that future you describe. You have given so much to improve humanity's lot, James. And now we must face the fact that, though our people have created a wondrous future, sadly… it is not for us."

Satnam eyed his old friend and comrade for a long moment, before asking, "So what do you think?"

"Ah think Ah should have taken the post of cabin boy and left ma wife in charge."

Back at the controls of his dropship, Corporal Thomas lifted from the ground and turned back towards the wormhole. All personnel and vehicles cleared the area, so that they were well out of the way when the raging white water jetted through the portal once more.

In the rear of the ship, Reiver growled. Natalie hushed and tried to comfort him, but he remained anxious. The seats and harnesses in the dropship were naturally designed for humans, so she held him on her lap – always fun with an agitated collie.

He growled again.

His out-of-touch two-leg put it down to being 'one of those things'.

As previously, the violent stream appeared out of nothingness. Thomas offered the little ship up to the wormhole carefully. Vicious buffeting made the operation precarious as he nosed into the flow. Dr Patel had explained that if he lost control of the ship and slewed sideways, there was a chance they would be forced back into real space. Alternatively, they might be cut in half and disintegrated. Unsurprisingly, it was the latter theory that most played on his mind as he increased engine output to overcome the kinetic energy of the water, but the real skill was in controlling pitch, roll and yaw as vortices within the main current battered their aerodynamic surfaces from all angles.

His last trip through the portal had been guided, and mostly powered, by the angry torrent of the river itself. This time was far more difficult and dangerous.

The engines roared, causing the little craft to surge forward. Thomas immediately eased off, striving for stability over speed.

"Steady, Corp," Douglas encouraged calmly, from the co-pilot's seat.

"Yes, sir."

Thomas increased power again, but more gently. The dropship

fought the twisting eddies to stay in line as she crept forward. The cockpit emerged back into real space, as white water surged over them. Flying entirely by instruments, Thomas goosed the throttle, bringing the rest of the ship forward to emerge into the mid-Cretaceous and to a place that would one day be Great Britain.

Once through, he immediately went for altitude to escape the ferocious torrent, though the rain beat his screen so hard, he wondered if he had. He landed a hundred metres south of the anomaly, atop the small hillock where he previously dropped Douglas' six-man team, what seemed like a lifetime ago.

In the rear compartment, Georgio Baccini gave their equipment one last check, while Douglas stepped through to take command. He opened the ship's rear hatch to the storm and, with reticence, ordered the machinery unloaded. They rolled the powerful magnetic field generators down the ramp on their flatbed trollies. Small wheels sank immediately into the saturated earth to bog down, while rain slashed at the miserable crew, drenching them instantly.

Pleased to be outside again, Reiver ran around, barking excitedly. With all the mockery of a planted quadruped, he seemed oblivious to the driving storm. Struggling to keep her feet, Natalie was compelled to take him back inside the ship before she tumbled down the bank herself, while trying to save him[1]. Upon re-entering the ship, Reiver calmed immediately, whatever was worrying him before, seemingly forgotten. Natalie returned quickly, leaning into the gale-force winds when a sudden gust shoved her into Douglas.

He caught her supportively, shouting over the howl of the wind, "OK, Georgio, you're our chief on this one. How do we set this up?"

"Remind me to thank Hiro for his confidence in me," Georgio called back, wretchedly. "We've calibrated the field generators to

---

1. In the way that cats need rescuing from the tree they just climbed with ease – humans like to feel relevant.

work at seven metres from each other, Captain."

"Several?"

"*Seven,* sir! We must place them se-*ven* metres apart."

Douglas relayed the order at the top of his voice, barely above the storm.

His small crew glared unhappily; merely getting their equipment off the ship's ramp had been a struggle. Fortunately, their grumblings did not carry. Eventually, having enlisted everyone on their short passenger list, the machines were set up under hastily constructed weatherproof canopies.

Reiver knew when to follow orders. Remaining dry, he barked encouragement from the open hatch.

Georgio stared balefully at him, before searching the hilltop for places where bedrock broke through the ferns. He found several and ordered rock bolts fired at strategic points to provide anchorage. Heavy straps were passed through securing loops between the bolts and the base of the machines themselves, for despite their mass, their aligned polarity would push them apart if left untethered. High winds and the storm's destabilisation of the subsoil also increased the likelihood of them sliding down the hillock and ruining their purpose.

Soaked and utterly miserable, Douglas' team re-embarked. He walked along the length of the ship, through its small cargo hold, to join Thomas in the cockpit. Behind him, the others reclaimed their seats along the sides. Georgio drew up the ramp and closed the rear hatch.

Thomas turned to greet him. "All sorted, Captain?"

Douglas nodded miserably. "Aye." He jabbed a thumb at his own chest. "But next time, *Ah'll* be flying the ship."

Thomas grinned. "Knock yourself out, Captain. I'm from Birmingham. It's always like this, mate. That's why we've got so many canals."

Douglas cracked a half-smile before dropping miserably into the co-pilot's seat.

Reiver yelped and growled.

"Sorry, laddie, Ah didnae see ye there – all cosy and warm," he added bitterly, as he gently brushed Reiver off the seat.

"Ar. I put the heated seat on for him, Captain. Day[2] want him getting cold, like, you know? But yoh can have it."

Douglas' initial response was lost in a convenient clap of thunder. "That's very thoughtful," he continued. "Look at this weather. And Ah thought the *Borders* had a good line in sudden squalls."

Reiver continued to growl. Douglas looked down in surprise; he had never known the dog to hold a grudge against him before, but Reiver was not looking at him. The collie stood, hackles raised, instead staring into the rear compartment. *This is new,* Douglas thought. Psychically sensitive as a block of wood, he also put it down to being one of those things.

Beck Mawar watched Reiver with interest, frowning with nebulous concern.

Natalie retrieved her best friend and tried ineffectually to calm him again.

Douglas thought it odd. Animals always have a reason for causing a fuss. Unfortunately, they lack nuance when reporting back, leaving the human nominally in charge to discern whether a leaf has just blown by, or there actually is a man standing at their back with a big knife. Douglas shook it off. "Take us up, Corp. We dinnae want to be near those generators when they fire up. Who knows what they'll do to the electronics on this bird."

"Aye, sir." Thomas took them to a safe distance and hovered several hundred metres above the ground. "Sending the activation signal, Captain." He glanced at Douglas. "Generator one is online. Hope this works."

Down on the rain-ripped hillock, the first machine hummed to life beneath its canopy.

---

2. In most West Midlands dialects (England), 'day' means 'didn't'. For example: 'Ar day do nuffin'' means 'I didn't do anything wrong' – to which parents, teachers, employers and policemen often reply, 'Yeah right, that'll be the day.'

99.2 million years into the future, give or take, Baines studied the wormhole closely, while the *New World*'s sensor suite recorded and analysed everything. The torrent seemed to take on a spiralling motion, like it was being shaken or moved. "Looks like it's working," she noted.

Meritus nodded. "Hopefully, this will give us a reliable doorway back to our people, while we fix the ship. If not…"

"If not," Baines completed for him, "we'll have flooded this ravine with trillions more Cretaceous microbes to add to the billions here already."

Meritus shook his head, sadly.

"What is it?"

"Just remembering when I accepted Schultz's offer. If I had known…"

Baines took his hand. "Our world *was* dying, Tobias – the evil old coot was right about that. It's what we do now that matters."

"That's what worries me. Honestly, if there was any way I could go back…"

She squeezed his hand. "Our best minds all seem to agree that criss-crossing our own personal timeline might prove even more disastrous… disastrouser? Whatever. The only way is through. Ha! Look. It's stopped."

The river raged along the single valley leading out from Crater Lake, but the wormhole was moving east, away from it – a weird, barely visible hole in reality, gliding through the jungle like a ghost. The electrons at its event horizon span slowly as it drifted, its own small magnetic field attracted to the machinery up on the hill via a process known as frame-dragging.

Presently, it climbed to within a few metres of the generator.

"Begin dialling down, Corporal," Douglas ordered, "and fire up the second machine."

Autopilot engaged, Thomas gave all his concentration to balancing the generators. Both were set up to attract the wormhole, which meant they would repel each other, so it was just a matter of encouraging the wormhole to drift halfway between, before it became distorted by the forces fighting to attract it.

"Powering down, sir."

"Nice job, Corp," Douglas congratulated. "Now, will it stay put?"

Thomas checked his instruments. "So far, no movement, sir." He turned to Douglas with a grin. "Looks like it worked!"

Douglas grinned back, rainwater dripping from his chin. "Excellent. Now activate the wee program Dr Patel wrote to keep it in position."

"Done, sir. If the wormhole drifts, the machines will reactivate and auto-balance it back into place."

Douglas breathed a deep sigh of relief and opened a channel. "Come in, *New World,* this is Douglas – over."

"*Reading you five-by, James,*" Baines answered immediately. "*Looks good from this end. We're already packing away the beach towels – over.*"

"Good. Couldn't send them our way, could ye? We're drenched! Ah can tell we're back in Britain!"

"*I don't know, James. I'm quite enjoying this Roman Warm Period we're living through.*"

Douglas grimaced, as water dripped from his hair down into his eyes. He wiped it irritably. "Glad tae hear it! Look, we're going to press on with the next stage of our journey, Jill. Make sure the wormhole remains heavily guarded. Who knows what sort of beasties are hiding from the rain in this jungle, and Ah dinnae want any further surprises from Heidi, either – out."

Thomas disengaged the autopilot and flew over the sharp pinnacles that soared high, surrounding Crater Lake. In less than a minute, they were landing alongside the *Newfoundland*'s rescue pod.

Just as he was about to touch down, the main hangar airlock opened, allowing him to creep forward and land inside. As the double set of massive steel doors closed behind them, Douglas, Thomas, Coleman and Bismarck stepped from the rear hatch

– Bismarck still on borrowed crutches from Dave Flannigan's sickbay.

Dr Brian Alba walked across the hangar with Sergeant Zimmermann. "So," he greeted brusquely, "*not* dead, then?"

Bismarck gave Douglas a wry smile before answering, "It seems not, Brian. Sorry."

"No need to apologise," Alba sniffed. "I didn't want your *admin* job anyway."

"It's nice to see you, too, Brian," Coleman acknowledged, "and you, Sergeant."

Distracted, Alba turned to her. "What? Oh, yes. Welcome back, Commander. We've all missed you, I'm sure."

"Yes," Zimmermann agreed, meaningfully, speaking for the first time. "We really have, ma'am."

Coleman chuckled. "I, and Captain Douglas' people, would appreciate a few towels, please, Sarge. It's been quite the morning."

"Yes, ma'am." Zimmermann saluted and left.

"So," Alba turned to Douglas, "here to turf us out, eh, Captain?"

"Not yet. We're on our way…" He tailed off. "Let's just say, we've another stop planned before we move out. Ma ship still has repairs to make, so ye have a little time, should ye want to take a last stroll through the fields of home."

"What, in this weather?"

Douglas dripped, standing in a personal puddle on the hangar's deck. "Ah hadnae noticed." He turned to Coleman. "Once we've dried ourselves, we'll take our leave of ye, Commander. Ah'm no' sure how long we'll be gone – it may be no time at all." He shrugged helplessly.

Coleman smiled. "I understand. Wormhole physics is *well* above my head, Captain." She pulled him aside. "But seriously, have you reached your final decision about us, sir?"

Douglas sighed. "Ah've no wish to take this away from you, Ally. Ah can see why ye want to stay for the weather alone! But Ah just cannae see another way. Leaving ye behind might cause no end of damage to the timeline."

"But we may already have caused that damage, sir."

"True, but leaving forty healthy human beings in the Cretaceous could be a disaster for the future. With just a little time, forty would soon become forty thousand, and then forty million, and on and on it goes. We're talking about a hundred million years, here, and yet, in just a few centuries you might change everything – mess it up so badly that we're never even born. Ye must see Ah cannae take that chance, lassie. Ah'm sorry."

"What if we guaranteed that couldn't happen, Captain?"

He stared at her. "What do you mean?"

"It's a relatively simple operation."

"And you could make that decision, for all yer people here? Ah couldnae even *ask* it of them."

"Perhaps not, but I could."

Douglas was shaking his head. "That's a dark journey, Commander. Ah've already seen it. Two dear friends of mine took the same option aboard the *Newfoundland*. Their crew survived a crash, even thrived to a degree, despite losing many to the local wildlife, but eventually there were just two – each terrified of leaving the other alone. It's no' something Ah'd wish on anyone."

"What happened to them?"

"We saved them – well, Ah say that. Actually, they saved us first, Jill and me. But ma point is, they were lucky. And any less desperate a measure could never work. You could never make any promises on behalf of your descendants – and they would never stick to them, if ye did!"

Coleman nodded, thoughtfully. "Will you let me think on it? There must be some third way."

Douglas reached out a hand, holding her shoulder gently. "At the very least, it'll be a fortnight before ma ship's ready to disembark. If ye can bring a case before me by then, Ah promise to consider it. We seem to have two-way communication with the *New World,* now – at least, unless anyone tinkers with the manifold while we're away – so if you need any advice from the experts on ma crew, you've ma permission to speak with them on this topic. It's all Ah can offer ye at this time."

She smiled again, but with sadness. "'At this time' is a loaded term, Captain, but thank you. I'll convene a meeting with my best people – and Dr Alba – and we'll think on it."

⌖

A shimmer appeared in the middle of *Factory Pod 4*'s hangar. "*USS New World, this is Captain Douglas. Does anyone read? Over.*"

"Captain, this is Major Ford White. Is that really you? Over."

Douglas' smile travelled with the signal, travelled through the wormhole and through unimaginable time to warm the hearts of people who had long ago given up on ever being reconnected with their own, or their time, again.

"*Aye, Ford, it's me. We're in a wee ship, waiting tae come through. Are we clear for landing?*"

White grinned. "Yes, Captain. Ever since Satnam left with Thomas, we marked the wormhole area with tape on the floor. We all got tired of being run over. Long story. Come on through!"

The dropship appeared from the air, slowly reintegrating, centimetre at a time. Thomas set them down gently and opened the rear hatch.

Before White had even finished speaking into his comm, people were running towards the ship from all directions. Some, like Lloyd, approached more cautiously – he was eighty-three, after all.

Still anxious, Reiver dashed from the open hatch, barking the place down. Immediately feeling better, he jumped in circles around Rose, Henry and the others. He had forgotten none of them. Even though their complex scents had changed over thirty years – altered and augmented by living conditions and age – to the discerning nose, such changes were mere acetate sheets laid over the original plans, barely obscuring the subject. No. Reiver knew them all, even sparing a tail wag and a *woof* for Lloyd as he dashed among the quickly growing group of reunited friends – the family of the *New World*.

Douglas met White with a handshake and a warm embrace. "It's good to see you, laddie."

"You too, Captain. We'd given up hope."

Douglas grinned. "Jill sends her love. She wanted to be here, but one of us had to stay with the ship. She's Jill Baines-Douglas now," he added proudly.

White grabbed him by the shoulders, exuberantly. "James, that's great! Congratulations! Thomas told me you have a new ship, too?"

"Aye. The UNS *New World.*" He looked around *Factory Pod 4*'s hangar, a place he remembered so well, as it nestled beneath the wreck of his once-mighty USS *New World.* "No disrespect, lassie, Ah just wanted to keep yer name alive."

White wore his usual lopsided grin with a touch of mischief. "Thomas tells me she looks like Thunderbird II."

Douglas sighed, exhaling his exasperation with a laugh. "Aye. So they keep telling me. Ah swear, Ah cannae see it masel'."

Tim, Clarrie, Woodsey, Rose and Henry went into an immediate huddle, lost in their own little world. "Man, you're old!" Woodsey cried as he grabbed his friends boisterously. "I'd better be careful I don't knock your walking sticks from under you!"

"Lucky for you I don't have one, or I'd wrap it around your head!" Rose retorted, happily, throwing her arms around the New Zealander. "I'm old enough to be your mum now, so watch it!"

"But you're real old," Clarrie repeated, almost disbelieving her own eyes. "You look like Dad!"

"Thanks, sis. Great to see you, too," Henry snorted.

Clarrie blinked and turned her attentions from the old to the new – more specifically to her new sister-in-law. "Rose! You're still crazy hot! Where have you been getting your make-up?"

"Dad's a chemist, remember? He reverse-engineered some of the slap mum left behind for me. She didn't leave much, I can tell you! Queen Elizabeth uses it, now, too. I told him he should market it, but he's committed to keeping a low profile. I wanted to go with the 'Tudor Rose Collection', but he wouldn't hear of it."

"Hey," Woodsey butted in, "what happened to the Cronopios?

I've missed those little fellas."

Rose soured as Henry's expression immediately morphed into one of chagrin. "Ah, yeah, we still have a few of those li'l guys around. Not from the original pack, of course. That was, like, thirty years ago, right? But—"

"A few?" Rose interrupted, tetchily. "They're running feral!"

By necessity, Henry Burnstein's pack of terrier-sized mammals, known as Cronopio denticutus, had been left behind in the 16th century when most of the crew stepped through the wormhole to the future. After three decades, and a lack of advanced veterinary intervention, they were now a thriving colony. Henry had had no idea what to do with them – at first – though a business plan soon formed in *his* mind, too. Showing less scruple than his father-in-law, he realised that wealthy ladies of the period often kept small lap dogs to 'keep their bellies warm'…

Jim Miller smiled at the group around his beloved daughter, reminded of how close he had recently come to losing her, forever. In fact, he *had* lost her, and was saved only by the fact that forever was not what it used to be. Not when a man had access to time travel.

He spotted Patricia Norris and greeted her with a warm hug and a kiss on the cheek. Looking up, he noticed Hank and Chelsea Burnstein, too, standing on the ramp with tears in their eyes as they gazed down upon their long-lost son – now a man of forty-eight, and only a little younger than themselves.

Henry was just about to ask his sister how they were, when he saw them. He took a step towards the couple and stopped, a tower of emotion pressing down on him. He had so much to ask, so much to tell. He was paralysed.

Chelsea Burnstein broke from her husband's side and leapt into her son's strong arms. Hank Snr followed more slowly, letting his wife have the moment she had been dreaming of for so many years. Losing Henry had changed him forever. By another incredible quirk of time travel, he, too, had lost everything, but in the end recovered his heart's desire. Now he saw the man his son had grown into, he was content. He seemed to float across the distance between them as though in a dream. Henry reached out his left arm to receive him, pulling his father into a crushing embrace. "Dad," he cried softly.

Natalie gave up trying to control Reiver; her own emotions were equally unrestrained as she squeezed the breath out of Mother Sarah.

"Careful with my old bones, ya hear?" Sarah laughed as she squeezed back, tears of joy streaming down her cheeks.

Georgio Baccini moved in to give the old priest a hug, too.

"Georgio!" she cried. "It's so good to see you, my boy. What a handsome fella you've become!"

He grinned ear to ear. "I always was, and *you* always had excellent taste. Can a man help it if he just keeps improving with age?"

Sarah laughed. "Is Chief Nassaki here, too?"

"No. He sent me to get-a drenched on his behalf!"

Sarah looked from Georgio to Natalie, quizzically.

"It's a long, soggy story," Natalie explained.

"But I'm sure Hiro will enjoy boring you with it when you do see him," Georgio added with a grin.

Bemused by the strong emotion and goodwill on display, Bess and David – more correctly known as Queen Elizabeth I and Lord Maxwell – kept themselves to the side.

Douglas walked over to them, giving each a respectful nod.

Maxwell offered his hand, as did Elizabeth, if rather more daintily.

"We're surprised to see ye again, Jimmy," Maxwell stated with a broad smile. "Ah'll bet ye're surprised we're no' dead, eh?" he laughed.

"Only the good die young, Davy," Douglas replied, cheerfully. "Yer Majesty, the paintings that survived into the future dinnae do you justice – ye look beautiful, radiant! What's yer secret?"

Bess smiled indulgently. "You old rogue. You sound like one of our courtiers. Come. You may embrace me."

Douglas was never a man to disobey an order. "Aye, it's so good to see ye – both of ye."

After greeting everyone, Beck Mawar walked away to be alone, opening her senses to a higher level of consciousness. Still so much darkness and fear in this time, so much power. Like a supernova lighting up on the dark spiritual plane, she immediately attracted attention. She took a sharp, involuntary breath, having not stood in that place for over a decade – three decades in the local time – and yet despite all those years, *he* was still there.

***

Heidi had two points on her agenda. If the first worked, the second would become irrelevant. At least, it might to anyone else, but not to Heidi, because the second was a matter of revenge. Once her first plan was set, she would double back and enact the second before it took effect. After all, some people had to pay for all this – twice, if she could manage it.

She smiled cruelly as she trudged through the darkness along the path beaten by their vehicles, months earlier. Nature was already reclaiming her own, but the trail was easy enough to follow.

The jungle never fell silent. Twice a day there was the changing of the watch from the nocturnal to the diurnal and back again. The chittering of insects was oppressively loud, made more terrifying by the near-total blackness. Heidi had courage – even her haters never doubted that – but she still knew fear. Invertebrates here grew horribly large, but what she feared the most were the cathemeral creatures. Those who hunted the day *and* the night – the ones she could never evade once they had her scent.

She paused to rub the recently healed wound on her calf. The bite suddenly throbbed, jogging her memory. Just a few hundred metres into the jungle and the moonlight was completely extinguished. The presence of Douglas' people forced Heidi to put some distance between herself and them, but stumbling further into the pitch black was foolish. The last thing she needed was a sprained ankle. She laid her pack to the side of the track and switched on her head torch. The armoured personnel carrier she discovered on the *Last Word*'s plateau had left a while ago. She heard it go, and assumed it left through the wormhole, but soon after, the sounds of several vehicles and human voices reinvaded the night, culminating with the *chop, chop* of the helicopter taking off. It sounded like a larger force was building, for what reason she could not guess, when all fell silent once more.

With man and his devices gone, the nightly chorus soon returned, doubling in strength. She unpacked a case from her rucksack, and in the torchlight assembled her new best friend – a high-powered assault rifle. Swinging it over her shoulder, she stripped the case of its mini toolkit and spare ammunition clips before ditching it in the underbrush.

Heidi took a deep, calming breath. With the power of death in her hands, she felt braver already and switched off the comforting light to don her night-vision goggles instead. Fear of the dark has always been a curiously human frailty. Few are completely immune. Now she could see in the dark, she was part of the night; that was a good thing, but shattered any illusion that she might be safe from it. Scanning her surroundings, she knew that, out there, the hunters were completely indifferent to any such anguish or delusion. Out there, they were stalking. Out there, they were coming.

No more tangible than the scent of a shadow, the knowledge that she was no longer alone was incredibly powerful. It was a primal scream in her mind. A jolt of adrenaline. A call to fight or flee. Yet, even with her technological advantage, she could see nothing. Just the trees and the ferns. Only experience warned her to pay heed to such feelings, and then she heard them.

The sounds of skittering and squawking were immediately familiar. Without hesitation, Heidi ran to the nearest tree that looked even halfway climbable and scrambled up it. The growls and calls were all around her now. She powered higher and higher, from handhold to foothold, to knot, to branch, not daring to look down. Three times her own height above the ground, she stopped for breath, listening. The raptors were gone. They had buzzed her and left.

Heidi scanned the forest floor from on high, up in the crow's nest, five metres above the ground. Branches and ferns obscured her view, but surely not enough for the creatures to be hidden completely. This smelt like a trap – reeked of it – and she should know, having set enough of them over the years. The clever little monsters were luring her back down. It was unbelievable, yet she must believe, or die.

Fortunately, among the collection of toys she procured from Heydrich were several multipurpose grenades. Time to set a trap of her own.

Having walked a little way from the reunited friends and families, Beck Mawar opened herself to the past. "*Rotmütze,*" Beck breathed the name like anathema. "Robin Rotmütze."

Back on home ground and confident, Redcap had dropped his cloak, enjoying the fear he sensed in the medium before him. "I did not expect to see you again, either, oh meddler with things she does not comprehend," the black spirit replied.

"Nice turn of phrase. Gone native, have we?" Beck replied, caustically. "I know how to drive you back now, remember?"

The shadowy figure seared the air around him; his empty, pitiless eyes glowed and faded to black, swelling and imploding to the rhythmic, hypnotic heartbeat of the damned. The Redcap creature laughed, bitterly. "You and that ancient priest? Still think the old girl's got it in her, do you? You know nothing."

"Would you like to find out?"

His smile faltered. He was extremely perplexed about his failure to travel back further in time through the wormhole with Heidi. It had prompted his return, as soon as he learned Douglas' intentions. Although he felt more secure, back in the 16th century where he had his powerbase, it paid to be cautious. Beck's and Mother Sarah's exorcism had been brutally damaging for him, all those decades ago. His recovery had taken years. Fortunately, he had all the time in the world. "You people… you just don't know when to leave, do you? I've a feeling we'll be seeing each other again in the future – or is it the past? I forget." His smile returned, though it was faked. Perhaps there were limits to how far back he could go? Perhaps it was impossible for him to revisit the time when he was 'made' – forged in the explosion of that satellite, detonated by the hated Jill Baines – but then, that in itself was interesting. Did it mean he could no longer travel to a time before man? Was it a power issue? He knew animal psyches provided little he could use, like trying to run a high-performance racing engine on diesel. If Heidi had travelled so far back, what could she be up to? He shook it off, returning to the moment. "In the meantime, my associate will soon be keeping a close eye on things here."

Beck's eyes narrowed. "Who?"

Redcap's eyes burned brightly again, all arrogance and malice. "I feel sure you'll know him, when he comes."

The psychic blast dropped Beck to her knees. She fell forward onto her hands, breathing deeply. *Help me…* Though internalised, her call was answered immediately. Despite the pain at her temples, Beck smiled. "Mario."

"*Mario,*" Rotmütze mocked. "Your *pet* can't save you from me!" he spat, viciously. "*Auf Wiedersehen.*"

Before Mario's shade could bridle at the insult, someone's pet, quite unironically, shot from nowhere, barking angrily and snapping at the air before her. Beck closed her eyes against the stabbing pain, seeing flashes. When she looked up, the darkness was gone. *So that's why the dog was so upset,* she pondered, understanding at last. *Had the sub-creature followed through the wormhole with Drs Patel and Reid?*

Getting back to her feet, she found Mario Baccini's spiritual form at her elbow – never far from her, nor his brother. "Are you OK, Beck?"

She nodded painfully. "Thank you for your strength." She bent to pat the collie's head, who was calm once more. "And that goes for you, too, little man. Good boy. Brave boy. I—"

A strangled cry cut her off. "*Mario?*"

Beck turned to see Georgio Baccini staring in shock, directly at his brother's ghost. "Georgio? You can see him? You can see Mario?"

Georgio staggered slightly. Dumbstruck, he simply nodded, not daring to break eye contact in case his brother disappeared again.

Mario smiled, but there was a sadness behind the eyes. "Hello, *Idiota.*"

"I... I can see you."

Mario grinned. "You lucky devil."

Foolishly, Georgio tried to hug his brother but grabbed only air. "How?" he managed.

Mario's expression grew serious. "There's a vast amount of psychic energy here in this time. Far more even than the last time we were here. It's mostly fear and anger, but it's powerful. Rotmütze is tapping into it, and – because we're so closely linked, brother – you're able to use it to tune in to me, the way Beck can. I think the dog senses it, too."

Reiver sat looking up at Mario, dusting the deck with his tail.

"What's causing it?" asked Georgio.

"You'd have to ask-a the locals, but I can sense something bad's happening. Or at least, everyone's afraid something bad *might* happen."

"Who are you talking with?" Mother Sarah interrupted, staring at Georgio strangely.

"I..." Georgio spluttered, unable to tear his eyes away from Mario, desperate to keep the connection.

"It's Mario," Beck explained. "He says there's an unusual amount of psychic power here – even for these times. What's happening outside, Sarah? Out in the world?"

Sarah peered, unable to see anything. "I'll have to take your word for it," she answered, sceptically.

Beck smiled. She was used to it. "Mario's laughing. He does that a lot," she explained fondly.

"See him all the time, do ya?"

"Pretty much."

Georgio grinned. "Not while you're in the shower, I hope, huh?"
Both brothers guffawed.

Beck blushed. "No. Mario would never…" She had not the heart
to be cross. Seeing the twins laughing together, like they were
always meant to, brought tears to her eyes.

"I think," Mother Sarah began, unintentionally disrupting the
moment, "that the psychic upheaval you're talking about might
be something to do with the Armada. You know, the Spanish
Armada? It's 1588 here. The attack failed, of course – just like in
the history books, largely thanks to Drake's fire ships, I understand
– but it took weeks for folks to hear it was even coming, so it'll
probably take weeks, or longer, for folks to hear about it going."

"That must be it," Mario agreed. "I can feel a terrible fear through
the ether."

"He says he thinks you're right, Sarah," Beck communicated.

"I miss you, brother," Georgio confessed, his eyes brimming.

"Of course you do. Who wouldn't miss-a me, eh?" Mario replied
conceitedly, laughing again. "I have to go now, brother. This is
hard work. I always had to work-a harder than you!"

"That's because I'm the one with the talent. Everything comes
easy to me," Georgio taunted right back.

They laughed again.

Mario reached out a hand for his brother's shoulder, though
Georgio could not feel it. "I'm always with you."

A sudden lump caught in Georgio's throat, making it difficult to
speak. "*Amo tuo, fratello.*"

Mario grinned. "Well, you're-a only human. Didn't you say that
at my funeral?"

Georgio blinked. "You were there?"

Mario tugged at an ethereal ear. "*Sì.*"

"How was it?"

"Weird. I'd recommend it to anyone, though. I particularly liked the wreath you made, and all the nice things you said about me. Of course, I always knew, but hey, it's-a nice to hear from the horse's mouth." Mario grinned again, and with that, he faded.

Georgio smiled, wiping tears from his eyes.

Beck placed an arm around his shoulder. "Glad Hiro sent you now?"

"Better not tell him. Remember the last time I heard from my brother's ghost? He almost fired me."

Chapter 16 | One

Heidi waited out the night. Her tree was as safe as anywhere else in Cretaceous Patagonia, so she caught what sleep she could, in short, fitful bites. Dawn came early, which suited her, because she was extremely uncomfortable. Moreover, daylight gave her the edge when dealing with predators. With just a little warning, her vastly superior mind would always win out – or so she hoped.

She must have made a tempting target for the pack of Buitreraptors – soft, slow and lacking any obvious defences. Naturally, they had no understanding of human intelligence, nor the human propensity for tool use and cruelty. They had cunning, of course; they were hunters. Nature had given them all the apparatus required to track and kill their intellectual inferiors, even when considerably outgunned physically. They had no idea what

467

they were in for.

Heidi had some idea what she was in for. She had lived there alone for many days, soon after the original *New World* arrived in the Cretaceous. She had no doubts at all that the pack were hiding, waiting for her to climb down.

She was wrong – or at least, *half* wrong. The pack were indeed in hiding, but the reason had nothing to do with her.

Her injured leg tingled again, doubtless from the recent injury. She tried to ignore it, believing the limb had gone to sleep metaphorically as she had literally. As the sensation returned, the tingling became more like tickling. She looked down and nearly fell from her branch. Climbing up her leg was the biggest spider she had ever seen, and by a great margin. Her grandfather's fortress, in what remained of the 22nd century rainforest, boasted nothing a tenth its size.

"*Eugh!*" She swiped it away with her rifle butt, scrambling to her feet to check herself over.

A loud, drawn-out grumbling, followed by wet smacking sounds and a sneeze drew her attention. Heidi's frantic moment of panic as she rubbed herself down ceased immediately, and she looked further down, below. Suddenly, the raptors' disappearance made sense.

A whine followed the sneeze. It sounded for all the world like one of her grandfather's hounds waking. Wrong again – or at least, *half* wrong again. What she heard was indeed an animal waking to greet the day with a yawn, a shake and a sneeze, but it was categorically no wolfhound.

The bushes swayed around the bottom of her tree as the undergrowth shuffled and parted or was flattened. A creak and a crack brought the branch just below Heidi's down. She waved her arms about for balance, dextrously taking two long strides along her own branch to secure herself against the trunk.

A massive head moved beneath her, followed by a vast body and culminating in a tail that seemed to go on without end. Heidi thought her horror must surely be complete. However, she turned out to be completely wrong about that, for when the creature stopped to sniff again, it turned to face her – literally.

The head rose, and rose again, to look her in the eye. Worse yet, Heidi recognised that face – recognised the scar that ran down the side of its snout, across the maxilla. She had tangled with this creature before on a lake shore, not far from where she hid now. At that time, she had been trying to get back from the abandoned *Newfoundland* to her long-lost *Heydrich,* before they limped the ancient ship thousands of miles north, to the islands that would one day become Great Britain. Although Heidi was not acquainted with the creature by name, she once again stared with forlorn disbelief into the eyes of Matilda, the Tyrannotitan – and Matilda stared right back.

Matilda's jaws parted, her lips drawing back into a sneer[1]. Theropod dinosaurs had exceptional olfactory senses, but whether they possessed the mental equipment to recall the scent of a previous adversary remains open for debate. In any case, it hardly mattered. Animals always live in the moment, and unless she acted quickly, that would be all Heidi had left.

She pulled the pin and launched the grenade, clutched tightly in her hand all night long, at the giant face. It bounced off Matilda's nose before it went off.

Heidi covered her ears and shut her eyes tight against the flash-bang. Even with her ears covered, it was loud enough to make her nauseous. Ears ringing, she risked opening her eyes.

Matilda was reeling. Head down, she staggered.

Recognising an opportunity, Heidi leapt onto the giant head and

---

1. Palaeontologists have, in recent years, begun to consider the possibility that some dinosaurs might have had lips. If true, then the traditionally terrifying, toothy visage of the classic *Tyrannosaurus rex* might well have been positively gawky when the animal was at rest. *That* is just not box office. So, for the purposes of this narrative, think of Matilda as twisting her lip into the full Dwayne Johnson – the full Elvis being the preserve of Reiver.

ran down Matilda's back as the dinosaur succumbed to dizziness and disorientation of her own. Eventually, she lay down and Heidi jumped the short distance remaining to hit the ground running. If she were lucky, Matilda might reconsider her early start and take the rest of the morning to lie in.

The lithe young woman belted along the trail, not stopping until she reached the river. Pulling up, she hid behind a tree near the ford. Heidi was fit and strong, but any human being would have found her pack heavy over a one-mile dash. The clash with Matilda had been unexpected and unwelcome, yet her next challenge might prove even worse.

She leaned forward, hands on knees, panting.

As her breathing regulated, she straightened and took a drink from her flask. The water was warm and unpleasant, but it hydrated her cells, even if it failed to refresh her palate. She shook her head. Most people had barely considered coffee and croissants by that time in the morning. She blew out a long, exasperated sigh, reminding herself why she was doing this.

The last time she walked across the ford, she was to lose most of her small band of followers. A pang struck her to the heart as she, once again, remembered Ben Jansen. He had been there then. Up until recently, he had always been there. She had not appreciated that enough. Perhaps he would not have turned against her if she had. She shook her head again. There was no benefit in going over old ground in her head – not while she still had so much old ground to go over with her feet. That was bad enough, but what really concerned her was going over the water.

The ford was not deep. It was a natural crossing point, used by the local fauna as it had been by the vehicles of her people. However, the river narrowed before and again after, the slow, sluggish water gouging deep into the earth and pooling to either side. It was, in fact, the perfect spot for amphibious killers to wait in ambush, and Cretaceous Patagonia had no shortage of those.

Peering across to the opposite bank, she considered. Despite the river's calm appearance, she was mindful of how they had received no warning last time. Not until they were halfway across, drastically slowed by thigh-high waters and treacherous footing. The riverbed was an obstacle course of smooth, slimy stones. It represented no serious challenge to the tracks of their armoured carriers, nor to the metre-wide, webbed feet of the *Oxalaia quilombensis* that hunted this stretch of river. Yes, Heidi certainly remembered them. She needed a distraction.

Sidling as close to the river's edge as she dared, she selected another grenade and waited. Standing perfectly still for several minutes, she finally saw it. The flash of silver.

The fish was enormous. Heidi did not recognise its species and it was gone in an instant, but that hardly mattered. She threw the grenade to where the creature dove, just a split second before.

The *splosh* it made upon entering the water was interesting, and the fish returned instantly, to snatch whatever bounty had fallen from the sky. Unlike the flash bomb used against Matilda, this was a true grenade, and Heidi dove behind the nearest tree just as the *boom* sounded from beneath the water. A plume of spray soared high into the air, crimson with blood and fish guts.

The effect was immediate. A sail emerged, towering above the sluggish waters, resplendent in every shade of blood red and fiery orange, and just ahead of it, a snout appeared, too.

Fish use their swim bladders to control buoyancy, but if filled with air at the point of death, the swim bladder causes the corpse to float upside down at the surface – perfect for the giant, *crocodilianesque* jaws of one of the local spinosauridae to collect it for breakfast. Indeed, the fish was large enough to keep the giant going for days.

He snatched it up and swam strongly for the shore to tear his meal into swallowable chunks.

Heidi watched him approach – she could hardly miss him. Oxalaia was one of the largest land predators of all time. She ran into waters heavy with silt and kept going, wading as quickly as she could until she was safely across, up the opposite bank, and back once more within the protection of the jungle.

Again, she stopped to rest, glancing back to check she was not followed. She need not have worried; Oxalaia certainly had bigger fish to fry. Heidi risked a more modest bite from a power bar. *I sincerely hope I do not have to do all this again, in reverse,* she mused in silence as she chewed. *Once is quite enough.*

⸎

Baines waited in her meeting room off the *New World*'s bridge. Hiro arrived first, as per her arrangement with The Sarge. She sat him down and explained about Aito's possible duplicity.

The chief sat in silence, giving little away, but she had to wonder what was going on beneath. Presently, she concluded her statement and pressed for a reaction. Hiro was not forthcoming, so she tried a different approach. "I've been wondering whether Aito might have been right to solicit Dr Hemmings' help…"

It was not exactly a question, more a lead in for him to flesh out with his own theories. Again, nothing.

"Hiro? What are you thinking?" she asked, eventually. Subtlety was rarely successful where her chief engineer was concerned.

"He betrayed me," he muttered, simply.

"I'm not so sure about that, either."

He looked up, suddenly focused, though he said nothing.

The vacuum created by Hiro's strenuous listening left Baines feeling that she should explain herself, if only to fill it. "What I mean is, I don't think he's working against your plan. Actually, I think he might, perhaps in a misguided way, be trying to help you. Though I, too, disapprove of his going behind your back and breaking our agreement."

Again, Hiro simply stared.

"You're angry. I understand. His end run might have potentially landed you in as much trouble as he's in. But I ask you to consider what he's been through. He was almost killed, more than once, and in his personal timeline, he's spent the better part of the last four years with the Schultzes. He's had to survive on his wits, Hiro."

472

"You think I should just let it go, because he has seen a few bad times, Captain?" he asked, suddenly. "Would you cut yourself so much slack, or me, or any of us?"

"I—"

Hiro cut her off. "I've been making excuses for him my whole life – covering up his behaviour from our father. He knew. My father missed nothing. But how did he repay us? He faked a horrible death and ran off with terrorists because he thought that would help him bring down the entire human race. I'm sorry, Captain, I have tried!"

"Well, when you put it like that," she replied, gently. "Still, you got your brother back – from the dead. He's a tearaway, I'll grant you that, but I genuinely think he wants your plan to work, like it's his way of making it up to you." She was unsure why she felt the need to defend Aito, though she suspected it was more to protect Hiro than his brother. He had been hurt enough, but Hiro could not be deflected.

"By involving *me* with his terrorist friends?"

Baines shrugged a certain acceptance to that. "Misguided, I'll grant you, but when I spoke to him, he seemed to genuinely believe your plan to draw the wormholes together in the… let me see if I have this right…" she spoke slowly, "the Oligocene Epoch of the Palaeogene Period, is dangerous. Maybe catastrophically dangerous. Did I get the names right?"

"It's what Tim called them. He's developed a proven record over the years."

"True, but Aito disagreed with you." It was not a question.

The chief brooded.

"Hiro?"

"Yes. He thinks we should risk creating an even bigger problem at the site of the 'Cretaceous Egypt to 1944 Germany' wormhole. The one that opened right in the middle of Munich!"

Baines considered. "How much damage could we do, if this went wrong?"

Hiro threw up his hands. "Blow up the planet? I don't know. No one does."

She glared at her chief engineer. "No need to sugarcoat it for me!"

"I'm sorry, Captain, perhaps you would prefer we do nothing and just leave hundreds of millions of years of Earth's history to mingle and blend to see what happens?"

"*That* was sarcasm," she accused.

"And you all thought I didn't get it."

Baines snorted. "OK, Hiro. I agree with you, we must do something, but *I'm* calling Anne Hemmings in on this now. Also, Satnam and that bland, balding fella, too."

"Dr Reid?"

"Yes. We may as well get every mind we have on the case. After all, it's only the future of everything at stake!"

"And the history of everything," he added, glumly.

"Right." The door chimed. "Come."

The Sarge ushered Aito Nassaki and Dr Anne Hemmings into the briefing room. "Take a seat, people. Sarge – you, too. I want you in on this."

They sat around the table. "Dr Hemmings, Aito already brought you up to speed on Hiro's plan, I understand? Good. I'll hear your thoughts now."

Heidi walked the whole day, often scaring away the wildlife. Just as often, dashing pell-mell for the nearest tree or cave to hide. The Cretaceous jungle was filled with marvels, but also dangers, so she could never let her guard down – it was exhausting. By early evening, the light was already fading fast beneath the canopy, and she began to look around for a likely tree in which to spend the night.

The trail, left many months ago by their APCs, had served her well – possibly taking a day or more off her journey – but she was spent, nevertheless. She staggered over a half-buried stone in her path and almost went down. Rubbing tiredness from her eyes, she leaned against a trunk. It was about the size and girth of the leg of a giant sauropod dinosaur. Even the colouration was close. In her weariness, she looked up and up again to check it was what she thought it was, before attempting a climb. No – just a tree. She should have known the notion was ridiculous. To penetrate so far in, what giant animals removed from the jungle was *the jungle,* but tiredness was playing tricks on her mind.

She waited and listened. Was she hearing things, too? The sudden silence was disconcerting. All day, she had been surrounded by the chirruping of amphibians, the buzzing of insects, the threats of violence that humans label quaintly as birdsong – even the occasional roar of larger creatures, complaining about their lot – but suddenly, there was nothing.

Like the flicking of a switch, the dayshift knocked off and the nightshift began. Instantly, the whole world was flooded with the chittering and call of every conceivable form of invertebrate – not to mention a good many she would rather not consider, especially as she was about to spend her second night up a tree.

Heidi slouched, leaning. She had never felt so weary and was about to begin her climb when a specific sound cut through the cacophony. Her ears pricked up immediately. It was a sound that was becoming all too familiar. Pulling her rifle from around her shoulders, she stood ready to defend herself. Raptors.

Where are you, you devils? she thought, trying to clear the fog of fatigue from her mind, but apart from the nocturnal insects, she could hear nothing. Instinct told her she was about to come under attack. Any second, they would close the trap and appear from everywhere and from nowhere. Each time she encountered Buitreraptors, they attacked in an organised fashion. They were many, they were skilled, they were ambush predators – and she was only one.

Deciding it was now or never, she scrambled up the tree, reaching into every knot and hanging on to every protrusion as her tired muscles pulled her upwards. The night before, she escaped them by the skin of her teeth. She had to believe she could do it again. As Heidi climbed, she wondered if it was the same pack, but pushed the thought aside. If they had been tracking her, they would have fallen on her earlier in the day. They would be unlikely to pursue prey for thirty klicks or more. There was plenty of other food in the jungle for small carnivores. That thought gave her hope. If this was indeed a separate pack, then they would have no knowledge of her tactics, nor any knowledge of humans. It barely occurred to her tired mind that they, too, might have their own unique tactics, completely apart from other, rival packs she had encountered before.

Her bubble burst when she felt something claw its way up her back and over her shoulders to jump on ahead, up to the next branch. She looked up to see one of the Buitreraptors staring down at her with the wide-eyed intensity of the berserker. The little creature opened its jaws wide, wagging its tail side to side in obvious anticipation. The claws on its hind legs bit into the bark, securing its perch with dexterity equal to any bird[2].

Heidi's were the wide eyes of panic as the pack swarmed around her, climbing with an ease that was embarrassing, to take up perches along the branches where she hoped to find refuge. "I may have miscalculated."

She half-slid, half-dropped to the jungle floor, immediately bringing her rifle to bear. Several raptors still on the ground leapt at her and she fired, dropping three of them. In an extraordinary display of gymnastic agility, the others twisted in the air to land lightly, already accelerating away as they hit the ground.

The shrieking and squawking from the branches above made her turn and point the weapon up into the canopy. She let go another short burst, shredding pine leaves and eviscerating the first unlucky climber in an eruption of screams, blood and feathers. It fell to earth with the wet thud of meat.

---

2. Birds: otherwise known as 'avian dinosaurs'. Food for thought, when resting on a park bench with a flask of coffee and half a loaf of stale bread, outnumbered a thousand-to-one by flying psychos.

Heidi was suddenly alone once more – not counting the dead. She quickly replaced the clip in her rifle and kissed its barrel, reverentially. Even Second Amendment sceptics would hold their tongues in the Cretaceous – and joy of joys, she had caught dinner.

One of the deadly critters would be more than ample to keep her going. She grabbed it around the neck like a large goose, when an idea struck. Heidi dropped it to the ground, fumbling in her pack for one of the hermetically sealable bags she used to keep her possessions dry and her rations fresh. They also prevented the scent of food from leaving her pack to get her killed.

She opened the bag out to its full extent and slipped the little creature into it. Very quickly, the bag was full of blood. Perfect. She sealed and tied it onto the rear of her pack – just in case she needed to ditch it in a hurry. She grabbed one of the other corpses and marched on, leaving the area rapidly, while the adrenaline rush lasted.

The two bodies she left behind would keep the pack busy for the evening, and she would do well to distance herself from the blood and carrion before other interested parties caught the scent.

She managed another couple of kilometres, reaching the T-junction with the road built by Douglas' people. It stretched away north to the lake and south to the *New World* enclosure.

Disappearing twenty metres into the darkened woods opposite, she collected wood and kindling. Judging by the climbing antics of the local raptors, fire would have to be her final redoubt, and she built it large, far larger than it needed to be to cook her meal. She did not want it to burn down while she slept, and she *needed* to sleep.

Douglas returned from the USS *New World* to the UNS *New World* replenished. For more than a decade he had carried the weight of leaving his friends behind. To see them all again and to provide them with hope was one of the most fulfilling experiences of his life. Every one of them accepted that they were stuck there, and that their contribution to the future was paramount, but they now knew for a fact that their plans were actually *working*. Completely reinvigorated by the fact that they were no longer alone in a strange time and would be allowed to see friends and loved ones again, they once more carried hope in their hearts.

Buoyed by his experience, Douglas decided that now was the time to grasp the nettle. He passed a couple of security personnel, returning their salutes casually as he came to a halt before detention suite 121. He pressed call.

The *Heydrich*'s crew, rescued from certain death after Heidi's nuclear strike on their facility in Cretaceous Egypt, were not exactly prisoners. They were not exactly guests, either. They straddled the uncomfortable line of the refugee that no one trusted and few wanted. Their every action was scrutinised or sanctioned by their hosts, their every word recorded.

Most bore it stoically, just glad to be alive. Others merely waited for the other shoe to drop. Heidi's final option – a nuclear strike intended to wipe them all out – had certainly solidified support for the Schultz sceptics. Even her most ardent supporters balked after that. Naturally, a few still believed Heinrich plotted a rescue mission, and would somehow reach out from 1940s Germany to save them – but then every movement has its fools.

As one of the known leaders of the anti-Schultz movement, Douglas had no doubts about where Anne Hemmings stood regarding her cousins' betrayal. He had been told that Heidi referred to Dr Hemmings as 'Two' and Reid as 'One', so it was hardly surprising that loyalties were shallow. He was less certain about where she stood when it came to the man who allegedly killed her daughter, and his conundrum only worsened from there, because he knew that he *had* killed her daughter, Lieutenant Elizabeth Hemmings. The fact that it was completely by accident and utterly beyond his control barely assuaged his guilt. He had no idea what to expect from the next few minutes. Though each was the enemy of their enemy, they were by no means friends.

The door slid open. "I was expecting you," Hemmings stated, unemotionally. Turning her back on him, she walked to her small dining table and sat, leaving the door open for Douglas to follow.

He stepped inside the small suite, the door sliding shut almost silently behind him. He gestured to the chair opposite her. "May Ah?"

She looked away, like she could not bear to look at him. "It's your ship," she replied, noncommittally.

He sighed, lightly. *What were ye expecting, Douglas, a fanfare?* he chided himself. "Aye, but for now, at least, these quarters are your home. Ah thought, a little respect…"

"I'm not paying you rent. Save it for the tourists. We both know I'm your prisoner."

He sighed again, taking the seat.

Without looking at him, Hemmings spoke in subdued tones. "Tell me, honestly, did you kill my daughter?"

Douglas had prepared himself for that. It had not helped. The memories of the young lieutenant's death haunted him still. "Ah…" he began.

When he tailed off, Hemmings looked up to glare at him. "Speak, man!"

"When the *Last Word* turned over, Ah…"

She slammed her fist on the table before them. "Tell me!" Her voice broke, eyes brimming with tears unspilled.

"Ah caused her death. When the *Last Word* turned over, Ah fell on her… from some height. It was pitch black. Ah didnae realise how serious her injuries were until…"

"When the *Last Word* turned over," she repeated, quietly. "So it was Captain Baines who killed her."

"No! It was war! A war we didnae start! Lieutenant Elizabeth Hemmings was a brave soldier, and a good woman. When we eventually got back to the future, Ah wrote a posthumous commendation to honour her sacrifice. UNASA have it on record. I vowed to let others know what she had done, everything she risked, to save humanity."

That seemed to take Hemmings by surprise. "What do you *mean?*"

Douglas blinked. "Ye didnae know?"

Her silence answered his question eloquently.

He took a deep breath and explained how her daughter had been working with Homeland Security, to bring down the Schultz regime from within after the murder of her husband.

Hemmings listened in silence. She had not known, but nor was she shocked by the revelation. Eventually, she said, "Heinrich never took people's feelings seriously. Comes of being an automaton, I suppose."

"He was a psychopath!" Douglas corrected, harshly.

She looked at him clearly for the first time since he had appeared at her door, all emotion now in check. "He probably still is. Who knows what he's up to in 1944."

Douglas sat back, taking her measure. "And how do ye feel about him now?"

"He ordered my daughter's execution. All that saved her was the *Last Word*'s departure. She was finally beyond his reach. If she had been alive when our Dawn Fleet caught up with you in the Cretaceous, I've no doubt he would have finished what he began. No one survives a death mark from Heinrich Schultz."

"Why did he no' have ye executed, after ye turned against him?"

"He's my cousin – or more specifically, my *second* cousin. Not that he's ever cared about that. We were stuck in the Cretaceous next to a world-killing wormhole and I knew more about it than most – more than him – but had Heidi not nuked our facility, leading to our capture by your wife, my time would have come."

Douglas leaned forward. "Well, ye'll no' be saddened to learn that his time came first, then, eh?"

She stared. "He's dead? How do you know this?"

"We were recently joined by an old friend of mine. He accidentally found himself in 1944 Munich, too, after chasing Heidi through a couple of wormholes. Apparently, Old Man Schultz met his end on live television. Quite the exit, by all accounts."

Her eyes narrowed. "You're sure of this? *How* did he die?"

"Eaten."

"In *Germany?* What the hell do they put in the sausages of that alternative timeline of yours?"

Douglas snorted gently. "No. A dinosaur also followed Heidi through the wormhole. Apparently, there were casualties," he added, regretfully, explaining what he knew.

Hemmings nodded thoughtfully. "I wish I had seen it. Just to watch him die, even once, would at least be something."

Douglas frowned. "Die once? He's dead, lassie. There's no round two. He's no' coming back."

She looked away again. "I wonder."

"Look, if there's something ye're no' telling me…?"

"Then you wouldn't be the least bit surprised."

He sat back, a smile tugging at his lips. "Touché."

She sighed. "As you know, I was one of Heidi's top scientists after she nominally took over from that old monster. Back in *our* 22nd century, Heinrich had people working on genetic control mechanisms. The work was incomplete, but we did get as far as creating nanites that made people trackable and recorded their memories, personalities – even their desires. Heinrich was attacked in Egypt. Not long after the *Heydrich* flew there – after Heidi's demented run on the moon with a comet! He was mauled by some kind of birds or pterosaurs. He barely survived being chased by a Bahariasaurus ingens, too – that's one of the giant theropod killers we found in ancient Egypt. Such a lovely place. After being stitched up, he required a lot of blood and Heidi made sure he got a little extra, too, along with the transfusion."

"She injected her own grandfather with nanites?"

"We're quite a family," she replied, sardonically. "She wanted to know exactly where he was, at all times. Wise, if you're related to Heinrich Schultz, believe me."

"Well, unless these nanites can rebuild him from scratch, Ah fail to see what we have to worry about."

"That, Captain, is merely a failure of imagination on your part."

Douglas bowed his head, deflating. "What are ye saying?"

"I'm not sure, but should anyone have access to his blood, and advanced cloning facilities, they could, in theory—"

Douglas sat back in his seat, his sigh of disgust cutting her off. "Even when we see them die, the Schultzes willnae stay down!"

Heidi awoke stiffly. After pushing herself hard the previous day, she was feeling it. The fire had banked overnight, but still burned. She threw more timber onto the flames, revitalising it. Warming herself gradually, she revitalised, too, by gently stretching and performing a few basic callisthenics to shake the stiffness from her muscles and joints.

There was cold meat left over for breakfast and she made best use of the fire to boil some water. Almost immediately, she began to feel better. It turned out that a steaming mug of English breakfast tea was as efficacious in the Cretaceous as it was for anyone surviving a monsoonal camping holiday in the Lake District.

She was about to face what might yet prove the most important, possibly even the most dangerous day of her life, but after her magic morning elixir, anything was possible.

She packed her things and strode south along the trail, leaving the campfire burning behind her. No camper in their right mind would have done such a thing, but this was not the Lake District and Heidi did not care. She had no plans to stay in her current time a moment longer than was necessary.

The air was fresh, the scenery magnificent. Ordinarily, Heidi cared little for such things, yet she had a spring in her stride that morning. So long as the terrifying monsters stayed far away, all was well.

"How did it go?" Baines asked Douglas when he returned to their quarters.

"Ah'm no' really sure. Ah dinnae think she blames me – no' directly, at least." He neglected to mention Hemmings' accusation that her daughter's death was Baines' fault. He knew his wife carried guilt enough over the deaths resulting from that long-ago night attack on the *Last Word*. "But Ah doubt she'll ever be a fan."

He sighed, sitting heavily.

"But will she help or hinder Hiro's plans to close the wormholes, I wonder?"

"Hard to say," Douglas admitted. "Ah think she's at war with herself."

Baines frowned. "What do you mean?"

"Ah believe she'll be only too happy to scupper Heidi's plans – on a *good* day. On a bad day, Ah dinnae think she cares whether she, or anyone else, lives or dies. Ah suppose losing a child must be like that – anger and despair vying for prominence. We've learned to consider the Schultzes evil, and some of them certainly are – or were – but it seems that even their family has nuance."

Baines nodded thoughtfully. "I've been thinking about their family. More specifically, about Heidi. James, I think we need to go after her."

He stroked his chin thoughtfully. "Aye, Ah've been thinking the same. She obviously went back to the Cretaceous with a plan. Ah'd rather find out what that is for maself, than wait for her next spectacular reveal. Especially if Heinrich's no' dead."

"*What?*" She straightened in alarm. "Arnold told us he saw him die. On TV!"

Douglas chuckled, gently. "Well, if it was on the news, it must be true – it's no' like they've ever lied tae us!" He tugged nervously at his ear.

She gave him a hard stare. "James...? He *is* dead, right?"

"Aye. About that..."

After a surprisingly pleasant walk through the forest, Heidi arrived at the large clearing where the *New World*'s earthworks still stood testimony to man's first ever built environment. She skirted the treeline – it was safer than exposing herself in the open. Most of the predators could outrun her, some by quite a margin. So far, even the trees proved less of a refuge than she hoped. What little security she had relied on cover.

Gazing east across the sunlit clearing, she ran her eye along the earthworks and palisade. Her *mind's* eye placed USS *New World* in the background. Relying on memory, she walked further round the clearing, until she was more or less at the location where she had lit a fire almost nine months earlier, in her personal timeline, to attract the attention of Bond's people aboard the ship. She remembered adding boric acid from a domestic cleaning fluid to make the fire burn green, thus distinguishing it from a natural event. Bond had replied with a signal in morse code.

Naturally, that was at night. It was now broad daylight, but the sense of timelines coming together in a collision was palpable. A smile spread slowly across her lips. Destiny was a fine thing, but that was no reason to accept it blindly. She intended to give it a second spin.

She was about to turn away when corner-of-the-eye movement caught her attention. Her jaw dropped. *Sneaky,* she thought, for just a few hundred metres to her left lay a sleeping behemoth – at least, she hoped it was still sleeping. She only saw it because it stirred, fitfully. The creature's camouflage was extraordinary under the edges of the canopy, but what really gave her pause was that she recognised the animal. Perhaps not the individual, but certainly her species. Heidi frowned. *What are you doing here?*

The animal was vast. In a world of terrors, it snoozed indolently, tail curled up around its nose in Smaugian comfort. Easily twenty metres in length, it was Spinosaurus aegyptiacus.

Heidi frowned, mildly perplexed. It made no sense. She knew the mighty Oxalaia hunted this part of the world – knew only too well, as they had hunted her, more than once. She had also seen the smaller Irritator challengeri living in and around the rivers, but Spinosaurus – at least, as far as she was aware – belonged in North Africa.

"Ha!" she exclaimed softly, as she realised she did know the animal, individually and personally. She knew that Douglas' people had captured the beast that followed her to AD2122 Egypt – she had extracted that information from Master Sergeant Badawi after capturing him. They must have dropped the animal off here. Her thoughts immediately raced to her cousin, Tim Norris. She smirked. *That must have given his obsessive–compulsive disorder quite the episode. I must ask him about it, shortly, when I see him again. It has to be the same creature. So… together again, my giant friend. I may have further work for you.*

Melting quietly back into the jungle, she searched the leafy shadows looking for a bed of igneous rock sticking up through the undergrowth. Taking her last remaining blast cap, Heidi tapped the steel bolt against the rock. She winced. The *bang* was unnaturally loud across the sunny glade, leading to a second explosion – this one of movement, as every jungle creature within a fifty-metre radius ran or flew for its life. The cap drove the steel bar into the rock, providing a technological anchor point in space–time for Heidi's wormhole device.

Silently, she moved back to the treeline to check on her giant companion. The Spinosaurus yawned hugely, but seemed otherwise untroubled by the unexpected detonation hundreds of metres away.

Heidi breathed a sigh of relief and unhitched the hermetically sealed food bag from her pack. Extremely carefully, she hung it from a low branch, just above head height. One nick and the scent would escape – and she would find herself in Hell's kitchen. The bloody remains of the dead Buitreraptor could be seen through the opaque material, but so far, the seal held the stench within.

With a knife, she carved a small hole into another nearby tree and inserted a camera. She stepped back. It was so tiny as to be invisible. Connecting via an encrypted link to her comm, she adjusted it to cover the area of the plain where she intended to meet with some long-lost shipmates.

All set, she took a last look around, checking everything was in order. Satisfied, she opened a channel. It was time to place a call.

Chapter 17 | Cow

The shuttle craft came in to land, sending the people of Yeavering Bell running for cover in panic. Douglas grimaced. "Probably should have sent Jones ahead with a forward party, to warn everyone."

"At least this will save time, Captain," Tim explained. "I think Chief Nassaki is champing at the bit to leave. He's had everyone working round the clock."

"Aye, but we've still much to do. For a start, Ah intend to track down that escaped sigi... sigil... that escaped dinosaur!"

"Sigilmassasaurus brevicollis?"

Douglas gave a half-smile. "The very same. Still, Ah'll no' deny the help all that combined brainpower we've managed to recruit recently has brought to the table – from all over the multiverse.

With Hiro's staff and all those extra physicists and engineers, our rate of progress has increased dramatically. We might just fix the ship and pull this off, yet. Ah want those wormholes closed. Forever."

"Yes, and based on our past record, I'm sure nothing will go wrong."

Douglas snorted, gently. "Sarcasm, perchance?"

Tim laid a theatrical hand upon his own chest. "*Moi?* No, not really, Captain. I'm just grateful we're able to leave Belle to begin a happy, new life, with plenty of grass."

The engines powered down and Douglas opened the side hatch. He and Sergeant Dewi Jones stepped out first, into glorious sunshine, the threatened rain of the previous evening gone without trace. Douglas looked up, high into the blue infinity, before taking a long look around. They had endured so much, but were at long last about to set out on the final leg of their journey. The natural beauty of their surroundings was a tonic that put a spring in his stride, and he took great lungfuls of healing.

He turned back to the fort to find the top of its mighty stone walls bristling with spears – perhaps unsurprisingly, after the nature of their entrance. His newfound positivity wavered. "Erm…"

"Alright or wha'," Jones called his unofficial-traditional Welsh–English salutation.

Cadwaladr pushed to the front. Recognising them, he smiled broadly and bellowed for men to open the gates.

Tim approached, placing a hand on Douglas' arm. "I do believe they're getting used to us, Captain."

Clarrie and Natalie followed them out of the shuttle, leading Belle the cow.

Yeavering Bell's diminutive king burst forth from his gates to exchange enthusiastic greetings with Douglas and Jones. Jones introduced Tim, Clarrie and Natalie, who were also warmly welcomed.

Tim was immediately struck dumb, completely awed by where he was and what he was doing – not to mention who he was meeting. It took him a while to find his voice. "I've been here before. It was the only place in Britain left unspoilt... I saw a red squirrel..." He tailed off, bashfully.

Jones clapped a heavy hand on his shoulder. "This is better, isn't it?"

Cadwaladr had not the first clue what Tim was gibbering about but invited them all in, jovially. The village inside its ring of stone was abuzz with sudden activity.

"I think we've been invited to a feast, Captain," Jones translated. "They must have been expecting us, after all."

"Oh, really? Ah'm no' sure we have the time—" He stopped mid-excuses when he saw the pleading looks on everyone's faces. "Er... Mapusaurus steaks again, is it?"

Jones laughed. "It tastes just like chicken, boy!"

Douglas was whisked away to sit in a place of honour next to Cadwaladr, centre stage in a scene spookily reminiscent of the conclusion to every Asterix the Gaul story he had ever read as a child. It was quite wonderful, and the smell of roasting meat and honey cakes made his stomach growl. In a moment of guilt, he remembered his comrades aboard ship, missing out, but it soon passed.

The little boy he had saved with modern medicine ran to him, reaching to be picked up. Douglas smiled down at the child, lifting him onto his knee to share some roast boar. His name, as best as Douglas could tell, was Mok, and he giggled gleefully while the UNS *New World*'s captain prattled some nonsense about trains and tunnels.

Douglas could remember few days, if any, when he had felt so content. He, too, had visited Yeavering Bell in a previous life. At least, had visited its ruins in the late 21st century. He could almost feel his father's presence at his shoulder, while the little boy bounced on his lap, laughing and playing with his food. In a moment of madness, he could have happily turned his back on a world of technology and terrorists forever, to begin a new, analogue life, right then and there. Going off-grid had never felt more appealing.

Would he miss his creature comforts? Not enough to matter. Only his sense of duty forbade him. His father would have understood that, too, for it was he who instilled it.

Mok chortled merrily as the honey cakes arrived, and Douglas felt the need to surreptitiously wipe a brimming tear before it fell.

Jones was experiencing pain of his own, as he did his best to describe how Belle was found and rescued to Cadwaladr, and how she had become known as the 'wedding present'.

After they had all eaten, Cadwaladr led the *New Worlders*, and Belle, towards the cattle pen they kept safely within their walls. With Jones' clumsy assistance, Natalie explained the virtues of Jersey milk, while Clarrie and Tim stroked Belle's nose.

Cadwaladr watched the scene with bemusement. His people's attitude towards potentially dangerous herd animals was one of careful respect; they valued them and were grateful for the gifts the beasts granted, but never before had he seen such tenderness for a cow. There were even a few tears. The king shook his head ruefully – Douglas' were a strange folk. Still, Belle was clearly an expensive animal. He had never before seen her like, and so accepted the gift gladly and graciously.

Douglas patted Belle's flank kindly. "She's from us all, Cadwaladr. Ah always believe in leaving something behind on a deal. Any bargain should always benefit all parties. Ye gave us shelter when we'd nowhere to go and she's a fine beastie, valuable, and needing a good home. A good deal all round. Thank ye."

Jones slumped beseechingly, but did his best to translate. Cadwaladr understood well enough, requiring no fine words, and promised Belle would be well looked after and not slaughtered. It was rough comfort, but Natalie and Clarrie bowed gratefully.

From Cadwaladr's perspective, the promise was no great dispensation. He owned several hundred head of cattle already. Belle, however, was unique, and that did indeed make her valuable – too valuable to place with the beef stock.

It was a decision made at first glance, but that did not prevent Natalie from bending Cadwaladr's – and Jones' – ear about how interbreeding Belle with his Highland cattle might improve milk yields and the quality of their dairy produce. Again, Jones did his best, but who knew if Cadwaladr really understood, or cared. He did understand that they were leaving and called for three large drinking horns, tipped and rimmed in decorative copper – fine tableware for the time.

He offered one to Douglas, as a leader and a peer, and another to Jones. Any warrior of Jones' stature automatically received lordly status within their culture. Even without his flying chariots and godlike powers, Cadwaladr would have rated Douglas highly indeed, simply for having such a man under his command. He waited for the captain to drink.

"Ah shouldnae really. No' while Ah'm flying. Ah mean, Ah…"

"Don't think there's anybody here to check your licence, isn'it," Jones encouraged with a smirk.

Douglas took the horn and clunked it together noisily with Cadwaladr's, sloshing the mead everywhere. He drank deeply, doubting he would do anything quite so manly, ever again.

***

Two millennia later…

During a freezing February in AD1559 they walked, no more than ten miles the first day, and with Allison Cocksedge complaining every step of the way. Erika Schmidt stole survival gear from the *New World* when they escaped, but it was always better to find a structure in which to shelter for the night where possible.

The barn was everything Cocksedge had always hoped never to see, and when Schmidt asked her to milk the cow with whom they shared their accommodation, she almost fainted away.

The mother's calf looked less than a year old, but still nuzzled, so Schmidt guessed the cow was probably nearing the end of her milking cycle. Charity was hardly a virtue in Henrich Schultz's inner circle, and she regarded Cocksedge balefully, drawing inevitable comparisons.

"Ah'll dae it," Aila offered, breaking the awkward silence. She grabbed a stool and bucket from the corner, easily getting down to work.

Schmidt nodded. "Allison, seriously, we should both take a turn. We must learn the skills of survival in these lands. As you yourself have stated, our destiny awaits, but it is a long way to London. A warm, nutritious drink whenever the opportunity arises will make the journey easier. Continue, Aila."

The disgust on Cocksedge's face spoke to a lifetime's aversion to manual labour. Physically, she had *always* kept a clean pair of hands. "Don't be ridiculous," she hissed, turning her back on Aila and lowering her voice. "That's what *she's* for. Why do you think I brought her, for the conversation?"

Schmidt eyed her coolly. "And if something happens to the girl? We should learn anything she can teach us. These are dangerous roads in dangerous times. Especially for women."

"That's why we have you, dear, to protect us," Cocksedge replied smoothly, placing a hand over Schmidt's and tapping it gently. "I'd hate to be the man who tried to press unwanted attentions on you."

"You are quite correct. Naturally, they will come for me first, and when they start dying, they will try for Aila next. The dogs who live in these hills show little discernment, it seems – they might even come for you."

The cow moaned while Aila milked.

When Douglas returned, he was physically and emotionally exhausted, in no condition to give a blow-by-blow account of the last few hours with Cadwaladr and his people. Though truly blessed to have a good woman waiting for him, ready to offer comfort and ease away the cares of his day, he also knew his good woman would demand he tell her everything – with no time off for being dead on his feet, and him with a full belly, too.

She sniffed, impolitely. "You've been drinking," she accused.

An auspicious beginning, Douglas. "No! Well, aye, just a wee dram – just to be sociable, ye ken." He allowed himself a brief, weary smile. "Our gift to Cadwaladr and his people was a great success." With the last of his strength, he straightened proudly, subconsciously tucking one hand inside his tunic, Nelson style. "No man's legacy is his own, it belongs tae those he leaves behind, and Ah—"

"That's nice, honey," she interrupted, discourteously. "Been rehearsing a distraction?"

He snorted. "Perhaps."

"I understand that what you actually left behind was a cow."

He bridled. "It was a wee bit more than that, lassie. We made a difference."

Douglas' comm beeped. He sighed, tiredly, but answered dutifully, as he always did. "Douglas."

"Captain, bridge here."

Douglas recognised Lieutenant-Commander Singh. "Go ahead, Sandy. What have you?"

"I have a… a call for you."

Douglas could tell from the awkwardness in Singh's voice that something was amiss. "A call? From whom?"

"You're not going to believe this, sir. It's Heidi Schultz."

An unwanted kick of adrenaline pushed any thoughts of rest away, as he stared at his wife in astonishment.

In record time, they arrived on the bridge. "Outside it's late September," Douglas declared, brusquely, "so Ah assume this isnae some kind of April Fool's caper, Sandy."

Singh shook his head, seriously. "If only, sir."

"What in the hell does she want?"

Singh seemed to slump slightly. "Tim. She wants Tim, sir. And she's giving us a choice."

Douglas and Baines stopped dead in their tracks, halfway across the bridge.

"Continue," Baines prompted, warily.

"She's offering to give herself up, but *only* to Tim Norris, otherwise—"

"Unacceptable!" Douglas bellowed.

Baines placed a restraining hand on his arm. "Wait, James. Go on, Sandy. Otherwise, what?"

"*Otherwise,* she's going to destroy the future. That's all she said, Captains. We have a comm frequency and we're to contact her in thirty minutes, or the deal's off." His brow furrowed in thought. "Although with the time differential between the wormholes, I'm not sure how that works exactly…"

"Sandy, it hardly matters. We'd better make sure we get back to her as agreed. We can worry about temporal dynamics later… so to speak. Or maybe we should just strike now, with overwhelming force. Make sure of her!"

Singh was shaking his head. "Her signal was bounced off a relay. We'd have to find her first. Doubt very much we'd get the drop on her that way, ma'am."

"Aye yi yi." Douglas shook his head, frustratedly, still trying to clear his mind of the effects of alcohol. "Fine! We'd better get the laddie up here, then."

Tim arrived within a few minutes, looking sheepish. The reasons for his discomfort followed him onto the bridge.

Douglas blinked in surprise. "Evening, Patricia, Clarrie," he greeted.

"We were having a nightcap together," Tim explained, slightly embarrassed.

Douglas watched with mild amusement as another young man fell under the wheels of wifely devotion. The poor lad had his mother with him, too. Very nasty. Had the situation not been so serious, he might have grinned.

"And we refused to let him come alone," Clarrie cut through his musings and to the heart of Tim's dilemma. "Now, what's this all about, Captain? What does that witch want with my husband?"

The new husband smiled apologetically.

"You're not letting that woman within a *light year* of my son again, James Douglas, you hear me?" Patricia added for good measure.

Outflanked from both sides, Douglas looked to Baines for assistance. He had not seen his wife smirk in quite a while. He soured. "You picked yer time!"

She snorted. "Come on, ladies, let's try to stay calm. We don't know the details yet – it's just a conversation."

"Over the comm?" Patricia demanded, hotly.

"Over the comm," Baines confirmed, reassuringly.

"For now," Singh muttered, darkly.

Baines glared at him. "*Sandy!*" she hissed. "You never miss, do you?"

Douglas tried to calm them. "Look, Jill's right. We must keep a level head and see what she has to say."

"You can't possibly believe she's going to give herself up, Captain," Clarrie scolded. "She's up to somethin'!"

"Maybe she's had enough of being out in the forever, alone," Singh suggested.

Baines was about to invite him to shut up again, when Douglas stated that Singh might have a point. "She's lost everything, even her psychotic, maniacal grandfather now, it seems."

"For now!" Baines borrowed Singh's phrase, spitting it more harshly than she intended.

Douglas smoothed over her outburst, not wishing to get bogged down in that direction, feeling it was best to deal with one resurrection at a time. "Perhaps she just wants to come back, whatever the consequences. Even prison must seem preferable to being out alone in the…"

"Forever?" Singh prompted.

"Ah was going to say cold."

"That's all very poetic," Baines noted, drily, "but I don't buy it, either. She must have a plan. Also, there's the little matter of revenge. She sees Tim as a traitor for coming back to us. Do any of us remember her as the forgiving kind o' gal?"

"Let's just see what she has to say," Douglas stressed. "About the only thing we *can* be sure of is that, if she's threatening to destroy the future we're trying to preserve, she might just have a way to do it. How long before the comms pass, Sandy?"

"Thirteen minutes, Captain."

"Lucky omen," Tim muttered. "Just long enough to go out of our minds."

"State yer request," Douglas invited, roughly.

There was a short crackle before Heidi spoke, but otherwise the signal was strong. "*My terms are simple,* Kapitän. *I will surrender myself, but only to my cousin, Tim Norris.*"

"What's this?" Patricia burst out. "James, what the hell is she talking about, 'cousin'?"

Silence fell like a house brick into a bowl of soup – breaking the bowl. Everyone froze.

After an awful moment, laughter came through the comm. "*Is that your adoptive mother, Timothy? My, my, you are almost as good at keeping secrets as I am. You truly* are *a Schultz. I see you survived the gunshot wound I gave you, Patricia. Good for you.*"

Patricia grabbed her son by the arms. "Tim, what's she talking about?"

"It's not true, Mum. That's why I never told you. After you were shot… I mean… look, there was just no point in upsetting you further. It's all lies." Tears welled in his eyes. He honestly did not know if he was telling her the truth or not. Absolute proof had been denied, exactly as Heinrich intended. He doubted even Heidi knew for certain. "Mum, it's a *lie,*" he repeated more forcefully.

Patricia bent double, holding her stomach, shock provoking the phantom pain to return like a second gut-shot. Suddenly, everything seemed surreal; she was sleepwalking through porridge, her mind groggy, her footing heavy and treacherous. Agonised, she looked around the bridge, one face at a time. "Who else knew? Did you all know? Did everyone?"

Baines placed an arm around her to offer support. "Very few people knew, Patricia. When we found out, you were desperately sick, after that witch nearly killed you. There was no point—"

"No point?" Tears streamed down Patricia's cheeks. "That was ten years ago!"

"No point at all," Baines repeated, firmly. "The Schultzes lie on an industrial scale. It's the one thing we know about them for certain. What little evidence we were able to find was far from concrete, and of course, the years went by…"

"Mum." Tim took her hands, gently. "We were unable to prove it one way or the other, and I just didn't want you to ever have doubts about me. I'm your son, in every way that matters – as I always was."

"Nothing would ever have changed that, Tim," she muttered softly, but the pain was clear in her eyes. "But this conspiracy… and for all these years. Am I the butt of some kind of joke aboard ship? The only one left in the dark? I can't believe you all kept this… this evil suggestion from me."

"*They* didn't, Mum," Tim explained. "I did. It was my decision and everyone respected it. I didn't leave it up for debate. Until there was actual, undeniable evidence, I didn't want it to hurt you, just in case…"

"Just in case it was true," Patricia completed for him, tonelessly.

"More in case it wasn't. I'd have inflicted the lie on you for nothing – constructing a doubt that could never be removed."

Patricia wiped her tears, hurt replaced by anger. "Is that *woman* saying that your real parents weren't who we were told they were? The records lied?"

"I don't know," he admitted, honestly this time. "It's probably all a twisted lie, as Jill said. I'm sorry, Mum, but I just didn't want you to have to live with this. It changes nothing… does it?"

"*This is all very touching*," Heidi drawled, "*but we have a transaction to conclude. Do I surrender to my cousin, or do I disappear to do my worst? Consider carefully*, Kapitän. *If I go, you will* never *find me, and that future you so desperately crave will die right here, right now. You have my word on it.*"

Douglas would never take Heidi's word on anything, but it

would be foolish to ignore the threat. After all, liars sometimes told the truth; that was what made them so dangerous.

"I'll go," Tim announced, stepping away from his mother.

"*No!*" Patricia grabbed him, pulling him back into her arms. "No," she sobbed.

"Dinnae worry, lassie," Douglas comforted. "If Heidi thinks she'll get her hands on Tim again, she's delusional!"

"*So… no deal?*"

"Wait!" Tim snapped. "Why do you want to see me, Heidi? Why me?"

"*We are kin. Of course I want to see you, cousin.*"

Tim tensed. "The truth, damnit! What do you want? To finish me off?"

"*On the contrary. I wish us to be together again. That is why I am willing to give myself up to you – but* only *to you. Surely none of you would want me in the wind, with all that I know, would you? It might surprise you to learn that I often remember our defence lessons on that island beach, off the coast of Africa. How close we became, for a time.*"

"You mean those beatings you gave me?"

"*You needed toughening up, cousin. It was a harsh world. I gave a harsh lesson. I was trying to save* you."

"Really?" The sarcasm in Tim's question was obvious.

"*So now you hate me, yes? Would you kill me, given the chance, Timothy?*"

"I would never want to kill *anyone*. That's what proves I'm no kin of yours!"

"*But could you?*"

Tim fell silent. The idea was abhorrent, not least because if she was a genuine, flesh and blood relative, how would he live with that afterwards? He sensed subtle psychology working against him but could not quite grasp what she was up to. In his heart, Tim knew he *would* feel the loss if she was killed. He would mourn, not the monster she had become, but what she might have been. Nothing would change the love he felt for his mum, but the fact remained, Heidi might actually be his only close, living relative. As for killing her… He shuddered, looking to Douglas for guidance.

"Heidi, stand by," Douglas ordered. He gestured for Singh to mute the connection. "Put that out of your mind, Tim. She's playing games. But that said, what do we do, people? Does anyone doubt she could destroy the future our friends in the 16th century managed to create?"

"Not for a second," Tim announced. "This might be our last chance to end it."

"No!" Clarrie pleaded. "She's a killer, Timmy!"

He nodded, accepting. "I know. And she's more than half insane, but just maybe she's telling the truth. After all, she really has lost everything. Even her madcap scientist is with us now. Maybe she just wants to come home."

"You're thinking like a normal human being," Baines warned. "Dangerous, Tim. Half-insane, huh? Let me tell you something, she's a *full-on* whack job, the proper article!"

"So?" he challenged her. "Who says I have to go alone?"

Douglas signalled for Singh to unmute. "Heidi, this is Douglas. Where exactly *are* ye?"

"I am in the Cretaceous – the last time frame the wormhole outside your ship led to."

"So ye did come through here," he acknowledged, gratified they had guessed correctly.

"I did. But if you are thinking of sending a strike team through to deal with me, think again. I am camped by the earthworks you built just after we arrived here – about fifty kilometres east of the portal."

Douglas was taken aback. Singh had warned that she would be difficult to locate near the wormhole, but fifty klicks? "How did ye get there?"

"Walked. How else?"

Douglas' eyebrows shot up, impressed.

"Stop stalling, Douglas. Do we have a deal? I surrender to my cousin, or I disappear – choose!"

"It will take us a wee while to get to ye—"

"You have one hour."

"We cannae travel that distance over rough ground in one hour. Be reasonable."

"Reasonable is your way, Kapitän, *not mine – and how has that been working out for you? I suggest you fly. I will allow you to send a pilot and one other – I do not expect you to send my soft cousin out on his own. One hour, Douglas, or the deal is off!"*

"Ah'll come with him."

"No. Not you, Douglas. Commander… forgive me, Captain *Baines may accompany him along with a pilot. No one else, clear?"*

"Ye cannae be serious?"

"Tick tock, Kapitän."

The combat chopper drove through the wormhole, powerful electric motors driving its landing wheels, while its rotors remained folded back for transport. Much larger than the small reconnaissance chopper flown by Gleeson, the blades, when extended, were too long to allow the aircraft to fly through the portal. It popped out into brilliant sunshine onto the *Last Word* plateau, behind an armoured vehicle sent on ahead to check the coast was clear.

Once more at the controls, Gleeson toggled the switch that opened the rotors, locking them into their five-way positions ready for flight. He looked to Baines in the co-pilot's seat. "This is it, Cap. Do we have a go for Operation This-is-a-bladdy-stupid-idea?"

She nodded moodily. "Let's get it over with, Commander."

"Yes, ma'am." He fired up the jet-fuelled engines. "All OK in the back, kids?"

"We're ready," The Sarge answered, seriously.

"No," Tim replied through the headset, "but like Jill said, let's just get it over with."

Gleeson turned one last time to Baines. "You really think we're gonna bring her in this time?"

"I think we're gonna try—"

"Or die!" Tim interrupted. "I don't know about all of you, but I'd like this to end now."

Baines nodded. "Do it, Commander," she ordered softly.

The chopper lifted and turned east towards the original *New World* settlement.

"This is craziest thing we've done yet," Douglas stewed, angrily. "There's no way she's on the level."

"What choice did we have, Captain?" Singh asked seriously. "If we did nothing, we'd be *guaranteeing* the worst outcome. At least this way there's a small chance she's playing straight with us, or, and this is more likely, we'll have one last chance to take her down before she does anything drastic."

"Considering where we are, and everything Heidi's already done," Douglas countered, "Ah'd rather not speculate about what 'drastic' might entail at this juncture!"

Patricia and Clarrie remained on the bridge, flat refusing to be removed from the action. "C-can The Sarge k-kill her?" Clarrie asked, nervousness making her teeth chatter.

Douglas studied the young woman, wishing desperately that he could protect her from the truth. She looked so afraid, ready to lash out to protect the one she loved, and her fears were certainly well founded. He felt the same way – along with Tim, his wife was out there, too. Eventually, he decided on, "He's the best we have, lassie. He'll no' let anything happen to them. And as for Commander Gleeson, he's the best kind of crazy."

"The best kind?" Singh queried.

"Aye. The kind that's on *our* side. Don't worry, ladies. Ah didnae tell Jill, but Ah'm sending backup through straight after them – two more combat 'copters with armoured ground support. They'll neutralise Heidi's transmitter on the other side and be ready to move in at a moment's notice."

"Why didn't you tell Jill?" asked Patricia.

"Plausible deniability." He winked. "Heidi will never know what's hit her!"

⌇

Heidi heard the *chop, chop* of the helicopter echoing around the mountains well before she saw it. Feeling adrenaline surge through her system, she set her hidden camera to record and broadcast. It would soon be over, and she would start again, completely afresh – this time holding *all* the cards. She knew Douglas would never trust her offer, but neither could he ignore it. He had no choice but to agree and see where it led. Neither of them could afford to pass up one last opportunity to end this.

She checked her wrist device a final time, making sure the coordinates were set and correct, and that it would precisely record the timestamp provided by the anchor cap she had buried in the rock at her feet. Time would be critical. Space would be critical. This would be, by far, the biggest risk she had ever taken.

The chopper flew in to circle the clearing at speed. It was an impressive machine, obviously built for war. Douglas was learning, and Heidi had no doubts that its full sensor suite was already sweeping the entire area, looking for her. She was under no illusion that they would hesitate if she granted them a clean shot with a missile – not with Baines in the mix. She backed a little further into the jungle, hiding behind one of the larger redwoods to confuse their scans.

Gleeson brought them down low, to hover a hundred metres from the treeline.

Two hundred metres north, Spinosaurus stood, growling her annoyance, but she was also afraid. Whenever the unnatural flying things came, she woke up somewhere new – and usually worse. Quickly taking stock of the situation, she decided that the place she had chosen for her mid-morning snooze was entirely too busy and too noisy. She sloped off to the river and slid beneath the waters into beatific silence.

Baines opened a channel. "Well, we're here."

"*I noticed. Nice gunship.*"

"Whatever. Are you coming out, or are we playing hide and seek?"

"*So you can incinerate me without placing so much as a wheel on the ground? I think not.*"

Baines looked to Gleeson, who raised his eyes to heaven. "She's scattering her comm signal. I can't pinpoint her."

Baines grimaced. "Of course she is." No one expected Heidi to make it easy for them. She opened the channel once more. "So what do you suggest?"

A crackle of analogue noise and Heidi's voice filled the cockpit again. "*I suggest you point those cannon away from the trees by turning your machine through ninety degrees north. You will land and fully power down. Then, and only then, shall we meet, at the treeline exactly due west of your position. Unless you plan on carving down the entire jungle to find me, Kapitänin?*"

Baines' expression soured further, wondering whether she could. After a moment's consideration, she nodded for Gleeson to follow the instructions.

Heidi moved back to her original location near the anchor cap fired into the stone. Hanging from a low branch above was the bag of putrefying raptor. Standing to the side, she took out a blade and slit the bag, letting its contents slop out onto the forest floor. Wrinkling her nose in disgust, she tracked further back into the jungle to wait.

Baines stepped out of the helicopter, ducking under the rotors' downwash before they came to rest. Tim made to follow. "You stay here," she commanded.

"No. I won't let you go alone, Jill. It's me—"

She silenced him with a nod to The Sarge, who pinned the younger man in place. "Do as the captain tells you, lad."

Baines took out her comm and sidearm. "Coming, ready or not!" She strode towards the edge of the clearing.

"The deal was, that I would surrender to my cousin," Heidi called from the trees as Baines drew near.

"And so you shall," Baines called back. "Once I'm certain you don't have any tricks for us."

"Tut, tut, *Kapitänin.* You are not keeping up your end of our bargain. I see you have not changed."

"Neither have you – you see the problem?"

Heidi laughed, girlishly. Arming herself with her last and only true friend through so many trials and tribulations, her trusty nine-millimetre, she stepped out from behind a tree and approached.

They faced each other, guns in hand.

"What the hell is that stench?" Baines asked, trying not to gag.

"The real world, *Kapitänin.* Death. Now, where is my cousin? I would like to finalise our agreement."

"Interesting choice of words."

Heidi rolled her eyes. "Are we here to discuss semantics? Keep our bargain, or I will execute my alternative plan. You prefer those words? Well, *Kapitänin,* what will it be?"

Baines glared at her. *Cow!* she thought. *She's up to something. The last time we squared up like this, James was taken prisoner aboard his own shuttle, removing any options I might have had. If I bring Tim forward, I'm risking a repeat.*

Her chest felt tight as she forced a calming breath. She was sorely tempted to just start shooting and leave the rest to fate. Letting the breath out slowly, she was about to speak when Heidi spoke first.

"You are considering shooting me?" she guessed, accurately.

"I never stopped!"

Again, Heidi laughed. "Seriously, Baines, bring Tim forward or I walk. As even you will have surmised, I already have contingencies in place, so I suggest you do not try… what is the phrase… winging it? Even if you succeeded with a lucky shot, rest assured, you would be left with a considerable consolation prize. You must know how much I would hate for you to go home empty-handed."

Wondering if the woman before her was bluffing, Baines raised her comm. Heidi immediately tensed to shoot, slowly relaxing once she was sure there was no attack.

"Twitchy, aren't we?" Baines taunted.

"The Cretaceous breeds caution, *Kapitänin*."

Baines narrowed her eyes, remembering the Permian–Triassic cataclysm – the greatest mass extinction event of the Phanerozoic Eon[1]. "I've seen worse places and worse catastrophes. Believe it or not, one of them wasn't even your fault." Raising her comm again – slowly this time – she spoke into it, "Commander, send Tim to me. You stay with the chopper."

That was code for The Sarge to stay hidden in the rear for now. He released Tim. "Good luck, lad. We'll be right behind you," he whispered, softly.

The rotors came to a full stop, drooping downwards at the ends, as Tim stepped out to walk beneath them. Slowly, he approached the two women. Baines had her back to him, keeping her eye very deliberately on the enemy.

She heard the crunch of his boots as he came to stand behind and just to the left of her.

"Hello, Heidi."

She nodded. "Hello, cousin. You have grown up."

"It was ten years ago – what did you expect?"

She smiled cruelly. "I expected you to die. When we fired on the *New World* over Crater Lake. After you betrayed me. Though I understand you have led a remarkable existence since. I look forward to learning all about it."

"Weren't you about to surrender?" Baines interrupted, harshly. "Tim's here. Get on with it! You can start by throwing down your

---

1. The Phanerozoic Eon stretches from 541 million years ago, all the way up to the Holocene Epoch in which these words are being typed – and with any luck, long after. It includes: the Palaeozoic Era, which saw the birth of complex life, through to the first truly large creatures – some of whom left the sea to claim the land alongside the new plants; the Mesozoic Era, broadly described as the reign of the dinosaurs; and the Cenozoic Era, being everything since. From the early days, sifting nutrients from silt, all the way to modernity, sifting meaning from memes, life goes on.

weapon."

"All in good time." Heidi approached them slowly, unthreateningly. "Tim, *unser Großvater* is dead. We are all who remain now."

"*Your* grandfather, Heidi. He was nothing to do with me. I heard about his death. Couldn't have happened to a nicer chap."

She giggled again, lowering her guard for an instant.

Baines saw an opportunity and swung, hitting Heidi in the jaw, the weight of her sidearm adding to the force of the connection.

It should have knocked her out cleanly, but Heidi's reactions were extraordinary, and she managed to turn her head away, sapping the force of the blow. She continued around in a clockwise spin to bring a roundhouse kick against Baines' head.

With a split second to bring her arms back up, Baines met it with a double block. Bracing herself against the force of the kick, she stopped Heidi's heel and calf with her forearms and, before Heidi could regain her balance, hooked her leg behind the younger woman's, pushing her to the ground.

Heidi barely landed. She used the momentum of Baines' thrust and immediately pirouetted back to her feet, firing two shots, almost point blank, into Baines' chest.

Baines flew backwards and went down without stirring.

"*Jill!*" Tim screamed, reaching for her.

Heidi grabbed him, spinning him round. "Come with me, cousin. We could rule the world, you and I. I will protect you. Teach you all that I know."

Unthinking, Tim simply reacted, catching Heidi with a roundhouse punch of his own. It was ungallant, but semi-effective.

A warrior of experience, Heidi saw the flash in his eyes and knew it was coming. She had no time to block and so relaxed and rolled with it, once again, taking the power out of the stroke. Effortlessly, she struck back, using the butt of her gun to knock Tim to the ground. She could easily have cracked his skull wide open, but tempered the stroke, making sure he remained conscious. She spoke without anger. "We are family, Timothy. Come with me."

"You and me, Hell's very own Blood Royal? You're not *family,* you're a monster!"

"*Timothy!*"

Tim reached for Baines' dropped weapon and pointed it at Heidi, hesitating.

"You shot me once before, remember?" Emotions were a foreign country for Heidi, but she mimicked the angst she had observed in others, drawing him in. By a quirk of time travel, they were of an age now, but Tim was still a child in her eyes.

Taking her sorrow at face value, Tim got to his feet, saving Heidi's life.

A hundred metres behind him, she caught movement and recognised The Sarge, outside the chopper now, aiming a sniper's rifle. As Tim stood, blocking his shot, he moved the barrel to the side and cursed.

Heidi screamed in frustration. She was out of time and could only hope that one final outrage would yield the reaction she sought from her weak cousin. Firing a gratuitous third round into the chest of Baines' lifeless form, she snatched her backpack from the ground, turned and leapt into a wormhole that shimmered to life behind her.

"*Nooooo!*" Tim cried, firing two shots after her.

The Sarge appeared at his side in moments, staring in disbelief as the wormhole vanished, leaving no sign it had ever been. "Check on the captain!" he bellowed. When Tim failed to respond, he slapped the younger man's arm with the butt of his rifle. "Wake up!"

Tim staggered, but obeyed, kneeling at Baines' side, while The Sarge kept watch on where the wormhole had been, just moments before. He knew better than to *ever* trust Heidi Schultz.

Gleeson appeared out of nowhere. "What the hell just happened? *Jeez!* What's that stink?"

The Sarge risked a glance at the commander. "Get back to the chopper! Only you can fly the bladdy thing! Stay behind the wheel – or whatever."

"You mean the stick…" But Gleeson was not really listening. He was staring, flabbergasted. The Sarge immediately snapped his attention back. The wormhole had reappeared, and Heidi tumbled through it to fall flat on her face, two bloody bullet holes in her back.

The Sarge leaned forward. "What's that in her hand, some kind of strap?"

"Must be the remains of the wormhole device that bladdy drongo Reid made for her," Gleeson answered absently, though he was more interested in the cause of death. "Nice grouping, mate," he commented, slightly stunned. "Straight through the heart. A shot in a million with *that* Sheila— Oh, bagger…"

Sergeant Jackson turned his attention back to his colleague, but this time Gleeson was looking up, and up again. The stench from Heidi's carrion bag may have lacked charm, but it had certainly worked like one, and she could not have hoped for a more impressive dinner guest than Spinosaurus aegyptiacus.

The Sarge gulped. "Oh, Turkish delight!"

The wormhole vanished again, but they hardly noticed.

Baines coughed as she regained consciousness. "I'm alright," she wheezed. "Kevlar." She rapped her knuckles hard against the breastplate sewn into her combat jacket, making her cough again. "Ow. Why did I just do that?"

"Up on your feet!" The Sarge bellowed at the top of his lungs. "Tim, help her – jump to it, lad!" He fired at the massive muzzle, grinning down at them, drooling disgustingly onto the ferns.

Tim was at sea, but dutifully wrapped Baines' arm around his shoulder and struggled her back to her feet. Gleeson grabbed her roughly by the other arm and they set off. Gleeson screamed, "*Ruuuuun!* She's invited her bladdy relos[2]!"

The Sarge fired again, but the single-shot, high-performance rifle did little more than agitate a creature already wondering

---

2. Australian slang for relations. Harsh, but fair, when considering the Schultz family.

what the hell was going on with her food. She *roared!* Part anger, part anguish – the bullet really stung. The running humans were deafened and terrified.

"What about Heidi's body?" Tim shouted above the raucous shouts and roars.

"Big 'un back there can keep it. She'll need a palate cleanser after that rotten corpse!" Gleeson hollered back.

"Big 'un's already got it!" The Sarge called from behind. "Run faster! Before she comes for dessert! I bladdy told you, you should have stayed at the wheel!"

Baines was struggling for breath, unsurprising after the beating she had endured from three nine-millimetre rounds to the chest at such close range, bulletproof vest or no. Virtually carried between the two men, she managed one step in four as she was dragged back to the helicopter.

Reaching the chopper, Tim turned as Gleeson half-helped, half-threw Baines into the rear seats. He saw Heidi's body lifted from the ground, almost delicately, as the giant *crocodilianesque* head tipped back. Spinosaurus threw the young woman's body high into the air, opened her jaws wide, and Heidi Schultz vanished.

Tim's breath caught in his throat. He had caused this. He had killed her. No matter what she had done, no matter what she had become, he would never forgive himself. His actions this day cost him a piece of his soul. She had taken it with her. Was that Heidi's revenge?

"Stop gawking, lad! Get in!" The Sarge shouted in his ear, thrusting him into the rear of the helicopter with Baines, as Gleeson fired up the engines. He span round to get into the co-pilot's seat and saw Spinosaurus bearing down on him. "Get us in the air!"

"I'm bladdy trying, I'm not a bladdy drongo!"

"Oh, my *Gooood!*" The Sarge cried in horror, as the massive predator crashed into rotors that had barely begun to spin, smashing them, one at a time.

"AAAARRRGGGHHH!" they all screamed together as the chopper lifted from the ground, but not under its own power. It began to tip.

"We're going over!" Gleeson shrieked.

"*We know!*" they hollered back as the machine crunched onto its side.

"Don't worry!" he assured them. "This is a warbird. She won't be able to crush us."

"That's easy for you to say," The Sarge roared. "It's my bladdy window she's got her nose up against! I knew I should have shot her when we had her drugged in the ship's hangar!"

Gleeson looked up at the grinning maw, filled with jagged ivory. "You think it's the same animal?"

"*Yes!*" they all called again.

Spinosaurus *roared.*

Inside, the crew screamed.

"*Captain Baines, come in – over.*"

The sudden radio communication shut them up, immediately. Gleeson reached for the comm with shaking hands as the damaged helicopter was rocked and shoved by the furious dinosaur.

"I'm sorry I shot you! OK?" The Sarge lamented. "Oh, Turkish delight – hang on!"

Another colossal thrust, and the chopper turned completely over, destroying the rotor mast and blades entirely.

"Bagger! Not even Nassaki will be able to fix that— *Whoaaa!*" Gleeson cried. None of them had had time to strap themselves in before they were attacked, and they all fell headfirst. Gleeson banged his head hard against the airframe, proving that, occasionally, one man's ceiling could become the *same* man's floor. He expressed his displeasure. "Ow! Bladdy hell!" Despite his panic, and being upside down, he somehow managed to operate the comm. "This is Commander Gleeson – over."

"*Commander, do you require assistance? Over.*"

"No, we're having the time of our bladdy lives! Are you going to shoot this ugly mongrel, or do I have to get out and throw bladdy stones at it?"

"Don't kill her!" Tim shouted from the back.

"Are you kidding?"

Two identical gunships came in to hover just above the altercation. Spinosaurus bellowed her wrath at the sky, but despite such terrible rage, she knew the odds had shifted. With a last roar of defiance, she made her way back to the cool, welcoming waters of the river.

Coast now clear, the backup helicopters landed and powered down, once more allowing peace to flow back into the world.

"She's gone." Tim muttered into the sudden silence. "I shot her, and now she's gone."

Gleeson turned to him. "You shot her as well? No wonder she was so bladdy angry."

"Not her. I mean… I *meant,* Heidi."

Gleeson struggled to right himself, now sitting on the chopper's canopy. "Yeah, but she came back," he replied, thoughtfully. "And here's the thing, she looked like she was already dead. I can't see how she made it."

"Maybe she didn't want to die alone, or thought we'd at least retrieve her body and bury it decently?" Baines suggested, rubbing the bruises she could feel blossoming across her chest.

"I think she was alone all her life," Tim added, morosely.

Holding her right arm painfully to her chest, Baines reached out to place her left around his shoulders, to comfort him. "Perhaps. It'll be OK, Tim. It's over now. By the way, it was good of James to tell me he was sending backup," she added, sarcastically. "If I know my husband, he'll spin me a line about plausible deniability, and so help me—"

"Good job he did," The Sarge cut her off. Moving himself into a sitting position on the chopper's ceiling, he looked back into the rear passenger compartment. "What happened back there, Captain? With Heidi, I mean."

"Yeah, it was a little strange," Gleeson reflected.

Baines glanced at him, around the upside-down pilot's seat. "Ya think? I'm curious – which bit stood out for ya?"

"Well, if *I've* learned anything about that woman, it's that we'll probably never know for sure," The Sarge asserted with a sigh. "Not unless Dr Flannigan wants to go through that monster's stool, in lieu of an autopsy." His eyes bored into Baines'. "Is it over? It is over, right?"

Baines shrugged, making herself wince. "I don't know, Sarge – but if it is, and Heidi's gone, then all we have to do now is destroy her wormholes and implement Hiro's plan to save the world from temporal catastrophe."

"Plain sailing from here, then," Gleeson chipped in, blood trickling down the side of his face. "Ow, my bladdy head!"

Tim sat in silence.

Chapter 18 | Another Fine Ness

Gleeson complained. Safely laid up in the *New World*'s med bay, he was feeling hard done by. Dr Dave Flannigan buzzed around, checking the contusion and mild concussion he sustained during their recent adventure. He had borne it stoically, until Flannigan explained that he was to remain on the ward for the next twenty-four hours, under observation.

"Oh, bladdy 'ell, mate! I've had my head looked at!"

"You don't say? Did it help?" Flannigan drawled, illustrating that doctors do not necessarily need pointy things to give people the needle.

"Captain," Gleeson called across the otherwise empty ward to Baines, pleading. "Tell him I'm fine, will ya?"

"Sure. Right after you tell him I'm fine, too!" It seemed like the whole day had been lost to Flannigan's scans as his team inspected her innards and monitored her bruises. She was bored, too.

"Alright, listen up." Flannigan turned to face them both. "Captain, you were shot, three times, point blank. We just need to make sure there're no internal injuries. You're staying here for twenty-four. Commander, you got a good crack to the noggin. Ditto on the twenty-four. Those are the facts. Any questions?"

"Can we get a second opinion?" Baines grumbled.

"Sure, I'll fetch Matron Runde…"

"No! Don't do that." Gleeson held out a hand beseechingly. "My backside's still smarting from that javelin she stuck me with. Don't know what the bladdy hell a bump on the head has to do with a needle up the—"

"Ah, that's where you're wrong." Flannigan brandished a reproving finger. "That contusion came with an abrasion, and *you* never checked in with me for your tetanus booster."

"Oh, so now we really get to it," Gleeson grumbled. "That's what this is all about, right? I can always file a complaint about abuse of power, y'know."

"Sure, the captain's right over there. You can file it in person."

"Oh, come on, Dave," Baines complained. "We're both absolutely fine."

"You don't say?"

"Have a heart," she implored. "That snapdragon even took my tablet away – and you *know* how my husband likes his reports."

Flannigan's eyebrow rose scornfully. "Not all tablets are medicine!"

"Was that a pun?"

"Jill, Matron took your tablet because you're meant to be resting! As for having a heart – I've already stated twenty-four hours."

Baines rolled her eyes. "And that's what, generous? Thanks, *Dad.*"

"Sure is. Captain Douglas suggested I make it seventy-two – to teach you guys a lesson." She made to object, but he waved her down. "Don't worry, Captain. All that scintillating paperwork will still be there when you get outta here. As for your husband, he's on his way down to sickbay right now. He was just waiting for me to check you guys out. Should be here any minute, if you wanna debate him? A couple o' days extra bedrest never hurt nobody, so I'll be happy to take his advisement, if—"

"No, we're fine!" Gleeson sounded out from the opposite row of beds. "Twenty-four is good. Careful, Captain, don't turn this into a bladdy auction! I'm alright. Got a thick head, mate."

"You don't say."

"Will you stop saying that?" Baines and Gleeson called together. Flannigan laughed.

"Just what the *hell* were you playing at?" Douglas erupted onto the ward.

Massaging her chest demonstrably, Baines groaned, raising herself as slowly as possible to an elbow as she faced him. "Calm down, honey. Take it gentle with me, OK? I'm feelin' real weak."

Flannigan gaped, scandalised by her performance, but made no comment.

Douglas was buying none of it. "Ye took a swing at Heidi Schultz? Engaged a deadly killer, hand-to-hand, while she was *armed?*"

"Our plan *was* to capture her, after all—"

"Since when?"

"Oh, come on, James. Unless you've undergone some kind of Damascene conversion in the last few hours, you know you never would've shot her in cold blood. Not when she looked like being talked down."

"Maybe, but Ah thought *ye* might!" He sighed, exasperated. "Look, we both agreed, many years ago, that we wouldn't let overprotectiveness interfere with our duties, but if that last shot had been just a couple of inches higher, ye'd have caught it in the throat." His voice cracked with emotion.

"Perhaps, but if it had been a few inches lower, I'd have lost my lunch, so it's all good."

"That's some line you walk! And was not the deal, Jill. When Ah agreed to yer mission with Tim, Ah—"

"James." She reached out for his hand. "Relax. It's over. She's dead." She grinned. "Better yet, I punched her hard enough to shake her eyeballs loose! I've been saving that right hook for ten years – ever since she took you hostage – and it was *glorious!*"

"Dead, ye say? There seems to be some confusion about that, tae."

She frowned. "What do you mean?"

"Ah mean, Tim might be bereft, thinking he took the life of possibly his only close, living blood relative – as disgusting as that sounds – but The Sarge is less sure."

"James, darling, Sarge Jackson is one of the best men I know, but we all saw the body. She leapt through the wormhole and came straight back with two bullet wounds in her back. According to Tim, that happened almost immediately after he fired. She must have known she was done for. We never got chance to check if she still lived, but it hardly mattered."

"Oh, did it no', indeed?"

"Not after that Spinosaurus, the one we freed, came back to claim her. That animal would never have even been in the southern hemisphere, if we hadn't captured it."

"What's your point?"

"Simply that not all interference is necessarily negative, honey."

Douglas waved a dismissive hand. "There would have been another giant predator stalking the area. There's hardly a shortage of them in that place!"

"Come on, James, let's take the win, huh? Heidi was swallowed whole, and good riddance! She's not coming back – she's not Boba Fett!"

"Who?"

"Never mind. Look, I was a little out of it, I confess, but Tim saw it all with his own eyes – and you know how observant that kid is."

"Oh, aye. It only took him ten years to marry the girl who was crazy about him since they were bairns!"

"*James…* calm down. It's over. At least, that part is over."

He sighed again, running his fingers through dark hair shot with just a little extra grey after his day of worry. "Ah hope you're right, lassie. But it seems to me that ye saw a *body*. Ah cannae help wondering whether it was the right body."

She pulled him down to sit beside her on the bed. "We can't let Heidi's ghost make us paranoid."

"Alright, I can see no one's gonna lie down just 'cause the senior medical officer says so!" Flannigan chided them. "But they do need to rest, James. I'm gonna have to ask you to keep this visit short."

Douglas nodded. "Ah will, Davey."

"Thank you, Captain. I'll leave you all to bicker about whose fault all this was, but then it's a rest cycle. That's an order. I'll check on you in one hour. Captain, Captain, Commander." Flannigan nodded to each as he turned to leave.

"Potted Hitler!" Baines called after him.

❧

The brush slipped. The painter cursed. His hands just would not stop shaking.

The order came two days ago, early in the morning. Now, there was a time, not so long ago, when he would have been ecstatic to receive such a profitable commission, but that was when he was chief signwriter to the Party. That had been dull work, but it always guaranteed his next salad. His passion for watercolours, particularly landscapes and architecture, rarely paid well, but this current commission was different. The fee offered was exorbitant, and while well outside his usual subject matter, contained elements of everything that would grant him, if not actual fame, then an infamy that would leave its indelible mark on history. It showed devastation, monsters and death.

He sighed. What a mess. So much for fine art. Tutting, he wiped away his mistake as best he could and began fleshing out the error, working back into it to describe piles of rubble that were once the Old Academy in Munich. He glanced at the large screen mounted on the table before his easel, in the bay window of his apartment at

Prinzregentenplatz 16. It displayed a still-frame, clipped from a news reel, showing an exquisitely dressed old man being torn apart by a vast, demonic creature from another world.

He knew that man. Heinrich Schultz. Had watched *other* videos, with him. Such things, Schultz had shown him, things from an alternative timeline that might yet, potentially, become his future – his destiny. Though all the films, weirdly, were from the old man's distant past, they had nevertheless given him the creeping horrors – real life ghost stories too horrible to believe, and yet they were all true. 'Were' being the operative word, for none of those atrocities had happened in his reality. Not yet. Perhaps, now the old man was dead, they never would.

He replaced his brush on the side and took a sip of his afternoon apple tea, laced with a nip of apple liquor, to help his poor digestion. He knew his latest patron, too. Reinhard Tristan Eugen Heydrich, the coldest, most frightening man he had ever met – until he met Heinrich Schultz. Now the one had commissioned a painting of the death of the other – and what a death.

He shuddered, replacing his cup clumsily on its saucer. He was the plaything of monsters, and yet had it within him to be the greatest monster of them all. After all, he had seen it. Visions that appalled him, yet he could not quite draw away from them.

His work with the Party had gone quiet in recent months, though his standard of living had improved dramatically. A poor artist knew better than to look too closely at where the good fortune was coming from, but he knew there would be a price. Now his previous employer was dead, too. Killed by the very same creature. Martin Bormann had been his main contact within the Party – would that mean an end to it all? Things had certainly ended badly for Schultz's *Führer* from the original timeline; would it end so for him? Or could he, *should* he, simply slip away quietly and forget all he had seen and heard? After all, he wanted so badly to be an artist. His application twice refused by the Academy of Fine Arts Vienna, perhaps a third time would bring him success?

He straightened. No. He was a man of destiny. Somehow, he had always known it, despite his failures with brush and easel.

The door opened behind, making him turn from his work. One of his handlers, Albert Speer entered, without knocking.

The artist acknowledged the unwelcome guest and returned to his painting. "The work is almost complete, *Herr* Speer," he explained stiffly.

"I bring news from *Herr* Heydrich. Your presence is requested and required."

Sighing deeply, the painter stepped back to view his canvas. He hated it. Never mind. It was not for him to like but for his patron – for him, it represented a living wage, nothing more. He lifted his brush, sloshing it irritably in a water jug before taking a little black pigment on the bristles. He signed the bottom right-hand corner of his work, *Adolf Hitler.*

"In my original timeline," Corporal Heinz Engel explained, "we had a popular moral quandary. If you could kill Hitler as a baby, knowing all the evil he would release upon the world, would you do it?"

"Spare us," Fritz Todt drawled. "Is that one of those dilemmas where – to remain fashionable – you are meant to say no, but everyone is thinking yes?"

Amusement played in Engel's eyes. "I believe you may have solved it, *Herr* Todt."

Todt stared down his nose at the corporal, snooty as a swan. "And you think this Hitler, this *painter,* is somehow important to our enemies?"

"Only if you believe lightning can strike twice. Perhaps if you saw some of the news reels from my alternative timeline—"

"It can and will strike twice," Colonel Hans Schultz stated with finality. "Heydrich will see to it. There is no way he will be able to resist the sort of power those news reels revealed."

"You think he is that insane… or evil?" asked Todt.

"All that and more. You have met the man. And you have also seen the film footage, Fritz. My *descendants,*" he placed an emphasis of disgust on the word, "made sure our leadership saw them, too. Heinrich Schultz knew that some would be turned immediately by greed and others would be forced to capitulate out of fear for their own safety, as all the sureties they had grown up with began to crumble around them. I don't doubt such a man would enjoy the perversion of otherwise liberal people most of all, while forcing them to commit acts of evil against their will. We must clean out the entire nest. You and I already discussed this at length – well before the Old Academy incident."

"Clean out the entire nest, is that all?" exclaimed Todt. "The *entire* party, or just the leadership?"

"If I may, let's just remain calm, gentlemen, and consider what we know," Engel continued, reasonably. "Both Heidi and Heinrich have been buddying up close with Reinhard Heydrich. If I know them – which unfortunately, I do – they will have offered him some incredibly powerful and advanced technology in exchange for assistance with their schemes. Now, you have mentioned that, in this timeline, Heydrich is a powerful industrialist and phenomenally wealthy—"

"And a total swine!" Todt affirmed.

"Sounds perfect," Engel noted wryly. "If it's any consolation, Heydrich probably won't survive the partnership. I'm more concerned about that technology coming to be, well before it was meant to. It could quite possibly mess up the positive future some of us have already seen. The world our friend, Master Sergeant Badawi, is from. Especially, as the colonel says, if the political class are perverted into taking a new and destructive path. And I promise you, it won't end with Germany. The Schultzes are masters of treachery, far aloof from any puppet governments. We'll soon find unelected global organisations running the world – for the common good! God help us. We must stop this before it begins."

"Good point," Colonel Schultz agreed. "And as you say, you know them better than any of us, Corporal, so what do you suggest?"

"Heidi has the technology to come and go, but it's my belief that, if she's still around, she'll want to get rid of H as a matter of business, so she can assume the persona of her fourth-great-grandaunt and slip in and out of the limelight at will. To what end, I don't know yet, but H's wealth will be a draw, too. Maybe we can use that?"

"She's milking Heydrich at the moment," Todt explained, "and as we have just stated, he is one of the richest men in the world."

"She may have Heydrich's backing for now, but independence is a fine thing," Engel persevered. "H may not be as rich as Heydrich, but she has enough. Heidi won't play second fiddle for long – if at all – and she won't let *our* removal trouble her, either. So I suggest we 'do unto others', sir, and do it first!"

Hans Schultz considered. "I was thinking about removing them all from power. Are you suggesting we remove them from the world?"

Engel shrugged. "It's the only way to be sure, sir."

Todt adjusted his collar uncomfortably. "Look, I have grown to know her over the last six months – on my way back and forth from Cretaceous Egypt, you will understand – and I have learned to hate her as much as the next man, but this is the real world, gentlemen. We are talking about murder, here – worse yet, terrorism."

"I would not go that far," the colonel replied, calmly. "More a strategic offensive. As the corporal said – and he is right – it is the only way to be sure."

Todt shook his head. "No. I understand there may be a military component to our solution, Hans, but we must remain true to who we are. Most of the Party leadership are just politicians – they will bend and sway with the prevailing wind. Widespread action will not be necessary. There should be no need to take down the Party in its entirety. I mean, what are you suggesting, we take one of Heidi's weapons of mass destruction and call down a nuclear strike? Oh, and by the way, has she not, somehow, already walked away from one of those?"

"If only we could build our allies, quietly," Schultz considered aloud for his audience. "If only we had a senior Party member and political figure among us…"

Everyone turned to Fritz Todt, Chief Engineer to the Party.

Todt sat back in his chair, appalled.

The colonel smiled, mercilessly. "Fritz, I understand you know Albert Speer?"

Engel almost choked on his drink. Turning to Todt, he spluttered, "Speer! But he replaced you! I mean, after Hitler had you murdered in that plane crash in '42."

"Thank you!" Todt snapped, waspishly. "You are all such pleasant company. It may have escaped your notice, Corporal, that no one in *this* reality has had me murdered – though my new circle of friends do seem determined to get me killed! Might I remind you all that we are on the run? You are confusing reality with one of the films by those Americans with the piano and the long flight of stairs! And let me tell you, the only Academy Award *we* are likely to win is a life sentence for blowing it up!"

A flicker of amusement crossed the colonel's face. "I think one of them is British, but I take your point." He knew what they were asking would be difficult and dangerous in the extreme, their status as people of interest, after the destruction of the Old Academy, only adding a further level of complexity to the interesting times that lay ahead.

After a good night's rest, Douglas felt human again – even in good humour. Just one final task before they left – catch the dinosaur.

Their recent success in rounding up and corralling the pack of Mapusaurus roseae, and sending them back to the Cretaceous, added to his confidence. There was but one Sigilmassasaurus brevicollis out there. How hard could it be?

Within minutes, he stood outside Lieutenant-Commander Singh's quarters. The younger man answered the door red-eyed with ruffled hair.

"Ah hope Ah didnae wake ye, Sandy?"

"No, of course not, sir," Singh lied, stifling a yawn. "Come in. Coffee?"

Douglas grinned as he entered. "Not for me, thanks, but please do have one yerself, Commander."

They sat at Singh's small dining table while he took his first breakfast tea of the day. Somehow, he still had his Delhi Daredevils mug.

Douglas was surprised to see it. "Ah thought ye'd lost that cup years ago, when we left Tudor England?"

"No, sir. You ordered we take only absolute necessities and only that which we could carry." He smiled his still-boyish grin. "Turns out, a mug's not that heavy. I'm glad I did, too. In the altered future they were called the Delhi Capitals, so…"

"That's just no' cricket, eh?" Douglas suggested, wryly.

"Let's just say I'm keeping the legend alive. I keep it safe in my quarters because…"

Douglas was intrigued. "Because?"

Singh looked uncomfortable.

"Go on, laddie, spill the beans."

"Well, it was Captain Baines, sir. She kept putting it in the dishwasher. Ruins the print."

Douglas threw back his head and laughed in what seemed like the first time in ages. "Did ye no' tell her?"

"Of course, sir." He leaned forward, conspiratorially. "The information just never seemed to take."

Douglas laughed again. "Well, I'm glad you kept it safe. Long live the Daredevils."

Singh raised his mug in salute and drank.

"Now, to the reason Ah'm here, Sandy. Remember that program you wrote for ma shuttle's sensor suite, years ago? The one that searched Cretaceous Patagonia for anything that might have resembled a man-made construct?"

Singh nodded, taking another sip of his hot beverage.

"Ah need ye to write a similar program to search for our missing dinosaur. The north of England and Scotland is a big area to search. We'll need a computer-aided approach."

Singh nursed his mug thoughtfully. "That shouldn't be too difficult, sir. We know exactly what we seek, after all. It's not like the parameters are likely to be confused with anything else out there. We could take a ship high, very high, almost into orbit, and snapshot the whole area, if the skies are clear."

Douglas winced. "If the skies are clear? Scotland, remember?"

"Roman Warm Period," Singh countered. "I'm told the weather is stable and even clement here. According to Thomas Beckett, in a few hundred years there will even be Roman vineyards in the Borders." He grinned. "He was disappointed we arrived early. So, shall I get to it, sir?"

Tim fastened the straps on his flight harness. His had been a small and impoverished childhood, limited by circumstance – especially after losing his father. Patricia Norris always did her best, but existence was a dire struggle on a single income in the 22nd century – even for a relatively well-paid professional. Consequently, flight, in those days, was a dream well outside their means. Joining the Mars Mission in 2112 changed all that forever – an opportunity orchestrated by Heinrich Schultz. That was what Tim had been told, and it rang true. He hated that. Difficult to refute, it made his relationship to the Schultzes not only possible, but likely, and in his darkest moments, he believed it.

Since that day, Tim had flown through the air, through space – even through time. Once more strapped in for take-off, he never took that for granted, nor did he ever forget where he came from. The Schultzes had unleashed the most dangerous forces known to man, and yet, cruelly, he owed them everything – he hated that, too.

Thoughts of his last meeting with Heidi haunted him. He had

shot her. He, Tim Norris, had shot someone, and not just anyone. He had shot his cousin. At least, that was what all the evidence suggested. Patricia finding out about Tim's lineage the way she had had been a disaster, too. He could never have hoped for a better mother, and yet, as an adult, he could see how adoptive parents might forever live with the ghosts of their child's biological mothers and fathers. To find out they may have been Schultzes was brutal. Even if they were defectors from the Schultz regime, it raised questions that could never be reburied, probably never answered.

Douglas glanced over, noting the sorrow etched into the younger man's face. After all they had been through, the cause might have been anything, yet Douglas was a perceptive man and guessed correctly that family matters, culminating in Heidi's death, were at the heart of Tim's woes.

He reached across to squeeze his shoulder. "Do ye know what Ah do, when the past willnae leave me alone? Ah focus on the present. There's usually enough of it to push *anything* from ma mind." He smiled, kindly.

Tim took a deep breath, his expression lifting. After all, he was about to fly again – and in search of a magnificent dinosaur, too.

Douglas' most fervent hope was that they sought the *only* dinosaur in that time[1]. He was eager to put everyone and everything back in their boxes, closing the lids once and for all. He internalised a sigh. Yes, it was time to take his own advice and focus on the present.

They took off in a roar of fire and rocket noise, their dropship shooting from the *New World*'s open hangar. Tim watched the landscape roll by from the navigator's seat at the rear of the cockpit. As everything grew smaller, his perspective grew so much larger. Quickly reaching an altitude of two hundred miles, he stared in wonderment, his eye following the Earth's curvature out of sight,

---

1. During the Iron Age, avian dinosaurs were simply known as birds, or occasionally – *omens.* Douglas felt well within his rights to discount them.

in a time when most believed it to be flat[2].

No, he would never take what he had been given for granted. Pushing his concerns aside, he allowed *this* moment to be one of contentment.

Lieutenant-Commander Singh activated the program that had taken him most of the morning to write and compile with the computer's assistance. It now hijacked the ship's entire sensor suite to search northern Britain for one solitary animal.

Their craft was a warship, her long-range camera equipment state of the art. Within minutes, Singh found their quarry, though the female Sigilmassasaurus had ranged considerably further north than expected. Douglas' hopes that she might find a pool local to the wormhole to dominate were dashed. There were no lakes or rivers deep enough to allow such an immense creature to live naturally anywhere near Yeavering Bell. So, the dinosaur had naturally continued her search north, looking for a place that looked like home, and was now well up into what would one day be known as Scotland. With her coordinates logged, Singh was able to zoom right in to see the animal loping across the low hills, due south of a large body of water.

"If she gets in there, we'll have huge problems retrieving her, Captain," Tim noted.

Douglas nodded, though he had a faraway look in his eyes.

Suddenly aware of Douglas' silence, Singh looked over from the pilot's seat. "What is it, sir?"

"A horrible suspicion."

Tim groaned.

Douglas focused on him, at last. "Are ye thinking what Ah'm thinking?"

---

2. Although documented as an idea in the 5th century BC, the first attempt to *prove* the Earth was a sphere was taking place, roughly, as Tim flew above it, by 3rd century BC Greek philosophers establishing Hellenistic astronomy – and yet, born thousands of years later, Douglas and his crew were *still* trying to figure out what made it go round.

Tim covered his eyes with a hand, nodding affirmative.

"Well, is anyone going to tell me?" Singh demanded, testily.

"Aye. Sorry, Sandy. *That,* unless Ah'm very much mistaken, is Loch Ness – heard of it?"

Singh stared a long, long way below, studying the recognisably long and narrow lake, as he considered Douglas' words and suspicions. "It couldn't be, could it? So you think that animal might be…?"

"It can," Tim stated from a rear seat, "and the way our luck usually goes, it will! We need to get down there, gents. Might be time to load the rifle with darts, Captain."

Far below, hunting wolves brought down a sheep at the lakeshore. Nothing for it but to save themselves, the rest of the flock had it away on their cloven, woolly toes. A savage bite to the throat from the matriarchal bitch killed the luckless sheep instantly, so his problems were over. Weirdly, it was now the wolves who were in trouble.

Watching from the next hill, the shepherd looked on furiously. He opened his mouth to call his dogs when the cry strangled in his throat. The man was no fool. He knew he was standing out against the skyline and instantly dropped flat to the earth, for approaching the hunters, stealthily downwind, was a monster – one of the old gods, it had to be.

The man clamped a hand across his own mouth, lest he whimper in terror and give himself away. He was not strictly wearing pants, but he peed what he *was* wearing.

Focused on the stench of blood directly ahead, Sigilmassasaurus brevicollis failed to notice the watcher on the hill. She walked low on all fours, stalking. Down in a dip, she was hidden but for the sail that ran tall along her back.

A young wolf looked behind. Too small and inexperienced to win a share of the choicest bites, he had only survived his first year by fighting over scraps with his brethren and clearing what the older wolves 'left behind'. However, one advantage of this system meant there was always someone on guard – and it had never mattered more than on that day.

Sigilmassasaurus popped up from the hollow, little more than her own length away from her next meal. Rising to her hind legs, she surged forward into a sprint.

The youngster, barely more than a cub, barked, yelped and span in circles, terrified. The pack elders immediately sensed that his was more than mere denial whining – they all knew the pecking order. Bloody, snarling mouths dropped the sheep and turned as one to bark and threaten.

It was not so much that Sigilmassasaurus was unimpressed; it was more that she barely noticed. She opened her vast jaws to *roar!*

Wolves have always survived on cunning and cooperation. So, as one, they ran like hell – faster than the dinosaur could have matched, even if she had a mind to. Their annoying barking and yelping was alien and hurt her ears, but quickly grew quieter and lower as they doppler shifted away. She cared not. The sheep would make a nice snack, a little instant energy before she took a soothing swim after her long march.

What remained of the carcass vanished down her gullet with a single swallow.

The shepherd watched in horrified fascination. Keeping his dogs close and quiet, he was frozen in place, neither able to move nor tear his gaze from the spectacle. He had never been more scared – until the sky fell. At least, that was how it seemed to him.

The dropship appeared on a rolling wave of sound.

Sigilmassasaurus was familiar with the roar of the flying things that were not food, from her life at Crater Lake. It hurt her ears far more than the recent barking. She mitigated her discomfort by slipping off the bank into the loch, disappearing instantly to its depths.

Hovering overhead, Douglas swore roundly and with feeling. As if the animal's disappearance were not enough, their ship had been spotted by a local tribesman. He swore again.

The moment Singh touched down, Douglas and Tim were out

of the rear hatch, rifles in hand, running for the lakeshore with a growing sense of dread.

Nothing.

Even the bubbles had dissipated, leaving no sign the giant had ever been.

Douglas fell to his knees. "Oh, this is another fine mess!"

The shepherd had also had enough. Dropping his crook, he ran for home as fast as his shaking legs would carry him, faithful hounds yapping at his heels. He had to warn everyone. He would certainly never go swimming again. Unidentified flying objects? A monster in the loch? Not if he told the story for the rest of time, would anyone ever believe him.

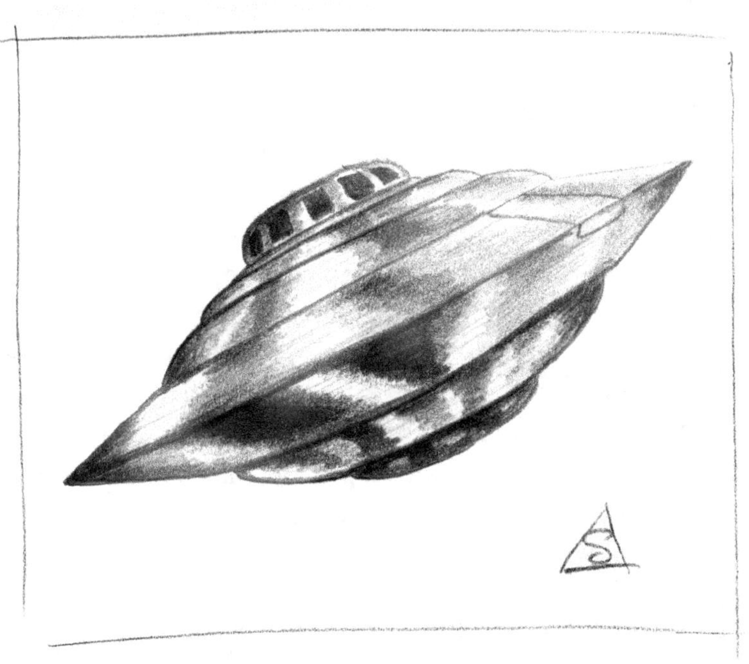

Chapter 19 | Try, Try, Triassic Again

Douglas was fuming, his wife's report only compounding his annoyance. While he was tracking the missing dinosaur, Baines had everyone not fixing the ship working in teams to clear up everything that washed through with the recent floods from Cretaceous Britain. It was impossible to completely sanitise the area, but they did what they could. One item proved particularly concerning.

"They found the remains of a giant fish – mostly eaten," she explained.

Douglas nodded, remembering. "Aye, the beastie we just lost in Loch Ness brought it through with him."

"Her."

"What?"

"She was— *is* female."

He shrugged. "OK."

"No K. It gets worse, James. She's pregnant."

"*What?*"

"Calm down, honey."

"Calm down? She's only the first single mother to be cast away alone, a hundred million years from home, that's all. This is a disaster, Jill[1] . How do we know she's pregnant?"

"Patricia Norris has been taking samples from the collected detritus, to make sure we're removing the right material. She's one smart lady. Apparently, she noted foreign blood on the dead fish. A DNA test showed that it was dinosaurian – not much of a stretch to work out which animal it came from. She postulates that the predator may have bitten into a major bone and lost or loosened a tooth, although we never found it. Anyhow, the blood also showed evidence of the heightened calcium usually associated with medullary bone. I'm not sure whether you're aware – Tim did explain this a while back. Basically, that's how birds and reptiles produce the extra calcium they need to make eggshell. It goes without saying that medullary material is only found in females, and only when pregnant."

Head in his hands, Douglas sighed. "Aye yi yi. Fascinating, Ah'll no' argue that, and ingenious, but this only reinforces how important it is for us to remove that animal from this time." Agitated, he got up to pace their quarters.

"Hmm."

Douglas turned back to his wife. "Ye disagree?"

"Well, I…"

He slumped. "Ah'm no' going tae like this, am Ah?"

"It's just that – and this is only a theory – maybe she was *meant* to come here. The dinosaur, I mean."

"Oh, come on, Jill."

---

1. With regards to pregnancy, Douglas had no inkling at that point as to the full horror of Heidi's plans.

It was Baines' turn to shrug. "No one's saying it, but we're all thinking it."

"Yer no' telling me ye think that monster might be Nessie?"

"Nessie's great-great-great-to-the-nth-degree-grandmother, maybe. How long do those creatures live, anyway?" She threw up her hands, forestalling him. "Hear me out. I've spoken with Tim, and he thinks the idea might have legs. Here's the thing. Traditional thinking has always considered that Nessie might be some form of plesiosaur. Pretty ridiculous, as they died out at the end of the Jurassic, some 155 million years ago."

"No' as ridiculous as it used tae be," Douglas countered, sourly.

"OK, point. There might be some flexibility in the timeline these days, I'll grant you, but there's still no way that any creature could live forever. Now take our friendly, neighbourhood spinosaur. She arrives, well into the time of man, not long before written history is introduced to these isles. If she does have young, it's plausible they might adapt and survive a couple of millennia into the era of photography, even with a restricted gene pool. You only have to look at the world-famous Chillingham cattle – one day, just over the way from here – to see how that might work."

"Well, she's living in a damned big pool now! What are you suggesting, we just leave her there?"

"I think we might have to, honey."

"Why? Surely we could just capture her when she comes out to sun herself on the shore?"

"I'm sure we could, but should we? Let's face it, despite the mindboggling array of game-changing inventions Scotland gave to the world, when it comes to much of that world, your homeland is practically synonymous with Nessie! If we capture her, we might change that. And that leads me to my next point."

"Go on."

"If we take her away, how many untold millions do you think that'll cost Scottish tourism?"

"You *are* kidding?"

"No, James. I'm not. We grew up with the legend of the Loch

Ness Monster, yet no one knows its true source. What if Saint Columba was *meant* to have the bejesus scared out of him in the sixth century?"

"You've been talking with Beckett again, too," he accused.

Baines sighed. "No. Well, OK, yes, but my point is we don't know what we're messing with. I honestly think we should let this be. We do have other things on our plate at the moment."

<hr>

The next day and 252 million years earlier…

The Earth has many plates. Constantly in motion, they forever move and stretch, or are crushed into subduction zones where they pass beneath one another.

Seated at a technical station on the *New World*'s bridge, Hiro watched in silence while Singh piloted them in over a particularly notable weakness in Laurasia's tectonic plate formation, just north of the equator. During their recent visit to those space–time coordinates, the entire region had erupted into a vast cauldron of magma, very nearly destroying the *New World* with all hands. Although 'visit' suggests a pleasure entirely at odds with the crew's lived experience. The fact that it took place just weeks *and* a quarter of a billion years earlier, also leaves the term 'recent' a little punch-drunk, too… and what a few weeks it had been.

Working doggedly every waking minute, Hiro had scarcely taken a proper meal break through any of it, dividing his attention between fixing their ship and removing man's interference from natural time. His ever-growing team of brilliant scientists and engineers were equally exhausted. Now all that remained was to unstick the past from the future, by eradicating the wormholes Heidi and Reid had unleashed upon the Earth – and more importantly, the collision of three hundred eras of Earth's history, all stitched together into a single time. Causality was in trouble. Anyone sane was terrified – a terror sublimated only by their fear of the cure they were about to implement.

Dissenting voices argued forcefully against Hiro's solution, including those of his brother, Aito, and Dr Hemmings, who advocated using the cross-dimensional weakness they had already created in Cretaceous Egypt. It already existed, after all, and certainly had the power they needed, without stressing the planet further. However, Patel had sided with Hiro, stating that the secant line drawn in 'space' through the outer core, and in 'time' between Cretaceous Egypt and 1940s Germany, had already created instability. He argued that any further prodding and poking might lead to unforeseen and uncontrollable consequences, especially as one end of the wormhole would reconnect to a major European city.

Douglas, like so many leaders throughout history, was left grappling with concepts well beyond him, while trying to make policy affecting the lives of millions – or in this case, the future lives of billions – based solely on what he could glean from two opposing scientific camps. In the end, he could only reason that unleashing their experiment – for such it was – in the heart of a city was a no-go. He also knew that, despite the reservations of others, Hiro had spent more time and effort on this problem than anyone. His chief engineer may have been distracted of late – largely due to his brother's presence and predicament – but he had never let his friends down. Douglas could do no less. So he would not cower; he would not pass the buck or allow the loudest voices to push him against his instincts. He would trust those who over the years had earned it. It was time to put his faith in his friends, and as far as Douglas was concerned, Hiro and Patel were the safest bets he could place in a totally unstable situation. That decision made, he ordered everyone to work with the options remaining to them – and most importantly, to work *together* – in the hope that space–time would do the decent thing and fall into line behind.

Accepting Douglas' decision, Dr Hemmings suggested a method for testing Hiro's idea before carrying out their plan. "After all," she continued, "if we are wrong, the consequences might be unthinkable. Especially when we consider the forces at work.

Added to that, once Chief Nassaki's 'single location theory' is proved, or disproved, my idea will also identify the *exact* region and time from which we might extract the greatest energy from the smallest area. Power at a point, ladies and gentlemen."

That was something Douglas *did* understand, and the cost in time and material was small, so there they were, hovering above the most destructive event in the last 450 million years[2].

Singh kept the *New World* high, well clear of the many hundreds of calderas below, all in full swing, working together to belch forth a new continent from the bowels of the Earth. To avoid paradox, they arrived just a few days after their first foray into the Triassic–Permian divide, and it was immediately obvious that the destruction below had advanced massively in that time. He sighed. *Extreme heat, extreme magnetism, extreme gravity – and that's just what we plan to add to the chaos down there. If we survive this one, Ah'm going to spend the rest of my life watching paint dry.*

"The missile is ready," Hiro interrupted his thoughts.

Douglas and Baines exchanged a meaningful glance.

Baines raised an eyebrow. "Shall we?"

"Ladies first."

She smiled. "That's right, put all this on me. Fire the weapon, Hiro."

"Missile away, ma'am."

The device was not a true weapon, not any more. Most of its

---

2. That is, 450 million years before the Permian extinction where the crew now found themselves again. In an event known as 'Snowball Earth', roughly 700 million years before mankind fretted about the weather, the entire planet became an ice-ball for approximately 100 million years. Fortunately, the microbial life that survived was given a helping hand, perhaps ironically in this context, by another, earlier era of extreme volcanism. Enough ice was melted to significantly reduce the amount of sunlight being reflected back into space. The result was a dramatic global warming event that created conditions ideal for the emergence of complex life. Without the combined effects of our local star and volcanism, we would not be here, but what the Earth giveth...

trinitrotoluene, or TNT, had been removed, leaving just enough to detonate the casing, so that its new payload could be distributed over as large an area as possible. The missile now carried a hundred tungsten bars, impregnated with uranium 235 at their core. Tungsten was chosen for its high melting point, some 3422 degrees Celsius, whereas the optimal heat generated by lava was a mere 1200 degrees Celsius. Dr Hemmings' plan relied on the hypothesis that at least some of the bars would survive being baked into the new Permian–Triassic boundary rock, and would carry their uranium payload well into the future. The power of the catastrophe below them, and the timescales involved, were breathtaking, but with the half-life of uranium being 700 million years, the chance of it enduring 222 million years into Hiro's chosen Oligocene Epoch of the Palaeogene Period was feasible.

"Package coming in over the target area, Captain," Hiro reported. "Detonation in ten, nine, eight…"

Baines leaned in close to her husband, seated in the commander's chair. She resisted the urge to take his hand while they were on duty. Listening to Hiro's count, she whispered, "Didn't all this begin with a countdown?"

Douglas winked. "It's nae over yet, lassie."

"Four, three, two, one, and… gone. Payload delivered."

There was no whoop of delight this time, just an anticlimactic message from the chief engineer, explaining that something relatively simple had worked as expected. The excitement was still to come.

Baines took a deep breath, letting it out slowly. "OK, Sandy. I take it you have the space–time coordinates logged?"

"Aye, aye, Captain."

"Very well. Plot a course to our next stop."

The UNS *New World* climbed out of the atmosphere into high orbit and kept going until she left the Earth far behind, eventually taking up a low orbit around the moon.

Borrowing from Heidi's own playbook, courtesy of Dr Reid, Singh brought them in, skipping the tops of the razor-sharp crags of Montes Apenninus. Within minutes, they were cruising just one hundred metres above the Mare Imbrium flats.

From an airlock in the *New World*'s portside, The Sarge launched a tungsten bar down to the moon's surface. Ship's gravity made it heavy to lift, but with lunar gravity at one-sixth Earth standard, it fell slowly once out of his control. He had another from the case, ready to drop, before it even impacted below. Slightly clumsy in his space suit, he slipped with the tongs and dropped the second radioactive bar. Not that it mattered; they were all going the same way.

The first hit the lunar surface. Resembling a stone splashing into water, it sent a plume of chalky dust unnaturally high into space, almost taking gravity by surprise in its leap for the stars. Inevitably, gravity had the final say, arresting its ballistic flight so that the cloud hung motionless for a while, before every grain was irresistibly recaptured in slow motion. Sergeant Jackson smiled. He had seen some incredible things on his journey, but what struck him most about his current assignment was how unchanging the moon appeared. Especially when contrasted with the Earth, hanging in the sky before him. The moon suffered none of the abrasive effects of wind and weather, nor the continental upheaval caused by the awesome power of an ever-moving molten core. The moon was frigid and still, but for the occasional impact – and most of those were small fry since the end of the late heavy bombardment – so there was little to challenge the tranquillity of the lunar sphere. Heidi would not slam a comet into it for another 150 million years, give or take, creating the remarkable rings of ice that had stunned the *New World*'s crew when they returned to the Cretaceous. He sighed with pleasure. *Yep, you've seen it all, me old son.*

He dropped a dozen bars in all, over a thousand-kilometre span, just in case a few of them did suffer an unfortunate meteor collision. Taking one last, lingering look around, he closed the hatch.

"I'm all done, here, Captain. Hatch secured and ready to go."

"*Thanks, Sarge,*" Baines answered.

The *New World* rose, quickly leaving the pockmarked surface behind. In no time at all, the pale grey-white ground became a pale grey-white sphere, and at 190,000 kilometres out – roughly midway between the Earth and the moon – Baines ordered a full stop.

Drs Reid and Hemmings, in conjunction with the *New World*'s science and engineering staff, had reconfigured the wormhole drive to mimic the operation they carried out aboard the *Heydrich* in Cretaceous Egypt. Holding a small wormhole open, they poured every bit of processing power the ship's state-of-the-art computers could spare into searching the future for a specific movement. Using the principles Heidi implemented to follow her Spinosaurus aegyptiacus from Cretaceous Egypt to 1943 Munich, the *New World* tracked the uranium isotopes dropped into the lava flow on Earth, triangulating them twice daily with the bars so recently left on the surface of the moon as it circled more than eighty-one billion times around the mother world. Over the next hour, they plotted their progress across many millions of years, and, as expected, tectonic plate movement within the Earth's crust gradually described a south-easterly drift. When compared with their original coordinates, this allowed the engineers to gauge when their markers reached the location of the Palaeogene super-volcano – approximately thirty million years before the time of man.

Existing geological charts accurately located the eruption in space, and now, having taken the long way round over 222 million years, their uranium isotopes arrived at the epicentre to give them the exact moment in time, too.

The locations were aligned.

The *New World* vanished.

Amaryllis
belladonna

Chapter 20 | If

A vast, black spaceship appeared from nothing, not exactly all at once, though that was how it would have appeared to any observer. Not that there was an observer. There was nothing at all.

"Sandy, report. Where are we?" Baines demanded.

"Working on it, ma'am. Oh *ffffiddlesticks!*"

"Problem?" asked Douglas.

"A small one, sir. Trouble with jumping through a wormhole in space is *we* are still physically where we were, but all the planets have moved around."

"Ah thought ye'd factored for that?"

"I did, sir, within certain parameters – didn't want us popping out in the middle of the Earth's core due to a rounding error."

"Makes sense."

Singh sighed, spinning his chair round to face Douglas and Baines. "Unfortunately, we're at the extreme range of that margin for error, Captains." He held out his hands, palms up. "With a two-hundred-and-twenty-million-year jump, there was always going to be an element of pot luck."

Douglas forced himself to breathe easily, releasing the tightness in his chest. It could have been worse. "How far out are we?"

"Two days, give or take," Singh replied, matter-of-fact. "Still…"

"Go on, Sandy," Baines encouraged.

"I was just thinking, we've pushed ourselves pretty hard the last few weeks." He glanced meaningfully at Hiro, who was oblivious and already wrapped up in his next task. "If there was ever a time to, erm, *order* some rest…"

Baines and Douglas followed his gaze, and his point. "A couple of days R and R sounds like just the thing," Baines agreed.

Tim kicked the ball, clumsily – sports were never really his thing. His opponent did not seem to mind, however, right up until the inevitable *pop!*

"Reiver!" he cried, remembering the last time he played this game – and how it had ended. Yet the moment did not play out exactly as it had all those years ago. This time there were witnesses.

Tim looked round, smiling sheepishly. "Sorry."

Reiver felt no need to apologise. He had simply improved the ball's ergonomics, so that it now fitted more easily into his mouth.

They shared the games court with Reiver's mistress, Natalie, and her husband, The Sarge; Woodsey, and one of Captain Meritus' staff sergeants, a stern brunette that he was desperately trying to impress; and most importantly of all, as far as Tim was concerned, his wife, Clarrie.

The game was going well, until it abruptly ended – though Reiver failed to grasp the rules in that regard, and saw no reason to give the ruined ball back. Suddenly man-of-the-match, he ran rings around the two-legs and their pathetic attempts to retake possession. In truth, *no one* seemed to have a firm grasp of the rules. There were no actual sides, let alone *off*sides, but there was plenty of laughter – a wonderful benefit when a sport devolves back into a game, and always completely free. Yet perhaps it *was* better that Reiver took the ball away, before play inevitably degenerated into boys against girls, and the deplorable cheating that would certainly have followed.

Breathless and giddy, the players decided to make for the ship's *other* recreational area instead.

As one would expect from a ship built in the 22nd century, the bar contained nothing so filthy as an ashtray, and for that reason alone, Natalie brought along Reiver's drinking bowl. He would do almost anything for a half of bitter – even let go of a burst ball.

The bar was filling up. Everyone understood they were about to bet the whole farm over the next few days, and yet, spirits were high. There was a real sense that the end was in sight – even if no one was completely sure what that end might look like.

Lieutenant-Commander Singh sat in a corner, quietly, smiling at his friends – his family. He remembered the last time they threw a party like this – quite different from Tim and Clarrie's wedding celebrations, which took the opportunity to look forward to all the wonders life could offer a young couple. This felt more like the time when they first landed in the Cretaceous, against all the odds surviving a near-deadly re-entry in a damaged ship, barely under control.

Oh, Singh remembered that moment well; over a hundred lives in his hands, but luck, or some would have it, talent, had been on his side and he had prevailed. Almost certainly the greatest test of his life so far, it still kept him awake sometimes, ten years on. Yet, once down – a hundred million years from home and in the middle of a terrific storm – the *New World*'s crew had remained fierce in the face of adversity and the dark days ahead, the relief that they still lived, a force to behold. This felt like that. They knew they were about to go into battle again, but they also believed they could win.

The Earth grew large in the front viewscreen. Even without magnification, the continents were clear, if not completely familiar. Thirty million BC saw them well divided into the world Douglas and the others knew well, yet there were differences. North America was closer to Eurasia; Africa was closer to South America, with the narrower Atlantic a lightning bolt of blue dividing them, but that was mere description. Less easy to define were the emotions that view inspired in the earthlings, as they looked down from space – a soulful beauty that could never be described in technicalities. She was majestic. Different, but magnificent. Home, but not quite home. Yet the one thing she never was, was commonplace.

Douglas unconsciously let go a long sigh. The mere sight of his world, unspoilt and perfect, left him, however fleeting, in a state of bliss. He could almost feel his blood pressure lowering – yes, she was still there, still beautiful; everything was going to be fine.

He had no idea Baines was watching him. Seeing him, even momentarily, shed the cares he had worn for so long was like a balm for her own soul. There was nothing like seeing the person she loved most enjoy a moment of total contentment. She only wished she could protect him from all the hurt, all the stress, from everything, but she knew that was not possible, for two reasons. Firstly, things just never worked out that way, and secondly, because he felt exactly the same way and would never stop throwing himself in harm's way for her, either – or for his crew, for that matter. Sometimes, it was enough to be grateful for what one had, because sometimes, that was a lot.

"What?" he asked, a secret smile on his lips.

Baines had drifted slightly, without realising he was now watching her. "Oh, nothing. Just admiring the view."

He nodded, missing the subtext. "Aye. Shall we be about our business here?"

"Yes, James, let's close those wormholes." Addressing the bridge crew, she continued, "It's been a hell of a ride. Forwards, backwards. History, prehistory. I think I'm just about ready to return to reality, thank you very much."

"It'll be quite the tale to tell, one day, Captain," Singh agreed.

Baines nodded. "Won't it ever. But before we descend, does anyone want to offer any stirring words about that story, or to usher in what comes next?"

Douglas smiled at his wife. "Aye. Ah've this tae say. It's about time…"

Re-entry was smooth and controlled and could not have contrasted more markedly with their experience a decade earlier. Singh felt that he could have landed them in his sleep, so impressive was the second *New World.* "We're coming in over our coordinates now, Captain," he announced. "There's a lot of activity down there, and a huge cloud of water vapour. Also, carbon dioxide, sulphur dioxide – along with trace quantities of hydrogen sulphide, carbon monoxide, hydrogen chloride, hydrogen fluoride, and others. I'd say she's ready to blow, sir."

"Good. Ah hate long waits," Douglas growled. "Well, this is it. Is everyone ready?"

The Sarge, recently returned to the bridge's security station, called affirmative. "All stations green across the board, Captain. Engineering have all their gizmos ready for deployment, sir."

Douglas gave him a half-smile. "All our ducks in line, eh, Sarge?"

"Couldn't have put it better, sir."

Despite the insanity of what they were attempting, there was an infectious positivity among the crew. They all felt it, like everything that had happened to them was about to culminate right there and then. A loaded term, though for most of their lives time had done her job adequately, quietly moving forward. Only in recent years had the clockwork of the universe proved a fickle mistress. Douglas could only wonder – would this final act restore trust?

Better not to dwell, he thought, privately. "Take us in, to a safe distance, Commander."

"Aye, sir."

The *New World* crept over the target zone, just as a colossal explosion sent shockwaves through the earth and the air.

"Kick off, sir," The Sarge reported.

"Wow," Singh commented softly. "The pressure on the gases dissolved within the magma is decreasing near the throat of the vent, causing them to explode, propelling lava… wow…"

"Sandy?" Baines queried.

"Sorry, Captain. I was going to say propelling lava close to fifteen hundred metres into the air. That's got to be a record. Most volcanic explosions don't send lava more than six hundred. Are we sure about this?"

"Not really the time for that conversation, Commander," Douglas admonished.

Hiro rejoined them on the bridge to sit once more at his science station, clearly preoccupied. "We're all set, Captain," he reported as an afterthought.

"OK. Sandy…" Douglas took a deep breath. "Open a wormhole to the magma flows of the Permian–Triassic boundary."

"Aye, sir," Singh repeated. Reconfigured for a third function, the wormhole drive opened the largest wormhole yet known to mankind.

The ship rocked as a massive explosion aft sent shockwaves through every deck. Douglas looked to his wife. "Alright, Jill, *now* Ah'm experiencing déjà vu!"

"Wormhole drive has exploded, sir," Hiro reported, sadly. "As expected. Fire suppression systems are active with containment teams moving in."

Douglas looked to Sergeant Jackson.

"No casualties, sir."

Douglas breathed a sigh of relief, unbidden thoughts of Mario Baccini's fate crowding his mind. "Do we have our wormhole,

Sandy?"

"*Oh,* yes. The mother of all wormholes, Captain."

"Aye, but is it enough? Sandy? Hiro? Anybody?"

"Still collecting data, sir," Hiro answered, tetchily. "Patience, please!"

Douglas raised a wry eyebrow, in spite of himself. That was him told. He should have known better than to interrupt the chief while he was concentrating.

Within moments, everyone was on the proverbial hot bricks. "*Hiro?*" Sandy yelled across the bridge.

"Wait a minute!"

"Wait a minute, *sir,*" Lieutenant-Commander Singh muttered huffily.

Douglas smiled. "If Ah didnae get a sir, good luck with that, laddie."

"Let me concentrate!" Hiro hissed.

Douglas grinned at Singh, placing a finger over his lips.

"IT'S WORKING!" Hiro bellowed, jumping to his feet and punching the air. "The secant line cut through the outer core is pulling magma from more than four hundred miles below the crust. The magnetic field is off the scale, sir!"

"Thank you," Douglas and Singh replied together.

Singh coughed with embarrassment. "And Heidi's wormhole devices?"

Hiro opened a channel to engineering. "Georgio, do Drs Reid and Hemmings have results for us?"

"*Just coming in, Chief. The permanent wormhole open at the Permian–Triassic boundary is exerting a vast magnetic pull that is being disseminated throughout the entire wormhole manifold, drawing all three hundred wormhole generators through to those space–time coordinates.*"

Hiro looked to Douglas. "You heard that, Captain?"

"Aye. Order Georgio to launch phase two. Sandy, take us in slowly, and Sandy…"

"Yes, sir?"

"Dinnae take us too close, laddie."

"Yes, sir."

The second part of their plan was even more dangerous, for it meant flying close to possibly the largest volcano the world had seen since the planet's earliest days, billions of years ago. Douglas only wished that was the limit of the insanity they were about to unleash on their home. They now knew that wormholes were affected dramatically by strong magnetic fields, but the small wormhole generators that Reid built existed *outside* time and space, locked into a fifth dimension. Like the familiar three dimensions of length, height and depth, the fifth was also a spatial dimension. Curved tightly in on itself, it took up less space than an atom and would ordinarily be invisible as far any human observer might be concerned. Consequently, a fifth dimension may only be recognised by its effects, and one of those effects was gravity.

However, via a fluke of wormhole physics, human observers *were* able to glimpse Reid's devices outside the four dimensions of space–time as they floated between dimensions, seemingly *within* the wormholes they generated. The titan magnetic forces, generated by the linked super-volcanoes, drew the tiny devices all into one place via Reid's manifold. All they now required was a mere *tug,* to bring them into real space.

Easier said than done. The artificial gravity generators aboard the *New World* were only designed to create the standard 9.807 m/s², or 1G, of force needed to prevent the crew from floating around when the ship went into space. Most human effort went into negating the effects of gravity, rather than increasing them. Even by the 22nd century, the physics was mostly theory. Fortunately, Heidi had stolen the one device on Earth powerful enough to exert limited control over the curve gravity *pressed* into space–time, whilst being small enough to suspend from a tungsten-steel cable over an active super-volcano. After decades of research, the scientists at Area 51 had found a way to switch the device on. Building on that limited, if rather vital foundation, Patel and Reid had worked out how to switch it on *and* reverse its effects, to create a small gravity well. When activated, the machine would further curve space–time in its immediate vicinity to pull Reid's wormhole generators back into the so-called real world of three dimensions.

They were about to find out whether their plan would deliver as hoped, ending Heidi's madness forever, or merely deliver their ship into a vast magma chamber very briefly.

"If…" Douglas swallowed nervously. "*If* this should fail, how sure are we of our plan B?"

"Not really the time for that conversation, sir," Singh rejoindered.

"Good point well made. Steady as she goes, Mr Singh."

Two kilometres below the *New World,* hanging from a slender cable, was a device built by an intelligence millennia ahead of the people now utilising its power. Whether it was alien, or from the future, was for the birds at that point. All that mattered was whether it would work.

Dr Satnam Patel and Dr Reid faced each other.

"So here we are," Patel announced anxiously, holding a remote controller in his hand. It was a simple device with just two buttons, one for 'on' and 'off', the other to reverse polarity.

"A wise man once said – friends and enemies, working together…" Reid tailed off, a gentle smile tugging at his lips as he repeated Patel's earlier words back to him.

"Together at last?" Patel suggested, holding out the device.

"Together at last," Reid repeated, and reaching out, they activated the gravity well together.

Far below, conditions were extreme. The cable glowed ruby red, while the alien artefact seemed aloof to the effects of millions of tons of exploding lava. Ever downward it descended, lower and lower towards what should have been Dantean oblivion, yet there were no outward sounds or effects. Nothing went *click.* As far as anyone could tell, the machine had no moving parts to make any sound at all. The only measurable and quantifiable indications ever observed were its unnatural influence over gravity, positive or negative, and extreme radiation. Killing radiation.

The latter was largely irrelevant in the throat of an exploding magma chamber. The effects of the former were yet to be felt.

Chapter 21 | Full Circle

**USS *New World,* 2000 hours, 31st July, AD2112 /
15th April, 99,198,017BC**
A young woman appeared from nothing in the middle of *Factory Pod 4*'s main hangar. Two sudden, powerful, invisible shoves sent her sprawling across the deserted deck, her backpack skidding alongside. All crew and passengers were either at their stations or strapped into their seats in embarkation, as she knew they would be. Indeed, she knew *exactly* where everyone would be. She had already lived these events and knew she would be alone.

The invisible hand that propelled the woman across the floor with such force knocked the breath from her. She hissed painfully, climbing to her feet and removing her flak jacket. There were two bullet holes, perfectly side-by-side, in the rear of the garment.

Kevlar armour prevented them from entering her body through her back to blow a hole out of her chest, taking most of her heart along with them. She nodded with frank admiration. "Nice grouping, cousin."

The wormhole closed with no assistance from her on this occasion – controlled by Lieutenant Singh up on the *New World*'s bridge, high above and a quarter of a kilometre ahead of her – for this was one of the fixed-point wormholes, etched into the very fabric of the universe by circumstance and destiny. Unlike the seven-metre diameter portal created by her wrist device, this wormhole was vast – large enough to pass a 550-metre-long spacecraft.

The *New World* emerged completely, back into real space. However, despite the wormhole's location being fixed, to an outside observer in space with no frame of reference, it appeared that it travelled along the ship's length, materialising her into existence like the galaxy's largest 3D printer. Once the ship was clear, the anomaly vanished. It was the wormhole of last resort for the young woman, so dangerous that any traveller would have to be insane to use it.

Fortunately, this presented no problem for Dr Heidi Schultz.

The slugs that knocked her to the deck were still in her jacket. She pocketed them, carefully. It was vital that she left no evidence of her passing. Having lived through this timeline, roughly nine months ago for her personally, she knew where to hide without being discovered. Now, with four and a half days to lie low, she would plan a new dawn.

Heidi knew her younger self was currently under deep cover, as were Del Bond and her other cohorts. She gritted her teeth over that. "Del Bond," she hissed his name disgustedly. "Your game is up, my friend, before it even gets going." Throwing her pack over one shoulder, she jogged to the nearest exit.

When she jumped into the wormhole – demonstrably fleeing Baines' team and her cousin, Tim Norris – the other end was a fixed point in space, originally 1,800,000 kilometres from Mars.

However, accounting for a time slip of almost 99.2 million years, the planets were completely realigned, and Mars was nowhere to be seen. Nothing more than blind good fortune had placed the *New World* mere days from Earth the last time – although technically, that was now *this* time.

Heidi felt a little woozy and lightheaded, not sure whether that was because of the paradox she was creating or because she had, just moments ago, been shot by Tim Norris. Fortunately, she had known where she would land, more or less – assuming she survived and her desperate gambit worked at all – because wormholes were scalable.

She stepped through from Cretaceous Patagonia, naturally, at ground level. The wormhole created by the *New World* was much larger, by necessity, yet she still appeared near its base – that being the main vehicular hangar aboard *Factory Pod 4,* slung beneath the *New World* herself.

Her wooziness continued and she stumbled. Dehydrated, she took a drink from her flask, replenishing herself as she checked her wrist device[1] to confirm the *New World's* coordinates. The locater beacon, blasted into a rock before her fateful reunion with Tim, was still broadcasting, its coordinates clearly plotted within the device's systems. It was good to know she could find her way back, should things go wrong. It was also comforting to know that she could place her hands on her own and her grandfather's clones – when the time was right. Heidi trusted Mengele to get on with the mad science – driven by twisted intrigue, he would be unable to help himself – but she would never *leave* them in the hands of such a creature. Nor his master.

She considered Reinhard Heydrich. If her plan worked, he would soon be father to her as-yet-unborn child. An incident of genetics,

---

1. A whole expansion level above merely 'checking the time'. Though the science was impressive, it was still possible to tip a drink down one's shirt while doing so, but then, wisdom often chases progress, desperate to get its attention. When it fails, the napkin of regret does what it can.

nothing more. He would come no closer than that, for he was another monster – and almost certainly the kind of man with whom her grandfather would have encouraged her to propagate. Heidi found that irritating. Even from beyond the grave he seemed to be pulling her strings. Taking away Heydrich's access, even his knowledge of the child, was a counterbalance and an act of defiance. *I pull* all *the strings from here, Opa,* she decided forcefully, as though her dead grandfather could hear her thoughts. Yes, better that she brought the Schultz family back together. They would be a family re-engineered, headed and shaped by her, and only her, and in tune with Heidi's own desires. There was just one person missing from that ideal, but she had a chance to fix that, too, this time around.

She synchronised her comm with the time displayed on a wall control unit. She would need to stay abreast of all that was happening, where and when, over the next few days. Thoughts of bringing the Schultz family back from the dead buoyed her as she ran through deserted corridors towards an emergency hidey hole she prepared the first time around, but never used. That made it even more perfect, because there would be no chance of running into herself, either. Though she was a little over nine months back, in her personal timeline, her younger self was still running around sabotaging the USS *New World* and murdering people. She must do nothing to change that. Not yet. Everything must play out as it had previously. For the next few days, Heidi had only time to kill.

Nineteen hours passed slowly, when Heidi's comm sounded an almost silent alarm; just enough to get her attention. Within the embarkation lounge, Douglas was about to give a speech to the passengers. Practically everyone would be there. It was time to go.

Donning a black ski mask, she ran to the closest hatch that led from *Factory Pod 4* to the *New World* and made for her own quarters. No one would be checking security footage or looking for an insurgent just yet. By the time they were, they would already be on the lookout for someone in a black ski mask, so if she happened to be spotted, her presence would only add to Douglas' conundrum while revealing nothing of value.

Arriving at her own door, she remembered the access code easily enough and let herself in. Quickly going through younger Heidi's linen basket, she found a slightly soiled uniform and quickly changed, placing her own clothes in a small bag. No longer bothering with the mask, she strode from her quarters like she belonged there – Pilot Officer Schultz reporting for duty.

Heidi's was a brisk, no-nonsense gait ordinarily, so she saw no need to hurry further. Within minutes, she was back aboard the life pod and making her way to the Norris quarters. As ship's surgeon, she was party to the *New World*'s emergency door override codes; it took but a moment for the door to slide open. She smiled. *Who needs an army when they have access to their enemy's security information?* she thought wryly. The blind, deaf and confused Douglas of this time was much more to her liking. She slipped in without notice.

There were two bedrooms allotted to the Norrises within their small but well-appointed accommodation. One was neat with a cupboard full of women's clothing, the other was obviously the room of a teenaged boy. There had not yet been time for Tim to make the room his own but it was already untidy, with belongings dumped where they fell.

Heidi tutted, appalled by such slovenliness from one she still believed to be of her blood. She donned a pair of surgical gloves and quickly found a hairbrush. Removing some loose hair, she captured it in a small, sterile bag and sealed it up, carefully replacing the brush where she had found it – back on the floor.

She took one last look around, checking for anything that might give further insight into her young cousin's life before she knew him. Heidi would have made a more thorough search, but time was short, and she already had what she came for. Quickly checking the corridor was still empty, she relocked the Norris quarters and slipped away, returning to her secret hideout.

⌇

Another four days and change passed slowly. Time dragged for Heidi, though explosions, vibrations, and frantic conversations held across the ship-wide comm left no doubt that the same could not be said for the *New World*'s crew. Indeed, she remembered causing much of their distress, culminating with the ship crashing into the planet's atmosphere. Yes, she had fully expected to die that day – had been prepared for it.

She smiled at the memories, wondering how she could have been so short-sighted, so trusting. By this time, her younger self – Pilot Officer Schultz – believed her entire mission to have failed and consequently worked to carry out her grandfather's contingency order: leave no survivors. Heidi knew she was out there, looking for a way to completely destroy the ship and herself with it. Despite a couple of failed attempts, she would not stop until she succeeded – she was a Schultz, after all. She remembered reasoning that, even if there were a way home, Heinrich would kill anyone who failed in such a vastly expensive enterprise, so she may as well die with honour. That was her belief.

Older Heidi knew better and intended to stop her now.

Her solution was beautifully low-tech and simple, though her scribbled note would also be understandably low on detail, and she remembered being baffled by it at the time. However, she had recognised and trusted its source enough to immediately begin changing her plans accordingly. Unfortunately, finding it the way she had – or more to the point, *where* she had – had appalled her, but was a small price to pay.

She shuddered at the memory as she crept from her hiding place.

The previous day, and despite incredible odds, Sandip Singh miraculously managed to land the *New World* in Cretaceous Gondwana. He was an enemy, yet she remembered feeling a grudging respect at the time. Knowing in advance that they would make it down safely made re-entry into Earth's atmosphere less stressful this time around – merely a matter of waiting for the ride to stop.

By this time, most of the crew and passengers were gathered in the main hangar, leaving just the ship's officers and repair crews abroad trying to fix the air-flow system. Another beautifully executed piece of sabotage, designed to force Douglas' people outside to their deaths. Again, she smiled at the memory as she crept stealthily through the deserted ship.

Within minutes, she entered Dave Flannigan's sickbay aboard the *New World*. All Heidi's access codes still worked because Pilot Officer Schultz was under no suspicion yet. As a medical doctor and surgeon prodigy, she was extremely valuable to her enemy and extremely low on their list of suspects. It was all so easy, and her timing was perfect.

On the floor lay Nurse Justin Smyth, right where younger Heidi had left him. The man with a neck injury lay in one of the beds, both where she had put him *and* left him. Ditto for Lieutenant Geoff Lloyd, still in a coma. There was but one occupant unaccounted for. She waited. Within seconds there was a thud against the door inside Flannigan's office.

Heidi's lip curled with satisfaction. Once again, her timing was perfect. She pushed the door open with effort, to find her younger self slumped against it, unconscious on the floor. She remembered injecting herself with sedative in just the right quantity to leave time for her to remove her gloves and collapse in Flannigan's office – well away from any evidence left by the 'intruder'.

Quickly scanning the small room, she located a pen and notepad. She tore off a page and bore down on Flannigan's desk to write a brief note, leaving no indentations on the pad for Douglas' wretched policeman, Drummond, to find.

Cease and desist. Last Word soon. No merit in M.

She stopped to think, desperate to reveal more, but it was too risky, and in any case, younger Heidi would not need the extra information if her own plan worked. This was merely to protect the *Factory Pod 4* asset from her younger self and provide insight *to* her younger self, should her schemes fall apart. Having been down this road before, everything should be cut and dried, but her very presence changed things – and she knew from bitter experience that Douglas and Baines were insufferable meddlers.

Heidi shook her head no; she would say no more. Rolling the paper up tightly, she applied a little Vaseline and tucked it where even her doctor would need a damned good reason to look, uninvited.

There, it was hidden, and all things considered, the experience had been no more enjoyable this time around, but at least she knew it would work. After all, it *had* worked. It was hardly surprising that she had never disclosed what caused her sudden change of heart and why she gave up on destroying the *New World*. Jansen had tried more than once to get that information from her. "Oh, Ben. If you only knew."

Pausing momentarily to wash her hands – with some distaste, it had to be said – she opened the doors to sickbay. Checking once more that the coast was clear, she ran back to her hiding place to wait for the next window where her schedule, and that of her younger self, would coincide.

A further two days passed. Heidi spent them with her comm, scrolling through Tim Norris' notes on Cretaceous Patagonia. It was a refresher, but also a chance to increase her understanding of a place and time firmly linked to her own fate and to which she kept returning. Her recent fifty-kilometre hike from the *Last Word* plateau to the *New World*'s vacated compound left no doubt that she needed to know more. The giant spider had been a particularly nasty surprise. She would be out there in the wild again soon enough and it paid to be prepared. Besides, she really had nothing better to do. The flora and fauna shared similarities with North Africa, where she had spent more time, but many variances waited to catch the unwary.

She checked the time. It was becoming a habit. Out there in the Pod, her younger self would be stealing survival equipment at that very moment. Every act was burned into Heidi's memory; her recollections, while offering a road map and comfort of sorts, were also strange and unsettling. Though she had masqueraded publicly as one of her own direct ancestors in 1940s Germany, she had never lived through a time where there were literally two of her before. By now, her younger self would know she was there, too – or at least, that she had *been* there. Yes, that was what she believed the first time around, that someone had delivered the message, somehow, and left. A message that just happened to be in her own handwriting. She blew out her cheeks. *When you are wrong, you are wrong.*

She had no doubt the other Heidi would have found her note almost immediately, after Flannigan brought her round from the sedative – an uncomfortable moment in so many ways. It was vital now that the other Heidi, the younger Heidi, believed the messenger to have left. Clearly, interference from the future last time had not worked or *she* would not be there, and that gave her pause.

Firstly, because she remembered every action her younger self carried out, including her foiled attempts to destroy the *New World* in space, in the air, and on the ground, she knew that, upon recognising her own handwriting, all further attempts would cease immediately. She would now wait for backup – she *had* altered her strategy to wait for backup. As the note advised, she had never trusted Meritus either, always keeping him on what she had believed was a short leash. Though the phrase 'no merit in M' may have been a mistake in hindsight.

She cursed. That potential flaw seemed to have passed her by for a second time. Why had she not seen it? While so vague as to mean anything or nothing to prying eyes, to Heidi it named the person and suggested incompetence – a faulty syllogism that hid the real problem, that he was not to be *trusted*. In effect, he was not truly her man. In contrast, she could always trust her grandfather to choose such operatives while keeping the full details of their background to himself.

Her anger flared and subsided. She had learned much in the last nine months, enough to re-evaluate her grandfather's choices. Weirdly, Douglas had completed her education. Now she understood how unthinking stooges, slaves to an ideology, rarely possess the flair necessary to be a true leader. Clearly, her grandfather had trusted Meritus to spearhead their capture of the *New World* because he was a man capable of breaking his programming when the situation called for it. He was also a man who wanted to live and had nowhere else to go. A Faustian bargain that suited both parties – or so it seemed at the time. *Dangerous, Opa. You should have warned me.* That got her to wondering just how much her grandfather had foreseen. *Could* he have known? She might go mad[2] speculating over that can of worms. After all, he had known he was dying, and now he was to be born again, under the wing of one of the most powerful and unscrupulous men in history.

Never mind. If her plan worked, Meritus would be dealt with, and her grandfather's clone would fall under *her* tutelage, rather than the other way around[3] . Heidi's second and more worrying concern was that her younger self had continued down the same road *at all*. Since stealing aboard the USS *New World* for the second time, she had remained so focused on stopping younger Heidi from destroying the ship and pod from under her, that she never

---

2. Some might say she was already there, but recognising one's own insanity is an extremely rare trait.

3. Some might say that was actually the *same* plan, the popular definition of insanity being the repetition of the same actions while expecting different outcomes – outbreaks of epiphany remain isolated.

considered the possibility of something going wrong with her own plan. It was almost like there was a recurring error built in. Was she destined to go round and round until doomsday?

No. There must be an opportunity for divergence – an off-ramp. It was for her to recognise and act upon it. It was her life and her success that mattered, not those of any younger, or even older self – assuming she was caught in a loop at all. She, personally, had only been round once before, so the data from which she could draw any conclusions was limited. Logic suggested she should, at the very least, take more care, perhaps even carry out her actions in a different way from her original plan. Maybe she should change her plans altogether? Despite knowing the past and the future, she found herself once more off the map. It was infuriating, especially when she had so little time to draw a new one.

Her comm pinged softly – time to leave her hiding place. Never had her coming actions mattered more. If successful, they would affect and effect everything.

Heidi waited, nervously checking the time every few seconds now. It was unlike her to show apprehension, but everything depended on her next moves going undetected.

She hid behind a lorry, one of the eight-wheeled behemoths originally designed to work opencast mines on Mars. At last, Flight Officer Schultz – her younger self – appeared at one of the pedestrian hatches situated along the opposite wall of the Pod's main hangar. With the Pod's main power still off due to younger Heidi's sabotage, most of the light came in through small portholes above the main vehicular airlock. Masked and all dressed in black, she might have been anyone – was barely even visible in the dismal gloom of minimal emergency lighting. Heidi watched herself shove a man into the hangar ahead of her. He was instantly recognisable – Chief Hiro Nassaki.

Still some hundred metres away, she watched her black-clad self retrieve a bicycle, loaded down with bulging paniers over its front and rear wheels. She grinned as the engineer was sent sprawling across the deck towards the pedestrian hatch. *I do have a way with people,* she noted proudly.

Although the quietly held, one-sided conversation did not travel across the hangar, she remembered well Nassaki's confusion about opening the hatch, and his pointing out the extraordinary dangers without. For her part, she had not spoken a word, yet every gesture – augmented with her nine-millimetre – was understood perfectly. Nassaki suddenly threw his hands up in surrender, bringing another smile to her lips as she recalled his terror, after the first attempt to open the hatch failed. Quickly, he redoubled his efforts, when the main lights came back on. Heidi blinked as clinical, omni-directional luminosity flooded the hangar.

Nassaki's hands were up again. "It wasn't me! That wasn't me!" he cried out, loudly enough for her to hear this time.

The black-clad figure pulled back the firing hammer, putting the weapon to Nassaki's head, free hand pointing to the exit hatch.

The engineer bent to his task, knowing his life depended upon it. The hatch slid open, and he immediately picked up the portable power supply to step into the airlock. He was out of sight, but she knew he was already working on the outer hatch.

With the lights on, this was a dangerous time for her. On the one hand, she could not risk being seen by her younger self, and on the other, she had no idea how long it had taken last time for help to arrive on the scene, because she had already left.

She balled her fists irritably. *Off the map again!* Heidi hated winging it, even though constant necessity had forced her to become rather good at it. Timing was essential, but she could only make a best guess, so she slung her backpack loosely over one shoulder, freeing herself to fight, if necessary, and ran for it. Moving silently from cover to cover, hiding behind vehicles, packing crates and anything else large enough to conceal her, she hoped no one would come looking for Nassaki before she got away. She had no reason to believe anyone would arrive at that moment, or that

Flight Officer Schultz would turn around to investigate – after all, she had not – but if she made a mistake or a sound, that might change, along with everything else. Although she planned to unravel this timeline, she did not want it to unravel yet.

Crouching behind a mini digger, she heard the soft *thud* of younger Heidi administering a blow to the back of the chief's head on her way out – almost immediately followed by a second, heavier thud as he collapsed to the deck. Next came the ratchet sound of a bicycle crank reversing to bring the pedals into position for mounting. She risked a quick glance around the corner into the airlock.

Facing away from her, Heidi's younger self climbed on and set off, riding away through the *New World's* incomplete outer compound. Douglas' people were yet to build the later palisade and gates.

Nassaki was down, as she remembered. So far, so good. However, the seconds flashing by for Heidi the cyclist, as she approached the large gap in the newly constructed earthworks, dragged interminably for Heidi the spectator. Her younger self would soon be out and heading for the treeline, not daring to look back.

This was her chance. Securing the pack around her shoulders and clipping the straps together for security, Heidi ran for it, out into the Cretaceous sunshine. She made the gap in the earthen walls at a sprint and once outside the ramparts, dove immediately left, down into the ditch left behind by construction crews as part of the new defences. Panting, she waited as long as she dared. This was the most dangerous time for her. She knew for a fact that her younger self would stop just inside the treeline to look back through binoculars, checking she was not followed. Added to that, Nassaki might be discovered at any moment. Frantic to get away, she dared not move. If younger Heidi spotted her, all would be ruined, and that was when she discovered the flaw in her plan, the one that had gnawed at her the last few days. She had her off-ramp, just not the one she had been looking for.

69.2 million years later…
Hanging below the UNS *New World* by a cable, the antigravity drive activated, its primary purpose inverted to *generate* gravity. A relatively tiny piece of technology, it nevertheless completely overpowered the attraction of an entire planet, creating a localised mass curvature in space–time – a second gravity well. The cable securing it to the ship's underbelly went slack, as the giant vessel was inexorable dragged back towards the alien device.

"Pour it on, Sandy!" Baines called out across the bridge, over a sudden eruption of alarms and warnings.

"Yes, ma'am." Gritting his teeth, Singh fed power into the main thrusters to counter the extraordinary force acting upon them. "Balancing. OK, we've stabilised… barely." He whistled. "Can we integrate that thing into *this* ship, please? It's playing with the *New World* like a toy. Wow!"

Outside, behind and below, magma continued to fly high into the air but with renewed vigour, creating an ever-growing ball of molten lava in the sky that burned like a second sun. Eventually, the core temperature became too much, even for the tungsten steel. It began to neck, near the point where it attached to the gravity device, and eventually snapped.

The *New World* shot forward. Close to full power, her crew were pressed into their seats to the point of blacking out before Singh could bring her back under control.

"What happened?" Douglas demanded.

"Cable snapped, sir," Singh replied. "Must have."

Douglas leaned forward slightly, his crash harness relaxing its grip on him, while his own tension spiked. "We've lost it, then?"

"No, sir." The answer came from behind and right of Douglas' command chair.

"What's happening, Chief?"

Hiro studied his readouts. "The ball of magma is still growing,

Captain. The device must still be…"

"Chief?" Douglas prompted, alarmed.

Hiro was shaking his head. "It's still running, sir. Floating completely within the grasp of its own gravity well. Bits of the Earth are being torn away, evidence that the whole planet is showing signs of creeping towards *it!* This is unbelievable!"

"What about our mission, Hiro?" Baines called. "I'm guessing that leaving that thing switched on for any length of time will be bad news for our world below – and can someone switch off those damned klaxons?"

The Sarge obliged, forcing them all to calm themselves in the relative quiet that followed.

"That's better," Baines noted with a sigh. "Well, Hiro, what about our mission?"

"All I can tell you is that the generator is still running. Its gravity is such that it's attracting more and more lava to itself – almost sucking it from the fissure in the crust. And like I said, when everything portable has shifted, it will begin to crack and attract parts of that crust, followed by the mantle—"

"Oh, let's not do that!" Baines interjected, nervously.

"Indeed, ma'am, and… oooh."

"Ooh? What's ooh?" Baines demanded.

"There's so much interference from the volcano… Give me a minute." Hiro tried to make sense of his readings. "I believe something's happening to the wormhole now… erm… erm."

One glorious, sunny day in the mid-Cretaceous…
The animal was a matriarch among Mapusaurus roseae. She was massive and terrifying. Heidi withered in her shadow. *Now I know why younger me continued down the same road. I failed. Oh, ich habe Mist gebaut!*

Safely within the treeline, younger Heidi sneered, replacing her binoculars in a jacket pocket. "Bad luck, Chief." She could see no humans following, but the giant theropod predator that sniffed around, just outside the *New World* compound, was impossible to miss. Killing Nassaki had not been her intention. After all, he was a man of intellect and ability – useful once she had control of Douglas' ship – but she would not lose any sleep over it.

Oblivious to the continued presence of her older self, she rode away, leaving the *New World* and, by an extraordinary feat of temporal dexterity, herself behind, too – and right in it.

Older Heidi was no stranger to this type of thing. In the last nine months, she had consistently survived similar scrapes more times than she cared or wished to remember. However, this was different. She was now interfering with her own timeline. She remembered receiving the note in her own handwriting, and based on the temporal dance that was her life, assumed it was from herself. At that time, she believed that was the end of the matter. Now, she knew why and swore, vehemently.

Mapusaurus showed no obvious signs of offence. Instead, she leaned closer, sniffing the morsel crouched before her. Cretaceous creatures were often intrigued by the strange sounds the human interlopers made. Like us – like animals generally – they tended to be curious about anything new, but that would not stall her for long.

"What if I told you there was a man over there – just lying there – and that he was much fatter and juicier than I am? Would that work for you? I have seen him eat – he is practically *made* from protein bars. Oh, what is the use!" Heidi snapped in frustration and fear. Suddenly furious, and lacking any serious alternative, she picked up a stone to launch it at the massive, grinning face. "Stupid animal!"

Not even registering the missile, Mapusaurus growled, opening her jaws wider.

It occurred to Heidi that, while there was indeed little she could do, a show of bantam aggression at that moment might actually push the 'stupid' more onto her side of the equation. The creature's breath alone nearly felled her. She dared not even fire her trusty sidearm. It would do little good and would alert *everyone* to her presence. *It cannot end like this,* she thought frantically. Rather than the ordinary fear of conflict that held her – even when confronted by such a powerful adversary – it was the sense of history repeating itself that sapped her spirit. Now she understood where the cease-and-desist note came from, it became clear there was no way out. She would never be heard from again and no one would even know what had happened to her.

All her hopes and ambitions flashed before her eyes. Her child would never be born. Tim Norris would never die by her hand for subverting her standing with their grandfather and would never be reborn in Mengele's lab from the DNA recently stolen from the hairbrush in his quarters. The world would *never* be at her feet[4].

"Nooo!" she screamed at the top of her lungs, her fists balled in fury.

Mapusaurus *roared!*

Violent egocentricity was the default setting for both these females – the matriarch and the murderess. No one in their right mind would have placed themselves between these women scorned.

Heidi knew she had died there – would die there. It was her destiny, but giving up was not the Schultz way. She jumped from her crouched position to circle left.

Mapusaurus circled right.

Heidi took the initiative and ducked under the giant's chin to dash between the tree-trunk legs, narrowly avoiding the enormous, muscular tail as it swished to counterbalance the predator's movements. With an ivory-shattering *clop,* Mapusaurus snapped the empty air, but reacted instantly, turning to pursue her

---

4. By this point, even Heidi's detractors probably agreed that she really had worked for it.

tricksy prey, all at once forgetting her annoyance – this was sport. Her excited roar made Heidi's ears ring, almost stunning her – she had only one place to run.

Scrambling up over the edge of the ditch, she dashed back into the compound, heavy footfalls shaking the ground in her wake. On her right was a mound of loose earth, left over from the construction of the enclosure's ramped inner face. She would pass close to it and logged the information, unsure of its importance.

Again, she wondered if this dance was a rerun. Her disregard for the natural order over the last nine months meant she could no longer be sure. If it was, then what could she do differently? *It would help if I knew exactly how it ended the last time,* she thought, desperately.

The moment came. Lithe as Heidi was, Mapusaurus gained on her and bobbed a giant head to snatch the woman from the ground, hoping to tear her in two. Out of options, out of ideas, she made the snap decision to behave erratically and simply fell to the ground. The dinosaur ran straight over her. Fortunately for Heidi, such a vast animal tracked at 1.8 metres across the hips, and Heidi managed to curl up between the footfalls, rolling out of the way as each giant claw fell.

Giving the hunter no time to work out what had happened, she sprinted for the mound of loose earth. Rushing around the back, she dug feverishly into it with her bare hands.

The heavy *thump, thump* of Mapusaurus' steps slowed as the colossus turned to search for her lost quarry. Mystified by Heidi's sudden disappearance, she scanned the compound, sniffing the air.

Heidi managed to pull a landslide of soil down upon herself. Buried alive, she gently fashioned a small airhole. Had the moment of her death passed? Would she now live? Would she be able to affect the future of her younger self after all? Everything depended on the efficacy of her hiding place – or so she believed.

Mapusaurus' confusion and disappointment over losing such a fun chew toy evaporated as she reacquired Heidi's scent. Retracing her steps back to the spoil heap, she clawed at the loose earth, eager to continue the game.

A third party stirred, changing the dynamics of the situation. Back at the entrance to *Factory Pod 4,* Hiro groaned.

The matriarch's head rose instantly, staring over the pile of earth. She squinted in the bright sunshine, eagle-sharp eyes focusing on the chief as he rolled over onto his back. He remained unconscious, head and one arm lolling across the threshold of the outer hatch.

The soil spilled down to cover Heidi even more completely. She held her breath, not daring to open another air hole. The creature's senses were extraordinary. Though Heidi's plunge to the ground and fast retreat confused the predator, she nevertheless walked straight to Heidi's location, despite the myriad' conflicting scents within the turned soil.

Heidi had no idea Hiro had just moved; she only knew she was not dead. Not yet. When the heavy footfalls moved away from her, more slowly this time, she felt them through the ground and almost whimpered with relief. Fortunately, buried with a mouthful of soil, any involuntary sounds were stifled.

She waited for the vibrations to diminish before cautiously removing some of the earth that covered her, forging a small breathing hole. Spitting dirt and gulping fresh air, she listened intently. The dinosaur seemed to have walked off, though from where she was, it was impossible to discern where.

She removed just enough soil to see clearly. There was no sign of Mapusaurus near the opening in the ramparts. Heidi considered; the dinosaur must have approached the *New World* again, behind her hiding place in the spoil heap. A memory surfaced from when *she* had been her younger self, and hope ballooned in her chest. Standing just within the treeline, she had said, 'Bad luck, Chief'. *At the risk of repeating myself,* she thought, realising what was happening.

Then came the shouting. It sounded like two men. To her ear, they sounded Australian. The dinosaur roared and several stun bolts were fired.

Time to go! Putting action to her thoughts, she ran like hell, using the mound in which she had hidden for cover, until she reached the opening in the earthworks. Having no choice, she dashed pell-mell between the banks, hoping no one saw her as she rolled once more down into the ditch. She came to a stop, panting hard.

Risking a look over the top, she watched the altercation taking place a hundred metres away, saw Sam Burton dive in to drag Chief Nassaki out of the dinosaur's reach by the heels and watched the hatch close, knocking the massive head to one side.

Mapusaurus roared again, incandescent now. Twice she had failed to secure a relatively easy snack and that door in the face was the last straw. Someone must pay.

Yep. Really *time to go!* Heidi raced for the treeline, fleeing like never before in her life. Cheating destiny, she was once again off the map, but this time it felt wonderful.

Chapter 22 | Greatest Hits

"Hiro!" Baines cried frustratedly.

"I'm trying to make sense of it, Captain. Oh…"

"The wormhole's gone!" Singh shouted from the pilot's seat. He span his seat to face them. "It's gone," he repeated, this time in an awestruck murmur.

They all turned to Hiro. "Is that what you were trying to impart, Hiro?" Baines demanded.

Hiro seemed to have lost the ability to speak. His mind was leaping to all kinds of theories and eventualities. Fortunately, he was saved by a comm call.

"*Bridge, this is Satnam Patel.*"

"Satnam, it's Jill. Go ahead."

"*Captain, according to our instruments, the wormhole has closed. We have no way of knowing whether our mission was successful, but I suggest that we invert the device once more into antigravity mode so that we may attempt to retrieve it."*

"Won't it still be in the middle of molten lava?" asked Douglas.

"No, Captain. Once inverted, the lava should fall into the waiting arms of the Earth's natural gravity, leaving our equipment free-floating. It obviously survived the intense heat. The current super-volcano should also return to its previous magnitude now no longer joined to the Triassic super-volcano."

"Very well. Do it," Douglas ordered. "Once the area is safe, we'll move in close enough to retrieve our equipment."

Hindsight was coming in handy. Heidi knew her younger self was ensconced high on a rocky ledge, within a convenient cave, and would make camp there for some days – long enough to safely weather the coming storm. Remembering her actions back then made it easy to avoid crossing paths. She checked the chrono on her comm and smiled at the memory. Younger Heidi would venture out from her cave several times over the coming days and nights. By this time tomorrow, she would be starting a wildfire a few miles north of the *New World*'s position, her plan, to flush out the larger and more dangerous animals. The fire would drive most of them east, away from the forested and mountainous west, in a massive stampede against Douglas' new enclosure. That had been unintentional but was no less amusing for it.

Returning to the moment, she beat her way through the jungle, just a few miles south to a place no one from the *New World* had yet explored. Going with what worked, she found a smaller outcrop with its own cave, partway up the north-east face.

Ten metres above the ground, it was a scramble. Worse, it was home to several small avians – some type of pterosaur she did not recognise – and a plethora of insect life further back. Securing a firm foothold, she reattached the silencer to her sidearm – another memory jogger; it had been a while since she had needed it. Killing one of the flying reptiles, she quickly turfed the rest out. They flew at her, screeching, but when another of their number fell from the air, seemingly without reason, they burst from their home and scattered.

Heidi moved in. The place stank of guano, but she had endured worse. Feeling around outside the cave mouth, she hung the little bodies of her kills like crows on a farmer's fence, as a warning to the others not to return. The climb was too difficult for any large predators and the cave too small. She was all set, though the view might have been more agreeable.

Her new, temporary home looked out over a fetid pool. Occasionally, a large, scaly body would surface for air and vanish again. "A charming neighbourhood," she noted, drily. Fortunately, the trees were smaller around the pool – perhaps the result of an earlier fire – so she at least had a reasonable view towards the *New World,* if she could not actually see it. Heidi discounted the idea of cooking one of the pterosaurs. She would have to do without a campfire, in case it drew attention. She may have cheated death, but she was not yet ready to irreparably change the timeline. It was important that certain events played out first.

Making the most of her downtime, she cleaned the cave up as best she could, removing any remaining insects and arachnids hiding in the darkness. Heidi did not fear them per se, but they were shocking; scorpions the size of domestic cats were enough to make anyone balk. With the invertebrates, she threw any she killed into the pool far below, after reading that certain species gave off a pheromone upon death that attracted others to swarm the threat. She had no idea if these were such creatures and no wish to find out.

Settling in for the evening, she nibbled half-heartedly on basic rations and tried to get some sleep.

Heidi awoke stiff, but relatively content, having not been attacked or bitten in the night. After a few gentle calisthenics, she passed the day lazily, using Tim's notes to identify some of the plants and animals that inhabited her hiding place. Appended to his palaeontological research, there were even a few observations from his time in the Cretaceous to offer comparison.

By the middle of the afternoon, she tired of reading and glanced up to look out over the treetops. In the north, a narrow smokestack rose high into the blue sky. She smiled, wryly. "Right on time. Little sister, I salute you."

Soon after, the black column thickened, and a deep rumble began to shake the ground. Soon after that, all hell broke loose. Even from a couple of miles away, she could hear the bellows, brays, roars and screams of a vast, mismatched menagerie on the move.

Heidi closed her eyes, remembering the higher vantage point where her younger self was currently encamped. It offered a commanding view over the stampede that was, even now, about to engulf the *New World,* breaking around its earthen enclosure like a wave. Leaning back casually against the cave wall, she remembered watching with bemusement through powerful binoculars, all those long months ago. Perhaps she would take a little nap now. After all, everything was proceeding as planned, and with her younger self doing most of the work, her new map was practically drawing itself.

***

69.2 million years later…
Douglas, Hiro, Patel and Reid stood around the rescued alien machinery in one of the *New World*'s smaller hangars. The heat still radiating from the device kept them well clear. Douglas held out his hand to get a better sense of it. "Ah take it that's just residual heat from the lava and we're no' going to get melted from radiation burns?"

"We're in no danger," Patel explained. "The device is deactivated."

"We think," muttered Reid.

Douglas took a small step back as he looked around his three companions. "Hmm. So, what now?"

"I've been thinking about that," Reid began. Still very much the outsider, he half-expected Douglas to shoot him down.

Hiro encouraged him. "Go on, Dr Reid."

Reid shrugged. "Well, I think we should proceed with the assumption that our plan worked, and if it did, then this is what I believe just happened…"

Ten minutes earlier…

The alien technology created a massive gravity well, just after the *New World* opened a vast wormhole conjoining the Palaeogene super-volcano with a region at the volcanic heart of the Permian–Triassic mass extinction event. The effects were greater than anything they expected, their destructive power surpassing even the worst-case scenarios generated by computer modelling.

The influence of magnetism on wormholes was known, but so powerful was the magnetic field generated by magma from such a deep cataract into the outer core, that it attracted every wormhole on Reid's manifold system all at once, literally sucking them through holes in space–time to a single fixed point where the permanent wormhole sat, at the Permian–Triassic boundary.

The manifolds essentially collapsed, leaving just one open wormhole that tunnelled a secant[1] line through the outer core between the Permian–Triassic and the Palaeogene Periods. Two points in time *technically* sharing the same space on the Earth's crust, this was only possible because the Earth's crust had shifted over 222 million years, allowing the creation of that secant line through the

---

1. A secant line is a straight, direct path between two points on a circle or sphere, rather than following the *curvature* of that circle or sphere. In effect, it's a shortcut, and in this context, a direct pathway that cuts through the outer core of the planet to arrive elsewhere on the Earth's crust. The crust is in constant motion, especially over millions of years, allowing this bilocation through time. In lieu of a diagram, perhaps an aspirin?

outer core, that is, through space, as it travelled through time.

The colossal eruption in the Palaeogene spewed so much iron ore and magnetite up to the surface of the Earth that it created what would one day be known as the Bermuda Triangle – still the most magnetic region on Earth, even thirty million years later.

The second part of Hiro's plan required the destruction of Reid's wormhole devices. Pulling them to one place was not sufficient. Still open, and now sharing one set of space–time coordinates, the ramifications, if left untended, might prove beyond the nightmares of physicists. The alien device, stolen from Area 51, created an intense gravitic draw that nudged Reid's tiny technologies from their protective fifth dimensional space and back into three-dimensional 'real space', where the immediate heat of the magma chamber destroyed them all instantly. With them closed the last remaining wormhole, sealing the integrity of the natural timeline once more. Cause would now lead to effect, leaving everyone and everything exactly where the universe intended them to be… almost.

Now…

"What do you mean, almost?" Douglas asked tersely as Reid's narrative ended abruptly. "If we succeeded, and the wormholes have now been closed, then surely there's nothing more to do?"

"No. Probably not," Reid muttered, pensively.

"Not helpful, Doctor!" Douglas roared.

"James, if I may," Patel interjected. "I believe that what Dr Reid is trying to say is that, if you are correct, and we were indeed successful in closing the wormholes, then there may be… *consequences.*"

Douglas frowned, not following.

"He means stragglers," Hiro explained wearily. "Things, people, animals, anything that crossed over to find itself out of place." He sighed, heavily. "Will this never be over?"

Douglas groaned as the penny dropped.

Mid-Cretaceous Patagonia

Six days passed, largely without incident. Heidi remembered the boredom of her first vigil, nine months ago. This time, she was content in her boredom, because this time, she knew what was coming next – and was in no hurry to meet it.

Dark clouds already gathered in the east. A storm was brewing over the baby Atlantic that would soon be heading her way, and it would be a monster. She sighed. The Cretaceous did everything 'large'. There was nothing she could do but hunker down and wait for it to pass.

Within the hour, the entire sky visible from her cave mouth turned black. It felt like the bright sunlight was being chased away as an unnatural gloom settled. Almost immediately, it began to rain heavily, beating hypnotically against the cliff face of her elevated hideout. The wind followed fast on its heels. A few tentative gusts tugged at her clothing, shunting her back. It was all the warning she received before she was lifted off her feet, bowled over and pinned to the rear cave wall. She had forgotten just how sudden and ferocious this storm had been – or more accurately, *was.* Just one more desperate drawback with her last-ditch, desperate plan. This was going to be awful.

Her cave curved slightly, just enough for a slender woman to tuck herself out of the horizontal rain, driven so hard by gusts touching 150 miles per hour that it struck like a spray of nails. Heidi cried out, silent in the storm, clinging to her backpack for dear life. Although waterproof, and offering limited shelter, the wind tore at it so hard that it was all she could do to hang on. She dared not move from her refuge, lest the hurricane sucked her straight out to plummet down the rock face to her death, or into the crocodile pool below – also to her death.

Regretting her choice of cave, she wished she had spent longer searching, and found one facing the opposite direction. It might have sacrificed a view towards the *New World,* but would have been far safer. Her principal concern, then, had been the threat from predators; now, it was the storm system that she knew would sit on them for at least two days, growling around the plains and valleys in circles. The only brief interval would come when the eye passed over her current location in approximately two hours' time. If she did not have a plan by then, she might yet make her date with destiny.

That gave her pause. *Had* she thwarted fate? Or was this actually the end she *thought* she had escaped – death by storm? There was no way she could cling on safely where she was for two days. The 'eye' would give her eight minutes of relative calm – and though she had been redrawing her map, what she really needed at that moment was a plan.

"Damn!" she cursed in vain, her voice and breath instantly snatched away.

It was a long two hours – long and torturous. When the wind finally dropped, and the sky outside brightened, Heidi collapsed into a puddle on the cave floor, every muscle aching and spent. Setting the stopwatch on her comm, she rubbed what life she could into weary limbs before climbing down to the ground. The large crocodilians that inhabited the pool below continued to hide beneath what remained of its murky depths. The pool was much shallower and smaller than it had been, and now sat within a ring of vile, stinking sludge, much of the water having blown away. She could see them, all grouped together, too stunned to posture or fight.

Safely down on the forest floor – for now – and with the coast semi-clear, she scrambled back into the forest, retracing her steps from several days earlier.

Briefly, she considered using her wrist device to take her to safety, but the only wormholes she could be sure of were commanded by Douglas' people. No. She was here, and here she must stay, if she was to ever create the future she wanted.

Her journey there had taken her past a hollow nestled within three intertwined tree trunks. At the time, she noted but disregarded it as a hiding place because, at ground level, it offered little protection from the wildlife. Now, she made for it, hoping the trees still stood.

Driving her exhausted muscles onwards, she ran back through the forest, trusting that she could find it again. Though it was not far, the detritus left by the earlier storm had blocked many of the animal tracks she traversed after leaving the *New World*. Moreover, it had changed the landscape. Everything looked different.

She sought three deciduous trees together. They stood out as an uncommon species for the area, but mostly because they were twisted around one another. Somehow, nature had seeded three trees to grow in the same spot, where they had fought for dominance ever since, surviving as one. Their shape provided considerable strength and stability – a natural shelter, where Heidi hoped to ride out the returning storm she knew would be terrible.

Hope surged for a split second as she spotted them. Indeed, the fact that the trees still stood, their shared vigour defying the storm, offered comfort, if short-lived. She tripped and fell, sliding down into a completely separate hollow created by a less fortunate tree, uprooted by the hurricane winds. Clawing at the sides, anxiety growing by the second, she pulled herself back up to ground level. The sky above the canopy was darkening once more. Her stopwatch chimed a repetitive *bong, bong, bong*. She was almost out of time.

Clambering over the top, her rucksack was caught by a sudden and colossal gust, and she flew, pinwheeling into bushes and brush bent double by the renewed onslaught.

Captured by the undergrowth, she hung as though from barbed wire, fighting ineffectually against the tangle as the storm's full force held her in place. Its ferocity made even inhaling hard work, tearing the breath from her mouth. Even more dangerous was the flying debris. Just about everything deposited by the storm, before the eye moved over, was in motion again. With desperate effort, she pulled her hands free and raised them to protect her face from flying vegetation, and even a few unfortunate creatures. The whole jungle bent and creaked ominously, so much so that Heidi could hear the strain on the world around her, despite the dreadful roar of the gale.

Frantic to untangle herself before she was hit by something more substantial, she cried out in fury and desperation. The wind was so powerful that even moving her arms was a battle. Eventually, she managed to free a knife from her belt. Using her left hand to protect her face, she took it in her right and began to cut away at the bushes ensnaring her legs.

It felt like the entire jungle was swaying in a violent dance. When the merest twig struck like a missile, it was only a matter of time before she was seriously injured. Heidi cried out soundlessly from blow after blow as she was assailed by falling branches and whipped by everything that flew past.

Something snapped. She could hear almost nothing above the mayhem, but she felt it. Suddenly, she could move. Left leg still pinned, she had regained enough mobility to begin working on her remaining bonds. It took every bit of strength she possessed to sit up and lean forward, but slowly, deliberately, she began sawing at the tough plant sinews. Finding it increasingly difficult to breathe, the exertion was causing black spots to swim before her eyes. When her leg pulled free, she was bowled over backwards, her backpack acting like a sail. Eventually, she came to a stop against a substantial tree trunk.

Viewed upside down, the world seemed even more chaotic. She considered crawling around the tree to hide in the lee of its smooth trunk, but the chances were that the vortex shedding taking place behind would either suck at her, sending her flying, batter her with detritus from the forest floor, or, judging by the way it was swaying side to side, tear the tree from its roots to fall on her. She had to find better shelter. Righting herself, she kept low and crawled for her original destination – the entwined trees.

She could see them, just ahead. Though stripped of much of their foliage, the nature of their entanglement was serving them well as they bore the brunt of the storm with far less movement than the trees around them. Through a haze of terror, the scientist in Heidi understood that their twisted form worked like the helical strake on a tall chimney, breaking up the oscillating high- and low-pressure zones that sucked at them, weakening the hurricane's effects.

Again, a violent gust caught her pack and she scrabbled desperately for some anchor or handhold to keep herself on the ground. She caught a strong root and hung on for dear life. Whatever had been attached to it was long gone, but it enabled Heidi to pull herself back to the ground and continue her brutal crawl. Briefly, she considered unclipping her backpack and letting it go, but without survival gear, how would she live after the storm?

No. Her mission was far from over and might yet end in failure. She needed her meagre belongings, and so, slowly, painfully, she crawled, inching forwards into the teeth of the storm. Her greatest regret, at that point, was not bringing a helmet. Several times she lost purchase and lurched backwards as she was forced to bring her arms up to protect her head. Hers was a journey of just a few metres, but it seemed like hours as Heidi fought and struggled for the cover she hoped would save her life. All the while, the little devil at the back of her mind kept repeating that destiny had decreed she must die, and not interfere with the future of her younger self. If that were so, it meant that in nine months' time, her younger self would end up exactly where she was now. The idea of being trapped in a doom-loop of failure urged her to fight even harder and eventually she got a hand to one of the exposed roots belonging to the trio of twisted trees. Knife now in her left, she dug it into the soil like an ice pick to help anchor her in place. Completely spent, she could do little more than hang on.

Taking a deep breath, she coughed violently, swallowing a mouthful of blown earth and pine needles. Heidi knew this was it, her last chance. Willing every joule of energy she had left into her grasp, she pulled herself onwards, edging closer to shelter, until she felt the force of the winds mercifully drop, just enough to allow her to scramble into the cleft between the trunks. Safely within the hollow, she coughed again before breathing deeply, at last.

She removed her pack, threading her arms through its straps to wear it across her chest for protection as she huddled, wedging herself in place. This would be rough – and dangerous – but at least she was shielded from the brunt of the wind's force. Now it was just a matter of waiting it out – a predicament shared with the trees themselves and every other living thing, as they clung on, collectively, waiting for the hurricane to abate. It was unlikely that any predators would threaten her hiding place during such a storm. They would be too busy hiding themselves. All life could do now was endure, and so, lodged firmly into the hollow, but fighting terrible exhaustion, she pulled a pair of tiny foam ear buds from a pocket. Opening the wrapper, she inserted them as the packaging was torn from her grasp. The dramatic reduction in sound made the storm seem further away and despite the raging winds, she fell asleep instantly.

⁂

Oligocene Epoch of the Palaeogene Period, approximately thirty million BC, Patagonia
Douglas scanned through the highlights of Hiro's damage report wearily. Its contents represented a lot of work, and following on from the weeks spent repairing the ship from damage sustained in their firefight over Area 51, made depressing reading. The wormhole they created, to join the super-volcano responsible for the Bermuda Triangle with the mass extinction event at the Permian–Triassic boundary, was larger and far more protracted than the *New World* had ever been designed to generate. Once again, perhaps unsurprisingly this time, their wormhole drive had been completely destroyed.

"Cheer up, honey," Baines interrupted his thoughts. "At least we have the equipment to rebuild it this time. *Those* parts and consumables were among the first things we loaded, if I remember correctly."

"Aye," he stated noncommittally.

"Something else bothering you?"

"No. Ah'm just tired of revisiting our greatest hits."

She smiled. "Don't worry, James. From here on in we'll write all new material."

"Not quite."

Her eyebrow rose quizzically.

"We still have to collect Meritus' fallen. Ah gave Tobias ma word Ah'd no' leave them behind. More even than that, we cannae abandon them at the *Last Word* plateau to contaminate the timeline, or the fossil record, or any other damned thing."

"Is that why you intend to take us back to mid-Cretaceous Patagonia?"

"Aye, eventually. Hiro believes our repairs can be carried out in orbit. Hopefully, he's right. It'll do nae harm to leave the Earth alone for a wee while. We'll cause less damage that way. It'll also keep us well away from the effects of that belching super-volcano. But before we begin our repairs, we've another drop to make first."

The UNS *New World* would not be wormhole-capable for a while, but she had no problems making for space. Settling her into a stable, high orbit around the planet, Chief Nassaki released the tungsten steel cables that once more tethered the gravity drive stolen from Area 51, setting it adrift. Satnam Patel had made a convincing case for the technology not to be left anywhere on the planet, where it might be found by future primitive cultures.

"Maybe we should destroy it," Reid suggested.

Hiro stared in disbelief.

Patel looked uncomfortable. "I have to admit, that thought crossed my mind, also."

Hiro could scarcely believe men of science would countenance the destruction of such a technological marvel, such godlike power. He glared at each in turn. The word 'blasphemy' did not strictly apply to his deus ex machina, but that was merely semantics to the

New World's chief engineer. "It's… it's the most important piece of tech any of us has ever seen!" he spluttered, finding his voice at last.

Douglas felt he should make his own position clear. "Ah agreed to this *only* because it will remain here, should we need it, or work out a way to fully unlock its secrets, and… well… that's it," he finished, weakly.

"Leave it, maybe, but talk of destroying it?" Hiro rebuked them all.

"Yes, it is important, Hiro, but it's not ours," Patel countered, reasonably. "Hopefully, this will keep it out of reach for any but those societies wise enough to at least understand what and just how important it *is*."

Hiro glanced pointedly at Reid and raised a wry eyebrow. "More likely, it will be found by a civilisation hell bent on throwing itself into the most devastating war in the history of our species. Personally, I think it should remain with us," he turned away, angrily, "but I see the captain agrees with you. So here we are."

With a sigh, he watched a camera feed show the deceptively tiny, yet incredibly powerful machinery grow smaller and smaller as the *New World* left it behind.

69.2 million years earlier, Patagonia

The storm raged for two further days, thankfully easing slightly through the cooler nights. With the backpack still in front of her, Heidi was able to access essential supplies of food and water. During a short window of relative calm, she was even able to free a rope and lash herself to one of the tree trunks – though answering the call of nature was a test of dexterity and nerve.

She remembered the nighttime lulls in the weather, where the hurricane wound back to merely gale-force. Somewhere out there in the jungle, her younger self was making use of those windows, leaving her cave hideaway to spy on the *New World,* each time hoping for a sign from Del Bond's group that they were ready for her to return. It had been incredibly dangerous and Heidi was glad that, for her at least, it was all in the past.

The worst of the storm blew out during the third night and the next day dawned peacefully. She removed her earplugs, enjoying a natural silence. It was time to leave, before she was discovered by anything large, anxious and hungry. Once again, hindsight served her well. She knew this was no lull in the storm; it had passed. That gave her an edge over every other living thing within her environment. They would all wait a while, before venturing from their hiding places.

Taking the advantage, she packed her things and walked north, eating a simple breakfast on the move. The fire, the stampede and the storm should have cleared her route back. If she was lucky, she would reach the *New World* before the Cretaceous forest came fully back to life.

Almost a fortnight had passed for her personally, since she placed the locator beacon in the bedrock near the treeline, just before Tim Norris shot her. She did so quite deliberately. Unaffected by the storm, she remembered the rock formation well, from its shape and from its view of the monstrous spacecraft in the centre of the clearing. She also placed it to make life easier for herself when the time came. After all, no one would choose to lug a heavy load far, especially through dense jungle, and she would soon have to carry her own weight across her back, into the clearing.

As often follows a storm, the weather was bright and fresh. Twice, since leaving the ship, she had scotched her own destiny. Despite the odds, she was alive, and on such a morning, it was hard not to feel invincible. The wildlife remained subdued, still not trusting that the storm was truly over, but the animals sharing her world would soon forget. Life would continue as it always had, until the next disaster.

However, for a short time, at least, Heidi had the world to herself. Aside from an occasional scurry though the undergrowth, very little moved, and she encountered no large creatures at all. Despite slaloming through storm wreckage here and there, she enjoyed her hour-long stroll through the Patagonian forests, the opportunity to stretch her limbs most welcome after the last, cramped couple of days.

Assuming the *New World*'s security were monitoring their surroundings, she kept well back into the trees. With so much vegetation to break up her lines, even infrared equipment would be unlikely to identify her. She had all day to find the perfect hiding place and wait for the evening to draw in.

She stared north, looking for threats. There were crocodiles in this area, much larger than the ones beneath the cave where she spent the last few days. Massive river-going Sarcosuchus hartti. No large animals were showing themselves yet, but she would remain vigilant. Most of the flooding was back in the river that ran through the clearing, though it remained swollen and up over its banks after the recent torrential rains.

At least she would not have to watch out for that enormous Spinosaurus – *she* was still swimming about in the rivers of North Africa in this time frame, and would be for another nine months or more. *What an incredible life I have led,* Heidi considered, in a rare moment of introspection.

Her memories strayed once more to Benedictus Jansen. Though he betrayed her, she had found it difficult to shoot him through the heart and leave him for dead. Even now, her feelings were unclear. Better to focus on his treachery.

Such thoughts naturally led her back to Tim Norris, her unwanted cousin, but those feelings had changed, too. She had meant it, when she offered him the world. He would have been her junior partner, naturally, but she *had* meant it, and that in itself surprised her.

Then there was her grandfather. She sighed. How unlucky she had been with the men in her life. Possibly the best man she had ever met was her arch enemy, Captain James Douglas. He was simply what he was, and what he was – she hated to admit – was often right.

Yes, it was time for a clean slate. Sometimes the world gets so messed up and insane that it simply needs a reboot. She smiled. *On the other hand, I could just take what I have and walk away – live in any time. Capitalising on my knowledge, it would be so easy to become wealthy and pampered. I could* rest...

Her last thought was heartfelt, for indeed, she was so tired, had lived through so much. Toying with the idea for mere moments, it already bored her. She smiled again – a hard smile, this time. *I can rest when I am dead, but that will not be today. Well... not strictly.*

A bass roar from deeper within the jungle made her turn sharply. Obviously, not everyone had cleared the area. *Better get your mind back on the task ahead, Dr Schultz, or you will be going round again!*

She found a suitable tree, where the foliage had survived the storm and was still thick, providing an excellent hiding place. There she passed a pleasant day watching a beautiful prehistoric world come back to life all around her, after the stresses of the last few days.

***

Nine months later...
UNS *New World* appeared in orbit around the Earth. Trapped in the Palaeogene Period, thirty million BC, it had taken over a month to rebuild the wormhole drive. When it came to choosing a shakedown destination for her return to service, Douglas opted to take them back still further, to the mid-Cretaceous, and to a time and place – for them, at least – with few surprises.

Singh's re-entry into atmosphere was practically humdrum, everything performing within expectations. Within minutes, the vast ship appeared in the sky above the ruined *Last Word*.

The *New World's* matt black surfaces were hard to observe, creating an effect not dissimilar to the way stars in the night sky can vanish when viewed directly, only to pop back out of the blind spot as corner-of-the-eye phenomena.

None of that mattered to the animals of the mid-Cretaceous. Far from appreciating the stealth technology, they were far more concerned with running away from the colossal roar of her engines.

She set down on the plateau, staying well clear of the weakened edge, further washed away by the recent floods.

"We're down, Captain," Singh reported. "Scanning for… for the bodies, sir."

Douglas felt rather than saw Meritus stiffen in the XO's seat Baines usually occupied at his side.

Singh rotated his pilot's seat to face them. "Some have been washed down the slope. Disarticulation suggests…"

"Go on, Commander," Meritus prompted, gently.

"Well, it suggests they may have been interfered with, sir. Scavengers, most likely."

Meritus swallowed. "James, I wonder if I might have a word in your private briefing room?"

<hr>

Nine months earlier…

Heidi's eyes snapped open, a sixth sense stirring her fully awake. The soporific afternoon sun had proven too much and now it was dark. A surge of adrenaline brought her immediately back to her senses as she checked her comm for the time. The evening was marching on. Any minute now…

She held her breath. Through the forest she could hear footsteps – light, graceful footsteps.

That must be me, she thought. Suddenly wide-eyed, she could scarcely believe what was happening and what she must do. I *am walking through the trees beneath me!*

She waited. Eventually, she heard a gentle rustle of twigs and brush being drawn together. Waiting until the builder of the campfire concentrated their full attention on their work, Heidi slipped silently from the tree. She stowed her pack where it could easily be found and moved forward.

Hunched over, younger Heidi bent to blow on the kindling. From nothing, the magic of fire leapt to life and flaming tongues soon licked at broken twigs, dried in the afternoon sun, to grow quickly. In seconds, she had a respectable campfire.

Older Heidi watched from the shadows. *Not yet. I must not make my presence known until exactly the right moment.*

It was a weird sensation, watching herself unpack a bottle of stolen disinfectant from her pack and pour it onto the flames, the boric acid making them burn with a green light. Nine months ago, in her personal time, *she* had built that fire. She remembered it clearly, though it seemed that her own 'older Heidi' had not made it. She knew that for certain, too, or she would not be here. It was a bizarre paradox, but it would end here and now.

The flashing light from the *New World* was easily visible to both Heidis – Del Bond's message to come forth. Another traitor, but he would soon be dealt with. Younger Heidi carried several stun rifles with her, retrieved from the archaeological dig site after they were lost in the recent storm.

Older Heidi waited for the message to be received twice, as she had the first time, and then took a deep breath. Suddenly paralysed by doubt, she froze. She had seen and experienced so much that was bizarre, but this was surely the pinnacle, and the worst.

Younger Heidi stood, backing away from the flames, when she froze, too. She had heard a sound from directly behind her.

Older Heidi had no idea what would happen if two versions of the same person shared the same reality at the same time for a protracted period, let alone if they spoke with each other. Would the universe end? Would it even matter? Her eyes narrowed. Ultimately, the only thing that certainly mattered was freeing herself from Douglas' interference, and to do that, a sacrifice was necessary.

"I am sorry, sister." She fired. Twice. The silencer masked the sound as the bullets pierced her younger self through the heart.

Before she fell, Heidi leapt forward to catch her, stopping her falling into the flames. She held the dying woman in her arms.

"Why?" she spoke in an agonised whisper.

"For the future. Take your rest, sister. I will carry the burden from here." But Heidi was not merely talking to *herself,* she was also talking to herself. Younger Heidi was already gone.

She stared at her a moment, so beautiful, even in death. Heidi the younger would grow no older. It had, indeed, been one hell of a week.Heidi

The last time she shed a flood of emotional tears, she had been no more than five years old. Her grandfather wasted no time in breaking her of that particular trait, but she shed them now. Having carried out many hits on his orders, committing every kind of homicide – committing suicide was a first. She blew out her breath, harshly, batting away her tears as she got to work. Time was suddenly against her once more.

Throwing the dead body over her shoulder, she made for the place where igneous bedrock poked up through the underbrush of the forest floor. Nine months into the future, she would drive her locator beacon into the stone, and at the exact space–time coordinates stored in her wrist device, a wormhole would appear very nearby.

Quickly, she stripped the dead woman and then stripped herself. When leaving the *New World,* she had dressed in the same combat fatigues she had been wearing when Tim shot her. Hastily swapping clothes with her dead self, she removed the Kevlar plates and tucked them into her pack, before checking the accuracy of the bullet holes Tim had left in her jacket with the wounds she had just inflicted. Almost perfect. She pressed the wounds, to soak the jacket in blood around the holes. *Good enough. Now just one final touch.*

She had been tempted to leave her wrist device with her younger self, but that really would mean putting all her eggs in one basket – and in the Cretaceous, who knew what might hatch. Instead, she removed her wormhole device and tore half the wrist strap away. She would have a new one attached when the *Last Word* arrived in just a few days' time. She stuffed it into dead-Heidi's fist, closing the fingers around it.

Lifting the corpse once more, she moved beyond the treeline into the large clearing to stand in the tenebrous moonlight. Dropping the dead woman onto her feet, Heidi held the body upright while she activated the wormhole device. A portal appeared before her, practically invisible in the light of the quarter moon, though she once again noted nebulous reflections from the daylight side. She turned the body around and let it fall through, into the future.

Quickly activating her comm, she scanned for the frequency of the camera she had hidden in a nearby tree. The signal came through loud and clear, allowing her to relive what, for her, had happened a fortnight ago.

She saw Sergeant Jackson glance at Commander Gleeson. "Get back to the chopper! Only you can fly the bladdy thing! Stay behind the wheel – or whatever."

"You mean the stick," Gleeson replied, absently. He was staring at the wormhole just as dead-Heidi fell through to collapse face down in front of them.

The Sarge leaned forward. "What's that in her hand, some kind of strap?"

"Must be the wormhole device that bladdy drongo Reid made for her," Gleeson answered, though he seemed more interested in the corpse. "Nice grouping, mate. Straight through the heart. A shot in a million with *that* Sheila— Oh, bagger…"

Via the hidden camera, Heidi saw the vast Spinosaurus aegyptiacus approach rapidly to leer over The Sarge and Gleeson. She smiled, satisfied. Her carrion bag had worked as expected, the stench of the dead Buitreraptor summoning the giant carnivore like she was on a string.

The Sarge appeared momentarily stunned. "Oh, Turkish delight!" he managed at last.

Heidi closed the connection. Entertaining though it was, she could not risk the dinosaur stepping through the open wormhole. They thought she was dead now and that was enough. She had to get away from there and retrieve the dead woman's belongings from the forest. Refocused within her own time, she glanced at the USS *New World,* glowing pale under the moon's minimal light.

If others noticed the green fire, they might become suspicious. Besides, she now had a gun run to make.

592

Chapter 23 | The First Deadly Sin...

"I have to go, Captain," Meritus explained, earnestly. "When the *Last Word* was destroyed, I lost sixty-three men and women out of a hundred and fifty-six. That was a deep cut, James, when even the loss of one would have been too many. And that's not counting the twenty-seven who were seriously injured." He paused, hanging his head. When he looked up, anger flared in his eyes. "Now they're denied even a respectful burial – torn apart by scavengers."

"But, Tobias, that was ten years ago. And most of those survivors ye mentioned are still with us. We've all lost people, and ye're part of *this* family now."

Meritus smiled sadly. "I know. And it's meant more to me than anything else in my life, really it has, but I never expected to find a way to undo what happened. Now, with an opportunity to act, to stop all those needless deaths, how can I just walk by? I must try. Surely you understand?"

Douglas massaged his temples. "So let me get this straight. You want to go back and talk your younger self into throwing in with us from the get-go?"

"That's my plan," Meritus lied. "When you offered yourself hostage, and Heidi delivered you into my brig, I should have seen you as an ally, rather than a threat. I intend to fix that." Those words were half-truth, half-wish, because he knew better than to think his younger self would buy into a story like that. He remembered that man – someone so jaded and distrustful of the Schultz regime that he would have assumed any such intervention was nothing more than a clumsy, last-minute loyalty test before they set out. Even if the messenger did look a dead ringer for an older version of himself.

Meritus' plan was simpler and more brazen than that, but he knew Douglas would never agree to it, especially if he believed it to be a one-way trip. The Scotsman was also right about family. It would break his heart to leave them, but he had to, even if it meant he could never return.

"We should discuss this with the others, Tobias. This is a big move."

"I know this must seem like a red flag, James, but—"

"Ah wouldnae swim near it – Ah can tell ye that! What about the future we created? Bringing those people back might change everything."

Meritus sighed. "Not necessarily. Besides, on the flip side, an extra sixty-three able bodies would have really helped ten years ago, the way I remember it. And with a guiding hand on the future, it will be like sending my younger self forward with a map – a map you will be able to use, James. As for discussing it with the others, I don't want a big song and dance about this. I especially don't want Jill involved."

Douglas frowned. "Why?"

"Because she blames herself, too. Wrongly, I might add. She did the only thing any leader could, when facing a threat like the

Last Word. We all have regrets, but those people were under *my* command."

Douglas nodded slowly. He understood, all too well. Honour, decency, respect for life; all laudable sentiments, but there was pride, too, and therein lay the problem.

"There's no need for her to take this on her shoulders," Meritus continued. He hated to lie to his old friend, but saw no other way. "Besides, I'll soon be back, right here, like nothing ever happened, right? We're outside our own timeline now, and I can take a copy of the wrist device Dr Reid provided. Apparently, with the exact time and space coordinates – which I have – it should work. I'll soon be back. *We* may always be outliers, but the rest of causality can continue along a better path."

"Aye, about that. Our wee sojourn into Tudor England is vital to that future we've sacrificed so much to protect. Like Ah said, what if you mess things up?"

"I can't deny there are risks, but if I can explain to *myself* that Schultz had a fault built into the Dawn Fleet's wormhole drives, making any return to the present impossible—"

"What if he decides not to go? Humanity waits to choke, back in 2112, in the final collapse of civilisation, all none the wiser? We need parts from the *Last Word* to escape the Cretaceous, remember?"

"He won't do that. *That* Captain Meritus joined to save as many as he could – as *I* could. Especially after the Canadian leadership began launching those secret operations in league with hostile states. With Uncle Sam's northern border exposed – thanks to traitors in *my* government – I knew they'd never offer me a place in NASA. That's why the Americans kicked us out of the Mars Project, remember?"

"Ah never agreed with that decision," Douglas acknowledged, sadly. "The people of Canada had nae part in it. Their wishes were ignored. They were also betrayed."

Meritus shrugged. "I can't change that, but if I could just convince the younger me to separate Schultz's fanatics from the rest of the crew on arrival, *that* would be something. If I can save them all, well, then…"

Douglas waited for his friend to find the words.

"What I mean to say is," he continued, "if I can save their lives, there might be a chance for me to also save them from themselves – break through their conditioning. The Captain Meritus of ten years ago will be well aware of who the zealots are, as I was. I'll convince him to open talks with the captain of the USS *New World.*" He smiled. "After all, I've found him to be a pretty reasonable guy, over the years. Between us, and with the power of the *Last Word,* we'll easily deal with the rest of Schultz's fleet when they arrive. Then Chief Nassaki will be able to strip my ship of the equipment he needs for the *New World* to jump forward to crash in 1558 – and round and around we go."

Douglas sat heavily. "Ah can see the merit in yer plan – nae pun intended."

Meritus grinned.

"But going without telling anyone… Ah don't know, Tobias. That's a lot tae ask."

"Problem is, I don't want to go, James. And seeing everyone will only make it harder. If anything does happen to me, you'll tell them what I tried to do?"

Douglas nodded, solemnly.

"And how much I care for them all?"

"Aye. Of course. Ah've yer promise now? That ye'll be right back, as soon as ye've spoken with him – that is, with *you?*"

Meritus smiled again, but this time it was tinged with sadness. "I won't let you down, James," he answered, obliquely. It was a promise of sorts. One he hoped he could keep.

Douglas held out his hand. "Good luck, ma friend. We'll be waiting for ye to come home."

Meritus shook it. "Thank you. For everything. Now, I'd better get an early night. Big day tomorrow."

The large auditorium functioned as the embarkation lounge once had, aboard the first *New World*. The floor was large and open at the centre, with a raised staging area at one end and four hundred tiered seats set into a horseshoe pattern around the other.

Still concerned after his conversation with Meritus, Douglas stepped up onto the stage. Looking for a distraction from his warring emotions, he plunged straight into his statement. "We have another terrible decision tae make, ma friends. Ah know how much we've all been looking forward tae returning tae the lives we made in 2122, but…" He sighed, his eye roaming around the faces before him. Could he really ask for more from them, after everything they had already been through?

He pinched the bridge of his nose, tiredly, before continuing, "Unfortunately, Heidi's *dabbling*, and the multiple wormholes she created, have left us with a few problems."

Again, he hesitated.

"It's OK, James, we can take it."

Douglas recognised the voice that called out and looked around for its owner. Just to his left, in the seats nearest the stage, he saw Hank Burnstein smile and nod.

Douglas snorted, gently. "What a journey we've all been on, eh? And how it's changed us. Look, what Ah have to tell ye, some of ye may have worked out already. Heidi opened three hundred permanent mini wormholes, criss-crossing hundreds of millions of years through Earth's past. We barely grasp the scope of all this, but thanks to the brilliance of our science and engineering team – especially Chief Hiro Nassaki, whose idea it was – we've successfully closed them. Every one of them."

A cheer erupted spontaneously from the gathered crew and passengers – now all *New World*ers.

Buoyed, Douglas straightened. What was he worrying about? Whatever lay ahead, they would deal with it, just like they always dealt with it, together. He smiled. "Thank ye, ma friends. However, although we cannae know for sure, we have tae assume that animals – even people, potentially – have found themselves displaced by these conduits through time. After all, we've seen animals travel into other periods with our own eyes – some of us, far more up close and personal than we ever wanted tae – so it's no' such a stretch."

Laughter.

He smiled again. "So, Ah propose that we stay here, in Patagonia, while we plan our next move. This could take a while, but fortunately, we have a time machine!"

More laughter. Douglas was surprised at the mood of his people. He expected them to be exhausted – and maybe they were – but no one was complaining about a delay in returning to the place they had made their home over the last decade, in AD2122. At least, not yet.

"Ah thank ye all for yer understanding – for everything ye've done and how hard ye've all worked to make this mission a success. Ah firmly believe we're on the home run, but we've a mess tae clean up. It's no' our mess, but we cannae back away from it. We're the ones who're here, so it falls tae us. There's no one else. We'll rescue all the stragglers and return them as best we can to their own times. Does anyone have any questions or anything tae add?"

He gave them a moment to respond, but no one did.

"Very well. That's how we see the medium term, so we'll call that decided. In the short term, we'll devise a strategy over the coming days, while others among us exhume the fallen from Captain Meritus' crew and take them to a place where they can receive a proper, permanent burial, with military honours. Ah thought the survivors from the *Last Word*'s crew would like to take that in hand themselves, with any and all support necessary from the rest of us."

A respectful, if less jubilant round of applause.

"Now, Ah'd like to talk to ye about our long-term future."

The auditorium fell completely still.

"Captain Meritus cannae be with us for this meeting, but just before we came in here, he said something that stuck in my mind. He called us 'outliers'."

Again, he looked around the faces before him, taking their measure. "He was right. Our time – our very timeline – is gone, and gone forever. The truth is, Ah'm no' really sure *where* we belong, so Ah've been considering options. Ah'll lay them out for ye now.

"One, we complete our mission and do indeed return to 2122, hoping everything's right where we left it, so we can live happily ever after. That sounds comforting but may be fraught with problems if any of a billion tiny changes have occurred during our time back in the Cretaceous – and other times. It needs careful consideration and may not necessarily be the obvious go-to that it seems.

"Two, we return to Crater Lake and the small settlement we set up there, now led – and led well, it seems – by Commander Ally Coleman. That will mean strict, almost draconian population control. We'd need tae put every precaution in place so that all evidence of our existence is erased over time. Ah'm no' fond of that option, but Ah offer it for consideration.

"Three, we return to 1588 and rejoin our friends from the original *New World.* Working together, we should be able to make sure the bright future we've already seen and shared comes tae pass. We've no idea what the effects of this would be on the future, although some have argued that we may be changing the course of history if we *don't* do this, now we have the capability. It's a minefield, ladies and gentlemen, but we must consider wisely before deciding.

"Four, we know that in the 22nd century of the new timeline, humanity used wormhole travel to settle other worlds, out among the stars. There are many worlds with non-sentient life earmarked for further colonies – we could sever our ties with the planet that gave us life and begin afresh, thus effectively taking ourselves off the grid. That way, the Earth's timeline would be safe from further interference. We could at least build a permanent base and settlement there, one with a future. Our only contact with Earth would be with our crewmates and families in Tudor England.

"It's a lot to take in – a hell of a lot, Ah know – but while we're catching our breath, Ah'd like ye all to consider these and any other options ye may have. Whatever happens, ma friends, whichever future we choose, our story will go on. That Ah *can* promise ye."

<hr />

Douglas kept Meritus' plan to himself as promised. Utterly drained, after his speech to the crew, he decided to sleep on the problem. When he awoke, it was with a start, his subconscious mind sending a jolt of certainty through him as he sat bolt upright in bed. He had made a mistake, and knew it.

Alone in their quarters, his wife having drawn the nightshift on the bridge, he threw off the covers and leapt out of bed to dress in a hurry.

In moments, he was running through the corridors that connected the crew quarters, making for Meritus' billet. Breathing heavily, he pressed 'call' on the door control panel and waited for his friend to appear on its small screen.

Nothing.

He pressed it a second time.

Again, nothing.

Douglas cursed. He hated to do it, but using his Commanding Officer codes, he let himself in. Meritus' quarters were empty, the bed made and unslept in. On the bed was a folded note.

Seething, he walked over to pick it up. It came as no surprise to see 'James' written on its outer leaf. He opened it cautiously, already guessing the contents.

James,
I couldn't take the chance that you might change your mind, so I left ahead of schedule. I'm truly sorry, but I have to do this and hope you'll understand. I'll be seeing you very soon.

Your friend, always,
Tobias Meritus, Captain.

Douglas swore and ran from the room.

Within minutes, he was outside the ship on the *Last Word*'s plateau. Many of his people were gathered near the edge, looking over towards the ruined ship below. No one seemed to be working.

Focused on the calamity about to unfold, Douglas failed to notice that he was no longer alone. A low growl sounded from behind him – more specifically, behind and *above* him.

He turned slowly, looking up into the grinning maw of Mapusaurus roseae. It was the giant alpha again, and if he was not mistaken, the same animal that had terrified the life out of him the very first time he stepped out into the Cretaceous all those years ago – although for the animal, just a little over nine months had passed.

Douglas scowled, drawing his sidearm. "You! Again!" he accused.

The dinosaur opened his jaws to leer down at him.

Douglas snarled, pointed his weapon upwards and fired ten shots in rapid succession. The bullets flew harmlessly into the air, but Mapusaurus roseae was only marginally better endowed in the forelimb department than the mighty Tyrannosaurus rex, and so had no option to cover his ears.

"Get tha hell outta here!" Douglas bellowed, firing another couple of shots that zinged right past the animal's giant face. "Go boil yer hid!"

Mapusaurus turned and, not exactly, ran away. His was more a dignified stalk, as he swished his tail angrily for Douglas' benefit. Not that Douglas would have followed. It would have been suicide. Anger abating slightly, he looked down at the gun in his now-shaking hand. "If only Ah'd had ye ten years ago!"

His comm binged, making him jump and almost drop his weapon. Fumbling nervously, he answered, "Douglas."

"Captain, it's Sandy. I've been scanning the area and there are a few dinosaurs close by. You should be careful, sir."

Douglas almost collapsed in a mixture of relief and amusement. "That's good advice, Commander. Ah'll definitely bear it in mind."

Taking a deep, steadying breath, he watched the massive

Mapusaurus vanish into the forest. Shaking his head ruefully, he turned and, on trembling legs, ran to join his people at the edge of the plateau.

They were all gawking at him as he chuffed over to them. Spotting an Australian construction worker he knew well, he called, "Bluey, what's going on?"

"Er… g'day, Captain," the builder answered, a grin slowly spreading across his face. His expression turning serious, he added, "They've all gone, mate."

"Who's all gone?"

"The bodies. All of Captain Meritus' people. They just vanished while we were digging them out! Bladdy madness!"

Douglas looked around, speechless. Tim Norris approached, shaking his head. "It's happened again."

"Tim? What's happened again?"

"I'm giving up on digging, *and* digs, Captain. Things keep disappearing on me!"

"Oh, no, no, no…" Douglas groaned. "Has anyone seen Captain Meritus? Anyone?" he repeated more loudly for everyone to hear.

"Never mind that," The Sarge called. "Has anyone seen the *Last Word?*"

"*What?*" Douglas shouted, running to the edge of the plateau and looking down the steep slope to the last resting place of nothing and no one. Utterly flabbergasted, he searched the faces of those around him for answers, then realised, *he* was the one with the answers. At least, he had one answer. *Oh, Tobias, what have ye done?*

The Sarge spat on the ground. "Here we go again. Turkish delight!"

A distortion appeared within the narrow alley, lost in the shadows of a back street in Baharan, Fars Province, Southern Iran. Meritus knew exactly where he was and that his younger self was about to meet with a Schultz contact in the town. According to his borrowed wrist device, it was the year AD2112, and within hours, the *Last Word* would begin her fateful voyage back to the Cretaceous. He coughed. He had forgotten how polluted the air was in this time, but having purposely arrived two hours prior to that meeting, he walked about town to find a barber, visiting several before he found one with a stylist.

He produced a photograph on his comm. "This is a style I wore ten years ago. I'd like it again, please."

The barber was impressed. "Ten years ago, huh? Very fashionable. It's a rare gift to be able to see the future, my friend. Maybe you should work for me – we could get a bigger shop in the city? I like your comm, by the way. Is it a new model?"

Meritus smiled. "Just something I picked up on my travels. Oh, and fix the grey at the temples, will you? I'm going for a whole new me."

The barber shrugged and began his work.

Half an hour later, Meritus left looking ten years younger. The meeting his younger self was about to hold with a *fellow* Schultz operative – that made him shudder – was in a seedy bar tucked away in another back street. The operative was named Elizabeth Hemmings, and she was there to deliver his final orders from Heinrich Schultz before joining as a lieutenant on his staff.

I can make sure all this ends differently for her, too, he thought, as he sweated through the merciless heat of the dusty desert town. *Just one more casualty I can prevent.*

Schultz's secret base was hidden in the mountains to the south, east of the remarkable Marharlu Lake – remarkable in that it was pink, due to its high salt content and evaporation cycle – but Meritus was not there for the sights. He was on a mission to change the world.

He bought a coif from a local street vendor. Wrapping it about his head, he used it to cover all but his eyes. Taking a deep breath, he entered the bar.

Inside was cooler than the street, barely, yet it was more unpleasant, too, stinking of sweat and illegal substances. He spotted his younger self and the female lieutenant in an instant. In such a dive, their crisp uniforms made them impossible to miss.

His people rarely left their base, but when they did, the locals knew enough to leave them alone. Both wore a sidearm.

Meritus spoke quietly with the bartender, who directed him to a shadowy figure in the corner, smoking some form of pipe. He approached the man, who glared up at him through the haze, like Meritus was something on his shoe.

He warmed when Meritus placed a souvenir from Cretaceous Patagonia in his palm – a nugget of pure gold. They conversed, Meritus in pidgin Farsi, his companion in pidgin English. Between them, they reached an understanding and waited.

Presently, his younger self left Lieutenant Hemmings alone at the bar. Remembering his visit to the lavatory before leaving, Meritus knew it was time to act.

Along with his new and most disreputable colleague, he followed himself into the toilets. Under no illusion that explaining the situation and the stakes would do any good, he simply knocked the younger Captain Meritus out from behind – an ungentlemanly act, though he wished himself no serious harm. If he knew *himself,* he would soon come round, realise what a mess he was in and be away across the border, to disappear from the Schultzes' orbit altogether. Heinrich would never forgive what was about to happen next.

Meritus swapped clothes with his younger self, secretly pleased that the clothes still fitted, and between them, he and the other man tied their victim, hands and feet, gagged him, and locked him in a foul-smelling cubicle.

"You keep him there," Meritus raised two fingers, Churchill-style, "two hours – yes?"

The man flipped the golden nugget, caught it, and pocketed it with a grin.

Meritus returned his smile with a grimace of his own. *It's all for the best,* he told himself.

He rejoined Lieutenant Hemmings at the bar. "We should go. We have a schedule to keep. I have a car."

She looked at him queerly for a moment. Appearing to shake off whatever had unsettled her, she allowed herself to be ushered to where his younger self had parked. They got in and drove south into the mountains.

Two hours was cutting it close, but he knew better than to trust his partner in the crime he had just committed for any longer than that.

With ten minutes to spare, they arrived at a compound in the middle of nowhere.

Though the perimeter fence was intact, there was nothing obvious inside it to guard. Meritus activated a device built into the vehicle, keyed to his voice.

"Open," he stated simply.

The technology analysed his voice patterns before opening a section of fence – actually a concealed gate. It slid to the side. He drove in, counting the metres on the car's odometer before coming to a stop.

Lieutenant Elizabeth Hemmings reacted with some alarm when the ground appeared to fall away.

Meritus chuckled, as he had the first time he drove her there, ten years earlier. His sense of déjà vu was sublimated only by his sense of destiny.

In true supervillain style, they were taken down into a vast underground hangar, their vehicular elevator coming to rest on the metal-plated floor.

Hemmings took another sharp breath, for standing in the centre of the hangar, brand new and immaculate, was the *Last Word*.

Meritus felt a pang of emotion. She was a technological wonder, after all, and this time she would be used for peace. He would take her on a mission to save the human race from extinction, rather than abandon it.

He beckoned Hemmings. "Quickly, we launch in…" he checked the chrono on his comm, "six minutes. When we arrive in our designated time, I wish to meet with you in private, Lieutenant."

She stared at him intently, trying to discern if there was some hidden meaning or trap behind his words. "Yes, sir."

Meritus knew Elizabeth Hemmings would technically betray him by helping Douglas escape, but felt sure they might come to an understanding this time around – one that would save many lives, including hers.

The roof parted at its centre, each half sliding open to spill tons of sand in great plumes, a hundred metres down to the hangar floor. The air was thick, coating the *Last Word* berthed below as she lifted in an explosion of light and noise.

The granular remains of prehistoric rock cascaded from her hull, turning to glass under the punishing heat of her thrusters. The hardened steel deck plates glowed cherry red as she left them behind, the pilot carefully lifting one of the most powerful battleships ever conceived from a vast hole in the ground. Soon, the hangar where she was made, and even the vast desert itself, was also left behind forever – the past, a lens that made everything smaller. A proof borne out as mountains became molehills and the sky became the curve of the world.

Captain Tobias Meritus knew every satellite and scanner their side of the planet would be locked onto and following them, and so ordered a wormhole jump immediately upon gaining high orbit – just as he had the first time.

His thoughts strayed to his friends aboard the *New World*, all waiting for his return. *I must see this through personally, James. Replacing myself on this mission was the only way to make sure everything's put right. I'm sorry for the deception. I hope you'll understand. Until we meet again, old friend…*

Patagonia, Mid-Cretaceous
Heidi waited in the darkness. For her, the *Last Word* had not even arrived yet, let alone vanished. Although she remembered its arrival well enough, all that was the future from where she crouched now.

The New World listed slightly to starboard after the recent flooding, providing a convenient hiding place under her port side. Bond's earlier Morse code message clearly stated the time and the place, and so, at the allotted hour, she made her way around the aft end of the ship – there were fewer portholes that way, and less chance of being spotted by the crew. It was difficult enough to move stealthily, carrying five stun rifles over her shoulder. Despite leaving her pack hidden within the treeline, she needed every advantage.

The pedestrian hatch slid open, unlit. A figure waited in the shadows.

"Good evening, Dr Hussain," she greeted.

She sensed, more than saw, him stiffen in the darkness. "How did you know it was me, Dr Schultz? There was nothing in our message…"

The hatch closed behind them, light instantly flooding the airlock.

Heidi's lip twitched, enigmatically. "I know everything now, Aabid."

Her words and demeanour clearly made Hussain uncomfortable, though he tried not to show it. "Follow me, please."

They walked across *Factory Pod 4*'s hangar towards the small room where Baines was held prisoner. After the shock of Heidi's return, their conversation passed word for word as it had the last time. Baines' barb about Heidi's failure to steal a hairbrush was no more amusing than it had been previously, but this time Heidi knew that if her hair *was* awry, it was small wonder after her survival of the last nine months' incredible adventures. She had visited deep time and deep space, seen Earth's story play out from the Triassic to the 22nd century, over three continents, created a cataclysm on the moon, lived with dinosaurs and within alternate timelines; there was so much to tell that there was nothing to say. Especially as she set out with foreknowledge to relive it all over again. The less others knew, the better. Her lip curled into a sneer. Baines would find out soon enough.

One thing was different, however. She had practically ignored Del Bond the first time around, treating him with contempt – as someone beneath her notice. This time she respected him enough to kill him, but not yet. Everything in good time.

During the altercation that followed, Douglas offered himself in exchange for Baines' life, as Heidi knew he would. She was about to board Douglas' shuttle with her captive and remaining insurgents, when someone shouted her name.

She sighed with the contentment of certain knowledge as she turned to see Commander Jill Baines, so recently promoted in the field to captain, striding towards her with intent.

The women faced each other. Baines' arm rose accusingly, pointing directly at Heidi, but she already knew what Baines was going to say and cut her off very simply. "*Auf Wiedersehen, Kapitänin.*" Her lip twitched into a smile. *Never let it be said I do not learn from my mistakes,* she thought as she turned on her heel, leaving Baines stamping in impotent rage outside as the hatch closed between them.

Heidi's chest swelled with pride as she considered her achievements over the last nine and a half months. She felt certain no one could stop her this time, because this time all unknowns were known, all pitfalls and betrayals foreseen. This time, she would replace Meritus immediately – she had no idea that he had already replaced himself. Through her vignette of hubris, she ignored what lurked at the corners of the picture she was painting, seeing only success as she told herself there would be no more mistakes – *could* be no more mistakes. She already knew it all. This time, it had to end differently, but then, maybe it always did end differently, and in this infinite universe of time and space, maybe it always would.

Epilogue

Not for the first time, a giant black spaceship appeared in orbit around the Earth. However, as far as human knowledge extends, it *was* the first time such a thing happened in AD1588.

Far beneath the interstellar craft, ships relied on the four winds to push them across the vast seas and oceans of the largely blue-green sphere their pilots called home. The spaceship was not so constrained, but true freedom is illusory, the ability to travel anywhere and any-when harnessed to consequence, and Douglas dreaded what he might find in the world below.

He had always loved the gods' eye view of his home world from space, but on that occasion, there was no joy, only apprehension. Indeed, there had been altogether too much playing God as far as he was concerned, and he suspected today might just be the first instalment of a terrible payback cycle.

He breathed a deep, shuddering sigh, his chest tight, for it seemed there was now no doubt that he, and all the *New Worlder*s, were orphans in time. If they were doomed to live outside the normal causes and effects that drove progress on the planet below, then he would see them leave this place, so that Nature could heal the harms inflicted by man's interference.

However, he must first learn what changes, if any, had occurred.

Meritus' potentially irrevocable intervention may have taken away many options remaining to Douglas, but then history was full of examples where one good man or woman made all the difference. Perhaps Meritus had even restored balance. It was possible. Added to the uncertainty surrounding the assumed deaths of Heidi and Heinrich Schultz, Douglas had no idea what the future might hold for his crew. All he really had at that point was hope.

There was only one way to find out.

He turned to his wife and closest friend. She smiled in return, a brittle confidence he knew she did not feel, but he appreciated her support, nonetheless.

"Sandy…" Douglas let the pilot's name hang for so long that Singh eventually looked round.

"Captain?"

Douglas took another steadying breath. He nodded. "Take us in on our predetermined flight path. Stick to the plan."

"Aye, sir."

Once again, Singh demonstrated a textbook re-entry, bringing them down over the Atlantic. Such things have no meaning in space, but once more in the world, they headed east.

The demonic shade of Robin Rotmütze sensed the *New World's* crew the moment their ship arrived in orbit. Summoning his henchman, the twisted spirit of Sir William de Soulis, he waited atop the highest mountain on the island of South Uist in the Scottish Outer Hebrides, Beinn Mhòr – the very spot where they recently witnessed a nuclear explosion out to sea, that killed all aboard the *San Juan de Sicilia* as she ran for home after the failed Spanish Armada. The wave created when Lloyd, Rose, Henry and Major White were forced to drop the bomb had also destroyed farms across the lowlands, in turn forcing the farmers to flee to other islands. South Uist was now uninhabited, but all that was about to change.

The UNS *New World* came in under the cover of darkness. Daylight hours were short in December, and Douglas hoped their arrival would go unnoticed – assuming there was anyone *to* notice.

Singh scanned the land below for a large enough, and roughly level enough, area where the bedrock was sufficiently close to the surface to bear the ship's vast weight. He landed her skilfully, straddling Locheynort and several other large pools, just south of the impressive five-metre-high standing stone monolith of Ad Carra, below the craggy ridge of Beinn Mhòr.

He powered down. "That's it, Captain, 1800 hours on the 24th of December, AD1588, as requested." He turned in happy surprise. "And it's *not* a Tuesday. Things are looking up already, Captain."

"Thanks, Sandy. Are there…" Douglas was about to ask if there were any signs of their people when curiosity got the better of him. "So what day *is* it?"

Singh's face lit up with his perfect, white, schoolboy grin. "According to the, ahem, *new* Gregorian calendar – before I raise the ire of Thomas Beckett again – it's a Saturday, sir. And Christmas Eve, too! That *has* to be a good omen, Captain."

Douglas smiled kindly at the pilot's enthusiasm. "Aye, what could go wrong, eh? Any radio chatter, or other signs of our people?"

Singh turned back to his station. "No, sir, but that may be because they're not making any transmissions at this time. Apart from each other, I doubt there's anyone else to communicate with – electronically, anyway."

"Very well. Let's hope they're listening, at least." He refrained from saying 'let's hope they're *there*'. "Open a channel to the USS *New World* and *Factory Pod 4*."

"Channel open, sir."

"*New World,* this is the…" He tailed off, ruefully. "This is the *New World,* come in – over."

"Nothing, sir."

"Did ye record the message?"

"Yes, sir."

"Broadcast it on loop. Maybe they're just no' listening at this time. Like you say, Sandy, they'll hardly be expecting radio messages in 1588."

"We could do a flyover, sir. Take a shuttle, maybe?"

"Perhaps, but no' yet. Ah dinnae want tae cause a panic, if it can in any way be avoided. For now, we wait."

"Aye, sir."

The doors opened behind them to admit Tim Norris. "Captain, Captain, Commander," he greeted the bridge crew.

Douglas stood to welcome the young man. "Tim – grab yourself a seat, laddie."

Tim sat, nervously. "Are they there?"

Douglas shook his head solemnly. "No response ye—"

A crackle across the comm cut him off. "New World, *this is* Factory Pod 4, *Major White speaking. Come in,* New World – *over.*"

They all jumped to their feet. "Answer that call, Commander!" Douglas cried.

The embarkation lounge aboard *Factory Pod 4* dripped with mistletoe, holly, ivy, yew and laurel – all the decoration of a Tudor Christmas. Off were the sterile white, 22nd century illumination panels. In their place, the cavernous auditorium was bathed in the warm, festive glow of many dozens of large candelabra, each holding several tall tallow candles.

Baines screamed with delight as she flew into the arms of Major White and Mother Sarah. Their reunion was joyful, chaotic and *loud* as friends and families, parted for thirty years in some cases, came together once more.

Douglas had no idea how any of that was possible. With Meritus' disappearance, all evidence of the *Last Word* vanished with him. All that remained to prove the Schultz fleet had ever existed were the two hundred souls from four destroyed capital ships that were now part of his own crew. He was at a loss to explain anything as he walked away to find a quiet corner, where he might take a moment to get his bearings and adjust.

Near the entrance to embarkation, he observed Mary Hutchins, the *New World*'s cook, cleaner and general dogsbody. They had been there all of five minutes and she was already pushing a drinks trolley around.

Douglas smiled wearily. *How that woman loves to take care of us all.*

Geoff Lloyd passed her, helping himself to something from the trolley and earning himself a peck on the cheek for his trouble.

Douglas chortled to himself.

He was soon joined by a black and white face he knew well. Reiver sat wagging his tail, looking up and waiting patiently to catch Douglas' eye.

"Good boy." He smiled down at the collie. "Up ye come, then."

He did not have to ask twice. Reiver jumped into the seat alongside him and immediately *leaned,* until Douglas got the message and responded with fuss.

"How's any of this possible?"

Douglas' mind was in such a whirl, he almost believed the dog had just spoken to him.

"Up here, James."

He raised his eyes to see Tim Norris standing before him, smiling. "I thought that, you know, when the *Last Word* disappeared..."

"Aye, Ah know. Ah thought the *New World* and *Factory Pod 4* must surely be gone, too – in this time, anyway. Ah thought it all might be gone. Everything. All we've seen and done, erased."

"And now this." Tim waved a hand around an embarkation lounge filled with love, friendship and Christmas cheer. "Apparently, we're even expecting a royal visitor – Good Queen Bess." He grinned. "Someone must have told her about Reid's time-travelling wrist devices. I've been told she's asking if she can meet Johnny Rotten! Even old David Maxwell is around here somewhere – still going strong. Last I saw him, he was dancing with my wife! James, I'm not dreaming, am I? This is real, right?"

Douglas snorted. "Damned if Ah know, laddie, but Ah'll take it. Let's no' forget though, we still have a lot of work before us, checking all the locations where Heidi and Reid dropped those wretched wormholes. There're bound to be people and animals still lost out of time. We cannae abandon them. Only we can fix it."

"Yes, and then there's Commander Coleman's people at Crater Lake."

"Aye, Ah'm still chewing over what to do with them. Ahh..."

He shrugged. "They're no' going anywhere. Whatever else has happened, and whatever Tobias Meritus did, everything here, at least, seems unchanged."

"That suggests he made some *big* changes back in the Cretaceous."

"Aye," Douglas repeated, tiredly. "Ah'm no' sure we'll ever know what really happened. Ah hope he's no' lost to us. Maybe he'll pop up again… somewhere."

At that point, they were joined by another, who came bearing three beautifully handcrafted tumblers from Mary's drinks trolley.

Left out, Reiver jumped down from his seat and *woofed*, indignantly.

Geoff Lloyd chuckled softly, handing Douglas and Tim a glass of Lord Maxwell's finest single malt. Having caught the end of their conversation, he suggested, "Shall we leave that story for another time? Merry Christmas, gentlemen."

Such a gesture from Lloyd surprised Douglas. Perhaps not everything was the same here. He stood, and taking the glass, raised it to *clink* with his old comrades. He smiled. "Aye, Ah'll drink tae that."

Advanced gravity–antigravity technology circled the Earth. It had for millions of years, until a chance collision with a small meteorite sent it off course. The tiny piece of rock, left over from the birth of our solar system, span off into the Earth's gravity well, flashing white-hot for the briefest moment as it vanished to oblivion – a mere blip in the ambient temperature within the atmosphere.

Deflected, the highly advanced machinery continued around the planet, falling lower and lower into a decaying orbit. Three days later, it too fell irresistibly to Earth, crashing in the desert eighty miles northwest of Roswell, New Mexico in July, AD1947.

Corporal Engel watched it hit the sands through a pair of field glasses. "At least that happened – and on time." He turned to his companion. "One building block back in place, eh? Perhaps someone out there still cares. That just leaves us another, er… *how many to go?*"

They remained hidden within a large boulder field as the area came to life, suddenly swarming with military personnel. He handed the binoculars to the blond woman at his side. "Looks like they got your message, too."

"Of course," she replied, in clipped Germanic tones.

Figures in the middle distance soon collected the crash debris and removed it to a secret facility, clearing all evidence that it had ever been. Certified non-terrestrial, it lay classified and denied for another seventy-six years, slowly becoming the stuff of folklore, until its existence was eventually and unexpectedly revealed via a televised presentation to Congress in AD2023. Strangely, there was little interest from the media, or the public, and its existence was later re-denied by the Pentagon. Predictability was returning. Time, though scarred, was healing, with history falling back into sequence. The future, once more, unknown.

✆

The fire still roared in the hearth, devouring winter logs with a crackle and pop that sent sparks pirouetting up the chimney. A border collie curled up, snoozing contentedly in the warmth and soothing light. The old man closed the book in his hands to peer over at his grandchildren on the rug at his feet. Both were seven years old. Both sat open-mouthed.

The little boy spoke first. "What happened next, Grandpa?"

"Tell us more about Queen Elizabeth!" the little girl demanded.

"I want more stories about Reiver!" his grandson argued.

The old man chuckled indulgently. "What happened next might take some time, Christian, but as for *your* question, Rosie, I'll tell you something Queen Bess once told me."

He sat back, his gaze defocused in recollection. "When I was your age, I was obsessed with dinosaurs." He chuckled again. "Still am. I was always reading. Always buried in some scientific text or another, so I never really bothered with what you might call 'literature'." He gestured with the time-honoured inverted comma bunnies. "Queen Bess, on the other hand, was very book-learned for her time – a remarkable woman, in so many ways. Well, one day, instead of learning from me, she decided to teach me a thing or two, starting with Geoffrey Chaucer. Now, he studied works from the Greek and Roman classical period, all written, oh, at least a thousand years or more before he was born, and Queen Bess read this quote to me – I've never forgotten it.

"For out of old fields, as men saith, cometh all this new corn from year to year – and out of old books, in good faith, cometh all this new science that men learn."

Rosie sat quietly, pondering its meaning.

Christian skewered his grandfather with a little boy's stare. "Are you trying to get us to read more, Grandpa?"

The old man threw back his head and laughed, for his grandchildren were gifted with very different types of intelligence, and he delighted in both. "The more we understand the past, the more we understand the present, maybe even the future, but yes, you're broadly correct. That is what I'm saying."

"But we like it better when you read to us, Grandpa," Christian implored.

"I'm sure you do, but it's time for bed, I'm afraid."

"*Ohhh,*" the children opined together.

"But here's the thing," the old man continued, leaning forward, eyes twinkling in the firelight. "You see that second old diary up on the shelf there?"

They looked and nodded, excitement bright in their faces. "If you go to bed – without a fuss, now – then we'll take that book down tomorrow evening, and I'll read you a few more of my memoirs from the *New World.* How would that be?"

Rosie leapt up, throwing her arms around the old man's neck, burying her head in his shoulder. "Wuv you, Grandpa Timmy."

"And I love you, too, both of you."

He held them, one in each arm. Unfortunately, he needed a third, as his faithful hound awoke at that moment, to barge in on the action between them. Tim grimaced good-naturedly as the inevitable wet tongue lapped up his cheek. Pinned in place, he giggled like a little boy himself, despite his discomfort. Dog breath was a small price to pay for love, loyalty and, when necessary, even courage so freely given.

He pushed back, gently, releasing the children. "Off to bed now. Time to dream about stories told and stories still to *be* told. And remember, like you, the universe is still very young, and no matter how dark parts of it may appear, all things are still possible."

The end of the beginning.

Our beleaguered band of bickering,
heroic travellers will return...

Author's Notes

The final *author's notes* of the series, where I try to remember everywhere I've taken liberties with history or science, or where the narrative didn't allow for full explanation. Actually, this time, it feels more like trying to make sure I haven't forgotten anything! With that in mind, I thought I'd start these notes with a couple of mentions.

Firstly, Geoff Lloyd used the phrase 'deaf as Drake's gunner', my respectful homage to the late, great Richard Carpenter, who wrote some of my favourite shows from the 70s and 80s. It's remarkable how some things can influence and stick with you. I actually wrote that line thinking it was my own but something about it gnawed at me and then I realised where I'd heard it before. I could have changed it, of course, but I thought I'd explain it in my notes instead, so that anyone reading this might look into some of Carpenter's work for themselves and maybe enjoy it as much as I did.

Secondly, I heartily recommend *When Life Nearly Died* by Michael J. Benton – a wonderful history of palaeontology from the 18th century onwards, which also seeks to establish the reasons for the end-of-Permian-Era extinction, 252 million years ago, and the greatest mass extinction of the Phanerozoic Eon of complex life on Earth (the last 542 million years, give or take a day or two). An excellent read for all those interested in the story of life (and death) on Earth. The Permian–Triassic boundary extinction probably took place over a protracted period, possibly even as long as 200,000 years. I had almost exactly 199,999.4 years less than that to write this book, so I hope readers will forgive any omissions or contractions on my part.

My last shout out, rather immodestly, is to my own Medieval Northumbria series. Inside Book 1, *The Apothecaries* (mentioned within my preface), you can read the other side of Heidi's and Reid's encounter with Harry-the-Cough and Matty in the darkened, wintry woods of medieval England. If you enjoy British comedy and/or historic fiction/fantasy, please give it a try. There will be at least two more books in that series to follow.

Right! The dinosaurs…
This being the final instalment, I just had to bring back my favourites from the series – the active, sometimes nurturing, often vicious, always fascinating terrors of the mid-Cretaceous, *Mapusaurus roseae*, *Carcharodontosaurus saharicus*, *Tyrannotitan chubutensis* (Matilda), *Spinosaurus aegyptiacus*, *Oxalaia quilombensis*, and the petite nightmares, *Buitreraptor gonzalezorum*. I've explained a little about these magnificent creatures within the author's notes sections of earlier books and hope their deadly reprises got the blood pumping for you again. Each became characters in their own right throughout the series, so there was little room to introduce new animals at this stage (although, for any dinosaur enthusiasts out there, my upcoming NEWFOUNDLAND will be full of similar creatures as well as many new ones). Obviously, in an action series we often imagine such animals at their very worst to work the plot, but I believe the important word there is 'animals' – not 'monsters'. So often dinosaurs are portrayed that way. Some may have behaved in ways that would terrify us, almost certainly, but they were no more monsters than a tiger, or a cow for that matter, both of whom also have the capacity to dispatch a man easily – and do. I try to write opposing philosophies in my characters to reflect humanity, and hopefully to avoid tiresome single agendas, but it's probably no secret that I've a deep respect for animals – may even have written about a few! I believe we can learn much from their behaviour, and if I occasionally anthropomorphise them, here and there, to aid the

narrative or work out a piece of comedy, my aim has always been to show them simply doing their best to survive good days and bad, just like the rest of us.

Talking of animals, sometimes, when I offer one of my own furry friends a little treat or reward for being good, I often suspect they understand full well that by sharing such moments they're rewarding me, too – also for being good, in their eyes. It's so often true that it's better to give than to receive, and we humans do like to feel important! They occasionally drive me up the wall, too, but the only time any have ever hurt me is when I've lost them, and those are scars I'll never forget. They remind me what a damned good job they did, every day of their lives, making my life better. I'd hate to live in a world without animals. Not that I'd want to be a dino-snack! Again, it's a matter of respect, and returning to dinosaurs, I did manage to cameo *Rebbachisaurus garasbae* this time. Barrel-bodied, *Rebbachisaurus* was a diplodocid – twenty metres and twenty tons of long-necked, long-tailed sauropod majesty, related to the even longer but lighter, and far more famous *Diplodocus longus* (any who have visited the Natural History Museum in London may be familiar with 'Dippy', the full-sized reproduction of the late-Jurassic herbivore who lived fifty million years before *Rebbachisaurus*). *Rebbachisaurus* were specifically differentiated by unusually tall dorsal vertebrae along their high backs, giving them pronounced ridges that set them apart from most other sauropods, and even from other diplodocidae cousins. The idea of *Rebbachisaurus* and the relatively tiny, three-ton *Ouranosaurus nigeriensis* joining forces to survive the nuclear wasteland was sweet, if sad. For all my fellow animal-lovers out there, fear not! Both made it safely back to their herds in the north, after Heidi and Captain Bessel rudely broke into the narrative and whisked us away to 1940s Germany, taking the granddaddy of all carcharodontosauridae with them!

The other animal I introduced to this story was an outlier, living many millions of years before the mid-Cretaceous and even the dinosaurs themselves in the late Permian Period, 259-252 million years ago. *Inostrancevia latifrons* was the largest gorgonopsian to live in Laurasia (the northern half of the supercontinent, Pangaea). They must have been truly frightening predators. Larger than Bengal tigers, with massive heads and wickedly large sabre-teeth in their powerful jaws, *Inostrancevia,* and gorgonopsians generally, were part of the synapsid clade, a major group of the tetrapods that include mammals. Consequently, they were far more mammal-like than the later dinosaurs, and are believed to be part of our own very distant mammalian ancestry. Whether they did indeed have any fur is as yet unclear, but to give an idea of what it would be like to meet one, I suggest watching the very first episode of the British TV show, Primeval, with Douglas Henshall (2007). The writers called the creature Gorgonopsid, but it's essentially the same beast. You really wouldn't want to bump into one while taking a stroll one day!

That's almost it for the animals – just my last old favourite to mention: *Sigilmassasaurus brevicollis* the spinosaur, and terror of Crater Lake. I had the idea of a throughline between that bad-tempered beastie in Cretaceous Britain and Nessie, several books ago. The idea of an animal surviving untold millions of years in a Scottish loch, a mere 10,000 years old (created by the last ice age) is, of course, perfectly ridiculous – and you could argue that my idea about a time-travelling interloper, laying eggs and raising her progeny to survive a couple of thousand years, isn't much better, but I couldn't resist! (NB: I'm not currently sponsored by VisitScotland, but remain open to a retrospective bribe). Naturally, if someone produces convincing new evidence proving the existence of the Loch Ness Monster after this book goes to press, I reserve the right to retract my 'perfectly ridiculous' comment and take on an air of smugness, while pretending that I knew all along – please arrange interviews through my publisher and agent; I have history in making up stories :-)

There's so much back and forth in this book, that I thought I'd try to go through the notes semi-chronologically where possible, and so, moving forward (a long way) to England's Tudor period, we meet some interesting new characters beginning with the Cout of Kielder…

The heath-bell blows where Keeldar flows,
By Tyne the primrose pale;
But now we ride on the Scottish side,
To hunt in Liddesdale.

Gin you will ride on the Scottish side,
Sore must thy Margaret mourn;
For Soulis abhorr'd is Lydall's lord,
And I fear you'll ne'er return.

(excerpt from *The Cout of Keeldar*, by John Leyden)

That cheery little snippet just about sums up the fate of Sir William de Soulis' enemies, of whom the Cout o' Kielder was reckoned one of the greatest of many (as the legend goes). A giant Englishman and Tynedale baron, who allegedly died in the early years of the 14th century – possibly late 13th. As mentioned in previous author's notes, I brought De Soulis forward to the middle 16th century so that I could include such an authentically historic supervillain within my tale of Hermitage Castle and the Borders (I write a little more about De Soulis and Geoff Lloyd, and their Yuletide antics, in GHOST – part of my New World Extra series).

Information about the cout is sketchy and often contradictory, but it seems he was lauded as a brave young hero type, much admired for his physical size and prowess. While out with a group of friends on a hunt, and who knows what sort of larks, he ignored the local legend about tempting fate when riding anticlockwise, or widdershins, around the Kielder stone (probably the medieval equivalent of reading from the book of the dead in a basement, or repeatedly saying Beetlejuice). Protected by magic armour (stay with me) he did indeed tempt fate. The rest is history, or more probably, legend. The friends were caught trespassing by De Soulis and invited to Hermitage Castle. Despite De Soulis treating the nobles respectfully, offering them Border hospitality, they began to suspect that he actually intended murder – that seemed to be just how he rolled. Strong and powerful, the cout fought off De Soulis and escaped with his comrades on horseback. De Soulis must have found that irritating, because he and his men pursued them immediately. Enter our friend Robin Redcap. De Soulis' tame demon helpfully explained that the Cout's magic armour would not in fact protect him in running water. Doubtless this was sage advice; after all, very few swimmers favour doing the breaststroke in mail! While trying to cross Hermitage Water – the river that ran through Liddesdale and alongside Hermitage Castle itself, and still does to this day – the cout stumbled and fell into a place where the river pooled (a place now known as Drowning Pool). Unable to climb out, the cout was held down by De Soulis' men with their 'lang spears' until he drowned. There's a grave just outside the small chapel a short walk from Hermitage Castle, marked *The Cout o' Kielder* (spelt Keilder on the marker). Against that backdrop, I hope Douglas' burial of a *Mapusaurus* thigh bone so that it could be found two millennia later sounds almost plausible. However, modern cynicism aside, these Border tales are a wonderful part of British history and legend, and are not so different from the historic/horror/fantasy fiction we write and consume today. I love them.

Moving on, I briefly introduced a chap named Captain Fear-God Barebone into this story (we'll hear more of him in REBIRTH – or a longhand title might be *Geoff Lloyd Saves the World* – coming soon). My character is not to be confused with the real 'Fear-God Barebone', a minor 17th century poet and brother to Anabaptist preacher 'Praise-God Barebone', who became a London councillor and member of Oliver Cromwell's Appointed Assembly – a body that became known as Barebone's Parliament (probably ironically) – almost a century later, after the civil war. He was imprisoned after the Restoration (the return of

Charles II), but was later released to live into old age. The only connection between my character and the man is his name – and what a name. It almost paints a thousand pictures! Ideal for the type of chap I had in mind. The reason I mention this curiosity in my notes is because the Barebone family penchant for uniquely descriptive names didn't stop with Fear-God. His brother, Praise-God Barebone, had at least two children. Are you ready for these? Jesus-Christ-Came-Into-The-World-To-Save Barebone and, the even longer typesetters' nightmare, If-Christ-Had-Not-Died-for-Thee-Thou-Hadst-Been-Damned Barebone – I kid you not. Unfortunately, the latter became known simply as 'Damned Barebone'. For some reason, he wasn't fond of that moniker, and went by Nicholas instead – parents, honestly! Still, he must have taken the fear of hellfire seriously enough, because he went on to found London's first fire insurance company and fire brigade. Having read about these men, I simply had to have a Barebone for my story[1]. Isn't history wild and wonderful?

While on the subject of wild and wonderful, this book alludes to a hearing with Congress on the subject of UFOs – or UAPs, as they're often termed (unidentified anomalous phenomena) – and the existence of alien technologies that may be in the possession of the US military at Area 53 (I went with Area 51 because it's

---

1. In the broadest of strokes, Anabaptists believe that baptism by water should take place when one is old enough to *choose* one's faith. Even when baptised as an infant, they are re-baptised upon reaching an age of maturity, if not actually majority. In Reformation England, such beliefs could be dangerous, dependent on the prevailing orthodoxy of the time and who happened to be on the throne. Most notably, during the Reformation of the 16th century, common folk were encouraged to read the word of God for themselves. Up until then, literacy had been mostly an elite privilege; even many churchmen were illiterate. Whatever anyone's views about religion, it's hard to overstate the importance of being encouraged to read – a truly pivotal moment in human history sadly, and yet thankfully, so often taken for granted today.

more widely known and so required no explanation). Once again, I feel the need to repeat: I kid you not. What I found astonishing, possibly even more so than the discussion itself, was how little the world seemed to care. Have things really become so bizarre over the last few years that real-life aliens are now humdrum? I have no answer to that, but here is a transcript from the news channel that broadcasted it live on the 26th July, 2023.

The U.S. House Committee on Oversight and Accountability heard explosive testimony Wednesday, not only about the mysterious craft that was beyond any known technological capabilities but also eyewitness accounts by former US military personnel.

The hearing entitled 'Unidentified Anomalous Phenomena: Implications on National Security, Public Safety, and Government Transparency' heard from: Ryan Graves, Executive Director of Americans for Safe Aerospace; Commander David Fravor (Ret.), Former Commanding Officer United States Navy; and David Grusch, Former National Reconnaissance Officer Representative, Unidentified Anomalous Phenomena Task Force, Department of Defense.

Grusch testified that both he and his wife witnessed 'non-human[2] ' entities doing harm to humans that he described as 'very disturbing'.

Graves testified that he had a pilot tell him he almost hit a UAP during take-off: 'One of these objects was completely stationary... It was right where all the jets were going on the eastern seaboard. The two aircraft flew within 50 feet of the object.'

Upon talking to the pilot after he landed, Graves said he found him with his 'mouth open' and that the pilot told him that 'he almost hit one of those darn things'. Graves said the pilot described the object as a 'dark cube inside of a clear sphere'.
Source: Global News

Is any of that real? Or true? Can it be true? Is it a hoax? Who knows?

---

2. I assume they didn't mean animals.

It all sounds rather surreal, and that's putting it mildly. Whether 'the truth is out there' remains uncertain, but the full hearing is out there on the Internet – you decide.

Finally, I come to something a little more tangible – volcanoes. The events here straddle some of the time periods described above, so I thought I'd just tag it on the end. Apologies if the chronology makes anyone twitch. The enormous volcanic event during the Oligocene Epoch of the Palaeogene Period, roughly thirty million years ago, really did happen and really did spew billions of tons of magnetite up from the mantle to create the strongly magnetic Bermuda Triangle – so we can hang on to that. Although, as I type the name 'Bermuda Triangle' after discussing UFOs, I feel like I'm disappearing down an entirely different but strangely similar rabbit hole! (Author's Notes is where I usually attempt to tie the story to real facts and events and discuss any deviances; however, on this occasion, I think reality may have upstaged my fiction.) I'll try again. The Permian–Triassic extinction, 252 million years ago, *definitely* happened. Almost everything on Earth died, therefore please note: creating a link between that event and the Oligocene eruption, the way Hiro Nassaki did, would probably not be a good thing… so with that, I'll end by saying 'don't try *any* of this at home' and most importantly of all, thank you so much for reading the New World series. It's been a wonderful journey for me as an author and I hope you've enjoyed it.

Until the next time…
Stephen Llewelyn

New World Extra

The New World Extra series of short stories:

ENGEL

Six people alone in a Cretaceous jungle. Ordered to make a threat assessment of their environment, Corporal Heinz Engel is at a loss where to begin. Between running and hiding from a most irascible spinosaur, his team find that foolish mistakes have bloody consequences, and while their predicament brings out the best in some, others show their true colours. By the end of the mission, Engel seeks only justice.

(A short story set during the early chapters of REVENGE.)

MAPUSAURUS

Boy is a baby Mapusaurus roseae who must grow up fast to survive in the mid-Cretaceous. After an adult Mapusaurus destroys his family, he runs for the debatable safety of the forest. Brushes with other creatures, including the crew of the USS New World, are all part of the learning curve as he strives to carve out a territory of his own and grow strong enough to eventually face down his arch nemesis.

(A short story set during DINOSAUR and REVENGE.)

GHOST

Christmas AD1558. A haunted castle in the Scottish Borders. Snowed in and trapped with the most ill-tempered member of their crew – not to mention a malevolent ghost – Major Ford White and Mother Sarah could really use a holiday.

(A short story set immediately after REMAINS – contains spoilers.)

DRUMMOND

When a young palaeontologist is abducted from a dig in Patagonia, Detective Sergeant Rick Drummond receives a call for help from an old friend. Four years previously, he and Detective Sofia Romero investigated an industrial espionage ring. The operation to retrieve stolen experimental drive schematics ended in failure, yet Romero is convinced the latest disappearance is linked with the same syndicate.

Before he knows it, Drummond is embroiled in something deadly as they travel the world without orders, jurisdiction or backup – but thousands of miles are as nothing to the final journey he must take… through time.

(A short story prequel to DINOSAUR.)

DRAGON
Coming soon.

All available to download free from stephenllewelyn.com

"When I first heard about 'Dinosaur' I immediately thought that it would be along the lines of 'Star Trek' meets 'Jurassic Park' with a soupcon of 'James Bond'. Well, I was wrong. It is much, much more than that. It is an excellent adventure story in its own right, packed with action, suspense, humour and emotional drama played out by a wonderful gallery of characters. There is no denying that the prospect of recording a 500 plus page novel with a very broad range of characters and hellish pronunciations was initially quite daunting, but the more we recorded, the more I relished the challenges of 'owning' the characters and bringing Mr Llewelyn's fantastic descriptions and observations off the page. It has been a great privilege to be involved in this project and I hope people enjoy listening to 'Dinosaur' as much as I enjoyed recording it!

Chris Barrie

BOOK 1
DINOSAUR

BOOK 2
REVENGE

BOOK 3
ALLEGIANCE

BOOK 4
REROUTE

BOOK 5
REMAINS

BOOK 6
CURSED

BOOK 7
COLLISION

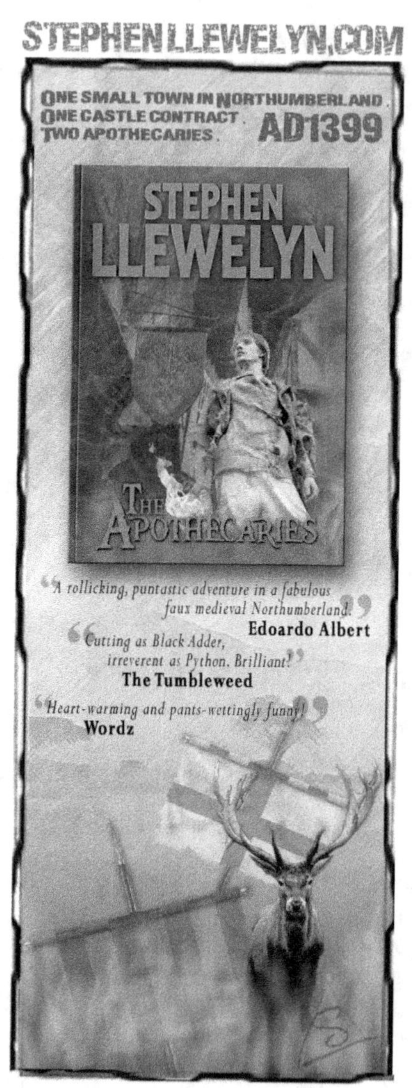

The Apothecaries – Medieval Northumberland Series Book 1
by Stephen Llewelyn